D1025647

THE IRON LANCE

VOLUME ONE OF THE CELTIC CRUSADES

STEPHEN R. LAWHEAD

ZondervanPublishingHouse
Grand Rapids, Michigan

A Division of HarperCollinsPublishers

The Iron Lance
Copyright © 1998 by Stephen R. Lawhead.

Requests for information should be addressed to:

ZondervanPublishingHouse
Grand Rapids, Michigan 49530

Library of Congress Cataloging-in-Publication Data

Lawhead, Steve.
   The iron lance / Stephen R. Lawhead.
     p.   cm. — (The celtic crusades; v. 1)
   ISBN 0-310-21782-8
   1. Crusades—First, 1096–1099—Fiction. 2. Scotland—History—1057–1603—
Fiction. I. Title. II. Series: Lawhead, Steve. Celtic crusades; v. 1.
PS3562.A865I76 1999
813'.54—dc21
                                     99-32360
                                      CIP

First US edition co-published by HarperPrism and ZondervanPublishingHouse, divisions of HarperCollins Publishers.

A hardcover edition of this book was published in Great Britain in 1998 by Voyager, an imprint of HarperCollins Publishers.

For information address:

HarperCollinsPublishers, 77–85
Fulham Palace Road, Hammersmith,
London W6 81B, Great Britain

First hardcover printing: December 1998
First softcover printing: July 1999

Printed in the United States of America

99 00 01 02 03 04 /❖ DC/ 10 9 8 7 6 5 4 3 2 1

THE IRON LANCE

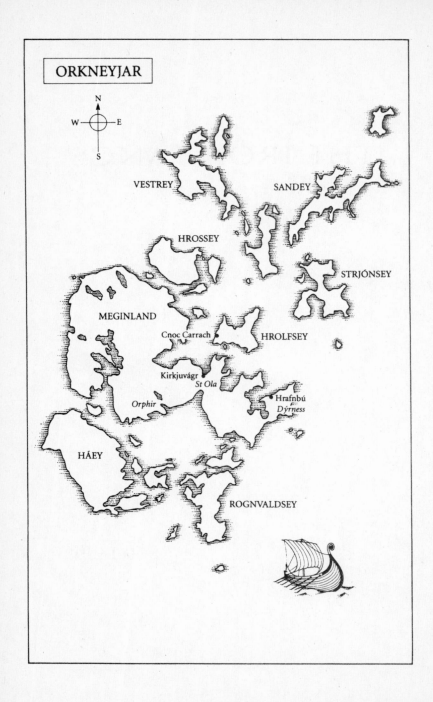

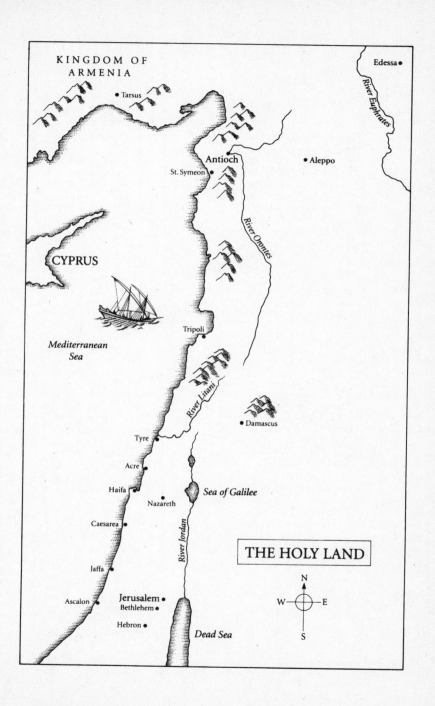

KINGDOM OF
ARMENIA

• Tarsus

• Edessa

River Euphrates

Antioch
St. Symeon •

• Aleppo

River Orontes

CYPRUS

Tripoli

Mediterranean
Sea

River Litani

• Damascus

Tyre

Acre

Haifa

• Nazareth

Sea of Galilee

Caesarea

River Jordan

Jaffa

Ascalon

Jerusalem •
Bethlehem •

Hebron •

Dead Sea

THE HOLY LAND

N
W — E
S

In memory of my Father
Robert E Lawhead

BOOK I

January 6, 1899: Edinburgh, Scotland

My name is of no importance.

It is enough to know that three nights ago I obtained to the Seventh Degree Initiation. Perforce, and I am now a member of the Inner Temple, and therefore privy to the secrets I am about to reveal.

Do not think for a moment that I intend to betray the trust which has been placed in me. I would gladly die before endangering the Brotherhood or its work. As it happens, much of what I shall set forth is already known; at least, any reasonably intelligent reader with an ounce of curiosity and a half-decent library can obtain it with patience and perseverance. The rest, however, is beyond all recovery, save by the methods which have been employed on my behalf. Those methods, like the knowledge so derived, is arcane beyond belief.

Indeed, were I not now among the chosen few, I would not believe it myself, nor would I be writing this at all. As to that, I have put it off long enough. The time has come to order the confusion of my thoughts and the extraordinary, nay *fantastic*, experiences of the last days. Perhaps in the writing I will begin to reassure myself that I am not insane. The events which I shall tell *did* happen, believe me.

I begin.

The summons came as it usually does – a single rap on the door of my study, and a note bearing neither seal nor signature, nor any message save the solitary word: *Tonight.*

Needless to say, I spent the rest of the day disengaging myself from my various commitments and, at the appropriate time, made my way to the appointed place of rendezvous. Forgive me if I do not divulge the location of our meeting place. Suffice to say that it is a simple church no great distance from the city, easily reached by hansom cab. As always, I paid the driver for his trouble, delivered instructions for his return, and proceeded the last two

3

or so miles on foot. Like my fellows, I vary the route each time, as well as the driver, so as not to arouse undue interest or suspicion.

Although the church appears nondescript – all sombre grey stone and suitably traditional appointments – I assure you it is quite ancient, and anything but traditional. Upon entering, I paused to pray in one of the chapel pews before retrieving my grey robe from the rack in the vestry, and making my way down the hidden steps behind the altar to the crypt where our more intimate convocations take place.

The lower room smells faintly of dust and dry decay. It is dark. We rely on candlelight alone, and that sparingly. I am not afraid; I have participated in many such gatherings of the Brotherhood for several years now, and am well acquainted with the various forms and functions of our group. Ordinarily, I am one of the first to arrive. Tonight, however, I can sense the others waiting for me as I stoop nearly double to enter the inner room. I make some small excuse for being late, but am reassured by Genotti (I should state here that *all* names encountered in this narrative have been altered to protect the anonymity of the members of the Brotherhood) – who tells me that I am not late, but that tonight's meeting is a special affair.

'We began our colloquy last night,' Genotti tells me. 'You were not required until this moment.'

'I see.'

Another voice speaks. 'You have been a faithful member of the Council of Brothers for six years, I believe.' It is Evans, our number two, or Second Principal. 'In that time, we have watched you ceaselessly for any hint or sign of impropriety, however small.'

'I hope I have not disappointed you.'

'On the contrary. You have impressed us greatly. Our admiration has only increased.'

A third voice speaks from the darkness. 'Many have been called to the Brotherhood before you.' It is Kutch; his Austrian accent is all his own. 'However, no one has proven worthy of higher honour . . . until now.'

At his use of the word 'honour', my senses prick. That word was used only once before on such an occasion – the night I was asked to join the Brotherhood.

'I was not aware any higher honour existed,' I reply.

'Martyrdom was an honour,' Zaccaria informs me calmly, 'to those who embraced it.'

4

'Am I to be a martyr?'

It is De Cardou who answers. 'We are *all* martyrs, my friend. It is only the cause which distinguishes one from another.'

I do not know what to say to this, so the silence stretches long. I have the sense that they are watching me, that they can see me in the dark even though I cannot see them.

It is Pemberton who speaks at last. This surprises me, for I expected one of the others – Evans, perhaps, or De Cardou. But, no, I know now that the unassuming Pemberton is our superior, our First Principal. 'If you would suffer martyrdom, as we have suffered it before you,' he says gently, 'you have but to step forward.'

I do so, and without a moment's hesitation. I have seen enough of the Brotherhood and its works to trust these men implicitly. I need no second invitation, and in any event I would not have received one. Thus, I accept, stepping forward the prescribed single step; and thus, the initiation begins.

At once I am seized by two members of the Inner Temple, one on either side; they stretch out my arms horizontally, while a third fastens a thick, padded band around my waist. I am led forward to a small table which has been set up in the centre of the crypt.

A solitary candle is lit, and in its glow I see that the table is covered with a spotless white cloth upon which a selection of objects has been assembled: a silver bowl of liquid, a white clay pipe of the kind used to smoke tobacco, a communion chalice, a golden plate containing something which looks like dried figs, a folded black cloth of a material which I assume to be silk, or satin, and lastly, a crude wooden cross set on a pedestal of gold.

I am brought to stand before the table, and my six initiators take their places on the other side, opposite me; they have covered their heads with their cowls so I may not see their faces. It does not matter, I know their voices like I know my own. Even so, the effect is unsettling.

'Seeker, stretch forth your hands.' The command is delivered by Pemberton, and I do as I am told. He picks up the silver bowl and places it on my palms. 'Take and drink.'

I raise the bowl to my lips and sip the liquid. It is sweet, tasting vaguely herbal, like a mixture of roses and anise; yet, there is strength in it, too. I feel the burn in my throat as I swallow. I lower the bowl and it is removed from me, only to be offered once more. 'Seeker, take and drink.'

I drink again, and feel an uncanny warmth spreading through my gullet and stomach. I lower the bowl once more, and once more I am instructed to drink. The strange warmth is filling me from the inside out, spreading from the pit of my stomach to my limbs.

After the third drink of the heady potion, I am allowed to replace the bowl, whereupon the cross is raised and offered to me. 'Seeker,' it is De Cardou, 'venerate the cross.'

At this, the cross is elevated and placed before my face for me to kiss. This I do, and the cross is replaced. De Cardou takes up the clay pipe and turns away. When he turns back, the pipe is lit and smoking – although this happens so quickly I do not see how he could have struck a match, let alone lit the pipe. 'Seeker, imbibe the Incense of Heaven.'

I take the end of the pipe into my mouth and draw upon it. The smoke is fragrant and fills my mouth. I blow it out, and draw again on the wonderful fragrance. After the third such puff, the pipe is, like the bowl, withdrawn and replaced on the table.

Genotti speaks next. 'Seeker,' he says in his soft Italian tones, raising the golden plate, 'take and eat.'

I choose one of the shrivelled brown objects from the offered plate. I put it into my mouth and chew. The flesh is soft and somewhat leathery – like that of dried fruit – but the taste is acrid, bitter. Tears start to my eyes, and I am overwhelmed by a desire to spit out this strange substance. The bitterness is so intense it seems to burn, and then to numb my mouth. My tongue loses all sensation, becoming an unfeeling lump of useless tissue which, unaccountably, seems to swell in my mouth. I fear I will choke. I cannot breathe.

Gasping, gagging, somehow I keep chewing the awful stuff, and am at last able to swallow it down. A new fear overtakes me: I will be made to eat from the plate again . . . but no, Genotti replaces the plate, and takes up the chalice. This is offered without a word, and I accept. I drink; it seems to be a cordial of some kind. I can detect no particular aroma or taste, but instantly feel my tongue and teeth and lips and the soft tissues of my throat begin to throb with a tingling sensation. I know not whether this comes from the dried fruit I have ingested, or from the cordial, but the tingling does not abate.

I am suddenly taken with a curious desire to laugh. I feel as if a bubble is rising inside me, growing larger as it ascends, and that

I must give birth to this bubble with a gale of laughter, otherwise I will burst. It is all I can do to keep from laughing out loud.

'Seeker,' says Genotti once more, 'imbibe the Incense of Heaven.'

The smoke calms me, and though my mouth still tingles I am no longer afflicted by the mad desire to laugh. Evans speaks next. 'Seeker, answer me: how sees a child of God?' he asks, his Welsh lilt falling easily on the ear.

'With the eyes of faith,' I reply. The question is a standard query posed to initiates at every degree.

'Then open your eyes, Seeker, and you shall see,' Evans commands. He takes up the folded cloth of black silk and, stepping around the table, raises the cloth to my face. He quickly binds my eyes, and, blindfolded, I am led by my right hand to another part of the room and made to lie down on my back on the floor.

I compose myself for whatever will happen next, and I hear a low scraping sound, like chalk dragging slowly across a blackboard. This goes on for a time, and then I feel cold air on the left side of my face – as if a door has opened to the draught. At the same time, ropes are attached to either side of the padded band around my waist, and then I am securely tied. The others are standing around me now, towering over me.

Suddenly, my feet are grasped and I am spun like a terrapin on my back. When my feet are released once more, I feel that there is nothing beneath them – my feet dangle over open space. I am allowed no time to reflect on this, for at almost the same instant I am gently pulled forward, allowing my feet, ankles, and legs to slide down into emptiness. My arms are taken up, the ropes pulled taut, and I feel myself slipping into the hole which has been opened in the floor.

Slowly, I descend into the void, dangling at the end of my ropes like a puppet.

The chamber into which I am lowered is immense. I cannot say how I know this – perhaps the size is suggested by the chill of the air and the sound of my breathing echoing back from unseen walls. My eyes are bound; I see nothing. Down and down I go.

At last, my feet touch solid ground once more; I gather my legs under me and stand. I cannot tell how far I have descended. The voice falling down to me from directly overhead reaches me as an echo merely: 'Seeker . . .' it is Pemberton, 'with the eyes of faith, I bid you seek . . . and may you truly find.'

7

At this, the ropes go slack as they are thrown in after me. This puppet's strings have been cut, as it were, and it is for me to find my own way, to seek. But what ... *what* am I seeking? What am I meant to find? None of my previous experiences with the Brotherhood have prepared me for this test. I will stand or fall by my own efforts.

As I am a seeker, I decide, I will do as I am told. Although the object of my search remains a mystery, I will have faith enough to believe that I shall recognize the prize when I find it.

Thus resolved, I take my first faltering steps into the cave – for that is how I think of it, an immense subterranean cavern, a vast hollow chamber of stone deep under the earth. I take three steps into the clinging darkness, and I stop. I am no longer steady on my feet. I feel light-headed, as if I am floating.

Nevertheless, I take a deep breath and proceed.

I turn slowly, first left, then right. I seem to feel the faintest breath of air on my cheek when I face the right, and so I decide to pursue the search in this direction. It is a whim, nothing more, but it is rewarded by the fact that after a dozen or so measured paces, I reach a step.

I stoop and feel the edge of the step with my hands; it rises to others behind it. I mount the first three, then three more, then another, and I am arrived upon a platform, which I take to be cut into the cavern wall.

I speak a word and judge by the reverberation of the sound that I have entered a smaller chamber, open to the larger – a vestibule of sorts. Stretching my hands before me like a blind man – truly, I *am* a blind man – I shuffle forward to explore the chamber to which I have ascended.

My head is spinning now. I have passed giddy and am actually growing dizzy. My senses remain acute. I feel as if I am glowing in the dark, giving off sparks. My hearing is sharp, but there is nothing to hear, save my own breathing. Since I have not been instructed otherwise, I decide to remove the blindfold.

As expected, there is no light. The subterranean darkness is complete. It covers me like a second skin, so close as to be part of me. Though I am blind still, my senses are alive and tingling with anticipation – or, more probably, the strange substances I have imbibed are beginning to work in me somehow. I feel as if I am flying.

I continue with my inspection. The walls of the vestibule, I discover, are rounded and smooth, cut, as I have surmised, into the walls of the cave. There is no impediment to my movement as I work my way around what I perceive to be the back wall of the vestibule, feeling with my hands. And then . . .

I brush the edge of the opening with my fingers. I feel the curved lip of a ledge, and quickly trace the opening in the wall with my hands. It is a niche, wider than it is high, and with a slightly projecting shelf. I reach in. It is not deep. I feel the back of the niche, and then begin running my fingers along the shelf.

My fingertips brush something cold and hard.

The object has been placed in the niche precisely. Indeed, I presume the niche and shelf have been constructed especial to hold the object it contains. Could this be what I was meant to find?

I continue my investigation of the object. It is long and thin, with a hardness and coldness that can only be metal. I take it into my hand and carefully remove it from its resting place, holding it lengthwise across my palms to judge its heft. From the weight, I suspect bronze, or iron; and from the length and shape, I imagine a rake handle. But no, it is too thin – the circumference is too small for any common tool or implement of that sort – and it is too heavy. The surface is rough, pitted, and without marking or ornamentation that I can discern.

Running my hand along the length of the metal rod, I perceive that it is not entirely straight – the metal bows and turns slightly as it gradually thickens towards its blunt, rounded end. I turn my attention to the opposite end, and find that the cylindrical shaft thins as it nears what I imagine to be the top, its roundness squared beneath a short, triangular-shaped head. There are three – what shall I call them? protrusions? – on the head: small vanes, if you will. These vanes are thin, and . . .

As I stand puzzling over the nature of the object I have found, I hear the whoosh of air, great volumes of air moving, yet I feel not the slightest movement on my skin. Sweat breaks out on my forehead.

All at once, it seems as if the floor beneath me is tilting. I reel forwards, clutching the metal rod. With my free hand, I grab for the edge of the niche, miss, and lurch awkwardly into the wall. The cavern is booming now, and I realize the sound is in my head – it is the rush of blood through my ears. Bracing myself against the wall, I try to turn, but find I can no longer stand.

I am panting like a dog. My breath comes in quick bursts and gasps, as if I have run ten miles. Sweat is pouring from my face. I hold to the wall, leaning against it, afraid to move lest I fall from the raised vestibule to the floor. Instead, keeping my back to the wall, I slide down slowly into a sitting position, clutching the metal rod, and gulping air like a fish caught on dry land.

The floor beneath me trembles; I feel the vibration seeping up through the stone floor and into my bones. My mouth is dry and tastes of sour milk. The sweat is pouring from me now. I press my head back against the solid rock and feel my poor heart thumping away wildly in my chest.

This is how I will die, I think.

There are dancing spots before my eyes – like fireflies, these errant beams glint and fade, appearing and reappearing in the vast emptiness of the cavern. Unlike fireflies, however, they are swarming, growing larger, gathering more substance. I see colours: bold, vibrant, shocking in their intensity. The light is growing stronger, coalescing into spheres.

It must be the last eruption of a dying brain, but no . . . I can see some of the cavern chamber illuminated in the light of the ever-shifting spheres. One of them drifts close to me, shedding a gentle glow of light over me. What is more, I can see something moving *inside* the sphere: the dim shapes of human figures.

The images inside the sphere are shifting, changing, filling my vision. It is all I can see now, and the light is growing stronger. Without warning the vision breaks over me. A sudden burst of light, and all at once, the cavern is ablaze with sparkling images. They fly past my dazzled eyes in a flurry of beams, a veritable blizzard of brilliance, each image a burning spark striking deep into the soft tissue of my brain. Each blazing particle is part of a greater whole, merging and coalescing as they accumulate in my mind.

Individual fragments are swallowed in the gradually emerging whole, and I begin to see – not broken images now, but a portrait entire. With the crystalline clarity of a dream, I see it all. More, I *behold*. I have become part of the dream, living it even as it is played out in my mind.

Still, the dazzling fragments, these scintillating shards of dream, fly at me, piercing my senses, embedding themselves deep in my perception. I am defenceless before the onslaught. I can but gape and surrender to the dizzying torrent. But there is so much! The scenes cascade into my consciousness, and I am a man drowning in the onrushing flood.

10

I can derive no sense or understanding of what I see; the dream is too vast, too chaotic, too wild. It is all I can do to take it in. Yet, there is meaning here. I feel it. This dream is no hollow hallucination, the shadow-play of a drugged and fevered brain. Indeed, irresistibly, I am impressed with a grave and terrible certainty that the things I am seeing, however bizarre and chaotic they may seem, actually happened. The dream is authentic. It *happened*.

Oddly, it is this awful certainty which overwhelms me in the end. I cannot endure the frenzied onslaught, and I fall back. A man drunk on an impossibly rich and heady elixir, I slump against the wall, blind and insensate. Resting the metal rod across my lap, I press the heels of my hands to my poor eyes. Instantly, the images cease. Upon releasing the rod, I have broken contact with the source of the dream, and am myself released to the blessed, soothing darkness of the cavern.

Oh, but it is a darkness lit by the flickering light of a strange and glorious magic. The dream is alive in me. Slowly, slowly, with ignorant, faltering steps I begin the first feeble attempt to impose some small order on the irreducible chaos of the thoughts and images whirling inside my mind.

Great God, I am lost!

The cry is scarcely uttered when the answer is revealed. There is a thread . . . a thread. Seize it, hold it, follow it, and it will lead through the twisted labyrinth of madness to sweet reason.

Carefully, carefully, I take up the thread.

ONE

Murdo raced down the long slope, his bare feet striking the soft turf so that the only sound to be heard was the hiss and swash of his legs through the coarse green bracken. Far behind him, a rider appeared on the crest of the hill and was quickly joined by two more. Murdo knew they were there; he had anticipated this moment of discovery, and the instant the hunters appeared he dived headlong to the ground to vanish among the quivering fronds where he continued his flight, scrambling forward on knees and elbows, first one way and then another.

The riders spurred their mounts and flew down the hillside, the blades of their spears gleaming in the early light. All three shouted as they came, voicing the ancient battlecry of the clan: 'Dubh a dearg!'

Murdo heard the shouts and froze fast, pressing himself to the damp earth. He felt the dew seeping through his siarc and breecs, and smelled the sharp tang of the bracken. The sky showed bright blue through leafy gaps above him and, heart pounding, he watched the empty air for the first glimpse of discovery.

The horses raced swiftly nearer, their hooves drumming fast and loud, and flinging the soft turf high over their broad backs. Murdo, flat beneath the bracken, every sense alert and twitching, listened to the swift-running horses and judged their distance. He also heard the liquid gurgle of a hidden burn a short distance ahead, lower down the slope.

Upon reaching the place where the youth had disappeared, the riders halted and began hacking into the dense brake with the butts of their spears. 'Out! Out!' they shouted. 'We have you! Declare and surrender!'

Murdo, ignoring the calls, lay still as death and tried to calm the rapid beating of his heart so the hunters would not hear him. They were very near. He held his breath and watched the patch of sky for sight or shadow of his pursuers.

The riders wheeled their mounts this way and that, spear shafts slashing at the fronds, their cries growing more irritated with each futile pass. 'Come out!' shouted the largest of the riders, a raw-boned, fair-haired young man named Torf. 'You cannot escape! Come out, damn you!'

'Give up!' shouted one of the others. Murdo recognized the voice; it belonged to a thick-shouldered bull of a youth named Skuli. 'Give up and face your punishment!'

'Surrender, you sneaking little weasel,' cried the last of the three. It was the dark-haired one called Paul. 'Surrender now and save yourself a hiding!'

Murdo knew his pursuers and knew them well. Two of them were his brothers, and the third was a cousin he had met for the first time only ten days ago. Even so, he had no intention of giving up; he knew, despite Paul's vague assurance, they would beat him anyway.

Instead, amidst the shouts and the brushy whack of the spears, Murdo calmly put two fingers beneath his belt and withdrew a tightly-wound skein of wool and deftly tied one end of the thread to the long bracken stem beside his head. Then, with the most subtle of movements, he began to crawl again, paying out the thread as he went.

Slowly, slowly, and with the icy cunning of a serpent, he moved, pausing to unwind more string and then slithering forward again, head low under the pungent green fronds, forcing himself to remain calm. To hurry now would mean certain disaster.

'We know you are here!' shouted Torf. 'We saw you. Stand and declare, coward! Hear me? You are a very coward, Murdo!'

'Surrender,' cried Paul, dangerously near. 'We will let you go free.'

'Give up, Stick!' added Skuli. 'You are caught!'

Murdo kept silent – and even when Paul's spear swept only a hair's breadth from his head, he did not break and run, but hunkered down and waited for the horse to move on. Reaching to the end of his thread ball, he lay still, trying to determine where and how far away were each of his pursuers. Satisfied that they were all at least ten or more paces away, he took a deep breath, pulled the woollen thread taut . . . and then gave a quick, sharp tug.

He waited, and jerked the string hard once more.

'There!' shouted Skuli. The other two whooped in triumph, wheeling their mounts and making for the place.

But Murdo had already released the thread and was slithering down the hill as fast as he could go. He reached the bank of the burn and risked a furtive look back at the riders: all three stood poised in the saddle with spears at the ready, shouting into the bracken for him to surrender.

Smiling, Murdo eased over the edge of the bank and lowered himself into the burn. The water was shallow, and cold on his bare feet, but he gritted his teeth and hastened on. While the riders demanded his surrender, Murdo made his escape along the low stream bed.

It was Niamh who finally caught him; he was sliding quietly around the corner of the barn, hoping to slip into the yard unobserved. 'Murdo! There you are,' she scolded, 'I have been looking for you.'

'My lady,' Murdo said, snapping himself straight. He turned to see her flying towards him, green skirts bunched in her fists, dark eyes flashing.

'A fine *my lady*! Look at you!' she said, exasperation making her sharp. 'Wet to the bone and muddy with it.' She seized him by the arm and pulled him roughly towards her. A head or more taller than the slender woman, he nevertheless delivered himself to her reproof. 'You have been at that cursed game again!'

'I am sorry, mam,' he replied, his man-voice breaking through the boyish apology. 'It's the last time, and –'

'Hare and hunter – at your age, Murdo!' she snapped, then looked at him and softened. 'Ah, my heart,' she sighed and released his arm. 'You should never let them treat you like that. It is neither meet nor fitting for any lord's son.'

'But they could not catch me,' Murdo protested. 'They never do.'

'The abbot is here,' Niamh said, tugging his damp, dirty siarc and brushing at it with her hands.

'I know. I saw the horses.'

'He will think you one of the servingmen, and who is to blame but yourself?'

'What of that?' Murdo replied sourly. 'It's never me that's going.'

15

'How should you be going? For all it is only ten and four you are.'

'Ten and five – in five months,' Murdo protested. 'Besides, I am taller than Paul, *and* stronger.' But his mother was already moving away. He stepped quickly beside her. 'Why is the abbot here?'

'Can you not guess?'

'It's the gathering,' Murdo answered.

'It is that.'

'When?'

'Ask the abbot,' replied Niamh. 'It's him you are greeting soon enough.'

They proceeded across the yard – a flat expanse of hard-packed earth enclosed on three sides by the barn and storehouses, and on the fourth by the great grey stone manor house itself. In all, Hrafnbú was as fine a manor farm as any in Orkney; the estate, or bú, had been in Murdo's family for five generations, and it was the best place Murdo knew.

Seven horses waited in the yard – the four clerics' and those of Torf, Skuli, and Paul, who had reached the bú well before Murdo, but just after the abbot. Lord Ranulf, flanked by his sons and nephew, stood in the centre of the yard, deep in conversation with the abbot and his monks.

Ignoring the clerics, Murdo's eyes went first to his father. The Lord of Hrafnbú towered above those around him. He was a big man, with large, strong hands – one of which gripped his elbow while the other stroked his heavy brown beard. Open-faced and naturally amiable, he was frowning now, his friendly dark eyes narrowed in a look which Murdo knew to betoken trouble.

His expression changed instantly when the lord glanced up at the approach of Murdo and his mother. 'Abbot Gerardus, my wife and last-born son.' Ranulf held out his hand, which his wife accepted with a minute bow.

'Lady Niamh,' the abbot said, inclining his head respectfully. 'God save you, my lady. I greet you in the name of Our Redeemer. I trust you are well.'

A gurry-mouthed Saecsen, thought Murdo darkly, stiffening at the abbot's accent. They hold themselves so superior and cannot even speak a proper word.

The young abbot's eyes swung easily to Murdo and, finding little enough to interest him, flicked away again. Murdo vowed vengeance for the slight.

'Good abbot,' said Lady Niamh, 'my husband would keep you talking the whole day long, but I will not. I am certain that whatever you have to say will be better spoken over the welcome cup. Come, you have ridden a fair distance already and the day is yet new.'

Murdo squirmed uncomfortably as his mother slipped easily into the speech and manner of the hated foreigner. Why did she always have to do that?

'You are most kind, my lady,' replied the abbot imperiously. 'I assure you my fellow priests and I would be delighted to attend you.'

'This way, friends,' said the lord, indicating the house with an expansive gesture. 'We will discuss our business over our cups.'

Lord Ranulf and the abbot started off, and Torf, Skuli, and Paul made to follow. 'See to the horses, you three,' Ranulf called over his shoulder, halting them in midstep. 'And give our friends' animals a good measure as well.'

The young men stared after the lord, suddenly chagrined at being left out of the discussion. Murdo allowed himself a smile of wicked glee at their dismay. Torf saw the smile and started for him, fists clenched, but Paul seized the older youth's arm and pulled him back, saying, 'If we hurry, we can still join them before the cup is dry.'

Torf growled and, turning on his heel, darted after the others. As the horses were led away, Murdo fell into place behind the trailing monks and the procession crossed the yard and entered the house. The monks were brought into the hall and given places at the lord's board.

Unlike Jarl Erlend's palace in Orphir, Ranulf's manor was very much the house of a working farmer, whose estate, though extensive, required constant vigilance and exacting care in order to produce even the modest wealth the lord and his vassals enjoyed. There were no golden bowls, no silver ornaments for visiting clerics, no gifts of coin for the church; the hall was not full of warriors with gleaming torcs and armbands awaiting the next raid, the next battle. Indeed, the master of Hrafnbú kept no fighting men, and at Yuletide and other holy days, his own family and friends more than filled the low-beamed hall; if any more visitors came, extra boards and trestles were set up in the yard. Still and all, Ranulf's ale was good and dark and sweet, and the fire at his wide hearth was as warm as any king's.

Murdo liked the hall and the solid stone house, and bristled at the way in which the abbot dismissed his surroundings with an indifferent glance. Ranulf failed to notice the snub, however, as he poured the monks' cups with his own hand. When the bowls were filled, he raised his, saying, 'Health and long life. Take your ease and be welcome in my house.' The holy men nodded in silence, and they all drank.

'Lord Ranulf,' remarked the abbot, lowering the cup at last, 'this is a rare pleasure for me, I assure you. I have long had it in mind to visit you, and I rejoice that the jarl's decision has provided this felicitous opportunity.'

'You honour me with your company, Abbot Gerardus,' replied Ranulf, reaching forward to refill the cups. He emptied the jar and made to replace it on the board but, seeing Murdo, gestured to his son. 'Here now, Murdo, fill the jar.'

Murdo leapt to the task so that he would not miss a single word. He dashed from the hall and into the kitchen to the vat in the corner, lifted the wooden cover and plunged the jar into the cool brown ale, pulled it up, and was away again before the cover slammed down. He brought the jar still dripping to the board and placed it beside his father.

'It is as I expected,' Ranulf was saying. Murdo noticed the frown was back on his father's face. 'Yet, I had hoped he would change his mind.'

'No doubt Jarl Erlend has many pressing concerns,' the abbot remarked judiciously.

'Nay,' replied Ranulf scornfully, 'the concerns of the Holy Church are the concerns of all good Christian men. What temporal duty can claim greater obligation?'

'Both the bishop and I agree, of course,' Abbot Gerardus said. 'And that is why we have interceded with the jarl – sadly, to no avail.' He allowed this sorrow to be duly felt, before brightening once more. 'Still, I am pleased to tell you that he has at least seen the wisdom of our appeal and allowed his decision to be moderated somewhat.' The abbot paused to indulge a smugly satisfied smile. 'When the interests of the church are at issue, I think you will find us most formidable adversaries.'

18

'I am certain of it,' answered Ranulf quickly, impatient to learn the answer he had been waiting for over two months to hear.

But the abbot was enjoying his diplomatic mission and would not be hurried. 'Of course, the jarl is a difficult man at best, and never easy to persuade. Truly, if it were not for the bishop's friendship with King Magnus, I do not believe –' he paused again. 'Ah, well, all that is done now, and I am pleased to tell you we have secured that which we sought – at least in part, as I say.'

'Yes?' coaxed Ranulf, leaning forward slightly.

Abbot Gerardus lifted his head as if he were delivering a benediction. 'Although Jarl Erlend remains firm in his decision, he has given his vow that he will neither hinder nor reprove any nobleman who chooses to follow the crusade.'

'Good!' cried Ranulf, slapping the board with his hand.

'God be praised,' the monks murmured, nodding contentedly.

'Indeed,' continued the abbot, 'each of the jarl's vassals is free to obey his own conviction in the matter.'

There was a movement beside the lord as his wife stepped beside him. Alone of those present, her expression was dour. Ranulf, oblivious to her disapproval and giddy with the prospect before him, took her hand into his. The abbot looked away primly.

'Naturally,' intoned the abbot after a moment, 'the jarl wishes it to be known that, inasmuch as he is not taking the cross himself, he will not be extending any material assistance to those who choose to go.'

'Nothing?' asked Ranulf, the smile fading from his face.

The abbot gave a slight shake of his head. Murdo could see how much the grey-robed cleric relished his position as emissary, and hated him the more. Self-important meddler, thought Murdo, and entertained himself with the vision of the abbot's backside covered in ripe, red boils.

'You see how it is,' Abbot Gerardus replied. 'The jarl has many claims on his properties and substance. It is enough that he will be deprived of the rightful tribute of his noblemen. Certainly, he cannot be expected to provide supplies and provisions for all.'

'But –' began Ranulf. His protest was stifled by the imperious abbot's upraised palm.

'It is the view of the church that those who follow the crusade are pilgrims and as such must meet the cost of the pilgrimage out of their own resources.' He looked around the room, as if assessing the value of its appointments. 'If one finds oneself unable to meet the cost, then perhaps one is unwise in pursuing the journey.'

'The tribute will be forgiven?' wondered Ranulf.

'Of course.'

'For the duration of the crusade?'

The abbot nodded. 'All tithes and taxes, too, yes – that is, until the pilgrim returns.'

Ranulf rubbed his chin, reckoning his savings.

'I would not like to think the love of mammon stood between any man and his sacred duty,' Abbot Gerardus continued. 'The spiritual rewards are not inconsiderable. As you know, all pilgrims will enjoy complete absolution for all sins committed while on crusade, and should death befall anyone who takes the cross, his soul is assured swift admission into paradise.'

'That much I have heard,' Ranulf replied.

Lady Niamh, grim and silent, stood with her arms crossed and her mouth pressed into a thin, hard line. Murdo knew the look, and rightly feared it.

The three young men entered the hall just then, eager to hear the abbot's news. They approached the board and Ranulf beckoned them close. 'We have our answer,' the lord informed his sons and nephew. 'Jarl Erlend will allow the crusade, but we cannot look to him for aid.'

'We can go?' asked Torf, glancing from his father to the abbot and back again.

'Aye, that we can,' Lord Ranulf answered.

'Then I take the cross!' declared Torf, thrusting forward.

'Torf-Einar!' exclaimed Lady Niamh. 'It is not for you to say.'

'I take the cross!' Skuli echoed, ignoring his mother.

Not to be outdone, Paul pushed forward. 'In the name of Christ, I take the cross!'

Ranulf stood, gazing resolutely at his wife. 'Tell Bishop Adalbert that Lord Ranulf of Dýrness and his sons will come before him to take the cross on the Saint John's Sabbath.'

Murdo heard this and his heart beat faster. Did his father mean to include him, too? Perhaps the lord had changed his mind, and he would be included after all. He held his breath.

The young abbot nodded. 'Trust that I will tell him. Of course, you will wish to place your lands under the protection of the church during your pilgrimage.'

'That will not be necessary,' Ranulf replied easily. 'Lady Niamh will remain in authority here. My son, Murdo, will be here to help her, of course, and as the jarl is to stay in Orkneyjar, we have nothing to fear.'

Murdo's face fell as the hope, so quickly kindled, died to ashes in his heart.

'That is your privilege, of course, Lord Ranulf,' remarked the abbot. 'But I advise you to pray and seek God's guidance in this matter. You can deliver your decision to the bishop on the Sabbath.'

'There is no need,' Ranulf assured him. 'I have made my decision, and I will not be changing it now.'

'Very well.' With that, the abbot rose, and Murdo received the distinct impression that, having made a dreadful blunder, they were all being abruptly dismissed.

Heads erect, hands folded before them, Abbot Gerardus and his brother monks left the hall, retracing their steps to the yard. The lord bade his sons to fetch the clerics' horses, and Murdo used the opportunity to loosen the cinch strap on the abbot's saddle – not enough so that the churchman should fall, but enough to make the saddle sway uneasily from side to side.

Back in the yard once more, the abbot accepted the reins from Murdo's hand and, without so much as a word of thanks, swung himself onto his mount. 'Pax vobiscum,' he intoned sourly.

'Pax vobiscum,' answered Ranulf, whereupon the abbot wheeled his horse and rode from the yard, followed by his three silent companions.

After supper the Lord of Dýrness and his lady wife exchanged sharp words. Late into the night their voices could be heard beyond the thick walls of their chamber. The servingmen had vanished just after clearing the supper board, lest they come foul of their lord's displeasure, and none were to be found anywhere. Murdo, sitting alone at the hearth, could not hear what they said, but the meaning was clear enough. Even the lord's grey wolfhound remained curled in a corner of the hearth, jowls resting on his great paws.

'What ails you, Jötun?' muttered Murdo, flicking a peat clod at the dog. 'It's *me* that has been forsaken.'

Murdo did not go to his bed that night; he was discouraged enough already without listening to the smug chatter of his brothers and cousin. Instead, he stalked the hill behind the house cursing his luck and railing against his untimely birth. He demanded of the heavens to know why he had been born last, but neither the stars, nor the pale half moon deigned to answer. They never did.

TWO

'Your horse has been saddled, basileus,' announced Nicetas. From his camp chair in the centre of the tent, Alexius Comnenus, Emperor of All Christendom, God's Co-Regent on Earth, Supreme Commander of the Imperial Army, rose and lifted his arms. Two young armour-bearers darted forward, one of them clutching the imperial sword, and the other the wide silver belt.

Together the two buckled the sword and then backed silently away while old Gerontius, Magister of the Chamber, shuffled forward holding the emperor's golden circlet on a small cushion of purple silk. Alexius lifted the circlet and placed it on his head, and then turned to his ageing servant. 'Are we ready, Gerontius?'

'The basileus is ready,' replied Gerontius with a bow.

'Come then, Nicetas,' said the emperor, stepping quickly to the door. 'We would not have the enemy believe we are cowering in our tent. We shall let them see us at the head of our troops, and they shall know Alexius fears nothing.'

The two men emerged from the imperial tent, and the emperor stepped onto the mounting block where his favourite stallion waited. Alexius raised his foot to the stirrup and swung easily into the saddle; he took up the reins and, with Nicetas, Captain of the Excubitori, the palace guard, mounted beside him, made his way slowly through the camp to the chorused shouts of acclaim from rank upon rank of soldiers.

'Listen to them, Nicetas. They are eager for the fight,' Alexius observed. 'That is good. We will whet their appetite a little more, so that tomorrow they will feast without restraint.'

'The blood of the enemy will be a rich sacrifice for God and his Holy Church,' the captain of the guard replied. 'Amen.'

'Amen.'

Upon reaching the edge of the camp, the two rode on, following a trail which led to a nearby hill where three men on horseback waited. 'Hail and welcome, basileus!' called the foremost of them, riding forward to greet his sovereign with a kiss. The other two offered the imperial salute and waited to be addressed.

'What have you to show us, Dalassenus?' the emperor asked. He rubbed his hands in anticipation, and regarded his kinsman fondly.

'This way, if you will, basileus,' replied Dalassenus, Grand Drungarius, Supreme Commander of the Imperial Fleet. The family resemblance was strong in the young commander: thick black curly hair and keen black eyes beneath even brows, he was short-limbed and muscular like all the Comneni men, and swarthy-skinned like his cousin; he differed only in that where his kinsmen displayed the Greek half of their heritage, his own features tended more towards the Syrian.

Reining in beside Alexius, he led the emperor up a winding rocky path towards the crest of the hill. The two rode together side by side, easy in one another's company. They had fought alongside one another many times, and both knew and respected the other's skill and courage.

As the emperor and his entourage gained the top of the hill called Levunium, the light from the setting sun struck them full like the blaze from victory fire. The sky, aglow with flaming reds and golds, shone with a brilliance exceeded only by the sun itself. The men, blinded for a few moments, shielded their eyes with their hands until they could see once more, and then looked down into the dusky valley below.

The extreme desperation of their predicament became apparent only gradually as they beheld the dark, spreading blotch rippling north and south from one promontory to the other, and stretching into the distance as far as the eye could see – like a vast black river whose waters were slowly filling the Maritsa valley with the flood of a vile and filthy sea.

Alexius stood in awe-stricken silence, gazing into the valley at the assembled enemy: Pechenegs and Bogomils in numbers beyond counting, tribe upon tribe, whole barbarian nations rising to the slaughter of the empire. Nor were these the greatest enemy bawling for the blood of Byzantium. They were merely the last in a long, long train of barbarian hordes seeking to enrich and aggrandize themselves through the plunder of the empire's legendary wealth.

Alexius, the light of the dying sun in his eyes, took in the unholy sight before him, and remembered all the other times he had gazed upon the enemy before a battle. In the last thirteen years he had faced Slavs and Goths and Huns, Bulgars and Magyars, Gepids and Uzz and Avars – all howling down across the windswept steppelands of the North; and in the south the wily, implacable Arabs: first the Saracens, and now the Seljuqs, a sturdy and energetic warrior race from the arid wastes of the East.

God in heaven, he thought, there are so many! Where does it end? Forcing down his dismay, he declared, 'The greater the enemy, the greater the victory. God be praised.' After a moment, he turned to his kinsman and asked, 'How many Cuman have pledged to fight for us?'

'Thirty thousand, basileus,' replied Dalassenus. 'They are camped just over there.' He indicated a series of rough hills, behind which a pall of smoke was gathering. 'Does the emperor wish to go to them?'

Alexius shook his head slowly. 'No.' He squared his shoulders and straightened his back. 'We have seen enough barbarians – they hold no fascination for us. We would rather speak to our soldiers. It is time to kindle the flame of courage so that it will burn brightly in the fight.'

He reined aside and departed the hilltop, returned to the Byzantine camp and commanded Nicetas to assemble the themes and scholae. While the soldiers were summoned, the emperor waited in his tent, kneeling before his chair, hands clasped tightly in prayer.

When Alexius emerged from his tent once more, the sun had set, and two stars gleamed in a sky the colour of the amethysts in his swordbelt. A raised platform had been erected beside the tent so that he might address his troops and, with the coming of night, torches had been lit and placed at each corner of the platform. Preceded by an excubitor bearing the vexillum, the ancient war standard of the Roman Legions, Alexius mounted the steps and walked to the edge of the platform to look out upon the assembled might of Byzantium – a force much reduced from its former size, but potent still.

The last of the ancient and honourable themes stood in ranks before him, their separate regiments marked out by the colour of their cloaks and tunics: the red of Thrace, the deep blue of Opsikion, the green of Bithynia, the gold of Phrygia, and the black of the

Hetairi. Rank on rank, upraised spears gleaming in the dusky twilight, they stood, fifty thousand strong, the last remnant of the finest soldiers the world had ever seen: the Immortals. Alexius' heart swelled with pride to see them.

'Tomorrow we fight for the Glory of God and the welfare of the empire,' the emperor declared. 'Tomorrow we fight. But tonight, my brave companions – tonight, above all nights, we pray!'

Alexius paced the edge of the platform, his golden breastplate glimmering like water in the torchlight. How many times had he addressed his troops in just this way, he wondered. How many more times must he exhort men to lay down their lives for the empire? When would it end? Great God, there must be an end.

'We pray, my friends, for victory over the enemy. We pray for strength, and courage, and endurance. We pray God's protection over us, and his deliverance in the heat and hate of battle.' So saying, Alexius, Elect of Heaven, Equal of the Apostles, fell on his knees and fifty thousand of the finest warriors the world had ever seen knelt with him.

Raising his hands to heaven, the emperor sent heartfelt words of supplication and entreaty winging to the throne of God. His voice rang out in the twilight stillness with all the passion of a commander who knows his troops woefully outnumbered and must trust their courage to sway the scales of war.

When at last the emperor finished, night had descended upon the camp. Alexius opened his eyes and stood to gaze in amazement at a most miraculous sight; it was as if the stars above had fallen to earth, and the plain before him now sparkled with all the glory of heaven itself. Each and every soldier had a lighted wax taper affixed to the blade of his spear – fifty thousand earthstars shining with bright-flecked rays, illuminating the camp with a clear and holy light.

The glow from that light sustained Alexius through the long, restless night, and was with him still when he rode out at the head of his troops before dawn. The imperial cavalry crossed the Maritsa a few miles upstream of the encamped enemy, formed the battalions, and waited for daybreak. They attacked from the east, with the light of the rising sun at their backs. To the sleep-sotted barbarians, it seemed as if the warhost of heaven was streaming down upon them from out of the sun.

Alexius struck the confused mass at the centre of the Pecheneg and Bogomil horde. It was a swift, sharp thrust into the belly of the beast, and he was away again before the barbarian battlehorns had sounded the call to arms. Having roused and enraged the enemy, he fell back -- just out of reach of their slings and spears -- and waited for them to make their counter attack.

The invaders, eager to avenge the assault, hastily formed a battleline and began their plodding advance. The imperial defenders looked out on a single vast, clotted mass of bellowing barbarians – less an ordered line than an enormous human tidal wave rolling across the land – and heard the deep jarring bone-rattling thump of the drums, the strident, sense-numbing blare of the huge, curved battlehorns, and the defiant cries of the warriors as they swept towards them with quickening pace.

It was a display calculated to produce terror in the beholder; it was their chief weapon, and one which served them well; with it, they had conquered tribe and nation, overrunning all they surveyed. The empire's soldiers had faced it before, however, and the sight and sound of barbarians massing for their attack no longer inspired shock or dismay, no longer quelled the heart in terror, or swallowed the senses in panic. The Immortals gazed with narrowed eyes and tightened their grip on lances and reins, calmed their horses with gently whispered words, and waited.

Flanked on either side by his standard-bearers – one lofting the purple banner of the Holy Roman Empire, the other the golden vexillum – Alexius looked across to his officers, the strategi, who anchored the long ranks at the centre of either wing. The foremost of these was a seasoned veteran of the Pecheneg wars, a man named Taticius, whose fearlessness and shrewdness had often saved lives and won battles. The emperor signalled his general, who sang out in a strong voice: 'Slow march!'

The trumpets sounded a single, shrill blast, and the troops started forth as one. The imperial formation -- two divisions, each made up of ten regiments in ranks, five deep, and a hundred riders to the rank – moved in close concert with one another; shoulder to shoulder and knee to knee, the riders formed a wall not easily breached or broken. Their long lances kept the foe out of reach of their horses, and themselves out of reach of barbarian axes and war hammers. Once in motion, there was little on the ground that could withstand a charge of mounted warriors.

Taticius gave the sign, the trumpets blared again, and the riders quickened their pace. The invaders met this with a shout, and came on. Fifty paces later, the trumpets sounded a third time, and the riders doubled their speed. The horses, trained to combat, strained at the reins, excited for the coming clash; but the riders held them back, waiting for the signal.

Faster and faster came the barbarians, the sound of their screams and drums and horns shaking the very earth and air, drowning out the thunder of the onrushing hooves. At the strategus' signal, the trumpets shrilled once more. Ten thousand lances swung level.

The two forces closed upon one another at speed. As the gap swiftly narrowed, the trumpets gave out a last signal and the horsemen put spurs to their mounts and let them run.

For the space of two heartbeats, the world was a churning chaos of blurred motion as the two onrushing armies fell upon each other. The clash sounded a mighty crack which echoed from the surrounding hills, and ten thousand barbarians fell. Many of these were trampled down and their brains dashed out beneath the iron hooves of the emperor's horses; the rest met death at the point of a Byzantine spear.

The charge carried the emperor and his troops deep into the barbarian mass. The screaming hordes, seeing the gleaming gold and purple standards, leapt over one another in their frenzy to strike down the Elect of Heaven. But Alexius, mindful of the danger of allowing the enemy to surround his division, had instructed Taticius to signal the retreat as soon as the assault foundered. Accordingly, the trumpets sounded above the barbarian shriek and, with practised ease, the imperial soldiers disengaged, fleeing back over the bodies of the dead and dying.

The enemy, seeing the horsemen turn away, pounded on in blood-blind pursuit, screaming as they ran. They chased the fleeing horse-men – only to be met with another measured charge by oncoming cavalry. The emperor, having had time to halt the retreat, had turned his troops and reformed the ranks; Alexius, with five thousand horse-men behind him, spurred his division into the centre of the oncoming barbarian battlehost.

The barbarians, neither so quick nor so tightly clumped as before, were more cautious this time. They tried to dodge the spears and hooves, to allow the horses to pass and stab at the riders as they swept by. The Byzantines had long acquaintance with this tactic, however, and were not easily outflanked. The ranks behind covered for the line ahead, and the barbarians could not close on those they sought to strike. Indeed, most were fortunate not to be cut down as they darted into position.

The charge ground to a halt, and the imperial troops made good their retreat, falling back the instant the attack faltered. They fled back across a battleground now deep with Pecheneg and Bogomil dead. This time, however, they did not regroup and charge again, but fled up the hill.

The enemy, believing they had beaten the Byzantines, quickly reformed the line. The drums began beating, and the horns blaring, and they marched ahead once more, but slowly this time. Two disastrous charges had taught them respect for the elusive horsemen.

Nicetas, who had been waiting on the hilltop, joined the emperor, and said, 'The Cuman are growing restless, basileus. They say that if they are not allowed to fight before midday, they will leave the battlefield.'

'It is a long time to midday,' Alexius replied. 'Their patience is soon rewarded. See here!' He pointed to the approaching horde. No longer a single amorphous line, the barbarians had separated themselves into three distinct bodies, each under the leadership of a battlechief. 'Tell our vengeful friends that we will soon deliver their enemies into their hands. Warn them to be vigilant.'

Nicetas saluted, turned his horse and galloped back to his position. The emperor returned to the head of his troops to lead the next assault. Aware that he was embarking on the most dangerous phase of the battle, Alexius uttered a brief prayer and crossed himself. Reining in among his standard-bearers once more, he signalled to Taticius, who turned and shouted the order: 'Slow march!'

The trumpets sounded, and the long ranks of horsemen stepped out. The invaders reacted to the movement by increasing the distance between their divisions. Alexius could see that if he gave them half a chance, the enemy would try to outflank him. Should the barbarian horde succeed, the balance of the battle would shift perilously.

Alexius watched the two enemy clusters moving farther out on either side of the central host. Behind the three advancing bodies, he could see the rest of the enemy horde taking up the positions vacated by the three advancing groups.

They were learning, he thought; their battles with the empire over the years was teaching them the rudiments of tactical warfare. Each encounter was more difficult to win, and more costly: all the more reason to make certain it ended here and now. He raised his hand and signalled his strategus. An instant later the trumpets sounded their high clarion call, and the imperial troops surged ahead.

As expected, the moment Alexius committed himself to his attack, the enemy's two flanking bodies turned and drove in on either side. At the same time, the greater host behind swept in to surround and crush the Immortals.

As before, the attack was halted by the dense numbers of foemen, who absorbed the assault with their shields and bodies. The horse soldiers abandoned their lances and took up swords to slash their way free of the enemy's grasp. Glancing quickly to the right and left, Alexius saw the enemy divisions closing swiftly. He gave Taticius the sign, and the trumpets sounded retreat.

Crouching low, Alexius jerked the reins back hard, wheeled his mount and led the Byzantines in full flight up the hill. The barbarians, amazed at the ease with which they had blunted the imperial attack, rushed forward to press their advantage. The three main bodies, followed by the great rolling wave – twenty thousand barbarians wide and twenty deep – swept on up the hill at a run, determined not to allow the Byzantines enough time to regroup for another charge.

With an earth-trembling roar, the barbarians rushed to the kill, their feet pounding the hillside, weapons gleaming in the bright sunlight. The Immortals, unable to order the ranks and prepare the charge, had no other choice but to retreat further up the hill. The trumpets shrilled the call to retreat.

Within moments, the imperial horsemen were fleeing the field, cresting the hill and disappearing over the other side. The barbarians, screaming in triumph, pounded after them, baying for blood.

Upon reaching the hilltop, the enemy saw the Immortals galloping down the far slope towards a loop of the river. Eager to catch the horsemen as they floundered through the ford, the barbarians flew after the retreating troops, shrieking in triumph.

Down and down they came, streaming headlong into the valley, racing for the river. As the first barbarians reached the fording place, however, ten thousand foot soldiers suddenly appeared on either flank. Hidden in the rushes at the water's edge, the imperial infantry rose up with a shout. At the same instant, the Immortals turned their horses and started back, throwing the barbarians into a howling panic.

Desperate now to retake the high ground lest they find themselves pinched between the two opposing forces, the foemen turned and fled back the way they had come.

It was then that the Cuman mercenaries appeared on the hilltop behind them: an entire barbarian nation, thirty thousand strong, and each and every one of them nursing a long-standing hatred of their Pecheneg and Bogomil neighbours.

The trap was sprung, and the slaughter commenced.

Alexius, confident of the outcome, withdrew from the battle. Summoning his Varangian bodyguard, he charged Dalassenus to bring word as soon as the victory was complete, then rode at once to his tent.

That was where the Grand Drungarius found the emperor, bathed, shaved, dressed in his clean robes, dictating a letter to the Magister Praepositus, who was taking Alexius' words and inscribing them on a wax tablet.

'Ah, Dalassenus! Enter!' he called as the young man appeared behind Gerontius. He waved the chief scribe away, saying, 'That is all – bring it to me to sign as soon as you are finished. It will be sent immediately.' The scribe bowed once and withdrew. 'Well? Tell me, how did the battle end?'

'As you predicted, basileus,' answered the commander.

'Indeed?'

'Down to the last detail. The Cuman auxiliary were merciless. Once they had the scent of blood in their nostrils, we had no need to engage the Immortals. We merely stood by to prevent the survivors escaping into the hills.' He paused, and added, 'There were no survivors.'

'Gerontius, did you hear?' called the emperor. 'Our victory is absolute! Pour the wine! Dalassenus and I will drink to the triumph.'

The elderly magister bent to the table, and turned a moment later bearing golden cups. The emperor lofted one of the cups and said, 'All praise to God, who has delivered our enemies into our hands, and driven them into the dust of death!'

'All praise to God,' the Grand Drungarius answered.

They drank together and Alexius, laying aside his cup quickly, said, 'See here, Dalassenus. I have already sent messengers back to the city. The ships will be ready to sail upon your arrival. It is a cruel thing to dispatch a man fresh from the battlefield, I know. But you will have a good few days' rest aboard ship.'

The young commander nodded. 'It is no hardship, basileus, I assure you.'

'It is not that I do not trust the Logothete or the Syneculla,' Alexius continued. 'Indeed, they will go with you. But this is primarily a military matter, and the Patriarch of Rome must know the importance I place on the victory we have achieved today, and how much I value his aid. Now that the northern border is secure, we can turn our attention to the south and east.'

The emperor began pacing back and forth, clenching his fists. 'We can begin taking back the lands the Arabs have stolen. At long last, all we have worked for is within our grasp. Think of it, Dalassenus!'

Alexius stopped, regaining control of his free-racing hopes. 'Alas, the army is not ready to meet the challenge.'

'Your troops fight well, basileus,' Dalassenus disagreed mildly. 'We could not ask for better soldiers, nor would we find them.'

'Do not misunderstand me. I agree: they are brave men – the most disciplined and courageous soldiers in the world – but they are too few. The constant warring has taken its toll, and we must begin rebuilding the themes. There is so much to be done, but it is within our very grasp now, and –'

The smile on Dalassenus' face arrested his kinsman's familiar tirade.

'Forgive me, cousin,' Alexius said, 'I am forgetting myself. You, who have been with me from the beginning, know it all as well as I. Better, perhaps, in many respects.'

Dalassenus turned to the table, refilled the emperor's cup and handed it to him. 'Let us savour the victory a moment longer, basileus.' Raising his cup, he said, 'For the glory of God, and the welfare of the empire.'

'Amen!' replied the emperor, adding, 'May the peace we have won this day last a thousand years.'

THREE

Murdo wilted under the abbot's interminable prayers and wished he was far away from Kirkjuvágr. His knees ached from kneeling so long, and the smoke from the incense made his empty stomach queasy. The dim interior of the great church reminded him of a cave: dank and cool and dark. Save for a smattering of candles around the altar, and a few tiny slit windows, he might have been deep in an earth-howe, or one of the ancient chambered tombs scattered among the low hills. Outside it was balmy midsummer, but here inside the cathedral it was, ever and always, dreary mid-November.

Craning his neck sharply to the right, he could see the stern countenances of saints Luke and John staring from the nearest wall in sharp disapproval at his fidgeting. Higher up, under the roof-tree, a frog-eyed gargoyle grinned down from a corbel – as if in merry mockery of Murdo's growing discomfort. To his left knelt his mother and father, and before him his brothers and cousin. None of them, he knew, shared his distress, which made it all the worse.

The Feast of Saint John was one of the few holy days Murdo truly enjoyed, and here he was spending it in the worst way possible. If he had been at the bú, the morning service would have been over long since and he would be filling himself with roast pork and barley wine. Instead, he was trapped in a damp, dark cavern of a church listening to some lickspit priest gabble on and on and on in irksome Latin.

Why, of all possible days, did it have to be this one? He moaned inwardly, contemplating the ruin of the day. The waste of a good feast-day was a mortal sin, yet the bishop, in typical ignorant clerical selfishness, had decreed the Feast of Saint John for the cross-taking. The only consolation, and it was cold comfort indeed, lay in the fact that at least Murdo was not alone in his misery.

Indeed, the entire church was full and so was the yard outside –

full of men and women of rank, as well as merchants and tenants of various holdings large and small, from many of Orkney's low-scattered isles: hundreds of islanders in clutches and knots, all of them kneeling, like himself, heads down, faces almost touching the clammy stone, intoning their dull responses in a low, mumbled drone. Murdo imagined they were each and every one praying that the abbot would, for God's sake, stop.

Seeing them like this, their backs all bent, put Murdo in mind of a field of boulders, and it was all he could do to stop himself leaping up and making his escape by skipping from one humped back to the next like stepping stones. Instead, he lowered his head once more, squeezed his eyes shut, and tried not to think of the succulent roast pork and sweet ale he was missing.

When at last the ox-brained abbot *did* stop, Murdo rose to his feet, almost faint with hunger. He stared glumly, forlornly ahead, as yet another black-robed cleric ascended to the pulpit high above the upturned faces of the overcrowded sanctuary. Bishop Adalbert stood for a time, gazing beatifically down from his lofty perch. Satisfied that every eye was upon him, he thrust out his hands and declared, 'This is the favourable day of the Lord!'

'Amen,' the congregation mumbled. The response sounded to Murdo like the sea when it lies uneasy on the shore.

Again, the bishop put forth his hands and proclaimed, 'This is the favourable day of the Lord!'

'Amen,' muttered the crowd, sounding more and more like a fretful sea.

'Amen!' cried the bishop triumphantly. 'For this day our Saviour King will receive into his service men of faith who will fight for him in the Holy Land.'

The cleric retrieved a square of parchment and made a show of unfolding and opening it. 'This,' he explained, 'has lately come into my hands: an epistle from our holy father, the Patriarch of Rome, bearing his seal.' He flourished the parchment to show the red blot of wax and the golden cord. Holding the letter before him, Adalbert began, 'I read it thus: "Bishop Urban, servant of servants, to all the faithful of Christ, both rulers and subjects: Greetings, grace, and apostolic blessing. We know you have already heard that the frenzy of the barbarians has devastated the churches of God, and has, shame to say, seized into slavery the sacred relics of our faith, those blessed objects of veneration by which we recognize and proclaim the truth of our salvation. Alas! Not content to destroy our churches, the infidel have seized the Holy City of Jerusalem itself and would prevent God's people their rightful worship."'

The good bishop paused to allow his listeners to more fully savour this dire state of affairs. '"Grieving in pious contemplation of this disaster,"' Adalbert continued, making Murdo squirm, '"we strongly urge the princes and people of every western land to work for the liberation of the Eastern Church. Who shall avenge these wrongs, who will recover the relics and lands if not you? You, my people, are the race upon whom God has bestowed glory in arms, greatness of spirit, physical energy, and the courage to humble the proud locks of all those who resist you."'

Adalbert looked up from his reading to gaze upon the assembly as if to say, *I, too, have seen this glory, greatness and courage.* He then cleared his throat and continued. '"We have heard that some of you desire to go to Jerusalem. Know then, that anyone who sets out on this journey, not out of lust for worldly advantage but only for the salvation of his soul and for the liberation of the Church, is remitted in entirety,"' the bishop paused so to repeat this astounding offer with appropriate weight, '"***remitted in entirety*** all penance for his sins, if he has made a true and perfect act of confession.

'"O, most valiant knights, descendants of unconquerable ancestors, remember the courageous faith of your forefathers and do not dishonour it. I urge you to become Soldiers of Christ and follow the cross whereby you have received your strong salvation. For this purpose and to this end, we have appointed this a year of jubilee to be celebrated in the pursuit of Godliness and righteousness, the culmination of which is to be a pilgrimage to free Jerusalem from the wicked oppressor under which the Holy City languishes even now.

'"Beloved in Christ, if God calls you to this task, know that this Most Holy Crusade will set out, with the aid of God, the day following the feast of the Assumption of the Blessed Virgin. May Almighty God strengthen you in His love and fear, and bring you free from all sins and errors to the contemplation of perfect charity and true piety through this pilgrimage of faith."'

Here the bishop laid aside the epistle and, gazing benevolently over his congregation, said, 'Brothers and sisters, the day has come to declare our intentions in this holy enterprise. Whosoever would become a soldier for Christ, let them come forward now and, before this devout assembly, let them take the cross!'

At this, Murdo braced himself against the surge as the congregation started towards the pulpit. All around him, men and women were clamouring for the cross, reaching, stretching out their hands and calling on God to hear their heartfelt vows. The canny bishop was ready for the rush which met his invitation. No fewer than a dozen senior monks appeared on the dais below the high pulpit, each with a bundle of white cloth in his arms.

Murdo saw the bundles and, despite himself, his heart beat faster. *The crosses!* He had heard about the white cloth crosses, of course, and the thought that his brothers should receive them while he must go without was almost unbearable. He watched in an agony of jealous torment as the monks proceeded to distribute the white cloth crosses to the eager throng. The commotion of voices echoed among the roof beams like the din of bells.

When the crosses had been distributed all around, Bishop Adalbert instructed every recipient to kneel. He then led them in a vow of allegiance whereby they all swore a sacred oath never to abandon the holy pilgrimage so long as Jerusalem remained captive. His pilgrims duly forsworn, the bishop then took up his crozier and offered the benediction. 'God bless you and keep you, and make his face to shine upon you, and be gracious unto you now and forever. May victory be swift, and trials few, and may God speed your safe return. Amen.'

'Amen!' shouted the newly-recruited soldiers of Christ.

Murdo glared darkly at Torf and Skuli, who remained blissfully unaware of their younger brother's poisonous stare as they fingered the white cloth crosses and argued with Paul over whether it was best to wear them on the front or back. The interminable service finally over, Lord Ranulf led his family out of the church. Murdo shuffled after them, head down, defeated, and collided with Paul when the family was halted just outside the door by a monk in a brown robe. The cleric exchanged a brief word with Ranulf, who made a courteous reply, and then turned and announced, 'We have all been invited to observe the feast at the bishop's table.'

Murdo heard this and hope rekindled in his heart. The bishop's board was renowned throughout the isles, and second only to the jarl's table. Murdo allowed himself a smile at his unexpected good fortune. The bishop's table! Such lavish bounty, such wild abundance – who could have foreseen it?

The monk led them across the crowded courtyard, through an arched doorway, and into a sunny, cloistered square where at least ten long tables had been erected on the green. There were a good many people already gathered here and, to Murdo's increasing dismay, more, and still more guests, were arriving by way of other doors along the cloisters.

As no one had been given leave to sit, everyone swarmed onto the green, eagerly awaiting the summons to dine. There were so many! Had the bishop invited the entire congregation? By even the most casual estimation, Murdo reckoned he would be fortunate indeed to get so much as a gravy-soaked crust. And this, a true feast-day – in Murdo's regard, second only to the Christ Mass at Yuletide. All the other festal days, so far as Murdo could see, were unutterably dull and tedious, requiring, as they did, mass and prayers and obscure observances of various kinds. And anyway they were not true feasts at all since no special food was ever laid on, and chores still had to be done despite spending the whole day in church, which meant that he often ended up working in the dark, a thing Murdo loathed.

Saint John's day, however, was different. Though he still had to go to church, that hardship was made more endurable by the fact that, however long the services – and they could be bone-achingly endless – there was the promise of good meat and ale and cakes afterwards. Occasionally, one or another of the priests was invited to Ranulf's board – an invitation, Murdo noticed, that was never, ever declined – and this made the festivities even better. Though Murdo resented the clerical intrusion, at least when monks were present the lord and lady tended to offer more lavish fare. Also, folk from neighbouring farms often joined in, bringing food and drink with them so that the resulting feast was a celebration worthy of the name. What is more, falling as it did at midsummer, the festivities of this special day would inevitably extend far into the long-lingering twilight.

But now . . . now it was all ruined. Murdo watched the multitude assembling and his heart sank; he could not see how so many people could be fed, let alone feasted. There were not enough cakes and ale in all Orkneyjar to fill them. His stomach rumbled and he abandoned any hope of an adequate meal.

He was still occupied with this grim thought when he heard someone hail his father, and glumly looked around to see who might be joining them at the table. He saw a man he knew – Lord Brusi Maddardson – striding purposefully towards them across the green with his family straggling along in his wake.

Like Lord Ranulf, the Maddardson clan farmed a large estate on the island of Hrolfsey and consequently attended the same councils as Murdo's father. What is more, Murdo's mother and Lady Ragnhild were childhood companions, and had maintained a warm friendship over many years. The lord of Hrolfsey had three sons, the youngest of which was Torf's age, and one daughter, Ragna, who was only a year or two older than Murdo.

Owing to his age, Murdo had never been of interest to the brothers Maddardson, who always preferred the company of Torf and Skuli to the point of excluding Murdo entirely – not that Murdo minded overmuch, for he found the older boys frivolous and loud, interested only in fighting, boasting, and besting one another.

Ah, but Lord Brusi's daughter was as different from her brothers as moonbeams from muck. She was, in Murdo's opinion, the sole saving grace of the entire Maddardson tribe. And this day, with its relentless indignities and insults, he had need of the sweet solace he always felt in her presence. Indeed, but one glance at the golden-haired Ragna approaching across the greensward, and the low dark clouds of despair parted and the sun shone full on Murdo again.

Tall and willowy, and with a fair and shapely form, the smooth-skinned Ragna embodied Murdo's idea of female charm. She possessed a kindly disposition, but was neither overly timid, nor too fastidiously female for Murdo's liking. Intelligent, and with a ready tongue to match, she held her own in any company, and Murdo respected that. To Murdo, her forthright demeanour seemed more boyish than maidenly, and it always struck him anew whenever they met; on those rare occasions, he wondered if it resulted from the fact that she was raised in a family of men, or whether her nature was in some way ordained by her childhood deformity.

The way Murdo heard it, she had been but a toddling babe when Lord Brusi's swineherd, upon hearing a squealing commotion, discovered her lifeless body in a field the pigs were gleaning. Upon driving off a recently-farrowed sow, he scooped up the child and, thinking only to wash away the mud and blood from the little mauled corpse, plunged her into the water trough. The cold shock revived her, whereupon the astonished swineherd ran with the screaming babe all the way back to the house where her wounds were swiftly tended. The damage was done, however; her badly-mangled foot had never straightened, resulting in a stutter-step limp. The horrid gash to her mouth had healed in time, and was not usually noticed until she smiled: the hair-thin scar lifted the corner of her lip slightly, making her appear always somewhat sly and subtly mocking.

None of this mattered to Murdo; he had never considered these flaws to mar her beauty. To him, she was good and kind and smart, and far, far better than her brothers, or his own. Those few and infrequent times when they were together, he always came away with a craving for more – as if a feast had been spread before him and he had received but a single taste.

He looked at her now, dressed in a gown of pale green, with a yellow mantle, and he thought she had never looked so womanly. His heart quickened. He drank in the sight of her, and felt a quiver of joy leap up within him; and the ruin of the day receded.

Then he remembered he was not alone. Murdo's gaze shifted quickly to where Torf, Skuli, and Paul stood, as yet unaware that they were about to be joined by the Maddardson tribe. Good, he thought, and breathed easier; they had not seen her.

Then Torf looked up, saw the approaching clan, and nudged Skuli; Paul turned his gaze to where the others were looking, and Murdo watched beastly grins appear on all three faces. Skuli made a crude gesture with his thumb and fingers, and then all three sniggered obscenely. Murdo, embarrassed beyond words, wished the ground would open and swallow them whole.

For her part, Ragna gazed steadily and placidly ahead, her clear hazel eyes untroubled beneath the delicate arches of her fine brows, her lips neither smiling nor frowning, her elegant features impassive to all that occurred around her. Indeed, it seemed to Murdo that though their feet touched the common turf, Ragna walked in flowered fields far beyond the cathedral's cloistered walls. Obviously, the dull proceedings around her were unworthy of her regard. And why not? Ragna was finer than any mere princess, after all.

Lord Brusi and Lady Ragnhild greeted his parents, and the Lord of Hrolfsey presented his sons to the Lord and Lady of Dýrness. Murdo could not help noticing that the men, lord and sons alike, clutched white cloth crosses. Torf and the others noticed, too, and joined their friends in noisy exultation of their high honour while both lords beamed proudly over their respective broods and pronounced upon the certain success of the pilgrimage. The ladies, meanwhile, exchanged more solemn words; Niamh led Ragnhild aside and the two stood head-to-head, clutching one another's hands and talking earnestly.

Murdo, unable to hear what they said, turned and found himself unexpectedly alone with Ragna. The shock made his poor empty stomach squirm and his hands grew moist.

'Greetings, Master Murdo,' she said, and, oh! her voice was like burned honey, all liquid sweetness and smoke.

Even if she were not a very vision in Murdo's eyes, he would still have found her ravishing for the sound of her voice alone. She had only to speak a single word and the rich, low, luscious tone sparked fire in his deepest heart. If to other ears Ragna's speech seemed a little too hoarse, perhaps, and lacking the natural mellifluence of a well-born maiden, Murdo considered that where other girls twittered, Ragna purred.

'It is a pleasant day, is it not?' Ragna inquired innocently. She looked at him from beneath her eyelashes and Murdo felt the blood rush to his face. His throat tightened, and he could not breathe.

Murdo opened his mouth to reply . . . only to discover he had misplaced the power of speech and was completely mute.

'I believe we are to observe the feast together,' she continued, unaware of his affliction. 'Or, so it would appear.'

'Very pleasant, indeed, Mistress Ragna.' The response surprised Murdo, who did not recognize the utterance as his own.

She regarded him demurely, and seemed to be expecting him to say something more. 'I have always liked Saint John,' he blurted, and instantly wished he had never been born.

'I like him, too,' Ragna laughed, and the sound drew the sting from his stupidity.

'The feast, I mean,' Murdo hastily corrected. 'It is my favourite feast-day – apart from the Christ Mass, I mean.' *Fool!* he shrieked inwardly. *I mean – I mean . . . Is that all you can say? Idiot!*

'Oh, indeed,' agreed Ragna happily, 'the Feast of Christ is by far the best. But I like Eastertide, too.'

40

There followed an awkward silence as Murdo struggled desperately to think of something else to say. Ragna rescued him. 'I see you do not carry a cross.'

Murdo gazed down at his empty hands in remorse. He shook his head. 'My brothers are going,' he admitted woodenly. 'I am to stay behind to help look after the bú.'

Although he expected Ragna to spurn him, now that the awful truth was known, his confession produced a wonderful result. The young woman hesitated, glanced left and right quickly, and leaned forward, boldly placing one long-fingered hand on his sleeve. The skin of his arm burned beneath her touch. 'Good! I am glad of it,' she whispered, adding a nod for emphasis.

Murdo did not know which astonished him more, her hand on his arm, or the conspiratorial glee with which she imparted her extraordinary assertion.

'Good?' wondered Murdo, his head spinning.

Ragna fixed him with a clear and steady eye. 'It is not a pilgrimage, but a *war*.' She said the word as if it were the worst thing she knew. 'That is what my mother says, and it is the truth.'

Murdo stared, unable to think what to say. *Of course it is a war!* he thought. There would be no point in going otherwise. But to speak that sentiment aloud would immediately place him outside the balmy warmth of Ragna's confidence and, having just acquired it, he was loath to abandon it so quickly. 'It is that,' he muttered vaguely, which satisfied her.

'My mother and I are staying, too,' Ragna informed him proudly. 'Perhaps we shall see one another again soon.'

Before he could reply, Lady Ragnhild noticed them talking and called her daughter to her. Without another word, Ragna spun on her heel and rejoined the women – but Murdo thought he saw her smile at him as she turned away.

FOUR

'A disaster of undeniable magnitude,' groaned Alexius.

'Certainly unforeseen, basileus,' offered Nicetas helpfully.

The emperor shook his head, venting another groan of mingled anger and despair. He stood with a small retinue of advisors – the sacrii consistori, and the commander of the palace guard – on the wall above the Golden Gate, looking out upon the dark ungainly flood creeping towards the city from the west with a strange, almost dreamlike lethargy.

For three days Constantinople had been receiving reports – often contradictory – regarding the size and direction of this slow-moving invasion, and now, for the first time, the invader could be seen. Ignoring the road for the most part, they simply sprawled across the plain in ragged clots and clumps, rolling recklessly over the land in an untidy mass.

At the sound of hurried footsteps, the emperor turned. 'Well, Dalassenus, what have you discovered?'

'They are indeed Franks, basileus,' he said, pausing to catch his breath. 'But they are peasants.'

'Peasants!'

'For the most part, basileus,' Dalassenus continued. 'There are but a handful of soldiers among them. Nevertheless, they insist they are coming at the Patriarch's behest, and what is more, they are on pilgrimage to the Holy Land.'

'Indeed?' Alexius turned his eyes once more towards the straggling flood. 'Pilgrims!' he shook his head in dismay. 'We cannot possibly protect them. Do they know that, Dalassenus?'

'They say they do not require our aid in any way,' the commander answered. 'They say God Almighty protects them.'

'Extraordinary,' sighed the emperor, shaking his head again. The dust from the feet of this rag-tag invasion rose into the clear summer

42

sky. The day would be hot; no doubt the pilgrims would welcome water before they reached the city walls. Alexius, already calculating how best to fend off the swarm, began arranging the distribution of water.

'There is more, basileus,' said the drungarius, breaking into the emperor's thoughts.

'Tell us, Dalassenus, what else?'

'They are led by a priest named Peter, who believes they have been commanded by the Patriarch of Rome to liberate Jerusalem from the rule of the infidel. It is their intention to do so.'

This pronouncement brought a laugh from Nicetas and some of the others on the wall. 'Liberate Jerusalem!' scoffed one of the advisors. 'Are they insane, these peasants?'

'They say Bishop Urban has called for every Christian to take the cross and go on pilgrimage to fight the Saracens.'

'The Saracens?' wondered Nicetas. 'We have not been troubled by the Saracens for more than thirty years.'

'Fifty years,' suggested another of his advisors.

Alexius had heard enough. 'Nicetas, find this Peter and bring him to us. We would speak to him and learn his true intentions.' The commander of the excubitori made a salute and departed on the run. The emperor, taking one last look at the slow-approaching horde, shook his head in disbelief, then hurried off to await the arrival of his unwelcome guest.

He did not have long to wait, for he had just finished donning his robes of state when word of Nicetas' return reached him. Moving from the inner chamber to the audience room, he mounted the dais and took his place on the throne, the Holy Scriptures beside him on a purple cushion; Grand Drungarius Dalassenus, together with the emperor's usual assortment of court officials and advisors, stood behind the dais, solemn and mirthless, exuding a sombre gravity befitting the seriousness of the extremity facing the empire.

Taking his place quickly, Alexius, nodding to the magister officiorum, said, 'Bring him.'

A moment later the magister struck the white marble floor with his rod of office, and the great gilded doors of the Salamos Hall swung open. In marched Nicetas, followed by four of the imperial guard – one at each corner – leading a large, thick-set shambling man, tonsured and barefoot, and dressed in the dun-coloured hooded cloak and ankle-length mantle of a rural Roman cleric.

Excubitor Nicetas, sweating from his ride in the heat of the day, advanced quickly to the foot of the throne, prostrated himself, and rose at his sovereign's command to say, 'Lord Basileus, I give you Peter of Amiens.'

The rustic priest, suitably awed by the wealth of his surroundings, gazed with wonder at the exalted being on the throne before him. Upon hearing his name, he pitched forward onto his face and seized the emperor by the foot, which he kissed respectfully, saying, 'Hail, Sovereign Lord, your willing servant salutes you.'

'Rise, and stand on your feet,' said Alexius sternly. The man rose, shaking his clothes back in the same motion; with his tattered cloak and filthy mantle he looked like a vagrant bird which, having bathed in the dust, now settled its bedraggled feathers.

'They tell us you are the leader of these pilgrim peasants,' the emperor said. 'Is this true?'

'By no means, Lord Emperor,' replied Peter. 'I am but a poor hermit granted by God and His Holiness Pope Urban the divine favour of going on pilgrimage to the Holy Land.'

'You know, of course, that martyrdom awaits you,' Alexius informed him, 'should you be so fortunate as to reach Jerusalem.'

At this the hermit priest drew himself up to full height. 'Lord and Emperor, it is our very great privilege to wrest the lands of our Saviour from the evil infidel. With Almighty God as our protector, this we will do.'

'The Arabs will oppose you,' the emperor stated, watching the man before him. 'How do you plan to win Jerusalem?'

'If necessary,' the hermit replied, 'we will fight.'

'It will most certainly become necessary – of that we can assure you,' Alexius said, feeling his anger stir within. 'The Arabs are fearless in battle, and their resolve is legendary. Where are your weapons? Where are your supplies? Have you any siege engines? Have you the tools to make bridges, dig wells, scale walls?'

'What we need,' answered the cleric placidly, 'the Good Lord provides.'

'And has the Good Lord provided any soldiers for your army?'

'He has, Lord Emperor,' answered Peter, shaking back his cloak once more. There was more than a touch of self-righteous defiance in his stance and tone.

'How many?'

'We have eight knights with us. They are led by the most devout Walter Sansavoir of Poissy.'

'Eight,' repeated Alexius. 'Did you hear that, Nicetas? They have eight mounted soldiers.' Turning once more to the priest, he asked, 'Do you know how many warriors Sultan Arslan commands?'

Peter, uncertain, hesitated.

'Too late you show a little wisdom, my friend,' the emperor said. 'Very well, I will tell you, shall I? The sultan has forty thousand in his private bodyguard alone. Forty thousand mounted warriors against your eight.'

'We are sixty thousand strong,' Peter proclaimed proudly. 'We are God's own army.'

'*We* command God's own army, priest!' cried Alexius, unable to control his anger any longer. '*You* are a rabble!'

The emperor's shout echoed in the hall like the crack of thunder. He leapt from his chair and stood towering over the unfortunate priest. 'What is more, you are a wayward and undisciplined rabble. We have heard how you have plundered your way through Dalmatia and Moesia, looting towns and settlements to provide yourselves with food and supplies.' He turned his head to the Captain of the Excubitori. 'We are not at war with Dalmatia and Moesia, are we, Nicetas?' he inquired with mock innocence.

'No, basileus,' the commander replied, 'the people there are citizens of the empire.'

'You see!' cried Alexius. 'You have attacked dutiful citizens whose only fault lay in the fact that they happened to live in the path of your thieving mob.'

'They were Jews,' Peter pointed out smugly. 'We have vowed before the Throne of Christ to rid the world of all God's enemies.'

'Your vow was ill-spoken, priest. You have neither right nor authority to swear such a thing. You are above yourself, and we will not suffer these transgressions lightly,' Alexius declared, glaring hard at the ignorant cleric. After a moment, he appeared to soften. 'Nevertheless, despite your flagrant and lamentable trespasses, we will make a bargain with you. In exchange for peace while within imperial borders, we will give you food and water while you are here in Constantinople; further, we will arrange safe conduct for you back the way you came.'

'With all respect, Emperor and Lord,' the hermit replied, 'that I cannot do, for we are sworn to liberate Jerusalem at all costs.'

'Then you must be prepared to pay that cost with your lives,' Alexius declared. 'For truly, you will not escape with less.' He paused, drumming his fingers on the arms of his throne. 'Is there nothing we can say to persuade you to turn back?'

The rustic priest made no reply.

'Very well,' conceded Alexius, 'we will see you safely across the Bosphorus, at least. And may God have mercy on you all.'

Humbled at last, the tattered hermit bowed and accepted his lord's generosity with simple thanks.

'Hear me, Peter of Amiens,' Alexius warned, 'you proceed at your peril. Take our advice and turn back. Without protection and supplies, your pilgrimage will fail.'

'As God wills,' he replied stiffly. 'We look to the Almighty for our aid and protection.'

Alexius, still fuming, glared at the mule-headed cleric and decided there was no point in prolonging the misery; with a flick of the imperial hand, he ended the audience and directed Nicetas to take him away. When they had gone, the emperor turned to Dalassenus. 'This is that incompetent Urban's doing, and he will bitterly regret it. His insufferable interference has brought us nothing but hardship . . . and now this!'

The emperor stared at his commander, his brow furrowed in thought. After a moment, he said, 'Can it be that he has misunderstood our intentions?'

'I do not see how that could be possible, basileus,' Dalassenus replied. 'Your letter was most explicit. He had it read out before his bishops, and you have received his favourable reply.'

'Even so, something has gone wrong,' Alexius declared. 'I asked for an army to help fill the ranks and restore the themes. I said nothing about a pilgrimage to the Holy Land.'

'No, basileus,' agreed Dalassenus firmly.

The emperor shook his head. 'I fear I must ask you to return to Rome, cousin. We must learn what that old meddler has done, and take measures to prevent any more citizens coming to harm. You will leave at once, and may God go with you.'

FIVE

'I have spoken to Guthorm Wry-Neck,' Lord Brusi was saying as Murdo drifted near, 'and he said the ship will leave Kirkjuvágr the day after the Feast of Saint James, God willing.'

'That soon?' His father sounded surprised. 'It cannot take so long to reach Lundein.'

Brusi only nodded. 'That is what he said.'

'But the harvest will not be finished,' Ranulf pointed out.

'Aye,' Brusi agreed. 'There is no help for it, I fear. We must reach Rouen by mid-August and no later if we are to travel with the king's men.'

'Yes, yes, I see that,' Lord Ranulf agreed. 'Still, I had not thought we would be leaving so soon.'

Their conversation was cut short by the arrival of Bishop Adalbert, who called his guests to table – the women to tables on the right, and men to the left. In the eager, but not undignified, rush which ensued, Murdo found himself squeezed onto a bench between two merchantmen of more than ample girth. The one on his left eyed him disapprovingly – as if he feared that Murdo's presence might turn feast into fast; but the man on the right winked at him and smiled. 'Going to Jerusalem are you, boy?'

'I am not, sir,' replied Murdo in a tone that dared his listener to pursue the matter further.

'Ah,' the merchant nodded sagely, and Murdo could not tell whether he thought this a good thing or not. 'I am Gundrun,' he said, 'and I give you good greeting, young man.'

'God be good to you, sir,' replied Murdo; he gave his name, and pointed out his father and brothers sitting a few places further down the bench, and identified them to his listener.

The merchant on the left took this in with a heavy grunt, where-upon Gundrun said, 'Do not mind him, Murdo Ranulfson; he is

47

always out of temper – is that not so, Dufnas? Never more so than on a feast-day following mass.' The man on the left grunted again and turned his surly attention elsewhere.

A monk appeared just then, carrying a tall stack of round, flat loaves of bread. He passed along the bench, placing a loaf before each guest. 'Here now,' said Gundrun, 'the food arrives.'

Murdo looked at the solitary loaf, and searched the length of the board in vain for anything resembling a bowl or cup, but saw none anywhere and knew his worst fears confirmed: nothing but dry bread for him today, and not so much as a sip of water to wash it down. Unable to keep his disappointment to himself any longer, he shared his gloomy opinion with his stout companion.

But Gundrun only winked at him again, and said, 'Have faith, my friend.'

As if in response to these hopeful words, there came a commotion across the square, and Murdo saw what he took to be a procession emerge from the cloisters. Pairs of monks – dozens of them, all carrying fully-laden trenchers between them – appeared on the green and proceeded at once to the tables, where they delivered their burdens and hastened away.

Almost before the starving Murdo could wonder whether a single platter would suffice for the entire table, two more appeared, and then two more, so that each trencher served a pair of guests either side of the board. While the monks scurried after more platters, still other clerics delivered silver bowls of salt to the table, placing them within reach of the diners.

Murdo gaped at the mound of food before him. Rarely had he seen such a profusion of roast fowl: quail, doves, grouse, and pheasant. Nor was that all, for there were quartered ducks, and the smaller carcasses of larks and blackbirds, and, scattered throughout, the eggs of each of these birds.

The platter had no sooner touched the board than Murdo's hands were reaching for the nearest bird. His fist closed on the leg of a small duck and he pulled it from the pile, loosening a quail, which tumbled onto the table before him. Gundrun, beside him, and the two diners opposite, helped themselves as well, and a singular hush fell upon the green. Murdo finished the duck and, grease dripping from chin and fingers, started on the quail.

'Good tuck, boy, no?' exclaimed Gundrun tossing bones behind him, and Murdo, mouth too full to reply, nodded enthusiastically.

Murdo finished the quail and helped himself to a pheasant, tearing long strips of meat from the breast of the bird with his teeth. He was thus employed when two monks arrived at his place with a steaming cauldron. Murdo watched with interest as a third monk dipped a cannikin into the larger pot and proceeded to pour the contents onto the flat bread before him, before moving on to Gundrun, and so on down the bench.

Murdo stared at the pottage; it was a deep red colour, which he had never seen in a stew before. 'Mawmenny,' sighed Gundrun contentedly. Lowering his face to the meal, he sniffed expertly. 'Ah, yes! Enchanting!'

Murdo had heard of the dish – said to be served in the halls of kings – but had never seen it. He put his head down and caught the mild, somewhat delicate scent of cherries. Dipping the tip of his finger into the sauce, he found it produced an unexpected, though not unpleasant, warm tingle on his tongue together with the taste of beef and plums.

Following Gundrun's example, he took a lump of meat between his fingers and thumb and chewed thoughtfully, savouring the rich intermingling of unusual flavours. He then proceeded to devour the rest of the mawmenny without lifting his face from the board until he had finished each succulent morsel. He was only prevented from licking the now-empty bread trencher by the abrupt appearance of a monk who took it up and replaced it with a fresh one.

What a splendid feast! thought Murdo, looking down the board to see the next delicacy just arriving. He saw his father, deep in conversation with Lord Brusi, and his brothers stuffing their faces and laughing loudly with Brusi's sons. Across the yard at one of the women's tables, he thought he saw his mother leaning across to Lady Ragnhild. Just as he made to look away again, his eye shifted and he caught sight of Ragna, gazing directly at him, her expression at once shrewd and thoughtful. She was watching him and he had caught her; but she did not look away, nor did her expression change. She continued staring at him, until two monks carrying a cauldron passed between them and removed her from his sight – but not before Murdo had seen, for the second time that day, the secret smile playing on those sly lips.

Distracted and confused, Murdo addressed himself once more to his meal and his companions. Gundrun proved himself not only an amiable table companion, but a veritable fountain of knowledge. He had travelled widely; his trade took him throughout the north and into Gaul. Once, he had even made a pilgrimage to Rome. Thus, when Murdo asked him where Rouen might be, the older man replied, 'Why, it is in Normandy, if I am not mistaken.'

'Who is king there?' wondered Murdo.

'That would be William Rufus, King of England,' Gundrun told him. 'Are you thinking of joining the pilgrimage after all?'

'No,' Murdo confessed. 'I heard my father talking about it. They are to go to Normandy and travel with the king's men.'

'Ah, no doubt you mean William's *son*, Duke Robert of Normandy,' corrected the merchant gently. 'It seems he is to lead the Normans and English to Jerusalem – along with some others, of course. There are very many knights and men-at-arms travelling together, you see. At least, that is what I have heard.'

This brought a snarl of disapproval from Dufnas, sitting next to Murdo. Gundrun replied, 'What is it to you, my friend, whether the Franks send a blind dog to lead the pilgrims to Jerusalem? You have no intention of going in any event.'

'Foolish waste,' Dufnas declared. Then, having found his voice, added, 'I would not set foot in that God-forsaken land for all the gold in Rome.'

Thus delivering himself of this sentiment, Dufnas turned once more to his neglected meal; seizing a pheasant, he broke it in two between his fists – as if to show what he thought of the pilgrimage – and then bit deeply into the half in his right hand.

'Pay him no heed,' Gundrun advised. 'He has been to Jerusalem.'

'Twice,' grumbled Dufnas.

'Twice,' confirmed his friend. 'He was robbed by Saracens the last time, and he has never forgiven them.'

Murdo turned wondering eyes upon the moody merchantman. He did not appear a likely pilgrim; but then, Murdo had never known anyone who had been as far as Lundein, much less Rome or Jerusalem. 'They say,' he ventured, 'that the Holy Land is surrounded by a desert, and that the sand burns with a fire that cannot be quenched. Is this so?'

Gundrun passed the question to Dufnas, saying, 'Well, my friend, you heard him – what about the desert?'

'Aye,' he agreed between bites, 'there is a desert right enough.'

'And does it burn?' persisted Murdo.

'Worse – it boils,' answered Dufnas, wiping his mouth with his sleeve. 'No one can cross it during the day. You must wait until the night when it freezes like ice.'

Murdo nodded, as if he had long suspected this to be the case. He tucked this nugget of information into his memory to bring out later and impress Torf and Skuli. He was about to ask Dufnas whether it was also true that the Saracens could take as many wives as they pleased, but the serving monks arrived with pitchers and beakers of wine just then, and everyone began filling their cups and drinking one another's health. Murdo joined in, and found that he liked wine, and the way it made him feel as if he were glowing inside.

All around the green, the feast took on a more convivial mood, as everyone awaited the appearance of the Saint John's bread, sweet little barley cakes taken with wine. When at last they arrived, the cakes brought gasps of delight from the celebrants, for, baked into each small round loaf was a silver coin. Murdo plucked the coin from his cake and cupped it in his palm. Though it was but a tiny coin, it was more money than he had ever held at once. He gazed at the coin and marvelled at the Bishop's generosity.

'The pilgrim's coin,' Gundrun told him. 'It is to pay the gattage.'

'The what?'

'The tax which the gatemen of Jerusalem demand of all pilgrims who enter the Holy City.'

'To carry it with you means that you will live to see the city of the Blessed Saviour.'

Dufnas grunted at this, and pressed his coin into Murdo's hand. 'There,' he said, 'now you can pay my tax, too, when you get there.'

Murdo thought to remind the disagreeable merchant that, in fact, he was not going to Jerusalem at all, but Dufnas was already draining his second beaker of wine and Murdo thought it best not to disturb him with such trifling matters. He tucked the coins into his belt, and turned his attention to the Saint John's bread and wine.

The wine, sweetened with honey and lightly spiced, quickly disappeared – most of it down Dufnas' gullet, it had to be said – so Murdo sipped his cautiously, fearing he would get no more. Yet, no sooner had the empty pitcher touched the board than it was refilled from one of the two tuns of wine the bishop had established at either end of the green. One glance at the broad oak vats supported on their iron stanchions, and Murdo drained his beaker and then thrust it out for Gundrun to refill.

'Thirsty, boy, eh?' he laughed. 'Well done!'

Dufnas nudged him with an elbow and nodded his grudging approval. 'We shall make a trencherman of you yet,' he declared.

There followed more barley cakes and spiced wine, and some time later a dish made from ground almonds, honey, eggs and milk all boiled together to produce a thick sweet confection which was eaten from bowls with spoons as if it were soup. Murdo had never tasted anything so sweet, and did not think he could finish his, until, following Dufnas' example, he alternated each spoonful with a healthy swig of wine, and found the combination produced a delectable flavour.

When Murdo at last looked up from his third bowlful, he was astonished to find that the day was fading; shadows were stealing across the green. Many of the celebrants had left the board – some to stroll arm in arm around the cloisters, others to be received by the bishop before making their way home. He looked for Ragna and her family, but could not see them anywhere.

He was still searching when he heard someone call his name; he turned and saw Skuli motioning to him to come, and then saw his father and mother among those awaiting a word with Bishop Adalbert. Murdo reluctantly rose to join them.

'Leaving us so soon?' inquired Gundrun, placing his hand affectionately on Murdo's shoulder.

'Alas,' replied Murdo, 'I must go, or get left behind.' He bade his dining companions farewell and thanked them for telling him about the Holy Land. Upon receiving their compliments, he turned and walked, on slightly wobbly legs, to where his father was just then stepping before the bishop.

Murdo arrived in time to hear the cleric say, '– so I have been informed. However, I had hoped, Lord Ranulf, that you might be persuaded to see the matter in a different light. It is a long journey and far from safe at the best of times. I am certain you would travel in better peace were your lands and possessions secure in our care.'

Ranulf smiled with genuine warmth. 'Your concern shows much

to your favour, bishop. Yet, the matter is settled. My lady wife is well able to look after the ordering of the farm. Indeed, she has been so accustomed these last twenty years.'

'Even the most accomplished overseers require help,' the bishop pointed out, nodding slightly towards the lady in question. Niamh smiled, but Murdo recognized the cat-like smile as that which usually preceded a stinging reply.

Before she drew breath, Lord Ranulf interposed swiftly, saying, 'Of course, bishop, that is why my son Murdo is staying behind. He is a steady young man, and knows his work. Also, our tenants will continue to provide their share of labour.' The lord glanced approvingly at his lady. 'I have given the matter a great deal of thought, as you can see,' he concluded. 'And, I am certain you will agree that since Jarl Erlend is to remain in Orkneyjar, my short absence will occasion but little remark. Also, I would not like to cause anyone the slightest hardship. I know you will have care enough to look after all the lands which will be delivered to your keeping. I could not rest easy in the thought that my affairs had become a burden on anyone.'

So saying, the lord bade the bishop good day; Lady Niamh added her farewell and thanks for a magnificent feast worthy of the name-sake saint. Bishop Adalbert delivered a benediction of parting, and, even as they turned to leave, added that should anything occur to change his mind, the lord would find him ready and willing to shoulder the responsibility of looking after his lands.

Torf and Skuli made their farewells, Murdo muttered his regards, and then they were escorted once more through the cathedral and outside the church wall. They made their way to the bay below the low church hill and boarded the boat for the homeward voyage. The wind was light, but steady out of the northeast and the seas calm; the sailing would be pleasant, and they would be home in no time at all.

Ranulf woke Peder, his boatman, who was asleep on the tiller bench, and ordered Torf and Skuli to ready the sail, while he and Murdo untied the boat and, taking up two long oars, pushed away from the quay. Then all four men rowed until, once clear of the other boats, they could turn around, whereupon Ranulf gave the command to raise the sail. The heavy fabric shook itself and puffed out nicely, and the small ship glided from the wide, shallow bay and proceeded on an easterly course to clear the headland, before turning south and coasting home.

Once past the headland, there was nothing for Murdo to do, so he propped himself up on the rail and watched the low hills and cliffs, the dark rocks glowing red and purple in the westering sun. Murdo settled to bask in the warm, long-lingering sunset. Perched on the rail, he could not help thinking that, all in all, it was a splendid end to a fine day.

He looked at his father, who had taken the tiller from Peder, and watched as Ranulf expertly guided the boat, eyes scanning the familiar coastal waters, his face ruddy in the red-gold light, his fine blue cloak slung back over his shoulders so that his strong arms might move more freely.

At that moment, it occurred to Murdo that he wanted nothing else in all the world but to be that very man, to one day assume the lordship of Dýrness and the protection of his family's lands. He looked across at his mother, serene and beautiful as she sat on her cushioned bench beside the tiller. One day, thought Murdo, he would also have a beautiful wife. He savoured the word inwardly – *wife* – and was not surprised when it conjured Ragna's face. She was, after all, the only person worthy of the thought.

He held her image in his mind and watched the pale silver crescent of the moon rising, as if out of the very sea, to begin its silent journey towards morning. The sky was filled with stars by the time they reached Hrafnbú Bay, and Murdo was asleep in the bottom of the boat. He woke when the hull ran aground on the pebbled shore of their gjá, the ravine-like bay carved deep into the high rock cliffs upon which their farmland lay. He roused himself, slipped over the side, and helped Peder and his brothers make the boat secure.

They then waded to shore, where they were met by Jötun and Balder. The two wolfhounds bounded along the strand, barking eagerly and splashing everyone. Ranulf greeted them, cuffed them both affectionately around the ears, and sent them racing back towards the house to announce their master's return.

The very next day, the manor began preparations for the pilgrims' departure. As the days went by, Murdo watched with increasing jealousy as his brothers and cousin assumed the manner of worldly-wise men who could not be bothered with the commonplace chores of the farm. They ordered the servingmen like they were kings delivering edicts of life-or-death import to uncomprehending slaves; they swaggered about like battlechiefs of vast renown, and remained aloof from all former labours. It was as if the impending pilgrimage had absolved them not only of sin, but of work, duty, and common decency, too. Murdo ground his teeth until his jaws ached, but kept his resentment to himself.

Then, before the next full moon shone over Orkney's smooth hills, the pilgrims were gone.

SIX

'Basileus Alexius wishes me to express his gratitude for your efforts on behalf of the empire,' Dalassenus said, placing the gift chalice on the table beside the throne. 'He sends me with this letter' – withdrawing the parchment square from the leather pouch at his belt, the young commander offered it to the cleric – 'along with his regrets that he could not come to Rome to discuss his concerns in person. However, matters have arisen since I was last with you which prevent the emperor from leaving the capital at this time.'

'Be assured I am only too aware of the burdens and difficulties besetting those in authority,' the pope replied, accepting the folded parchment and placing it in his lap. He sat back, placidly regarding the man before him; thick muscled and compact, his dark curly hair and large dark eyes gave him the strong, virile semblance of a young bull.

'Please tell our dear brother that I have caused prayers to be said in order that he may prevail in every way against the devil's wiles. Tell him, too, that I hope for the day when he and I can sit down together and discuss our common affairs. Still, I am pleased to welcome his emissary. After our last meeting, I have often had cause to praise your sagacity and tact, drungarius. The emperor is fortunate indeed to have such an envoy.' He watched as the immaculate Dalassenus bowed with perfect courtesy – neither too shallow, which would be a slight, nor too deep, which would be servile. 'Agreeable though your presence undoubtedly is, I am intrigued to know why I am favoured to receive your attentions so soon upon the heels of your last visit.'

'Your Holiness flatters me,' Dalassenus answered smoothly. 'Perhaps you will permit me to say that the basileus has sent his kinsman and servant so that you may know the high regard he has placed on your counsel, and the eagerness with which he awaits your reply.'

56

Urban regarded the emperor's letter, bound with ribands of gold and sealed in purple. Could it be that now, at long last, his adversary was accepting the peace he had laboured so diligently to achieve? Healing the generations-old fracture had been one of the chief aims of his papal tenure and, if he understood Dalassenus correctly, that selfsame reconciliation was now delivered into his grasp.

Dalassenus continued, 'Also, the basileus would have it known that, after a lengthy investigation into the matter, it has at last come to light that the name of the Patriarch of Rome had been omitted from the diptych not by any canonical decision but, as it were, from carelessness. Rest assured this highly unfortunate oversight has been corrected.'

The pope moved to secure the peace at once. 'I rejoice to hear it,' Urban replied, smiling benignly at his guest. 'Tonight we will dine together you and I, and discuss the preparations for a celebration to mark the resumption of friendly relations between Rome and Byzantium.'

'Nothing would please me more, Bishop Urban. Unfortunately, my stay must be brief; Basileus Alexius expects my imminent return.'

'Then tell me your errand, my friend,' the pope said, 'and I will do my best to accommodate you however I may.'

'It is simply this,' Dalassenus replied and, using every grain of discretion at his command, inquired whether the pope had seen fit to reply to the emperor's request for troops to help restore the themes for the coming campaign to recover the imperial territories lost to the Arabs.

'As to the matter of the emperor's enquiry,' Urban answered happily, 'you may tell our brother and friend, that I did indeed take his entreaty to heart. What is more, I wasted not a moment, but acted on it without delay. You see, I myself have but recently returned from the field of battle, so to speak.'

The pope went on to describe what he called his inspiration in convening a council of bishops to discuss the need for aiding the empire, and to decide what form this aid might take. 'I am pleased to relate that the council has seen the wisdom of protecting the cradle of our salvation from heathen predation. Moreover, I have sent letters to all the bishops under my authority to preach Crusade.'

'Crusade?' Dalassenus had never heard the word before, but knew his worst fears confirmed.

'It is to be a pilgrimage like no other,' the pope explained. 'I have called upon the lords of the West to raise up an army of holy warriors to defend the Holy Land.'

'Then it is true,' the young commander confirmed. 'You are sending an army into Byzantium.'

Allowing himself a smile of quiet satisfaction, the Bishop of Rome answered, 'The idea was not original, I assure you. Confidentially, far too many of our noblemen are preoccupied with petty wars among themselves. Think you it pleases God to see his children wasting life and substance fighting each other when godless heathen occupy the Holy City, and stain the very stones where Jesu walked with the blood of the righteous? It is nothing less than an abomination.'

'Of course, Lord Bishop,' agreed Dalassenus quickly, 'but –'

'This I have preached, and the call has been answered. God be praised! Even now the lords of the West, mighty men of faith one and all, are raising armies to march against the infidel. I only wish that I could lead them myself,' he sighed, then pressed on with enthusiasm: 'Still, may it please God, I have delegated the task to one of my bishops – Adhemar of Le Puy enjoys my full authority so far as the disposition of the pilgrimage is concerned.'

'Bishop Adhemar,' the drungarius repeated dully.

'Do you know him?'

'Alas, no.'

'A wonderful man – solid of faith and rich in good works, a saint unflagging in zeal and courage.'

'Be that as it may,' Dalassenus said, 'it appears your intentions have been anticipated somewhat.' He then told the pope about Peter the Hermit and his pilgrim horde, and their unruly excursion through imperial lands.

Bishop Urban shook his head sadly. 'It is unfortunate, I agree, but I do not see how it can be prevented. God calls who he will. Are we to judge who may take the cross, and who must refrain? It is the instrument of salvation for many, and no earthly power has the right to deny it.'

'When will these –' Dalassenus hesitated. To avoid needless antagonism, he said, 'These *crusaders* – they will pass through

Constantinople, no doubt? In that event, it would be useful to know how many we might expect to receive.'

The pope's eyes went wide at the question. 'I have no idea! It is God's will, my friend. He alone knows the number. Yet, I can tell you the call was most enthusiastically received.'

'When might we expect them?'

'I have decreed that those wishing to follow Bishop Adhemar on pilgrimage must be ready to depart no later than August of this year. God willing, you may expect their arrival by the Christ Mass, if not before.'

'The emperor will be delighted to hear it,' the young commander replied, trying not to let dismay colour his tone.

'Good,' the pope answered. 'So be it.'

'Now, if you will excuse me, I must make arrangements for my departure.'

'Such devotion to duty is laudable, Drungarius Dalassenus. But must you leave Rome so soon? I had hoped you would dine with us here in the palace. These are exciting times, and there is much to discuss.'

'I am sorry. As much as I might wish otherwise, I am compelled to rejoin the basileus as soon as possible.'

'As you will.' Urban, Patriarch of Rome, extended his hand for the kiss, and the young commander brushed the papal ring with his lips. 'Farewell, my son. Greet the emperor in my name, and tell him he is remembered daily in prayer, as are all our brothers in the east.'

'Thank you, I will indeed tell him,' Dalassenus answered. 'Fare well, Bishop Urban.'

The young commander turned on his heel and departed the audience room. Urban sat for a long time, contemplating the incredible event which had just taken place. Then, when he had set the thing properly in his mind, he called his abbot to him and, giving him the emperor's letter, commanded him to read it aloud. The priest broke the seal, unfolded the heavy parchment square and, in a high, thin, reedy voice, began to read.

'Slowly, Brother Marcus,' the pope chided, 'slowly – and in Latin, please. My Greek has never been more than adequate. Begin again, my friend, if you please.'

As the abbot began once more, Pope Urban leaned back in his chair, folded his hands over his stomach, and closed his eyes. Yes, he thought, the long hoped-for reconciliation had come; what is more, thanks to the tremendous response to his call to Crusade, it was now proceeding more swiftly than he would have dared dream possible.

SEVEN

Harvest time sped by Murdo in a dull blur of sweat and fatigue. Day after day, he dragged his aching body out of bed at first light, pulled on his clothes, and was in the fields by dawn, where he laboured until long into the radiant northern twilight, pausing only to break fast at midday, and then again for supper. He took his meals in the field with the vassals and, like his father, worked elbow to elbow with them, never allowing himself even so much as a swallow of water unless he could offer them the same.

By the time the last sheaf of grain had been gathered and the last lonely kernel gleaned, Murdo knew deep in every bone and sinew that he had never worked so hard, nor accomplished so much. The fact that the final three rows were harvested under black, threatening skies with the rumble of thunder in the distance only increased his sense of triumph. When the last wagon trundled into the yard and the oxen were led to the barn, he stood and gazed proudly at the great stacks of yellow grain, marvelling at the achievement. When his mother came and put her arm around his shoulder in a gentle hug, Murdo could not have been more delighted if heaps of gold had been mined and stored away.

'You have done well, Murdo,' his mother told him. 'I cannot remember a richer harvest. Your father could not have done better, and he would tell you the same if he were here.'

'The weather remained dry, and that helped,' he replied sagely. Casting an eye towards the dark clouds overhead, he added, 'I feared the storm would take the last, but it can rain from now until Yuletide and I will not breathe a word of complaint.'

'A harvest like this deserves a feast,' Niamh suggested. 'Tomorrow we will celebrate. Tell the tenants and vassals, and then choose a pig – oh, and one of the yearling calves, too. We will make it a fine harvest celebration.'

As his mother hurried off to begin ordering the preparations,

Murdo stood for a time admiring his handiwork. Then, adopting the manner of the absent lord himself, he strode into the barn where the workers were placing the last sheaves onto the stack, and began praising the men for their diligence and hard work. 'Tomorrow will be a feast-day at Hrafnbú farm,' he told them, and bade them bring wives, children and their old ones to help observe the festivities properly. Leaving the others to finish in the barn, Murdo and Fossi went to the cattle pens to choose the calf and pig for the feast.

Fossi was the family's oldest and most trusted servingman. Though his hair had grown grey in the service of Lord Ranulf's father, he still moved with the spry step of a man twenty years younger; his eye was as clear and his hand as steady as Murdo's. Never one to speak two words where one would do, that one word was worth ten of anyone else's. Old Fossi could be relied on to say what he thought without regard to rank or favour.

'What think you, Fossi?' asked Murdo as they leaned on the enclosure fence.

'The gathering-in?'

'Yes. How do you mark it?'

'I marks it right fair.'

They stood a little in silence before Murdo coaxed some more out of him. 'I am thinking it is better than last year,' Murdo suggested.

'Oh, aye,' agreed Fossi.

'We shall have enough to plant the new field, I think,' Murdo ventured. Lord Ranulf had cleared a patch of ground to the south of the present barley field earlier in the summer, and it was Murdo's plan to sow it in the spring as his father intended.

'Aye,' Fossi concurred, 'we will.'

Satisfied with this, Murdo chose a fine, fat calf from among the yearlings, and one of the pigs. 'Mind you do not take Red William by mistake,' Murdo warned. 'He is for the Yule board.'

Fossi frowned and regarded Murdo with dark disapproval for impugning his abilities, but said nothing. Leaving Fossi to oversee the butchering, Murdo walked back to the house, tired in every muscle, but glowing with a contentment he would have envied in anyone else. The first drops of rain splashed into the dust at his feet as he reached the yard; he paused and stood as the rain pattered down around him, feeling the cool splashes on his upturned face.

'*Come winds and rain and winter cold,*' he hummed to himself, reciting the words to the song. *'my hearth is warm and my house is dry, and I shall not stir until the sun does rise on blessed Easter morning.'*

The good weather held long enough for the folk of Hrafnbú to enjoy their feast the next day, but after that a gale broke in full across the isles. The golden autumn dissolved in a rainy haze that did not lift, giving way instead to cold, grey days of rain and snow. Winter came early and stayed long, but the great house and its inhabitants remained in good spirits, passing a fine, if somewhat subdued, Yuletide with guests from the neighbouring farms.

Murdo reluctantly returned to his wintertime pursuit of Latin, and made steady progress in both reading and speech. His natal day passed uneventfully and unmarked, save for his mother's thoughtful present of one of Lord Ranulf's best hunting spears – one which Murdo had secretly coveted for some time. True, it was not the swordtaking he would have wished, but it would have to do until his father returned. He prized the spear, and alternated his Latin with hunting from then on.

Following the turn of the year, he and his mother, along with some of the neighbours, rode to the church at Saint Mary's for the Feast of the Virgin. They stayed seven nights at Borgvík, the estate of Jarl Erlend's younger sister, Cecilia, and her family. There were many young people, but no one Murdo's age, and while the older people made vague attempts to include him in their conversations, all the talk of fishing and farming soon grew wearisome and he decided to play games with the children instead.

Upon their return to the bú, Murdo began the task of repairing the tools and equipment for the spring planting. Besides that, there was the lambing to think about, but mostly the days remained uncluttered and he had time to himself. He occupied himself with riding the estate, often taking the spear and, with two or three of the tenants' sons, trying his hand at hunting for the table. The woods at the end of the valley yielded a young stag, and though they often saw wild pigs, they were never able to get close enough to one for a good cast.

Often on these excursions Murdo pretended he was on pilgrimage fighting Saracens. With every throw and thrust of the spear, he struck a decisive blow for Christendom. From time to time, he wondered about his father and brothers. He had no idea how far distant Jerusalem might be, but he thought they must soon be returning. How long could it take to liberate the Holy Land from the slack grasp of a few vexatious Arabs?

According to common opinion, the pilgrims would make short work of it so that they could return to the comforts of home as soon as possible. Murdo decided that his father and brothers would be back well before the next harvest, and he would not have to undertake that chore alone.

Thus the months passed, and winter grudgingly receded. The days grew longer and warmer, and the rains less fierce. As spring firmed its hold on the land, Murdo frequently found himself weighing the possibility of paying a visit to Lord Brusi's estate to see how Lady Ragnhild and her daughter were bearing the lord's absence. Try as he might, however, he could find neither a convenient nor convincing excuse to go to Hrolfsey. Sailing from one island to another was not difficult, but it was not a thing one did casually, and it was not in the way of a simple day's outing. His mother would have to know, and he had no satisfactory means of explaining his sudden interest in the welfare of the Hrolfsey farming estates.

He decided instead to make certain he and his mother attended the Eastertide ceremonies at the cathedral – in the hope that Lady Ragnhild would do the same. It took him several days to work up his courage to broach the subject with her, and then several more to find just the right opportunity to introduce it naturally into the conversation so that she would not suspect him of plotting anything. His chance came one night when, after their supper, he and Lady Niamh were sitting in their chairs before the hearth. His mother was mending a siarc, and he was stropping a knife on a length of leather when his mother said, 'We will soon begin our Lenten observances.'

'Is Eastertide so near?' he wondered, assuming an air of astonishment. 'I suppose it must be. What with the planting and all, I had completely forgotten.'

This statement, uttered with innocent sincerity, caused his mother to look up from her needle to regard him curiously. Murdo continued stropping the knife, aware of her glance, but betraying no sign. After a moment, Lady Niamh resumed her sewing. 'We must give a thought to Eastertide preparations,' she said.

'Did we go to the cathedral last year?' Murdo asked. 'I have forgotten.'

'Oh, Murdo, of course we did,' his mother informed him with quiet exasperation. 'You forget because it is beneath your regard to remember. You have so little heart for the church, I wonder you go at all, Murdo.'

I would *not* go, he thought to himself, if I was not forever pestered into going. Adopting a suitably contrite tone, he admitted, 'It is not often uppermost in my thoughts, it is true. But I did enjoy the Saint John's feast, and I would be happy to hear Easter Mass at the cathedral – if that is what you wish.'

Oh, that was well done. He had deftly turned the entire affair into a matter of pleasing his mother. Murdo commended himself on his shrewdness and aplomb.

His exultation was short-lived, however, for his mother downed her needlework to stare at him – as if unable to determine whether it was indeed her son sitting beside her, or a sly impostor. 'As it happens,' she said, 'I have already made other plans. We are to spend Eastertide elsewhere.'

Murdo felt his heart sink. After all his cunning and careful planning, he was not to go to the cathedral at all. In desperation he said, 'Yet the cathedral is a splendid sight on Easter – what with all the gold and finery. Could we not hear the mass, at least, before chasing off somewhere else? I do so like it there.'

Lady Niamh frowned and shook her head. 'You are a wonder. I had no idea you held such strong opinions on the matter.' She paused, considering what to do. After a moment, she said, 'Honestly, I wish you had spoken sooner, Murdo. Lady Ragnhild has invited us to join them, and I have accepted. I do not see how I can tell her that we will not come after all – they will have made many preparations for us.' She paused again. 'But, if you are determined, we might –'

'Lady Ragnhild – wife of Lord Brusi . . .' Murdo interrupted quickly.

'Yes, the same – and if you tell me you cannot remember *them*, Murdo, I will thump you with a broom.'

'I remember them right well,' Murdo replied truthfully. 'But I do not recall seeing a messenger hereabouts.'

'Messenger? Whatever do you mean? There was never any messenger.'

'Then how –?'

65

His mother regarded him with frank exasperation and clucked her tongue. 'Ragnhild herself invited us at the Feast of Saint John. She knew we would be alone – as she would be herself – with the menfolk gone on pilgrimage. I told her we would be honoured and delighted to observe the holy days with them.'

Murdo, adopting a philosophical air, replied, 'Well, I am never one to disappoint a body. In light of all the preparations the good lady will have made on our behalf, it would ill behove us to spurn an invitation already accepted. I fear we shall have to make the best of it.' He sighed heavily to show that, though his sentiments were firmly elsewhere, he was nevertheless capable of sacrificing his own happiness for that of others.

'The things you say, Murdo,' Niamh said, shaking her head slowly. 'One would almost believe you had another purpose in mind.'

'My only wish is to please you, Mother,' Murdo replied, trying to sound hurt and dignified at the same time. 'Is that wrong?'

Lady Niamh rolled a sceptical eye at him and took up her needlework once more. Murdo turned his attention to the knife in his hand with what he considered an attitude of silent forbearance, all the time hoping against hope that his mother would overlook his ill-timed insistence on attending mass in Kirkjuvágr, now the last place he wanted to go.

'Then it is settled,' Niamh mused after a time. 'We shall go to Cnoc Carrach as we have planned.' She paused, thinking of the impending visit. 'It will be good to spend a few days with Ragnhild again; it's a long time since we stayed with one another.'

Murdo, feeling he had said more than enough, wisely kept his mouth shut, as if accepting his mother's final decree. That night he lay awake imagining what he would say to Ragna when he saw her, and wondering whether some sort of gift might be required for the occasion. He determined to give the matter serious consideration, and fell asleep dreaming of her pleasantly surprised reaction to his affection and generosity.

In the days to follow, it took all of Murdo's cunning to appear indifferent to the impending visit. He contrived to help Peder ready the boat; after wintering on the shore, there was always a deal of work to get the craft seaworthy once more, and the old sailor was most exacting about how the various chores were done. Peder had collected a supply of pitch to be mixed together with a little wool, the compound to be pressed into the seams and any cracks which had opened during the cold months. Then, the hull would be scraped with pumice stone and a fresh layer of pitch applied. Also, during the long winter, Peder fashioned lengths of rope from twisted hemp; these would have to be stretched and soaked, stretched and soaked again, and then spliced together to make good stout seaworthy lines – an arduous process, but, as Peder never tired of pointing out, at sea a man's life hung by each and every strand of seaman's thread.

Save for the smell of hot pitch, Murdo did not mind the work. He preferred the sailing to farming anyway, and Peder's rambling talk took his mind off the aching anticipation of seeing Ragna again. The thought tormented him like an inflamed itch, and he could not wait for the day. Easter had gradually assumed a towering significance for Murdo, and he began to fear he would not live to see it. The incomparable day hung over him like doom itself, and he even considered praying that God would allow him the blessing of behold-ing the lovely Ragna once more. If I can but see her dressed in her Easter finery before I die, he thought, I can depart this world a contented soul. And if, by some miracle, he was granted the favour of a kiss, he would meet judgement day a happy, happy man.

Despite his feelings, however, Murdo made no prayers. He felt it beneath his dignity to honour that distant tyrant with his reverence, and he certainly did not care to enter into any bargains which might require him to atone in some disagreeable way, or attend church more often than he already did. He bore his affliction as best he could, working hard and taking long walks at dusk when his thoughts inevitably turned towards the forthcoming journey . . . and the inef-fable delight which lay at the end of it.

When the day of their departure finally dawned, Murdo was awake and ready before the cock had finished crowing. For the life of him, he could not understand why, this day of all days, everyone had suddenly become so sluggish and slow. It was not as if they were taking the entire holding with them; besides his mother, Murdo was the only other person going, along with Peder, of course, and Hin, one of the younger servingmen, who was to help with the boat. But there were numerous baskets and bundles of food, and several chests of clothing and other belongings to be loaded onto the wagon and carried down to the boat, and stowed aboard.

'We are not settling unknown territory,' Murdo observed tartly. 'Why do we need all this – this tack?'

'Is it impatient you are?' his mother cooed sweetly. 'Ah, heart of my heart, you will see your Ragna again soon enough.'

Murdo gaped at his mother. All this time he had been so careful – how did she know? How *could* she know?

He could feel his cheeks burning, and turned away quickly. 'I was only thinking of the weather,' he said vehemently. 'Peder says we will have a good wind to begin, but it will grow tassy by midday.'

'Listen to you now,' Niamh said, her eyes glinting mischievously as she stepped near, 'going on about the weather, when the merest mention of her name brings the colour to your cheeks . . . or was that the wind as well?'

He glared at his mother, but held his tongue lest he make the thing worse.

'Murdo,' she coaxed, 'you have been stalking around here like a caged bear ever since we decided to go to Cnoc Carrach – did you really think I would not guess the reason? I have been the mother of sons for a fair few years; there is very little I do not ken of menfolk.'

Murdo softened under her gentle reproof. He shrugged, and said, 'Well, we have been shut up here all winter, after all. I know how eager you are to see your friend again.'

Lady Niamh put her hand on her son's shoulder. 'Hear me, my soul,' she said, 'Ragna is a splendid young woman, and nothing would make me happier than seeing you take her to wife. Your father feels the same, I know. We are both noble families, and there is a great deal to be said for binding our houses together. I have good reason to believe Lord Brusi would welcome the match.'

'Mother,' he said, mystified, 'why are you telling me this?'

She smiled. 'So that you will feel free to follow your heart in the matter.' She lifted her hand and lightly touched his cheek. 'I have seen the way you look at her. Truly, a love match is a rare thing, my light. Your father and I have been fortunate, but many – nay most – are not so blessed.' She paused. 'As it happens, I have also seen the way Ragna looks at *you*.'

Murdo jerked his head back in disbelief.

'Oh, aye,' his mother assured him, 'she likes you, Murdo. She surely does.'

Unable to endure any more of this talk, Murdo turned away, seized the nearest basket, and strode from the room as quickly as his wilted dignity allowed. 'You could do worse, dear son of mine,' Niamh called after him. 'Just you ponder that!'

EIGHT

The boat made landfall in the narrow cove below Cnoc Carrach on the western side of Hrolfsey. The house was built on the southeastern side of the cnoc, or hill, so that it might not be seen from the sea, but Murdo knew where it was, and his heart quickened at the thought that Ragna was so near. To his dismay, he found his hands trembled on the tiller as Peder and Hin readied the pole and anchor in preparation of coming alongside Lord Brusi's timber quay.

No one appeared to notice his excitement, however, and Murdo quickly busied himself with helping unload the boat. They were still about this chore when two servingmen and an ox-drawn cart appeared on the winding track leading down to the cove. 'We saw your boat in the narrows,' the elder servant explained. 'Lady Ragnhild sent us to help you.' Addressing Niamh, he said, 'If it pleases you, my lady, you might go ahead to the house. It's for us to see to your possessions.'

Murdo's mother thanked the servants, but declined, saying, 'There is no hurry. We will stay and help you.' She then directed Murdo to assist the servingmen, while Peder and Hin secured the ship. Owing to the steepness of the cliff, the cart could not reach the quay and so all the chests and baskets had to be carried half-way up the hill to the waiting wagon. This simple task seemed to take forever, and the sun was already disappearing behind the shoulder of the hills by the time the cart was loaded and the oxen prodded into motion.

The visitors climbed the hill and walked the short distance to the house, and by the time they reached the yard, Murdo was almost faint with anticipation. His heart pounded in his chest and his vision swam; it was all he could do to keep from falling over at every step.

Ah, but his expectation was not misplaced. For no sooner had the cart come to a halt than the door to the great house opened and Ragna emerged, bearing a golden cup on a wooden tray. She stepped lightly into the yard, her limp visible only in the slight tilt and jiggle of the tray she carried. To Murdo, however, she seemed not so much to walk, as to glide a little above the ground.

Dressed in a simple white mantle edged with gleaming blue embroidery, and wearing a blue-embroidered girdle around her slender waist, she appeared taller than Murdo remembered, and even more beautiful. *She is always new,* he thought, *and always better than herself.* Indeed, her fair features seemed to glow in the setting sun, and her hair glinted red-gold in the dusky light. She was a creature of radiance and grace. Murdo drank in the sight of her in one prolonged gawk of amazed delight, and swore on his life that he had never seen anything so handsome, or so fine.

Ragna did not deign to glance at him, however, but directed her steps to his mother. 'Welcome, Lady Niamh,' she said nicely. 'We have been eagerly awaiting your arrival. Please,' she lifted the tray, 'be refreshed after your journey.'

Lady Niamh inclined her head regally, accepted the offered cup, and raised it to her lips. She sipped elegantly and thanked Ragna for her kindness and courtesy. Only then did the young woman turn to address Murdo. 'Be welcome, Master Murdo,' she said, offering him the tray; 'the freedom of our hearth is yours for as long as you care to stay.'

'I thank you, Mistress Ragna,' he replied, ducking his head as he took up the cup. He drank down a gulp of the sweet mead and replaced the golden vessel on the tray, whereupon Ragna, her lips twitching with private pleasure, turned once more to his mother.

'Lady Ragnhild is ready to receive you,' she said. Indicating the elder of the servants at the cart, she added, 'Roli will see that your men are well settled in the servants' house. Would you like to follow me? I will take you to my lady's chamber.' With that, she led them into the house.

They entered a long, wood-panelled vestibule, off which two wide doors opened. Ragna chose the door on the left and showed them into the room where the Lady of Cnoc Carrach waited to welcome her visitors. The chamber was comfortable, with lime-washed walls to which ochre had been added for colour, and a rug of woven wool on the smooth timbered floor; an oak screen closed off one corner of the room, and there was a small needlework tapestry hanging on the wall. Ragnhild, dressed in a rose-red cloak and mantle, was sitting in a chair beside the window, which was open to make the most of the failing light. Although the day had been balmy for the season, a small fire of coals burned in a brazier to ward off the chill which was seeping into the air with the coming of night. She glanced up from a tiny book she was reading, and smiled as her visitors entered the room; closing the book, she placed it on the window ledge and then opened her arms to greet her childhood friend.

The two women kissed, and embraced one another with a warmth of affection that made Murdo squirm slightly. But Ragna, having placed the tray and cup upon a nearby table, watched with obvious delight.

'Nia,' said Ragnhild, 'it is happiness itself to see you again. I do hope your journey was not too arduous.'

'Oh, Ragni – Ragni, dear friend,' replied his mother, – Murdo was surprised to hear them speak so familiarly to one another – 'it is so good to be here. It has pleased me greatly to think we might spend these days together, and now that I am here, I am delighted.'

They hugged one another again, and Murdo averted his eyes. When he looked again, Lady Ragnhild was turning towards him. 'And who is this handsome young man?' she inquired, as if she did not know who could be accompanying her friend. 'This cannot be young Murdo! But of course, it is!'

She stepped before him, extending her arm. Murdo bowed politely and kissed her hand. 'Murdo, greetings and welcome. It is so good of you to allow your mother and me the opportunity to see one another again.' She spoke as if he were the lord upon whose whim the celebration depended and, for all it was a simple device, Murdo found that he liked it.

'My lady, the pleasure is entirely mine,' he replied gallantly.

Whereupon, Lady Ragnhild endeared herself further by saying, 'As you will be the only man among us, you shall have the lord's place while you are here.'

The only man, thought Murdo; that had not occurred to him.

'I do so hope you will not become bored with our female chatter. I have instructed my daughter to do whatever she can to make your stay more pleasant.'

Although Murdo would have given his left arm to see Ragna's

reaction to this announcement, he dared not glance her way. Instead, he forced himself to look straight into Lady Ragnhild's eyes and reply in what he hoped was his most winsome manner. 'You are most considerate, my lady. But I beg you, take no thought for me. I am certain I shall find the company here endlessly agreeable,' he told her, thinking he had acquitted himself very well.

The Lady of Cnoc Carrach gave him a pleasant smile, and turned once more to his mother. 'I know you have had a long day, and that you must be tired from your journey. Therefore, we will not presume upon you for supper. Instead, we will allow you to dine alone tonight, so that you may rest and restore yourselves.'

Murdo's heart sank. After waiting so long to be here, the thought that he would have to wait yet one more night to be with Ragna was beyond endurance. Desperately, he tried to think of some way to divert this disaster, but his mind refused to yield any suitable reply.

His mother redeemed the day.

'How kind you are, Ragni,' she offered smoothly, 'and how thoughtful. But we would consider the pleasure of your company the best restorative of all.' She deferred to Murdo with a slight tilt of her chin. 'Unless my son prefers otherwise, we would be pleased to take supper with you tonight.'

'By all means,' added Murdo, hoping he did not sound over-eager. He glimpsed Ragna out of the corner of his eye – was she laughing at him?

'Splendid!' cried Lady Ragnhild, as if this were the very thing she yearned to hear. 'I will instruct the cooks. Meanwhile, Ragna will take you to your rooms, and I will have my servingmaids bring your belongings shortly.'

Ragna led them from the room then, and they proceeded further down the long vestibule to the end where a turret of steps spiralled up to the floor above. Upon climbing the stairs, they discovered a chamber faced with three wooden doors. 'Your room, Lady Niamh,' she said, indicating the door directly before them. 'This will be your room,' she continued, indicating the left-hand door for Murdo. 'And my room is there,' she said, lifting her hand to the right-hand door. 'Now then, if there is nothing you require, I will leave you to rest before supper.'

When Ragna had gone, Murdo's mother turned to him and said,

'I am glad we have come. You will not mind being the only man, will you?' Tilting her head in Ragna's direction, she said, 'No doubt Ragna will help you find a way to enjoy your stay.'

Murdo, embarrassed to have his most intimate sentiments announced so blatantly, turned swiftly to his door and pushed it open. 'I think I shall be content here,' he agreed distantly, peering into the room.

'Oh, aye, I am certain of it.' His mother bade him take a moment's rest, and went into her room, leaving Murdo to himself. He stepped over the threshold and closed the door behind him. The room was mostly in shadow now; there was a fireplace and many candles, but none of them were lit. The high-sided bed was built into the wall directly across from him; the linen appeared clean, and the curtain was drawn back. A small round table stood in the centre of the room, and there was a three-legged stool beside the bed. The walls were limed to make the most of the scant light through the small, square window. There were iron sconces on the wall, and a sheepskin before the bare hearth.

All in all, the room was not so different from his own at home. Yes, he thought, I shall be content here – especially knowing that Ragna is sleeping only a few paces away. As he was not particularly tired, he decided to have a look around, and so crept from his room and back down the stairs. He found his way to the vestibule and walked outside.

The sun was down, but the sky was still light, the few clouds violet-tinted in the twilight. Two or three stars were already glowing low on the horizon; the breeze was rising out of the west and it smelled of rain. There was no one about as Murdo proceeded through the yard, looking at the various buildings; he stopped before the barn, but it was dark inside so he did not go in, continuing around the house instead. There were two fields hard by the house, and in one of these ploughing had begun for the spring planting. Other fields and grazing lands lay further off, and more, no doubt, were scattered among the surrounding hills. He saw pens for sheep and cattle – though none for pigs – and, glimmering darkly at the foot of the nearest hill, a pond for ducks and geese.

Lord Brusi's farm, though larger, was much like his father's, Murdo concluded, and wondered how much land Brusi owned, and how many vassals Cnoc Carrach maintained. As his circular path brought him once more into the yard, the scent of wood smoke told him the hearth fires had been lit, and it would soon be time to eat. There was a low stone trough a few paces from the door, so he took a drink and, remembering that he was an honoured guest, washed his hands before going inside.

Candles had been lit in the vestibule and, curious about what lay behind the right-hand door, he lifted the wooden latch, pushed the door open a crack and looked inside. It was the great hall, and the size of it gratified Murdo, for it seemed at least twice as large as his father's hall at Hrafnbú. The ceiling was high and open, and there were iron sconces hanging from the beams and rooftrees. The hearth alone took up the whole of the further wall and it was laid with a single immense slab of stone; three more huge slabs formed the opening, looking like the uprights and lintel of the doorway to a cavern. The lintel was handsome grey-green slate which had been chiselled smooth, and carved with the intertwined knotwork of the old Celts.

Two long black boards on trestles ran side-by-side the length of the hall to end at a third, shorter board before the hearth. Both long tables had benches either side, but the short table had benches only on the side nearest the hearth. Iron sconces lined either wall, and iron candletrees and candleholders of various kinds were scattered around the room in profusion. New straw had been laid on the floor, filling the room with the fresh scent of the field.

'The hall is being readied for the feast,' said a soft voice behind him.

Murdo turned quickly. 'Ragna, I –'

It was not Ragna who stood before him, however, but one of the servingmaids: slight and dark, her hair pulled back and bound in a length of white cloth. She was holding a trencher on which lay a small loaf of bread and bowl of salt. 'You are to sup in my lady's chamber tonight,' the maid explained cheerfully.

'I see,' he replied.

The two stood for a moment looking at one another, and Murdo, unused to such bold scrutiny from female servants, shifted uneasily from one foot to the other.

'You are Murdo,' the maid informed him.

'Yes.'

'I am called Tailtiu,' she said. 'I serve Mistress Ragna, and my mother served Lady Ragnhild – until she has died two years ago.

75

One day, Mistress Ragna will be a lady, and I will serve her just like my mother before me, you see.'

'Yes,' Murdo answered; then, fearing he was repeating himself, added, 'I see.'

'You are from Dýrness,' the maid blithely continued, 'and your father is one of Jarl Erlend's noblemen – just like Lord Brusi.'

'He is that.'

'Lord Brusi and his sons has gone on the pilgrimage to the Holy Land with your father and brothers,' she said, warming to the discussion. 'You were not allowed to go, for you has not taken arms yet, for all you are too young.'

'I am sixteen summers now,' Murdo announced haughtily. He stared hard at the impertinent creature, and wondered how she had come by her information and whether he should send her away. But she was not his to command, so he stood firm and hoped his scowl would drive her off.

'Mistress Ragna is good to me,' Tailtiu continued. 'She is very beautiful, too, and she has given me many gifts, for I am her maid.'

'So you have said,' replied Murdo.

'You do not look like a Dane,' the maid observed.

'My father's line is descended from Sigurd the Stout,' Murdo declared. 'My mother's people are blood kin of King Malcolm of Scotland.'

'My father was a Dane, too,' the girl countered, as if the illustrious Sigurd were no more to her than an itinerant farmhand. 'My mother was of the Irish. She was brought here as a wee girl no bigger than a cricket – is what she used to say. One day I will go to Ireland, too. They say it is a fine land – an island, it is, and much bigger than all of Orkneyjar.'

'That is what they say,' agreed Murdo wearily.

Footsteps in the vestibule alerted them just then, and they turned to see Ragna approaching. 'There you are, Tailtiu,' she chided. 'I am certain Master Murdo has better things to do than listen to your chatter all night.'

'Yes, Mistress Ragna,' Tailtiu said, not chastened in the least.

'I will take this,' Ragna said, reaching for the tray, 'and you can return to the kitchen.'

Ragna took the tray and the maid departed, casting a lingering mischievous glance at Murdo as she went. 'The chamber is ready,'

Ragna told him, moving towards the door. 'You can come in if you like.'

'Thank you,' he said, following her.

Ragna turned and met him at the threshold with the trencher of bread and salt. 'You must take a bit of bread and dip it in the salt,' Ragna explained. 'It is the custom of the king's court.'

Murdo pinched a chunk of bread from the loaf and pressed it into the salt. He held it for a moment, uncertain what to do next. 'And then?' he asked.

'You must eat it,' Ragna answered. The laughter in her voice charmed rather than shamed him, and he laughed, too.

'Why must I eat it?' he asked, to prolong the pleasantry.

'It is a sign of hospitality by which honoured guests are received in this house,' she told him. 'My father learned of it in King Olaf's court.'

Murdo put the bread into his mouth, and Ragna indicated that he should go into the room. He stepped across the threshold, and caught the warm scent of her as he passed – slightly sweet, like heather, or a spice of some kind. She followed him into the chamber, which had been transformed into a dining room. A table had been set up before the hearth, where a fire now crackled, making the room warm and welcoming.

Ragna placed the trencher on the table, and turned to the hearth where a pitcher and cups were waiting. She took up one of the cups, and brought it to Murdo. 'A drink while you wait,' she said.

Murdo sniffed the warm liquid and caught the same scent of spice which he had smelled on Ragna, though he did not know what it might be. He put the cup to his lips and sipped. It was metheglin, and although Murdo had drunk it but twice in his life before now, he pronounced it very good indeed. His commendation brought a smile to Ragna's lips. 'Did you make this?' he asked.

'I did,' she answered. 'How did you know?'

Lady Ragnhild entered the chamber at that moment, and Murdo turned to greet her. She joined them at the hearth and accepted a cup from her daughter. 'I see Ragna has made you properly welcome,' she said. 'As the hall is being prepared for the Easter festivities, I thought we might enjoy ourselves better here.'

'It is a good room,' Murdo agreed, then remembering his manners, he lifted his cup. 'Here's health to you, my lady.'

They drank together, and Murdo, the temporary lord, felt pleased with his thoughtfulness. When Lady Niamh joined them a few moments later, he proposed her health as well, and the evening began. Tailtiu and one of the kitchen servants brought a succession of dishes to the table, beginning with braised fish, and then roast fowl and turnips. There was ale to drink, and flat bread, both soft and hard.

Over meat, the formality of their reception fell away, inspiring in Murdo the hope that he would not be suffocated by the strictures of polite custom. When talk turned to the absent lords, his mother said, 'I am most eager to hear how you have fared since your menfolk left. It cannot be easy for two women alone.'

'No,' allowed Ragnhild, 'but I am growing used to the extra demands. The vassals undertake the difficult chores, of course, and we have many loyal servants. It is not easy, no, but we are making our way.'

'It is the same with us,' Niamh said, and went on to explain how they had worked themselves half to death during harvest time. Murdo listened happily to his mother's account, luxuriating in her luminous appraisal of his many labours and successes.

After that, talk passed to other things and the evening proceeded pleasantly. When they finally rose from the board, the candles had burned down, and the fire was a heap of embers on the hearth. Taking a taper from the nearest sconce, Ragna led them up the spiral steps to their rooms and bade them a pleasant and restful sleep, before disappearing into her own room. Only then did Murdo realize he had said none of the things to Ragna that he had wanted to say.

He bade his mother a good night and went into his room. The candles in their sconces were lit, and a fire burned brightly on the hearth. The servants had placed a candletree beside his bed, and Murdo sat on the stool before the hearth and pulled off his boots, vowing not to let another day go by before he found a way to get Ragna to himself alone. But the next day the household was upside down in preparation for the impending celebration, and the day after that was Passion Day, a fast day, and the beginning of the Eastertide observances; everyone spent, as it seemed to Murdo, the entire day in the little chapel the monks maintained on the island. If not for the ride to and from the chapel, Murdo would likely not have had a single opportunity to see Ragna at all. The next day was also a fast day, so there were no meals to be taken and, as Murdo himself was now fully occupied with helping prepare for the feast, he had to content himself with the few glimpses he got of her as they went about their respective chores.

Thus, it was not until Easter day that he found the opportunity to speak to Ragna at length again – and then the house was awash with the boisterous tide of kinsmen and friends which had swept over Cnoc Carrach, and it was impossible for Murdo to see her alone. Some of Ragna's female cousins had come to partake of the festivities, so he had to content himself with sitting across the board from them and exchanging mild pleasantries of only the most general and insipid kind.

After the first of several meals had been served, however, many of the younger people, having taken the edge off their hunger, went out in search of diversion. Some had begun a game of skilty in the yard, and Murdo wandered out to see how they fared. He had played skilty from the time he was a child, and now considered himself above its modest pleasures. Still, as the rest of the young people were making such a fuss about it, he decided to join in, and even caught two of the fleeing hares before he saw Ragna watching him from the doorway of the cookhouse behind the kitchen. She motioned him to her before disappearing inside.

Murdo played but a moment or two longer, and then allowed himself to be caught and removed himself from the ring of participants. Then, with the stealth of a hunter, he stalked across the yard to the cookhouse and slipped unseen through the door.

The interior of the hut was warm and smelled of bread. Ragna was standing at a large table, shaping a great mound of butter with a small wooden paddle. She glanced up as he came to the board, and smiled. 'Good Easter to you, Murdo,' she purred lightly, drawing the paddle across the pale yellow mound. He thrilled to the sound of her voice.

'Good Easter, Ragna,' he said, promptly forgetting all the things he had planned to say to her when they were alone again.

'Are you enjoying the feast?' she asked, after a moment.

'Aye,' he replied. 'It is a fine feast – passing fine.' He looked at her for a moment, dressed in a new rose-coloured mantle, her golden hair brushed until it gleamed, plaited with threads of silver into a thick braid which hung over one slender shoulder. She was a very vision, he thought, of beauty and womanly perfection.

He took a step towards her and she met him. They stood looking at one another for a long moment, neither speaking, and then Ragna placed the butter paddle on the table, and Murdo, his hand nearby, moved his fingers to meet hers. It was only a fleeting brush, but Murdo felt as if his fingertips had been singed in the flame that was kindled in that touch.

Ragna gave a little gasp of surprise, but her eyes never left his face. Her wide-eyed stare drank in his features and his heart beat fast to see the love and desire glowing there. He knew he should speak, but could think of nothing to say. 'I, ah – I mean, Ragna, I –' he began, badly.

She raised a slim finger to his lips. 'Shh,' she whispered, 'say nothing . . . my love . . .' The last words were spoken with the lightest exhalation of breath, so faint as to be inaudible, yet Murdo heard them as if she had shouted from the hilltop.

Transfixed by the moment, they stood without moving, the heat from their bodies burning across the small distance between them. Murdo wanted nothing more than to fold her into his arms and carry her away with him – to a place where they could be together always and for ever. She drew her face nearer; her lips readied for a kiss . . .

The door to the cookhouse opened just then, and one of the kitchen maids entered, saw them standing together and said, 'Üfda! Oh, it is you, Mistress Ragna, I was –'

'Here now,' said Ragna, bending quickly to the butter dish, 'it is heavy though. Mind you do not drop it.' So saying, she lifted the small mountain of butter and placed the dish in Murdo's hands. 'Hurry! They are waiting for it in the kitchen.'

Murdo took the dish and carried it to the door, moving past the maid, who turned and held the door open for him. The last thing he heard as he stepped outside was Ragna telling her maid, 'Run ahead of him and see the kitchen door is opened so he does not put the dish aside. The blame is yours if it gets so much as one fleck of dust on it. Go now!'

That was the only time Murdo spoke to Ragna alone for the remainder of their stay. A few days later, he and his mother joined Peder and Hin at the wharf where their boat was waiting for the return voyage home. Lady Ragnhild, her daughter, and a few servants accompanied their departing guests down to the cove to bid them fare well and see them away. There were two other boats in the cove, waiting to make sail, and Peder, anxious to cast off, called Murdo into the boat the moment his feet touched the planking.

The two women embraced one another and made their farewells. Ragnhild, smiling happily, said, 'Truly, it was good to have you here, Nia. I would invite you to join us for midsummer, but our husbands will no doubt have returned by then.'

'No doubt,' agreed Niamh. 'Even so, we can persuade them to observe the festivities together. And this time, you must come to us and allow us to return the hospitality we have so enjoyed.'

Murdo, preparing to cast off, heard this and looked up to see what Lady Ragnhild's response would be. Say yes, he thought, his heart quickening at the thought that in just a few months he would see Ragna again.

'Very well,' agreed Ragnhild, 'it is decided.' She and Niamh embraced one another warmly, whereupon Niamh took her place in the boat and Peder gave the nod to Hin and Murdo to cast off. The boat slid away from the wharf and Peder, working the tiller oar, turned the vessel with practiced ease.

Murdo took up his oar, and looked one last time to where Ragna stood; as the boat swung about, he saw her raise a hand to her lips, and then toward him in farewell – a brief gesture for him alone. He lifted a hand from the oar and returned her farewell, his heart soaring.

Until midsummer, he thought, feeling the delicious ache of anticipation begin again. He pulled hard on the oar, watching the slender white figure on the wharf until the black shoulder of the headland took her from view. And then, as Hin raised the sail, Murdo shipped his oar and filled his mind with Ragna's image even as the wind filled the white expanse of cloth.

NINE

Murdo stood on the clifftop, gazing down at Hrafnbú in the near distance. The sun was low, and the shadow of the long hill to the west cast most of the yard in darkness. There was no one about. Though all was quiet and, apparently, in order, the hair on the back of his neck prickled.

His mother, coming up behind him, saw him halt on the path. 'Murdo?' she said. 'What do you see?'

When he did not reply, she asked again, and this time he turned to her and said, 'Someone is at the house.'

'How do you know?' gasped Lady Niamh.

'Jötun is not here to greet us,' he replied. Turning to where Peder and Hin were working with the boat on the beach below, he shouted down to them, 'Peder, keep the boat ready! Hin, come with me!'

Niamh clutched at his sleeve. 'Murdo, take care!'

'I will, Mam,' he promised. 'Stay here with Peder until I return.'

'I will go with you.'

'Stay here, Mother,' he insisted, removing her hand gently from his arm. 'We will just go and see, and then come back.'

Niamh relented. 'Very well, but look you be careful, son.'

Hin joined them then. 'Follow me,' Murdo commanded, and the two of them set off at an easy loping run, skirting the path and coming at the house from across the empty field behind.

Niamh stood rooted to the clifftop, watching her youngest son as he ran, unarmed, into danger, and wondering when he had grown so tall and strong.

Peder called up from the beach to know what was happening, and she told him simply to wait, and then whispered to herself, 'Holy Michael, Angel of Might, guard my son with your fiery sword. Shield him, guide him, and lead him safely back.' She then made the sign of the cross, and folded her arms over her breast to wait.

Upon coming within shouting distance of the house, Murdo and Hin crouched down and proceeded slowly towards the first of the farm's outbuildings, alert to the slightest sign of trouble. They reached the tool hut without incident and, crawling cautiously around the side, entered the yard.

They halted at the edge of the hut, and waited for a moment, watching and listening. The house was quiet, and there did not seem to be anyone about. 'This way,' whispered Murdo and, flitting from the tool hut to the barn, disappeared inside.

The barn was dark and quiet, and Murdo had no sooner stepped inside than he caught a familiar, sick-sweet scent. Hin, darting in behind him, took a breath and whispered, 'Blood.'

Yet, there did not seem to be anything amiss. They moved silently to the great barn door, which was closed. Putting his face to a gap between door and post, Murdo looked out. The yard was empty still. He pushed through the breach and stood watching the house for any movement while Hin squeezed through behind him.

'They must be inside,' Murdo said softly. 'You stay here. I will go –'

He saw Hin's face freeze, and turned to see what had drawn his attention. Hanging on the door behind them was the body of a man. The wretch had been stabbed in the belly and chest, and then nailed to the door and left to bleed to death in agony.

Murdo moved to the corpse, stretched his hand towards a pale limb. The flesh was cold and hard, not like skin at all. He bent down and looked up into the dead man's features.

'It is Fossi,' said Hin, his voice hollow.

Murdo looked at the face, frozen in its final anguish, mouth open, eyes staring, and confirmed that it was indeed Fossi. The front of his siarc was black, and stiff with dried blood. There were wounds in both arms and legs and where the nails had gone in.

'He was still alive when they hung him here,' Murdo concluded sadly.

'What should we do?' asked Hin, his voice growing small and frail. Turning his eyes from the corpse, he glanced quickly around the yard.

Before Murdo could think what to say, there came the sound of a dog – half-growling, half-whining – as if the animal were being mistreated. 'Jötun!' whispered Murdo.

At that moment, a tall, fair-haired man entered the yard, pulling the resisting hound with a rope. He was dressed in leather breecs, tall boots of soft leather, and a tunic of undyed wool; he carried a stick in his hand, and every time Jötun tried to pull away, he struck the dog sharply on the back.

'You there!' shouted Murdo stepping away from the door. 'Stop that!'

The man spun towards the sound, took in Murdo at a glance, and said, 'Who are you to tell me what to do?'

'Let the dog loose,' Murdo said.

In response to this, the man, without moving, raised his voice and shouted at the house. 'Björn! Kali! Come here!'

A moment later, two men emerged from the house. Like the first, they were dressed in leather breecs and tunics; one was fair-haired, and the other dark, but both were tall and armed with swords and knives, the blades of which were thrust through their wide brown belts.

Hin took one look at the swords and backed towards the barn, ready to flee.

The two men regarded the newcomers impassively, but before either of them could speak, Murdo demanded, 'Who are you, and what is your business here?'

The dark-haired intruder answered. 'Keep a respectful tongue, boy,' he said quietly. 'What is your name?'

'I am Lord Ranulf's son,' Murdo replied, his voice loud in defiance. 'It is his land you are trespassing, and his hound you are beating.' Gesturing behind him at the barn door, he added, 'And it is Lord Ranulf's men you are murdering.'

'Björn! Do not let him –' the man with the stick began.

'Quiet, Arn,' the dark-haired man muttered, and stood eyeing Murdo cautiously.

'These lands belong to Prince Sigurd now,' the intruder told him, taking a slow step forward. 'We have taken them in the prince's name.'

'Jarl Erlend will hear of this!' Murdo charged. 'If you do not leave at once, I will go to the jarl and tell him what you have done. He will send his house carles against you.'

'No,' the one called Björn said, taking another step closer, 'I do not think he will do as you say. Hear now, King Magnus has taken possession of Orkneyjar unto himself and he has given the rule of the islands to his son.'

'Liar!' cried Murdo, anger rising within him like a tight-balled fist. 'Jarl Erlend would raise the war host against anyone who tried to steal these lands.'

The two fair-haired Norsemen laughed, but their dark-haired comrade gazed solemnly at the boy before him. 'I am telling you the truth,' he said. 'The jarl gave up without a fight. He and his worthless brother Paul have been taken hostage to the king's court in Norway. Prince Sigurd rules here now, and he has given the lands hereabouts to our lord.'

Murdo could not believe what he was hearing. How was it possible such momentous events should take place without his knowing?

'You are lying,' Murdo declared again. 'Who is this lord of yours?'

'Our lord is Orin Broad-Foot, advisor to Prince Sigurd,' Björn told him, taking another slow step nearer. 'He has gone to Kirkjuvágr to establish his claim of possession to Dýrness and its holdings. But he has commanded me to make an offer of peace with any who should come after.'

'What offer?' demanded Murdo, suspicion making his voice shrill. 'The same offer you gave *him*?' He pointed to poor dead Fossi nailed to the door.

'Aye, he had his chance, but took it into his head to fight,' the dark-haired intruder replied. 'Do not make the same mistake. Swear fealty to King Magnus, and you will live.'

'And if we should refuse?' sneered Murdo.

'Then, like the man on yonder door, you will die,' Björn answered indifferently. 'Now, it does not have to be that way. Lord Orin needs workers; vassals are no good to him dead.'

Stung by the cruel injustice of the demand, Murdo could not speak. To become vassals on the land they rightly owned and ruled – the thing was unthinkable.

'It is the land he wants, not blood, boy,' Björn said. 'Just you come with us, and we will see you are treated right.'

'We mean you no harm,' insisted Arn, holding tight to Jötun's collar. 'Come along peaceful and quiet now. We will go see Lord Orin and you can talk to him about it.'

'To the devil with you all,' growled Murdo.

Björn, having narrowed the distance between himself and his prey, leaped forward with an agility that surprised Murdo. But the younger man was the quicker, and Murdo ducked, driving his shoulder into the intruder's stomach as he lunged. To Murdo's amazement, the dark-haired man was lifted off his feet and thrown backward. 'Get him!' he screamed at his comrades, who stood looking on in flat-footed wonder.

The one called Kali ran at Murdo and made a clumsy grab, which the young man easily eluded. Murdo dodged aside and made to run between Kali and the fallen warrior, but Björn kicked out as he darted past, sweeping Murdo's legs from under him. Murdo landed on his side in the dirt, and Kali was on him instantly.

Hard hands seized him and he was jerked roughly to his feet. Björn rose up before him, drew back his arm and struck Murdo on the face with the back of his hand. Murdo's teeth rattled with the force of the blow and red-and-black fireballs spun before his eyes. His legs lost strength and he slumped to his knees.

Björn, cursing the boy's audacity, raised his arm to strike again. Kali, gripping his arms, hauled him upright, and Murdo braced himself for the blow. The hand started forward, but faltered half-way to the mark as Jötun, seeing his master in trouble, pulled free from his captor's grasp. Arn darted after him, but the great wolf-hound took two bounds, leapt, and seized the offending arm in his teeth.

Murdo heard a shriek of pain as Björn was yanked sideways and down. Kali, in his haste to help his companion, abandoned his charge and shoved Murdo aside; he drew his sword and ran to where the hound was doing his best to wrest the dark-haired intruder's arm from his shoulder.

'Jötun!' shouted Murdo, desperate to draw the dog away before Kali could strike. 'Here, Jötun!' But the fair-haired warrior stepped in and the sword, clutched tight in both hands, swung up over his head.

Then, even as the sword descended, Kali was struck from behind and thrown forward, losing his balance. The blow fell awry, striking the big dog a glancing stroke on the shoulder.

Murdo sensed a rush of motion towards him. Suddenly Hin was there, lifting him to his feet. 'Run, Master Murdo! Run!'

His ears still ringing from the blow to his face, Murdo shook his head to clear it. 'This way!' he said, dashing for the barn. 'Jötun, come!'

The hound obeyed and all three ran for the gap in the door, leaving the three intruders stumbling in momentary confusion. Björn quickly came to his senses, however; clutching his bleeding arm he shouted for Kali and Arn to give chase. Then, turning towards the house, Björn bellowed for help.

Murdo glanced back over his shoulder as they disappeared into the darkened interior of the barn, and his heart sank to see four more Norsemen emerge from the house. Without a quiver of hesitation Murdo made for the far wall of the huge barn, dodging around the grain wagons and carefully stacked bundles of straw.

He reached the back wall and crouched down, searching for a small door – little more than a flap of wood hinged with leather – cut in the back wall of the barn some time in the past to allow pigs to get in out of the rain. It was unused now, but Murdo remembered it, and thought that if they could reach it before the warriors saw them, they might gain a few precious moments to make their escape. He ran along the wall for a few paces, found the door, and pushed it open.

'This way,' he said, shoving Hin through ahead of him.

Murdo ducked through next and held the flap for Jötun. Shouts from inside the barn told him their secret would soon be discovered. 'Run for the boat,' said Hin, breathless with fear.

'No,' Murdo warned, 'they would see us and follow us to the bay. Even if we outran them, we would never cast off in time.'

'What, then?' whispered Hin desperately.

'This way.' Murdo dashed for the corner of the barn, reached it, and slid around to the other side. He then ran along the side of the barn to the yard. As he expected, all the warriors had joined the pursuit and were now inside the barn. He and Hin darted across the yard to the side of the house and disappeared around the corner, Jötun following at their heels.

'Listen, to me now,' Murdo said. 'The old barrow – south of the bay – do you know it?'

Hin nodded. 'I know it, yes. I think so.'

'Make for it. You can hide there and they will never find you.'

'Inside the grave mound?'

'There is nothing to fear,' Murdo told him, thinking of the hunting game he and his brothers had played for years. 'I have done it a hundred times.' He slapped Hin on the shoulder to awaken his courage. 'Go now. Take Jötun with you and wait for me. I will meet you there.'

'Meet me?' wondered Hin worriedly. 'But where are you going?'

'I must lead them a false trail or they will go directly to the bay,' Murdo explained. 'Go now. I will join you at the barrow, and we will take the cliff trail to the bay. Hurry! before they see you.'

Hin, shaking with fear, spoke a command to the hound and, putting his hand to the dog's heavy collar, started off across the field behind the house at a run. Murdo waited until he was well away, then crept back along the side of the house and peered around the corner. The yard was empty, so he started across – as if he meant to escape down the track leading to the house.

He reached the entrance to the yard and heard Björn's voice cry out behind him. Without so much as a backward glance, Murdo started off, smiling to himself. The chase was on.

TEN

The old grave mound had been raised by the first inhabitants of Dýrness in times past remembering. It was a single long chamber marked out and roofed over with great slabs of stone and covered with earth. Its low entrance opened onto the sea, and from any distance its shallow hump appeared as nothing more than a hillock of grassy turf.

There was an old tale that the People of the Otter had built the mound as a tomb for their revered dead; there might have been something in this, so far as Murdo knew, for some men near Orphir had once found skulls and leg bones, beads, and carved stones in a similar mound; even so, he had never found anything but bits of shell and a few otter teeth, and he had been inside many times.

By the time he reached the tumulus, Murdo was out of breath. He had led the intruders a furious chase, allowing them tantalizing glimpses of him as he drew them further and further away from the coast, before losing them in the bracken of the valley. He then doubled back to the hill and, when he was certain he was not followed any longer, raced along the cliff track to the barrow.

'Hin,' he called softly, kneeling at the small dark entrance. 'Jötun.'

He waited a moment. When he did not receive any reply, he called again. Again, there was no answer, so Murdo knelt down and, cursing Hin's stupidity, wormed his way into the mound. The interior was cool and still as any cavern. He knew, before opening his mouth to call for the third and last time, that Hin was not there.

He backed out and climbed to the top of the mound and lay down on his stomach, scanning the fields between the cliff-top and the house. There was no sign of Hin, nor was there any sign of Lord Orin's men.

The devil take him, thought Murdo angrily, as he slid down the rounded rump of the mound. He had little choice now but to make for the cove and hope that Hin, having grown tired of waiting, had ignored his instructions and gone there instead.

Murdo struck off along the coast track, adopting a peculiar low trot which, though uncomfortable, would keep him out of sight from the house and surrounding fields. Upon reaching the bay a short while later, he looked down to the strand below, saw the boat, Peder, and his mother standing nearby – but neither Hin nor Jötun were anywhere to be seen.

He scrambled down the stepped path. 'Where is Hin?' he called as soon as his feet touched the sand.

'He went with you and has not returned,' his mother replied, hurrying to meet him. 'Why? What has happened, Murdo?'

'Intruders have taken the house,' he informed her. 'They killed Fossi –'

'No!'

'Yes – killed with the sword. The intruders chased us, but we got away,' Murdo explained. 'I told Hin to wait for me at the barrow. I was just there, but could not find him.'

'Why would they kill Fossi?' asked Niamh, struggling to keep her voice steady as the shock of his words struck her.

'I will explain it later.' With that he turned and started away again. 'Stay here.'

'Murdo, no!' she cried, even as she marvelled at her son's courage.

'I am going to find Hin,' he shouted behind him. 'Help Peder make ready to sail. Put to sea as soon as you see us on the cliff.'

Murdo reached the tumulus and, once again, called for Hin. Receiving no reply, he edged around the side of the mound and looked back towards the bú. As his eyes swept the expanse of empty fields, he heard a shout in the distance, looked in the direction of the sound and saw Hin running to meet him, Jötun loping easily at his side.

Stepping quickly from behind the mound, Murdo put his hands to his mouth and urged them to hurry. Even as his shout hung in the air, the intruders appeared – four big men, armed with spears.

They were gaining on Hin, but Murdo reckoned he would reach the cove before the intruders could catch him. 'Run!' he cried. 'They are onto you, man! Run for your life!'

Hin put his head down and ran the harder. Seeing his master, Jötun, too, increased his pace. Murdo thought to run back to help ready the boat for their escape, but could not tear himself away from the chase before him. He could not help Hin by staying; neither could he leave. 'Faster!' he cried.

Murdo glanced across the cliff-top towards the hidden cove, torn between going and staying. He looked back to the chase just in time to see Hin stumble and fall headlong to the ground. 'Get up!' cried Murdo, dashing towards his fallen friend.

Hin regained his feet in an instant, and started running again. The wild whoops of the pursuers pierced the air, and Murdo, crying encouragement, raced empty-handed to the rescue.

He had taken but a dozen steps, however, when the hapless Hin, risking a look behind him, tangled his feet and went down again. He sprang up and ran on – but not as fast as before, his gait laboured. One of the foremost pursuers, seeing a chance, put back his arm and, with a mighty heave, loosed his spear into the air. The shaft landed only a few paces behind the struggling Hin.

Murdo cursed the brute's cowardly heart, and shouted for Hin to hurry. The second spear was in the air before Murdo drew breath again. He watched the deadly thing arc and fall beside his friend. Hin ran on.

'Hin! Jötun!' cried Murdo. He could see Hin's face now, and knew he was injured. 'Come, you both! The boat is waiting!'

Murdo did not see the third spear thrown – merely the cruel glint of the blade in the air as it dropped, and then Hin's face as he felt it strike home. The force of the blow carried him forward a few steps before he fell.

Murdo halted and stood gazing in horror at the spearshaft protruding from Hin's back. Jötun, too, sensing the terrible distress of the human with him, turned and began pulling at the wooden shaft as if he would draw it with his teeth.

Hin made to rise. He pushed himself up on stiff arms and looked to Murdo. White-faced, eyes wide and bulging, the unlucky youth opened his mouth to call out, but collapsed as the foemen rushed upon him.

Murdo spun away and did not look back – not even when he heard the cheers of the victors. The world became a blur around him – grass, rocks, sea, sky – everything melted and merged, and Murdo ran as he had never run in all his life, rage and fear lending speed to his flight. He ran, tears in his eyes and a curse between his teeth. Upon reaching the cove, he flung himself headlong down the cliff-side, shouting, 'Go! Go! Go!'

The boat was in the water a few dozen paces from the shore. Peder had already turned the vessel; the prow was pointing seaward.

'Go!' Murdo shouted, and saw the oars strike the water. 'Row!'

The invaders gained the top of the promontory and started down the narrow trail. Murdo leapt the last few steps, and fell sprawling on elbows and knees in the deep sand.

He heard his mother scream, and he scrambled forward, crab-like, hands and feet churning. In the same instant, a spear struck the sand in the very place he had landed. Half-rolling, half-running, he struggled on, the soft sand dragging at his feet.

'Row!' cried Murdo. 'Row, Peder!'

Behind him, Orin's men, having sighted the boat and its passengers, loosed wild whoops and flew down the cliff-side trail.

Murdo gained the water's edge and splashed to his knees in two bounds, then lunged into a dive and came up swimming, all the time shouting 'Row, Peder! Row!'

The boat had increased its distance from the shore, and was moving more quickly now as Peder's swift sure oar-strokes carried it forward. For an awful moment, Murdo thought he would not be able to swim fast enough to catch it. Tired from his run, he could already feel the strength ebbing from his arms and legs. His lungs burned and he felt himself sinking lower in the water.

Closing his eyes, Murdo swam until he thought his heart would burst. He heard a voice call out to him, and felt something hard strike him and wrap him in stiff coils. He opened his eyes to see that his mother had thrown a rope. He grabbed it and felt himself drawn through the water.

Three heartbeats later, he bumped against the side of the boat, reached up a hand and somehow grasped the rail. Then his mother's hands were on him, hauling him up from the sea; he kicked his legs and was dragged over the rail. He slid into the bottom of the boat and lay gasping and panting like a landed salmon.

His mother, bending over him, brushed the water from his face and searched him with her eyes. 'I – I,' he wheezed, 'I am – not hurt.'

There came a raw cry from the beach and Niamh turned towards the sound. Murdo, pushing himself up, leaned against the side of the boat and looked back at the beach to see a dark mass streaking across the sand towards the water.

'Jötun!' cried Murdo.

As if in answer to his name, the great hound barked once and sped between two Norsemen. One of the men lunged at the dog with his spear, missed, and fell onto his knees as the animal raced by.

'Come, Jötun!' shouted Murdo, dragging himself up. 'Jötun! Here!'

All four Norsemen were on the beach now, and two were wading into the water as if they might give chase. The dog, swimming mightily, passed out of reach, but the intruders, having lost the boat and its passengers, appeared reluctant to allow the animal to get away, too. Picking up stones from the beach, they threw them at the dog and at the retreating boat, venting their frustration in curses and crude abuse.

Gripping the rail, Murdo leaned over the water and called encouragement to the hound. Jötun paddled with renewed fervor, but it was clear the animal could not overtake the boat. 'Stop rowing, Peder!' called Murdo. 'He cannot reach us.'

So saying, Murdo, rope in hand, plunged over the side once more and swam to meet the dog.

'Murdo!' screamed Niamh, striking the rail with the flats of her hands. 'He'll drag you down, son!'

The invaders, seeing Murdo in the water once more, redoubled their efforts. The stones came thick and fast. One of the foemen dived into the sea and began swimming towards the youth and his dog.

Ignoring his mother and the commotion on the beach, Murdo swam to Jötun, seized a handful of wet fur at the nape of the beast's neck, and shouted, 'Pull us in!'

Upon reaching the boat, Murdo gripped the rail and tried to lift the dog out of the water; the animal was too heavy – it took both Peder and Lady Niamh to drag the soggy hound into the boat. Murdo followed, slithering over the side like an eel. He then had to brave Jötun's wet and happy welcome, while Peder and his mother stood looking on.

As the dog licked his master's face with great lashes of his tongue, Murdo took his head in both hands and tried to hold him back. 'Down! Jötun, down!'

Suddenly, a tremendous splash sent water cascading over the rail. 'They's on the cliff!' shouted Peder, taking up the oars once more.

Murdo raised his eyes to the promontory high above them and saw three Norsemen raising an enormous chunk of stone. They swung it once . . . twice . . . and let it go. The rock tumbled slowly as it sank, striking the cliff-face and spinning out into the air to smash into the cove a mere hairsbreadth from the stern.

'Row!' shouted Murdo, leaping to the bench. Settling himself beside Peder, he took an oar and began pulling with all his might.

By the time the third stone struck the water, the boat was moving again, slowly, edging away from the cliff. Two more stones were thrown – each further away than the last, and Murdo knew they were finally out of reach.

They gained the mouth of the cove and Peder, shipping his oar, dashed to the tiller, calling, 'Up sail, boy!'

Murdo leapt to the mast, quickly untied the loosely-secured line, and dragged it towards the prow. The yard rose slowly and came around as the sail unfurled; he then pulled for all he was worth, and when the yard gained the top of the mast, he quickly ran to secure the line once more. For a few agonizing moments, the sail flapped idly, slapping the mast in an uncertain wind. Peder gave a few mighty heaves on the oars, and the boat came clear of the cove. All at once the lank sail snapped smart, filled, and the boat lurched forward, the prow biting deep into the swell.

'Hruha!' cried Peder. 'Hruha-hey!'

Murdo, sweating and exhausted, stood and watched the figures on the shore and sea ridge dwindle away, and even when he could no longer see them, he still watched. Niamh came to stand beside him. Neither one spoke, until Peder, manning the tiller, called out to know what course he should set.

'Hrolfsey,' Niamh told him. 'We will return to Cnoc Carrach, and hope we can warn them in time.'

'They will have taken those lands, too,' Murdo pointed out. 'They have taken everything.'

'Maybe,' allowed his mother. 'But I do not see what else we can do.'

ELEVEN

Hugh, Count of Vermandois, arrived in Constantinople well ahead of his army. Owing to a nasty shipwreck, the unfortunate young lord had lost his horse, armour, a few hundred good men, and most of his coin, and was therefore relieved when an imperial escort arrived two days later. While he was borne swiftly to the capital, his army – reprovisioned at the emperor's expense, and led by a regiment of Pecheneg mercenaries – undertook the long march through Macedonia and Thrace.

The excubitori hastened their noble charge along the Egnatian Way, sweeping through the Golden Gate and into the streets of the most magnificent city Count Hugh had ever seen. There were buildings of such size and grandeur as to make the castles of his brother, Philip, King of the Franks, appear little more than cow byres.

He saw men wearing long robes of costly material, and women aglitter with gold and jewels, walking about unattended and unarmed. He saw men astride elegant horses, and beautiful dark-haired women borne through the streets in chairs, their slaves better arrayed than himself. Everywhere he looked a new wonder met the eye: churches with domes of gleaming copper, topped with crosses of silver and gold; basilicas of glazed brick; statues of emperors, some carved in stone, others cast in bronze; victory columns and triumphal arches erected to celebrate commanders and conquests unknown in the west; long, broad avenues paved with stone radiating out from circular plazas in every direction as far as the eye could see.

Count Hugh was given no time to savour these sights, but was conveyed straight away to the emperor's palace, where, still breathless from the relentless chase of the last days, and dazzled by the prodigious wealth and power he saw all around him, he was led stiff-legged with wonder into the imperial throne room. There, seated on an enormous chair of solid gold, he was received by God's Vice-

Regent, the Equal of the Apostles and Emperor of All Christendom, Alexius Comnenus.

The magister officiorum indicated that the young count was to prostrate himself before the throne. He did so, pressing his fevered brow to the cool marble floor with a profound sense of relief and thanksgiving.

'Rise, Lord Hugh, and stand before us,' Alexius commanded genially in impeccable Latin. 'Word of your recent misfortune has reached our ears. Perhaps you would allow us to offer you a small expression of our commiseration over your loss.'

Lifting a hand, the emperor summoned a half-dozen Varangi, who stepped forward, each bearing an item of armour, which they placed at the much-impressed Count Hugh's feet. He saw a fine new mail hauberk and steel helm; there was a splendid sword, belt, and scabbard, and a handsome dagger to match, and a long spear with a gleaming new blade. A sturdy round shield with spiked silver boss was laid atop the rest.

'Lord Emperor, I thank you,' Hugh gushed. 'Indeed, I am overwhelmed by your generosity and thoughtfulness.'

'Perhaps you would bestow on us the inestimable honour of being our guest during your stay in the city,' Alexius said.

'I am your servant, Lord Emperor,' Hugh replied, not quite believing his remarkable good fortune. After a disastrous beginning, it appeared his pilgrimage was at last coming right. 'But, if it please you, lord, a humble bed in a nearby abbey or monastery would suit me. My needs are simple.'

'Come now,' the emperor cajoled gently. 'You are our esteemed guest. We cannot allow you to wander the streets alone. You will, of course, reside here in the palace with us.'

Hugh acquiesced with good grace. 'Nothing would please me more, Lord Emperor.'

'So be it,' Alexius said. 'Magister, conduct our friend to the apartment prepared for him. We will expect to see him at table tonight where we will share wine, and he will relate the tale of his recent adventures.'

Hugh, still overcome by this surprising turn of events, bowed low and backed away from the throne. Upon reaching the carved marble screen before the door, he turned and followed the magister officiorum from the reception hall.

When he had gone and the doors were closed once more, Grand Drungarius Dalassenus stepped beside the throne. 'Do you trust him, basileus?'

Alexius pressed his fingertips together and leaned back in his great chair. 'I think so, but time will tell,' he replied, tapping his fingers against his lips thoughtfully. 'Still, if I have an ally among the western lords, it will be easier to deal with those who come after. This one is harmless, I think. He is the Frankish king's brother; he has lost everything in the shipwreck and is therefore needy. We will make him beholden to us, and see if he will repay his debt.' Turning to his commander, the emperor asked, 'How many soldiers remain to him?'

'Only a few thousand,' answered Dalassenus. The emperor glanced at him sharply, so he amended his reply accordingly. 'Four thousand mounted troops, and maybe half again as many on foot. They should arrive in Constantinople sometime in the next three or four weeks.'

'The others will have arrived long since,' Alexius observed dismally.

'Yes, basileus,' Dalassenus concurred. 'Our Pecheneg watchers tell us they are but ten days' march from here.'

'Ten days . . .' Alexius frowned. It was not much time. 'Well, there is nothing to be done about it. We must take them as they come and, God help us, deal with them as best we can.'

Two days later, after receiving numerous gifts of gold, as well as a handsome and well-trained horse from the emperor's own stables, the all-but delirious Count Hugh, having been feasted and shown the treasures of Byzantium, was once more summoned before the throne. He entered to find the emperor dressed in purple and surrounded by a contingent of Varangian guardsmen wearing helmets with horsetail plumes, and carrying spears with broad leaf-shaped blades.

'Greetings, in Christ's name, Lord Hugh,' the emperor said. 'Come closer, friend, and learn the subject of our latest meditations.'

'If it pleases you, Lord Emperor,' replied Hugh, utterly beguiled by the affable and compact Alexius. He stepped to the very foot of the throne and awaited his benefactor's sage reflections, glancing now and again at the fearsome Varangi, standing tall and silent in their ranks a few paces behind the throne.

'We have been thinking about this pilgrimage, this Holy Crusade which the pope has decreed,' the emperor began. 'It would seem to us a difficult task to bring so many men from so many different nations to Jerusalem.'

'It is our duty and our joy,' replied Hugh confidently. 'As good Christians we happily obey God's will.'

'Of course,' agreed Alexius, 'and it is laudable that so many have answered the call of this duty – laudable, yes, but difficult nonetheless.'

'The hardships are insignificant in view of the glory to be obtained,' Hugh remarked. 'What are earthly travails compared to Heaven's treasures?'

'Indeed,' said the emperor. 'Yet, we find we have the power to alleviate a few of those hardships for you. The matter of supply and provisioning, for example, weighs heavily on all competent commanders. Soldiers and animals must be fed and watered, after all. Weapons and equipment must be maintained. We have ready stores of grain and oil, wine and meat, and so forth. These could be made available to the armies that pass through imperial lands.'

'It would be a blessing, Lord Emperor,' replied Hugh, impressed yet again by the emperor's incomparable largesse.

'Good,' cried Alexius jubilantly. 'We will cause orders to be given to establish provisioning stations along the way for the armies yet to come. Further, some arrangement must be made to promote harmony and unity of purpose among men arriving from such diverse lands and realms. It would seem that as we assume the burden for supplying these armies, we also accept the responsibility for encouraging their accord.' The emperor regarded his guest placidly. 'Is that not reasonable?'

'Entirely reasonable, Lord Emperor,' replied Hugh readily. 'It is wisdom itself.'

'What better way to bind the disparate members of this unruly body,' Alexius continued, 'and remind them of their common purpose, than to bring them under the authority of the one who shoulders the burden and responsibility?'

Hugh, entirely agreeable, nodded his support for the notion.

'Therefore, we propose a declaration of allegiance, recognizing the supremacy of the imperial throne,' Alexius concluded. He smoothed his purple robe with battle-hardened hands and gazed benignly upon his guest.

'Does the emperor envision the form this declaration might take?'

Alexius pressed his mouth into a thin line and held his head to one side – as if considering this question for the first time. 'A simple oath of fealty should suffice,' he answered equably, then added a satisfied: 'Yes, that should serve us nicely.'

Before Hugh could reply, the emperor continued, 'Naturally, the noblemen who lead this pilgrimage, and benefit from the empire's protection and provision, would take the oath, binding them one to another under the dominion of the imperial throne.'

Recognizing what was required of him, Count Hugh happily complied. 'Might I beg a boon, Lord Emperor? I would deem it an honour if I were allowed to be the first to take this oath.'

'Oh, indeed, Lord Hugh,' the emperor replied. 'Take it, you shall.'

TWELVE

Murdo recognized every twist in the muddy track rising from the harbour to the cathedral. Retracing his steps for the sixth time in as many weeks, each lump and puddle had the tediously familiar look of a much-detested chore. A chill rain splattered down over him as he slogged along beside his mother, the low grey sky making for a day as dismal as his mood. In five attempts they had yet to obtain an audience with the bishop; even the abbot was so overwhelmed by the imperative duties of his office that he could not fight free long enough to discuss their petition.

Still, Lady Niamh was determined to enlist the church's aid in regaining their estate. It was said, and widely believed, that King Magnus and his son, Prince Sigurd, were God-fearing men, baptized into the faith, and generous supporters of the church. Indeed, on two of their five visits the bishop could not attend his usual office of supplication because he was closeted with the young prince, who was receiving Christian catechism from the senior churchman himself.

'We will not leave,' Niamh vowed, for the fourth time since starting out, 'until we have spoken to Bishop Adalbert in the very flesh, and he has heard our petition.'

Murdo made no reply. It seemed to him an empty vow. Five times they had come, and five times failed. He saw no reason to think that this visit would be any different. The bishop, he decided, was avoiding them. This neither surprised nor dismayed him. He had long since relegated the church and its leaders to the perdition preserved for grasping clerics and their smarmy ilk who preyed on the credulous and gullible. His mother, he knew, was neither gullible nor credulous, and this was precisely why the churchmen refused to see her. What Murdo could not understand was why she insisted the bishop should be involved in this dispute.

The track rose sharply as it joined the path leading to the sanctuary entrance. The great doors were closed, but the smaller entry cut out of the right-hand panel was open. They entered the dim, shadowed vestibule and paused, allowing their eyes to grow accustomed to the murky interior. The tall pillars stretched up into the darkness above, their broad bases lit by pools of quivering candlelight. A few monks chanted away near the altar, their voices echoing from the cavernous vaults of the roof, making it seem as if moaning angels hovered far, far overhead like desultory doves.

On their previous visits, Lady Niamh had presented herself to the first monk who met them, and requested an audience with the bishop. On each occasion, the entreaty was duly channelled along lines of proper authority and they were politely conducted to the cloistered gallery outside the chapter house where the bishop held consultation with those members of his flock seeking his advice on matters both temporal and spiritual. There they were asked to wait until the bishop could receive them.

Five times they had sat and waited, and five times they had departed without so much as a glimpse of the elusive churchman. The first three times, after a lengthy wait, a monk had come to inform them that the bishop's previous consultations had run overlong and that he begged to be pardoned but he would not be able to see them. They were, with all cordiality, invited to please come again next week; the bishop would certainly see them then. On their fourth visit, they were informed, after another long and tedious wait, that Bishop Adalbert had been suddenly called away on a matter of utmost urgency and that he would not return for several days. Then, last week, after waiting through most of the day, they had at last been forced to leave when the bells rang vespers and the cathedral was closed to visitors. No explanation was offered for the bishop's failure to see them.

With each disappointment, Murdo watched his mother's fortitude weaken a little more. It hurt him to see her losing her resolve, and he determined that he would not allow her dignity to be stolen, too. The waiting, he concluded, was meant to wear them down, to make them so grateful for their audience, should they finally receive it, that they would gladly accept whatever sop the bishop deigned to offer them.

Now, here they were, for the sixth time, and Murdo decided it would be the last.

As before, they were met by a monk who conducted them to the chapter house door where they were asked to wait. The monk bade them sit and indicated the wooden bench, then turned, opened the door, and made to step inside. Murdo, however, moved in swiftly, seized the door and held it open. 'I think we have waited long enough,' he told the monk.

'Please! Please! This is a holy place. You cannot force –'

Murdo shoved the door wider. 'Coming, Mother?'

Niamh, overcoming her reluctance, joined her son. 'Yes, I think we have waited long enough,' she told the monk. To her son, she whispered, 'Be careful, Murdo,' and gave him a sharp warning glance as she passed.

They entered a long dark cell. A single narrow window high up in the wall allowed a little sunlight into the room; otherwise, the few candles scattered here and there provided the only light. Five or six clerics toiled at a large table beneath the window; they looked up as the visitors entered, but then resumed their work. To Murdo, the scratching of their quills sounded like rats scrabbling in the dry husks in the barn; and there was something decidedly vermin-like about the brown-robed clerics and their bristly, half-shaven heads and narrow eyes held close to their work.

'Where is the bishop?' asked Murdo, his voice loud in the thick silence of the room. 'We want to see him *now*.'

The monk made no reply, but his eyes shifted towards one of the two doors at the farther end of the room. 'In there, is he?' asked Murdo, already moving towards the door. He lifted the latch and pushed it open even as the monk hurried to stop him. Stepping into the room, he saw a cleric sitting at a table piled high with loose scrolls. The man was hunched over his work, and looked up as Murdo walked quickly to the table.

'Ah, young Ranulfson – is it not?' Abbot Gerardus said, his voice flat, expressing neither surprise nor concern.

Murdo frowned. The smarmy abbot was the last person Murdo wanted to meet. 'We have come to see the bishop,' he told the abbot coldly. 'Where is he?'

'We?' the abbot asked, his smile thin and self-amused.

'My mother and I –' began Murdo, gesturing behind him as Lady Niamh entered the room, the ineffectual monk darting in behind her.

'I am sorry, abbot – they would not wait,' the monk began, but the abbot silenced him.

'Never mind, Brother Gerald,' said the abbot, rising from his chair. 'They are here now; I will see them myself.'

'It is the bishop we have come to see,' Murdo repeated.

'That is not convenient,' the abbot said, turning to Murdo, his eyes hard. 'Perhaps if you had made proper application –'

'We have been coming here for five weeks!' Murdo snapped. 'Each time we make *proper application*, and each time we wait and wait, and we go away without seeing anyone! This time, we *will* see the bishop. I do not care whether it is *convenient* or not!'

The abbot bristled. His eyes narrowed, and he glared at the young man before him, his mouth tight with unexpressed loathing.

'Abbot Gerardus,' Niamh said, stepping briskly forward, 'I will ask you to forgive my son's bad manners. He seems to have forgotten himself in his impatience.'

'Of course, Lady Niamh,' said the abbot, inclining his head in a modest bow, instantly the self-effacing cleric once more. 'I am your servant. How may I help you?'

'It is as my son has said: we have come to see the bishop, and in light of our previous attempts, I must insist we see him today.'

'Then I fear you will be disappointed yet again,' the abbot replied with a small gesture of helplessness – as if to say that the matter was in the hands of an authority much greater than his own. 'You see, the bishop has given instruction that he is not to be disturbed for any reason. Perhaps you will allow me to help you in his stead.'

'Show us where he is,' Murdo demanded. 'That will help us best.'

Laying a hand on her son's arm, Niamh said, 'Peace, Murdo. It may be that once we have explained our purpose, the abbot will intercede for us.' She turned to the abbot for confirmation of this assertion, but the abbot merely smiled wanly back.

Murdo wanted nothing more than to shove his fist into the abbot's smirking face, but refrained for his mother's sake, and for the sake of Hrafnbú.

'As you will know,' Lady Niamh began, moving a step nearer the table, 'the rule of the islands has passed from Jarls Erlend and Paul, to Prince Sigurd, son of Magnus, King of Norway.'

'Certainly,' Abbot Gerardus replied, 'we are only too aware of the upheaval this has caused. This is precisely the reason why you have found it so difficult to gain audience with the bishop these last weeks.'

'In consequence,' Niamh continued, 'our lands have been taken from us. Two of my servants were killed, and we have escaped with only our lives.'

The abbot pressed his mouth into a firm line. After a moment, he said, 'Most distressing, to be sure. Yet, I cannot see what you expect the church to do about it.'

Niamh stared at him in amazement. 'This injustice must be remedied as swiftly as possible,' she said. 'Our estate has been seized and given to one called Orin Broad-Foot, a nobleman said to be an advisor to Prince Sigurd. The bishop must intercede for us with the prince. He must demand the return of our lands – on pain of excommunication, if need be.'

'Would that we could wield such power as you imagine us to possess,' Abbot Gerardus said with a show of weary resignation. 'In truth, we have no such authority. The bishop would tell you the same.'

'Then let him tell us face to face,' growled Murdo.

'If only that were possible,' replied the abbot.

'Do you refuse to allow us an audience?' demanded Niamh.

'Alas, it is not within my sway to allow *or* refuse,' the churchman said. 'It is the bishop's command. We all must obey.'

'My husband is on pilgrimage,' Niamh said pointedly. 'He is fighting for the church – and you ask me to believe that the bishop, at whose insistence he took the cross, cannot now find the time to address a wicked violation of the peace which he himself upholds.'

'Again,' the abbot replied, 'you think us more powerful than we are. The church has no authority to compel the compliance with –'

The abbot broke off suddenly as the door behind him opened and all turned to see the bishop himself emerge from his audience chamber. 'It is well, abbot,' Adalbert said in a kindly voice. 'I heard voices and thought to interrupt my meditations if I might be of service.' He smiled benevolently and, turning to his visitors, said, 'Lady Niamh, it is so good to see you. Tell me now, daughter, how may I help you?'

While the abbot stood frowning, Niamh stepped to the bishop and quickly explained the theft of their land and the predicament forced upon them. Murdo watched in growing disbelief as the bishop, nodding in heartfelt sympathy replied, 'It is most distressing. Yes, most distressing. Believe me, I wish there was something we could do.'

'But you can intercede for us,' Niamh insisted. 'You are the sole authority of the church in Orkneyjar. There has been a dire mistake. On pain of excommunication, you can force them to relinquish the land they have stolen.'

The bishop, still sympathetic, replied, 'Lady, I cannot.' He seemed to reconsider his reply then; raising a finger, he asked, 'What was the name of the man who has assumed ownership of your estate?'

'He is one of Prince Sigurd's house carles – a nobleman called Orin.' Niamh glanced at Murdo for confirmation; he nodded curtly, suspicion swarming around him like wasps.

The bishop appeared to hesitate, as if drawn up short by the name. 'Lord Orin Broad-Foot?'

'The same, yes,' Niamh answered. 'Do you know him?'

'Alas,' sighed the bishop, 'would that you had said any name but that. Was I not holding audience with that man in this very room, Gerardus?'

'Indeed, yes, Bishop Adalbert,' replied the abbot, who seemed to Murdo to have become curiously complacent about the proceedings.

'Then you know that what I have said is true,' Lady Niamh declared.

'Dear lady,' rejoined the bishop, 'I have never doubted you for a moment.'

'Then you will help us.'

'I have already told you that I would if I could,' Adalbert maintained. 'But Lord Orin has followed his king's leading and has taken the cross.'

Murdo felt a sick dread stealing over him. He could feel the knife sliding into his gut, though he had not yet seen the blade.

'Indeed, he, like so many of our island sons, is to become a pilgrim,' the bishop continued. 'In view of the upcoming journey, he has availed himself of the pope's decree regarding the guardianship of the land.'

Niamh stared at the bishop. 'You mean . . .' She faltered, unable to make herself say the words.

'The Holy Church of Christ has pledged protection for the estate,' the bishop replied. 'The pertinent documents have been signed and are now on their way to Jorvik for safekeeping. So you see, it is too late.'

'When did this take place?' Niamh's voice had gone cold.

'Two days ago,' said the abbot, almost gloating with triumph.

'Two days!' shouted Murdo. 'Two days! Yet, you *knew* we had been here seeking audience every week for five weeks! You knew it and did nothing!'

'Calm yourself, son. Your anger is misplaced. As it happens, the assumption of Prince Sigurd has brought about many sudden and unexpected changes, as you can imagine. We have been kept busy from dawn to dusk merely to keep pace with the demands which, like your own, have arisen in the wake of the jarls' removal. I assure you, we knew nothing of your plight until you told us just now.'

'Hrafnbú is *ours!*' shouted Murdo; fists balled, he stepped towards the bishop. 'It is ours and you knew it!'

'Yes!' Adalbert snapped, anger flickering to life. 'And I tried to make your father see reason, but he refused. So be it. Now you must live with the consequence of his stupidity.' Glancing at Niamh, he quickly added, 'I am sorry to be so blunt, good lady, but there is nothing I can do.'

Abbot Gerardus moved to the bishop's side. 'If Lord Ranulf had not been so covetous of his rents, the estate would sooner have been under our control, and you would still have a home.'

Murdo gave a strangled cry and started for the abbot, who backed away swiftly.

'Murdo!' his mother shouted, her voice sharp as a slap. She drew him back, saying, 'Come away, son. We will not weary these church-men further with our trifling grievance. They must have other sheep in their flock to look after – it seems it is the shearing season after all.'

'Lady Niamh,' protested the bishop, 'I fear you have taken my meaning amiss.'

'Have I?' she challenged tartly. 'Covetous of his rents . . . the estate under our control . . .' She paused, eyes ablaze. When she spoke again, her voice was low, barely audible. 'I believe I understood your meaning very well, proud priest.'

The bishop frowned. 'Please, you must be patient. No doubt the matter can be disentangled when the claimants have returned from pilgrimage to resume the governance of their estates.'

'What would you have us do until then?' demanded Niamh. 'Beg in the marketplace like paupers?'

'The convent is ever –' began the abbot.

But Niamh was no longer listening. 'Come away, Murdo. There is no justice for us here.'

She turned her back on the churchmen, and walked to the door. Murdo glared at the men with all the hate his soul could muster, and felt the awful impotence of frustrated rage. 'You will curse the day you slandered my father and sided against us,' he said, his voice trembling with fury. 'Hear me! Murdo Ranulfson makes this vow.'

'Come away, Murdo,' his mother called from the door. 'Do not waste your breath on them.'

Murdo, still glaring at the clerics, took a slow step backwards. 'You know well the worth of a vow made on holy ground. Mark me, and remember.'

The abbot made to speak, but the bishop waved him silent, and Murdo and his mother stepped into the anteroom. Murdo saw the table where the abbot had been sitting – two other monks now hovered over the document the abbot had been studying. Murdo strode to the table, snatched up the ink pot and dashed it over the parchment. Black ink splashed everywhere. The horrified monks shrieked, one threw his hands above his head, while the other began pawing at the ruined manuscript in a desperate effort to save it.

Murdo, allowing his anger full rein, raised his foot, put his boot against the table, and shoved with all his might. The sturdy thing tilted and slammed to the floor with a colossal crash, scattering documents and smashing the ink pot.

Other monks, hearing the commotion, rushed into the room, saw the overturned table, and flew at Murdo. He dodged aside, but one of them seized him by the arm, and the others fell on him.

'Remove him!' shouted the abbot from the doorway.

The monks hauled Murdo to his feet and dragged him away.

'Let him go!' cried Niamh, rushing to his aid.

One of the clerics, in his excitement, put out his hand and pushed her aside. Murdo saw her fall and, gripping his captors' arms tightly, swung both feet into the hapless cleric's face. His foot struck the man squarely on the chin. The man's head snapped back on his shoulders and he dropped like a felled tree. Meanwhile, the force of Murdo's kick unbalanced the monks who held him and they all collapsed in a heap on the floor, taking the boy with them.

'Get him out of here!' Abbot Gerardus shouted again, hoarse with rage.

The monks, still clasping their prisoner tightly, jerked him to his feet once more. The abbot stepped swiftly to where they struggled. 'You stupid, insolent little –' He drew back his hand to strike.

'Enough!' shouted the bishop. He stood in the doorway, his face livid, but his manner composed. 'Enough, I say. This is a house of God and you are behaving shamefully.' He thrust his hand towards the door. 'Lady Niamh, I must ask you to leave this place at once.'

'We are going,' Niamh said tersely. 'Come away, Murdo.'

Murdo shook off his captors' grip, and joined his mother. 'You call this a house of God,' Murdo spat, 'but I see only thieves and cowards.'

The monks started for him again, but Niamh took his arm and drew him quickly away. They hastily retraced their steps back through the cloisters and church, and did not stop again until they were standing in the muddy track outside the cathedral. 'Worse than vipers, the lot of them,' Murdo muttered, still shaking with anger.

'We *will* have our lands back, never fear,' Niamh assured him. 'When your father returns, we will –'

'What are we to do until then?' asked Murdo. 'What if they do not return until next summer – or even the summer after that? How long must we wait to reclaim what is ours?'

'We can stay at Cnoc Carrach. Ragnhild has offered –'

'*You* stay at Cnoc Carrach with Ragnhild,' Murdo told her harshly. 'I will not spend another day waiting – not while our home is held by thieves and greedy priests.'

Niamh regarded her son silently for a moment. 'What is in your mind, Murdo?'

'If we cannot take back what is ours until Lord Ranulf returns, then I will go and bring him back.'

'No,' Niamh told him firmly. 'Think what you are saying, son; you cannot go to the Holy Land.'

'Why not? Everyone else is going – even Orin Broad-Foot. Perhaps I will go with him!'

In truth, his thoughts had been scattered and confused. Yet, the moment he spoke the words, everything became clear and simple. Murdo knew what he would do.

Niamh saw the light of grim determination come up in his grey eyes, and recognized in the set of his jaw the stubborn resolve of Lord Ranulf himself. 'No, Murdo,' she repeated. Turning, she started down the track to the harbour where Peder was waiting with the boat. 'I will not hear it.'

She walked a dozen paces and, when Murdo made no attempt to follow, she turned back. 'Stop behaving like a child.'

'Fare well, Mother.'

'Murdo, listen to me.' She walked back to where he stood, and Murdo knew he had won his way. 'You cannot go – not like this. It is impossible.'

'I *am* going.'

'You must have provisions and money – you cannot simply go off as if it was a market fair. You must be prepared.'

Murdo said nothing, but gazed impassively at his mother.

'Please,' Niamh continued, 'come back to Cnoc Carrach at least, and we will make proper preparation for the journey.'

'Very well,' agreed Murdo at last. 'But when Orin Broad-Foot sets sail for Jerusalem, I will be on that boat.'

THIRTEEN

Night lay heavy on the house and on Murdo's soul. He stared into the darkness, unable to sleep for the ceaseless whirling of his mind. He thought about the journey to come and the trials he might endure, and how he would find his father. Niamh had written a detailed and passionate plea for Ranulf's return, but Murdo reckoned the campaign would probably be finished by the time he reached Jerusalem, and anyway, he would have little difficulty convincing his father and brothers to hasten home and redress the outrage practiced against them in their absence.

He thought about the wickedness of Bishop Adalbert, and Abbot Gerardus; he cursed them breath and bones. He thought about how he would get himself a place aboard one of King Magnus' ships. Most of all he thought about Ragna. Tomorrow he was leaving Cnoc Carrach, and he did not know when he would return. After being near her every day for the last many weeks, the prospect of not seeing her as she went about her chores, not hearing her voice in the morning as they broke fast together, not being near her and knowing he might catch sight of her at any moment – to be so deprived seemed an almost insufferable hardship.

As if in answer to his thoughts, he heard the creak of a floorboard outside his room, and an instant later the latch of his door lifted. He sat up in bed. The candle had burned low, but he took it up and stood; unable to sleep, he had not bothered to undress. The door swung open and Ragna stepped into the room, pulling the door shut silently behind her.

She saw him standing with the candle, as if he knew she would come and was waiting for her; she smiled and moved quickly to his side, her limping step more prominent with bare feet.

'Ragna, what do you –' he began.

She lay a finger to his lips. 'Shh! Not so loud. Someone will hear us.'

'What are you doing here?'

'Do you want me to leave?'

'No – no.' He looked at her wide eyes and long unbraided hair, the gentle swell of her breasts under her nightdress, and desire welled up inside him. 'Stay,' he said. 'I could not sleep.'

'Neither could I,' she told him. 'This is your last night and after tomorrow I will not see you anymore.'

'I will come back,' he pointed out hopefully.

'I know.' She bent her head unhappily. 'But then everything will be different. You will go back to Hrafnbú and I will stay here, and . . .'

'No,' he said, and surprised himself with this reply. Ragna glanced up quickly, her eyes shining in the candlelight. 'We will be together,' he suggested.

'Do you think so? I would like that, Murdo. I would like that very much.' Suddenly embarrassed by her own audacity, she hesitated and looked away. 'You must think me wicked,' she said softly.

'Never,' Murdo protested gently. 'I think you . . . beautiful.'

She smiled again. 'I brought you something.' From a fold in her mantle she brought out a slender dagger and held it up in the candlelight. 'It belonged to my mother, but she gave it to me last Yuletide.'

He took the knife and hefted it in his hand. The blade was thin and the handle light; it was a woman's weapon, but exceedingly well made: the edge was straight and sharp and the tip pointed as a serpent's tooth. It was obviously very expensive. 'Are you sure you want me to take this?'

Ragna nodded. 'I thought if you kept it inside your siarc it would help keep you safe.'

'Thank you.' He looked at the knife for a moment, and then at Ragna. 'I have nothing for you,' he confessed.

She lay her hand over his. 'I have everything I want – at least, I will when you return. Promise me you will come back for me, Murdo.'

'That I will, Ragna.'

'Promise,' she insisted.

Murdo nodded solemnly at the young woman who held him with her burning eyes. 'With all my heart, I promise: I will come back to you. Murdo Ranulfson makes this vow.'

She put her hand to the back of his head, drew his face near, and kissed him. Her lips were warm and he wished he might linger there forever. Never had leaving seemed such a bleak and daunting prospect as it did then.

After a moment, Ragna pulled away and held her cheek against his. 'I will wait for you, my love,' she whispered in his ear. 'Pray God, let not that wait be long.'

Rising, she turned and stepped from the bed, casting a last glance over her shoulder. She hesitated, and Murdo, seeing the hesitation, reached out and caught her by the hand. 'Stay,' he said.

She looked at him, her eyes wide, then glanced towards the door hesitantly.

'Please,' he said, swallowing hard.

She came into his arms in a rush. They fell back onto the bed together, their bodies entwined, mouths searching, kissing hungrily. Murdo's hands stroked her body, feeling the warm and willing flesh through the thin stuff of her nightdress. He gave a groan and sat up all at once.

Ragna rolled away. 'What is wrong?'

'Nothing,' he said. 'Wait.'

He slid off the bed and went to the chest where he had placed his belt and pouch. Taking up the belt, he unfastened the pouch and withdrew the small silver pilgrim's coin the merchant Dufnas had given him for the gattage at Jerusalem. Returning to the bed, he took up the knife Ragna had given him and pressed the sharp edge into the small disc of silver.

Ragna, on her knees now, watched him, her heart beating so fast and hard in her breast she could not speak.

Laying aside the knife, Murdo took the silver coin between the thumb and first finger of either hand, bent it and, bringing all his strength to bear, tore the coin in two. He offered one of the halves to Ragna, saying, 'As this is torn, so shall our souls be torn when we are parted.'

Ragna took the coin and, holding it out towards Murdo's half, reunited the two pieces. 'As this is joined, so shall our souls be joined.'

They then clasped hands over the coin and said together, 'From this night, and henceforth, forever.'

Murdo drew her to him once more and they kissed to seal the vow. Ragna threw aside the bedclothes, and pulled Murdo down with her into their marriage bed. Their first lovemaking fled past Murdo in a blind frenzy of heat and aching need. Afterwards, they lay panting in one another's embrace.

'They might –' Murdo began when he could speak again. 'They might try to challenge our vow –'

'Hush,' Ragna whispered. 'We are hand-fasted, and joined in the eyes of God. No one can separate us now. When you return we will confirm our vows before the altar.'

'I will never set foot in that cathedral again.'

'In our chapel, then,' Ragna suggested.

'Very well,' he agreed, 'in your chapel.' He bent his head to kiss her once more. 'I wish I did not have to go. But it will be morning soon and –'

She placed a fingertip to his lips. 'Speak no word of leaving. This is our wedding night.' So saying, she sat up and, taking the hem of her nightdress, lifted it over her head. Murdo saw the exquisite fullness of her breasts and the supple curve of her hip as she bent to extinguish the candle. And then she was beside him again, kissing him, caressing him, guiding his hands in their discovery of her body. Their second lovemaking was slower, and sweeter, and Murdo wished it would never end; but it did, leaving Murdo's heart cleft in two for the beauty of Ragna's giving of herself to him.

They slept then, their faces close, breathing one breath, their bodies sharing one space, one warmth. Ragna rose and slipped from his room just before dawn, and Murdo knew he would never be whole unto himself again. Part of him would remain with Ragna forever.

Later, after breaking fast, Niamh, Ragnhild, and Ragna walked down to the cove with Murdo. Peder and two of Lord Brusi's men were waiting at the boat. The early morning sun had burned away the low-hanging mist, and the day was coming clear. 'A good wind out of the north,' Peder called as they approached. 'We shall have a fair run to Inbhir Ness.'

Niamh halted on the path. 'You *will* turn back if there is trouble,' she said.

'As I have told you.'

'Or, if you cannot get a place on one of the ships,' she added.

'Mother,' answered Murdo with gentle, but firm resolve, 'we have talked about this a hundred times. I am no pilgrim. I will not fight. I mean to find my father and bring him home. That is all.'

'And your brothers,' added Niamh.

'Of course.' He gave a gently exasperated sigh.

Niamh halted on the path. 'It's just that you are the only one left to me. If anything should happen to you, Murdo, I do not think I could –'

Embarrassed to be overheard by Ragna and her mother, he turned and quickly reassured her. 'Nothing is going to happen to me. I am not going alone. I will be travelling with a large warband, after all. Nothing will happen. I promise.'

They started walking again. 'I will be home again before you know it,' Murdo said, trying to lighten the sombre mood settling around him. Now that the moment of leaving was upon him, he was far less eager for it than he had been even the day before. Indeed, after his night with Ragna, he wanted nothing more than to stay in Orkneyjar and for the two of them to remain together always.

If he stayed, however, that would never happen. The way Murdo saw it, his only hope of making a life for himself and Ragna was to regain possession of Hrafnbú. The only way to do that was to find his father and bring him home.

If his zeal for the journey had waned, these thoughts reminded him that there was even more at stake than recovering stolen property; his future happiness was at risk so long as intruders held their lands. So, Murdo put iron to his resolve and set his face to the sea.

His mother continued to offer advice and elicit his promises to be vigilant and careful, but Murdo was no longer listening. The sooner he was away, the sooner he could return, and his heart was set on a swift returning.

Upon reaching the shingle, Murdo turned at the water's edge and thanked Lady Ragnhild for her continued care and hospitality of both himself and his mother, and thanked her, too for the fine new clothes he was wearing – a handsome red-brown cloak of wool; a pair of sturdy breecs of the same cloth and colour with a wide belt and soft boots of new leather; and a long siarc of yellow linen. He also thanked her for the money she had given him to aid his travels, and promised to repay it at the first opportunity.

'It is nothing I would not do for my own blood kin,' Ragnhild told him; her emphasis on the last words, along with the lift of her eyebrow and not altogether approving gaze gave him to know that Ragna must have told her mother what had passed between them

114

during the night. 'Your mother and I are more than sisters,' Ragnhild continued, 'I do welcome her company, all the more so with the menfolk away. We will be safe here, never fear. Look to yourself, Murdo, and God speed your return.'

He then embraced his mother for the last time while Ragnhild and her daughter stood a little apart, looking on. When Niamh had finished her farewells, she moved aside and Ragna stepped quickly before Murdo and kissed him chastely on the cheek. 'Come back to me, Murdo,' she whispered.

'I will,' he murmured, longing to take her in his arms again, and crush her willing body to his own.

'God speed you, my soul,' Ragna said, already moving away. Before he could reply, she had rejoined her mother. There was so much he wanted to say to her, but that was impossible with everyone looking on. So, pressing his hand to the dagger beneath his siarc, he silently pledged his love to her; she saw the gesture, and answered him with her eyes.

Promising yet once more to return with all haste, Murdo stepped into the sea and waded out to where Peder was waiting at the oars. He pulled himself up over the rail and took his place at the prow, while the two servingmen turned the boat in the water and gave it a push to send it off. Murdo shouted farewell one last time as Peder plied the oars and the boat moved out into the bay. He did not take his eyes from the figures on the shore, but stood and watched them dwindle away to mere coloured flecks against the grey rock of the cove.

Presently, Peder called for him to raise the sail, which he did. When he turned back, the cove had disappeared behind a rocky shoulder and the watchers could no longer be seen. Still, he lifted his hand in a final farewell, and then returned to his work.

BOOK II

January 12, 1899: Edinburgh, Scotland

I was born in the Year of Our Lord 1856, in the tidy industrial town of Witney in Oxfordshire, to parents of good old Scottish blood. My father, who had left his beloved Highlands to further the family interests in the wool trade, eventually put the business on a solid footing, hired a manager and moved back north to 'God's ane countrie,' as he liked to call it.

Thus, on the cusp of my sixth year of life, I was yanked, roots and all, from the humming bustle of a prosperous Cotswold town, and transplanted to a rude hamlet in what to my inexperienced eye appeared a drizzly, heather-covered moor in the remote Scottish wilds. Surrounded by sheep and gorse, I began my education in the tiny village school where I found both the teachers and my fellow classmates not only brusque to the point of rudeness, but incomprehensible. I spent the whole of my first year's lessons in a state of teary agitation, vowing at the end of each day never to return to that accursed school.

It fell to my patient grandmother to soothe my schoolboy woes. 'Nivver fret, laddie buck,' she would say. 'All will be well in God's good time.' She was right, of course. I finished my schooling and graduated from St Andrews University, having pursued a double course of study in History and Classics.

Favouring a life of professionary indolence over the blustery routine of a work-a-day wool purveyor like my father, however prosperous and thriving, I hastily signed on as a clerk at one of Edinburgh's reputable legal firms, and was plunged straight away into an amiable, yet tedious, drudgery copying drafts and opinions, writs and grants and summary judgements, for my learned superiors. After a few weeks of this occupation, I began to suspect that the life I had chosen did not suit me as closely as I had imagined. I began to drink – only in moderation, and only after hours with others of my ilk – frittering away my evenings with good talk, cheap whisky, and cheaper cigars in one of Auld Reekie's many excellent pubs – which would have horrified my dear old Gran no end.

Still, I was young, unattached, and reckless. My needs were simple, and easily met. One of my fellow scribes and imbibers, it soon transpired, was an inveterate walker who thought nothing of sailing off down the road to one distant destination or another with nothing more than a stout stick and half-a-sixpence. He was a true Son o' the Heather through and through, and gloried in the name Alisdair Angus McTavot. A splendid fellow, Angus – he detested the name Alisdair and would allow no one to use it in his presence – possessed an absolutely infectious enthusiasm, and I soon found myself tramping around the damp countryside with him at week's end and holidays.

We spent many a squall huddled in the doorway of a cow byre waiting for the rain to move off, and as happens on such occasions, we began to speak of our families. It turned out that the McTavot clan enjoyed some tenuous connections with the lapsed Scottish aristocracy. His father was a baronet, whatever that is, and though the title was no longer a sinecure for great wealth, there was yet a modicum of prestige to be wrung from it. If nothing else, his uppercrusty heritage had given Angus a taste for pomp and tradition of an obscure kind. He revelled in all manner of old fashioned notions, and indulged a penchant for the arcana of Celtic history, especially as it touched primitive royalty.

It was through Angus that I was introduced to the Ancient and Honourable Order of the Highland Stag – otherwise known as a gentleman's club. In its prime, the Old Stag as it was affectionately known to its intimates, boasted such illustrious members as Cameron Brodie and Arthur Pitcairn Grant, and such notorious brigands as Drummond 'Black' Douglas, and Judge Buchanan. Sir Walter Scott was an honorary member, as was Robert Louis Stephenson, and Captain Lawrie of Krakatoa fame. Although still eminently respectable, the club had come down somewhat in latter years and no longer attracted the blue-bloods and patricians in the numbers it once boasted – which, I suppose, is how Angus and I were able to gain entrance. Some few of our legal brethren were also members as it was considered a good way for a young man of discreet ambition to advance himself.

I found in the Old Stag a refuge from the increasingly dissipate life of the smoking and drinking set. It was easier in many ways to beg off an invitation to a Friday night's binge with a smile and a 'Love to, chaps, but I've a do at the club. Sorry.'

So it was that I found myself sitting alone in the smoking room one rainy Friday night. It had just passed eight, and most of the other members had gone through to dinner by the time I arrived, so I had the place to myself. I was nursing a pre-prandial single malt, while waiting for a very late Angus, when a tall, distinguished-looking fellow in a quietly expensive suit sat down in the leather armchair directly opposite me. He had a newspaper with him, but it remained folded on his lap while he passed a perfunctory eye over my rather ordinary person.

I assumed he was waiting for me to offer my name – a thing routinely expected of younger members as it allows the elder a chance to vet the newcomers without waiting for a proper introduction. No offence is taken; we are all *members*, after all. Before I could present my name, however, he said, 'Excuse me, I have no wish to intrude, but you are a friend of young McTavot, I believe.'

'Precisely,' I replied. 'Indeed, the very fellow I am waiting for now.'

'Yes,' said the stranger, 'he will be detained a few minutes. I thought we might take the opportunity to talk.'

This aroused my curiosity, I confess.

'Allow me,' said the man, extending a gold cigar case towards me.

I selected one of the fellow's panatellas, thanked him, and sat back. 'You know Angus, I take it?' I inquired, trying to sound nonchalant.

'Know his father,' answered the man. 'I knew your father, as well. A fine, upstanding man he was, too. Admired him tremendously.' He struck a match to light his cigar. 'I don't mind telling you that I miss him very much.'

'I beg your pardon, sir,' I said, 'but I think you might have me mistaken for someone else. You see, my father is still very much alive – at least, he was last time I checked.'

The man froze, the match hovering in the air. His eyes grew keen as he looked me up and down. 'Good Lord! William Murray still alive? I attended his funeral . . . or thought I did.'

The mistake came clear. 'William was my *grandfather*,' I explained. 'Thomas is my father.'

The man slumped back in the chair as if he had been walloped on the jaw. He waved out the match, and stared at me, lost, his eyes searching.

'Oh, I *am* sorry,' he said, coming to himself once more. 'I seem to have got myself into something of a muddle. You are his grandson . . . Of course! Of course you are. Do forgive me. It is, I fear, one of the burdens of old age. Truly, it is all I can do to remember which century I am in, let alone which year.'

'Think nothing of it,' I offered. 'Happens to me all the time.'

He lit another match, touched the tip of his cigar, and puffed thoughtfully. 'Thomas . . . yes, of course,' he murmured to himself. 'How silly.' He extended the box of matches to me.

'You knew my grandfather, then.' I selected a match, struck it, and occupied myself with my smoke, giving him time to reply as he would.

'Not half as well as I should have liked,' he answered. 'Met him once or twice at business functions, social wrangles, and the like. William was the friend of a friend, you see.' He paused, puffed, and added, 'McTavot was more in my circle of influence.'

'I see.' We talked of the McTavots and he asked me how Alisdair and I had come to be acquainted. I explained that we laboured in the same law firm, and how Angus had taken me under his wing and introduced me to some of Edinburgh's finer points. 'I'd never have known about the Old Stag, if not for him,' I concluded.

'That's much the best way,' the gent replied amiably. 'Friends of friends.'

Angus arrived in a lather just then, bursting into the room, shaking rainwater all over the expensive leather upholstery. 'Dreadfully sorry,' he apologized. 'I've been trying to get a cab for a half hour. The least little whiff of rain and they all run for cover. I'm soaking. What's this?' He picked up my glass, sniffed, and bolted down the contents. 'Whew!' he puffed out his cheeks. 'That's better.'

'Sit down,' invited the old gent. 'Care for a smoke?'

'Thanks.' He took one of the slim cigars, lit it, and said, 'I see you two have met. Good.' He rubbed his hands together. 'I'm starved.' To the older gent, he said, 'We were about to go in to dinner. Would you care to join us? There's haggis stalking the moors tonight, I'm told.'

The tall gentleman stood. 'Very kind of you, but I'm afraid I've made other arrangements this evening. Some other time, perhaps.' He bade us both good evening and walked away, quiet and confident, like a cat having got the cream.

'What a strange man,' I remarked, when he had gone.

'Pembers?' wondered Angus. 'Why do you say that?'

I told him about the misunderstanding over my father, and how he had made light of it. 'The strange thing is, I had the distinct impression he really *didn't* know which century he was in, if you can believe it. He seemed completely lost for a moment. And another thing: I did not give him my name – he already knew it.'

'So? It's not exactly a secret is it?' Angus countered, pulling his watch out of his pocket for a quick glance. 'Someone in the club must have mentioned it to him. Relax, Pembers is all right.'

'Pembers? Is that his name? He never said.'

'Pemberton,' McTavot informed me. 'He has been a friend of the family for I don't know how long. Known him all my life, I suppose.' We started towards the door to the dining room.

'What does Pemberton do?'

'For a living?' He shrugged. 'Landed gentry, I expect. Why do you ask?'

'Just wondering.'

We entered the large, dark-panelled room and I saw many familiar faces among the diners, but my attention was instantly arrested by the liberal sprinkling of women in glittery evening dress scattered among the tables. It was Ladies Night – the Old Stag hosted them on occasion – consequently, there were fewer tables available than usual, and most of them sported lighted candles. I spied a small empty table near the sideboard, and made my way to it. Some of the older members were already at the cheese.

I made to seat myself, whereupon Angus took one look at my selection, and said, 'Won't do, I'm afraid. Won't do at all. Let's try this one over here.'

He moved to a nearby table – set for four and with unlighted candles. 'This one is reserved,' I pointed out as he drew out his chair.

'It is, yes,' he agreed, sitting down. 'For us.'

'You reserved a table for us?'

'I did, yes. I have a surprise for you.' He gawked around the room. 'I hope it hasn't got hung up somewhere.'

'I'm intrigued,' I said. 'Tell me more.'

'All in good time.'

A white-jacketed waiter appeared to inform us of the evening's selections and then departed, leaving us to our contemplation of the club's estimable and extensive wine list.

'You know, there was something else,' I said, leaning forward conspiratorially.

'Something else? What are you babbling about?'

'You said you had been waiting for a cab for half an hour. That's not the kind of thing anyone else could know about, is it?'

'Not unless they were with me, naturally.'

'Naturally,' I conceded. 'But Pemberton knew. He also knew I was waiting for you.'

'You must have told him.'

'On the contrary. *He* told *me*. "You are a friend of young McTavot, I believe." He said it just like that, and I said I was waiting for you.'

'There you are, you see?'

'And then he informed me that you would be detained a few minutes, and that we might as well have a chat.'

'Well, you said yourself you were waiting for me. Anyone could see I was delayed.'

'Not *delayed*,' I told him firmly. 'Detained – that was the exact word. It made me think that he had . . . well, arranged it somehow.'

'Nonsense,' he scoffed. 'I was waiting for a cab, and trying –'

'Yes? Trying to what?'

'Never you mind,' he said evasively. 'Anyway, why would old Pemberton wish to detain me?'

'So he and I could talk.'

'He could talk to you anytime he wanted,' Angus laughed. 'He didn't have to *arrange* anything. You must have taken it all the wrong way.'

'Possibly,' I conceded, 'although I don't see why he –'

Before I could finish, Angus shot out of his chair and stood to rigid attention, beaming like a cherub. I turned to see what he was looking at and saw two absolutely stunning young women entering the dining room. Led by the head waiter, they were causing conversations to hush and heads to turn as they passed: one dark haired and slim, the other with long auburn locks, slightly taller, and with a fuller, more rounded figure, they were gorgeous in glimmering satin. Moreover, they were making right for us.

Angus intercepted the dark-haired one in two bounds, thanking the waiter and guiding her towards the table in one sweeping motion. 'Libby, darling! You look ravishing.'

So this was Libby. I had heard the name often enough – Angus was perpetually writing to this certain someone on the continent – but I had no idea she had returned from her travels, nor imagined that Angus might have known anyone of such dazzling description.

Turning to me, he said, 'May I present to you, my fiancé, Elizabeth Gowan, and her cousin, Caitlin Charmody.' He smiled as the auburn lovely offered her hand to me. 'Ladies, I give you my oldest and dearest friend, Gordon Murray.'

He made it sound as if we had known one another for several lifetimes, but if the slight exaggeration secured the benefit of the alluring creatures' company even for a moment, who was I to complain? 'Ladies, I am charmed.' Raising the young woman's hand, I brushed it gallantly with my lips. 'I am very happy to meet you, Miss Charmody.'

'I am pleased to make your acquaintance, Mister Murray,' she purred in a low, melodious voice.

'Allow me.' Leaning close, I withdrew her chair. Her delicate perfume filled my senses with delicious hints of exotic nectar, and I instantly wondered what it would be like to kiss her. 'Angus said he had a surprise for me, and I am delighted to say it is indeed a surprise – and of the most agreeable kind.'

That was probably the last rational thing I said that night, I fear. For, at the ladies' appearance, the waiter produced a bucket of chilled champagne and we all drank a toast to the public announcement of Angus and Elizabeth's wedding engagement, much to the amusement of all the members looking on.

Thus the evening passed in a brilliant haze of candlelight, perfume, wine and laughter. When we rose to leave, the dining room was dark and everyone else, including the waiters, had long ago departed. We walked along the river then, we four, and we must have walked for hours. I cannot think what I said, but the russet-haired beauty on my arm seemed to hang on every word, so I spoke just to keep her there, dreading the moment when we would part. I talked like a blithering fool to forestall the impending disaster.

But the moment would not be held off forever, and we said good-night, and then Angus bundled the ladies into a carriage, paid the driver, and sent them off. I stood in the street, bereft, watching the love of my life fade into the foggy mist. I felt as if life itself – at least any life hereafter worth living – had been cruelly torn from me. To make matters worse, it suddenly occurred to me that I had allowed her to leave without arranging to call on her again, or securing even a fragment of her address.

Angus, awash in love and benevolence, took one look at my face and said, 'Cheer up, old son. You'll see her again.'

'When?' I said, my voice a miserable bleat in the night.

'Why, tomorrow, I should think. We're all going out to Queen's Ferry for a Sunday picnic. It's all arranged. Have you forgotten?'

'All of us? You mean – I thought it was just you and Lizzy –'

'Libby.'

'All of us? Really? I thought . . . but that's just fantastic. It's tremendous!'

'Steady on.' He laid a hand to my arm. 'Come along, then.' He started off down the street. 'Let's see if we can find one more damned elusive cab.'

Thus, the two most significant events of my life occurred on the same evening. Within moments of each other, two meetings took place – Pemberton, and Miss Caitlin Charmody – meetings which were to alter the entire course of my life, the first no less than the second.

FOURTEEN

'By order of Alexius, Supreme Ruler of the Holy Roman Empire, Elect of Heaven, Equal of the Apostles, it is decreed that you shall not enter the city with your armies, but you shall establish your camp in this place and here you shall wait until the basileus receives you.' Nicetas paused, looking up from the rolled parchment in his hand. 'Do you understand what has been read to you?'

Godfrey, Duke of Bouillon, inclined his head slowly, but his brother Prince Baldwin made bold to reply. 'How long must we wait?'

'You will wait,' explained the commander patiently, 'until the basileus summons you.'

'Do you hear, brother?' Baldwin said, his voice thick with indignation. 'We are to be made to wait here outside the walls like a pack of lepers!'

'Wait however you like,' replied Nicetas placidly, 'but wait you will – until the basileus desires your company.'

'It is intolerable!' sneered Baldwin.

'It is so decreed,' concluded the young commander. He passed the document to the elder of the two brothers, turned and mounted his horse. The emperor's Varangi looked on without expression, as equally prepared to fight as to withdraw.

'After all we have endured on our journey,' Baldwin fumed, 'to be confined to our camps like a beggar band – it is an insult!'

'Perhaps the Christian citizens of Selymbria would have preferred such an insult,' replied Nicetas sharply.

'That was a mistake,' sniffed Godfrey, 'which we deeply regret.'

'I am certain Selymbria will rejoice to hear it,' Nicetas intoned. 'No doubt the survivors will feast in your honour. Would that your contrition extended to more material expression, however; the orphans and widows may find it difficult to feed themselves on word of your regret.'

'Come down off that horse, you impudent ass,' Baldwin roared. 'We command an army of forty thousand! We will not be –'

'Oh, we have seen what your glorious army can do,' Nicetas informed him coldly, 'when attacking the innocent and defenceless. If you find the emperor's greeting too harsh, I can only suggest that you might have considered whether slaughtering his subjects was likely to increase his joy at your arrival.'

Baldwin made a strangled cry and started forward. The Varangi spears swung level as they prepared to attack.

'Peace!' Godfrey said, putting out a hand to hold off his brother. To the commander of the palace guard, he said, 'We will abide. You will please convey our promise to the emperor, along with our highest regards.'

Nicetas lifted the reins, turned his mount, and rode away, followed by the excubitori. Upon reaching the military gate, the riders passed quickly through and the gate was sealed once more behind them. The commander returned to Blachernae Palace and was admitted directly into Alexius' private audience chamber, where the basileus was waiting to receive him.

'Well?' demanded the emperor. 'Tell me, Nicetas, what did you make of them?'

'They are Franks, basileus,' the commander replied with a shrug. 'They are arrogant hot-heads without the slightest intelligence.'

'Did they deny the attack?'

'They said it was a deeply regretted mistake.'

Alexius nodded thoughtfully. 'That is something, at least. Even so, we will send the Varangi to search out the stragglers and escort them at once to Constantinople. We will not suffer further attacks on people and properties under imperial protection. See to it, Nicetas.'

'It shall be done, basileus.' The commander of the palace troops acknowledged the order with a bow. 'Regarding those already arrived, they have been ordered to confine themselves to the camps outside the walls as you have decreed. Do you wish me to arrange an audience with their leaders?'

'Soon, Nicetas, but not yet,' answered Alexius. 'Perhaps once their hot heads have cooled sufficiently, they will recover some part of their sanity. A season of sober reflection is in order. Therefore, we will let them wait.'

'And the provisions, basileus?'

'We will grant the newcomers the same supplies we have extended to Count Hugh,' the emperor replied impatiently. 'Nothing more.'

Nicetas acknowledged the plan, but questioned the efficacy. 'Is it enough, basileus?'

'It is more than they gave the people of Selymbria,' replied Alexius tartly.

'Forgive me, basileus, but there *are* a great many of them.'

'How many, Nicetas?'

'The scouts say –'

'We know what the scouts say,' the emperor told him. 'We are asking *you*, Nicetas. You have seen them, what do you make it?'

'Perhaps twenty thousand, and more are arriving all the time.' He paused, as if unwilling to impart the bad news. 'The lords boast twice that number.'

'Forty thousand,' groaned Alexius, calculating how much it would take to feed so many mouths.

'That is just the soldiers,' Nicetas said. 'There are women and children with them, too.'

'God help us,' sighed Alexius. What madmen these crusaders were: bringing women and children into war. What possessed them? That they should arrive wholly unprepared for the rigours ahead – that was folly enough; that they should inflict such horror on their wives and offspring passed all understanding.

Alas, he reflected ruefully, they paid the highest price for their folly: the hermit Peter of Amiens and his peasant army had been cut down by the Seljuqs outside Antioch. Of the sixty thousand that left Constantinople, seven thousand were spared and taken into slavery; all the rest were slaughtered. On a single afternoon, fifty-three thousand misguided Christians sacrificed themselves to the folly of the Bishop of Rome. Indeed, it passed all understanding.

'God help us all,' sighed Alexius. He ended the audience then, dismissing the commander to his duties. When Nicetas had gone, the basileus called for the magister of the chamber. 'Gerontius!' he said as the man appeared. 'Bring us our riding cloak and cap. When we have gone, you may inform the magister officiorum that we have left the palace.'

'Certainly, basileus,' replied the elderly servant. 'Shall I summon the drungarius to attend the basileus?'

'No,' Alexius replied, 'we wish to ride alone today.'

The request for his cloak and cap had long been the emperor's coded way of saying he wished to go out into the capital unattended by his retinue of imperial bodyguards and advisors – something he often did, especially when he wished to learn the true humour of the people. Alexius wore no other disguise, having learned long ago that, without the elaborate pomp and ceremony that normally accompanied his slightest movements, he could easily go among the citizenry without attracting the least attention. Alexius, with his compact stature and bald, unassuming appearance, was not much remarked upon; dressed in rustic homespun, he could easily pass for one of his own subjects.

When he had put off his imperial robes, and donned the common cloak and drab cap of a stablehand, the Elect of Heaven, Co-Regent of God, walked quickly from the palace, using one of the hidden gates. Unlocking the low, narrow door, he ducked out quickly, passing between two high walls and into a close, winding street which backed onto a jumbled row of market stalls. He could hear the hubbub of the market in the street beyond. Stepping into the street, he looked to see if there was anyone about, but saw only two skinny dogs nosing in a garbage heap.

Pulling the cap down further, he hurried off along the backstreet, turned the nearest corner and passed unobserved into the market and melted into the crowd. He walked along for a time, taking in the sights and sounds of the market; he paused to buy a bag of dates from an elderly merchant, and then directed his steps towards the Wall of Theodosius.

Alexius moved easily among his subjects, eating dates and plotting recompense for the witless destruction of Selymbria. These arrogant princes must be brought to heel, and he would see justice satisfied before any of them returned home. First, however, he must get the measure of these petty potentates who dared ride roughshod through his realm in the name of God.

Upon reaching the wall, he turned and walked along the wide, busy street which ran the length of the western defences. Between the street and the wall, crude huts of cast-off wood and cloth had been erected by the poor – little more than lean-to dwellings to keep off the rain. Like so much within the capital, the basileus saw in this circumstance a symbol of the empire, where the massive wall was the strong rule of imperial law and civilizing faith, and the mean hovels were the fragile lives of the citizens which leaned in pitiable dependence upon the empire's great strength for their ever-tenuous survival.

Now and then, a wretch would hobble from a hovel to beg, and Alexius always obliged, giving a coin and a blessing to any who asked. When he ran out of coins, he gave away his dates.

He came to a crossroads which formed a wide square before the massive Charisius Gate, last of the old gates. Later emperors had constructed further defences just beyond the Wall of Theodosius, but in this part of the city, the older walls towered above the newer, forever proclaiming the glory that had been. Passing quickly through the entrances, he found himself in a quarter of smiths and artisans of innumerable variety, each practising his particular trade in a rough wooden stall behind which the craftsman lived in a few small rooms with his family. Judging strictly from the sound, every last smith was toiling away with utmost industry amidst the drifting smoke from their foundry fires. The clatter of hammer on metal, wood, and stone, the clamour of men shouting to one another for tools and materials, rose to a cacophony, not unlike that of battle.

Alexius liked the noise and commotion; he appreciated men who could make a living with the skill of their own two hands. He paused often to praise the finer examples of one craftsman or another, but did not allow himself to become involved in conversations which would, he knew, lead to bargaining for the wares he had just admired.

He pressed on to his destination, and came to the end of the Artisans' Quarter where he stopped for his first view of the pilgrim camp which lay on the other side of a wide expanse of waste ground – part of an old salt marsh that had long since been drained. The low dark tents sprawled across the land like an untidy flood, stretching back and back into the distance, rising up to overflow the banks of the Golden Horn. The smoke of their cooking fires hung in a dull haze above, making it seem to Alexius as if he were gazing upon a range of diminutive dark mountains wrapped in dirty clouds. What is more, this strange mountain range seemed to spread out north and west as far as the eye could see. There were thousands of them – tens of thousands! And, according to the scouts and spies working back and forth along the coasts and roads of western borders, these were but the first of several groups on the move across the empire, and all of them were headed for the capital.

Alexius moved closer. At the outer perimeter of the camp, he could just make out the long lines of the horse pickets as a thin brown line snaking off into the heat haze. Indeed, even though he could not see the animals, he could smell them – even at this remove, the pungent aroma of horse manure was unmistakable. Closer, the stink would be almost suffocating. Nevertheless, the emperor steeled himself for a closer look and started across the waste land; he wanted to see these mad Romans in the flesh.

Not that he was a stranger to the sight: as a young man, his first battles as emperor had been fought against just these sorts of men. In fact, he had traded victories with the wily Robert Guiscard for several years before the stubborn king had at last given up the fight and died following a brief struggle with typhoid. With the old king's death, his sons had fallen to squabbling among themselves for supremacy, thus leaving the empire free to concentrate on the defence of its northern borders, as well as the new and growing threat posed by the latest Arab terror, the Seljuq Turks.

Now the Romans, as they styled themselves, were back – and the fact that this time they were here to help him win back the Holy Land did not cheer him as much as they might have expected. He had seen in Robert Guiscard the naked face of the West, and he had good reason to fear and despise it. For the welfare of the empire, however, he would not allow personal rancour to dictate his conduct towards the pilgrim lords. He would receive them; he would even welcome them, but he would not believe them, and he would never trust them.

As Alexius neared the first ranks of tents that formed the perimeter, he noticed a fair number of merchants had gathered to offer their goods to the pilgrims – everything from precious gems, and rolls of the brilliant silken cloth for which the weavers of Byzantium were justly famous, to cabbages, boiled eggs, and flat bread. Closer, he heard in the bickering tones of trade a somewhat strident note, and quickly discerned that the bargaining was not flowing with the usual harmony of purpose. Seeing several disgruntled merchants – their handcarts filled with unsold produce – leaving the proceedings, the emperor hailed one of the men and asked what ailed him.

'Agh!' The merchant rolled his eyes. 'By the Pure Light of Heaven, these Romans are worse than barbarians! They want everything but will not pay. There is no talking to them. I am finished.'

Before the emperor could reply, the man demanded, 'Do they think us fools, that we should give away our wares? Look at these melons!' He plucked a round ripe melon from the neatly-arranged stack. 'Did you ever see such beautiful melons? And these apricots! Here, try one. Did you ever taste such an apricot?'

No, the emperor said, he had certainly never tasted such a wonderful apricot.

'Of course not!' cried the merchant. 'I grow all this with my own two hands! Food fit for the basileus himself! And what do they do? They blow their noses at me!' Taking up the handles of his cart once more, the man continued on his way. 'Theotokis is finished with them! Let them remember that when they are starving! Agh!'

Other merchants voiced similar complaints: the Romans had gold enough, but refused to part with it. They seemed to believe that, along with the grain and water the emperor provided, anything else they wanted should be given to them, too. For the merchants, that was bad enough; worse, however, was the Romans' inexplicable disdain. The abuse pouring out of the mouths of the visitors first embarrassed the emperor, then bewildered him. To a man, the Latin knights appeared to hold their Byzantine brothers in lowest contempt, reviling them, cursing them, even as they clamoured and cajoled for their goods.

'Pig! Over here!' they called, making sounds like hogs snuffling. 'Here, pig! You call this bread, pig? I would not give you a turd for it.'

Or, again: 'What! Think you I would touch this cloth after you've had your filthy hands all over it? Get it away from me, you shit-eating dog!'

This litany of crude abuse was repeated wherever the merchants clustered. And if it was worrying to the tradesmen, Alexius found it alarming. Encamped before him was a vast army of fighting men who did not recognize the simple unity of their common faith and brotherhood, who considered themselves superior to their eastern kinsmen, and moreover exempt from the obligations of ordinary human decency and goodwill.

What the produce merchant had said was true: these Romans *were* worse than barbarians. The benighted barbarian only wanted whatever valuables he might carry away. These men wanted the world – and, indeed, saw themselves ruling it. That notion, Alexius

133

determined, would be soundly squelched at first opportunity. Yes, but it must be defeated subtly, quietly, and without overt antagonism.

He strolled along the perimeter of the immense camp, watching the knights and footmen. They were, almost without exception, big men: tall, long-limbed, heavy of shoulder, belly, and thigh, hard-handed and thick-muscled; when they walked, their heels struck the earth with solid purpose, their movements ponderous rather than lithe. Their skin was pale, without natural colour, resembling raw dough in both texture and consistency. Alexius entertained the notion that his slightest touch would leave a lingering impression on such pasty flesh.

Their faces were broad, with thick lips and large noses; their eyes wide-set, but small beneath heavy brows. Alexius could not imagine any woman finding such horse-like features attractive. Worst of all, they wore their hair long – like maidens' hair – and like that of young women, it hung loosely about their necks in desultory curls; curiously, however, except for the occasional broad moustache, they kept themselves clean-shaven. The combination of long hair and smooth chins and jowls appeared odd to the Byzantine eye; it struck Alexius as somewhat obscene – as if the foreigners perversely insisted on covering that which should be revealed, and revealing that which should be covered.

Their garments were coarse and heavy, sombre coloured. Most wore an outer coat over a knee-length tunic cinched at the waist by a wide leather belt from which hung their knives. Some few, he noticed, did possess an outer cloak of better fabric, sewn with bright squares or stripes of contrasting colours – red and green, yellow and blue, black and white. But, whether cloak or mantle, tunic, or leggings, all were made for a clime much colder and more changeable than that to which they had come, and, God help them, far colder still than that to which they were going.

Their feet were covered with tall leather boots, or shoes of the old Roman style with tough soles and thick uppers which laced up the leg with stout leather thongs. In this, at least, they showed a little wisdom; the ground of the Holy Land was rough and arid, more rock than soil, and a soldier who could not walk or run could not fight. Too many good men died because their shoes could not take the strain of the march, let alone the fight, Alexius reflected; the emperor set great store by a soldier's footwear.

In manner, the westerners were much as he expected: haughty, insolent, and rude. They swaggered insufferably as they walked, hailing one another with uncouth gestures, their talk broken by coarse and raucous laughter. Loud in speech, brash in action, they were, in a word, crude; on the whole, they behaved as if they had neither a grain of civility in their souls, nor a redeeming thought in their heads. They were uninvited guests in a land far from home; for the love of Christ, did that mean nothing to them?

The arrogance and ambition of their leaders might be expected, but the casual cruelty of the average fighting man was definitely a startling and nasty surprise. Alexius saw in it the ugly shape of a malignant wickedness – a vile sinfulness which proceeded from a core of hate and ignorance and greed.

Having seen enough, the emperor turned away in disgust and hastened back to the palace to call his advisors and prepare for the battle to come. By the time he slipped once again through the hidden gate, Alexius had devised the first strike. It would come, he decided, in the form of a gift – or, better still, many gifts – the more gaudy and expensive the better.

FIFTEEN

The emperor kept his unruly visitors waiting for nine days, then despatched the Commander of the Imperial Excubitori with a summons. 'The emperor will receive you,' Nicetas informed the brother lords icily. 'Make yourselves ready. An escort will be sent to conduct you to the palace tomorrow morning.'

The next day, Godfrey, Duke of Bouillon, and Baldwin, Prince of Boulogne, each attended by numerous noblemen and vassals, were led into the great reception room of Blachernae Palace. The two lords and their entourage walked in open-mouthed awe of their peerless surroundings. Marble floors of palest green, polished to mirror-brightness, stretched away on every side beneath a gilded ceiling which glimmered overhead like a firmament of gold, supported by a forest of graceful pillars of marble so pure and white they seemed to shine with the radiance of the moon.

Led by the magister officiorum – stately, regal, holding high his ebony rod of authority – the Romans passed through two enormous doors of burnished copper which opened silently on hidden hinges to admit them into a vast cavern of a room possessed of even greater opulence than anything they had yet seen. The rarest blue and green marbles, imported at unthinkable expense from the farthest reaches of the empire, lined the walls and floor, gleaming and radiant in the light from a hundred perfumed wax tapers set in candletrees of gold all around the room.

Before them on a raised dais of expensive porphyry, dressed in his purple robes, wearing a crown of gold inset with rubies and pearls, sat Basileus Alexius Comnenus, Elect of Heaven, Supreme Ruler of All Christendom, God's Vice-Regent on Earth, Equal of the Apostles. If their first glimpse of the most powerful man alive did not impress them, the sight of his throne of solid gold thrilled them to their souls. Nor did they fail to appreciate the formidable presence of the triple ranks of the emperor's Varangian bodyguard, all of them carrying axes and shields of silver, and wearing helms set with lapis lazuli and breastplates sheathed in gold.

Godfrey and Baldwin were astounded, excited, fascinated, and delighted by all they saw. Though they might disregard the man, they could not dismiss his wealth, or the might at his command. In short, they each imagined themselves firmly ensconced in marble palaces, holding court on thrones of gold, and leading ranks of seven-foot tall warriors arrayed in gems and precious metals.

The possibility was so fitting, so unarguably proper to men of their rank and status, that neither lord foresaw any impediment to the early acquisition of this exalted state. Though they might be sojourners in a realm of riches beyond anything they had ever dreamed possible, they were still men of royal birth and therefore rightful heirs to all that kings could desire. Moreover, it was all theirs for the taking.

The magister led the party to the foot of the throne, where he thumped the floor three times with his silver-tipped rod, and announced, 'Bringing before your majesty his servants Godfrey of Bouillon and Baldwin of Boulogne, and their many retainers.'

He then prostrated himself, indicating that the bedazzled worthies should follow his example. Alexius let them lie on the floor for a long moment before he raised a hand and said, 'You may stand.'

The lords obeyed, rising to find themselves under the scrutiny of two keen dark eyes set in a shrewd, calculating face. Godfrey, the senior of the two, spoke first. 'Lord and Emperor,' he said, employing his best Latin, 'we greet you in the name of our Lord Jesus Christ. May his blessing be upon you. We bring greetings, also, from his Holiness, Pope Urban, who sends his highest regards, and begs the emperor to receive your brothers with felicitous good-will.'

'We accept your greetings,' Alexius replied, 'and stand ready to extend our friendship to you and all those under your command. No doubt,' the emperor observed, 'you have received the gifts which we have sent as a token of the friendship awaiting those who pledge faith with this throne.'

'Indeed, we have, Lord Emperor,' Godfrey replied. 'Our thanks are as boundless as your generosity.'

Alexius inclined his head regally. 'We assume also, that you have received the provisions we have caused to be delivered to your camps for the refreshment of your troops.'

'Again, we are in your debt, my lord,' the duke answered.

'It is a debt easily discharged,' the emperor told him. 'We require but one thing in return.'

'Your majesty has but to name it,' replied Godfrey expansively, 'and it will be accomplished with all speed.'

'We are pleased to hear it.' The emperor lifted his hand and beckoned one of the half-dozen black robed officials forward. The man, in a red cap as flat and square as a mason's board, stepped beside the throne. Bowing from the waist, the Logothete of the Symponus extended a parchment square on his outstretched palms. The emperor took up the document, unfolded it and began to read.

The two noble brothers listened, growing increasingly uncomfortable as the document spelled out in no uncertain terms their duties and responsibilities while guests of the empire. When Alexius came to the oath of loyalty they were expected to swear, recognizing the emperor as the supreme sovereign whose authority the lords of the West held above all other earthly claims, they were aghast.

'Lord and Emperor,' pleaded Godfrey, 'begging your imperial pardon, we cannot possibly swear by such an oath.'

Alexius frowned. Godfrey hastened to explain. 'It is most unfortunate, lord, but we have already sworn fealty to the Emperor of the West: William, King of England. We cannot by any means swear fealty to another, less yet hold *two* sovereigns supreme. Therefore, we must beg to be excused this condition.'

'But you will *not* be excused, Godfrey of Bouillon,' Alexius said, his voice quiet with the awful weight of his disapproval. 'As God is One, there is but one Holy Roman Empire and Constantinople is its capital. There is but one sovereign lord upon the throne, the same lord you see before you; there are no others. We care not what the lords of the West may do in their own lands, but when they come to the capital of the empire which has given them life and nurture, they will swear an oath of allegiance to the sovereign under whose protection they thrive.'

The lords were dumbstruck. Never had they anticipated such an ungracious reception. They had travelled nine months and endured countless hardships in order to lend their aid to save the failing empire – only to have their noblest intentions thrown back in their faces over a trivial matter of loyalty. Come to that, did the emperor actually expect them to sign his contemptible document?

'Emperor Alexius,' Godfrey began, somewhat uncertainly, 'we find ourselves unable to abide by your request.'

'Do you refuse?' enquired the emperor.

'In no way,' Godfrey blustered, 'but it is simply not possible for us to sign the document you propose.'

Baldwin found his voice then, and added, 'Our word is our honour, Lord Emperor – and that is good enough for any man.'

Alexius bristled. 'Honour? We will not hear you debase that exalted word in our presence. We have seen enough of your honour to know that your word, so easily given – when it aids your purpose – is thrice easily broken when it suits you. In short, there is nothing to which you will not swear; likewise, there is nothing you will not forswear when the tide of circumstance begins to run against you.'

The emperor glared mightily at the two uncertain noblemen before him, and vowed, 'Truly, we will have your signatures on this treaty of allegiance, or you will never see Jerusalem.'

The brothers looked at one another hopelessly, but remained unmoved. Alexius decided to allow them time to reconsider. 'Go,' he said wearily. 'Return to your camps and hold council with your advisors. We will send for your reply two days' hence.'

With that, lords Godfrey and Baldwin were led from the emperor's presence. They walked as men condemned, for they saw all the glittering treasures they had claimed for themselves receding swiftly from their grasp. Desolate and confused, they very soon found themselves cast out from the opulent palace and thrown back into the stinking camps where they sat in forlorn contemplation of the inexplicable treachery of the devious Easterners.

Thus began a battle of wills which was to endure for many weeks. Upon the pilgrims' repeated refusal to sign the oath of allegiance, the emperor finally discontinued the delivery of supplies and provisions. From time to time, Alexius would send Count Hugh of Vermandois, as his personal envoy, to the crusader camp to try to persuade the lords to swear the oath of fealty so that their troops could enjoy the fresh provisions of food and wine awaiting them. Each time, they would decline the oath, and grimly watch the level of their remaining supplies dip ever lower.

The first warning that it was time to force the stubborn brothers' surrender came to Alexius with the return of the Varangian regiment assigned to conduct stray pilgrims to the capital. The commander of the regiment sought out the drungarius and quickly passed on a letter from the emperor's nephew, John, the Exarch of Dyrrachium. Dalassenus thanked the man, and hastened to the emperor, whom he found with his family at prayers in the palace chapel.

He entered quietly, approached the altar, knelt behind his kinsman and waited for Alexius to finish. When the archbishop concluded the prayer, the royal family rose and turned to see who had joined them. 'Dalassenus!' exclaimed the empress. Irene, a tall and elegant woman, smiled graciously and extended her hand to one of her favourite courtiers. 'We have seen so little of you these last days. I hope you will observe Easter Mass with us – and the feast afterwards, of course.'

'It would be my pleasure, basilissa,' he said, bending his head to kiss her extended hand.

'If you will excuse us now,' the emperor said, 'I believe Dalassenus has come on urgent business.'

'All these interminable discussions,' Irene chided. 'Whenever will it end? Come, children,' she said, gathering her brood, 'your lessons await.'

Alexius bade farewell to his wife and children, and then turned to Dalassenus. 'The Varangi have returned. The patrician brought this for you,' he said, passing the letter to the emperor.

Alexius broke the seal, unfolded the document and scanned the contents quickly. Dalassenus, observing the change in the emperor's demeanour, inquired, 'Ill tidings, basileus?'

'At least two more crusader armies have crossed our borders; they are on their way to the capital even as we speak,' Alexius said. He frowned and added, 'It seems one of these armies is under the command of our former adversary, Bohemond of Taranto.'

'Him!' growled the drungarius, 'I thought we had seen the last of Guiscard's miserable misbegotten son.'

'So had I, cousin,' the emperor agreed.

'And the other army?' the drungarius wondered.

'It is under the command of a man called Raymond, Count of Toulouse. They landed at Dyrrachium on the Ides of March, and John moved them quickly on. They could arrive at any time.'

Dalassenus fought down his growing rancour. 'I will alert the Pecheneg theme to watch the roads and bring word as soon as they are sighted. That should give us warning enough –'

'Better still,' suggested Alexius, 'instruct them to escort the Count and his troops to the capital at once. I do not want these marauding pilgrims pillaging any more towns along the way.'

'It will be done, basileus,' the young commander replied. 'Does the exarch indicate how many we can expect to –'

Before he could say more, the Captain of the Excubitori appeared at the door. He coughed politely, and when Alexius beckoned him to approach, he said, 'Forgive the intrusion, basileus, but there may be a problem,' Nicetas announced. 'A riot has broken out in one of the markets outside the walls. The city scholae are dealing with it, but I thought you should know. Also, it appears the Romans are moving their camps further up the Golden Horn. They may be preparing an attack on the city.'

The emperor's frown deepened; he rubbed a hand over his face.

'What can they be thinking?' said Dalassenus, his brow lowering with exasperation.

Alexius drew a steadying breath and said, 'It may come to nothing. Nevertheless, we will be ready. Call out the archers, and have the Varangi man the walls.' To Dalassenus he said, 'Summon the Immortals.'

'Do you wish us to engage the pilgrims, basileus?' asked Nicetas.

'No,' he decided, 'at least not yet. If they approach the gates, tell the archers to shoot over their heads. Go now, both of you. We will join you on the wall.'

The emperor rose and left the chapel, hastening to the royal apartments where he called Gerontius to summon his armour bearers. 'We will show these quarrelsome lords the folly of making war on their emperor.'

While his servants dressed him for battle, he instructed the magister to send for the Logothete of the Symponus. The elderly official came puffing into his presence, clutching the document the emperor had requested. Alexius relieved him of the parchment and, buckling on his sword, made his way quickly to the wall. He was met on the steps by Nicetas.

'Eleven dead, basileus,' the commander reported. 'Twenty-seven wounded and injured.'

'Among the citizens – how many?'

'Eighteen, basileus,' the commander replied. 'Three merchants, six market traders and one or two artisans; the rest were women and children.'

Dismissing his commander to his duties, the emperor proceeded up the last of the long series of steps to the top of the wall where Dalassenus was waiting for him.

'The fighting continues, basileus. The Romans have pillaged the markets closest to their camps,' the Grand Drungarius informed him. 'They appear to be readying an attack on the gate.'

'Where are their commanders?' wondered Alexius, gazing down into the swirling mass of armoured men swarming the bridge before the gate. Like so many barbarian hordes before them, these mad Latins believed they could conquer the empire by beating down the gates of Constantinople.

'It does not appear to be an organized assault, basileus,' the young general informed him. 'Indeed, the main body of the force seems to be retreating.' He pointed to the river where the crusaders were moving along the southern bank. Across the waste ground, whole districts of the crusader tent city had been removed, and more were going. The pilgrim army was on the march.

'It may be they will try to establish siege points,' Dalassenus suggested. 'Or, perhaps they think to ford the river upstream and attack the city from the east.'

'Across the river?' Alexius shook his head. 'It makes no sense.'

'Nevertheless,' Dalassenus replied, 'we could defeat the force at the gate before the others knew of the attack.'

Just then a strategus approached on the run. 'The archers are ready, basileus,' he said. 'They await your command.'

The emperor turned away from the gate and looked out over the site of the affray. A dull haze of smoke hung low over the market square where the conflict had broken out. The market – what was left of it – stood in disarray; the traders' ramshackle wooden stalls had been smashed, broken up, and the pieces scattered over the empty square; ruined produce and wasted merchandise had been trampled into the dust; there were walking wounded hobbling, dazed, over the destruction, and two or three bodies still lay unattended, although several others had been collected in carts which were now hastening towards a nearby church.

'Shall I give the order to attack?'

'Send a few flights over their heads,' Alexius said. 'Drive them away from the gate.' Turning to one of the excubitori behind him, he said, 'We will need a horse, and one for the drungarius. Bring word when the Immortals have arrived.'

'Basileus?' wondered the drungarius. 'The Immortals can take them with ease. There is no need to put yourself in danger. Allow me to send word when we have secured the Romans' surrender.'

'No, Dalassenus, I want the Romans to see me leading the charge so that they will know who demands their allegiance. We will defeat them in their own camp, and they will sign the oath of loyalty,' he said, placing the parchment into his kinsman's hands. Turning his eyes once more towards the river, he looked at the long lines of crusaders moving along the banks, shaking his head in bewilderment. 'This is troublesome. I wish I knew what it meant.'

A few moments later, word came that the Immortals had arrived and were waiting at the gate below. Alexius and Dalassenus descended to join the élite scholae. Taking his place at the head of the troops, the emperor delivered final orders; then, turning to the wall, he signalled to the strategus, who gave the order to let fly the arrows. 'Open the gates!' commanded Alexius. The gatemen began plying the winches and there came a groaning sound as the huge doors ground open slowly.

Accompanied by his commander and a hundred mounted Immortals, and seventy-five Varangi on foot, Alexius charged into the fray. The pilgrims, having been forced away from the gate by the archers, were massed together at the end of the bridge over the dry ditch before the outer wall. The instant the gate was opened, they all surged forward, only to be thrown back upon themselves by the sudden appearance of the mounted soldiers.

As the horses thundered onto the bridge, the crusaders halted. Angry battle-cries turned instantly to screams of terror as the fore-ranks, squeezed by the multitude pressing in from behind, found themselves unable to escape. The fortunate few on the outer sides threw themselves off the bridge and into the ditch below to avoid the imperial lances. The rest were ridden down as the riders swept out into the chaotic mass of crusaders.

Alexius struck and struck again, using the butt of his spear as often as the blade. Even as the weapon rose and fell in his hand, he scanned the battleground for any sign that their attack would be met and matched by a sudden surge of knights. But he saw no sign of mounted resistance, and so carried the charge forward.

The pilgrims, disoriented and dismayed, fled in droves before the imperial assault. Although the emperor had given orders that his own troops were not to pursue opportunities for combat with individuals, the pilgrim ranks were in such disarray that the scholae could not help cutting them down as they ran. Even so, far more died in the crush, trampled to death by their own comrades desperate to flee the onrushing horses.

The imperial scholae cut a wide swathe through the scattering crusaders and proceeded swiftly towards the river, and the exposed flank of the crusader army as it moved along the bank. As they drew near, they were met by a body of defenders – perhaps a hundred hastily-ordered knights, and several hundred footmen – who formed a rough battle line between the emperor's force and their own directly behind them. Poised to fight, yet waiting for the Byzantines to make the first move, they appeared irresolute and uncertain.

'Halt!' Alexius cried, pulling hard on the reins. His horse reared and plunged to a stop within a dozen paces of the front rank of knights. Instantly, his bodyguard reined up beside him while the Immortals ranged themselves in two long wings of double ranks on either side, forming an intimidating wall before the reluctant knights.

Staring down the length of his spear, Alexius brought its point to the throat of the foremost knight. 'I am Alexius, Supreme Sovereign of the Holy Roman Empire. Do you understand what I am saying to you?' he asked, speaking in unadorned Latin so that there should be no mistaking his meaning.

'I understand,' replied the truculent soldier. The man's age and the scar on the side of his neck signified him to be a veteran of battle. Wisely, he made no move to raise his sword.

'Where are your lords?' Alexius demanded.

The pilgrim jerked his head sideways, indicating that they were up ahead, leading the march. 'Go and find them,' the emperor ordered. 'We will await them here.'

Seeing that the Greeks did not appear interested in offering battle, the knight nodded to the man beside him. The second warrior put spurs to his mount and rode quickly away. There followed a long, tense interval as the two opposing forces waited for the arrival of the crusader lords, eyeing one another across the short distance separating them.

All at once there came a commotion from the rearward ranks. A way parted and Alexius saw a number of riders making their way towards the front line. He waited until they had come within the sound of his voice, and then said, 'So! Tell me, how stood the fearsome merchants before your mighty swords? Did the children and their mothers offer stout resistance to your massed attack? The victory is yours – how well the glory sits upon your valiant shoulders!'

Duke Godfrey, a puzzled look on his face, drew himself up to speak, but Alexius continued, 'Why do you repay the empire's generosity with treachery? Not even wild dogs bite the hand that feeds them.'

Alexius glowered at the assembled knights, who shifted uneasily, looking to their leaders to defend their honour against the emperor's inexplicable wrath. 'Shame!' he cried. 'The blood of the defenceless demands justice. We charge you to make reparation out of your own treasuries to the families of those you have slain.'

'Lord Emperor,' said Godfrey defensively, 'I profess before God and all gathered here, I know nothing of what you speak.'

'Ignorance ill becomes you, lord,' Alexius replied tartly. 'Heed then, we will enlighten you.' He then told the disgraced nobleman about the riot and attack on the marketplace, and demanded, 'Where were you when your troops violated the peace and friendship between our peoples?'

'Our supplies have run out,' answered the duke, evading the question. 'The people are hungry – they starve. They have had nothing but stale bread for weeks.'

'Fresh provisions await your people – as you well know,' the emperor told him. 'It only requires your oath of fealty to secure all the food you need.' Having vented his anger, Alexius pressed on to secure his primary purpose. 'This day,' he said, assuming a more conciliatory tone, 'is the day appointed for the signing of the oath of loyalty. We will have your answer. What is it to be?'

Godfrey looked upon the imperial troops ranged before him, and hesitated. There came a movement from the rear, and Baldwin burst suddenly into the front line. 'This demand is an insult!' he shouted, thrusting himself forward. 'I say we will *not* sign!'

Alexius gazed on him without expression. 'Give us your pledge, or give us your life. The choice is yours, friend, but we will have one or the other before this day is run.'

'The Devil take your oath!' Baldwin said, drawing his blade. Several of the knights looking on shouted support for this sentiment. The air tingled with the sound of swords sliding from scabbards.

'Peace, Baldwin!' his brother roared. 'Put up your sword. We will abide the emperor's request.' To Alexius, he said, 'The attack on the marketplace was ill-judged. On my honour, those who led the raid will be punished.' His eyes shifted unhappily from Baldwin to several of the leading knights, who had gone very quiet. To the emperor he said, 'We deeply regret the destruction and loss, and will make suitable reparation as you command.'

'We urge you to be generous,' Alexius told him. 'For the measure you use for others will be used for you.'

'It will be done,' Godfrey replied. 'Moreover, we stand ready to sign the pledge of loyalty at the time and place of your choosing.'

'So be it,' declared the emperor. 'We will see it signed here and now.' He held out his hand to Dalassenus, who promptly delivered into the emperor's outstretched palm the parchment square, which Alexius unfolded. 'Come here,' he commanded the brother lords; they dismounted and stood before him.

'Read it out,' instructed the emperor.

Reluctantly, Godfrey read out the oath, promising to keep faith with the emperor and recognizing his sovereign authority in all matters pertaining to the governance of the empire and its citizens, and further, to return to imperial rule all lands or cities – and any concomitant treasures, relics, or holy objects – formerly belonging to the empire which might fall to the crusaders' advance.

Having read the oath, Godfrey owned the vow, whereupon Dalassenus produced a quill and a vial of red ink which he proffered to Godfrey.

Dour and unsmiling, the lord dipped the point of the quill into the vial and signed his name with a defiant flourish. Handing the document and quill to his brother, he said, 'Affix your name beneath mine, dear brother, and let us remember we have come to fight the infidel, not to make war on friends.'

Baldwin sneered at the last word, but signed the document in scribbled haste and passed it contemptuously to the emperor, who looked at the signatures, and then delivered the document into the hands of the Grand Drungarius for safe-keeping.

'The promised food supplies will be delivered at once,' the emperor informed the lords. 'In a few days' time we expect to receive Count Bohemond of Taranto, who will also sign the oath of loyalty. When that formality has been accomplished, we will meet together to lay plans for shipping your people, horses, and supplies across the Bosphorus.' He paused to allow the significance of his words to penetrate their understanding, and then said, 'As your time in Constantinople grows short, we would have you enjoy something of the city's treasures and delights. Therefore, we have arranged for you and your men to visit the principal sights of the capital.'

'You are very kind, Lord Emperor,' Godfrey said, accepting the invitation by way of a peace offering. 'We would enjoy nothing more.'

Baldwin frowned, but held his tongue for once.

'So that you should not come to grief in a city so large and unknown to you, we will provide an escort of our own bodyguard to serve as guides. Thus, you need have no fear of becoming lost, or falling into harm.'

'Again,' said Godfrey, 'your thoughtfulness is laudable. We thank you, and will anticipate with all eagerness the council you propose.'

The lord made a small bow, whereupon the emperor bade them farewell, and detailed the Grand Drungarius, two strategi, and fifty Varangian guardsmen to see to the reparation settlement and conduct the lords and the noblemen of their company on a tour of the city. He then returned to Blachernae Palace to prepare to meet his old enemy's bellicose son, Bohemond of Taranto.

SIXTEEN

The settlement at Inbhir Ness was much larger than Murdo expected, and far more squalid. Tight clusters of low huts with high-peaked roofs of coarse thatch huddled close together over narrow footpaths that seamed through the town in every direction, like a bare earth web. Smoke from a multitude of hearthfires hung over the place so that even in the bright sun, Inbhir Ness appeared dark and uninviting.

The river mouth itself was wide enough, but only a handful of small boats, and three or four ships, were moored along the muddy banks. Aside from a large monastery on the hill high above the firth, the place seemed old, derelict, and forlorn, which surprised Murdo. Even sleepy Kirkjuvágr boasted more bustle and commerce. When he mentioned this fact to Peder, the elder seaman simply told him to wait and see. They proceeded through a pinched and narrow channel, and into another, smaller firth, which continued inland a fair distance to the mouth of the Ness which formed a wide and shallow harbour so full of craft of various sizes that it took all Peder's skill to manoeuvre their own small boat to shore.

'Put in!' Murdo called from the prow. 'Put in!'

'Aye,' Peder agreed. 'We will – when I see a good place.'

The voyage had been good, the winds favourable and the seas calm. But after the better part of three days and two nights on the water, Murdo was in no mood to wait: *any* place would do. 'There! See it?' He pointed to a narrow berth between two stout, high-sided cogs. 'Put in there!'

Peder eyed the place and frowned at the look of it, but did as he was told and nosed the boat towards the place. 'Strike the sail,' he called, 'and pick up the oars. Row us in.'

Murdo hopped to his chores and soon they were gliding into the space between the ships. No sooner had the keel bumped against the earthen bank, than Murdo leapt out onto dry land. Peder threw him a rope, which Murdo secured to a stump atop the raised-earth bank.

'You run on, Master Murdo, and see can you find Orin's ship,' the old seaman said, clambering onto dry land. 'I shall keep with the boat.'

Murdo did not hesitate, but hurried off along the bank. He worked his way around the inlet, looking at the ships and trying to determine if this one or that might belong to Lord Orin. He eventually arrived at a wide place at the farthest end of the anchorage, a square of sorts, where the harbour and main settlement met. Here the wagons and carts of the provisioners called to deliver their goods, and here the sailors met to drink ale and talk.

An inn – the first Murdo had ever seen – fronted this muddy square: a low, dark, rambling house with a small mountain of wooden casks, kegs, and tuns stacked high outside the entrance. Upon reaching the inn, he paused and savoured the toothsome aroma of roasting meat wafting out the wide and open door; the smell brought the water to his mouth and made his empty stomach squirm in anticipation. While he was yet surveying the square, a man in a leather apron emerged from the inn behind him and took up one of the kegs from the heap a few paces from where Murdo stood.

'I beg your pardon,' said Murdo, putting on his most polite demeanour. The man glanced at him and started back into the inn. 'I am looking for Orin Broad-Foot's ship. Can you tell me where it is?'

The fellow grunted at Murdo, but did not turn aside. 'Am I the harbour master now?' he growled without looking back. 'Get you gone!'

Rebuffed by the fellow's unaccountable rudeness, Murdo nevertheless seized upon the notion of searching out the harbour master. He continued his circumnavigation of the square, moving along the edge, watching all that passed before him, but failed to see anyone who might be called the master of the port and its disorderly commerce.

There were, he determined, a hundred or more men – many in clumps of three or four together, a fair few in larger groups, and the rest hastening about their errands alone; but, whether talking loudly and drinking freely, or pursuing their various chores, everyone seemed wholly preoccupied and oblivious to Murdo's presence as he walked here and there, apparently idly, but listening all the while to each group for the accents of speech that would tell him he had found the Norsemen.

Upon reaching the earthen bank once more – here built up and faced with timber to better accommodate the loading and unloading of larger ships – Murdo saw a group of seven big men talking loudly and drinking ale from a large stoup. Behind them, eight others were shifting a small mountain of bundles, bales, and wooden boxes from the bank to the deck of a sleek, low-hulled, longship. The high stern and prow swept up gracefully from the knife-sharp keel; the prow was carved with the head of a dragon with round staring eyes painted red, and long curved teeth painted white.

The men working and drinking were dressed in leather and homespun, and most wore their long hair tied and braided. Murdo slowed to hear better, and the sing-song lilt of their voices confirmed what he already knew: Norsemen, without a doubt.

He paused for a moment to decide how best to approach them, and was still trying to work out what to say, when one of the group – a brawny bare-chested seaman with a thick braid over his shoulder, saw him. 'You there!' the man growled. 'You find something funny to look at maybe, hey?'

The man's accent was so thick that, though Murdo recognized the words, it took him a moment to work out what he meant. 'Beg pardon?' he muttered.

'He deaf maybe,' suggested another of the group as they all turned to stare at him.

'Please,' said Murdo, plucking up his nerve and stepping forward. 'I am looking for Lord Orin Broad-Foot's ship. Could you tell me if it is here?'

The men looked at one another, but appeared reluctant to reply. Murdo was about to ask again when a voice boomed out behind him. 'Who is it that asks of Orin Broad-Foot?'

'I do, myself,' replied Murdo quickly.

He turned around to see who had addressed him, and saw a swarthy, bull-necked Norseman with arms as big as hams stuffed through a sleeveless tunic of undyed leather. His breecs were heavy sailcloth dyed the colour of rust, the legs of which were rolled to the tops of his tall boots – made from boar's hide which still displayed the hair of the beast. A large purse hung from a wide belt made of the same stuff. His beard was long and dark and, like most seagoing men, he kept his hair out of his face by tying it back with a leather string. He wore a broad-linked chain of silver on his neck, and a fat gold ring on the first finger of his left hand.

The eyes that watched him were clear and keen beneath a high smooth, sun-browned brow. Good straight teeth flashed white as the newcomer demanded, 'What's your business with Broad-Foot?'

Wary of revealing too much, Murdo replied, 'It is said Lord Orin is sailing for Jerusalem.'

'Aye, he goes with his king on pilgrimage.' The man regarded Murdo, looking him slowly up and down – as if placing a value on a beast of burden, and that value was not high. 'What is it to you, boy?'

The man was blunt, Murdo decided, but not malicious. 'I also am pledged to go to the Holy Land,' Murdo announced boldly. 'I have come to ask a place in his boat. I know about ships, and I can work. Also, I have a little silver; I can pay my way, if need be.'

'Can you now!' the man said, his mood lightening somewhat.

'I would thank you kindly if you could tell me where I might find Lord Orin – or his ship, at least.'

The dark-haired man drew himself up full height. He was a big full-fleshed man, and his shoulders were wide and strong. 'You come looking for Orin Broad-Foot, and you come to the right place,' he declared, 'but you come too late. He sailed two days ago on the morning tide.'

Murdo's heart sank, and he felt bleak futility descending over him. He thanked the man, turned away, and began walking back to where Peder waited with the boat.

'Pilgrim!' the man called after him. 'How much silver?'

Murdo turned, not certain he had heard correctly. 'What?'

'You have silver,' the Norseman said. 'How much?'

Murdo hesitated, uncertain what to answer. The seaman eyed him shrewdly, awaiting his reply. 'Ten – ten marks.'

'Bah!' the man said, flapping a huge hand at him. 'Go away, liar.'

'No, wait!' Murdo protested. 'It is true – I have ten marks.'

'Let me see it,' the man demanded.

Murdo, against his better judgement, reached into his shirt and tugged out the little leather bag. He started to untie it, but the Norseman snatched the bag from his fingers. 'Stop!' cried Murdo. 'Give it back!'

'If there is ten marks in here,' the rough seaman told him, 'you have nothing to fear. If there is more, or less, I keep the silver and cut out your tongue for a liar.'

Murdo, smouldering with rage, watched as the man opened the bag and poured the coins into his fist; he then counted them back into the bag one by one.

'Ten marks,' the Norseman confirmed.

'I am no liar,' Murdo told him. 'Now, give it back.'

'I thought you wanted to go to Jerusalem,' the seaman said, bouncing the purse on his palm. 'Ten marks pays your passage.'

Murdo, outraged at being robbed, and aghast at the audacity of the thief, sputtered in protest.

'Stay or go – the choice is yours, but it must be made quickly,' the Norseman told him. '*Skidbladnir* is ready, and the tide is on to turning.'

Murdo regarded the ship: a goodly-sized vessel of the kind the Norsemen excelled at building – sleek and low, easily manoeuvred and fast; it could hold thirty fighting men. From where he stood, he could see that many of the rowing benches had been removed to accommodate the small mountain of cargo, and the tented platform behind the mast.

'I will go with you,' Murdo answered, making up his mind. 'But I will give you five marks only.'

'Impossible,' replied the seaman. 'Seven, or you stay behind.'

'Six,' countered Murdo confidently.

The Norseman hesitated, hefting the bag in his hand.

'The tide is running, and you are leaving,' Murdo pointed out. 'It is the last silver you will see until Jerusalem.'

'You are not so stupid, I think,' the Norseman allowed, extending his hand. 'Six marks it is.'

Murdo took the offered hand. 'Three marks now, and three when we reach Jerusalem.'

'Done!' said the Norseman. He counted out three marks and tossed the bag to Murdo.

'I must fetch my belongings,' Murdo said. Tucking the purse quickly out of sight, he started off along the bank.

'Here now!' The seaman called him back. 'If you are sailing on my ship, we can come to an understanding first.'

'Very well,' Murdo agreed.

'Hear me: I am King Magnus' man, and I am joining his fleet as soon as we quit this harbour. I will gladly cleave you crown to chin if you cause me trouble,' the seaman vowed, fondling the hilt of the very large knife in his belt. 'But just you stay out of trouble, and you will find me a most agreeable companion.' Crossing his arms over his chest, he said, 'This is my pledge to you. What is your pledge to me?'

'You will never have cause to raise your voice to me, much less your blade,' Murdo told him solemnly. 'I will cause you no trouble, and do as I am told. This I pledge you.'

'You'll do, boy!' The big man grinned suddenly, and Murdo saw that one of his lower front teeth was missing, and a fine, almost invisible scar creased his lip and chin, making his smile a wry, lop-sided, yet curiously compelling thing. Murdo smiled, too, in response, and felt his heart lift for the first time in many days.

'I am Jon Wing,' he said, clapping a huge hand to Murdo's back, 'and I mean to watch you like Odin's eagle.'

'Though you watch me night and day, you will find nothing you do not expect to see,' Murdo told him. 'I mean to make myself useful.'

'Be about it then,' Jon Wing said, and turned to the men on the bank and began calling commands. Turning back to Murdo he said, 'Well? Get on, boy! The tide is flowing, and we are away with it.'

Murdo raced along the top of the earthen bank to rejoin Peder, who was sitting on a stump, braiding the ends of a length of rope. He hailed the old seaman, and hastened to explain. 'The king has already sailed,' he said, 'but one of his men is still in harbour. The ship is called *Skidbladnir*, and the master has agreed to take me.'

Peder nodded. 'A good name for a ship. When do you sail?'

'On the tide,' Murdo answered.

'Then farewell it is,' Peder replied, rising from the stump. Descending the bank and climbing into the boat, he stooped and hefted up the bundle Murdo had left behind. 'Here now,' he said, passing the bundle to Murdo over the side. 'As the tide is running, I will be going myself. Give us a push, Master Murdo, and I am away.'

Murdo untied the rope from the stump, coiled it quickly, and tossed it into the boat. Then, he put his shoulder to the prow and shoved the boat away as Peder settled himself at the oars. Murdo called farewell, and watched the old seaman work the oars, turning the boat with deft, efficient strokes.

'Tell my mother the journey is well begun,' Murdo called. 'Take care of her, Peder. See she does not worry overmuch.'

'Oh, aye,' vowed the old helmsman. 'Never fear. Just you keep a sharp weather eye, lad.'

'That I will,' answered Murdo, not wanting to take his eyes off Peder or the boat until both were out of sight. A long, rising whistle from the direction of Jon Wing's ship called him away, however, and Murdo took up his bundle and ran to secure his place aboard the waiting ship. Four rowers, long oars in hand, pushed the craft away from the bank as Murdo clambered over the rail.

He found a place among the rowers, took up an oar from the holder, and settled himself on his bench. He fell into the easy rhythm of rowing and watched the settlement of Inbhir Ness slip slowly away as the ship moved out onto the estuary.

Murdo saw Peder again a little while later as the ship entered the wider water of the firth. Murdo called across the water and exchanged a last farewell with the old pilot as the larger ship overtook the smaller. A short while later, *Skidbladnir* turned, heading east along the coast, and the Orkney boat continued its northerly course. A small square of buff-coloured sail was the last Murdo saw of the boat and its lone occupant. He then turned his face to the dragonheaded prow and looked out on seas and lands unknown to him — merely the first of many he would gaze upon in the days to come.

SEVENTEEN

Bohemond, astride his dun-coloured stallion, lifted a hand to the vast camp and the enormous walls towering over it. 'See here, Tancred! This is how I remember the city.' Rising beyond the walls, three of Constantinople's fabled seven hills could be seen, white palaces gleaming in the midday sun. 'It is just like the last time I saw it.'

Lord Tancred, reining in his favourite bay mare, gazed upon the jubilant rush of men towards the imposing walls of Constantinople. 'Your father's siege was not successful, I believe,' he replied dryly, lifting his voice above the shouts and cheers of the soldiers.

'Alas, no. He ran afoul of the infernal Venetians who believe they own the sea. He beat them back at the cost of half his fleet, and came on to Byzantium in the spring.' The prince paused, thinking back over the years.

'It was fever took him in the end, was it not?'

Bohemond nodded without taking his eyes from the glimmering hills. 'Fever broke out in the camp. I myself was taken ill and sent home to recover. In the end, the count was forced to abandon the siege. He died soon after.'

'A pity,' remarked Tancred. 'Especially as he had so much to gain.'

'Yes,' agreed Bohemond, 'and now I have returned to claim what he could not. Come, let us learn the measure of this Emperor Alexius.'

Godfrey and Baldwin rode out to greet the newcomers, and conducted them to their tents where a small feast had been prepared along with two or three tuns of wine to help the newly-arrived wash the dust of the arid Byzantine hills from their throats. The princes and lords, and their upper-ranking noblemen, ate and drank and regaled one another with tales of their travels. The two brother lords entertained their noble guests with the best of the limited hospitality at their command, falling over themselves to relate all they had seen of the city in the past two days.

'You have no idea of the wealth amassed in this place,' Baldwin assured them. 'It is far more than you can imagine.'

'Truly,' Godfrey added, 'and if Constantinople's riches stir you, just think what treasures await us in Jerusalem.'

'You have met this Alexius, I presume?' Bohemond inquired. Oh, yes, the brothers replied enthusiastically, they had met with the emperor: twice, once in his palace, and once in this very camp. They knew the emperor well, and held him in highest esteem. 'Tell me about him,' invited the Prince of Taranto.

'He is a shrewd and cunning dog,' Baldwin replied. 'His fortunes are beyond counting, yet he goes about a very beggar by comparison. He is a small, pig-eyed man with a skin like an Ethiope.'

'Be that as it may, he has nevertheless agreed to provision us,' Godfrey pointed out benevolently. 'And that – what with upwards of a hundred thousand men and forty thousand horses – is no small matter. He asks nothing in return, save that you sign an oath of loyalty recognizing him as emperor, and agreeing to return any conquered lands and such to the empire.'

'Sign an oath of loyalty!' hooted Bohemond. 'On my word, I will do no such thing.'

The duke shrugged. 'That is up to you, of course, Bohemond, dear friend. But the benefits of doing so are not inconsiderable.'

'Did you sign it – this oath of loyalty?'

'We did,' Godfrey declared, 'and gladly.'

Baldwin frowned, but said nothing. There was no need to mention the unfortunate riot in the marketplace, and the resultant loss of fifty-six men.

'The Greeks are infamous for their treachery,' Bohemond observed. 'There is certain to be some deception in it. I will go to the devil before I pledge fealty to that black dog of an emperor.'

Godfrey glared at Bohemond, who stared back in fierce defiance, as if it was *he* and not Alexius insisting on the pledge.

'This hot, and it is but April,' complained Tancred, lifting his cup and draining it. Holding the empty vessel at arm's length, he instructed his steward to refill the cup and to keep the jug full and ready. 'At least,' he mused, returning the cup to his mouth, 'the emperor's wine is better than his reputation.'

Baldwin and some of the noblemen laughed, easing the strain of the moment.

'The duplicity of the Greeks is well known, of course,' sniffed Godfrey peevishly. 'But as we are only to remain in Byzantium a day or two longer at most, I saw no harm in signing the oath. He *is* the emperor, after all.'

'We have only just arrived,' Bohemond said imperiously. 'I have no intention of rushing off so soon. The men are exhausted, and the horses must be rested. We have been on the march continuously since Avlona. It will take more than a day or two before we can consider moving on.'

'The emperor is even now devising plans to help us move our armies across the Bosphorus where a camp has been prepared at Pelecanum,' Godfrey informed the prince, happy to see him squirm. 'Our armies have been waiting weeks now, and our men are more than ready to press on to the Holy Land.'

'Perhaps,' suggested Baldwin, 'you might persuade the emperor to allow you to wait until Count Raymond and Duke Robert arrive.'

'I wonder they are not here already,' Tancred mused. 'What the devil can have happened to them?'

'Ah,' Godfrey replied, 'I have it that they tarried a while in Rome – at the pope's request. Apparently, Urban, despite his zeal for the success of the pilgrimage, is not well enough to undertake the journey himself. Thus, he has appointed a legate to lead the crusade in his stead.'

Bohemond stiffened. 'Do we know this legate?' wondered the prince in a slightly strained voice.

'We do not,' admitted Godfrey. 'But he is said to be a churchman – a bishop, I believe – of scrupulous honour and highest repute.'

'Well,' allowed the prince, growing easy once again, 'so long as he keeps his reputable nose out of affairs that do not concern him, I have no objection.' Raising his cup, he cried, 'God prosper us, my lords! Hey!'

'God prosper us!' replied the assembled noblemen. They all drank then, and the feast proceeded in good spirit – so good in fact, that the arrival of a messenger with a summons for Bohemond to attend the emperor went unremarked and unresented. The prince allowed himself to be conducted to Blachernae Palace alone and unaccompanied by any but Tancred and eight of his closest noblemen.

Alexius received the son of his former enemy in the Salamos Hall of Blachernae Palace from which he had removed all its portable furnishings and treasures. Any that could not be moved, he had hidden beneath tasteful, but not unduly ornate Damasc-cloth coverings. He desired the room to present a suitably imposing, yet somewhat austere display, so as not to inflame his visitor's notorious greed.

For the reception, the emperor arrayed himself in his best ceremonial robes, but added to the imperial purple his breastplate, sword, dagger, and greaves: not the high-polished gilt armour he used for formal occasions, but the battered pieces he wore on the field. Alexius remembered, and dreaded, Bohemond's superior size and height, and wished to even the scales as much as possible by showing himself a man of daring and action. Likewise, he commanded the full complement of palace excubitori to attend him in battle gear used in previous campaigns. In this way, he hoped to gently remind his rogue of a guest that the emperor was a commander of armies, and well-used to the harsh fortunes of war.

So, when the two latest arrivals and their vassal lords were brought into his presence, they found the emperor standing before his throne and looking as if he expected to mount his horse at any moment and charge into battle. His manner, like his surroundings, bespoke an able ruler in full command of his faculties, passions, and authority. Tancred decided, before he had moved a dozen paces into the room, that he would happily sign the oath of fealty to this emperor.

Bohemond, however, appeared impervious to Alexius' sly design. Ever the arrogant prince, he walked with his customary swagger across the marble floor to stand directly before the throne and look God's Ruler on Earth in the eye.

'So, Bohemond, here you are again,' said the emperor, unable to bring himself to utter words of false welcome. 'You always wished to gain entrance to our palace; at long last it would appear you have achieved your ambition – unlike the last time you were here.'

Bohemond's smile was broad and genuine. 'Hail, Alexius! God be good to you, I hope.' He looked around the room, filling his eyes with the grand and stately architecture; even in its subdued condition, the room was still far more magnificent than any royal apartment he had ever known. 'To think,' he said amiably, 'I have achieved in friendship what could not be gained by force of arms.'

'You call yourself our friend,' remarked Alexius. 'Do we discern a change of heart?'

'I stand before you, Lord Emperor, your humble servant,' replied Bohemond, spreading his empty hands before him. Alexius remarked how large were those hands, and how powerful those arms. 'As you see me, so I am.'

'We do see you, Prince Bohemond,' the emperor intoned, 'but the sight does not entirely expunge the memory of our last exchange.' Even as he spoke the words, Alexius judged the changes in the man before him; twelve years had done much for old Robert's son. A tall, rangy youth, he had put muscle to his lanky bones; broad of shoulder and narrow of hip, he stood on long sturdy legs, with not the least hint of meekness in his clear blue eyes. Both chin and cheek were smooth from the razor, and his hair, unlike that of so many Franks, was cut even to his shoulders. He moved easily, and with confidence, alert to all around him. If not for the fellow's insufferable arrogance, pride, and over-reaching ambition, Alexius might have found it in himself to befriend the top-lofty prince.

'But that was a long time ago, Lord Emperor,' Bohemond was saying, still smiling. 'Then, I was merely a vassal in the command of my father. Today, however, I come freely of my own volition, responding purely out of Christian duty to see our common enemy vanquished, and the lands hallowed by our Lord and Saviour returned to the rightful occupation and veneration of God's faithful people.'

'Be assured all Heaven rejoices to hear it,' Alexius replied, moving swiftly to the moment of anticipated difficulty. 'We are always glad to welcome men of such high-minded resolve into our confidence – in observance of which we have prepared a small token of our regard.' He lifted a hand to the magister officiorum, who stepped forward with a lacquered tray bearing two fine golden bowls set with rubies and sapphires.

Alexius allowed his guests to fill their eyes with the prizes, and then, with a nod to Theodosius, Logothete of the Symponus, who advanced bearing the parchment square containing the oath of loyalty which Hugh, Godfrey, and Baldwin had already signed, the emperor said, 'So that we may all be of one accord, and enjoy the benefits of our newfound friendship, it only remains for you to join your fellow pilgrims in the recognition of our imperial sovereignty.'

Tancred, wishing to express his independence and secure the emperor's favour forthwith, spoke first. 'I will delay only so long as it takes to pare reed and dip pen,' he said, inclining his head. Whereupon the magister unfolded the document and, placing it on a board bearing a pot of ink and a prepared quill, offered it to the young nobleman, who affixed his signature beneath those of Godfrey and Baldwin while the magister held the board.

'Your readiness shames me, Tancred,' Bohemond observed. 'But I will write my name large so that our friend and emperor will know at a glance who it is that he has clasped to his bosom in friendship.' Taking up the quill pen he dipped the tip in the pot and with an elaborate flourish wrote his name in letters twice the size of all the others. He replaced the quill and, still smiling, inclined his head in submission.

The emperor, unable to believe the ease with which he had secured Bohemond's vow, said, 'Come, Nicetas, present the gifts to our esteemed guests.'

Tancred eagerly received the offered bowl; it was definitely worth the cost of travelling to Constantinople. Bohemond did not lift a hand to the tray, however, but remained with his hands clasped before him, smiling as he had since entering the throne room. 'Do not think I shun your gift, Lord and Emperor,' the prince said. 'If I refrain, it is not from scorn, but rather out of forbearance.'

Alexius stared at the haughty prince and tried to imagine Bohemond exercising this particular virtue. Certainly, he possessed all of his father's insatiable passions, and old Robert Guiscard had never abstained from anything the entire length of his life.

'You have some other token in mind, perhaps,' the emperor decided at last.

'Ah, you have hit on the very thing, lord,' replied Bohemond. 'As it happens, the pilgrimage we have undertaken is one in which the warrior arts must, alas, also play their part. It would mean more to me than treasures of gold to receive the imperial blessing on our mutual enterprise.'

'Our blessing,' echoed Alexius, smelling a trap, but unable to discern what it might be. 'Of course, Prince Bohemond, we ever offer prayers and blessings for the success of God's endeavours, and for those who carry out our Heavenly Father's designs on earth. What form might this blessing take?'

Bohemond's smile widened even further, showing his strong white teeth. 'Mere words,' the prince replied. 'A title only.'

'Have you a title in mind?' inquired the emperor, suspicion making him wary.

'Since you ask, it would please me to become Grand Domestic of the Imperial Armies.' Bohemond spoke simply, humbly – as if this were a thing of no consequence which had only just come into his mind.

The emperor felt the full implications of the request instantly. 'You are a bold schemer, Bohemond. Any man who doubts it does so to his regret and dismay.'

The shrewd prince watched the emperor carefully. 'Do you refuse my request?'

'We do not,' answered Alexius, choosing his words carefully. He knew full well the danger of denying Bohemond; at the same time, he could not possibly give the prince authority over the crusader armies. 'On the contrary, Bold Prince, we deem it a sound and sensible appointment. We doubt the leadership of the pilgrim forces could be placed in better hands. Indeed, we are only sorry that we cannot accede to your desires at this very moment. You will understand the difficulty if we are seen to favour one nobleman over another before all have arrived. Still, we are happy to offer you every assurance that when the time becomes appropriate, the title you seek will be swiftly granted.'

Bohemond, much to the emperor's relief and gratitude, accepted this answer with good grace. 'I leave it to your discretion, Emperor Alexius. When the time is ripe, you will find me eager to take up my new responsibilities.'

'We will await the day with keen anticipation. Until then,' said the emperor, almost hugging himself with joy for the way in which he had brought the difficult prince to heel, 'please accept the bowl as a small emblem of the treasures awaiting those who persevere in faith and,' he added pointedly, 'loyalty.'

EIGHTEEN

Murdo glowered at the white-haired monk before him. Why did it have to be priests, he wondered, and nosey ones at that? 'I was hoping to go to Jerusalem with King Magnus,' he muttered thickly, 'but I did not reach the ships in time.' The thought of sharing ship space with them filled him with despair – and all the way to Jerusalem!

'How extraordinary!' remarked the tallest of the three clerics. Somewhat older than the others, he appeared to be the leader of the group. His curly white hair was thick and close cut, making him appear to be wearing a fleece on his head.

'Extraordinary!' agreed the other two, regarding Murdo with a benign interest that made his skin crawl.

'That is exactly what happened to us,' the tall monk said. 'It took longer to reach Inbhir Ness than we knew. We arrived too late and missed the king's fleet.' The three fell to squabbling about how narrowly they had missed the boat – was it one day, or two, or more? They could not agree; but then, agreement seemed the furthest thing from their intentions.

Without a doubt, Murdo reflected sourly, these were the least likely churchmen he had ever encountered: dressed in long robes of undyed wool, the hems of which were tattered and bedraggled with mud; the hoods of their cowls hung down their backs almost touching the ground, and their sleeves were absurdly wide and ample. They were bare-footed, dirty-fingered, and reeking with the odour of lamb fat which Murdo could smell from where he stood.

Huge, worn, leather satchels hung at their sides from straps over their shoulders and, although they were aboard a ship in the middle of the sea, each one carried a well-worn wooden staff made from a rowan sapling. Their foreheads were shaved from ear to ear, save for a thin circlet of close-cropped hair resembling a crown at the brow.

Despite his aversion to clerics, Murdo could not take his eyes from them. As he looked on, it occurred to him that they were like ancient Druids – those weird and mysterious figures who inhabited the tales his grandmother used to tell. 'The druid-kind are wise and powerful seers, Murdo-boy,' she would tell him. 'They know all things men can know, for they do peer through the veil of time. They know the pathways that lead beyond the walls of this world and, as we might go to Kirkjuvágr, they roam the Otherworld.'

Could they be druids? Murdo wondered. But then he saw the large wooden crosses on leather loops around their necks, and decided that, perhaps they were priests after all – but of some obscure variety unknown to him. One tall and rangy, one narrow-faced and round-shouldered, one short and fat, with their filthy and dishevelled appearance, battered satchels and absurd staffs and chunky wooden crosses, they were, if possible, even more odious than the ordinary kind Murdo knew and loathed. Had he possessed a lump of dung, Murdo would have cheerfully pelted them with it.

It was just past dawn, and all the rest of the ship's crew, save the pilot – a grizzled hank of bone and hair named Gorm Far-Seer – were still asleep. Murdo had just woken from his place at the prow, when the three emerged from the tented platform behind the mast where they had, apparently, been sleeping off the effects of too much Inbhir Ness ale. They then proceeded to hobble up one side of the ship and down the other – not once only, but three times – slowly. They walked with their rowan staffs in their right hands, left hands raised above their foreheads, chanting with high reedy voices in a language that Murdo could not understand.

Upon the completion of their third circuit of the ship, they had come to stand before Murdo to greet him and make his acquaintance. He had not encouraged their questions, but these strange clerics seemed oblivious to his resentment.

'Maybe he has been unforeseeably detained,' the fat one was saying. He spoke his Latin in an odd lilting tongue, strangely accented – more like singing than speaking. 'That is exactly what I said: "He has been detained" – did I not?'

'And I replied, "I fear your hope is mistaken, brother," remember?' answered the thin one in a fine, faintly accented intonation. 'It was, if you will reconsider, precisely explained to us that the king had been there already. The master of the harbour was most emphatic about that.'

'Ah, but there was no harbour,' pointed out the tall one; his speech danced, too, but in a way slightly different to the others. 'Unless the rudimentary timber mooring on the river could in some way be considered a harbour.'

'Of course there was no harbour,' replied the thin-faced monk. 'I merely meant that which serves *in place of* a harbour for the good folk of Inbhir Ness.'

'If there was no harbour, there could not be a harbour master,' the tall monk rejoined. 'Ergo, the man you spoke to may not, in fact, have possessed the necessary authority to provide satisfactory answer to our inquiry.'

'There may be something in what you say,' allowed the fat priest. 'Yet, I feel duty bound to point out that the man's authority was never at issue. Rather, it was his perspicacity. Any man with wit enough –'

Murdo, astonished that they should recount in word-for-word detail their inane argument of two days ago, shook his head in disbelief. 'But how else were we to get to Jerusalem?' wondered the round-shouldered one. 'That is the question before us, brothers.'

'How indeed?' mused the tall monk. 'If not for the Great King's providential intervention, we might yet be pondering that very question.'

'We might have walked,' suggested the thin-faced monk. 'Many illustrious persons have done so in the past, much to their spiritual improvement. After all,' he added, 'it is the means of conveyance our Lord Christ himself chose when travelling abroad the land.'

'Verily, brother, verily,' agreed the elder cleric amiably. 'Well said.'

'I have no objection to it whatever,' said the fat one. 'I would only offer the observation that Jerusalem may be, according to many and various accounts, rather a great distance from our own green and pleasant shores. Therefore, a journey by foot could conceivably take somewhat longer than we anticipate. The crusade might indeed have achieved its end long before we reached the Holy Land, it must be said.'

'Alas, I fear you may be right,' sighed the thin one, suddenly disheartened by the thought.

Murdo, annoyed by their vaunted blather, decided they were harmless enough, if somewhat tedious. He was about to leave them to their pointless debate when the fat one looked up and grinned at him, his round face shining with simple good will. 'Brothers, see here! We are forgetting ourselves. Our young friend has no interest in our trifling suppositions.' The monk inclined his head in acknowledgement of Murdo's patience. 'Like you, we are on pilgrimage. It was arranged for us to join King Magnus' fleet at Inbhir Ness and take passage with him.' Smiling happily, he cheerfully confided, 'We are to be his advisors – in spiritual matters, that is – for the duration of the pilgrimage.'

'My brothers,' announced the tall monk suddenly, 'this is a most auspicious meeting, and one deserving of proper – and, I dare suggest, hallowed – recognition. The Good Lord has placed this young man in our path as a friend for the journey. Let us acknowledge this glad meeting with a drink!'

'Ale!' cried the fat monk. 'We must have ale!'

'The very cry of my heart,' remarked the tall cleric. 'Yes, yes, you and Fionn fetch us all some ale. We will celebrate the Almighty's wondrous providence.'

The two clerics tottered off along the rail, returning from their tent a few moments later bearing jars of frothy brown ale which they handed around.

'Hail, Brave Wanderer!' proclaimed the fat monk, thrusting a jar into Murdo's hands. 'May the Lord of Hosts be good to you; may the Lord of Peace richly bless you; may the Lord of Grace grant you your heart's desire.' Raising his jar in salute, he cried, 'Sláinte!'

'Sláinte!' echoed the other two, eagerly raising their jars.

Murdo recognized the word as Gaelic, a language many of Orkneyjar's older families still maintained, and one his mother often employed when more mundane words failed her. Consequently, Murdo knew enough of it to make himself understood. 'Sláinte mor!' he said, which brought smiles and nods of approval from the clerics.

'A man blessed of Heaven's own tongue!' declared the thin-faced monk. 'It is myself, Brother Fionn mac Enda, at your service. May I know your name, my friend?'

'I am Murdo Ranulfson of Dýrness in Orkneyjar,' he answered, straightening himself and squaring his shoulders so as to be worthy of his father's name.

'We drink to you, Murdo Ranulfson!' said the monk called Fionn, and all three raised their cups and began slurping noisily. Murdo followed their example, and for a moment they occupied themselves wholly with their cups.

When the clerics finally came up for a breath, the fat one, beaming like a happy cherub, announced, 'I am called Emlyn ap Hygwyd, and I am pleased to meet you, Murdo. I believe we shall be good friends, you and I.'

Although the prospect seemed unlikely in light of Murdo's avowed enmity toward priests, the rotund cleric spoke with such sincerity, Murdo could not bring himself to openly disagree.

'If you please, good Murdo,' Emlyn continued, 'allow me to present our esteemed superior, Brother Ronan macDiarmuid.'

The tallest monk bowed his head humbly. 'Superior in years only,' he replied with gentle dignity, 'not, I hasten to assure you, in zeal for our Lord, devotion, or holiness.'

Murdo repeated the monks names, whereupon they all drank again, and declared the ale a blessing of the highest virtue – in consideration of which they would all be guilty of gross impiety if they did not instantly avail themselves of a second helping. Accordingly, they drained the cups quickly, and Emlyn and Fionn hastened to refill them, returning in a short while, loudly praising the brewer's remarkable skill and generosity.

After they had guzzled from their jars, Ronan said, 'Now then, if I may be so bold as to suggest, I find it astonishing that a man of your tender years should be undertaking pilgrimage alone – commendable to be sure, even laudable – but astonishing nonetheless.'

'Many people from Orkneyjar have taken the cross,' Murdo assured him quickly. 'My father and brothers have gone before me – they travel in company with Duke Robert of Normandy, and many other noblemen. I am going to join them.'

'Ah, yes,' remarked the monk, as if Murdo had supplied the solution to a longstanding mystery.

'Extraordinary!' the other two declared.

Eager to avoid further questions, Murdo said, 'How is it that you come to follow King Magnus?'

'As it happens,' Ronan answered, 'our abbey occupies lands granted to Lord Magnus by Malcolm, High King of the Scots some years ago – near Thorsa. Do you know it?'

Before Murdo could answer, Fionn broke in, saying, 'When we learned that the good king had taken the cross and intended following the crusade, we made entreaty for the privilege of accompanying our monarch and benefactor on pilgrimage to the Holy Land.'

'Our bishop kindly granted our petition,' explained Emlyn, 'and it was arranged that we should accompany King Magnus to Jerusalem. I can only think that something must have gone amiss, otherwise he would not have sailed without us.'

'We were,' offered Ronan, resuming his story, 'to be the king's guides and counsellors in all matters pertaining to the Holy Land and its environs – leaving, of course, any actual combat to the more militarily inclined among the king's retinue.'

'I have never touched a sword,' Emlyn proclaimed cheerfully. 'I am certain I would cut off my own foot before ever coming so much as a stone's throw from a Saracen.'

'He would,' confirmed Fionn. 'Indeed, he would – we all would. We are not warlike in the least.'

Murdo considered this pronouncement a pathetic confession of weakness, thinking that if he owned such a defect, he would not tell another soul; certainly, he would not boast about it with the pride these confused clerics appeared to enjoy.

'Well, I suppose the king has warriors enough already. No doubt he needs priests, too,' Murdo allowed, although why anybody should want three such garrulous clerics was a mystery – especially when even *one* priest was a priest too many in Murdo's reckoning.

Still, the mention of King Malcolm's name piqued his interest. That these monks should have some association with his mother's kin intrigued Murdo. What, he wondered, had the King of the Scots to do with the King of Norway? And why should either of them be giving lands to this curious breed of cleric? Clearly, there was more here than he knew, and he determined to find out.

The sun was a foul yellow flare directly overhead when *Skidbladnir* came in sight of the jutting peninsula called Andredeswald by the Angles who lived there. 'That is where we shall put in for supplies,' Jon Wing announced.

The weather had been fair and the winds good for many days, allowing the knife-hulled ship to soar over the gentle sea swell as it made its way down along the eastern coast, bearing its crew and passengers swiftly southward. They made landfall now and then at safe havens to refresh the water skins and stoups, always moving swiftly on. Murdo, anxious to reach the Holy Land, resented stopping now – especially since they seemed to have plenty of provisions already.

But Jon would have it no other way but that they put in to shore. 'Dofras is the last good market this side of the strait,' he explained. 'Where we fetch up next, I cannot say. Better to take with us what we can.'

The monks agreed this seemed the wisest course. 'The voyage could be long,' Emlyn told him.

'How long?' asked Murdo suspiciously.

'A year, perhaps even longer – or so I have heard,' replied the priest.

'A year!' challenged Murdo. No place could be so far away that it could take so long. He imagined a few more weeks would be more than sufficient.

'Oh, yes,' agreed Fionn. 'What with winter harbourage, it could well take longer.'

This information cast Murdo into such a dismal mood that he lost all interest in going into the town. As soon as the boat touched the strand, the monks scampered away to the market to secure the needed supplies. Jon, having no wish to visit the settlement himself, allowed his men to go and enjoy a brief diversion. 'I will stay and look after the ship,' he told them. 'You go on without me, but try not to get too drunk.' Turning to Murdo he advised, 'You should go, too. We will not see another familiar settlement in a very long time, nor get any öl.'

'I left the last familiar settlement behind long ago,' Murdo told him. 'As I have no wish to drink öl in the marketplace, I will stay to help you with the boat.'

Jon shrugged, and proceeded to undertake an examination of his vessel, searching the craft prow to stern and rail to keel for anything requiring his attention; finding nothing particularly troublesome, he turned his scrutiny to the ropes and tiller and mast. Meanwhile, Murdo slipped over the side and waded to shore. The strand was flat and wide here, the settlement a fair distance from the sea, sheltering beneath towering cliffs of white stone. He walked a while along the sand, returning some time later to find Jon Wing wading around the hull of the ship, feeling the planking with his hands. Every now and then, he would take a deep breath and dive underwater, surfacing again in a moment to resume his inspection.

Murdo sat down on a low rock to watch, and approved of the precautions Jon was taking. He had quickly learned to respect the Norseman's seamanship, and that of his crew. They all worked well together, rarely provoking one another; each seemed to anticipate what the other would do so that Jon had little need to call commands or raise his voice in reprimand. Murdo knew enough about sailing to know that it was not as easy as Jon Wing and his crew made it appear. He concluded that this accord had been gained through long experience; probably they had sailed with one another for a few years at least.

The first of the evening stars were glowing when the monks and seamen returned, staggering over the strand, toting casks of ale, and sacks of grain, and numerous other bundles, including an entire side of smoked pork. The monks had purchased an enormous heap of common foodstuffs – so much, in fact, that Jon Wing complained that his ship would sink beneath the weight at the first contrary wave.

The monks merely shrugged and said that the market was so well-stocked with delicacies they could not help themselves. Apparently, restraint was not, Murdo reflected, a priestly virtue these curious clerics recognized.

Nevertheless, the supplies were quickly stowed, and Murdo, after a dull and tiresome day ashore, fairly itched to see the sail raised and the dragonhead prow slicing deep waves once again. But Jon Wing chose a snug little bay just a stone's throw down the coast and coved the boat for the night. 'After this, there is no more land for many days,' he said, when Murdo voiced his frustration. 'We will sleep on solid ground tonight. You should enjoy it while you can.'

The monks seemed overjoyed to have a night on dry land, and busied themselves with making a fire and preparing the evening meal. Despite his initial annoyance, supper that night was an extravagance Murdo welcomed. He watched hungrily while the clerics brought forth the victuals and set to work, as deft and clever in their movements as weavers. The seamen were amazed at the monks' proficiency with provisions. After securing the boat for the night, they settled before the campfire to gaze with increasing admiration at the master-ful display.

Various raw ingredients appeared and were nimbly dispatched to pot and pan and skewer. The three worked efficiently, rarely speaking, wielding knives and spoons with the adroit agility of jugglers. Their craft, and the rising esteem of the onlookers, was augmented by the very good ale which they quaffed liberally and shared all around, 'To restore the inner man,' as Brother Emlyn put it.

The monks prepared food enough for a hundred footweary pil-grims: pease porridge and new brown bread; smoked fish cooked in milk and butter and onions; chops of pork roasted slowly above the fire, and over which, from time to time, they sprinkled a concoction of dried herbs; and apples, cored and cooked in cream and honey.

Ordinary fare, but exquisitely prepared, and Murdo, after devouring one bowl of porridge and two chops, began to see a side of monastery life previously unknown to him. Priests were still a bane and a blight – deceitful as snakes, and just as poisonous – but these, he reflected once again, were of a wholly different stripe than any he had seen or heard tell of before. He wondered what other talents they possessed.

The seamen were equally impressed. Jon Wing could not help asking, 'Do you eat like this all the time in the monkery?'

'We are on pilgrimage,' Ronan cheerfully explained. 'It is for-bidden for pilgrims to fast.'

By the time the last bowl was licked clean and the last bone tossed away, the moon had risen and stars could be seen reflecting on the smooth surface of the bay. Fionn banked the fire for the night, and the good brothers fell to discussing whether the soul of a sinner was heavier than that of a saint – being burdened down, as it was, with the dross of iniquity. The exchange was good-natured, and Murdo followed their musical speech as best he could until, full of good food and ale, he grew too drowsy to keep his eyes open anymore. Rolling himself in his cloak, he was soon asleep with the murmur of monks droning pleasantly in his ear, and dreams of Ragna floating through his head.

He was roused the next morning well before dawn by a cup of cold water dashed over him. Murdo leaped up, spluttering and swing-ing his fists. 'Here now,' Jon said, 'and I thought you were eager for leaving.'

Murdo shook the water out of his eyes and, with a grumble about the coarseness of the jest, fell to helping the others fill the water skins; meanwhile, the monks, yawning and scratching themselves, stowed their cooking utensils, and within a few moments of rising, the crew and passengers were aboard and rowing the boat towards the open sea once more. Murdo nestled himself among the grain bags in the centre of the ship and leaned against the mast; he watched the early-morning mist swirling over the water and listened to the birdcalls in the trees along the river. He must have fallen asleep again, for the next thing he knew, he was rolling on the bottom of the boat.

Scrambling to his feet, he grabbed the rail and looked out to see low, green, cloud-covered hills far behind, and nothing but empty sea and sky ahead. The sail snapped sharply and the ship plunged into the swell again. Jon Wing, pulling hard on the tiller oar, turned onto a new heading, and the ship began to run smoothly before the wind.

Murdo felt the sheer exhilaration of the chase stirring his blood. Somewhere out there, across the grey and vasty sea, his father and brothers were fighting the cunning Saracen, and he, Murdo, would find them and bring them back. It would happen; it must. He would make it happen.

He spared no kindly thought for the pope or his innumerable lackeys, nor for the sacred duty of the pilgrimage. Whether the crusade succeeded or failed was all one to Murdo; he could not have cared less one way or the other. His heart was filled with a single desire and had no room for anything else: to see the lands of his fathers restored. His life, his future, his happiness with Ragna – *everything* depended on saving Hrafnbú. *That* meant more to him than all the empire's gold – and certainly, far, far more than the pointless protection of a handful of churches and a few dusty relics no one he knew had ever seen.

'You are very grim for a young man,' Emlyn observed cheerfully.

Murdo turned his head to see the round-shouldered monk reclining on his elbows against the rail. 'I was thinking.' He shifted on the grain sacks for a better look at the jovial priest.

'About the crusade, yes?'

Murdo heard the word, but the crusade was so far from his thoughts that for a moment he could not make sense of what the

171

cleric was saying. 'No, not that,' he answered at last. 'I was thinking about my farm – home, I mean.'

'You are wishing you had not left home perhaps,' suggested the monk. 'Ah, *fy enaid*,' he sighed wistfully. 'I, too, sometimes grow melancholy thinking of my home in blessed Dyfed.'

Murdo had never heard of the place and said so.

'Never heard of Dyfed!' cried the monk, aghast. 'Why, it is the best place on earth. God has showered every gift on that fair realm and the people there are the happiest to be found under Heaven's bright vault. How not? The land abounds in streams and lakes and springs of every kind – all of them flowing with water sweet and good to drink, water that makes the lightest, most delightful ale ever known, water that makes the thirsty kine content and the lambs' wool fine as silk.

'Truly, the weather is never harsh, and the breeze is soft as a mother's breath upon the cheek of her dearling child. The days are warm and the sky always blue as the lark's egg. Never does the stormcloud threaten, less yet conceal the glorious sun, for it rains only at night and then but gently, gently, wetting the land with dew as mild as milk. Thus, every good thing grows in abundance, and one has only to scatter the grainseed wherever he will to reap a bounteous harvest. Everywhere the grass is green and lush, fattening the cattle most remarkably well.'

The rapturous monk gulped down a breath, and plunged on in praise of his magical home. 'The women of Dyfed are beauty and elegance made flesh, and the men are bards and warriors every one. They live together in peaceful harmony, never speaking rudely to one another, much less raising their voices in anger. They spend their days making songs which are the envy of the angels themselves. Indeed, it has often been known that a bard will sing a song before his lord, and that night be taken up to Paradise so that he may teach the Heavenly Choir the blessed refrains he has composed.

'The wealth so coveted by other nations is wholly despised by the Cymry. Gold and silver are mere enticements for craftsmen to take up their tools and practice their masterly arts. The trifles they fashion become adornment for kings and queens, and even children are skilled in making the most wondrous and delicate designs. And . . . and . . .'

Overcome by the memory, Emlyn lapsed into an enraptured

silence. Murdo gazed at the man and thought again how odd these monks appeared. Were they, as they professed to be, truly clerics? If so, the church they served must be different by far from the one Murdo knew.

'It seems a most remarkable realm, the way you tell it,' Murdo observed.

Emlyn nodded solemnly. 'I tell you the truth: when Eden was lost to Adam's race, our Kind Creator took pity on his wayward children and gave them Ynys Prydein, and Dyfed is the finest corner of our beloved isle.'

'If it is as you say, I wonder anyone should ever leave it at all.'

'Oh, but that is the very heart and soul of our predicament,' the monk wagged his head sadly from side to side. 'For the Cymry, blessed of the Gifting Giver with all the highest boons, were also given a solitary affliction lest men of other realms and races eat out their hearts in hopeless envy. Heaven's Most Favoured were endowed with an irresistible taithchwant so that they might not become too proud in the enjoyment of their many-splendoured homeland.'

Emlyn spoke with such a soulful longing, that Murdo's heart was moved to hear it. 'What is this tai – taith –'

'Taithchwant,' the monk repeated. 'Oh, it is less an affliction than a cruel travail. It is a kind of wanderlust, but more potent than any yearning known to humankind. It is that gnawing discontent which drives a man beyond the walls of paradise to see what lies over the next hill, or to discover where the river ends, or to follow the road to its furthest destination. Truly, there is nothing more powerful, and only one thing that is known to be its equal.'

'What is that?' wondered Murdo, entirely taken in by the monk's sincerity.

'It is the hiraeth,' answered the monk. 'That is, the home-yearning – an aching desire for the green hills of your native land, a matchless longing for the sound of a kinsman's voice, a greedy hunger only satisfied by the food first eaten at your mother's hearth. Alas, the hiraeth is a hankering torment so strong it can bring tears to a man's eyes and make him forget all other loves, and even life itself.'

He sighed. 'So, you see? We are forever pinched between the two most formidable cravings men can know, and therefore we cannot ever be happy to remain in one place very long.'

Murdo admitted that it did seem a very shame, at which thought the cleric brightened once more, and said, 'God is good. He has made us his special messengers, equipping us to take his pure and shining light to a world benighted and lost in darkness. We are the Célé Dé,' he proclaimed proudly, 'the Servants of the High King of Heaven, who has abundantly bestowed his grace and favour upon us.' Emlyn leaned close as if to confide a secret; he lowered his voice accordingly. 'Hear me: we are the Keepers of the Holy Light, and the Guardians of the True Path.'

NINETEEN

Raymond of Saint-Gilles, Count of Toulouse and Provence, arrived at Constantinople the day before Bohemond's army was to depart. Having wintered in Rome, where he had been joined by the papal legate Adhemar, Bishop of Le Puy, the count had crossed the Adriatic and landed his army at Dyrrachium. Then, hastened on their way by the governor, the count and bishop had begun the long, uncomfortable climb up through the rough Macedonian hills.

The journey had proven blessedly uneventful, with only a few minor lapses of discipline among troops – unfortunate misunderstandings which resulted in the pillage and destruction of several unsuspecting Byzantine towns, and the temporary imprisonment of Bishop Adhemar by the stern Pecheneg escort the emperor had sent to help speed their journey to its destination. Nevertheless, the troops, though tired, were in good spirits and eager to savour the delights of Byzantium.

Upon reaching the capital, the newcomers saw the armies of Bohemond and Tancred encamped before the great western wall – a city of tents spread upon the plain like an enormous multicoloured cloak flung out to dry on the uneven ground. The first ranks of the straggling warrior host saw their comrades and surged forth in a giddy rush and, unable to hold back their knights and foot soldiers any longer, the leading lords gave the men leave to join their fellow pilgrims in enthusiastic celebration of the successful completion of the first leg of their journey.

Leaving their servants and footmen to pitch the tents and prepare their camp, Raymond and Bishop Adhemar proceeded to Bohemond's enclave. They were greeted by noblemen of the prince's retinue, who welcomed them in their lord's absence.

'Bohemond not here?' demanded Raymond. 'We have been in the

saddle for three months without rest. We have come from the pope himself.'

'With all respect, lord,' the foremost knight replied, 'we did not know you would arrive today.' The knight, a kinsman of Bohemond's named Rainuld of Salerno, gestured toward the prince's tent. 'Even so, wine awaits. We will raise cups while –'

'Where is Bohemond?' Adhemar interrupted, frowning at the manifest thoughtlessness of the prince.

'He is in consultation with the emperor, Lord Bishop,' Rainuld answered. 'The prince and his family, along with Tancred and some others, are dining at the palace today. They are not expected to return until tonight. But, please, you are most welcome to remain here and take your ease while your own camp is established.'

Raymond, peeved at this lacklustre welcome, sniffed. 'We will take our ease on the day we ride victorious through the gates of Jerusalem – and not before.'

'Does our Lord Christ *take his ease* while the salvation of the world hangs in the balance?' inquired Adhemar tartly.

'Pray forgive me, lords,' Rainuld replied stiffly. 'I seem to have offended your most noble sentiments. I assure you, I merely thought to make you welcome.'

'We see what manner of welcome the prince provides,' the bishop told him. 'We will return to our camp and trouble you no further.'

With that, they turned and rode back to where their tents were being erected a little to the south and east of Bohemond's forces. Upon arrival, they found an imperial delegation waiting to conduct them to the palace forthwith.

The armies of Hugh, Godfrey, and Baldwin had been shipped across the Bosphorus at last, and Alexius was determined that the latest arrivals should depart as soon as possible. Accordingly, he wasted not a moment in employing the same method with Raymond that had worked so successfully with Bohemond and Tancred: he offered them expensive gifts and provisions for their troops, and promised to assume the cost of conveying their armies across the Bosphorus – in return for their signatures on the oath of allegiance.

But, where the unpredictable Prince of Taranto had proven remarkably compliant and reasonable, the solid and pious Count of Toulouse and Provence demonstrated an inflexibility normally associated only with four-footed pack animals, and bluntly refused to sign any document which might compromise the special authority granted him by the pope.

'As the first nobleman to take the cross,' Raymond explained patiently, 'I have been honoured to receive my commission from the hand of Pope Urban himself. Therefore, I must respectfully decline the oath you propose.'

Bishop Adhemar, the pope's legate and special envoy, nodded smugly and smiled in righteous superiority. 'The vow you propose, Emperor Alexius, is unnecessary,' he declared grandly. 'A nobleman who has sworn on the Cross of Christ no longer heeds any earthly sovereign, but is answerable to God alone.'

Alexius, almost speechless with anger and dismay – and wearied beyond words by the unrelenting arrogance of the crusaders, gazed down from his throne upon the recalcitrant lords before him. Attended by his drungarius, two magisters, a phalanx of palace Varangi, and assorted excubitori, the Emperor of All Christendom on his golden throne presented an impressive spectacle. Nevertheless, Raymond, hands gripping his swordbelt, remained unmoved.

'Are we to understand,' the emperor intoned, 'that this commission of yours prevents you from acknowledging the superior authority of the Imperial Throne?'

'In no way, Lord Emperor,' Raymond replied graciously. 'I do freely acknowledge it in all areas pertinent to its domain, save one – the leadership of the pilgrimage itself. This honour, as I have explained, has been granted me by His Holiness Pope Urban.'

'We might remind you, Count Raymond, that even Bishop Urban holds his position by our sufferance,' the emperor replied, turning his gaze from the count to Bishop Adhemar. 'Any authority the Patriarch of Rome enjoys derives and flows from this throne. Therefore, the oath which we require in no way subverts or denies your special commission.'

Raymond, gaunt and tall, stared sternly ahead, his face dour and expressionless. 'Be that as it may, it is rumoured in the camps that the emperor has raised Bohemond of Taranto to a position of high authority in the empire. It is said he is to become Grand Domestic of the Imperial Armies.'

At last, thought Alexius with an inward sigh of relief, *we come to the source of this prince's pride: he is jealous of Bohemond.*

'At the risk of inspiring the emperor's wrath,' Adhemar remarked, 'I would point out that Prince Taranto does not possess His Holiness' sanction and blessing. This has been granted to Count Raymond alone, and I, in my capacity as the pope's legate, have been given a special authority in such matters as –'

'These rumours you mention,' the emperor said, interrupting the tedious Adhemar, 'are founded on Bohemond's ambition. While it is true that he has asked for high recognition within the imperial army, we hasten to reassure you, Lord Raymond, we have not acquiesced to Lord Bohemond's hopes of elevation.'

'Be that as it may,' Raymond observed woodenly, 'the crusade must have a leader. As I have been chosen by him who first summoned the valiant to take arms in this holy endeavour, I see no reason to relinquish the small authority I have been granted.' Seeing the colour rising to the emperor's face, the gaunt lord thought to amend his position. 'Naturally,' he added hastily, 'if the emperor was to assume personal leadership of the crusade, he would find me a most loyal and trustworthy vassal.'

'Alas, the untimely inception of this enterprise renders that possibility impractical,' Alexius told him firmly. 'Owing to the press of the imperial affairs, we will not be assuming direct command of the crusade, however much we might wish to do so.'

'Then I have no other choice,' Raymond replied, as if gallantly acquiescing to the inevitable, 'but to honour the pope's command and persevere in the position of leadership to which I have been called.'

Adhemar's smile deepened. He tucked his arms inside the sleeves of his bishop's robe and almost hugged himself with satisfaction.

'Oh, but we think you too hasty, Lord Toulouse,' remarked Alexius. He rose slowly and took up the parchment bearing the oath and names of his previous guests. 'Perhaps we can broaden your range of alternatives. See here: bind your allegiance to us, your rightful sovereign, or cling to the pope and retire from the crusade. The Bishop of Rome serves *this* throne, not otherwise, and we will have our authority upheld by all who would shelter beneath it. Lead the crusade – if you are thus determined – but you will do so at our pleasure, and with our permission.'

Raymond, already rigid with stubbornness, stiffened yet further. The emperor, seeing he had pressed the matter far enough for the present, decided to let the headstrong count ponder his choice.

'Tomorrow,' he said, 'the armies of Bohemond and Tancred will be conducted by the imperial fleet across the Bosphorus to join the armies of Hugh and Godfrey at Pelecanum, and resume their march to Jerusalem.'

He paused and regarded the Count of Toulouse sternly. 'You, however, will remain behind.'

'How long, Lord Emperor, must I wait?'

Was the stony-headed knight softening already? 'That is for you to decide,' Alexius answered. 'Sign the oath and you shall rejoin the others without delay. Refuse your emperor, and you will wait. For, without your signature on this oath –' he snapped the proffered parchment with his fingertips, 'you will not be allowed to move a single step beyond the walls of this city. Thus, any authority you possess will perforce fall to another.'

Alexius dismissed his guests, who were immediately returned to their camp to ponder the implications of the emperor's decree. As soon as the great doors closed on the Salamos Hall, the commander of the imperial fleet turned to his kinsman and said, 'Do you think he will sign it?'

'Who can say?' wondered the emperor. 'We have met many proud men in our day, Dalassenus, but none more haughty than Raymond of Toulouse. He is a wilful man who believes himself chosen of God to lead his rabble of an army to glory. He considers it an honour of the highest regard, and he is jealous of it.'

'And now he fears he may lose it,' Dalassenus mused. 'That was very shrewd, basileus.'

'Perhaps,' Alexius allowed cautiously. 'We shall see which is stronger – his fear or his jealousy.'

TWENTY

For eight days, Count Raymond of Toulouse held fast to his resolve and refused to add his signature to the oath of loyalty the emperor required. Instead, he stood by and watched the huge troop ships of the emperor's fleet ceaselessly plying the waters of the Bosphorus, ferrying the armies of Bohemond and Tancred across to Pelecanum and speeding them on their way. Meanwhile, merchant vessels of every kind and description arrived in port fully laden with supplies of grain, oil, wine, and livestock, for the provisioning of the crusaders. From morning to night, the busy waterway heaved and surged with a barely-contained tumult. At times there were so many boats out on the water the count thought a knight could have galloped from one shore to the other on shipdeck.

Every day, pilgrims in their thousands made their slow way down to the river landings on the Golden Horn, leading horses and pulling wagons overflowing with equipment and camp clutter. The horses were boarded first – a laborious chore which slowed an already sluggish operation to a tedious crawl; and when the animals were secure, the wagons, which had been disassembled on shore, were put aboard, followed by the weapons, supplies, and equipment the wagons had been carrying. Only when the ships could hold no more baggage, were the people allowed to come aboard – knights and their footmen first, and then the camp followers: the priests and churchmen of various kinds, the wives of the crusaders, and their children.

Fully laden, a troop ship could carry fifty horses, twenty wagons, and from three to four hundred people. The emperor had provided eleven of these large ships for the operation, and each ship could make two trips a day. Thus, while Count Raymond and Bishop Adhemar stood idly by, the numbers on the shore dwindled away with startling rapidity, until, after eight days, the sun set on an almost deserted quay.

The ninth day saw the arrival of Robert, Duke of Normandy, son of William Rufus, King of England; his cousin, Robert, Count of Flanders; and his brother-in-law, Count Stephen of Blois. Their combined forces ran to more than forty thousand men, including a small regiment led by the bellicose cleric, Bishop Odo of Bayeux.

Despite a slight difficulty with the Adriatic crossing, which resulted in the regrettable drowning of four hundred soldiers, all in all the journey to Constantinople had proved a highly satisfactory beginning to the pilgrimage, and the new arrivals were eager to cross the Bosphorus and engage the godless enemy. Like the others before them, the Latin Lords were immediately summoned to an audience with the emperor. Unlike some of their predecessors, however, they happily pledged allegiance to Alexius, and promised to return all lands, relics, peoples, and treasures to imperial rule.

The man largely responsible for their swift and gracious submission was Count Stephen, who appeared to enjoy a measure of influence with the others on account of his good-natured selflessness and genuine piety. Once the emperor learned of the high esteem in which Stephen was held by his comrades, he wasted not a moment in recruiting the young lord to the cause of inducing Raymond to sign the oath.

No sooner had Lord Blois replaced the quill upon the tray, than did Alexius remark how glad he was to have that formality behind them and how he would instantly command provisions to be delivered to the newcomers' hungry troops, whereupon the imperial ships would begin transporting them to Pelecanum to join their pilgrim comrades. Duke Robert, relieved and grateful, expressed his eagerness to resume the pilgrimage, whereupon the emperor mentioned what a dreadful shame it was that Count Raymond of Toulouse would not be joining them on the crusade.

The western lords glanced at one another wonderingly. Count Raymond's army was the largest and best supplied, and they were counting on his leadership. 'But, Lord Emperor, why should Raymond stay behind?' inquired Stephen respectfully.

'We can only assume that our friend has decided to abandon the crusade,' replied Alexius.

'Truly?' wondered Count Robert of Flanders.

'So it would appear.'

'Forgive me, Emperor Alexius,' said the Duke of Normandy, 'but

I find this most difficult to believe. The Count of Toulouse is known to be a most ardent pilgrim. Indeed, his army stands ready even now to depart. There must be some other explanation. No doubt a mistake has been made.'

'There has been no mistake,' the emperor assured him. 'The only impediment to his departure is the oath which you and your comrades have just signed. Count Raymond has been in Constantinople nine days; each day he is presented with the oath, and each day he refuses to sign.' Alexius' voice became hard. 'As he cannot continue to the Holy Land until the document is acknowledged, we can only conclude that he has decided to forsake the crusade.'

Stephen, frowning with concern, nodded sympathetically. 'I begin to understand,' he replied. 'Perhaps the emperor might allow me a space in which to try to change his mind. With your consent, Emperor, I will speak to him.'

'Please, by all means, speak to him,' said Alexius with the air of a man who has exhausted every possibility. 'We will pray God grants you every success, and swiftly. The ships will begin transporting your troops the day after the Easter Mass and the oath must be signed before any soldiers are allowed to make the crossing.'

'But Easter is tomorrow!' Stephen gasped.

'It is,' agreed the emperor. 'Thus, you begin to see the way of things.'

'By your leave, Lord Emperor, I will speak to him without delay.'

The tenth day after Raymond arrived in Constantinople, bells of the great city's churches broke the dawn silence with a clanging cacophony to herald the Eastertide Mass. The western noblemen and their families – for all except Stephen had brought wives and children with them – were invited to sit with the imperial family in the royal gallery in the Church of the Holy Wisdom. There, among Saint Sophia's gold-encrusted icons and immaculate mosaics of the Risen Christ, the visitors were offered a glimpse of the glory they had solemnly vowed to preserve. After the church service, while the emperor's party returned to the palace for a day of feasting, interspersed with prayers and worship, the pilgrims were conducted back to their stark and barren camps to reflect on the grandeur of what they had experienced.

Early the next morning, the imperial ships began moving the troops of Normandy and Flanders across the Bosphorus to join those of Hugh, Godfrey, and Bohemond awaiting them on the other side. For ten days the great troop ships traversed the narrow strait in waves as relentless as the tide, ceaselessly loading and unloading the crusaders and their paraphernalia of war. Still, the proud Lord of Toulouse refused the oath.

When the last horse and footman had been ferried across, the emperor gave orders to remove the imperial fleet from the quay to the centre of the Golden Horn so that the increasingly anxious Franks left behind would not be tempted to take them by force. He instructed his admiral to allow the ships to remain in full sight, however, so as to provide stubborn Lord Raymond and his wilful bishop a continual reminder of how little stood between them and their departure, and how swiftly they might be hastened on their way.

Lord Stephen, who had sent his troops on ahead with the others, remained behind to help persuade the toplofty count; he counselled, coaxed, and cajoled, and by dint of his genuine good nature succeeded, at last in softening Raymond's resolve. Thus, three days after the last troop ship had sailed, Count Toulouse and Bishop Adhemar appeared with Stephen at Blachernae Palace seeking audience with the emperor.

Alexius graciously agreed to see them as soon as possible, and then went casually about his affairs: reviewed the palace guard; strolled through the imperial stables and paused to watch the Master of Horse put the yearlings through their paces; observed mass; met with the magister officiorum and the quaestor sacri palatii to discuss the following week's register of state functions; dined with the empress at midday, following which he enjoyed a rare, if brief, nap in the garden; and signed a dozen or so documents relating to the promotion of several deserving military commanders and their requisite pay increases. Meanwhile, he had given the fleet commander orders to have the troop ships moved from the centre of the Golden Horn around to Hormisdas Harbour so that the crusaders should see them departing.

When Alexius had finished his chores, and could think of nothing else to do, he called the magister to him and asked if there was anything he had neglected to do that day. 'By your leave, basileus,' the magister answered, 'allow me to remind your highness that the Latin lords await an audience with the emperor. They are standing in the anteroom even now.'

'Ah, so they are,' agreed Alexius affably. 'Have they waited long?'

'Reasonably long, basileus. They arrived early this morning.'

'Well then, if there is nothing else, allow them to come in. We will see them now.'

'At your command, basileus.' The magister backed away from the throne, reached the screen and indicated to the guardsmen to open the door. A few moments later, he led two very anxious and unhappy noblemen, and an irate bishop, into the emperor's private audience chamber.

Alexius greeted them warmly as they came to stand before him, and asked why they had come. The two lords glanced at one another, and Raymond, at Stephen's prompting, replied, 'I have come to make my pledge, Lord Emperor.'

'Well and good,' Alexius replied, 'but we fear it is too late.'

'Too late?' wondered Raymond. His eyes shifted accusingly to Stephen.

'Forgive me, Lord Emperor,' said Stephen, speaking up. 'But I was given to believe that if I could persuade Lord Raymond to take the oath, we would be able to continue the pilgrimage.'

'That is so,' answered the emperor. 'But if you will recall, we said the oath must be signed before the ships finished the crossing.' Turning to the magister officiorum, the emperor asked, 'Is that not what we said, magister?'

The magister consulted the wax tablet on which he recorded all official transactions, replied, 'It is so, basileus. That is what was said.'

'We are sorry,' Alexius said placidly. 'If only you had come to us sooner.'

'We have waited all day!' exclaimed Bishop Adhemar, unable to contain himself any longer. 'This is intolerable.'

Alexius grew steely. 'And yet it will be tolerated. Lord Raymond has had ample time in which to make up his mind. Or did you think the world would wait for his decision? I assure you, the world waits for no man.'

'I stand ready to make my pledge now,' Raymond insisted, the colour rising to his face.

'And we are telling you it is too late.'

'Too late!' growled Raymond.

'The ships are needed elsewhere. We have compromised the protection of other provinces in order to accommodate the demands of the crusade, but that cannot continue indefinitely.' The emperor gazed implacably at the three before him. 'The fleet requires maintenance and repair; the ships must be readied for their departure. Any delay would be too costly to contemplate.'

Raymond, speechless with frustration, glared rancorously at the emperor. Adhemar drew breath to speak again, but the cooler-tempered Stephen prevailed.

'If you please, Lord Emperor,' said Stephen quickly, 'perhaps I might suggest a remedy.'

'If you know any,' Alexius replied, 'we would welcome it.'

'If the imperial fleet's departure could be postponed a few days, we might hire the ships to take our armies across. We can pay in gold.'

The emperor frowned. 'We have gold aplenty. What we lack is ships to keep the imperial waters safe.' He stared at the noblemen, and drummed his fingers on the armrests of his throne. 'Something else comes to mind,' Alexius said slowly, as if considering it for the first time.

'Yes, Lord Emperor?'

'It occurs to us that we have made good on promises to provision and transport the pilgrims through imperial lands and beyond, and borne the cost out of our own treasury. This we have been happy to do for the liberation of the Holy Land, and for the sake of the lands to be returned to the empire if you are successful.'

'With God's help,' Bishop Adhemar declared, 'we *will* be victorious.'

'We pray for your every victory, lord bishop,' Alexius told him. 'In view of that, it seems only fair that we should have an imperial emissary to lend aid to the enterprise, and attend to matters arising from the reinstatement of imperial rule.'

Stephen understood the offer the emperor was making and, before his companions could object, happily agreed. 'Of course, in recognition of the emperor's generosity in extending the use of imperial ships, we would be pleased to welcome an envoy of the emperor's choosing to offer counsel, and look after the special interests of the empire. I am embarrassed we did not suggest it ourselves.'

Raymond stiffened; he did not like the notion of an imperial factotum nosing around in the affairs of the crusaders.

'Good.' Alexius gestured to the magister. 'We accept your offer to hire the ships, and to include our imperial emissary among your advisors.' Extending his hand towards the magister, Alexius took up the parchment containing the oath which all the other crusading lords had signed, and passed it to Raymond.

The reluctant lord stood clutching the document, but made no move to unfold it. Instead, he looked helplessly to Stephen.

'As it happens, Lord Emperor,' Count Blois began hesitantly, 'I was meaning to suggest that Lord Raymond should be allowed to pledge an oath of his own devising.'

Alexius stared at the two noblemen. Was there no end to their impudence? At last, he said, 'We should have you bound in chains and dropped in the Bosphorus, except that we are curious to know why you think Raymond should be allowed this singular distinction –' his voice rose as he spoke, 'when all the other lords, including yourself, have seen the wisdom of compliance. Illuminate us if you can.'

Stephen shifted uneasily on his feet. 'The suggestion arises out of the unique position which Lord Raymond enjoys as leader of the pilgrimage. If I may speak for him, it is that he feels placing himself under loyalty to the emperor would be an abrogation of the fealty already sworn before the papal throne.'

'So we have heard.' Alexius waved the objection aside with an impatient flick of his hand.

'Therefore,' Stephen continued hurriedly, 'I have proposed to Count Toulouse that he make the pledge his countrymen use when affirming their devotion to an acknowledged superior.'

The Emperor of All Christendom, Elite of the Elect, and Equal of the Apostles, frowned as he contemplated his choices. If he sent the bothersome lord away, he would only make more trouble for the empire – more than two thousand citizens had been inadvertently killed on the march already, before the Pecheneg escort put a stop to it. On the other hand, if Raymond and his rabble were allowed to resume the pilgrimage, the problem might go away – at least for a time, and perhaps forever, if the Seljuqs defeated them, which in all likelihood they would.

If, by a miracle, the crusaders should emerge victorious, the cost of exterminating the Seljuq pestilence would have been well worth the price – although, Alexius concluded gloomily, the more he saw of the pilgrims passing through his realm, that miracle seemed ever more remote. So far, it appeared he was merely making the best of an increasingly poor bargain.

The emperor regarded the tall, gaunt nobleman before him. Hard-eyed, his jaw set, doubtless he had never willingly surrendered anything to anyone in all his life and was not about to begin now. Thus, Stephen's suggestion represented the best offer Alexius would receive from the proud and principled Count of Toulouse and Provence. With an air of weary resignation, he wisely accepted. 'What is this oath of his countrymen?' Alexius asked, wanting nothing more than to see the backs of the pilgrims once and for all.

'Allow me, Lord Emperor,' Raymond interrupted, and began to speak out a wordy vow which amounted to a promise to honour the emperor, respecting his life and rank, never maligning him, nor causing him to come to injury or harm, whether in word or deed, through any action, or inaction, on doughty Lord Raymond's part.

'Do you also pledge to honour the interests of the emperor in all matters pertaining to the recovery of lands, properties, treasures, and relics belonging to the empire?' demanded Alexius when the lord had finished.

'This I also pledge,' answered Raymond solemnly.

'And do you make this vow in fear of forfeiting your soul's eternal happiness, should you fail to discharge it faithfully?'

Bishop Adhemar opened his mouth to object, but Stephen wisely prevented him, grasping the disagreeable cleric by the arm and squeezing hard.

'I do so right and well, Lord Emperor,' answered Raymond readily, and without guile.

'Then we accept your vow in place of the oath which all other Christian noblemen have sworn,' the emperor said, unable to keep the reprimand to himself. 'Go now and assemble your troops. The commander of the fleet will be informed to begin the transport of your armies. The charge will be assessed at a cost of twenty marks a day for each ship required; this you will repay to the imperial treasury. Further, we will assemble a company of Immortals under the command of Taticius, who will serve as our emissary to offer counsel and look after our interests in our absence. You are to treat our envoy as you would the emperor himself. Do you understand?'

'Perfectly, Lord Emperor,' answered Raymond, much relieved to have settled the matter satisfactorily.

'Then we wish you God's speed, and swift victory over our common adversaries,' Alexius said. 'My lords, we commend you to your course.'

'Pax Vobiscum,' replied the western lords.

Before they stepped away from the throne, the emperor said, 'May we offer you a word of friendly warning?'

'Of course, Lord Emperor,' replied Stephen happily. 'Your instruction would be most welcome.'

'The Seljuqs are formidable, and they are fearless,' Alexius said, becoming the wily commander once again. 'They fight on horseback using the bow; they will harry you all day with feints and charges, seeking to wear down your numbers with their incessant arrows. Yet, they will not stand to battle. Do not mistake this for cowardice; it is nothing of the kind. Rather, it is their nature.

'We advise you, therefore, that when you are attacked you must close on them at once. Make them fight. Most likely, they will retreat, rather than meet you face to face. Should they flee, you must not give chase; their horses are faster than yours and they will easily outdistance you. Under no circumstance must you allow your mounted soldiers to become separated from those on foot. The Arab races are skilled horsemen, and can regroup in the twinkling of an eye. They like nothing better than turning on their pursuers, and taking them unawares, or circling back to attack the unguarded infantry. The same can be said of ambush and treachery.'

He watched the lords and saw that his words were having little effect on the two before him, so he concluded, saying, 'We beg you to remember, it is not courage which will win against the Seljuq, it is cunning.'

A sneer of disdain appeared on Raymond's face. 'We have heard your counsel, and thank you for it. But with all respect, Lord Emperor,' he replied, 'the Saracen will soon learn to fear crusader steel. With God and truth on our side, we have no need of cunning.'

'Then go with God, my friends.' The emperor dismissed them, and watched as they backed away from the throne. When the two had gone, Alexius turned to his kinsman, and said, 'What do you think, cousin?'

'I think the imperial treasury will soon flow with pilgrim gold,' Dalassenus replied. 'But why send the troop ships away, only to return them at hire? I cannot think you did it to save the cost of transport.'

'That?' wondered Alexius with mild surprise. 'I merely wished to teach them something about power, and their dependence on the empire. Whether they like it or not, they need us if they are to successfully achieve their conquest of Jerusalem.'

'I see,' answered the commander. 'I was thinking you had a different reason: that the gold was better given to you now, than plundered by the Seljuq later.'

'You hold their chances as poor as that, do you?'

'I am being optimistic, basileus,' the commander assured him. 'How they have made it this far is a mystery to me. But, from what I have seen of the Seljuqs, I know these pilgrims will never set foot in Jerusalem. As you have said, if courage alone had sufficed, we would have conquered them long ago.'

Alexius, brooding now, folded his hands beneath his chin and stared before him, as if into a dark and frightening future.

'These men – these *commanders* know nothing of what awaits them. They do not know the land; they have no idea of distances or terrain. They lack all understanding of the Arab – none of them have even *seen* a Seljuq, let alone fought an *amir's* army. To say that they will never see Jerusalem is, I think, no more than a realistic assessment. Taking all they lack in knowledge and provision, I believe most will never even see Antioch.'

'Yes,' agreed Alexius gloomily, 'and that is a very great shame. I greatly pity the soldiers of the line. As always, they will pay for the ignorance and folly of their leaders, and the cost will be fearfully great indeed.' He paused for a moment, as if trying to imagine the enormity of the sacrifice. 'And yet,' he said, after a moment. He lifted his head and looked at Dalassenus, 'and yet, despite all they lack, they possess one incalculable benefit.'

'What is that, basileus?'

'Belief,' answered the emperor. 'They believe they have been chosen by God to recover the Holy Land and regain Jerusalem.'

'A belief inspired by ignorance,' the drungarius remarked. 'Such beliefs are nothing more than foolishness.'

'You are forgetting, Dalassenus,' the emperor chided, 'God ever confounds the wisdom of men. And these ignorant, arrogant men are filled with the belief that they can achieve what they have set out to do. I ask you, cousin, what wisdom can stand against such exalted foolishness?'

Dalassenus nodded, accepting the emperor's observation. 'Unfortunately,' he added, 'it is neither wisdom nor folly they must meet on the field of battle – it is the might of Sultan Qilij Arslan, and that of the Seljuq amirs. God help them, I say.'

'Amen,' agreed Alexius. 'He is the only one who can.'

TWENTY-ONE

Jon Wing remarked often on the weather. Every two or three weeks, he proclaimed it a wonder. It was, he maintained, the best sailing he had seen in seven years – *twice* seven years, even. The days were bright and long, and the winds fair. 'This is a lucky omen,' he insisted. 'We will certainly make our fortune in Jerusalem.'

The vast treasure awaiting them in the Holy Land was something else Jon often remarked upon. At first, Murdo took this as a sign that they must be nearing their destination. Each day he waited for one of the crewmen to sing out with the news that Jerusalem was in sight; each day ended with Murdo closing his eyes on yet another strange and nameless lump of foreign coastline. Yet, despite the continual frustration of his expectation, Murdo awoke the next day all the more certain that *this* would be the day the Holy Land hove into view. After all, how much further could it be?

But, as the days ran to weeks, and the weeks turned to months, and still Jerusalem failed to appear on the horizon, Murdo at last began to take seriously the suggestion that the voyage might indeed take longer than he expected. In the meantime, they continually scanned the wide and empty sea for any sign of King Magnus' fleet.

The king's ships proved as elusive as the Holy City, however; although they sometimes saw a strange sail or two there was never so much as a glimpse of King Magnus' fleet. 'It is fifteen ships,' Jon declared. 'Fifteen cannot sail as swiftly as one! We will find them yet.'

All the while, the seasons, and the seas, grew slowly warmer. The grey-green waters of the north gave way to the green-blue waters of the south, and spring gave way to summer, and then autumn, as *Skidbladnir* slipped down and down along the coast. They passed Normandy and Frankland, and then places Murdo had never heard of: Navarre, León and Castile, Portugal, and still on and on, south and ever south.

As the journey wore on, the daily routine became established habit and small diversions loomed large with the longship's crew and passengers. From the stories they told, and the amusements they contrived, it became clear to Murdo that Jon Wing and his men were used to lengthy sea voyages in strange, if not hostile, waters. Murdo listened to their talk and learned what manner of men his fellow pilgrims were.

Although the crewmen were Norsemen one and all, Murdo discovered that none of them had seen their homeland in many years. Five had lived in Eìre: Hallvard, Hogni, Tiggi, Vestein, and Svidur; and five had lived in Scotland: Fafnir, Sturli, Raefil, Nial, and Oski; three had lived in Normandy: Olaf, Ymir, and Digri; and two had lived in both England and Frankland: Amund, and Arnor. All sixteen, including Jon Wing, had sailed with King Magnus on various expeditions, and spoke well of him. Murdo was impressed by the respect the king commanded, even in his absence.

He also began to unravel the complicated system of loyalties which bound the crew to one another, and to the ship – which they considered second to none in the king's fleet. *Skidbladnir,* he discovered, belonged not to Magnus, but to Jon Wing, who had agreed to provide his ship and crew to support the king on his pilgrimage, in return for the plunder they would receive. The crew and their master were not ordinary vassals of the king, but mercenaries who had taken oaths of fealty for the duration of the voyage.

When the crew discovered that it was Murdo's first voyage beyond sight of his island home, they undertook to teach him all they knew of the seaman's craft. They taught Murdo how to steer a longship – how to rig the sail, and which guide stars were most useful. And when Murdo proved a ready pupil, they delighted in teaching him other things as well: how to catch fish ten different ways, how to read the water for signs of trouble, how to forecast the weather by the smell of the air, and how to take care of his fair skin.

Unfortunately, this last lesson came only after Murdo had fallen asleep in the hot southern sun. He awoke feeling sick to his stomach, and as evening came on, began to experience a most remarkable agony. He felt as if hot pitch had been tipped over his back and shoulders and then set to the torch; he could not stand to have his clothes touch him, and the slightest movement brought rushes of pain cascading over him.

After the sailors had a good laugh over his calamity, they took pity on him and showed him how to take the fiery sting out of the sunburn with an unguent made from seaweed, and thereafter – until his skin developed its own protection – how to avoid getting another nasty burn.

Rarely out of sight of land, they put in to shore for fresh water as often as necessary, but seldom camped overnight; they much preferred lying at anchor in a calm bay or hidden cove. The few times they did sleep on solid ground, Jon made certain it was far from any human habitation; he said he did not trust folk from foreign lands. Once, however, after coming ashore for water they found themselves near a small farming settlement; after dark some of the crew went off for firewood, returning some while later with three sheep and a clutch of duck eggs.

The sailors claimed the sheep were strays they had discovered wandering lonely in the woods, but Murdo noticed that one of the men had a vicious gash on his leg not unlike a dog bite, and another displayed an unexplained lump on his forehead. Jon Wing seemed uninterested in further explanations, and everyone, even the mildly disapproving monks, enjoyed the mutton for the next few days.

As the endless succession of days stretched on, Murdo accustomed himself to the ceaselessly bouncing boat, and grew to enjoy sleeping under the night sky with its endless, wheeling canopy of stars. Often, when the wind was fine and the night good, Jon let the ship run through the night, steering by starlight and moonglow. The Norsemen took it in turns to stand the tiller, and Jon allowed Murdo to try his hand. Though the ship was larger than any he had sailed, Murdo found the skills much the same and soon became as accomplished as any of them, priding himself in his ability to keep the sail filled and the prow true.

To augment the nightly meal of porridge, hardtack, and salt pork, Murdo and the monks fished. At dusk, when the sun had sunk in a blood-red mist in the west, and the mackerel were flayed, spitted, and sizzling over the charcoal brazier, and night stained the far-off coastal hills in shades of purple and blue – *that* was the part of the day Murdo liked best. For then he would settle himself against one of the grain bags, drink his ration of ale with the monks and listen to their chatter as they cooked supper. Much of their talk was vaunted nonsense, so far as Murdo could tell: what was the proper hierarchy of the five senses; whether cherubs ever grew into angels; if the moon was full of devils . . . and such like.

Often, after their meal, Emlyn was prevailed upon to tell a story. He possessed a fine, expressive voice and a seemingly inexhaustible trove of tales from which he drew extraordinary stories – some of them lasting two or three nights altogether. They were, he said, just old stories of his people – some of which he had undertaken to put down in writing in the Abbey's scriptorium – and old they undoubtedly were. Yet, they produced a curious effect in Murdo, who felt drawn to them, and fascinated by them in a way he would have been embarrassed to admit to anyone aloud.

The Briton told them well, adapting his supple voice easily to the various tones of the tales – now hushed with fear or sorrow, now shaking with anger, or ringing with triumph. Emlyn also sang, and that was even more peculiar, for he sang the most beautiful songs in an impossibly obscure tongue; and though Murdo could not understand a single word, he found himself moved to his very soul by the power of expression alone.

If, when the song was finished, Murdo asked what it was about, Emlyn would say something like, 'Ah, that is Rhiannon's Birds . . .' or, 'That was Branwen's lament for the loss of her poor child . . .' or, again, 'That was Llew Silver Hand's triumph over the Cythrawl . . .' and Murdo would agree that yes, he had heard the birds, and plumbed the depth of Branwen's grief, and had indeed taken flight on the wings of Llew's exultation.

As the months passed, the intermittent songs and tales began to produce in Murdo a curious and potent longing – a yearning after something he did not know. It was as if he had been allowed the taste of an unimaginably pleasurable elixir, only to have it snatched away again while the cup was at his lips.

Occasionally, he caught the familiar echo of something his mother might have said, and then it was as if he had heard a call from the Otherworld – a voice reaching out to him from across the abyss of years, a distant shout, faint as a whisper and intimate as a kiss – and the shock of recognition made the hair stand up on the nape of his neck, and his heart beat faster.

One night, he listened to Emlyn sing a tale called *Rhonabwy's Dream*, and for days afterwards he felt empty, yet oddly stirred. He felt restless within himself, and fidgeted so much that Jon Wing, noticing his agitation, told him he was merely growing impatient with the close confines of the ship. 'It will pass,' Jon assured him. 'It is best not to think about it.' But Murdo knew his disquiet had less to do with confinement than with the queer world Emlyn's stories described.

If anyone else was likewise affected, Murdo never learned. He kept his yearning to himself, hiding it deep within, clutching it tightly as a rare gem lest anyone try to steal it. He went about his chores as one bearing an illness that produced both pain and rapture in equal measure, gladly suffering the torment for the sweetness of the affliction.

On and on they sailed, further and further from the lands he knew, and with each sea league, the place described by Emlyn's songs became more real to Murdo, slowly usurping the features of his native homeland in his memory. Whether by day or night, Murdo looked out at the all-encircling sea and dreamed of that enchanted realm, the Region of the Summer Stars, of which the round-faced Briton sang. Slowly, Murdo began to feel that he belonged there.

One night, despite the clamour of the Norsemen for a song, Emlyn professed himself to be out of voice. 'Singen! Singen!' they insisted. 'We are wanting to hear the *Battle of the Trees*!'

'Ah, now that is a fine tale – a splendid tale indeed. Tomorrow maybe I will sing it,' he told them, and said he must rest himself for a tale so exuberant and profound.

They let it go at that and, as the sailors returned to their ale cups, Murdo crept close to Emlyn, who was sitting with his feet propped on the rail, staring out into the west as the last glimmer of a violet sunset faded into twilight. He settled himself beside the monk, but said nothing. After a time, Emlyn sighed.

'Is it the hiraeth?' Murdo asked. 'The home-yearning?'

'Oh, you know it is,' he replied. 'And it has taken the heart out of me this time.'

Murdo nodded sympathetically. He had begun to feel something of the same thing himself. They sat in silence, listening to the smooth-rippling waves against the hull, and staring into the gathering gloom as night deepened around them. After a time, Murdo said, 'The clear light – what is it?'

The monk turned his round face towards Murdo. 'However did you come to hear of that?'

'*You* told me,' Murdo replied. 'You said you were the keeper of the clear light, remember?'

'*Sanctus Clarus* – the *Holy* Light,' the monk corrected. 'We are the Keepers of the Holy Light, and Guardians of the True Path.'

'Yes, that was it,' Murdo agreed. 'But what does it mean?'

'Ah, well now,' answered Emlyn, 'it is not a thing we tell just anyone.' He paused, and Murdo feared he would say no more, then added, 'Still, I see no harm in telling you a little.' He settled back, folding his hands across his paunch. 'Where to begin, that is the problem.'

He thought for a moment, and then said, 'Before the sainted Padraic established his hut among the wild tribes of Èire, before blessed Colm Cille took the rock of Hý for his abbey, the learned brotherhood of Britain and Gaul have held to the Holy Light: the inspired teaching of Jesu the Christ. This teaching was kept by the apostles themselves, and passed down and down through the years from one generation of priestly believers to the next.'

'The teaching of the church?' wondered Murdo, his heart sinking. He had hoped for a better explanation than this.

'No,' Emlyn allowed. 'At least, not as any would know it in this benighted day and age.'

'Then, what –'

'Just listen, boy. Listen, now, and learn.'

Composing himself once more, the monk began. 'Padraic was not the first to learn of the True Path, no – nor was he the last. Far from it. But he was a tireless servant of the Holy Light, and he –'

'Is the Holy Light the same as the True Path, then?' wondered Murdo.

'No, the Holy Light is the *knowledge* – the knowledge derived from the teaching. The True Path is the *practise*, see – the use of that knowledge day by day. The first –'

'Why did you say it was a secret?'

'What, and we are to have endless interruptions now?' Emlyn huffed. 'I did not say it was a secret. I said it was a thing we do not tell those who are not ready to hear it.'

'I was just –'

'If you will but hold your tongue between one breath and the next, we will reach an explanation.' He pursed his lips and closed his eyes. Murdo waited, itchy with expectation. After a moment, the monk said, 'This is the way of it: Padraic was not the first, and he was not alone. There were others before and after, as I say – men like the Champion Colm Cille, and the venerable Adamnan – men of courage and long obedience who kept the flame burning bright through many long and bitter years.

'But the Darkness is greedy. It is insatiable. Ever and always, it seeks to devour more and more, and the more it devours, the greater it grows, and the greater it grows, the more powerful it becomes, and the hungrier. There is but one thing strong enough to stand against this all-consuming darkness: the Holy Light. Indeed, it is the most mighty thing on earth, and therefore we guard it with our lives.'

Murdo could not let this assertion go unchallenged. 'If it is as powerful as you say, why does it have to be guarded at all?'

Emlyn clucked his tongue in disapproval. 'Tch! To even ask such a question shows how little you understand of the higher things. Still, I am not surprised. How could you know? For you have spent the whole of your young life in error and confusion. You, like all the rest, have been led astray, like those poor sheep wandering lost in the night.'

'Those were stolen,' Murdo pointed out.

'Yes,' agreed Emlyn absently, 'I suppose they were. But they were lost just the same. Tell me, are the sheep to blame if their shepherds are lazy, ignorant, and deceitful? If the sheep could keep from wandering, there would be no need for shepherds.'

'And if sheep could fly,' suggested Murdo, 'we would call them birds.'

'Scoff if you must,' Emlyn replied, 'I expect no less. We of the Célé Dé have grown accustomed to mockery. Derision is the refuge of threatened ignorance, after all.'

Murdo, chastened by this rebuke, apologized for his outburst. 'All this talk of sheep and shepherds – it seemed funny to me. Please, tell me about the True Path. Why do you call it that?'

'Because it *is* a path,' the fat cleric insisted, 'a path of truth and understanding, leading back and back to the beginning – to the very first day when Our Lord called the Twelve to be his faithful servants. From that day, the teaching of Our Lord has been passed from one servant to the next in a single, narrow, unbroken line of succession.

'As it is written: "O, my people, hear my teaching; listen to the words of my mouth. I will open my mouth in parables; I will utter hidden things, teachings from the creation of the world – what we have heard from our fathers." And also: "When Jesu was alone, the Twelve asked him about the parables. The Lord told them, 'The secret of the Kingdom of Heaven has been given to you. But to those on the outside everything is said in parables so that they may be ever seeing, but never perceiving, and ever hearing, but never under-standing.'" Thus, it has been since the beginning. The path stretches back and back, unbroken to this day.'

'But what is this teaching?' asked Murdo; he was intrigued, but growing impatient with the monk's vague explanation. 'It does not sound much different from what the bishop says back home.'

'That is where you are wrong. For, unlike so many of our dear brothers and sisters in the faith, we do not wander in error and confusion. Yet, the teaching can only be given to one who is willing to hear, and I do not think you are ready to receive it yet.' Murdo opened his mouth to protest, but Emlyn said, 'Still, I will tell you something about it, and perhaps discernment will begin to grow. The darkness is greedy, as I have said, and it is insidious. Even in those first days it was seeking what it might devour, but the presence of Our Lord kept it at bay.

'When he ascended to Heaven to begin his eternal reign, the Great Darkness sought out the weak and unwary; those it would destroy, it first led astray. Thus, even as the faith itself began to blossom and grow, darkness sowed its own seeds of error and confusion as well. Many have been deceived, and many destroyed.

'Alas! The holy church, the great fortress of the faith, has been breached, and all its bulwarks desecrated. Those who shelter within its walls – whether sheep or shepherds,' Emlyn cast a sidelong glance at Murdo, 'leaders or followers, from the highest patriarch to the most lowly scribe – all have been tainted by the darkness, and all are bereft of the Holy Light. The eyes of their hearts have withered and they glimpse the truth but dimly if they even see it at all.

'Listen to me, I make no selfish boast. Do you think I rejoice in the certain destruction of my fellow churchmen? Do you think I could derive any pleasure from the sight of the multitudes these blind guides lead astray? The loss of dear friends and the waste of souls is more bitter to me than anything I know.

'Yet, not even for their sake could I give up that which has been entrusted to me – even if that were possible. We are Keepers of the Holy Light, and we serve Him, and Him alone, who makes the light to shine. For so long as we live, we hold to the Holy Light, and we protect it against the darkness until the Day of the Redeemer.'

The monk fell silent, and after a moment Murdo asked, 'Why is it that you three are the only ones who know about all this?'

'Few, we may be,' the monk allowed, 'but not *that* few. No, we are not the only ones; although, with each passing year there are fewer, it is true. But your question is a good one: why us and not someone else?

'I think God has chosen the Célé Dé to be the keepers, because we are different from all our brothers in certain respects. The sainted Padraic used to say that God chose the Celts to guard the True Path because we live on the edge of the world – far away from the pitiless intrigues of the east.

'I have often thought about it, and I believe Old Padraic was right. The faith was first taught by Our Lord to the humble people of this world; poor folk – shepherds and farmers and potters and fishermen – were blessed of God to be first to hear and believe. Only much later was the faith taken up by the kings and princes of this world – the high and mighty, the governors and rulers of nations.

'So, when God began to look around for someone to be his Keepers and Guardians, his eye fell naturally upon the Celt – a race as much like those who first heard the faith as makes no difference: simple people who live close to the land and close to one another. Our homes are huts of mud and twig built in green and sheltered valleys, not great golden cities filled with hosts of strangers. Our lords are our own clansmen, men of our own tribe, not governors appointed by an emperor in a glittering palace far away. Our church is the simple expression of a naturally noble people, a folk who know nothing of religious philosophies, or ecclesiastical hierarchies, but feel in their hearts the joy of a song well sung, and the beauty of a mist-covered mountain in the pearl-like dawn of a new day.'

Murdo felt a thrill ripple through him as the cleric spoke these words – the sensation produced by the sudden recognition of a truth long suspected but never uttered aloud.

'Thus,' the priest continued, 'the Good Lord saw to it that the blessed spark was passed to the Celt, and we have kept it burning ever since. For all, we are a crafty and a cunning race, and tenacious in the deep matters of the heart and soul. Though our mother church has not escaped the ravages of the Great Darkness, her youngest offspring – tucked out of sight on the edge of the world, and beset on every side by barbarian strife and troubles such as would make the very stones weep – the youngest of our Great Mother's unruly brood has grown strong in the service of the light. The rest of the church that bears Our Lord's name may fall into disrepute and ruin, brought low by schemes and plots and scandals of every kind in the futile struggle for power and position, but we, the true Célé Dé, remain steadfast, holding still to the True Path.'

Emlyn paused, and after a moment sighed. 'Ah, fy enaid,' he said, his voice sinking into the night. 'I fear I have said too much.'

'Not at all,' Murdo assured him. 'I begin to understand – I think. But what if you are wrong? What if there is no Holy Light, no True Path?'

'I, too, have wondered this,' the cleric replied thoughtfully. 'I have pondered long and hard over it. And I think it comes down to this: if we are wrong in our belief, what is the worst? Well, at worst a handful of misguided monks have deluded themselves into thinking they had a special duty, nothing more.'

This reply did more to endear the rotund priest to Murdo than anything he had said, or could have said. He had never heard a cleric admit even the least shadow of doubt or uncertainty. Here was a monk who not only acknowledged it, but reckoned the likelihood in his thinking.

'But if we are *right*, what then?' continued Emlyn. 'Then the future of the faith and the souls of mankind are in our hands – given to us for safekeeping. So you see, whether we are right or wrong, we dare not lay aside our charge.'

'I see,' Murdo replied. 'But if no one will show us the True Path, how will anyone ever become ready to receive the teaching? And why must it remain secret?'

'We are neither high nor mighty in the eyes of the world, and that is both our blessing and our curse,' the monk declared. 'Our weapons are the weapons of the weak: wit, stealth, and secrecy. These we possess in prodigious supply, and have become proficient in their many uses. Make no mistake, our enemies are mighty and they are many – the Pope in Rome chief among them. For almost six hundred

years, Rome has sought the death of the Célé Dé, yet we remain –
a remnant only, it is true, but enough to ensure the continuation of
our line. Secrecy is our protection, and we cling to it.'

Murdo thought about this for a moment, then asked, 'If this
secrecy is so important, why do you tell me?'

'I have told you only as much as I would tell anyone who asked
and was willing to listen. It is the teaching itself that is secret, not
the means or purpose.'

Murdo regarded the monk sadly. Whatever else they might be,
the Célé Dé were madmen, obviously – roaming the wilderness
reaches of the world with their shabby little secret, bending the ear
of anyone idiot enough to give them a listening. He liked Emlyn,
and felt sorry for him. Still, all this talk of paths and lights and secret
teachings made him tetchy and impatient; and he regretted having
become entangled in such a futile conversation. Also, he felt foolish
for allowing the monk to beguile him into the hope, however fleetingly glimpsed, that there might be something in what he said, something important, something real, something worth giving his life to
learn and protect.

Even as he framed the thought, he remembered his own shabby
little secret – that he was no crusader at all. He had not taken the
cross, and had no intention of fighting for the liberation of the Holy
Land. He thought of this, and softened his harsh opinion somewhat.
After all, if he regarded his own secret as too precious and dangerous
to be told, he could at least appreciate how the monks must feel.

TWENTY-TWO

'Five weeks – six, perhaps – no more,' declared Count Raymond of Toulouse confidently. 'The distances between cities is not great, and the way is well marked. We will be in Jerusalem long before summer.'

'But the guides say the roads are uncertain at best,' Hugh pointed out. 'Also, the enemy may have destroyed the old provisioning places along the way. It may take longer than we anticipate.'

With the fresh conquest of Nicaea behind them, the lords had gathered around the board in Count Raymond's expansive tent to drink wine and study the map prepared for them in Rome at the pope's behest. Full of their good fortune, the noblemen stood clutching their cups and gazing at the unrolled goatskin with its thin meandering lines and spidery inscriptions.

From ancient times, there had always been but three ways across the great upland plateau of Anatolia. Each route offered the traveller particular benefits as well as challenges. With the coming of the Seljuq, however, the difficulties had swallowed any benefits. It was no longer a matter of passage, but of endurance, and even the most informed and enlightened pilgrim would have found it impossible to say which route offered the best hope of success, for the land had passed out of imperial dominion more than a generation ago and no one knew the condition of the roads anymore. Nor could anyone say what the pilgrims might encounter on the way. And which of the old towns and settlements remained? Where would they find watering places? What was the enemy strength in the sprawling interior?

'The guides you trust so highly are spies,' Raymond hissed, his gaunt face hardening. 'Spies in the employ of that craven coward of an emperor. He would see us fail so that he can claim the spoils for himself. Did you see how quickly he swooped upon surrendered Nicaea? He had it in his grip before the blood had dried in the streets.'

'There was no blood in the streets,' Stephen corrected mildly, 'and in any event, we had already decided to give it to him so that we might press on in all haste. The season grows hotter by the day, and we must move quickly – the summer heat will kill us, if the enemy does not.'

'Bah!' cried Raymond. 'Listen to your bleating! My lords,' he said sternly, 'with our own eyes we have seen how easily the Saracens are defeated. If the Greeks were but half the soldiers we are, they would have driven them into the sea years ago.'

'The Saracens are a pestering irritation,' declared Baldwin into his cup, 'nothing more.'

'Seljuqs,' Stephen reminded them. 'They are not Saracens, but *Seljuqs*. There is a difference, I believe.'

'There is *no* difference,' growled Raymond.

'I agree,' put in Bohemond indifferently. 'Stick them and they bleed; cut off their heads and they die.'

'They are infidel, and they will be exterminated like vermin.' Baldwin glanced around the board, gathering agreement for this sentiment. 'We took Nicaea without breaking a sweat; the rest will fall to us likewise.'

'But if the guides say –' Hugh began again, desperate to have his concern taken seriously.

'Hang the guides!' roared Raymond, slamming his hand down on the board. 'I am sick to the teeth hearing about them. These scheming Greeks are part of the emperor's deceitful designs. I warn you, Vermandois, trust them at your peril. The maps given us by the pope are more than adequate for the task at hand. We have only to keep to the old military road and we are assured swift passage to Jerusalem.'

Straightening to his full height, he placed his hands on his hips and glared around the table at his comrades. 'On to Antioch, I say, and devil take the hindmost!'

The next day, the largest force assembled since the golden days of Rome's glory trundled off on the broken road. Moving in long columns, staggered to keep out of one another's dust, the crusaders looked their last upon the conquered city, and set their faces towards Jerusalem.

Nicaea had been their first real test, and they had come through it handsomely. The victory was no less sweet for the ease with which it had been accomplished. The outcome had been in doubt right up to the moment of surrender – owing chiefly to the fact that when the siege was begun, the crusaders' fighting force had not yet reached its full strength.

The last pilgrims to join – Duke Robert and his noble kinsmen, and their respective contingents of English, Norman, Scottish, and Flemish knights – had not reached their comrades until the eve of the fall of Nicaea. Like the others before them, they had taken the oath of allegiance in Constantinople, then crossed the Bosphorus in the emperor's ships and disembarked in Pelecanum where they made their way along the gulf to Nicomedia, the last city in Anatolia remaining to the empire. There they were joined by a regiment of Immortals which the emperor had ordered to accompany the pilgrims. Eager to join the pilgrimage, the western lords pressed on to Nicaea, led by the Byzantine regiment, who were in turn led by their commander, the strategus Taticius.

Though they remained alert and wary of attack, they saw no sign of the enemy, and were thus able to travel at speed – owing to Taticius and their imperial guides, and the fact that the other crusaders had already passed through and chased any adversaries away. Even so, by the time the latecomers arrived, Nicaea had been under siege for almost a month. Chosen by Sultan Arslan to be his primary fortress, Nicaea sat like a gigantic boulder in the pilgrims' path. They could not advance until the city had been taken. However, situated on a lake and defended by high stone walls and stout, iron-bound gates, Nicaea easily resisted every attack by the crusaders, and appeared happy to go on doing so indefinitely.

As the latest pilgrims came within sight of the besieged city, however, a great cry went up from the enemy warriors massed atop the walls. The arriving crusaders assumed that it was the cowardly Seljuq giving in to their dismay at the sudden appearance of so great a force of excellent horsemen and infantry soldiers arriving fresh to the fight. They exulted in the revelation of fear their imposing presence was inspiring in their quaking adversary, until realizing that the cries were actually shouts of triumph raised for the return of Sultan Qilij Arslan, who was at that very moment sweeping down upon them from the north.

The sultan, they quickly discovered, had been on a raiding campaign and was away from Nicaea when the first Latins arrived. Upon seeing the crusaders encamped around the walls of his capital, Arslan determined to break through the besieging armies and liberate his people without delay. Duke Robert, assuming command of his troops, quickly marshalled the knights and formed the battleline. Pulling the footmen back behind the line to offer support, he waited while the Seljuqs charged. Seeing that the invaders were adamant, and that their own force – a light raiding party only – had lost the small benefit of surprise, the sultan decided not to pursue the attack and broke off after a few half-hearted charges.

At first sight of the enemy retreat, the pilgrims gave chase and succeeded in cutting down a few stragglers before the sultan and his warband disappeared over the hills once more. Miraculously, the first skirmish with the infidel was won at the cost of only one Christian life – a hapless footman who had been struck by a wayward arrow that glanced off a knight's shield and struck him in the neck. The crusaders thanked God for his mercy and joined the siege.

Count Raymond, impatient with the resistance, and worried that the sultan would soon return with a greater force, had commanded siege towers to be constructed so that the crusaders could get men over the walls. They laboured for three days and nights, raising timber frames and bulwarks, in a frantic effort to capture the city before Sultan Arslan reappeared.

The furious industry of the invaders alarmed the population of Nicaea. Each day they watched with growing dread as the towers neared completion. Having seen their sultan run off by these strange new Romans, and fearing the impending slaughter should they take the walls by force, the amir of Nicaea sent an envoy under cover of night to negotiate a peace settlement with the Byzantine commander. The envoy slipped out from the city by way of a water gate on the lake, returning the same way with an escort of imperial troops.

The next morning, when the crusaders rose to begin work on the siege towers, they saw the imperial banner flying above the gate. Raymond, furious over this betrayal, summoned Taticius to his tent and demanded an explanation.

'They wished to surrender,' he said simply. 'As the city formerly belonged to the basileus, they sought imperial protection. Naturally, I have taken the precaution of manning the garrison and relieving the enemy of their weapons.'

'This is treachery!' Raymond charged, leaping from his chair.

'In what way?' the strategus asked.

'The surrender belongs to *me*,' the count told him, striking himself on the chest. 'The towers are nearly finished. We were ready to overrun the city. The victory was *mine*.'

The wily soldier regarded the tall, thin knight. 'I do not understand your anger,' he replied. 'I thought the object of our exercise was to obtain the surrender of the city, not its destruction. Diplomacy is better than bloodshed.' Tacitus paused, eyeing Raymond with undisguised contempt. 'Perhaps it was the bloodshed you wanted.'

'Get out!' shrieked Raymond, slamming his hand down hard on the board. 'Get out!'

The strategus bowed stiffly, turned on his heel, and departed, leaving Raymond fuming at the ignominious way in which the surrender had been achieved and his glory stolen from him. His anger was quickly forgotten, however, once the assembled lords set about taking control of the city, and the problems began to multiply. For the noblemen could not agree how best to proceed, who should oversee the collection of the tribute, nor even how much the payment should be. Nor did they know what to do with Nicaea itself now that they had conquered it.

Clearly, the city would have to be protected from now on, lest it fall back into the hands of Sultan Arslan; since it had been his capital, he would certainly attempt to recover such a valuable and strategic asset. Also, one of his favourite wives and some of his children were now captives of the crusaders, and the sultan would no doubt try to free them and revenge himself on those who had embarrassed and humiliated him.

Duke Godfrey argued for leaving a contingent of soldiers behind to man the garrison. 'For the sake of those travelling on, the city must remain secure,' he argued. 'We cannot allow the enemy to cut off our communication with Constantinople. Nor would I care to have these Saracen devils on our tails all the way to Jerusalem.'

Bishop Adhemar agreed. 'God has granted us this first of many great victories as a sign of his favour, and of the high esteem in which he holds our holy enterprise. It would be disrespectful to throw away that which God has so freely given. The city must be claimed for the pope and the church.'

Bohemond and Tancred had other concerns. 'The reconquest of the Holy Land is only begun,' Bohemond pointed out. 'We will need every soldier in the days to come. The protection of this city would take far too many men, and I am loath to give up a single one.'

'Prince Bohemond is right,' declared Hugh of Vermandois. 'It would be foolish to divide our forces now, so far away from Jerusalem.' The lords of Flanders and Normandy, along with various other noblemen, agreed, adding their voices to Hugh's.

There the thing rested. Clearly, the city required their continued presence to ensure that it remained securely in the crusader's possession. Just as clearly, no one wanted to remove able-bodied fighting men from the campaign when the main objective was still to be accomplished. Also, no one was willing to remain behind in any event, thereby allowing the others all the glory and plunder to be won in the battles to come. The stalemate persisted for a day and a night – until Count Stephen offered the suggestion that a messenger might be sent back to Constantinople informing the emperor that Nicaea had been recaptured and returned to the empire.

'It might be,' Stephen proposed, 'that the Byzantines can spare the troops to secure the city. If they agreed to occupy it, we could continue on our way.'

The idea was instantly accepted by one and all, and messengers were hastening back to Constantinople before the ink had dried on the parchment. The Latin lords then set about installing themselves in the city. Since the siege camps were already established, the troops remained outside the walls. The lords, however, desired better accommodation for their wives and families, so proceeded to confiscate the best houses in the city for themselves.

The emperor did not wait for the couriers to arrive, however, but set out the moment his spies assured him the city was on the point of surrender. Sailing swiftly south to a bay on the nearby coast, Alexius rode the short distance inland with two divisions of Opsikion and Anatolian troops to oversee the city's surrender. To the utter surprise of the crusaders, the emperor arrived while they were still trying to decide which of Nicaea's palaces they should plunder first.

As the Latin lords squabbled over who should take control of Nicaea's wealth, Taticius led his regiment of Immortals to the abandoned garrison and placed it under their authority. They then secured the gate, and welcomed the emperor's bodyguard. The soldiers took up positions along the city's central street to greet the emperor while the crusaders stood in flat-footed amazement as Alexius rode in triumph through the gates of the city.

The emperor assembled the pilgrims to commend them on their

victory. 'You have done well, my friends,' he said, his voice ringing expansively. 'In capturing Nicaea, you have returned a prized property to the empire, and removed Sultan Arslan's capital. Long has the Seljuq sultan plagued Constantinople, making his incessant attacks beneath the very gates of the empire. But no more. From this day the sultan has no home but his tent, and with God's help that, too, shall soon be taken from him.'

So there should be no confusion over his intentions, Alexius continued, adding, 'We would have each nobleman here bear witness to our gratitude in accepting the return of this city to the empire. So that you may speedily continue on your way, we will reassume its administration and relieve you of its protection.'

He then granted the sultana and her servants and children safe conduct to Constantinople until word could be taken to Qilij Arslan, asking the sultan where he wished his wife to join him. The western lords were aghast at this extraordinary charity to an enemy. Lest the pilgrims harbour hard feelings over this settlement, Alexius promptly gave orders for the sultan's treasury to be opened and the entire contents shared out in equal measure among the crusade leaders; and further, that all the grain and produce of the markets to be distributed to the troops. The emperor took nothing for himself, save Nicaea.

While the emperor concerned himself with restoring the much valued city, the crusaders resumed their journey to the Holy Land in good spirits. Following the council in Raymond's tent, they departed Nicaea the next morning with highest hopes for a swift completion of the crusade – despite repeated warnings from Taticius and his guides that they had not seen the last of Sultan Arslan.

In the days to follow, they passed through deserted villages and abandoned towns – places that had once been flourishing market towns and important centres of local trade. The empty hills were strewn with ruined farms, and all along the road the habitations had been burned to their foundations. Wells and vineyards, fields and forests, had all been destroyed; bridges had been broken, and cisterns and dams smashed, left to bleed out their life-giving contents to the desert-parched land. The few stream beds they encountered were dust-dry, rock-filled ditches. The further they journeyed inland, the more arid the ground became.

After only five days the water supply began to dwindle, and it was decided that the army must be split into two divisions in order to lessen the burden on the foraging parties which were having to range ever greater distances to find fodder and water. One division – consisting of the combined troops of Godfrey and Baldwin, Hugh, and all the Franks, under the leadership of Count Raymond – would range north of the road; the other – comprised of the armies of Robert of Flanders, and Robert of Normandy, Tancred and Stephen, along with the rest of the Normans and English, under the leadership of Prince Bohemond – would assume a parallel course seven miles to the south of the road.

This they did, and advanced through the low Bythinian mountains, encountering nothing more fierce than a few Seljuq raiding parties, which they promptly chased away without incident. Once through the mountains, Prince Bohemond's division found itself on a broad upland plain of low, rolling hills in sight of the Thymbres River, and a short distance from the ancient and now-ruined city of Dorylaeum.

Almost delirious with thirst, the parched pilgrims flocked in droves to the riverside. They threw themselves headlong down the banks and stumbled into the water, sinking to their knees in the cool mud. They jostled one another to put their faces into the water, the last climbing over the first, and all of them sucking down the life-giving liquid. The horses, getting the scent in their nostrils, plunged chest-deep into the river where they stood with their noses sunk in the water.

When every last pilgrim had drunk as much as he could hold, they all turned their attention to replenishing every cask and butt and skin with fresh water. Then the children were joined by their elders as they bathed and frolicked in the shallows, splashing cool water over their blistered, sun-burnt bodies, making the nearby ruins echo with glad shouts and the sound of laughter.

As the meadow was full and green – the first good pasturage they had seen since leaving Constantinople – Prince Bohemond gave the order to halt and make camp. They grazed the animals on the wide rivermead and enjoyed a comfortable night. The next morning, after another swim and soak in the river, the crusaders moved on reluctantly.

They had only just reformed the line and begun the day's march when Sultan Arslan and the massed Seljuq warhost attacked and cut the crusader army to small, bloody pieces.

BOOK III

BOOK III

January 16, 1899: Edinburgh, Scotland

Caitlin and I were married in the spring of 1871. A few weeks after Angus and Libby were wed, my lovely Cait and I tied the knot and began a long and mostly sunny life together. I still saw Angus at the office, of course, and we still went to the club on the rare occasion, but we were both soon too preoccupied with the demands – financial and otherwise – of our burgeoning families to resume our old bachelor ways.

Our second wedding anniversaries saw two couples very much in love, and looking hopefully towards a prosperous and happy future. Then, only three short months later, Angus was dead.

Like so many others, he succumbed to the influenza epidemic which swept all of Europe that year. I knew nothing about his illness. I vaguely recall that he did not appear at work on Friday, and I did not see him over the week's end. By Monday morning, he was gone, having passed in the early hours of the night.

I was devastated. My best friend, gone for ever, and I never had the chance to say good-bye, to tell him how much his friendship meant to me. After the funeral, Libby and the child – they had a little girl less than a year old – moved back to Perth, where her mother and father lived; and though she and Caitlin kept up a regular correspondence, it was never to be the same.

I bring all this up now, because, as I think on it, Angus' funeral was the turning point. I took part in the service, naturally, and as I read out the eulogy, I happened to look up from my reading to see someone standing alone at the back of the chapel. It was Pemberton. Grim and tall in a black suit, his coat over his shoulders like a cape, he was standing with his hands folded before him, his eyes downcast.

But just as I noticed him, he raised his head slowly and looked at me. Not, I mean, as one does when being addressed from a pulpit – I was delivering the eulogy, after all – but . . . and how can I describe this? He raised his eyes and fixed me with a most extraordinary stare. Although he was at the back of the chapel and

I at the front, his gaze penetrated straight to my very soul and filled me with such sadness that I was instantly overcome and was forced to break off my prepared speech. I fear I muttered something incomprehensible in conclusion and sat down as a great crushing wave of grief washed over me.

Afterwards, when I had collected myself somewhat, I looked for Pemberton at the reception, but he failed to appear. Six months later we met again. Caitlin had taken the sprog – we now had a delightful little cherub named Annie to amuse and amaze us – to her aunt's house for a summer visit. I could not get away from the office to go with them, so stayed home, fending for myself. I was sitting in the smoking room at the club, reading the paper, and waiting for the dinner gong, when I became aware that someone was watching me. Glancing up, I saw Pemberton sitting across from me, and looking very much the way he had looked the day I'd seen him at the funeral.

'Are you alone this evening?' he asked, politely, but without preamble.

'Mr Pemberton,' I said, 'what a pleasant surprise. I did not hear you sit down. Yes, I am dining alone this evening – wife off to the country for a fortnight. I'm sick of my own cooking, so thought I might pop round to see if the Old Stag still provides a decent haunch of an evening.'

'Oh, excellent as ever, I assure you,' he replied. 'In fact, I would be most gratified if you would join me for dinner. I have been wanting to talk to you for some time.'

'How very kind of you. I would be delighted, sir.'

The gong sounded at that moment, and the tall gentleman stood. 'I asked to have a table waiting. I hope you don't mind if we go right in. We have much to talk about, I think.'

Talk we did, to be sure. We spoke briefly of poor Angus' untimely death, as I expected we would, and he said, 'I was very touched by your tribute to Alisdair at his funeral. I know his parents were very grateful for your friendship with him,' he paused, and added, 'as was I.'

Conversation then passed to other things. Our discussion ranged the length and breadth of the British Empire, I think: Egypt, the Sudan, India, Hong Kong, and a few dozen other countries I can't remember. He seemed to know about, or have interests in, all these places, and spoke not as a casual observer, but as one with an intimate familiarity.

Much of what he said that night I found incredible. Indeed, I went home thinking I had passed the evening with a madman. Harmless, perhaps, but mad as a hatter. Definitely.

In the weeks and months that followed, however, I found myself returning time and again to something he had told me – a peculiar phrase he'd used, or startling observation he'd made – and little by little it began to make sense. Curiosity took hold of me, and I found myself wondering what else he knew.

I determined to see him again. As I did not know any other way to get in touch with him, I left a note at the Old Stag, thinking that if he came to the club more regularly than I, the porter could give it to him next time he popped in. Sure enough, within a fortnight I received a reply. It came on gold-trimmed, cream-coloured stationery, very expensive, and said, simply: 'Delighted to see you again. Would dinner on the sixteenth suit? Best regards, Pemberton.'

Taking this to mean that we would meet at the club, I turned up on the night just before eight, and settled into my customary chair. By eight-thirty, I was beginning to think I'd missed the boat, when he came striding in. Looking neither left nor right, he marched to where I was sitting and shook me by the hand, apologized for being late, and pulled me with him into the dining room where, as before, he had a table waiting.

Our talk that night was no less wide-ranging than previously, but this time I listened most intently to all he said, and tried very hard to remember any detail he might mention about himself. At the end of the evening, I had learned very much about maritime exploration in Polynesia, and Renaissance philosophy in France, but almost nothing about my host. As we made our farewells, he took me by the hand and looked straight into my eyes, and said, 'I wonder if you would care to make the acquaintance of two of my closest friends.'

This took me off guard, and I must have hesitated, for he said, 'I see I've made you uncomfortable. Forgive me. It was only a thought.'

'No, no,' I protested, 'I would be honoured to meet your friends, Mr Pemberton. Truly, I –'

'Pembers, please. I feel we know each other well enough, don't you, Gordon?'

'Of course,' I agreed; and it seemed he had taken me into his confidence – an intimacy I was certain he did not bestow lightly.

'Splendid,' he said. We arranged a time for our next meeting, and bade one another good evening.

In the cab on the way home that night, I thought about what had taken place over dinner. Nothing of import, certainly. In fact, I felt distinctly let down. I suppose I had been expecting something extraordinary, and had to settle for the merely ordinary instead. Nor did our eventual dinner with his two friends seem remarkable in any way. They were agreeable enough gentlemen: one a short, well-upholstered Welshman named Evans, and the other a slender, grey-haired chap of French extraction by the name of De Cardou. Both were slightly 'olde worlde' in a pleasant sort of way, and, like our host, refined and voluble, eager and able to talk about anything and everything, yet never giving away the tiniest detail of their personal lives.

I, on the other hand, despite my best efforts, seemed utterly incapable of holding back anything. The ease with which they pulled out of me the minutia of my existence – from my boyhood days to the workaday office routine – was astonishing. The end result was that they learned a very great deal about me, and I almost nothing about any of them. Nevertheless, we seemed to have passed some unseen gate that night, for from then on I was the recipient of Pemberton's cordial attention. That is to say, I found myself increasingly in the orbit of his affairs.

There was, it seemed, no one he did not know, and whose good opinion he had not secured by some kindly act. The net result of this closer acquaintance was that my personal fortunes increased rapidly, if discreetly. Owing to a downturn in the wool trade at the time of my father's passing a few years earlier, I had inherited the unenviable position of satisfying several outstanding bills of credit. While I had been dutifully, if doggedly, paying off the creditors little by little, within a year of that watershed meeting, the previously limited horizons of my position had expanded dramatically. Promotions and advancements came my way with remarkable rapidity, *and* with commensurate financial reward. Caitlin and I at last began to entertain some hope that we might yet attain to some small standard of luxury in which we might have the leisure to travel.

About this time, too, I began increasingly to have the feeling that I was being watched. Do not take from this that the feeling was disagreeable or malign in any way. Indeed, I hasten to assure you that it was not – much the reverse, in fact. I felt protected, as if unseen angels stood guard around myself, Caitlin and the children, ever ready to aid and defend us.

Nor was I mistaken. But it was not until many years later that I was to learn the fearful cost of this security paid out on my behalf.

In the following months and years, the curious friendship between Pemberton and myself was to develop in unforeseen ways as I gradually discovered him to be the hidden architect of my continued good fortune. At length, and quite by accident, I learned my secret benefactor was a widower long alone in the world. Thenceforth, I seized every opportunity to repay his philanthropy by including him in the small celebrations of our family life.

In short, Pemberton became an unseen presence in our household. Upon the birth of our second child, Alexander, I asked him to stand as godparent. He accepted with great enthusiasm, and turned up at the christening with a case of port for the lad's coming of age, and a silver spoon engraved with his name and a family crest. 'It is the Murray crest,' he pointed out when Caitlin asked.

'Murray crest? You didn't tell me you were aristocratic, darling,' she replied light-heartedly.

'Believe me, I had no idea,' I answered.

Whereupon Pemberton became very serious. 'Obscure it may be,' he said. 'Yet, the Murray is one of the most ancient and honourable clans in the bloody history of our contentious race.' To the infant Alexander, nestled in Caitlin's arms, he said, 'You can be proud of your heritage, lad.' Then, as if searching back through the mists of time, he placed his hand on the babe's forehead, and said, 'May the holy light illumine your journey, and may your feet never stray from the true path.'

A curious benediction, you may think, but no more so than many of the things people are apt to say on such occasions, and offered with such sincerity that we did not remark on it at the time. As I came to know him better, and spent more time in his company, I found that he was often given to spouting strange little prophecies.

It would happen like this: a comment in passing, or an item in the evening newspaper, would catch his attention and he would offer a pithy forecast of the outcome – if it was in doubt – or the likely result of certain actions being carried forward into the future. In time, I came to heed his predictions and warnings for the simple reason that they most often came to pass exactly as he said they would. I do not mean to make him sound like a carnival fortune-teller reading the future; it was nothing so crude as that. In fact, prophecy is my word; he merely called them 'projections', meaning that he guessed.

Yet, his guesses, if not inspired, were at least the product of an exhaustive knowledge and a wide-ranging, not to say boundless, intelligence. Concealed behind his proper, elegant, but self-effacing demeanour was an intellect of considerable acumen and power. The more I came to know him, the more I respected and trusted him. Although the details of his past life and even his day-to-day existence were shadowy at best – I never learned where he grew up, for example, where he went to school, or how he had come by the considerable wealth he apparently possessed – the sterling quality of his character was abundantly clear.

In all his dealings, I never found him less than kind and considerate. He was not only unfailingly honest, but deferential, patient, generous, and fair. If he showed himself a shrewd and ruthless judge of worldly events and the failings of men, yet never a cruel or derisive word passed his lips. His capacity for understanding and forgiving his fellow creatures was, I truly believe, well nigh infinite.

Do not imagine this mildness concealed cowardice; it did not. There was nothing of the craven's wish to avoid unpleasantness or conflict, much less fear, in his conduct. His convictions were often at odds with the prevailing attitude of the day, yet he held to them without vacillation. If this put him in contention with the mass of society, so be it. I never saw him waver. Pemberton, as I came to know and trust him, was that rarest of human beings: a good man.

That is why, on the evening when he asked me to join the Brothers of the Temple, I agreed without hesitation.

This singular event took place, as so often happened, in the lounge at the Old Stag. He had, as was his custom, treated me to a delicious meal, and we were lingering over our whisky and cigars when he said, 'Gordon, my friend, I have a proposition for your consideration.'

'I would be pleased to give it my fullest attention,' I declared expansively. When I saw that he was quite serious, I added, 'Feel free to ask me anything.'

'I have known you for some years now, and I like to think that in that time you have come to know me a little also. Indeed, I like to think that our association has not been without its modest rewards.' I swiftly assured him that our friendship was of great importance to me. He smiled, and said, 'Then please, for the sake of our friendship, I will ask you to keep what I shall say in the strictest confidence. Will you do that?'

'Said and done.' I leaned forward eagerly. Never had I known him to be so clandestine.

'As you may have surmised, I have many involvements and interests with which I occupy my time. But there is one I would like to recommend to you. Knowing you as I do, I think you would find it very stimulating.' He glanced at me to see whether I wished him to proceed.

'Do go on. I'm listening.'

'The situation I describe is a strictly private organization, and very exclusive.'

He had become so serious, I sought to lighten the mood somewhat. 'A secret society? Pemberton, you do surprise me.'

'A society, definitely,' he said. 'Secret? Let us just say that, living in uncertain times as we do, we cannot be overly careful about those to whom we extend our invitations.'

'Forgive me, Pemberton, but are we talking about the Masonic Order?'

'Freemasons?' He looked genuinely shocked. At once his customary decorum gave way, and I caught a rare glimpse of the real man. 'Don't be absurd! We have nothing to do with that mumbo jumbo – nothing at all, thank God. As far as I'm concerned the Masons are a miserable tribe of sad little men muttering gibberish and flouncing around in the dark in their mothers' aprons. They are, quite frankly, priests of a long-dead religion venerating all the wrong bones.'

'I see.'

'No, our organization is quite far removed from that sort of thing. While we guard our traditions no less jealously than our masonic comrades, our roots lie in different soil, so to speak. It is known by its initiates as the Benevolent Order, and is wholly given to good works of various kinds. I have been a member for close to forty years, and we are always looking for men of integrity who could benefit from an association of this type.' He paused and smiled. 'It would be my very great honour to sponsor you for membership.'

'It would be my very great pleasure to accept,' I told him.

'Good,' he said, well satisfied with my enthusiastic response.

'Good. I will make the necessary arrangements, and you will hear from me shortly.'

A few weeks later, I was inducted into the order, and began to discover a side of society that had heretofore escaped my notice completely. Among the membership of Temple XX – which is what our local meeting hall was called – I was surprised to find several acquaintances, men I knew from my professional life, and two men who were members of the congregation of my church. Consequently, I felt very much at home from the beginning, and found it a convivial, if not utterly inspiring, group.

True to Pemberton's word, the Benevolent Order occupied itself with good works: gifts of books to libraries, wheeled chairs for the crippled, medicine for the invalided, shoes for the indigent, orphanages, and what not. Necessary stuff, and very much welcomed by the recipients, but a tad sleepy all the same. When not organizing deliveries of books or medicine, we were instructed by well-meaning lecturers in the lore of the order, history, and social issues.

My first impression was that the Benevolent Order of the Brothers of Solomon's Temple – to give it its official name – apparently derived much of its impetus and rationale from Freemasonry. We wore white monks' robes with strange insignia, and advanced through various degrees of initiation the stations of which were indicated by the colours of our belts and cowls. We had secret passwords for recognition, and were made to memorize patterns and liturgies of legendary ritual which we observed from time to time.

Despite Pemberton's protest to the contrary, I imagined that the Brothers of the Temple had been founded, at least partly, in response to the Masonic movement, perhaps even by disaffected former members of that better-known secret society. It was not until I had been a member for several years that I even began to suspect there might be something more to the Order than a bunch of cater-cousin freemasons running around in bedsheets, calling one another Brother Novitiate, Brother Warden, or Brother Preceptor.

The existence of the Brotherhood took me by surprise, I confess. But then, I suppose I had been lulled by the innocuous nature of the larger charitable organization. Certainly, the notion of a second order hidden behind the first was nothing new, but in all the time I had been a member of the Benevolent Order, I had never been given any reason to think that all I saw, was *not* all there was.

However, once I learned of the Brotherhood's existence, the object of the Benevolent Order became abundantly, and astonishingly, clear: it was to be the sorting shed, the clearing house, if you will, for its older, more clandestine associate. In other words, the Benevolent Order, while enjoying its own stodgy purposes, had actually been formed to serve the Brotherhood, and not the other way around.

I also discovered, to my compounded amazement, that only those fortunate enough to be elected to its number were vouchsafed knowledge of the Brotherhood. Thus, within a fortnight of receiving this manifold revelation, I found myself kneeling on the floor of a crypt at midnight on All Hallows Eve, repeating sacred vows, and kissing the blade of a sword – after which I exchanged my monk's robe and cowl for a black cape lined with crimson satin. I was also given a talisman: a blackened finger bone from the hand of one of the founders of our secret order, a Scottish lord who, rather than betray the Brotherhood, had been burned at the stake.

TWENTY-THREE

Ragna smoothed her hands over the gentle swell of her stomach. She had been able to hide the growing fullness for a time, but no longer. Soon the other women around her would notice what she had already told Tailtiu, her handmaid – not that she could have hidden anything from that bright-eyed magpie of a girl. She knew almost before Ragna herself was certain.

'If you tell anyone, Tailtiu,' Ragna warned her, 'I will not hesitate to cut out your tongue so you will never be able to tell another secret to anyone for the rest of your life.'

The threat did not distress the servingmaid in the least. 'What will you use? The knife you gave to our Murdo?'

'He is not *our* Murdo,' Ragna replied crisply. 'How did you know about the knife?'

'It is no longer in your keep-chest,' Tailtiu answered cheerfully. 'It is gone and so is Master Murdo. I cannot think he would steal it, so it must be you has given it to him. And he has given a child to you.'

'Listen to me, Tailtiu,' Ragna said, taking the girl by the shoulders, 'no one is to know of this until *I* choose to tell them.'

'You are afeared your mother will be angry with you?'

'I am not ashamed of what I did,' Ragna said sternly. 'But I will not have it treated as something lewd, to be whispered over by every lustful hinny in Kirkjuvágr. Do you understand?'

'I like him. He is good and kind. You do love him, too, I can tell. Will your father allow the marriage? I think he will be a fine husband.'

'Tailtiu, I mean what I say,' Ragna gave the girl a shake for emphasis. 'I will *not* have this brought into disgrace. Do you understand me?'

'I understand, my lady. It shall be our secret.'

'See that it remains so.'

That had been a few months ago, and beyond all expectation the chatter-happy Tailtiu had kept her mouth shut about her mistress' condition – not even so much as to whisper it between themselves. This had allowed Ragna to wait and hope, and when she was at last certain, ready herself to reveal the secret in her own time.

She would tell her mother first, and then Lady Niamh. The three of them would decide together what to do about announcing the birth. That, Ragna reckoned, would be the most difficult part. There would be no problem with baptizing the baby; when the time came, it could be done in their own chapel. The birth could be recorded there, and it would not have to be entered on the cathedral rolls until the child was two years old. By then, Murdo would be back and they would be properly married. If she stayed on Hrolfsey until Murdo returned, all would be well. No one outside their own family and vassals need learn about the child until the marriage was duly formalized and recognized by the church.

Through the long summer day, Ragna occupied herself with little chores, waiting for just the right moment to present itself. That moment came when Lady Ragnhild strolled into the herb garden outside the kitchen to cut fennel for the cooks to use in the evening meal. The lowering sun stretched the shadows long among the close-tended rows of plants as Ragna approached her mother. The warmth of the day and the honeyed light gave Ragna a pleasantly mellow feeling.

'It has been a good summer for the gardens,' her mother observed. 'The best I can remember for many years.'

'Perhaps it bodes well for a mild winter,' Ragna offered.

'Winter!' Lady Ragnhild stooped to snip a stunted, discoloured stalk from among the tall green forest before her. 'Please, summer is short enough without hastening it on its way. We have harvest to think about first, and that is upon us soon enough.'

'Our men will be home by then,' Ragna replied. She plucked a fragrant leaf from a nearby branch, raised it to her nose, then began twirling it between her fingers.

'Our men,' echoed her mother. 'It must be Murdo you are talking about. I cannot think you would speak about your father and brothers that way.'

'I miss him, Mother,' Ragna said quietly.

'Aye,' sighed Ragnhild, 'I miss your father, too. It is a hard, hard thing to stay behind.'

'It has been good having Niamh here. I am sorry about their lands, but she has been a help to us. I like her.'

'That is good,' observed Ragnhild absently, trimming the severed stalk further.

'It seems to me,' Ragna continued, 'that a bride should esteem her husband's mother as her own – and that is not always so easy, I think.'

The trimmer hesitated only an instant, and then . . . snip – another stalk fell. 'All this talk of brides and husbands,' Ragnhild mused. 'Am I to think a wedding is anticipated in this house?' She straightened and looked her daughter in the eye. 'Or has the marriage already taken place?'

'For a truth, it has. We were hand-fasted before he left.'

Ragnhild nodded and turned back to her work. 'Had it been anyone else, your father would have the man flogged through the streets of every town from here to Jorvik.' She paused. 'He might do that still, who knows?'

'Father would never oppose the match,' Ragna maintained, a wariness edging into her voice. 'He has never said anything against Murdo. He would never refuse us.'

'Nay,' Lady Ragnhild softened. 'How could he? Lord Ranulf is a nobleman of rank, and a longtime friend. Your father respects him, and values his friendship. Anyway, the deed is done and we must all make the best of it.' The trimmer neatly lopped the stalk into her basket. 'Bishop Adalbert should be your greatest worry. He can refuse to acknowledge the hand-fasting, you know, and your children would be born into perdition.'

'We have time yet.' Ragna bent her head. Her eyes filled with tears. 'Until the Christ Mass, at least.'

Ragnhild paused and regarded her daughter thoughtfully. She put down the basket and opened her arms. Ragna stepped into her mother's embrace and the two women stood for a time without speaking.

'Oh, Ragna, if you could have waited . . .' she sighed, leaving the thought unfinished.

'He will be a good husband, Mother,' Ragna said after a while; she sniffed and rubbed the tears from her cheeks. 'He has never been anything but kind to me, and I love him for it – I think I always have. We will confirm our vows in our own chapel when he returns.'

'And if he does *not* return?'

'Mother! I will not hear you speak so.'

'I *do* speak so. Daughter, they are at war. You know as well as I, that men who go away to war do not always come home again. Of all those who leave home and family, only a few will return. Men die in battle and there is nothing we can do about it. That is hard, but that is the truth.'

'Murdo did not go to fight,' Ragna pointed out. 'He went only to bring Lord Ranulf home, not to fight.'

'That is something, at least,' her mother allowed, tenderness and pity mingled in her gaze. 'Oh, Ragna, I would that it were different for you.' After a moment she said, 'We must tell Niamh, of course; she will want to know soon.'

'Tonight, I thought,' Ragna replied. 'I will not be able to keep it from her much longer in any event.'

Lady Ragnhild raised a hand to her daughter's head, and touched it gently.

'Crusade will end long before winter comes,' Ragna told her, forcing conviction to her voice. 'The men will have returned, and we will be married before the baby is born.'

'Pray that is so,' Ragnhild said, stroking her daughter's long golden hair. 'Pray your Murdo returns soon. Pray they *all* return soon . . . hale and unharmed.'

After supper that night, Ragnhild suggested that Niamh join them for a walk in the long-lingering twilight. 'These few fine days at the last of summer almost repay winter's dark and cold,' she said as they strolled the path behind the house. The sky was flushed with pink and purple, and the few low clouds were red and orange against a sky of deepening blue. The sea breeze was warm out of the south, and the evening star gleamed just above the line of the hills beyond the ripening fields.

'It has always been my favourite time of year,' Niamh agreed placidly. 'The cattle have calved and the young are growing. It is nicest before the tumult of harvest.'

'Ragna was saying that she hoped the men would be home for the harvest,' Ragnhild said.

'I hope so, too,' Niamh replied. 'But I think we must not expect it. Whatever the next months bring, I fear we must prepare to face it without our menfolk.'

One of the servingmaids called Lady Ragnhild away just then, leaving Ragna and Niamh together for a moment. They walked a while, enjoying the mild evening. 'You have been quiet tonight,' Niamh observed. 'It is not like you. Are you feeling well?'

'Very well, indeed,' Ragna answered. 'If I am quiet, it is that I have been trying to find the right words to say what I must tell you.'

'Just say what is in your mind,' Niamh suggested amiably. 'I am certain there is nothing you could say that I would not like to hear.'

Ragna nodded. 'You are kind, Lady Niamh –'

'Let it be Niá between us,' she replied quickly. 'We are friends enough for that, I think.'

'We are,' agreed Ragna, 'and it is that very friendship I fear losing.'

'Whyever should you lose it?' Niamh stopped walking and turned to Ragna. 'My heart, what is wrong?'

The young woman lifted her head. 'Murdo and I are hand-fasted. I am carrying his child.'

'I see,' replied Niamh quietly.

When no further reaction seemed forthcoming, Ragna accepted her reproach. 'I do not blame you for withholding your blessing,' she said, bending her head. 'No doubt you hoped to make a better match for your son.'

In two steps, Niamh was beside Ragna, gathering the young woman to her breast. 'Never say it,' she soothed. 'Ah, Ragna . . . Ragna. I chose you for him the first day ever I saw you. I have made the match a thousand times in my heart. I have never breathed a word of this to Murdo, mind; but I prayed he would one day see for himself what I saw in you.' She held Ragna at arm's length. 'I am happy for you, and for him, too. If I hold any sadness at all, it is for the fact that I fear for your future together –'

'Because of the church? I thought of that. We can confirm –'

Niamh shook her head. 'No, the church will be the least of your worries. Rather it is because we have lost our lands, child. Murdo will have nothing, and that is a sorry way to begin a life together.'

'But you will get your lands back,' Ragna said. 'When Lord Ranulf and your sons return – you *will* reclaim Hrafnbú. I know it.'

'I wish I could be so certain. The truth is, there is much against us, and even if Lord Ranulf were here now, it might go ill with us.' Niamh paused. 'We must not trust too highly in our hopes, for the whims of kings thwart all desires but their own.'

'Would you forbid our marriage for lack of land?' Ragna asked, not unkindly.

'My heart, I would forbid you nothing,' Niamh replied. 'I wish you the world, and my dear son with it. And if he were standing here before you now, Ranulf would say the same. Your own father might take a different view. He might consider a landless match beneath his only daughter; he might feel he could do better for you elsewhere. And it would be his right.'

'I want nothing else,' Ragna declared, anger flaring instantly. 'And I will have the father of my child to husband, or I will have no one. They will put me in my grave before I wed another.'

'Shh,' soothed Niamh gently. 'To speak so is to arouse the Devil's regard. Let us pray instead that the Good Lord will grant you your heart's desire.'

Ragna smiled. 'Despite those selfish kings.'

'Of course,' agreed Niamh, 'despite all those selfish kings. They are but flesh and blood, and not angels after all.'

She took Ragna's arm, and they strolled on. 'Now then, we must begin to prepare for the infant's arrival. We have clothes to make —'

'Warm clothes,' added Ragna, 'for it will be midwinter.'

They walked arm-in-arm in the gathering dusk, and talked of the preparations to be made in the next months. That night Ragna went to her empty bed with her soul more settled than it had been for a very long time. She fell asleep with a prayer on her lips. 'Lord of Hosts,' she whispered, 'send seventy angels to guard my Murdo, and bring him home to me with all speed. If you but do this for me, you shall never lack for a more faithful servant.'

TWENTY-FOUR

Skidbladnir passed between the Pillars of Hercules and entered the warm blue waters of what the monks called the *Mare Mediterraneus*. 'The Sea of Middle Earth?' wondered Murdo, thinking he must have heard it wrong.

'Exactly,' Fionn told him. 'We have come to the sea in the centre of the Earth. Of all the seas in the world, this is the best. It is the most peaceful and tranquil, and the fishing here is better than anywhere else.'

This boast was put to the test at once, and as the days went by Fionn's assertion did gather substance. Several places they coved for the night provided remarkable catches of fine-tasting fish of several kinds – some of which no one had ever seen before; one time they even caught crabs, which Murdo enjoyed, as they reminded him of Orkney.

A scant three weeks after entering this calm sea, however, the season changed; the good weather deserted them. The days grew colder and the winds increasingly harsh and fickle, and Jon Wing decided it was time to begin searching for winter harbourage. Accordingly, they searched the coastline for a suitable port, eventually settling on the small inland town of Arles, an ancient walled settlement on the southern coast of Gaul in the Kingdom of Burgundy. Jon Wing chose the town especially – rejecting larger port towns like Toulon and Narbonne, which were too big, he said: 'Too many people, too many ships, also too many snares for unwary sailors.' He liked Arles, however, because it was small and quiet; moreover, it was a much cheaper place to stay. Little Arles lay upriver a short distance from the sea, yet possessed a bay and harbour large enough to serve many sea-going trading vessels – a fair number of which had also chosen the inland town for their wintering.

The monks were pleased with the choice; they were more than

happy to spend the cold, rainy days in prayer and discussion with the local clerics at the Cathedral and Priory of Saint Trophime. Their mighty disputations were enhanced with the liberal application of the region's good red wine, which they praised and consumed with equal ardour. The rest of the crew divided their time between the several drinking halls and brothels of the harbour precinct, indulging one desire while contemplating the other.

The enforced idleness hung heavily on Murdo, however; he found little in the town to interest him. Having no itch to enrich the whores of the town, nor thirst enough to keep the brewers busy – neither did the allure of learned debate with Gaulish monks tempt him – he instead occupied himself with climbing the hills beyond the town, or tramping along the quiet river. The hills were green with winter rain, and he liked the scent given off by the low-growing shrubs, but there was little else to recommend them, and he soon turned to exploring the ancient town.

The streets of Arles were narrow and the houses close and crabbed, and shut against the wind gusting chilly and damp out of the north and west. When the sun shone, Murdo strolled the twisting pathways. There were many peculiar-looking buildings: some had been built by the Romans, Brother Fionn told him; the rest were made by the Moors. The Moorish buildings were strange to the eye; with their white walls, and tall, slender columns, curious onion-shaped arches, bulbous towers, and high narrow windows covered with hundreds of squares of glass, Murdo always thought they looked like palaces out of a dream.

The most remarkable of these was an imposing white building which stood on one side of the market square. The market itself was a forlorn place on rainy winter market days; inasmuch as there was little produce to be had, few people bothered to come and, save for a few forlorn sellers of eggs and cheese, Murdo often had the place to himself.

On one of his rambles, he discovered that the quiet little town boasted an armourer. There were two other smiths, he knew, and both supplied the port and farming trade, making fittings for ships and ploughs, and such like. But the third smithy was on the other side of the town, away from the port and market. Murdo stumbled upon the place one day while trying to circumnavigate the town by way of the wall. Drawn by the gusty whoosh of the bellows and the ring of hammer on anvil, he had found a low, dark dwelling built into the old Roman wall. Once a gatehouse, the gate had long since been sealed with stone; the house – little more than a covered recess excavated in the wall – now served a man skilled in making weapons.

The smithy was a warm place to stop on a dark, windy day, and as the craftsmen did not seem to mind his presence, Murdo paused to watch.

'Here now!' called the smith upon noticing the tall young man loitering at the open door. 'You like to work with iron, eh? Maybe you want to be a smith like me.'

Murdo explained that he was a pilgrim in the company of a warband bound for the Holy Land. 'Our ship is wintering here,' he said. 'We will sail again in the spring.'

'Ah, you are from the longship!' answered the smith, his Latin crude, but expressive. 'Very fierce warriors, these Norsemen, I am told. Good weapons they have, too – but mine are better. Come, I will show you something.' He beckoned Murdo into the hut, which was almost completely filled by the enormous central hearth and forge. Taking a glowing stub of iron from the red coals, he said, 'This will be a sword. It does not look like much now, perhaps – but soon! Soon it will fit the hand of a lord in Avignon.'

Murdo learned that the smith – a blunt, sweaty, black-fingered man named Bezu – had two apprentices and, owing to the increased demand for arms and armour brought about by the pope's crusade, two was not enough. Bezu was looking for a third man to help him meet the rising flood of orders for his wares. 'A strong boy like you would make a good smith. I could teach you. I could talk to your father maybe; I think we might come to an agreement.'

Murdo politely declined the offer, but the smithy became the place he visited most often. Indeed, Murdo became such a familiar onlooker that one day they invited him to share their midday meal of salt beef, cheese, and bread; in return for this kindness, he stayed to help with some of the smaller chores. When they had finished for the day, Bezu told him he was welcome to come and work and eat with them the next day.

Murdo happily agreed, and was soon spending much of his time with the armourer and his apprentices. The three worked together in a convivial haze of heat and smoke and earthy conversation, and Murdo enjoyed their camaraderie as much as he enjoyed watching them hammer the glowing red iron into sword-blades, spearheads, and shield-bosses. Bezu let Murdo try his hand at the bellows, and when he professed to enjoy this labour, the smith asked him whether he would like to learn how to make a spear.

'First, we must select the iron,' Bezu said, pawing through a stack of long, flat lengths of the black metal, some almost as long as Murdo was high. This amazed Murdo, who had imagined the head of a spear to be more properly fashioned from a short, thick square.

'Ah, this is where you are wrong, young Murdo. We are making this lance in the old Roman way,' the armourer told him. Laying a finger beside his nose, he added, 'It is a secret my family has kept for ten generations.'

'And you will tell me?' wondered Murdo, flattered by this unexpected confidence. 'Why?'

Bezu shrugged. 'Perhaps I show you, and you change your mind and stay to learn my craft.' He smiled. 'Also, what good is a secret if you cannot tell it once in a while?' Bending to the stack of iron, he pulled out a long, thin strap, as wobbly as a snake. 'Here!' he cried, handing the iron to Murdo. 'This for you!'

Murdo grasped the cold shank of rusty metal, regarding the wobbly length dubiously. 'It does not seem much to you now maybe,' the armourer suggested. 'But soon – a spear fit for the hand of a lord.'

Bezu then began showing his new pupil the long process of shaping the strap of iron: heating it in the forge, flattening it, folding it, squaring it, and then gently rounding the upper half, a third portion of which was folded over upon itself, squared and flattened once more, leaving a ridge in the centre and flaring the edges to form a stubby, leaf-shaped blade. Murdo liked working the iron, but regarded his handiwork as more of a curiosity than a weapon. Certainly, an iron spear was too heavy to throw, and the blade was too short and blunt to do much more than puncture.

'Just wait until you put the shank into the wooden shaft,' Bezu told him, showing how the long iron core would be inserted into a shaped haft of ash or oak. 'Like so, eh? The blade cannot become separated from the shaft, and the core makes the shaft as strong as iron. When it is finished, you have a spear which cannot be broken! *That* is the Roman way.'

Thus, Murdo occupied the wet winter months, coming early to

the smithy most days and working until dusk, often spending the night beside the hearth as well. When the closeness of the smithy stifled rather than warmed, Murdo would go out and perch himself on the old Roman harbour wall and spend the day wrapped in his cloak gazing out across the low-lying countryside towards the sea. Rain or sun – it made no difference to Murdo. The damp spates of wind and rain which the realm of Burgundy suffered were balmy as summer showers compared to the howling, spitting, bone-cracking winter storms of Orkneyjar.

On these occasions, and much of the rest of the time as well, he thought of Ragna, and what he would do when next he saw her; he thought about the two of them making love, making a home, making a life together. He thought of Hrafnbú, and how he and his father and brothers would win it back from the treacherous usurper Orin Broad-Foot. He thought of his mother, and he hoped she was well and not worrying about him. He took great solace from the fact that she was with Ragna; that the two of them should be together enjoying one another's company warmed his thoughts on dismal days.

As the wheel of the year turned slowly around to spring once more, he grew restless to resume the voyage. Day after day, he watched the low clouds sailing southward, and wondered when Jon Wing would summon the crew and cast off. He went to the harbour often and almost always found the sea lord and two or three crewmen tending to small chores: braiding ropes, mending the sail, repairing oars, and such like. Murdo guessed the time was fast approaching when they would leave, yet whenever he asked, the ship's master would squint up at the sky, taste the breeze, and announce, 'Not today.' Jon would shake his head slowly. 'Tomorrow maybe. You have one more day on dry land.'

Tomorrow would come and the answer would be the same. Then, just when Murdo was beginning to think they would never sail again, Jon looked at the sky and pointed to the north-flying clouds. 'Today we buy provisions. Tomorrow we sail.' He then ordered Murdo to go and fetch the crew from whatever hall or brothel they were to be found, and bring them to the ship.

The chore was quickly accomplished; most of the men, having squandered all their silver long ago, were now eager to sail on. Brothers Ronan, Fionn, and Emlyn were dragged from the cathedral cloisters where they were holding forth, and were despatched to the grain merchant, brewer, and butcher for provisions – this was because no wheedling tradesman ever got the better of the shrewd clerics when it came to striking a bargain.

While the monks were gathering the necessary victuals, the rest of the crew undertook to make certain the longship was sea-worthy. The mild winter had left the hull in fine condition – with no water freezing in the joints and ropes, and no raging gales to batter the mast and rudder – so only scrubbing and cleaning was needed. They raised the tent over the platform behind the mast, and by the end of the day, when the casks and bags and boxes of provisions began arriving at the quay, the ship was fit for the seas once more.

Jon Wing, pleased with the work, released the crew to the drinking hall for one last revel in port, and Murdo went off with them. He did not go to the nearby hall, however, but to the smithy to bid farewell to his friends.

'If you stayed a little longer,' Bezu told him, 'we might have made an armourer of you yet.' Producing Murdo's spear, he gave it to him, saying, 'I think you might have need of this where you are going.'

'But I have nothing to give you for it.'

'No matter,' Bezu replied. 'It is my gift to you.'

'I meant to finish it,' Murdo said, regarding the naked length of hammered iron. Crudely worked, and lacking any appearance of lethal power, it was, in Murdo's estimation, handsome nonetheless. 'I wish I had something to give you.'

'Take it – finish it,' the armourer insisted. 'And when men ask you where you came by such a fine and fearsome weapon, you will tell them Bezu, the Master Armourer of Arles, will make them one just as good. Agreed?'

'Agreed.' Murdo thanked him for the gift, and told them all that if they ever came to Orkneyjar, they would receive a hearty welcome. Bezu walked with him part way down the street, and then, looking up at the sky, eyes asquint in the quickly fading daylight, wished him a good journey and hurried back to his hovel. Murdo retraced his steps to the harbour and climbed aboard the longship.

'What is that you have there?' asked Jon Wing as he clambered aboard.

'It is a spear I've been making,' Murdo answered, holding the length of black iron out for admiration.

'Is it?' chuckled Jon. 'It does not look much like a spear. Are you sure it is not a pole for prodding pigs?'

'It is not finished yet,' Murdo replied sourly. 'It needs wood for the shaft, and then it must be sharpened.'

The seaman laughed. 'So this is what you have been doing all this time! I thought you had a girl in the town.' Pointing at the lance, he said, 'From the looks of this, maybe you should try your luck with the girls next time.'

Not caring to provoke any more mirth at his own expense, Murdo retreated to his customary place at the prow where he quickly tucked the unfinished weapon up under the ship's rail before anyone else should see it. The crewmen returned late that night, and the next morning at dawn Jon Wing roused them and gave the command to cast off. The longship was rowed into the bay and down the river. Once past the headland, they raised the sail and caught the first wind; the sail snapped taut, bellied out, and the *Skidbladnir*, as if delighted to be free once more, surged forward, cleaving the waves and throwing spray either side of the prow.

The journey resumed, and so too the search for King Magnus' ships. Murdo was certain that any day they would find the king's fleet – only the pilgrimage would be over and the ships would be sailing home. Nevertheless, as they slowly worked their way along the coast, pushing ever east and south, they began hearing news of the crusaders' progress. The Genoese, whose ships supplied the armies, brought back stories, and these were passed on in the ports where they stopped for water and supplies.

Although they always asked if anyone had seen the Norse fleet, the answer was always negative: no one had seen or heard of King Magnus or his ships. One scrap of information did prove useful, however. They learned from the harbour master in Trapani that the crusaders were not in Jerusalem at all, but on their way to Antioch, an inland city some distance to the north of the Holy Land. What is more, this report, he said, was very recent: not more than eight or ten weeks old.

'Antioch!' Murdo exclaimed when he found out. He had heard the name once or twice before and, though he had no idea where it might be, it sounded like a needless delay to him. 'Why would they go there? It must be a mistake.'

'Not at all,' Ronan corrected gently. 'Antioch is a great city, with formidable defences. Any war host moving overland would have to pass Antioch in order to reach Jerusalem. Indeed, the merchants have been supplying grain and wine to the camps, and they are saying the crusader armies are encamped before the walls of Antioch even now.'

'Antioch is closer than Jerusalem,' Fionn said. 'No doubt we will find King Magnus there.'

They sailed on, and the days grew longer. The sea, deep blue and alive with porpoises and small fish that skittered over the waves, grew warmer, and the islands smaller and more numerous. To Murdo, who was used to the low, smooth, green humps of the Dark Islands, the isles of the Middle Sea seemed to be mostly sharp escarpments of bare rock with tufts of grey-green thorny brush clinging precariously to life. Consequently, the arid islands, with their glistening white towns glimpsed among the blue coves and vine-covered clefts of valleys, held little appeal for him; he thought them impossibly dry, dust-filled, and sleepy, and could not imagine anything of interest ever happening. Unlike the monks, who enjoyed wandering around the tiny, fly-blown settlements, talking Greek to the inhabitants, Murdo considered every moment spent ashore a moment wasted. He could not wait to get to Antioch to find his father.

Some weeks later, they heard from a fisherman in Paphos on the island of Creta, who had heard from another fisherman, who had heard from an olive oil merchant who conducted trade between several of the many islands, that some Norse ships had indeed been seen in southern waters. Although he could not be certain, it was thought the fleet of ships was making for Cyprus.

They heard no more about this until reaching Kyrenia on the island of Cyprus, when this story was confirmed. 'They say the longships passed by here two or three weeks ago,' Ronan explained. 'One of the traders said he heard a fleet of Norse ships put in for water and supplies a few leagues up the coast on the mainland – at a place called Korykos.'

Jon Wing nodded. 'Three weeks ago,' he mused, looking at the cloudless sky and stroking his beard thoughtfully. 'They will have joined the siege, I think.'

'Indeed,' the elder cleric agreed, 'the merchant said it is but two or three days from here – four at most, if the wind is contrary.'

Murdo heard this and his heart beat faster. He could be with his father in two or three days!

Having come so far, to be this close – it was all he could do to contain himself while Jon Wing and Ronan walked down the quayside to consult the master of one of the trading vessels about the best way to reach Antioch. They returned after a lengthy conversation, and Jon began shouting orders to the crew sitting and lying on the wharf. In an effort to speed their departure, Murdo dashed everywhere at once, helping with the ropes, readying the sails, unbinding the oars. Ronan, meanwhile, retraced his steps into the town to summon his brother priests, who were lingering in the marketplace.

Soon *Skidbladnir* was ready to push away from the wharf, and Murdo had just volunteered to go in search of the monks, when they appeared, hastening for the ship as fast as their burdens of wine, goat's cheese, and olives allowed. They handed their bundles down, and dropped into the boat. Taking up an oar, Murdo helped push away from the wharf, and then settled himself on a rowing bench and rowed as if he would single-handedly propel the ship from the harbour. As soon as they were clear of the other craft, Jon called 'up sails,' and Murdo was there to lend a hand with that, too.

It took a while for the wind to find them, but as they came out of the windshadow of the headland to the west, the sails rippled and filled, and the dragonhead prow began to slice blue water once again. They shipped their oars and bound them once more, and Murdo found himself at the rail searching the horizon with an air of expectation he had not felt in many, many days. Emlyn, moving back to the tented platform behind the mast, passed by him; in his exuberance, Murdo remarked aloud, 'In three days we will be in Antioch, and I will find my father.'

'So I have heard,' Emlyn replied; he stopped and leaned against the rail. 'I am glad for you. It has been a very long trip – a good one, but very long.' He paused, regarding Murdo amiably. 'Have you thought about how you will go about finding your father and brothers?'

'That will not be difficult,' Murdo answered confidently. 'They are with the Duke of Normandy. As the city is under siege, I have only to look for the duke's camp and that is where they will be.'

TWENTY-FIVE

The hills rising from the sea, misty purple in the dawnlight, showed no sign of either port or harbour – less yet a city besieged by a hundred thousand warrior pilgrims. Although Murdo had been told that Antioch lay a few leagues inland, he still hoped he might catch a glimpse of it from the sea. Instead, the empty, rock-filled coast stretched out to either side – no towns, no settlements, no holdings of any kind, much less anything resembling the great and ancient city of Antioch. Neither did he see the port of Saint Symeon, which Ronan had said they would find upon reaching the mainland coast.

He folded his arms across his chest and stared out upon the all but featureless coastline. Somewhere on the barren stretch of pale grey rock and dust-coloured brush ahead, King Magnus had put ashore. The best harbourage, they had been told, was to be found at the port town of Saint Symeon. But, save for a single tiny fishing village now glinting small and white in the early morning sun, there was no other human habitation anywhere.

Stepping over the sleeping bodies of his shipmates, Murdo made his way back to the tiller to speak to Sturli, who had taken the last watch on the helm. 'We must have strayed in the night,' Murdo observed sourly. 'There is no port here.'

'Hey-hey,' agreed Sturli. 'But I do not think we drifted off course.'

'We should be able to see the harbour by now,' Murdo told him. He shoved a hand towards the empty hills, now pink in the rising sun. 'Do you see a city anywhere?'

'Nay,' said Sturli, unperturbed by the apparent mistake. 'But I do not think we drifted off course.'

'We must have!' Murdo insisted.

'I do not think so,' Sturli replied, shaking his head. 'We had a clear night and good stars. I know how to steer a ship. Maybe it is *you* that is mistaken, hey?'

Murdo – angry now, as well as disappointed – stomped away and slumped onto his bench once more. He hung over the rail and watched the dull hillscape draw slowly closer, and his mind began to wander; he thought about the journey. It had, as Emlyn said, been a good voyage, all in all. Still, the wheel of the year had turned round once already, and there was still no sight of Jerusalem! It would be another year *at least* before he would see Ragna again.

The thought proved so discouraging, he pushed it firmly from him, and turned instead to thinking about the triumphant day when he and Lord Ranulf would stride boldly into the bishop's lair, and obtain the return of their lands. He imagined the larcenous old cleric down on his knees, weeping his repentance and pleading for his life. He could feel the swordblade in his hand as the point pressed into the thieving bishop's fat throat.

This vision consoled him for a long time as the ship turned and began making its way slowly along the coast. A little while later, they passed a jutting promontory, whereupon Sturli shouted from the tiller, 'The king's ships!'

Murdo was on his feet in an instant, straining for a glimpse of King Magnus' fleet. He scanned the shoreline to the right and left, but saw nothing. 'Where?' he demanded of Hallvard, the sailor beside him on the rail.

'There! The king's ships! I see them!' cried Nial, his arm around the throat of the dragon. He stood on the rail, stabbing a finger at a small cluster of gleaming white buildings clinging to the hillside above a small, rock-sided bay. Murdo squinted his eyes and saw what appeared to be a dark mass on the shining water of the little bay below the town. Rising from this dark mass, like so many headless spears, were the masts of the longships. At long last, they had caught the ever-elusive fleet. Where there were longships, Norsemen could not be far away.

By the time *Skidbladnir* slid into the cove, Murdo was more than ready to face the entire Saracen warhost all by himself. He did not wait for the keel to bump the small stone quay at the end of the village, but jumped into the shallow water and waded to shore.

'There is no one here,' he called to the others splashing up onto the strand behind him. Jon Wing and the three monks came ashore at the quay, and Murdo ran to where they stood. 'The place is deserted.'

The seaman scanned the quiet village's empty footpaths and by-ways and replied, 'We shall see.'

Proceeding on, they paused at the place where the town's single street met the harbour path. Putting two fingers into his mouth, Jon gave a long, shrill whistle. He whistled twice more, and on the third, a door opened at one of the nearby houses and a tall, fair-haired Norseman staggered out. He took one look at the newcomers and shouted something over his shoulder to someone inside the house, then came running down to the shore to meet them.

'Olvar Three-Toes!' shouted Jon Wing. 'We find you at last.'

'Hey-hey,' replied the Norseman, rubbing sleep from his eyes. 'You have found us, Jon Wing. What has taken you so long?'

'We can only sail as fast as the wind allows,' replied Jon.

'No doubt you have stopped for plunder in every town you passed,' replied the sailor named Olvar with a smile. 'This is what has taken you so long, I think.'

'Nay,' answered Jon Wing happily. 'We have these monks with us,' he indicated Ronan, Fionn, and Emlyn coming up behind him, 'so we could not plunder a single town.'

Three more Norsemen emerged from the house and made their way down to the shore, calling noisy greetings to the crewmen they knew. 'Is it just the four of you, then?' asked Jon.

'Hey-hey,' replied Olvar. 'Us four, and six others. We drew lots, and the losers had to stay behind to guard the ships. All the rest have gone to join the siege.'

'Is the city far?' asked Ronan.

'Three leagues – maybe a little more.' Olvar shrugged. 'That is what I heard.'

'What of the villagers here?' asked Emlyn. 'Are they friendly?'

'I think so. Most of them have gone to tend the fields up in the hills. Only a few old ones are left behind, and they keep to themselves mostly, but they give us eggs and cheese.'

'Have you seen any Saracens?' wondered Fionn, staring at the dry, brush-covered hills rising behind the village.

'Nay,' replied Olvar. 'They have all run to the mountains to hide. They are Greeks here anyway.' Turning back to Jon, he said, 'Did you bring any öl? They have only wine in this place, and we are thirsty.'

Jon expressed his regrets, and said that he did not have any ale, either. He then called to some of his crewmen to bring the arms and armour ashore, secure the boat, and prepare to set off.

'You are not staying?' Olvar said, disappointment darkening his sunny features.

'We must hurry to Antioch before the city is taken,' replied Jon, 'otherwise we will get no plunder. Also, the king is waiting for his counsellors.'

As the weapons were unloaded and carried ashore, the six other guardsmen emerged from another house and came to greet their comrades. Weapons were then distributed among the men. Unaccustomed to carrying a heavy shield, Murdo took only a spear for himself; the blade was somewhat rusty from the voyage, but the edge and point were sharp still, and the ashwood shaft was sound. When they were ready, the Norsemen walked with them past the fields beyond the village and showed them which road to follow. Jon and his seafarers, now transformed into a warrior band, bade their comrades farewell, promising to send them ale from Antioch as soon as the city fell.

Murdo, eager to be reunited with his father and brothers, took his place just behind Jon and Ronan, leading the party, and settled into his stride. After so many months at sea, the solid ground felt strange under his feet; he kept expecting the earth to arch and plunge, and continually braced himself for the swell that never came. As they climbed the first low hills beyond the village, he began to notice the smell of the air – heavy and dense as the earth itself, and filled with a hundred heady scents of sun-baked rock and clay and brush and summer flowers.

The morning, already warm, grew steadily warmer the further into the hills they travelled, and Murdo, regretting the times he had complained of the cramped space on deck, began to long for the cooling sea breeze always present aboard the ship. Upon reaching the crest of the highest hill, he turned to look back briefly at the sea glittering flat and calm, and the tiny bay and village already disappearing behind them. Then, shouldering his spear, Murdo turned his face towards the east, and did not look back again.

The sun was directly overhead when they reached the hills above the river plain. Murdo, eyes downcast and squinting against the white-hot light, could feel the skin on the back of his brown neck beginning to sizzle; where the sun struck the top of his head, it felt as if his hair was on fire; the soles of his feet were burning through his leather boots; his heavy siarc, wet through with sweat, stuck to his skin and chafed as he trudged along. Even the monks, who ordinarily made no concession to the weather, gathered up their long robes and tucked the hems into their belts.

The long walk had been hot and tiring, but wholly uneventful. The fierce Syrian sun was beginning its long slow slide into the west when the forerunners sang out that their destination had been sighted. Along with the rest of the war band, Murdo picked up his feet and hastened the last few paces up the long slope to the top of the hill, and the city came into view, rising before them across the Orontes valley like the immense cloudbank of a storm looming on the horizon.

The sight halted the company in their tracks.

The monks had said it was a large city, an important city, a great city – but nothing they said had prepared any of them for the towering magnitude of the place: walls eighty feet high and two leagues long were guarded by three hundred towers, some of which protected the citadel occupying the highest promontory on the eastern wall. The walls on the lower section rose sheer from the slow-flowing river, while those of the upper section were carved out of the mountain itself, allowing the high citadel a commanding view of the valley all the way to the sea on one hand, and the Tarsus mountains on the other.

Murdo gaped in awe. Not only was Antioch the largest, most strongly fortified city he had ever seen, it was also the most beautiful. Looking at it rising across the valley, the straight high walls and towers adazzle in the blinding light, it seemed less a city than an enormous jewel: a monstrous ornament carved of whitest ivory and nestled against the black surrounding mountains, or a colossal milk-coloured moonstone set upon the dusty green of the valley to shimmer gently in the heat haze of a blistering summer day.

Crops and grazing land spread in irregular blotches over the river plain; here and there, Murdo could see men working with teams of oxen. Two roads, passing either way along the river, met at a bridge below the main gate, and there were a few people straggling on the roads, some with ox-carts bearing goods into the city. White birds soared in the air over the fields and above the towering walls.

An air of peaceful, if not oppressive, tranquillity pervaded the valley, and even as Murdo marvelled at the impressive city, his heart fell. He looked left and right along the walls and plains, scanning the hills and fields and river below – if only to confirm what he already knew: there were no tents, no horse pickets, no besieging armies, no defiant banners streaming from the walltops and tower battlements. The crusaders were gone.

He stood and gazed into the placid, empty valley, and felt the frustration uncoiling within him. The pilgrims had not come to Antioch after all; or, if they had, they were not there now. Either way, the search would have to continue. Even as bitter disappointment crushed him down, however, Brother Ronan said, 'The siege is ended. They have taken the city.'

Of course, thought Murdo, *they have taken the city! They are all inside the conquered walls.*

Suddenly, he could not wait to be there, too. Within three heart-beats, Murdo, and all the rest of the Norsemen, were flying down the hill towards the plain. It was not long before their steps became more cautious, however. 'See here!' shouted Fafnir, a little way ahead of the group. Murdo saw him stoop and bring up a broken sword from the long, dry grass. Almost at once, Vestein, no more than a dozen paces away, produced half of a shield and the broken haft of a spear. 'There was a battle here, I think,' said Fafnir.

They proceeded on, but more slowly, and the further they went, the more they found: battered war helms of a strange, pointed kind; lightweight oval shields made of boiled leather; arrows by the score, most of them broken. And scattered in amongst the remnants of battle, they found the remains of the warriors. Murdo bent down to retrieve a finely curved piece of a bow, and discovered the weapon was still attached to the hand that had last employed it. Both hand and arm came away as Murdo lifted it. There arose a fearsome, stinging stench, and he caught a glimpse of white maggots wriggling from a brown mass by his feet as he dropped the bow and jumped back with a shout.

The corpse was so far decomposed that it no longer looked human; Murdo had simply not seen it when he bent down. He saw it now for what it was and, realizing what lay before him, he began to see others as well. They had come to the part of the battleground where the fighting had been the fiercest, and the dead were lying where they had fallen.

Once fine clothes and cloaks were filthy, rotting rags; flesh and muscle were blasted black by the sun, and withered hard like old leather. Many of the bodies had been attacked by birds and beasts, and, more and more, Murdo caught the glint of smooth white bone gleaming dully from the long grass round about. Once, he stepped over what appeared to be the lower torso of a man and his foot struck what he thought was a stone. The stone rolled, however, and Murdo found himself staring down into a withered brown, worm-ravaged face, whose empty eye sockets gazed darkly up past him and into the sun-bright heavens above.

Murdo clamped a hand over his nose and mouth, and moved on, no longer looking either right or left. It occurred to him as he trudged along that he saw no carcasses of horses, and he wondered about this. Unless the battle had been fought entirely on foot, which he very much doubted, there must certainly have been some horses killed, too. What could have happened to them?

Upon reaching the plain, they passed through several grain fields and proceeded towards the entrance to the city, meeting no challenge until, upon crossing the bridge, they came to the huge, open gate. Six guards in loose, light-coloured mantles – three at either of the enormous doors – noticed their weapons and stopped them. 'You there! Halt!'

Murdo was surprised to hear these dark-skinned men speaking Latin. 'What is your business here?' demanded the foremost guard; he held a long, flat-bladed lance, and carried a short sword in his belt. A large man, he nevertheless looked ill-fed and haggard; those with him appeared even less robust. Murdo decided they looked like men dragged from their sickbeds and forced to stand guard.

Ronan answered. 'Pax Vobiscum!' he declared benevolently, raising his hands in priestly blessing. 'Greetings in the name of Our Lord Christ. My friend, we are pilgrims on our way to Jerusalem. We were told that this city was yet under siege, but it appears we were ill-informed.'

'The siege is over long since,' replied the soldier, eyeing them with tired suspicion. 'The armies have moved on.'

'Ah, yes,' answered Ronan, nodding sympathetically. 'As it happens, my brothers and I are priests, as you can see, and we travel in the company of vassals belonging to Magnus, King of Norway, whom we were hoping to meet here. We were told he has come to Antioch, I hope we are not mistaken.'

'Oh, him,' said the soldier, relaxing at last. 'He is here. You may enter.' He motioned them through with the head of his spear.

'You know him! Good. Could you tell us where we might find the king?' asked Ronan hopefully.

'All the lords are received at the citadel,' the guardsman said. 'That is all I know.'

The elder priest thanked the man for his help, gave him a blessing, and they continued on their way, passing between the great, iron-bound timber doors, and into the cool, shadowed darkness of the gate-tower. The respite was all too brief, however; a moment later, they were stepping once more into the harsh sunlight striking off the stone pavements all around. Momentarily blinded, Murdo put up his hand to shade his eyes; when he looked again, he found he was standing in the middle of a street, the like of which he had never encountered.

Stretching as far as the eye could see was a wide, stone-paved avenue lined with tall, graceful columns either side; moreover, these columns supported a second row of columns bearing a vine-covered roof to shelter the walkway below. The civility of this feature amazed Murdo when he realized that the people of the city were not forced to walk in the street with the carts and animals, but beneath a leaf-shaded arbour which kept the hot sun off their heads.

Rising from the broad, flat river bluff on which the city was founded, this remarkable double colonnade swept gracefully towards the heights of the cliffs and mountains, whose peaks could be seen soaring above the rooftops and domes just beyond the city to the south. Straight as a rod along its entire length, the broad street passed the ruin of an old Roman amphitheatre, an enormous basilica, and an elegant palace faced with glowing yellow marble. There were so many churches that Murdo soon lost count and interest, delighting himself instead with the profusion of palm trees, and brightly-coloured flowers growing in massive earthenware tubs everywhere.

Up the street they went, passing along the stately row of columns, past gleaming white houses with pierced-screen windows and bronze-figured doors. In niches high up in the walls of some of the more elaborate houses, statues looked gravely down upon the passing troop. Perhaps due to the heat of the day, the newcomers had the street and shaded walkway mostly to themselves. Apart from a few ragged water vendors pushing carts laden with clay jars there were few citizens about. They passed likewise empty sidestreets, and a vacant marketplace sweltering in the sun.

Over all the city, a quiet lethargy hung like a pall draped upon a gilded tomb. Murdo had imagined that a city of such size and grandeur must be thronging with people day and night, and the scarcity of citizens surprised him so that he began to wonder at it. Where was everyone? And where were the crusaders? Even if the whole population had been driven off, there should have been pilgrims aplenty to crowd the streets and marketplaces.

But, save for the occasional creak of a wagon wheel, or the rushing flap of pigeon wings as they passed another empty square, the city was quiet. The Norsemen noticed this, too, and their jovial exuberance grew more and more muted and subdued the further up the street they walked, until no one spoke at all, and they passed by the dark and silent houses in a bristling hush.

The wide central street ended at the citadel in the upper part of the city; the final climb to the fortress was the steepest part of the walk, and it left the seafaring warriors winded by the time they reached the square fronting the stronghold. On the left-hand side of the square, beneath the stronghold, four pairs of low, wide doors marked out the stables. The foremost pair of doors gaped open, and from stone troughs on either side, twin vines grew and spread to form a bower before the entrance where five or six men sat lolling in the drowsy shade.

At the approach of the newcomers, one of the men stood and came forward a few steps. He turned and called behind him to someone inside, then came on to meet them. He raised his hand to halt them as five or six more men tumbled out of the stable doorway behind him. The company stopped uncertainly, and waited.

The man spoke to them in a tongue which none of them could understand. When he received no reply, he spoke again, in Latin this time. 'What is your purpose here?' he demanded, hand on the knife in his belt.

'We have come to join Magnus, King of the Norsemen,' replied Brother Ronan crisply. 'Is the king to be found here?'

Before the guard could answer, one of the men behind him pushed forward suddenly. 'Jon Wing!' cried the man in loud Norsespeak. 'So! You come dragging in at last.'

'Hey-hey!' replied Jon happily. 'Here we are. And who is the first person we should meet?' Turning to the others just behind him, Jon called, 'See here! If they are letting a skull-breaker like Hakon

Fork-Beard prowl the streets in broad daylight, I know we have come to the right place.'

The two men clapped one another on the back and embraced like kinsmen. They began talking loudly together. More men were staggering out of the stables to join them; the priests, and some of the other crewmen gathered around, happily exchanging greetings with the others like long-lost kinsmen. Murdo stood looking on, suddenly very aware that the moment he had long awaited was upon him, and that his carefully nurtured resolve was swiftly deserting him.

'Come, wayward Sea Wolves!' said the man, his voice booming in the quiet square. 'The king will be glad to know his priests and pirates have arrived. Follow me!'

He led them to the door of the stables where he was met on the threshold by another Norseman – taller, younger, and dressed in breecs of brown leather, and a fine new linen siarc. His hair was long and fair, his braid thick. The two exchanged a word, and the one called Hakon motioned them inside, while the stranger stepped aside to greet the newcomers as they passed.

Murdo took his place behind Oski and Ymir at the end of the line. He hung his head and tried to creep by, hoping he would not be noticed. This hope died in vain, for as he came to the doorway, the fair-haired Norseman saw him, and put a hand to his chest and stopped him. 'Here now!' he said. 'Who is this with his bold glance?' He moved the hand to Murdo's chin and raised his face. 'Where did these Sea Wolves get you, boy?'

Since he had no other choice, Murdo squared his shoulders, raised his head, and looked the man straight in the eye. 'My name is Murdo Ranulfson,' he answered forthrightly. 'I came aboard with the priests at Inbhir Ness.'

'Did you now!' The man eyed him up and down. 'Why would you do that?'

Brother Ronan appeared at the Norseman's shoulder. 'Murdo here has taken the cross and has come to join his father and brothers who are also on pilgrimage to the Holy Land.'

The fair-haired man accepted this with a nod. 'Where is your home, boy?'

'Orkneyjar, my lord,' Murdo answered, and inwardly cringed. Why had he said that?

'Orkneyjar!' repeated the man, much impressed. 'I have lands in the Dark Isles, too. It seems we are fellow countrymen, you and I. Greetings and welcome, Murdo Bold-Eye.' He offered his hand in friendship.

Murdo grasped the offered hand, and grinned at his new name: Murdo Bold-Eye. He liked that very much.

'We Orkneyingar should watch out for one another, hey?'

'Just so,' agreed Murdo readily, forgetting his wariness.

'If you find yourself in trouble, just sing out for Orin Broad-Foot, and you will have a stout sword at your side before you can turn around.' The lord slapped him on the back, and bade him enter and partake of the welcome cup.

Murdo stumbled forward into the cool darkness of the room, feeling lost and confused. He had just accepted the friendship and protection of his avowed and hated enemy.

TWENTY-SIX

In the short time King Magnus had been in residence, the main room of the citadel's stables had been turned into something which at first sight more closely resembled a drinking hall than a horse barn. Seven long boards with benches either side had been erected in the centre of the great room, and the former stalls were filled with fresh straw to serve as sleeping places for the warriors.

Murdo sat at the end of the long board by himself, his head in his hands, his cup untouched. The realization that he had just pledged friendship to his worst enemy plunged Murdo into a sulky dejection. It would have been far easier to hate him if Orin Broad-Foot had revealed himself to be the pig-eyed, greedy, hump-backed brute Murdo had so often imagined him. That Lord Orin was a friendly and gracious – perhaps even honourable and trustworthy – nobleman would make it that much harder to betray him when the time came.

I have lands in Orkneyjar, too, Orin had said. Murdo groaned at his own stupidity. How could he have missed that? He *knew* he was coming into the enemy's lair. He had foreseen this day a thousand times since leaving home. He should have been on his guard; he should have been ready. *Stupid, stupid, boy!* Why, oh why, had he allowed himself to be taken in by the amiable lord?

It took all Murdo's considerable stubbornness and determination to rekindle some small remnant of his enmity. It was only when he reminded himself that he was now at long last among the very men who had conspired to steal his family's lands and deprive him of his birthright – it was only when he remembered Ragna, and the unthinkably barren future without her, that he was able to regain some portion of his former animosity.

Beware, Murdo! he told himself. *These men are not your friends. They have robbed you and your family. Do not be distracted by their winsome ways. They would destroy you without a thought. Guard yourself against them. Remain vigilant. Your chance to avenge the wrong will come.*

Still, he felt ill-used and vaguely cheated – as if he had been offered a boon of considerable comfort and value, but forced on principle to refuse it. He sat glumly by himself and watched the rest of the company as glad welcome turned into revel. He felt alone and angry with himself, and his hard circumstance.

The fact that his father and brothers were no longer in Antioch did not help improve his spirits. That hope had been dashed the very moment he set foot in the citadel stable, for Jon Wing, turning to Lord Orin entering behind him, had asked, 'Where are all the people? Is the city deserted then?'

'Almost,' replied Orin. 'Those who did not die in the battle were killed by the plague which followed the siege. We saw nothing of this, mind you – it was some months ago. The fighting and sickness was long over by the time we got here. The pilgrims were gone, too.'

'All of them?' wondered Jon. 'Who holds the city now? King Magnus?'

'Nay,' Orin replied, 'it belongs to one called Bohemond – a Frankish prince.' He then went on to explain how the crusaders had marched on to Jerusalem only a day or two before their arrival, and how this Bohemond had hired King Magnus and his men to help guard the city.

Murdo, hearing enough, had then slunk away to the end of the furthest bench where he now sat, gazing into his shallow cup as if it were the end of the world he saw glimmering dully within. He sat aloof from the others, and hardened himself against those he must now deceive for the sake of his vow. Brother Emlyn, seeing his friend sitting alone, begged him to come and join them. Murdo declined, saying that he was tired from the long walk, and wished only to rest.

'Come now, Murdo!' Fionn called, lofting the bowl. 'A wee sip of wine before lying down.'

Still, Murdo refused. Placing his spear beside the others lined against the wall, he dragged himself off to a quiet corner and collapsed into it. He closed his eyes and pressed his hot back and shoulders against the cool stone, feeling the delicious shock of the chill against his skin.

He sat for a while, listening to the clamour of voices across the vaulted room and wishing he could join in the revelry. Instead, he crossed his arms across his chest and pretended to sleep – all the while grinding his teeth against the malicious tricks of an indifferent God – always giving with one hand, while snatching away with the other. The injustice of this bitter observation occupied him until the members of the king's foraging party trooped noisily into the stables, bearing the day's findings: sacks of greens and flat bread. Close on their heels came the rest of the king's men – over two hundred in all – returning from their duties at the garrison in the lower city. In the commotion caused by their arrival, Murdo slipped out of the stable and into the dusky light of a dying day.

Though the sun had set in a murky white haze in the west, and the streets were sinking into shadow, heat still streamed from the pavements and stonework of the buildings all around. Murdo began walking, passing along a path so narrow he could have touched the buildings on either side with outstretched hands, and so low that the doors of the houses could only be reached by high stone steps set in the pavements. Shuttered windows fronted the street; the shutters were open now that the sun was gone, and strange smells reached him from open windows above; the scents of flowers, and food cooking, and fragrant smoke mingled to produce ineffably exotic aromas.

The street opened just ahead, and he soon came to a marketplace – deserted now, its only occupant a skinny dog nosing in a heap of dung and refuse off to one side of the square. The miserable dog slunk away the moment the lanky human appeared, head low, tail between its legs. And then Murdo had the place all to himself.

The square was bounded on one side by a stone breastwork, and Murdo wandered over to see the entire city of Antioch spread out beneath him in a haphazard jumble of rooftops: flat squares beyond number, all falling away in dizzying terraces down the steep-sloped streets towards the all-encompassing walls.

Softened by smoke and evening light, the colour fading into the gentler hues of night, the close-crowded chaos took on a friendlier aspect. On most of the rooftops he could see small trees and leafy shrubs growing, and even the smallest had a vine or two forming an arbour for shade; on many of the rooftops he saw people going about their chores, taking in the day's washing, perhaps, or cooking their evening meals; the smoke from the countless braziers drifted like silver threads in the still, heavy air. He could hear the voices of the people – shouts of children echoing unseen in the streets, and somewhere a baby was crying.

What must it be like, he wondered, to live so close to so many others? What manner of people built such cities as this? Did they never yearn for the clean, empty sweep of sea and sky, or the softly-rounded hills progressing in their gentle undulations towards the far distant horizon?

He gazed out across the jumbled rooftops. Countless domes bulged among and above the flat roofs of the houses. Some of the domes boasted odd round towers beside them; from the tops of these he could see curious standards in the shape of crescent moons. Many more of the domes, however, bore crosses, identifying them as churches; Murdo began counting the crosses, but soon lost count and turned his attention instead to the many-towered walls and the land beyond. A handful of stars glimmered low in the swiftly-darkening skies above the Tarsus mountains to the north. Away to the west lay the sea, and to the east, the dark meandering thread of the dull Orontes river.

It was not a place he would choose to live, he decided. Even in such an enormous place as Antioch, Murdo felt the great walls looming, pressing in; the closeness of the city's houses and churches seemed to clutch at him. Feeling suddenly cramped and confined, he turned and walked from the square, returning to the citadel as the last light faded from the sky overhead.

The sound of raucous laughter spilled out from inside the stables and Murdo entered, hoping to creep back into his corner unnoticed. It was not to be, however, for Orin Broad-Foot saw him and called out, 'Come, Murdo! I would have you meet your lord and king.'

Murdo took a deep breath, turned, and crossed the room to where the king and his noblemen sat at table. Jon Wing sat at the king's right hand, and Orin Broad-Foot on the left; the three monks, happy to be reunited with their benefactor, sat beaming beside Jon, and others Murdo did not know filled the rest of the places. But it was the sovereign alone who held Murdo's interest.

King Magnus, while not as tall as Orin, nor as well-muscled as Jon Wing, nevertheless possessed a powerful presence that com-manded the regard, if not the respect, of all who came under his sway. His beard and hair were plaited, the dark braids oiled so they glistened; his eyes were pale as the Skandian sky, alert and intelligent.

His smile was a sunflash of brilliant goodwill, and his manner at once casual and dignified.

As Murdo approached, taking the measure of the Norse king, he heard Orin say, 'Here now, my lord, I give you one of your own – an Orkneyingar by the name of Murdo Bold-Eye.'

'So!' cried the king in good-natured surprise. 'Hail and welcome, friend. How is it that one so young is to be numbered among my warrior host?'

Murdo was saved having to give an explanation by Jon Wing, who at that very moment leapt up from his chair and climbed onto the table, his cup in his hand. 'Hear! Hear!' he called, lofting his cup. 'Hail, King Magnus!' he cried, and began loudly pledging his loyalty to the king while the men all around pounded the boards with their fists, or the handles of their knives. The newcomers all drank the health of the king, whereupon others, not to be outdone, also rose to renew their vows of fealty and offer up compliments to the king.

Murdo did not stand waiting long, but took the first opportunity to slink away. He found a place at one of the tables and settled in between Tiggi and Arnor. There was bread in baskets before him, and soup in a small tun. Taking up an empty bowl, he dipped it into the tun, helped himself to a piece of flat bread, and began to eat. The soup, made from the greens collected earlier, was thin and tasteless, and the bread tough; still, after the day's walk, he was glad to get something warm inside him. He ate two bowls of soup, and three pieces of bread before stealing away again to one of the stalls to sleep.

He had just scraped together enough straw to make a bed when Emlyn appeared with a bowl, which he pressed into his hands. The wine was sweet and pleasantly cool. Murdo drank a deep draught, thanked the priest and handed back the cup, whereupon Emlyn sat down beside him. 'Ah, mo croidh,' he sighed. 'I do not think I will last very long in this land. All the saints bear witness, it is so *hot*!'

'You would not feel it so much if you were not so fat,' Murdo told him.

'Have you heard what they are saying?' asked the monk, sipping from the cup. 'They are saying a miracle happened here.'

'What kind of miracle?' Murdo took the cup and drank again.

'Something to do with an earthquake, and the discovery of the Holy Lance,' the priest replied. 'They say that was how they were able to defeat the Saracens, but inasmuch as none of them were here at the time, they cannot say more.'

The comment did not seem to require any reply from Murdo, so he lifted the cup to his mouth and drank some more. Miracles, so far as he could tell, always happened to someone else at some other time and in some other place.

'Also,' the breathless monk continued, 'it seems the Patriarch of Antioch has been restored to his position, and the church of Saint Peter has been reconsecrated. We are going there tomorrow, so we will ask the priests what they know of this miracle. Come with us, Murdo. It is a very ancient and venerable church. You should see it.'

Murdo shrugged. 'I have seen old churches before.' He drank again.

'Antioch, Murdo!' the monk exclaimed suddenly. 'This is the city where the followers of Jesu received the name Christian. Think of it! Here the apostle Paul and the blessed Barnabas preached and taught in the earliest days of our faith. Saint Peter himself ordained the first bishop, and commanded the church to be built on the very place where Paul stood in the market and proclaimed the Risen Lord to the Greeks and Jews of this land. It is a very holy place.'

Murdo nodded and passed the cup to Emlyn, and leaned his head against the cool wall. 'How long must we stay here?'

'Who can say?' replied the priest. 'King Magnus has agreed to help Prince Bohemond defend the city. In return he has been given a hundred thousand marks in silver, and this,' he gestured expansively to the room, 'the former stables, for his retinue. The king has rooms above, and –'

'Why does this Prince Bohemond need the king's help?' Murdo interrupted. He could see no reason why they should not simply press on to Jerusalem.

The monk explained that, owing to the cruel predations of the Syrian campaign, Prince Bohemond now found himself in desperate need of mercenaries to help hold his newly-won city. So many of his own knights and footmen had succumbed to starvation, plague, and Seljuq arrows, that his formerly great army was reduced in size to that of a merely respectable regiment.

'Indeed, they are saying that more than twenty thousand followed the prince from Taranto, but only nine hundred remain,' Emlyn told him, adding that many of these were yet recovering from the fever that had swept the city in the wake of the crusader victory. Hence, fit fighting men were of such value, the wily prince had granted the lately-arrived Norsemen not only a vast quantity of silver, but also the best of food and shelter he had to offer as well – all in exchange for their vaunted battleskill and eagerness for plunder.

'I thought now that we were all together, we would go on to Jerusalem to join the pilgrimage.'

'I suppose we shall,' answered Emlyn. 'But there is a time for everything, Murdo, and a season for every purpose under Heaven. We will get to Jerusalem in God's good time, never fear. But we are *here* now – so enjoy!' The monk raised the cup and drained it in a long, guzzling swallow.

Murdo frowned. The whole world, it seemed, was travelling to Jerusalem and here he was, stranded in Antioch. It beggared belief.

'This cup is empty,' Emlyn declared. Heaving himself onto unsteady legs, he staggered off in search of more wine.

'Enjoy,' muttered Murdo darkly.

Despite the merrymaking, the day's exertion and the wine combined to give Murdo a good night's sleep. He awoke early – just in time to see the three monks leaving for their dawn service. He kept his head down until they left so he would not have to decline the inevitable invitation to go with them, then rose quickly and hurried off, intending to stay out of the king's sight as much as possible to save having to explain his presence.

Taking a piece of bread from last night's supper with him, he gnawed the loaf and walked again to the square he had visited the night before. The city looked far different in the morning light, but no better for it, he thought. Most of the back streets were beaten earth, and powdered dust coated every surface, making the bottom half of all the buildings the same pale, yellow-grey colour.

As he passed one house, an old woman emerged with a bundle of twigs and began sweeping off the step before her door. She stared at Murdo as he walked by, muttering at him, and crossing herself with the bundle of twigs in her hand.

Although the sun was newly risen, he could feel the heat of the day already mounting in the square. The valley beyond the walls was hung in a thick bluish haze, and the sun, white as a hot poker, burned through a dead pale sky. Even as he stood looking out across the city, the first of the merchants began arriving to erect their stalls in the empty square. Murdo watched as the men and women went about their work, and quickly found himself admiring the clothing they wore. All of them were dressed in billowy flowing mantles that reached from neck to feet, gathered at the waist with a girdle of winding cloth – and all in a wild profusion of colours: blood red and blue stripes; glistening emerald green; deep yellow the hue of egg-yolk; rich brown with purple stripes and tiny silver threads between; pale ivory white, and sky blue; rose pink, and scarlet, and gold, and indigo so blue it was almost black.

Their extravagant clothes made Murdo aware of his own drab appearance. He looked down his length at what he was wearing. Both siarc and breecs were threadbare, and showing through at elbows and knees. Boots and belt were in good condition yet, but his once-handsome red-brown cloak was now faded and travel-stained, and ragged at the edges.

While far from persuaded to adopt the attire of the inhabitants of Antioch, he decided that perhaps he might buy a new siarc at least, and so lingered at the edge of the market while more and more merchants arrived and began busily erecting their cloth-framed shelters, and arranging their various wares, which they placed in baskets, or on mats of woven grass, or strips of cloth on the ground. Many of the traders had donkeys to carry their burdens, others lugged the baskets themselves. Murdo had never seen a donkey before, but thought the small, fuzzy horselike creatures absurd and amusing.

As the marketplace began to fill, Murdo strolled into the square for a closer look at the various wares, and was instantly assailed by a dozen or more brown children, who ran up to him and began tugging on his clothing, and gibbering at him in a strange, chirpy tongue. Some merely held out their hands in gestures of supplication, but others rubbed their stomachs and pointed to their empty mouths.

As he had no intention of giving them anything, he resented their noisy insistence, but tried to extricate himself gracefully – to no avail. The diminutive mob followed him, clinging to him, grasping at him. When he felt a small hand inside his shirt, snatching at the knife Ragna had given him, he became angry.

'Get away from me!' he shouted, seizing the hand and squeezing it hard so that it released the knife. 'Get away!' He stomped his feet at them, and they scattered, only to watch and follow him a few paces further away. His outburst succeeded in drawing the notice of some of the merchants, who likewise began clamouring for his attention. The closer ones came running to him, beseeching him in their strange language, vying for his patronage.

'No! No!' he shouted, walking briskly away. This merely provoked them all the more, and they shouted even more loudly, putting their hands on him, touching him, tugging at him.

Murdo could not abide the commotion. Desperate to flee, he rushed from the square down the nearest street, and kept running. When he was certain he was no longer followed, he stopped to look around and found that not only had he lost the grasping merchants and his beggar escort, he had lost himself. Nothing looked familiar, nor could he tell in which direction he had come, or which way he might be going.

No matter, he told himself, he could easily retrace his steps to the market square. So, he turned around and started back, but soon came to a place where the narrow way divided; the paths diverged to the left and right of a huge stone water basin, now dry and empty. Both pathways looked exactly alike to Murdo, and he had no idea which one he had used before. He chose the right-hand path and proceeded down it with the idea that if he did not recognize it, he could quickly retrace his steps and take the other way. But the street wound around and, upon retracing his steps, he returned only to find that it was not the place he remembered at all.

The divide was gone, and in the place where he imagined the water basin should be was a small domed hut with a crude wooden cross above its door. He turned around and stared down the narrow street, but it all looked strange to him. Had he passed this way? Two men appeared and came towards him. Murdo hailed them in his best Latin, and asked if they could help him find his way. Both men frowned at him and passed by quickly.

Disgusted – as much with himself and his own foolishness, as with Antioch's unhelpful citizenry – he turned and began walking back the way he had come. Again, the street turned on itself somehow and, after a time, Murdo found himself once more before the little chapel.

Frantic now, he set off down the opposite path, almost running. After a time, he heard what he thought must be the sound of the marketplace – the confused babble of voices as the merchants squabbled over customers, and buyers haggled with the sellers. He rushed towards the sound, turned one corner, then another, proceeded down a street that looked somewhat familiar, and . . . found himself standing yet once more before the tiny hut-like chapel.

Fighting down the rising panic, he turned away, intending to retrace his steps yet again. He had not taken more than five steps, however, when he heard a bell chime behind him. He stopped and looked back over his shoulder. The low wooden door was open now, and appeared inviting. He walked to the door and stepped inside.

The room was dark, save for a single small window above the tiny altar. He stood for a moment, allowing his eyes to adjust to the darkness.

'Pax Vobiscum,' said a kindly voice. 'You are welcome here, friend.'

'Pax Vobiscum,' Murdo answered, much relieved to hear a language he could understand. He looked into the darkened interior and a man emerged from the shadows behind the altar. Dressed in monk's robes of white, the figure beckoned him.

'You are new to this city,' the priest observed, moving closer.

'Yes,' Murdo replied. 'We arrived yesterday.'

The man stepped nearer. Murdo saw that he was a young man – at least, his appearance was youthful – with a kindly face. His black hair and beard were cut short, and their curly texture reminded Murdo of lamb's fleece. The teeth revealed in the smile were white and straight. His dark eyes glittered in the weak light from the door; his glance was keen and disturbingly direct.

He regarded Murdo for a moment, then said, 'What is it that you want, my son?'

Absurdly, the first thought to spring into his mind was that he wanted to be home – in Orkneyjar, at Hrafnbú, with Ragna, and the rest of his family around him, and all of them safe and happy for ever. In that instant, he saw himself amongst people in a cool, green valley surrounded by high, handsome hills under a wide open northern sky. Though occupying the briefest of instants – the small space between one heartbeat and the next – this thought produced a pang of yearning so powerful that it took his breath away. He stared at the priest, unable to speak.

'Do not be afraid,' the monk said, lifting his hand in a consoling gesture. 'You are safe here. Tell me, what is it you seek?'

Murdo swallowed, and his voice returned. 'I seem to have lost my way,' he said simply. 'I am trying to find the citadel.'

The priest smiled. 'Take heart. You are closer than you know.'

He stepped nearer. 'Come, I will show you.' The priest brushed past him, and Murdo felt a peculiar sensation on his skin – like the tingling he felt when watching a storm sweeping in off the sea – and he caught a faint whiff of icy, storm-riven air. It was as if something of his homeland had touched him, however fleetingly, and was gone just as quickly.

The white monk led him outside into the street once more. Pointing to the pathway on the right, he said, 'This is the way you must go. At the end of the street, you will find the market and the citadel is beyond.'

Murdo nodded, his heart sinking. He had tried this pathway before – twice, at least – and had not come within shouting distance of the square. Nevertheless, he thanked the monk and made to take his leave.

'Remember: the True Path is narrow, and few enter there,' the priest told him, and oh, the look in those keen dark eyes was like lightning flashing from a clear sky. 'But fortunate are you among men. For to you is given the Holy Light to guide your way. Go with God, my friend.'

Murdo gaped in amazement, unable to comprehend what the mysterious priest had just said to him. The white monk made the sign of the cross over him, and then moved back into the chapel. The door closed and, overcome with the strangeness of the incident, Murdo began walking quickly down the path. Before he knew it the tiny street ended and he was standing at the edge of the busy market square.

He stopped and looked back. The distance was so small – a matter of a few hundred paces. On a sudden impulse, he carefully retraced his steps, and soon arrived at the little crossroads once more. He saw the wider street leading away before him, and the other path which formed the divide angling off on the opposite side. But the chapel was nowhere to be seen, and in its place was the empty stone water basin he had seen before.

He stood for a moment, gazing at the dry basin, a queasy sensation snaking through his bowels. He could not have taken another wrong turning! What had become of the chapel?

And then his eye fell upon something he had not noticed before: a stone plaque set in the wall above the basin, bearing the image of a cross, and on one side of the cross was what appeared to be a spear, and on the other side was a footed bowl. Murdo stared at the image, and traced it with his fingers. Once again, he caught the scent of frigid, storm-driven, rain-washed northern air.

'Take heart,' he whispered, repeating the white monk's words, 'you are closer than you know.' Then, overcome by the strangeness of what had happened to him, he turned and ran back to the square, through the market, and did not stop running until he reached the citadel.

TWENTY-SEVEN

Murdo returned to the citadel to find the place in turmoil. The streets outside the fortress were awash with men and horses and wagons. Soldiers – mostly Franks, by the look of them, but a good few Norsemen as well – were scurrying everywhere, carrying armfuls of weapons, sacks of grain, baskets of foodstuffs; wagons were being readied, and horses saddled, and everyone seemed to be shouting at once. Dodging through the tumult, Murdo pushed his way into the stables.

'There you are!' cried Emlyn as he stepped inside. 'I have been looking for you, Murdo.'

'I walked to the market,' he explained. Indicating the confusion around him, he asked, 'Are we under attack?'

'Magnus is moving the fleet to Jaffa,' the monk said quickly. He made to dart away again. 'We are all making ready to leave.'

'I thought we must stay here to help defend the city,' Murdo pointed out. 'You said –'

'Yes, yes,' replied Emlyn impatiently, 'but Prince Bohemond has been summoned to Jerusalem.'

'Why?'

'The siege has begun. The liberation of the Holy City is at hand!' the cleric proclaimed, raising his hands in praise. 'Let all Heaven and Earth rejoice!'

In spite of himself, Murdo felt a shiver of excitement. At long last . . . Jerusalem!

'We leave at once,' explained the monk. 'It is a ten-day march overland, but only five days by ship. If we hurry, we can get back to the fleet before sunset, and sail tonight. There is Fionn!' the priest declared, and rushed away to speak to his brother monk.

Remembering the long hot walk from the harbour at Saint Symeon, Murdo prepared himself for the return as best he could. He filled a bowl with water and drank it down, then filled and drank another. He then fell in with the others, helping to make ready their departure. The tumult around him resolved itself quickly; the Norsemen were soon pushing through the massed chaos around the citadel and were trooping noisily down the broad colonnaded central street to the gate. With Magnus in the lead, the king's war band crossed the bridge and walked out onto the plain, past the road leading down to the port of Saint Symeon, and on until striking the footpath by which they had come; they were soon climbing the arid, scrub-covered hills, and leaving the city behind.

Upon reaching the top of the first hill, Murdo paused for a last look at Antioch; he gazed back across the valley at the city, its great stone walls white and shimmering in the summer heat. 'Ah, it is a splendid sight,' sighed Emlyn, toiling up beside him. 'I would have liked a few more days to know the place better. Mark me, there are mighty things taking place in that city. God is working there.'

'Did you learn anything more of the miracle?' Murdo asked, more out of idle curiosity than interest.

'Did we learn anything?' hooted Emlyn gently. His face was glistening with sweat, and his breath came in quick gasps, but his stride was easy and strong. He stabbed at the path ahead with his tall rowan staff, the leather pouch swinging at his side. 'We heard a wonder, my doubting young friend. What is more, we heard it all from men who were there – men who saw it with their own eyes.'

'What did they see?' demanded Murdo.

'They saw . . .' said the monk, lifting his eyes towards the sky, as if he might also glimpse a miracle, 'they saw the Holy Lance.'

'What Holy Lance?'

'The spear of the crucifixion!' answered the monk, aghast that Murdo should even wonder, let alone ask such a thing. 'Do you not know of it?'

'I know of it,' he answered, his tone implying that he had been expecting something slightly more remarkable.

'It is nothing less than the spear which pierced Our Lord's precious side and proved before the world and all his enemies that the Blessed Jesu was dead. *That* is the Holy Lance I mean, and it is the holiest, most sacred relic to come down to us,' Emlyn intoned solemnly, 'save one thing alone.'

'What is that?'

'The cup of the Passover Supper,' said the priest. 'That is more holy still. But it is lost long since, and only the spear remains.'

'I suppose that makes the spear the most holy thing after all,' observed Murdo.

Emlyn did not deign to notice the remark. 'The spear was lost, too, until they found it – only a few months ago.'

'They found it?'

'Is that not what I am telling you, Murdo?'

'You are telling very little it seems to me,' Murdo protested. 'First you said they only *saw* it – now you say they *found* it. Which is it?'

Emlyn drew a deep breath. 'I will begin again.'

'And start from the beginning this time,' Murdo instructed.

'Yes, yes,' the monk agreed. 'One of the Roman soldiers present at the execution of our Lord was a centurion by the name of Longinus. As the commander of the execution, it was his duty to see the crucifixion carried out properly and in accordance with the law of the day.

'It was a Friday, as we know, and when the scribes and Pharisees began clamouring that the execution must be completed before sun had set – for it is an abomination to the Jews for a criminal to be killed on the Sabbath – one of this young centurion's soldiers offered to break the legs of the condemned men so as to hasten their deaths.'

Emlyn, warming to his tale, began to embellish the telling, and Murdo came under the spell of the monk's voice as he had so many times aboard the ship. As the priest related the events of long ago, Murdo, tramping through the heat and dust on his way to the Holy City, began to feel the awful oppression of that black day. For the first time in his life it seemed to him more than merely a story.

'Well now,' the monk continued, 'this is the way of it: the centurion sees the Jews growing more agitated as the day wastes away. Wishing to avoid any further trouble, he agrees to end the criminals' suffering, and the order is duly given. "Break their legs," he says. The command is duly carried out, but when the soldier with the hammer comes to Jesu, he observes that Our Lord is already dead. "How can this be?" they say. "There has not been enough time." Death by crucifixion is seldom swift, you see, and it is far from painless. I have heard it said that such a death can often take several days – days of unbearable agony before the wretch succumbs and breathes his last.

'"Do not touch him! He is dead already!" some declare. "No!" shout others. "He has only fainted. Revive him, and you will see!"

'The crowd begins to argue. "Did you not hear him scream his death agony? He is dead."

'"No, no, he is alive still. Break his legs. Kill him!"

'The bloody execution of three men is not enough for them. They begin to fight amongst themselves. Longinus, striving to keep order, decides to settle the matter once and for all. Taking up his spear, he steps to the foot of the cross, and calls for silence. Then up thrusts the spear! Up! Up under the Blessed Saviour's ribs and into his heart. Water and blood gush from the wound. Everyone sees, and knows beyond all doubt the Son of the Living God is dead.'

The round-faced priest fell silent for a moment, and Murdo realized they had both stopped walking, and that he had been holding his breath waiting for the monk to continue. He exhaled, and the two resumed their march.

'Well, and well,' Emlyn sighed, his voice taking on a weight of sadness, 'they take Our Jesu down from the cross and lay him in the tomb lent by Joseph of Arimathea, a rich merchant of the city and a secret follower of the Christ. But the enemies of God are not finished yet. No sooner is the body wrapped in a winding shroud and taken away by the mourners than the venomous Pharisees seek audience with Governor Pilate. They rush in to the governor, saying, "This man you have killed – the ignorant people believe him to be a very great magician. Indeed, he has often been heard to boast how he will rise again from the dead."

'Does Pilate encourage their invidious intrigues? No, he does not! The governor wishes only to eat his supper in peace. "Is this so?" he replies. "Well then, we shall see what manner of man he was. Be gone! I want nothing more to do with you."

'But the Pharisees will not leave him alone. "It is not so easy as that," they say, "would that it were! No, you see, we have overheard a plot by some of this criminal's followers who are planning to steal the body from the tomb tonight. If they should succeed they would be able to boast that he has risen from the grave. Think of the trouble they could make."

'"Let them do what they like," growls Pilate, growing angry at last – he has lost a night's sleep to bad dreams and a painful conscience. "Whatever they say will be shown to be a lie and that will be the end of it. They are nothing but fishermen and shepherds. You make them more than they are."

'"Oh, to be so confident and trusting," marvel the sly Pharisees. "Alas, the truth is that these are very dangerous men who will stop at nothing. What is more, they have gained the sympathy of the rabble. Think what will happen when these brigands begin spreading their falsehoods among the people. There could be riots – and worse. We are only thinking of your position, O Mighty Governor. Of course, all this could be easily avoided."

'"What would you suggest?" asks Pilate, hearing the voice of the serpent hissing in his ear.

'"Place a cohort of your excellent soldiers around the tomb for a few days," the wicked Pharisees advise. "The outlaws would not dare try their devious tricks with Roman legionaries guarding the tomb."

'Pilate, watching his supper growing cold, extracts a promise. "If I send the soldiers, do I have your assurance that you will trouble me no more with your petty plots and conspiracies? Will you, in fact, show me the same measure of support you insist upon for yourselves?"

'The Jews pretend to be aghast at the suggestion that they have ever been anything other than loyal citizens of the empire, but they agree nevertheless, and the soldiers are sent out to guard the tomb – the same soldiers, as it happens, that conducted the crucifixion. Longinus is in command, and the centurion is there, standing guard with his men, when the earth shakes and the tomb opens wide to release its captive.

'Soon the whole world learns of the resurrection. Can anyone stop the sun from rising? Longinus, witness at the tomb, becomes a believer, and word of what he saw on that glorious morning spreads like fire through the dry tinder of the jaded legions. Whenever the centurion encounters anyone who doubts the veracity of his testimony, faithful Longinus produces the iron lance: "With this spear, I pierced his heart," he tells them. "Two days later, that same man walked out of the tomb. I was there. I saw it."

'Many years pass, and a church is erected over the site of the tomb, and Longinus' spear is placed inside the tomb for pilgrims to see and, seeing, believe in the Eternal Truth. Alas, Jerusalem fell to the Saracens,' Emlyn concluded, 'and the spear was lost in the terrible desecrations that followed.'

Murdo, enthralled by the tale, could not help asking, 'What *did* become of the spear?'

'Some say it was carried off into Egypt; others say it found its way to Baghdat as a trinket for the Caliph. I have even heard that it was destroyed – its iron melted down and made into a chain for Christian slaves. But no one really knew.'

'If no one knew what happened to it,' Murdo said, doubt creeping into his question, 'how did they know to look for it in Antioch?'

'Truly, no one knew,' Emlyn assured him. 'They had to be shown.'

'Who showed them?' demanded Murdo, openly suspicious once again. After all, if somebody showed the crusaders where to look, then *somebody* knew.

'No, no, no,' the monk protested. 'You are getting the wrong idea here. This is the way of it, you see – '

'How do you know?' Murdo said. 'None of us were there.'

'Tch!' chided the monk. 'How do I know? Have I not already told you? I talked to the priests. I also talked to men who were there – men who helped raise the siege and fought to regain the city. I listened to what they said, and now I am telling you. What is so difficult about that?'

Murdo grunted, but made no further protest.

'By your leave, O Head of Wisdom, I continue. This is the way of it: no sooner was Antioch liberated, than the enemy tried to recapture it. Sultan Kerbogha – the Seljuq chieftain of this region – gathered his armies and those of his vassal lords, and together they surrounded the city. Four days after marching through the gates in victory, our brother crusaders were trapped inside the very walls they had just freed from the enemy. Why, they had not even time enough to replenish the stores of grain and water depleted by their own long siege.

'No food. No water. The pilgrims were starving, and fever broke out. Men were dying by the score, and the army was growing weaker with each passing day. Many gathered in the church to pray God's deliverance. They prayed three days and nights, and during the night one of the priests in Count Raymond's retinue – Peter Bartholomew by name – was visited by a vision in which he was instructed to search for the Lance of Christ.'

'Who told him?' asked Murdo, a queasy feeling beginning to steal over him. 'Did they tell him where to search?'

'It seems Peter was visited by a young priest dressed all in white – he did not know who it was at that time – and this white priest told him that when they found the Holy Lance, the crusaders should carry it before them into battle, and their faith would be rewarded by a very great victory.'

At the mention of the white priest, Murdo's scalp prickled.

'It seems Brother Peter duly reported his vision to the count,' Emlyn said.

'And that was when they started searching?'

'Alas, no,' the monk answered. 'Count Raymond ignored him. Some people are always having visions, you know, and unfortunately Peter is one of these. No one listened to him. And the more he insisted, the less they believed him.'

'Then how –'

'If you will keep your tongue from flapping, I will tell you,' the priest chided. 'As it happens, two nights later another pilgrim had the same vision – *then* the lords began to take an interest. This second man – by name of Stephen of Valence, a chaplain to one of the lords, and by all accounts as humble, pious, and upright as Brother Peter is rascal – decides to hold a prayer vigil in the church, to seek holy wisdom. He gathers with some of the faithful in the Church of Saint Peter, and, lo and behold! in the middle of the night he is visited by an unknown monk dressed in white. "Dig!" urges the White Monk. "Dig and find! O, men of small belief, do you not know that victory is assured if you carry the Lance of Christ before you into battle?"

'So now, how can he keep this to himself? At once he runs to his lord and says that he, too, has seen the mysterious priest in white who tells him the battle will be won if only they recover the Holy Lance. The lord demands to know where they should search for the spear. "Seek the lance in the Church of Saint Peter. That is where it will be found." That is what he tells them.

'So, they begin searching. But can they find it? No, they cannot. They look here and there; they search the vaults and catacombs, they begin to dig beneath the floor. Three days they dig! Some of the lords abandon the search – they did not believe anyway. And even Raymond, who has faith, tires of the search and says they must desist, for the troops are growing discouraged. He turns from the excavation – they have begun digging beneath the altar – and walks to the door. He is not well; the fever has got hold of him. Raymond reaches the threshold and what should he hear?

'Here it is! We have found it! He turns and sees Brother Peter standing in the trench, pointing to the discovery. Lord Hugh of Vermandois is there; he leaps down into the pit and, while the object is yet embedded in the earth, presses his lips to the Holy Lance. Then Brother Peter raises up the spear.'

'What does it look like?'

'It is a Roman spear,' answered the monk, wiping the sweat from his face. 'Those who have seen it say it is a long, thin piece of hand-forged iron with a short, narrow blade. A wooden haft would have encased the lower portion, and indeed, the remnant of just such a wooden haft still clings to the base of the spear. But, mostly, all that is left is the rusted iron blade and shaft.'

'Where is it now?'

'Patience, boy,' the monk told him. 'All in good time. Where was I?'

'They take up the lance.'

'Yes, yes, they lay hold of the lance. But finding the spear is only half of the vision – now they must make their attack. The lords met that very night and battle plan was decided. At dawn the next morning, they rode out from the main gate and routed the Seljuqs. Forty thousand were slain, and the rest driven off. It was a magnificent victory, just as the vision foretold.'

Emlyn gulped a breath, his flabby chin shaking with excitement. 'Think of it, Murdo! The most valuable treasure of our faith has been recovered, and even now goes before us into Jerusalem to prepare the way for the restoration of the Holy City. The defeat of our enemies is certain. We will return the Sacred Lance to its rightful place in the sepulchre of Our Lord. Who could have imagined such a thing when we first began?'

Murdo agreed that it was a very miracle. 'But what of this vision?' he asked. 'You said the chaplain saw a priest in white who spoke to him. Did he say who this might have been?'

'Did I not say it already? It was none other than Saint Andrew, the apostle, brother to Saint Peter, and the same who as a tireless missionary sowed the seeds of many churches, including the church at Constantinople.'

'Saint Andrew . . .' Murdo murmured, and wondered whether he should tell Emlyn that he had seen a white priest, too.

But no, he decided, his encounter had been no dream in the night; it had happened in the clear light of day. Lost and confused, he had stumbled on the little chapel purely by accident – inasmuch as he could not find the street to the market, why wonder that he could not find the chapel again when he looked for it? The streets were baffling, the city strange and unknown, and he, desperate to escape the harassment of the beggars and merchants had not been looking where he was going. Where was the mystery in that?

'You have become very quiet, Murdo,' observed Emlyn. 'Do you doubt the tale even now?'

'No – no,' Murdo replied quickly. 'I was only thinking. By Heaven, it is hot though!' he said quickly. 'My feet are on fire already, and we have only begun.'

'Verily,' answered Emlyn, puffing out his cheeks. 'If it were not for the sake of Jerusalem, I do not think I could endure this heat.'

Murdo then suggested that perhaps it was better to conserve their strength and talk no more. In truth, he wanted a space to contemplate what he had just heard. He loped along, head down, his long legs swinging easily. Gradually, the monk fell further and further behind, and Murdo was alone with his thoughts.

By the time they reached the little fishing village on the coast, he had convinced himself that the discovery of the Holy Lance, however it might have happened, was nothing to do with him. Moreover, nothing else mattered but that he should find his father at the first opportunity.

The monks followed Lord Magnus onto his ship and, since no one told him otherwise, Murdo followed the monks. One of the crusaders now, he joined in with a will. He picked up an oar and rowed, desperate now to be in Jerusalem. All around him, men talked about the battles and, from the things they said, he gathered that the pilgrims had suffered greatly in their skirmishes with the enemy. Of all those who had begun the pilgrimage, they said, fewer than half now remained.

Murdo did not allow himself to contemplate the possibility that his father might be among the dead. Instead, he clung to the certainty that Ranulf was alive. I *will* find him, Murdo vowed with every stroke of the oar. I *will* bring him home.

The Norsemen used the days aboard ship to prepare their weapons and armour for battle. They honed, sharpened, and stropped their swords, spearblades, and axes; burnished their shield rims, war helms, and hauberks; repaired or renewed all the leather fastenings, bindings, straps, and ties; then polished everything until, upon reaching the port town of Jaffa on the Palestinian coast, King Magnus' war band – nearly four hundred fearsome Vikings – fairly gleamed and glittered with battle-keen ferocity.

Magnus secured his fleet in the Jaffa harbour, newly reconquered by the sailors of the Genoese merchant guild, which the wily king paid to keep watch over his ships so that he would not have to leave any men behind. They paused only long enough to assemble the wagons and load the supplies and water casks, then set off for the Holy City, two days' march inland.

They were yet half a day away when they saw the smoke rolling heavenward in a heavy black column. The Norsemen reached Jerusalem at midday to find that the northwestern wall had been breached and the rape of Jerusalem begun.

TWENTY-EIGHT

Jerusalem's high walls were breached on the fifteenth of July, 1099. The initial combat had been fierce. The crusaders suffered terribly under a constant rain of arrows and Greek fire as they laboured to fill the deep ditch at the foot of the wall so that the siege towers could be wheeled into position. Despite heavy losses, Godfrey, commanding from the top of one of the towers, had succeeded in lowering a bridge from his tower to the wall top. The first man across the bridge forced a way onto the battlement and somehow remained on his feet long enough to enable others to scramble in behind him.

Godfrey joined the fray, bearing the Holy Lance into battle once more. Emboldened by his example, other knights swarmed after him. Soon the courageous crusaders had secured a section of the wall, and Godfrey ordered scaling ladders to be brought up, enabling more attackers to join the fight. While his knights cut their way into the gate tower, Godfrey lofted the Holy Lance and urged more and more warriors up the ladders and onto the battlements. Meanwhile, his initial contingent of knights fought their way down to the gate itself, where the Arabs made a valiant stand. Crusaders were pouring into the city through the gate tower, however; the defenders were slaughtered and the Gate of the Column opened wide to allow the main attacking force to enter at a run.

Once through the gate, the crusaders made straight for the citadel, meeting little resistance on the way. Thus, they had the good fortune to surround David's Tower before Amir Iftikhar knew they were inside the city. The amir had no time to order a proper defence. Cut off from the main force of defenders on the northern wall, he had only his bodyguard at his command, and though they put up a desperate fight, Raymond's forces far outnumbered them and they had little choice but to withdraw to the protection of the citadel.

Once the northern wall and gates were lost, the Arab defenders regrouped and hastened to the Haram al-Sharif, the temple precinct, to mount their last defence. They retreated to the Al-Aqsa Mosq, which now occupied the site of Great Solomon's temple, hard by the Qubat Al-Shakhra, the Dome of the Rock.

Tancred, leading a large force of knights, pursued the fleeing Arabs to the Temple Mount and promptly surrounded the mosq. The defenders climbed onto the roof of the holy building and loosed arrows into the upturned faces of their attackers. This caused only momentary vexation, however, as the crusaders simply fell back and waited until the arrows were spent. Lacking the weapons and supplies to endure a lengthy siege, the Arab defenders threw themselves upon the mercy of their Christian conquerors. Tancred accepted the surrender of the infidel, and commanded his banner to be flown from the top of the temple as a protection to those sheltering within.

Elsewhere, the wily amir, high in David's Tower, sent word to Count Raymond that he was ready to deliver the city to the crusaders, but would do so only under Count Raymond's personal pledge of honour. In exchange for this pledge, Amir Iftikhar promised to pay a heavy ransom for himself and the men with him. Raymond accepted the conditions of surrender and, after receiving a considerable amount of treasure, escorted the amir and his bodyguard out of the city and saw them safely on the road to Ascalon.

With the departure of the amir, all resistance ceased, leaving Jerusalem and its citizens unprotected.

At first, few guessed the danger. While the Muhammedans cowered behind barred doors, the Armenian and Greek Christians were glad to welcome their western brothers, and threw open the windows and doors of their houses to shower flower petals and rose water upon the heads of the liberators. The Jews were less enthusiastic, to be sure, but not overly concerned. It was their city, after all – a claim which every occupying force from the Persians to the Muslims had recognized.

Then the slaughter commenced.

Unable to tell Armenian from Muhammedan, Greek from Jew or Byzantine, and unwilling to barter peace – after their long ordeal across the Syrian and Judean deserts, after their suffering at Dorylaeum and Antioch, after their grim endurance of countless privations, disease, and death since leaving their homes – the triumphant pilgrims would not be satisfied with anything less than blood.

Crusaders fresh to the fight poured into the city by way of the gates on the north and west. They ran through the streets, breaking into the houses and putting the inhabitants to the sword, before sacking the dwellings and carrying off any treasure they found. The terrified people fled before the onslaught, abandoning their homes for the safety of the southern half of the city where the attackers had not yet penetrated. There, they hoped to escape through one of the southern gates below Mount Zion.

King Magnus and his Norse battle host arrived at Jerusalem just as the pillage reached its climax in the northern part of the city, and was beginning to spread to the southern quarter.

Murdo squatted on the hillside in the shade of an olive tree, sweating from the long climb up through the hills. He gazed out upon the Holy City perched on a high rock escarpment, its massive walls rising sheer from the Hinnom Valley, soaring above the crusader camps spread like rumpled skins along the valley floor. From where he knelt, Murdo could see the vast stone curtain stretching away to the north, following the upward sweep to the heights of Mount Moriah to the east, and cresting Mount Ophel and Mount Zion to the south above the Vale of Kidron. Smoke, dirty and dark, filled the air from ground to sky, casting all below in a filthy brown, foul-smelling haze.

The Jaffa Gate gaped open, allowing a steady stream of crusaders into and out of the city. Shouts and cries, and the clashing sounds of battle, could be heard from various quarters, mingling with an eerie ululating wail that rose and fell with the wind, coursing hot and dry in fitful gusts through the valley. The sun shone as a dull blood-brown ember burning through the thick pall of smoke, bathing the city in a strange and lurid light. Murdo put his hand to his purse and shook out the small gattage coin onto his palm. Looking at the bit of silver glinting in the fevered light and, suddenly feeling foolish for having carried it so long, he tossed it away. He would not need it now.

All around him, Norse warriors chafed the dust-dry earth with the butts of their spears, and boasted to one another how much plunder they would get, and how many foemen they would kill. King Magnus, though eager as the next man for his share of the city's spoils, at least paused long enough to acquaint himself with the lay of the land. The monks, familiar with the Holy Land through long study, had prepared a simple drawing of the city for the king; Fionn held the crude map while Ronan pointed out the foremost features of the city and surrounding countryside.

Murdo, ignoring the vacuous banter around him, strained to hear what the elder cleric was saying. 'Before us is the main entrance – the Jaffa Gate,' Ronan explained, indicating the great timber doors on the western side. The priest's finger moved to the clustered domes directly over the entrance. 'There is David's Tower – which is what they call the citadel.' The finger moved to another cluster of domes rising high above the rest of the city. 'That is the temple precinct on Mount Moriah. That is where the Muhammedans have built their mosq.'

Brother Ronan went on to indicate other landmarks for King Magnus and his battlechiefs. Murdo crowded closer to hear. Little remained of the original temple, the priest told them; the ancient walls had been razed by the Romans, rebuilt by the Byzantines, and taken over by the Muhammedans. Murdo could see the golden dome gleaming through the smoke haze, and the mosq's towers, or minarets, still stately and grand above the city.

'The Mount of Olives is on the southern side of the city,' Ronan continued. 'We cannot see it from where we are standing.'

'I think we can see Golgotha from here,' Fionn suggested, looking up from the map. 'It might be that small hill there.' He squinted at one of the lumpy mounds in the distance. 'Or, maybe the one next to it.'

'The Church of the Holy Sepulchre is inside the walls,' Emlyn added helpfully. 'Many believe Our Lord was never buried there anyway, but was laid to rest in the Garden Tomb, which is outside the walls.' Pointing east along the valley, he said, 'Is that the Church of Saint Mary I see? If it is, the tomb must be –'

'But you are mistaken, brother,' Fionn interrupted. 'That is certainly the Church of Saint Stephen which you see on the hillside. The Church of Saint Mary is on Mount Zion.' He pointed to the hump of rock rising to the south of the city.

'You are right, of course,' agreed Emlyn placidly. 'Yet, I believe the Chapel of the Garden Tomb lies between us and the church. This was the point I wished to make.'

'And I am grateful for it,' said King Magnus, speaking up quickly. 'But the day is speeding from us.' Turning to Ronan, he said, 'Unless you have anything else to tell us, we will join the battle.'

'I have told all I know,' Ronan said, nodding thoughtfully. 'Yes, I believe that is all.'

King Magnus thanked his wise counsellor, and declared he would make for the temple precinct. If any fighting continued, it would be there, he reckoned, where resistance was bound to be most fierce. The king turned, raised his sword, and cried, 'For Christ and Glory!' He then led his men into battle.

They descended the hill and quickly crossed the narrow valley. Upon reaching the gate, they did not hesitate, but rushed directly into the smoke-filled streets to join their fellow crusaders in sacking the city. Murdo and the monks followed close behind, until coming to the entrance. There, amidst the commotion of warriors hastening both into and out of the city, the monks halted. 'We will remain outside the walls until the city is delivered. We can be of more use caring for the wounded,' Ronan said. 'Stay with us, Murdo. It seems the fighting is nearly over. Lord Magnus will not require your spear today; I will tell him you remained behind to help us.'

'My father and brothers are here,' Murdo told him. 'I am going to find them.'

'Wait but a little,' Emlyn pleaded. 'We will help you find them when Jerusalem is won.'

'No,' Murdo turned away brusquely, 'I have waited long enough. I am going to find them now.'

The monks did not try to dissuade him further, but gave Murdo a blessing instead. Raising his hands, Ronan said, 'Great of Heaven, send an angel to go before our brother, an angel to go behind, an angel above, an angel below, and an angel on either side to guard and protect him through all things, and bring him safely to your peace.' Ronan made the sign of the cross over Murdo and said, 'Come to us when your search is completed. We will uphold you in our prayers until we see you again.'

Murdo nodded once in acknowledgement of the monk's request, then joined the soldiers thronging through the gate. More tunnel than doorway, the entrance was dark and full of smoke; Murdo took a deep breath and, clutching his spear tightly, entered the city. The last thing he heard was Emlyn's voice telling him to be careful.

He emerged beneath the gate tower. Bodies of both crusaders and infidel lay smashed on the stone pavement where they had fallen from the breastwork high above. The pooled blood of these unfortunates was now scattered in a hundred thousand dark footprints radiating into the Holy City by way of its tight, impossibly tangled pathways.

Distracted by the corpses heaped around the gate, Murdo started down the street before him ... only to realize that he no longer recognized anyone around him. Turning around, he pushed back through the crowd, quickly retracing his steps; yet, by the time he reached the gate once more, the Norsemen were nowhere to be seen. Still, he heard the clatter of arms and the echo of voices down one of the streets to his left. Putting his head down, he ran as fast as he could, following the sound.

The street twisted and turned, crossing one path, and then another. Murdo thought he would see his comrades at any moment – he would round the next bend, and there they would be. But the further he ran, the fainter grew the sounds.

He paused to catch his breath and look around. The street was deserted. The houses were silent. He did not know whether to go back the way he had come, or to proceed.

As he was trying to make up his mind, there came a tremendous crash from further up the street. He made for the sound, thinking that if he did not find his lost companions, he might at least find someone who could tell him how to reach the Temple Mount.

The street turned, and turned again, and he entered a wider way, lined with trees and larger houses. Up ahead he saw a number of crusaders darting from house to house, or from one side street to another. He hastened to join them. Upon passing the first of the fine houses, he heard the crack of splintering wood overhead and glanced up just in time to avoid being struck by a wooden chest which was hurled from an upper window onto the street below.

The chest landed with a colossal thud at his feet It was swiftly followed by another, smaller box, which smashed on impact, spilling a horde of silver coins which bounced and rolled over the paving stones. 'You there!' cried a voice from the upper window. Murdo glanced up to see an angry face glaring down at him. The soldier shouted something, and when Murdo failed to respond, repeated in Latin: 'Get away! That's ours!'

Murdo was still staring up at the face when two crusaders ran out from the house and began scooping up the coins by the fistful. They were quickly joined by two more, who seized the larger chest, raised it over their heads and threw it down – once, twice, and again, before the chest split, scattering treasure into the street. Murdo caught a flash of silver and gold as cups and bowls, plates, bracelets and chains, rolled and spun in every direction. The crusaders shrieked at their good fortune, and dived to retrieve the plunder, snatching up the valuables and stuffing them into their siarcs.

When they had grabbed it all, one of the pilgrims peered around guiltily, saw Murdo watching, and turned on him. 'You!' he yelled. 'I told you to get away from here!' The man made a clumsy lurch towards him, but Murdo was already running away.

He knew the Norsemen were making for the temple precinct, and decided that was where he would find them – and even if not, he stood a good chance of finding his father and brothers – so he hurried on, following the street where it led, hoping to reach a place where he could get a glimpse of the Temple Mount to know which direction he must go.

From the side streets he glimpsed grim evidence of the conquest: to the right, four crusaders standing to their knees in white-robed bodies were stabbing into the pile with their spears; to the left, two warriors holding an old man between them while a third executed him – the man was shouting in Latin as the spear sank into his stomach. Murdo averted his eyes quickly, and from then on looked only at the street ahead. The pathway turned and turned again, and grew narrower until it ended in an enclosed courtyard. There, Murdo halted.

Fresh corpses covered the entire surface of the square three and four deep, rising to two separate mounds stacked ten or fifteen high. Murdo stared at the bizarre welter of bodies – many of them battered and mutilated beyond recognition – unable to comprehend how such slaughter could have been accomplished. He decided that either they had taken refuge in the courtyard, or had been driven there by the crusaders who then blocked the narrow entrance and began butchering them. In their terror, the victims must have climbed the ever-increasing heaps, standing on the corpses of their kinsmen in a futile effort to escape, while the crusaders struck them down, killing and killing as the mound grew ever higher.

He felt something damp seeping through his boots, and looked down to see that he was standing in a spreading pool of blood which was creeping slowly out into the street. Sickened, he turned and fled back the way he had come, shaking the vile stuff from his boots as he ran.

Upon reaching the larger street once more, he tried another way. This time, he struck a narrow pathway between large houses. Murdo could hear shouts ahead, and followed the voices to discover that the pathway led into a covered market. Holding tightly to his spear, he jumped over the bodies slumped at the entrance and entered the cool darkness of the suq. From somewhere amidst the maze of stalls and pathways, he could hear the triumphant shouts of the victors as they pillaged. Everywhere, goods and wares of all kinds were spilled and spoiled; in many places, what could not be carried off had been set on fire.

He looked down one dim pathway and saw a light at the end. The passageway was filled with what he took to be a multitude of stones strewn over the ground. Closer examination, however, revealed these to be loaves of bread, thrown down and trodden under foot. He started towards the light, but had not walked a dozen paces when, upon glancing into one of the many empty and ruined stalls, he saw a small huddle of bodies – those of a merchant family, perhaps, who had taken shelter in the suq.

The man had been gutted like a pig from navel to chin, his entrails pulled out and wrapped around his neck to strangle him. Two with long black hair – women, the man's wife and daughter, he supposed – had been beaten to death; their faces were a squashed mass of splintered bone and blood, no longer recognizably human. A small boy and a dog had been decapitated and their heads exchanged on the bodies.

All this was glimpsed in a fleeting instant, but Murdo felt the gorge rise in his throat. Bitter bile gushed up into his mouth and he turned away, retching. He lurched a few steps, then leaned on his spear and vomited on the ground.

Steeling himself, he staggered on, looking neither left nor right until he emerged into the filthy light at the far end of the passage. Murdo paused to catch his breath and look around. Here, in this quarter, the houses were larger, and more substantial, the people obviously wealthier. Here also, it seemed the conquest was still in progress. A ragged scream echoed from inside one of the houses; further up the street, flames leapt from the upper windows of several others. The stone-paved street was strewn with broken objects –

items of furniture, casks, chests, kitchen utensils, clothing – which had been stripped from the houses and thrown into the streets. Rising above the rooftops, Murdo saw the topmost section of a high-soaring wall some distance away; he scanned the length of stone curtain and caught the dull glint of a golden dome rising above the rim of the wall.

Picking his way around the debris, he moved on cautiously, keeping his eye on the upper wall. Upon passing a large stone house with two marble columns he heard a terrified shriek and froze in his steps. An instant later, a woman in a yellow robe broke into the street directly ahead of him, carrying a pale bundle beneath each arm. Right behind raced three pilgrims with white crosses on their mantles and red-streaked swords in their hands. One of them seized the woman by the hair and yanked her backwards off her feet. The bundles fell to the street, and Murdo realized they were babies. The infants lay crying, holding up their tiny hands, as the soldiers fell upon them and began chopping with their blades.

The woman screamed and lunged at her attackers, begging for mercy. Heedless, the crusaders turned their blades on her. The swords slashed and slashed again, the sharp steel biting deep into the smooth, rounded flesh of her white arms, hewing through muscle and bone, opening wicked red gashes; one of the swords found her neck, releasing a torrent of blood. In a moment, the screaming stopped and all three lay silent. The soldiers glanced around at Murdo, wild glee dancing on their smoke-smeared faces.

One of them shouted at him in a tongue Murdo did not understand. He replied in Latin, saying, 'I mean no harm. I am searching for my father.'

The pilgrims glanced at one another, and two of them stepped towards him. The first crusader spoke again, and pointed at him – thrusting his finger again and again insistently. He seemed to be demanding something, but Murdo could not tell what it might be. The two nearest took another step towards him, holding their dripping swords before them.

Murdo repeated his answer in Latin, stepping slowly backwards. The two muttered something to one another. Murdo took another backward step. His foot struck something and he fell. With a shout the three soldiers rushed upon him.

The two nearest reached him first. Murdo, flat on his back, slashed the air with his spear. The blade struck steel and one of the attackers leapt back with a yelp as his sword spun from his hand. Murdo jabbed the spear into the face of the other pilgrim, and the man darted aside, allowing Murdo to roll onto his knees.

The leader of the three gave a loud shout and charged with lofted sword – perhaps expecting the youth to turn tail and run. Murdo remained on his knees, however, and brought the weapon up sharply as the man closed on him. Murdo did not feel the blade enter the man's belly, and probably his adversary did not feel it either – at first. For he took another step, and struggled for another, before glancing down to see the long haft of the spear protruding from his gut.

A bewildered look appeared on his face. He dropped the sword, and his hands fastened on the spearshaft. He turned his face towards his comrades, and uttered a loud cry. Gripping the shaft, he tried to pull it from him, but Murdo held tight. The man gave another cry, which ended in a cough as a gush of dark blood bubbled up from his throat and spilled over his teeth and chin.

Spewing blood, the man crashed onto his knees, gasping for breath. Murdo, terrified the other two would attack him, yet not daring to release his hold on the spear, tightened his grip on the shaft and held on. The two faced one another on their knees – both clutching the same weapon. Then all at once, the crusader gave a little whimper and slumped onto his side.

Murdo yanked the spear free and turned to meet the two remaining soldiers. He did not wait for them to attack, but charged into them, the bloody blade streaming before him. The two turned as one and fled, leaving their dead comrade behind. Murdo ran after them, and they disappeared around the corner of the nearest house. Murdo, not caring to come upon them unawares, halted. Only then did he realize he had been screaming at the top of his lungs.

He returned to the man he had killed, and stood over the body for a moment. The corpse lay on its side, face against the street; blood had pooled at the open mouth – not as much blood, Murdo thought grimly, as that shed by the poor woman and her babies. Murdo had no regret for what he had done – only that he had not done it sooner. Perhaps the mother and her children would still be alive if he had acted more swiftly.

Then again, maybe it would be himself lying empty-eyed in the street now with a seeping hole below his ribs. His mind squirmed at the thought, and he turned away. Even as he turned, he caught a glint of white out of the corner of his eye . . . the crusader cross.

It came to him then why the man had been pointing at him: he had no cross. With nothing to identify himself as a pilgrim, the soldiers had mistaken him for yet another infidel to be murdered.

Murdo regarded the crusader's mantle, and the bold white cross sewn onto the shoulder. He hesitated only a moment, then, fearing the man's two comrades might recover their courage and return at any moment, he stooped, heaved the body into a sitting position, and quickly began stripping off the corpse's mantle.

TWENTY-NINE

Murdo drew the dead man's mantle over his head. It was wet with sweat, and reeked. The lower front was sticky where the blood had soaked through around the ragged hole made by his spear. Using his discarded siarc, Murdo rubbed off as much of the stuff as he could, then wiped his hands clean, threw down the tainted garment and picked up his spear. He glanced at the white cross now emblazoned on his shoulder. No one now would mistake him for an infidel, he thought, and hastened on.

Further along, the street bent around, rising towards the Temple Mount. Murdo entered a wider thoroughfare and stopped in his tracks. The street was choked with bodies. There were corpses strewn everywhere, some dressed in the white of Turks and Saracens and some in the darker clothing of the Jews, and all of them lying each by other, so that the bodies of the slain appeared to be accompanied by their own dead shadows.

At the far end of the street, Murdo could see the wall surrounding the temple precinct and the ample eastern gate. The gate was open, the heavy doors splintered, battered off their huge iron hinges. Even as he stood looking, an enormous wailing cry went up; it was answered and drowned by a rousing shout that sounded like: 'Deus Volt!' . . . *God wills!*

As if drawn by the sound, he stumbled forth, slowly picking his way through the jumble of bodies, step-by-step. Upon reaching the gate, he stopped to look inside and saw a vast courtyard filled with pilgrims, each one crying God's judgement upon the unbelievers. In the centre of the courtyard stood a squat, square building with a bulging top. Far off to the right, he could see a much larger building with a round tower, and a great golden dome. A Frankish banner flew from the dome's pinnacle. This then, was what the monks called the Al-Aqsa Mosq; the smaller of the two buildings, he decided, must be the Dome of the Rock.

The shrieking wail was coming from inside the mosq.

Murdo crept through the gate and into the courtyard. His heart quickened with the hope that he might find his father here. That hope died as swiftly as it was born, however; for as he waded into the throng, he realized the futility of his task. There were simply too many people, too much confusion, too much noise. Even if his father and brothers *were* here, he would never see them in the crush of soldiers.

Overcome by the futility of his task, he faltered. Dazed, confused, the shouts of the screaming mob loud in his ears, he turned and struggled back through the tight-pressed crowd – only to be swept forwards by a sudden surge. He fought to keep his feet, and escaped being trampled by the use of his spear to hold himself upright against the tide-rush.

The mob seemed intent on the mosq; every face was turned towards the golden dome. At first Murdo could not discern what it was that held their attention so firmly . . . then, above the heads of the mob, he glimpsed pale yellow fingers of flame just beginning to creep up the walls of the temple; flames were also sprouting from the base of the tower.

The cries from inside the burning building grew louder and more urgent. Murdo put his head down and began elbowing his way along, pushing, shoving, thrusting himself through the crowd. This time he reached the perimeter of the courtyard, and squeezed past the last of the crusaders.

There came another battle cry behind him, and he looked back, catching a glimpse of the temple entrance; the tall narrow door cracked open and black smoke billowed out and up as a mass of white-turbaned Arabs staggered from the burning building and into the waiting swords and spears.

Murdo's stomach convulsed into a hard ball in his gut, and he shuddered with a spasm of revulsion as the crusaders hewed at the wretches trying to escape the fire. Some, choosing martyrdom rather than the flames, threw themselves upon the blades with cries of 'Allah akbar!' Others crawled on hands and knees, whimpering, pleading for mercy. But there was no mercy. The mob stood jeering as they cut them down. Blood splashed upon the stones of the temple courtyard. The cruel blades flashed relentlessly, methodically, casually, carelessly, ceaselessly. The pilgrim soldiers roared with demented delight.

The flames burned higher and hotter. Beaten back by the heat, the mob retreated with a surge that carried Murdo towards the gate. He could feel the flames on his back as he fought free of the crowd.

Upon reaching the gate, he glanced back over his shoulder to see that the blaze had driven the throng into a wide ring around the burning building. Arabs still tried to escape, but those staggering through the smoke now were themselves aflame, their clothes and hair burning. They collapsed and rolled upon the ground in agony, much to the enjoyment of the crusaders.

The flames cracked and roared, forcing the onlookers back and back in an ever greater circle. There came a great groaning sigh from above, and the golden dome began to sag. The crusaders cheered as the mosq began to crumble inwardly upon the heads of the doomed Muhammedans whose dying screams rent the searing air.

Murdo could endure no more. He ran from the courtyard, fleeing back the way he had come. The golden dome of the Al-Aqsa Mosq collapsed with a mighty crash that echoed down the street behind him, but he did not look back again.

The path by which he had reached the Temple Mount sloped sharply down, and Murdo was soon running, gaining speed with every step. He ran with no thought in his head but to get away from the atrocity he had seen. On and on he ran; his breath grew laboured, and he could hear nothing but the dull thump of his own heartbeat in his ears. His lungs burned and his sides ached, but still he ran – flying down the hill as fast as his legs could move. The slap, slap, slap – quick and sharp – of his flying feet striking well worn pavements of Jesu's city mocked him. He felt afraid and ashamed.

The street grew narrower and began meandering sharply, bending away to the right and taking him with it. His breath came in ragged gasps and he tasted blood in his mouth, yet he ran on. He did not notice when the street began rising sharply once more, nor did he see the first wine-dark trickle of blood coursing down among the paving stones. He saw nothing but the dark faces of the Arabs screaming as they burned.

The steep incline of the path began to tell on him. He slowed his pace, but struggled on. It came to him that his last few paces had been accompanied by the sound of splashing. He took another step, lost his footing, and fell, sprawling forward on hands and knees. His spear skidded across blood-slick stones.

He jumped to his feet, his hands dripping, his sleeves and the knees of his breecs sodden now. He stood for a moment, staring at his bloody hands as dread stole over him. His empty stomach knotted and squirmed. The trickle of blood had become a very stream, coursing in frothy freshets down the footpath, pooling in bright red puddles and running on, branching and twining as it went, the meaty smell rich where it ran.

Desperate to escape, Murdo fled up another street. But there was no relief. Here, too, the well-worn path was awash in reeking blood. There were bodies, too – dozens, scores, hundreds – their white and yellow robes red-stained and dripping still. He kept his eyes on the path ahead, refusing to look at the blood.

But there was so much! Everywhere his eye happened to light there was blood, and still more blood – in such ghastly profusion, in such absolute abundance of quantity that he could not ignore it and began at last to see nothing else . . . blood pooling thick and black in the streets . . . spurting hot and dark from the wounds of the dying . . . blood stinking foul in the hot sun . . . staining stone and wood and dirt with its rich red-brown patina of extinguished life . . . blood oozing purple from neck stumps of headless victims . . . blood in glimmering puddles surrounded by six starving cats that crouched at their grisly feast with their tongues lapping, lapping . . . blood splattered on the walls of the houses, and on the steps, trickling from the windows, and out through the doors . . . blood sluicing in slow rivers down the dirty streets, a dusty grey membrane caking thick upon the turgid surface . . . blood sticky under foot and curdling in the fierce summer sun . . . blood wafting the sweet suffocating stench of death into the hot dead air . . . a never-ending flood-tide of blood gushing through the streets in wider, ever more prodigious streams . . .

The blood . . . God have mercy! There was so much!

Sickened, wretched, he turned his back and fled the sight. Heedless of all else save the need to escape, he ran until he could run no longer. When at last he stopped to look around he saw that the shadows stretched long across an empty square, and the pathways were dark. Corpses strewed the paths and byways, and lay heaped on the doorsteps of the houses – whole families, slain in defence of their homes and of one another.

Pressing a hand to his side, he moved across the square, and passed a building surmounted by a six-sided star of bronze. Someone had written 'Isu Regni' in blood over the doorway. The words brought him up short. As he was standing there, he felt a feather-soft touch on his face and hair and looked up. Falling from the sky all around him, black ash, fine as snow was drifting gently into the silent streets.

Thirsty now, and sweating from his exertion, Murdo walked on. The further he walked, the thicker grew the ash. He saw grey smoke filling the street ahead, but continued on and soon came to the flaming wreckage of a huge building. The roof had fallen in and little remained of the walls; a few of the larger timbers yet burned, but mostly the flames had died to embers. The smoke was bitter, and stank of burning fat; it stung Murdo's eyes and made a putrid taste in his dry mouth.

He wondered at the reason for this, and then saw that what he had taken to be mounds of smouldering debris were in fact the charred bodies. Murdo looked with dull eyes upon the great mass of twisted, blackened husks, frozen in the rictus of death, limbs deformed by agony and fire.

The heat of their still-smouldering corpses parched Murdo's skin even as the ash from their clothes and flesh settled over him. The carcasses crackled as the fiery embers continued to devour them. The air was rank with the odour of scorched grease and burned meat; every now and then one of the corpses would burst, spilling its stewed internal organs into the embers to sizzle and stink.

When at last he turned away, his eyes were hot and his lips cracked. He walked on with aimless steps, and the sky overhead – when it could be glimpsed through the drifting tatters of smoke – took on the colours of a ruddy dusk. Murdo wondered how it was the sun yet continued on its accustomed round, moving through its course, undeflected and unchanged.

The strangeness of this occupied him until he arrived in yet another quarter. There were, he noticed without interest, domes on some of the buildings and these bore wooden crosses. By this he knew he had come to one of the Christian districts. Perhaps, he thought, this quarter had escaped the worst ravages of the fighting, and he might find water here. He licked his dry lips, and stumbled on.

After a while, he found himself in another yard – the courtyard of a grand house. Near the house stood a stone basin of the kind used to water animals; Murdo moved towards it, thinking he might get a mouthful of water there, and indeed the basin was full, but the body of a drowned child floated just below the surface. He stood and gazed at the little corpse, staring up at him through the water, its mouth rounded in a soundless word. A swirl of black hair framed the little face, and bubbles nestled beneath the tiny chin and in the corner of each wide eye.

Whether boy or girl, he could not tell, but Murdo marvelled at the calm serenity in that small face. How could it be that the child should express a peace so greatly at odds with the violence of its death? He stood long, gazing at the child, and gradually became aware of screams and coarse laughter coming from around the side of the house. Probably, the commotion had been going on for a time, but, absorbed in his unthinking contemplation of the child, he had not attended it.

He walked to the corner of the house and looked: five soldiers were standing before a wall – two held an infant between them, and two others grasped a frantic woman by the arms; the fifth soldier stood behind the woman with a sword in his hand. The woman's clothing was ripped and rent, and she was screaming for her babe, which was squalling in the soldiers' grip. A man sat with his back against the wall, head down, unmoving, the front of his robe a solid mass of blood.

The soldiers holding the baby offered the infant to its mother. They said something to her and she struggled forward, but was held fast and could not move. Again they offered the infant, and again she struggled forth, only to have the babe snatched away. This time, however, the soldiers turned and, with a mighty heave, dashed the infant head first against the wall.

The babe slid silent to the ground.

In the same instant, the two brutes holding the mother released their grip. The woman lurched forward to retrieve her child. Even as she started forth, the soldier behind her swung his sword. The blow caught her on the back of the neck. Her scream stopped abruptly as her head came away from her shoulders. She crumpled in midstep, pitching awkwardly forward, her head spinning to the ground in a crimson arc, and rolling to a stop between the legs of her dead husband.

Murdo turned and ran from the yard, the sound of the soldiers' laughter grating in his ears. When at last he stopped running, he walked. But he moved like a man in a dream, heedless of his steps, seeing all, yet attending nothing, feeling nothing, stumbling forward, falling, picking himself up and staggering on, his heart a dull aching bruise inside him.

Sick to his soul at all he had seen, he thought: *This day I have walked in hell.*

Murdo carried the thought for a long time, listening to the words echo and reverberate inside his head. Some time later, long after nightfall, he finally reached the Jaffa Gate and made his way out of Jerusalem. As he stumbled out through the great doors, he paused to shed his borrowed mantle. He pulled the garment over his head and held it up to see the white cross glimmering in the pale, smoke-fretted moonlight.

Overcome by revulsion, he wadded the garment between his hands and hurled it away from him with all his might. He then stripped off his breecs and boots as well, and threw them away, too, before walking free from the Holy City.

He did not sleep that night, but roamed the darksome valley outside the walls, moving from camp to camp, restless in his search. However, Murdo no longer remembered why he searched, no longer knew what he hoped to find.

THIRTY

The fever raged for two days and nights, releasing its grip as a murky, windswept dawn seeped into the troubled eastern sky. Niamh, who had spent the last days and nights at her friend's bedside, felt the fierce heat slowly leave the hands beneath her own. She roused herself from her numb half-sleep and removed the cloth from Ragnhild's forehead, dipped it in the basin, wrung it out, and replaced it.

At the touch of the cool cloth, Ragnhild's eyelids opened. Her cracked lips parted and she made to speak.

'Wait,' said Niamh softly; she brought a bowl to the stricken woman's lips. 'Drink a little. It will help you.'

Ragnhild swallowed some of the water, and tried to speak again. 'Ragna . . .' she said, her voice a dry rasp deep in her throat.

'She is near. I will bring her.'

Niamh left the bed, and hurried to the room beyond, where Ragna was asleep in a chair beside the hearth. The young woman came awake at Niamh's touch. 'The fever is gone, and she is asking for you.'

Ragna struggled up from the chair, pressing her hand to the small of her back as she steadied herself on her feet. Niamh took her arm and led her to her mother's room.

'You go in,' Niamh directed. 'I will remain here if you need me.'

Ragna nodded and stepped through the doorway. The fire was low on the hearth in the corner; the room was cool, but close, the air dead. She went to the bedside and, settling her ungainly bulk on the stool, took her mother's hand in her own. 'I am here, Mother,' she said quietly.

Ragnhild opened her eyes, saw her daughter, and smiled feebly. 'Ragna, my heart,' she said, barely speaking above a whisper. 'Is the baby born?'

'Not yet, Mother,' the young woman answered. 'But soon – any day now. You must rest and get better so you can attend the birth.'

Lady Ragnhild nodded. She closed her eyes again. 'I am so tired . . . so very tired.'

Ragna waited until her mother was asleep, and then crept from the bedside. 'I think you are right,' she said to Niamh as she stepped from the room. 'The fever has gone. She is sleeping now.'

Lifting a hand to Ragna's face, Niamh touched her cheek. The skin was cool beneath her fingertips. 'How do *you* feel?'

'I feel as big as an ox,' she answered; her hands traced the outline of her bulging belly. 'Still,' she smiled wearily, 'I am well.'

'For the sake of the child, you should rest now.' Taking Ragna's elbow, she led the pregnant young woman away. 'I will have Tailtiu bring you something to eat, and then you must sleep.'

'What about you, Niá – when do you rest?'

'Do not worry about me,' Niamh replied. 'I am not the one having a baby. Go on and do as I say. I will stay with Ragni and wake you if she asks for you again.'

'Very well,' Ragna agreed, and allowed herself to be put to bed.

Returning to the sick woman's chamber, Niamh built up the fire to take the chill off the room and settled once more on the low stool. She closed her eyes, folded her hands, and began to pray softly to herself. Ragnhild murmured in her sleep, but did not wake, and after a moment gave out a little sigh.

Niamh broke off her prayers when she found that she was listening for Ragnhild to inhale again. 'Dear God in Heaven, please, no,' she gasped, but Lady Ragnhild was already dead.

The next day, Niamh and Ragna, and a score of Cnoc Carrach's vassals watched as the priest sprinkled holy water over the wooden box containing Lady Ragnhild's mortal remains. Taking up his censer, the priest swung it three times in the air above the coffin, before lowering it into the hole which had been dug beside the altar. He then began to chant, dipping the smoking orb each time he came to the Kyrie Eleison.

When he finished, he replaced the censer on the altar, and removed the stole from the coffin. He then summoned the four farmhands waiting at the side of the chapel to come forward with their ropes. They moved hesitantly to the altar, genuflected stiffly, and took their places, two at either end of the oblong box. Passing their ropes under the coffin, they lifted it and shuffled over to the hole in the floor, where they began paying out the rope.

The coffin slowly descended into the grave, and all went well until one of the men lost his grip and allowed the rope to slide through his hands. The coffin landed with a thump of such solid finality that Ragna, who had braved all to that moment, crumpled and began to weep. Niamh, standing beside her, gathered the young woman into her arms and held her, stroking her hair, while the priest began another round of prayers and his helpers began slowly shovelling dirt back into the hole.

Niamh clung to Ragna as if to stifle the sobs shaking her body, and breathed a last, silent farewell to her childhood friend as the dirt was tamped down and the floor slab replaced. The great flagstone slid home with a grating thud, and silence descended upon the chapel.

The priest departed, and the vassals filed out quietly, mumbling their respects to Ragna as they passed. The two women stood for a long time, clinging to one another, listening to the quiet hiss of the damp candles. Then, without either prompting the other, they turned and walked slowly from the little stone church.

Their grief was all but banished three days later when Ragna's birth pangs began. The first quivers started in the night, and by morning she was certain the baby was going to be born. Two of the estate's more experienced older women were summoned to help with the birth and, at Niamh's instruction, began to prepare the young woman for the ordeal ahead. They dressed her in a loose gown and took the bedclothes away, replacing them with rags and straw.

They filled four basins with water, two of which they warmed at the hearth; they made a potion of chamomile and lavender, which they gave Ragna to drink, and chafed the young woman's wrists and ankles. They prepared a salve of goosefat and rose oil which they rubbed on her back, legs, and thighs. All the while, they talked to Ragna about what to expect when the birthing began, and what they would do.

As the birth pains increased in frequency and severity, they held her hands, speaking soothing words and encouragements. They told her how beautiful the child would be, and how happy she would be when she saw the fruit of her body which God, in his boundless grace, had granted her. And, when the moment of birth came, they gathered close and held her upright, supporting her back and legs so that she should not injure herself straining too hard.

The baby, a boy, was born in the evening, and the whole estate gathered in the chapel to give thanks and celebrate the infant's safe arrival.

'He is beautiful,' Ragna sighed as she held the babe to her breast for the first time.

'He looks just like Murdo did the day he was born,' Niamh told her. 'He had long feet just like this one.' Taking a tiny hand in her own, she stretched out the little fingers with her fingertips. 'His fingers are long like his father's, too.'

'I wish Murdo could see him,' Ragna said. 'He would be so proud to know he had a son.' She paused, sadness creeping into her voice. 'One life is taken, and another given. Very strange, is it not?'

'Have you decided what he will be called?'

'I had thought to call him Murdo, after his father,' Ragna answered. 'But now that I see him, I think he should have a name he can make his own. Do you think Murdo would mind if his son had a different name?'

'I think men care less about such things than they let on.' Niamh brushed the tiny round head with its pale fluff of hair. 'A mother can be trusted to know what is best for her child.'

'Then I will call him Eirik,' declared Ragna.

'A good name,' mused Niamh. 'A name of strength and eminence. I like it!'

'It is the name of my great-grandfather – the first man of our people to be baptized a Christian.' Ragna cradled her baby, and whispered his name to him for the first time. 'Eirik,' she said. 'Do you like it, my darling?'

The two women sat for a time, cosy in one another's company, whereupon Ragna, exhausted from her labour, drifted off to sleep. Niamh pulled the bedclothes around the new mother and her infant, and then lay down beside them herself. Night folded itself around them and they slept soundly and peacefully, stirring only when the babe stirred.

It was Ragna who heard the commotion in the yard: voices raised, people shouting, the dogs barking, and the sound of horses stamping in the midwinter cold. She came awake with a start and saw Niamh resting beside her.

'Wake up, Niá.' She gently shook the older woman's shoulder. 'Someone is here.' Even as she spoke the words, her heart leapt in her breast. 'Wake up! The men! I think the men have returned!'

Niamh came awake at once. 'What? The men, you say?' She hastened to the single narrow window, rubbed the small square of glass with her hand, and peered out.

'Can you see?' Ragna sat up excitedly, waking the baby, who started and cried out, his tiny voice no bigger than a bird's cackle. 'Hush, my lovely,' soothed his mother. 'All is well.'

'It is still dark,' Niamh reported. 'I cannot see who it is. They have horses – three or four of them, I think . . .'

'Is it them? Is Murdo with them?'

'I cannot say.'

There came a crash as the bolted door burst open and the voices from outside spilled into the house. Then came the rapid thump of feet on the wooden stairs. 'They are coming up here!'

Niamh stooped and retrieved a poker from the hearth and stepped to the bedside. There came the sound of other doors banging open and, a heartbeat later, the door to their room opened and a man's head and shoulders thrust through the gap. Niamh tightened her grip and raised the iron poker.

The intruder saw the women, and called to someone behind him, 'Here they are! I've found them!' He pushed the door open wider, but did not come into the room.

Instead, he stepped aside and was quickly joined by two others, one of whom was a priest in a cowl and long brown robe. The foremost intruder was a tall, fair-haired knight of princely bearing; he regarded the women placidly, his expression firm, but not threatening. 'My lady,' he said, inclining his head. He looked from Ragna to Niamh, as if he was not certain which to address by that title.

'Who are you?' Niamh demanded, lowering the poker, but holding it across her body as a warning.

'I am Hakon Kol, my lady, house carle to Prince Sigurd.'

'What do you mean by disturbing the peace of this house?'

'I am sorry, my lady,' the warrior answered. 'We have come from Bishop Adalbert, who has . . .' He glanced uneasily at the young woman in the bed holding tightly to her infant, and his nerve began to desert him. '. . . the bishop has . . .'

The priest, seeing his envoy falter, pushed the knight aside impatiently. 'The bishop has placed this house, and all its lands and chattels, under the protection of the church.' Looking from Niamh to Ragna, he said, 'Are you Lord Brusi's daughter?'

'Yes, but –'

'Do you deny that Lady Ragnhild died and was buried four days ago?'

'I deny nothing.' Ragna replied, her fright giving way to disbelief and confusion. 'But the bishop knows full well that –'

The priest withdrew a rolled parchment from the pouch in the sleeve of his robe. Unrolling it, he began to read. 'Be it here known that for the good husbandry of these lands, Bishop Adalbert of Orkneyjar does hereby exercise the right of possession granted by Lord Brusi of Hrolfsey in the signing of the papal decree of remission and conveyance.'

'We are well aware of the decree,' said Niamh angrily. 'Yet, it does seem passing strange that you should choose this time to remind us of this fact.'

The cleric, ignoring her remark, resumed reading. 'For the protection of any and all Lord Brusi's surviving kinfolk, wards, dependants, and vassals, the bishop in accordance with the grant of rights has decreed that all said inhabitants shall be removed from these lands forthwith.'

'For our protection?' Niamh advanced. 'Speak plainly, priest! You are taking away our home, and casting us out into the cold.'

Folding the parchment carefully, the priest replaced it in his sleeve pouch. 'Adequate provision has been made for you elsewhere.'

'My father is on pilgrimage,' Ragna said, fighting to keep her voice steady. 'When he returns he will take up the lordship of his lands once more.'

The priest regarded her coldly. '*If* he should return.'

'This is our home,' Ragna pleaded. 'We have every right to stay here.'

'The bishop is responsible for your welfare, and is ever zealous to ensure your protection.'

'The bishop is ever zealous for his own gain.' Niamh advanced another step. 'To think that you would use the sad death of Lady

Ragnhild to cover your thievery. Shame! Shame on you and all your viper brood.'

The knight shifted uneasily, as if he would distance himself from the stinging accusation.

'You will be taken from here to a place where you can be cared for until such time as the final disposition of these lands shall be completed.' With a flick of his hand, the priest directed his now reluctant henchman to his duty. 'Take them out.'

Eyes imploring, apologizing, begging pardon for the hateful thing he was being made to do, the warrior moved a step forward. 'My lady,' he murmured softly. 'Please.' He made a small supplicating gesture with his hands.

Niamh made no move, but stood glaring defiantly at the priest.

'Take them away!' growled the priest.

The warrior hesitated, his frown deepening. The priest shouted his command again, and still the warrior balked.

Seeing his order defied, the priest rushed forward; taking Niamh roughly by the arm, he tried to wrest the poker from her hands. When her grasp proved the stronger, he raised his hand to strike.

As the blow fell, the warrior reached out, seized the priest by the wrist and jerked the hand aside, squeezing hard. The priest gave out a little shriek of pain and released his hold on Niamh, seeking instead to free himself from the knight's crushing grip.

The warrior bent the priest's arm and forced his hand behind his back. 'She is a lady!' Hakon said, his voice low, but filled with menace. 'Remember that.' He shoved the priest aside.

The priest staggered back, shaking with impotent rage. 'You will do as you are told,' he gasped, rubbing his wrist. 'You will perform your duty, or the bishop will hear of this.'

'I am Prince Sigurd's man, not yours!' the knight countered.

The priest turned and fled the room. In a moment, they could hear him calling for others to come and help him remove the women.

Turning once more to Niamh, the knight held out his hand. 'Please, my lady. Give us no trouble, and I will see no harm comes to you, or the young lady and her child.'

Niamh looked to Ragna, clutching the infant to her breast. Footsteps sounded in the room below as more men pounded up the stairs. 'My lady?'

'Very well,' Niamh relented, delivering the poker to her captor. She moved to the bed and put her arms around Ragna, who was sobbing softly. 'Be strong,' she soothed. 'We cannot prevent this, but we must do now what is best for the child.'

Three more men burst into the room with drawn swords. They made to fall upon the women, but the knight put out his arm as they tried to rush past. 'Stand aside!' he warned. 'I have given them safe conduct. Touch a hair of their heads, and you will answer to me. Is that understood?'

The men glanced from Hakon to the priest, seeking direction.

'Is that understood?' demanded the knight, his voice filling the room suddenly.

The soldiers nodded, put up their swords, and stepped aside. Hakon turned to the priest. 'Go and prepare the wagon. I will bring the women with me when they are ready.'

'You do not command me!' the priest objected.

Ignoring his protest, the knight signalled to the other warriors to leave the room – which they did quickly, relieved not to have to cross swords with their leader and friend. The priest followed them out, shouting at them to rouse their courage and perform their duty.

When the others had gone, the knight also departed. 'I will leave you to gather your belongings for the journey,' he told them, moving towards the door.

'Where are we being taken?' asked Niamh.

'I do not know, my lady. There is much about this that we were not told.'

'I see.'

'I will guard the door so that you will not be disturbed,' he said. 'Gather your things and come out when you are ready. I will conduct you to the ship.'

'Thank you, Hakon,' Niamh told him. 'Thank you for helping us.'

The knight made no reply, but inclined his head as he closed the door, leaving the women to themselves.

Ragna bent her head and began sobbing again. 'Come, daughter, save your tears,' Niamh said firmly. 'The time for weeping is not yet. I need your help now.' She opened the wooden chest at the foot of the bed, and began pulling clothing from it. 'The winter wind is cold, and we may have far to go. We must think carefully what to bring for the days ahead.'

Niamh emptied the chest, and then, coaxing help from Ragna, began to fill the box once more with the things they would need for their journey. When that was finished, Niamh helped dress Ragna in her warmest clothes, and bundled the babe in winding cloths. That finished, she dressed herself quickly, helped Ragna to her feet, and then summoned Hakon.

'We are ready,' she told him when he opened the door. Indicating the chest, she said, 'I would be grateful if you would have your men bring the box.'

'Certainly, my lady.'

The two started towards the door. Ragna, unsteady after childbirth and three days in bed, swayed on her feet and staggered backwards. The knight was beside her in two strides. 'Would you allow me?' he asked, holding out his hands for the child.

Niamh took the infant and gave him to the warrior. He turned and started from the room. 'Wait,' said Niamh; she stooped and retrieved a sheep's fleece from the hearth, crossed to the knight, and wrapped the sheepskin around the babe. 'Go,' she said. 'We will follow.'

Together the two women made their way slowly down the stairs and outside to the waiting wagon. A watery grey dawnlight glowed low on the horizon, and a few flakes of snow fluttered on the gusting wind. A group of vassals were standing in the yard, one of them bleeding from his nose and forehead; some of the women were crying. A few of them called out to Ragna as she was helped into the wagon, but, unable to bring herself to answer them, she raised her hand in silent farewell instead.

The two men bearing the chest came out into the yard. As they made to heave the wooden box into the wagon, the priest emerged from the house and stopped them, demanding to know what the chest contained. 'Open it!' he ordered. 'The bishop has commanded that nothing is to be removed from this place.'

Handing the infant to Ragna, Hakon turned to the priest. 'Leave it alone.'

'They might be taking valuables.'

The knight grabbed hold of the monk's robes and pulled him up close. 'You take the roof over their heads in the dead of winter, priest. Do you begrudge them the clothes on their backs as well?'

The priest made to reply, thought better of it and held his tongue.

Hakon released the priest and, to the men holding the chest, shouted, 'On the wagon with it.' Then, taking the horse by the bridle, he led the wagon from the yard and down the path to the waiting ship.

THIRTY-ONE

Murdo roamed aimlessly around the walls of Jerusalem, oblivious to his surroundings. The burning sun scorched his flesh, and the thorns of the desert brush scratched his bare legs bloody. Upon leaving the Holy City, he had stripped off his blood-stained clothes and thrown them away, keeping only his knife and belt, which he carried over his shoulder. He neither ate nor drank, nor stopped to rest, but walked day and night, his mind filled with horrific visions of carnage and butchery.

This is how Brother Emlyn found him two days later: naked and lost, his legs and feet bleeding, his red, inflamed skin blistered and peeling from his shoulders, forehead, and lips, dazed, unable to speak.

'Murdo!' cried the priest, running up to him. 'Oh, fy enaid, what have they done to you?'

Removing his own mantle, the much-relieved monk spread the garment gently over Murdo's sunburned shoulders. 'Here, now, let us get you out of the heat. Come, the hospital is just beyond that hill – not far. Can you walk, or should I carry you? Oh, Murdo, what has happened? No, do not say a word. There will be time to talk later. Save your strength. Come with me, my son; you are safe now. I will take care of you.'

Gently, gently, the good brother turned Murdo and led him by the hand up the hill to a nearby olive grove where the crusader lords had established a camp for the care of the wounded and sick. There, in the shade of the olive trees, priests and women – the wives and widows of the soldiers – moved quietly among the rows of tents, tending their charges. Despite the calming presence of the monks, the camp throbbed like a restless sea with uneasy sounds: the ceaseless moaning of the wounded over their injuries, the cries and whimpers of the dying, the juddering shrieks of the afflicted in their nightmares.

Emlyn led the unresisting Murdo to a place on the edge of the camp, and sat him down beneath the leafy branches of a low-growing tree. 'Rest here, and do not move,' he instructed. 'I will bring you some water.'

The cleric hastened away, and returned a few moments later, red-faced and puffing, bearing a gourd full of water, which he lifted to Murdo's mouth. 'Drink you now. Open your mouth, and wet your tongue.' Murdo did as he was told. 'Here now, drink a little.'

The water filled his mouth and he swallowed it down, and then began to drink in long, gasping, greedy draughts. 'Slowly, slowly now,' Emlyn warned, pulling the gourd away. 'Take your time, lad; there is plenty.'

Murdo put his hand to the gourd and brought it back to his mouth. 'The Saracens have poisoned every well and spring for many leagues around the city,' Emlyn told him. 'Until yesterday, the water must be fetched from the heights of Palestine, and beyond. We can get it from the city now, so drink it all.'

When at last Murdo pushed the gourd away, the monk sat back on his heels. 'Look at you, my friend. What has happened to you? Ronan and Fionn will be happy to know that you are safe once more. We worried when you did not return with the others after the city was taken. I shall tell them the glad news as soon as they return – they are with King Magnus at the council. I was given leave to search for you. Are you hurt?' Without waiting for a reply, he began examining Murdo's limbs and torso. 'I do not see any serious injuries –' he announced at last, 'save that you have been too long in the sun. I can make something for that, I think.'

Laying the gourd aside, Emlyn hurried off once more. Murdo leaned back, felt the cool shade on his sun-beaten head. All at once the water he'd drunk came surging up once more; he felt it swirl inside him and then it filled his mouth. He leaned forward on his hands and vomited. He felt better instantly and lay back, closed his eyes and fell asleep.

Though it seemed only a moment, when he awoke again the grove was in deep shade. Across the valley, the walls of the Holy City glowed with the golden light of the westering sun. Murdo lay for a time, unable to think where he was, or what had happened to him. But as he gazed at the shining walls and the dark smoke billowing up in gilded columns, the whole terrible ordeal came winging back to him as if from a very great distance.

The tears came at once to his eyes, and Murdo wept. He saw again the poor drowned child, the helpless murdered babies, the burned Jews in their temple, and tears flowed down his cheeks and splashed onto his stomach and thighs. He gasped for breath and tried to stem the flood of sorrow, but it bore him up and carried him away, and he was powerless to resist. His body began to shake, and he was convulsed by loud racking sobs which tore up from his throat as if loosed from the bottomless black pit that was his soul. Great ocean waves of grief and shame rolled over him, and he, a rag tossed up and dragged under with each new surge, wept and wept – until oblivion claimed him once more, and he slept again.

It was late the next day when Murdo woke and looked up through the leafy branches of the olive tree to a yellowing sky. He yawned and wondered how long he had been asleep – one day? Two? He had a vague memory of being roused from time to time and made to drink sweetened water, but no real sense of how much time had passed. As he pondered this, he became aware of a peculiar sound and realized it had awakened him: a droning, incessant, sharp-edged crackle falling from somewhere high above.

Turning his eyes to the sky, he saw that the crackling sound came from an enormous whirling dark cloud across the valley: thousands upon thousands of crows and ravens and, higher still, innumerable vultures and eagles.

Murdo gazed in awe at the endlessly swirling, squawking mass. He followed the downward spiral of their flight to a triple-peaked mound beside the road – the corpses of the crusaders' victims heaped into a pale mountain outside the northern wall. The mountain was alive with carrion birds.

Turning away from the sight, he sat up – wincing from the pain of his blistered skin. He touched his chest, and his fingertips came away slick and greasy. Looking around, he discovered that he lay on a mat of woven grass, naked beneath a thin cloth; his belt and knife lay beside him – along with Emlyn's mantle, neatly folded, and a gourd full of water which he took up at once and drained in long gulps.

His back and shoulders felt as if he had been scourged and then dragged by wild horses through flaming coals. There was a gnawing

301

ache in his empty stomach, and his eyes and lips throbbed. But it was not until he tried to stand up, that the fiery pain in his feet burst upon him. He fell back whimpering; the soles of his feet were gashed and torn, the skin hanging from them in shreds.

He groaned, squeezing his eyes tight against the pain and breathing in quick, panting gasps. This awakened Emlyn, who was lying behind him on the other side of the olive tree. 'Murdo!' he cried, rolling to his knees. 'You have come back to us! How do you feel?'

Before he could answer, the priest said, 'Are you hungry? There is bread and broth; I will get some for you.' He darted away before Murdo could think to call him back.

Unable to lie down again for the pain, Murdo leaned on his elbow and looked out towards the city. The shadow of the hillside stretched across the valley, and the ferocious heat of the day was abating. He could see men and wagons moving on the roads outside the city. Although he could remember all too vividly what he had witnessed in Jerusalem, he could not recall what had happened when he left the city, nor how he had come to be in the olive grove.

He pondered this until Emlyn returned a little while later, bearing a big wooden bowl and two flat loaves under his arm. 'The pilgrims here have been starving for months,' he said, 'but now that the city is free, food is more plentiful.'

Yes, thought Murdo grimly, *and I know why: the dead eat very little.*

Settling himself beside the tree, the monk helped Murdo sit up, and placed the bowl in his lap. Tearing a piece of bread from the loaf, he put it in the broth to soften it. 'Ronan and Fionn were here for a while today. They helped me prepare the unguent for your burns and cuts.'

'Where are my clothes?' Murdo asked in a voice as dry and rough as gravel. Taking up the spoon, he began to eat.

Emlyn shook his head. 'God knows,' he said. 'You are as I found you. I feared you had been set upon by Saracens. You were dazed by the sun, I think, and could not speak.' The priest looked at him with large, sympathetic eyes. 'Were you attacked?'

Murdo, his mouth full of soggy bread, only shook his head.

'Some of the things they are saying ... terrible things ... I cannot ...' the monk broke off and turned his face away. Murdo glanced up and saw Emlyn's eyes full of tears.

Murdo felt his throat tighten and his own tears welled up. He bent his head and began to weep anew. Huge salty tears fell from his eyes and into the bowl in his lap; ragged sobs seized him and he began to shake as the grief and shame descended all over again.

Emlyn, kneeling beside him, took the bowl away then and Murdo felt the priest's arms encircling him. Emlyn cradled Murdo to his breast, and whispered, 'Let it go, Murdo. Let it all come out. Give it to God, my son. Let the Good Lord bear it away.'

Murdo gave himself to his sorrow. As before, he was helpless against the deluge. The waves of remorse tossed him to and fro, battering him without mercy.

Emlyn held him, stroking his head, and after a while began to chant in a low murmuring voice: 'The Good God is my shepherd, I nothing want. In green pastures he makes me lie, and leads me beside the waters of peace; he renews my soul within me, and for the sake of his good name guides me along the right path. Even though I walk through the death-dark valley, I fear no evil thing, for you, O Lord, are with me, and your crook and staff are my very present comfort . . .'

When he finished the psalm, the monk began another, and then another – until at last the grief began to ebb. Murdo pushed the heels of his hands into his eyes and smeared the last of the tears across his blistered cheeks. Emlyn released him and took up the gourd; seeing it was empty, he went to refill it, and returned to find Murdo with the bowl raised to his mouth, spooning broth into his mouth. He accepted the gourd gratefully, and drank deeply.

They sat together in the growing twilight, silent in one another's company, watching the campfires spark to life across the valley. Then, with the monk's help, Murdo rolled onto his side, put his head down, and closed his eyes. The last thing he heard was Emlyn's promise to stay with him and watch over him.

Murdo woke twice during the night to the sound of his own screams. The atrocities and brutality stalked him in his dreams, and he imagined himself trapped in the burning mosq, or fighting for his last breath with a spear through his gut. Each time, Emlyn was there to comfort him and soothe him back to sleep with a psalm.

The next morning Emlyn was nowhere to be seen, so Murdo lay

back and dozed. In a little while he heard the soft footfall of someone hastening towards the tree. He lifted his head. 'Emlyn?'

'Murdo, I was coming to wake you,' he said, his voice shaking slightly. 'You must come quickly.'

'Why? What has happened?'

'Fionn has just come. It may be that he has found your father.' Emlyn took up his mantle, shook it out and began helping Murdo into the oversized garment. 'We must hurry.'

'Where is he?' Murdo asked, painfully drawing his arms into the sleeves. The coarse cloth was savage next to his sore skin. 'Is it far?'

'Not far. Fionn has gone in search of a donkey for you.'

'I can walk.' Murdo made to get up at once. His skin was still raw and sore from the sunburn, but it was his feet which hurt him more – cut and battered as they were, they had swollen and he could not put his weight on them. 'Agh!' he cried, sitting down quickly. 'No, it hurts too much.'

'Let me help you.' Taking the edge of his cloak, Emlyn tore strips from it and began wrapping the bands around Murdo's feet.

'Cannot my father come here?' asked Murdo. He saw from the priest's expression that he could not. 'Is he wounded then?'

'I fear he is,' Emlyn confirmed.

'How badly?'

'I cannot say.'

'How badly, Emlyn?'

'Truly, Fionn did not tell me. He said we must come quickly. Ronan is with him.'

While he was binding Murdo's feet, Fionn returned with the donkey, and hastened to help them. 'We must hurry, Master Murdo,' Fionn told him. 'Your father – if it *is* your father – is very ill. Are you ready? Put your arm around my neck.'

Together, the priests took him gently under the arms, lifted, and stood up. But even with his weight resting on the monks' shoulders it was still too painful. Murdo groaned and bit his lip to keep from crying out. Black spots spun before his eyes, and sweat broke out on his forehead. The monks steadied him, and then carried him the two steps to the waiting donkey and boosted him onto the animal's back.

Fionn led them higher up the hillside, passing through the hospital camp. Murdo was appalled and sickened afresh by what he saw: men were everywhere scattered on the ground, the blood of their wounds staining the earth dark beneath them. The fighting had been short, but fierce; many soldiers lost hands and arms to Seljuq blades, and others bore deep gashes and terrible slashes; most, however, had been pierced by arrows. The Turks routinely tipped their arrows with poison, so their victims lingered in agony for a goodly while before they died.

Of all the wounded Murdo saw, only a fortunate few had so much as a grass mat or cloth on which to lay, and fewer still had tents. Consequently, many tried to escape the blistering heat of the sun by making shelters out of their shields, or flinging their cloaks on low-hanging branches to create sun-breaks for themselves.

Some of the wounded men watched him with sick, pain-filled eyes as he passed, but for the most part each pilgrim was too preoccupied with his own dying to notice anyone else. No one spoke and, save for the constant murmur of moans or the occasional death rattle, the hospital camp was unnaturally quiet.

Fionn led them to a small tent near the top of the hill. At their arrival, Brother Ronan stepped from the tent, his face solemn. 'Good,' he said. 'I have told him you were coming. He is anxious to speak to you, Murdo. Are you ready?'

Murdo nodded, and the monks helped him dismount from the donkey; Emlyn took his arm and supported him as he hobbled inside. The sick-sweet stink of a festering wound permeated the close air of the tent. Murdo gagged and choked back bile as the good brothers lowered him down next to a raised pallet covered by a crudely-made matt of grass. On this bed lay a man Murdo did not know.

'We will stay near,' said Ronan as the monks left the tent. 'You have but to call out if you need us.'

Murdo made to protest that they had brought him to the wrong man, when the body next to him said, 'Is it you, Murdo?'

He looked again, and with a shock recognized in the pale, haggard face of the wretch beside him, the much-altered visage of his father. 'My lord?'

'I have been praying one of my sons would come,' Ranulf said, his voice both raw and hushed – little more than a croaking whisper. 'I did not know it would be you, Murdo. How is it you are here?'

305

'I have been searching for you,' Murdo told him. His eyes fell to the stump of his father's right arm. Bound in bloody rags, the arm was missing below the elbow; the stench emanating from the wound gave Murdo to know that it was rotten. Bleak despair swarmed over him and he felt a sensation like falling. 'Is it bad?'

'Bad enough . . .' he closed his eyes, then opened them again, suddenly agitated. 'You must hear it!' Ranulf said, rising from his pallet. He seized Murdo by the shoulder. Murdo winced from the pain to his sunburned skin. 'You must hear it, and tell others how it was. Take word back to the islands – tell them what happened.'

'I am listening,' Murdo said, trying to soothe. 'Rest now. I am here.'

He made to remove his father's hand, but Ranulf clung on, squeezing hard. 'Promise me, boy. Promise you will tell them.'

'I will tell them,' Murdo replied. He turned his head to call to the priests, but his father released him and slumped back, breathing hard, exhausted.

'Good,' he said, his breath coming in clotted gasps. 'Good.' With the tip of his finger, he indicated a waterskin on the ground beside the pallet.

Murdo took it up and gave him to suck at the opening, watching him as he drank. The face of his father was deeply lined, the eyes sunken, the flesh pale and yellow like old linen. The high, noble brow was waxy and damp, the dark eyes fevered. The once-strong jaw was grey with whiskers, and the lips were dry and cracked, the features pinched with pain.

But the lines eased as the lord drank and the pain released its grip; the fever-bright eyes dulled. Murdo guessed there was some kind of drug in the water. Turning his face from the waterskin, he regarded Murdo for a moment, and the ghost of a smile touched his mouth. Ranulf seemed to improve somewhat. 'I never thought to see you again, Murdo. But here you are.'

'Yes, lord.'

'I am glad,' he said. A spasm of pain coursed through him and he stiffened against it. After a moment the pain passed, and he said, 'Listen to me, now. You must tell them . . . everything.' His voice grew sharp with insistence. 'Everything – hear?'

'I am listening,' Murdo answered, swallowing the lump in his throat. 'And I will tell them, never fear.'

His father lay his head back and appeared to compose himself, marshalling his strength. Murdo waited, leaning forward to catch each word as it came to his father's lips, fearing these would be the last. After a moment, Lord Ranulf began to speak.

THIRTY-TWO

'It was bad for us at Antioch,' Ranulf said, 'but Dorylaeum was worse. By God, it was worse.'

Murdo had not heard of the place, but committed the name to memory, repeating it softly to himself. 'Dorylaeum.'

'Duke Robert's army was the last to arrive in Constantinople,' Ranulf continued, 'and the last to cross the Bosphorus. We were put aboard the ships so fast we got but a bare glance at the Golden City, and then we were on the march again.

'Nicaea was already under siege by the time we got there, and indeed, fell the next day, no thanks to us. Seeing how Amir Kerbogha was away and most of the city's defenders with him, the infidel governor surrendered without a fight. We secured the city and returned it to the emperor's rule, as we were foresworn to do, for all we were that eager to move on to Jerusalem.

'They told us we would be in Jerusalem before summer. Six weeks, they said. Blessed Jesu, it took a year!'

The outburst brought on such a fit of coughing that Murdo pleaded with his father to break off his recitation. 'Here, rest a little,' he said. 'You can tell me more later.'

Ranulf refused, saying, 'It passes . . . it passes.' He swallowed some more of his elixir and continued. 'So that is that. We leave Nicaea to the emperor and we march on. What do we find? The Turks have destroyed everything: settlements deserted, towns and farms abandoned. Whole forests have been burned, and any source of water has been spoiled – no well, but what it has been fouled; no stream, but what it has been filled with rocks. Truly, it is a God-forsaken place.

'It is not so long – a few days only – and our water is already gone, for we have not been able to get fresh water anywhere. So, it is decided to make two divisions, and each will fend for itself. We draw lots, and it falls that one division will be under Raymond's

308

authority – that is Godfrey, Baldwin, Hugh, and the rest of the Franks – and this one will fare seven miles north of the road.

'The other division is to be led by Prince Bohemond – that is, all the rest of us – and we fare south of the road. We make good marches, meeting no resistance. God help us, but it is dry! We thirst, and people begin to talk of turning back. The commanders push on, and the ranging parties cannot find provender or water – the little they find disappears too quickly, and we are no better for it.

'We come to the mountains – they are small mountains only, not too rough, or too high – and it is a little better for us. The air is not so hot, and we can find a few rock springs still dripping from the rains. There are Turks in the mountains, too, but they cannot get at us with their arrows, so mostly they leave us alone.

'And then all at once the mountains give way to a plain that stretches as far as the eye can see. This plain is full of hills and, God be praised, a river!

'There are no Turks around, so we make for the river as fast as we can, and come upon the ruins of Dorylaeum – it is all broken walls and heaps of rubble so there is nothing to fear. As soon as Bohemond gives the order to halt and make camp, we all flock like geese to the riverside to drink our fill, and oh! the water is sweet and good. We wallow like pigs in it, and spend the rest of the day filling casks and butts and skins with fresh water. We tether the horses on the meadow and spend a peaceful night.'

Lord Ranulf paused, and swallowed hard. The pain came back into his eyes as he continued, 'Next morning, we break camp. We have not seen Count Raymond's division, but he cannot be far away. No doubt they have seen the river, too, and stopped to refresh themselves as we have done. One of the lords says, "We should wait for them." Another says, "We should send scouts to find them." Bohemond will not hear it; he is all for pushing on before it gets too hot. We move on.

'We are marching past the ruined city now . . . the sun is in our eyes . . . it is just coming up over the hills and, by God, it is already hot!

'Lord Brusi is riding beside me. We are talking of this and that. Torf and Skuli are behind us, and Paul and Brusi's boys are but spitting distance. Brusi raises his head and says, "Here now! What is this?"'

'We look up and see four scouts flying back along the column. "The enemy approaches!" they shout. "Less than two leagues away."

'We ride to where Bohemond and Tancred have dismounted. The lords of Flanders and Normandy and all the other noblemen hasten to join us. Less than two leagues! We will not even have time to arm ourselves properly. Brave Bohemond is not stirred. "How many?" Taranto asks; he is always ready for a fight.

'The scouts are uneasy. They do not want to say. "It looks to be the sultan's war host," says the scout, avoiding the prince's stare.

'"Answer me!" demands Bohemond, his big voice shaking them out of their fright. "How many?"

'"Sixty . . . perhaps seventy thousand, my lord," the scout replies. "Maybe more."

'Seventy thousand! We can hardly believe our ears. We have maybe eighteen thousand knights, and thirty thousand footmen – the rest are women and children, priests, and the like who do not fight. Sultan Arslan's troops are all horsed – the Saracens keep no footmen, mind.

'But the prince is not dismayed. "Ride to the other column," he commands the scouts. "Tell Count Raymond we will meet the attack here. He is to join battle at once. Get you gone, by God!"

'The scouts wheel their horses and gallop away while Bohemond instructs his standard bearer to sound the call to arms. Meanwhile, the nobles hold council to order the battleranks.

'The field is not good. We are exposed on all sides, with but a marshy place a little down from where we stand. "The reeds and shrubs will provide the best cover," says Taranto. "We will put the camp there. The knights will form the line in front of the camp." The prince points to a low rise just ahead of where the camp will be. The rise stands at the mouth of a valley formed by a low-sloping ridge which curves around the marshland like a bowl. Heaven help us, it is a sorry place to mount a defence, but there is no time to search out a better one.

'"The Saracens overmatch us for numbers," the prince tells us, "but not for strength. One knight in battledress is worth ten Saracens. We have but to wait until they close on us, and then we will take them with our spears and drive them back up the hill."

'So it is agreed. The horns give out their blast and we are racing

away in all directions to form the line. Knights are everywhere struggling into hauberk and war cap, and strapping on greaves and sword-
belts. Slinging our shields over our shoulders, we remount our horses
and hurry to our places behind our battlechiefs.

'The battle line is only half-formed when the sultan's army appears
over the ridge: a hundred thousand strong. Either the scouts have
made a poor count, or the Saracen host is growing as more join it
from the nearby towns. We pull together as quick as may be – Lord
Brusi with his sons, and I with mine, and most of the Scots fall in
with Bohemond's troops – but there are big gaps in the line. We
tighten our grip on our spears and await the charge. But it does not
come.

'Would to God that it did! But, no, Sultan Arslan's warriors do
not charge like true fighting men. Instead, they skirt the battlefield
in swift, ever-moving swarms. They buzz around us like wasps. They
draw near to loose their stinging arrows and feint away again, only
to reappear and harass the line somewhere else.

'Still, we hold our ground. We keep our shields between us and
the arrows – the few that get by the shields – are easily deflected by
our good ring-mail hauberks. We stand our ground, unafraid. Let
them swarm and buzz! Where is the hurt?

'Ah, but there are so many of them, and every now and then one
of us slumps in the saddle and falls. More often a horse will be
struck from under its rider, and that unlucky knight becomes a
footman. Yet, though we bide our time, the enemy will not charge.

'Clearly, we cannot endure this abuse forever. It makes no sense
to stand by while they slay us man by man. So, after a goodly time,
the commanders demand another council. "They will not stand!"
bellows Stephen in his rage. "How, in God's Holy name, can you
fight an enemy who will not stand?"

'Once his mind is set, Bohemond is not easily shifted. "We have
but to wait until they grow tired of this spineless ruse and make
their attack. Then we shall cut them down like saplings."

'"How long must we wait?" shrieks Count Robert. "We stand our
ground and they cut us down with those infernal arrows. I say we
charge!" The Duke of Normandy agrees: "Make an attack – break
through and scatter the dogs, I say. Cut them as they run!"

'"Bohemond commands here," Tancred reminds them. He says
little, this Tancred, but he is shrewd and tough as his cousin. "If

Lord Taranto says we wait, my lords, then we will wait until Judgement Day."

'The bold prince flings his hand at the swarming mass of infidel. "Look! See how many the sultan commands. They would swallow us whole. We must hold the line until Raymond's forces join us. *Then* we will make our attack – not before." Bohemond glares around him; he does not like our position any better than the rest, but what else can we do?

'So the lords return to their troops on the line. Brusi and I tell our Scots and Orkneyingar what the prince has decided, and we all hunker down to wait for the rest of their army to join us so the real fighting can begin. But the day is getting on before us; already the sun is passing midday and there is no sign of Raymond's armies. Where are they? But a few leagues separate us – what can be taking them so long?

'Meanwhile, the Seljuq archers are growing increasingly daring and, though it is difficult to tell, it seems more infidel take the field with every assault. We begin to fear the enemy is refreshing itself from an even greater number of warriors than we have yet seen. Bohemond rides up and down the line, calling out exhortations, keeping our courage high.

'All the while, the enemy flies at us – always swarming, swarming like wasps, like hornets shaken from the nest to sting and sting again. We stand firm. The day passes, and still Raymond's army does not appear. God have mercy! Where are they? Why have they deserted us?'

The question became an anguished cry as Ranulf, reliving the battle anew, felt again the hopelessness of that terrible day. He struggled upright, and the movement brought convulsions of pain and coughing. Murdo sitting rapt at his father's side, brought up the waterskin and gave his father to drink. 'Peace,' he said, trying to soothe. 'It is done and over; there is nothing to fear.'

Ranulf took a long pull on the waterskin, then pushed it away. 'I look down the line,' he said, falling back onto his sweat-soaked pallet. 'The gaps in the ranks are larger now. The battleline is growing ragged. The men are clumping together, seeking shelter from the arrows under one another's shields – the first sign of an army feeling its defeat, mark me.

'Bohemond is riding back and forth, shouting for the knights to reform the line, and all at once a great shout rises up. I see Bohemond turn in the saddle, and I turn, too. Duke Robert has broken from the line and is leading a charge into the nearest swarm of Turks. Lord Brusi and his sons have gone with them. We had vowed to stand together with the prince, and the fool has followed the Normandy knights into battle.

'But wait! They have caught the enemy by surprise. The Turks are thrown backward upon themselves – those coming up from behind are driven back by warriors fleeing the charge. All at once they are confounded. Turks scatter in all directions, and it seems the knights will make good the attack. Others are calling now to be released to join the charge.

'Bohemond is wary. He calls for us to stand our ground, but no one heeds him any more. They think they see the chance we have been waiting for, and are desperate to seize it and make an end of the slaughter.

'With a shout for God and glory, they put spurs to their mounts and charge into them. The Flemish and English troops join the attack, and they are quickly followed by Stephen and Tancred and their warriors. Even Bohemond's knights strain after the others, but the prince holds us back. "Stand, men!" he cries, racing back and forth along the line. "Hold your ground!"

'Those of us left behind cry out to be allowed to join the assault. It is all I can do to keep Torf and Skuli at my side – they are eager to take the battle to the infidel. Everyone is shouting to attack, but the stubborn prince refuses. He shouts us down with his big voice and forces us to obey on pain of death. "I will flay alive any man who defies me!" he bellows, standing in his stirrups at the head of his troops.

'So, we have no choice but to stand and watch as our comrades pursue the enemy over the low hills.' Ranulf paused, swallowed hard, and then continued, his voice growing taut. 'God save us, the knights passed from sight over the hilltops, riding hard, and we see them no more. For the space of four heartbeats we hear nothing ... suddenly, the Seljuqs reappear. The treacherous dogs have circled around from behind. Oh, their horses are lighter and faster. The Turks are able to move like the wind over the hills, vanishing and appearing at will.

'It is but the blink of an eye, and already the attacking force is

313

surrounded. The enemy presses in on all sides, rending the air with their war cry of "Allah akbar! Allah akbar!" We stand and watch, but can offer no help. All the while, the short steel-tipped arrows fall upon our comrades like killing rain. We watch our kinsmen tumble from the saddle. God save us, their bodies cover the hillside, and still they fall!

'The knights try to rally. Duke Robert leads them and they drive again and again into the whirling enemy. A small gap appears in the Turkish line. The knights try to break through. I see the duke fighting his way to the place, only to see it close again before he can reach it. He drives on, regardless. Two Seljuq archers come before his face; they draw their bows and let fly. The first arrow strikes the rim of his shield and glances away; the second hits him in the chest, but he charges on.

'One of the archers has already darted away, but the duke catches the other squarely in the middle of the back as the fellow turns to flee. The force of the blow carries the slender Seljuq out of the saddle and he slams to the earth with the spear in his back. The duke's sword is in his hand before the hapless Turk touches the ground, and fifty more knights charge into the breach their fearless commander has forced.

'A heartbeat later, the crusaders are streaming through and the enemy cannot prevent their escape. The knights gallop back to the line which Bohemond has succeeded in holding all alone. "Join us here," the prince commands. "Reform the line! For the sake of Christ, reform the lines!"

'"They are very devils!" shouts the duke as he pulls the arrow from his hauberk. Knights are thundering back to resume their places. There are far fewer than before. I look, but I cannot see Lord Brusi. The other sorties have fared less well than Robert's. Tancred and Stephen, having run aground at the top of the hill, are scarcely able to slash their way back to the line. Good men and horses fall around them every step of the way. Once a knight is unhorsed, the Seljuqs fall upon him and cut him to pieces with their thin swords – three and four of them, hacking like butchers, until the knight is dead.

'The Count of Flanders and a great number of knights have become surrounded, and only escape when the enemy archers run out of arrows and must break off the attack. Before the sultan's troops enclose them again, the Flemish gather up their wounded and fly back to the line leaving a trail of bodies as they go. It is a slaughter, God knows, and we can do nothing but stand and watch it happen.

'The prince and lords are angry now, and desperate. "Where, for the love of Christ, is Raymond?" bellows Duke Robert. You could have heard him all the way to the sultan's camp.

'"Maybe he is attacked, too," says Stephen, rubbing sweat and blood from his eyes. "Maybe he cannot reach us."

'"Get back to your troops!" Bohemond roars – angry at the fools for breaking ranks. They have wasted good men in their folly, and the prince is in no humour to listen to them. "Regroup and reform the line."

'But the lords are discouraged. "What is the use?" demands Count Robert. "There *is* no line – we are surrounded on every side. There is nowhere to turn."

'Bohemond is adamant. He is furious. "I say we will hold the line until the Devil himself comes to take us."

'"We will die!" shouts the count, and the others agree.

'"Then say your prayers," Bohemond roars, "and die as faithful knights of the cross."

'They glower at him, and curse his name, but Bohemond will not be turned. "Get you back to your men. Dismount and put your horses behind you. Lock shields and stand behind your lances." Turning to Stephen, he cries, "Send men to the camp and tell the footmen and women to bring water to the line."

'Well, it is over for us,' said Ranulf, after another drink from the drugged waterskin, 'the sun moves across the sky, and the battle continues. The women and foot soldiers hurry back and forth to the line bearing jars and buckets of water. The Seljuq swoop and swirl, filling the burning air with arrows and their hateful, jeering cry, "Allah akbar! Allah akbar!" God is great! God is great!

'Then, above the triumphant cries of the infidel and the thunder of their horses, I hear a wail arising from the marshy land behind us. We all turn to see the camp followers fleeing towards us. The Turks have at last overcome the foot soldiers guarding the camp and are plundering the tents and wagons, and slaughtering the defenceless women and children who are trying to escape into the reeds and mud of the marsh.

'I look and see two Turks ride down a young woman from behind

– one of them splits her skull, and the other tramples her body under the hooves of his horse. They whoop in triumph as they murder her, and then turn their horses and ride back into the screaming mass to kill again.

'Bohemond is alight with rage. He is a very berserker! Look at him! Screaming in defiance, he springs to the saddle, bellowing for his troops to fall back and protect the camp. The other lords are to fill in behind us and hold the line. Before his orders can spread to the flanks, the prince is already racing back to camp. Alas! The other troops see the centre of the line collapse, and they retreat.

'Oh, the fools! The fools! All at once, the whole army is in motion. War band after war band withdraws – falling away from the line by scores and hundreds. Since no one had been ordered to cover the mistaken withdrawal, the retreat swiftly becomes a rout. The Turks, seeing the line crumble at last, believe that the moment for the attack has come. They draw their swords and charge, riding us down from behind. Cutting us to pieces with their swords. The screams of the dying fill the air.

'The battle is lost. The end of the crusade is at hand.'

Lord Ranulf fell silent. He lay back sweating, his breath coming in gasps from the effort of telling his story. Murdo, kneeling at his side, leaned close and offered another drink. After a moment, he lowered the skin from his father's lips and asked, his voice small against the horror of the battle, 'What happened next?'

THIRTY-THREE

'The battle is lost,' said Ranulf after a time. The drug that kept the pain at bay began to make his voice thick. He spoke, and the words seemed to struggle up from the depths of torment, as from a deep well. 'We stand on our feet and make the sign of the cross over ourselves. We prepare to die.

'But Bohemond is not defeated. He struggles forward through the onrushing tide of retreating troops, striving to turn them to battle. Duke Robert and Count Stephen follow his lead – they gather what is left of their armies and take their places either side of Bohemond.

'We can hardly stand. Our swords are heavy in our hands.

'The sultan sees the victory now.

'They come at us. By the thousands they come. For the first time all that long day, we have a solid force before us. We grip our spears and meet the charge, making good account of the weapons in our hands. We are fighting for our lives!

'The sound is deafening. I hear nothing but a growling roar like angry thunder. Faces swim before me out of a mist of sweat and blood. I grip my spear but the haft grows slippery in my grasp, and it is soon carried away. I fumble for my sword . . . God help me! I cannot find it! My sword!

'There! I have it! I make to pull it free from the scabbard and I feel a sharp pain in my arm. I look to see blood spurting from a gash above my wrist. The infidel's sword is quick. It strikes again before I can defend myself. I see the curved blade flick out, and feel the sting again – it bites to the bone.

'My fingers will not close on the hilt. The blade spins from my grasp. I cover myself with my shield and await the final blow.

'But my attacker is gone! God in heaven, they are falling away. I look down the line to see the infidel fleeing the field. Why? What can this mean?

'There! Streaming down the hill! See them? They come! They come! Raymond and the other lords have found us at last. God be praised! We are saved!

'I see crusaders sweeping down the hillside. Who is it? Is it Duke Godfrey? It is! His column is first over the ridge. Riding at the head of his troops, he leads them into the unsuspecting Turks.

'The other lords ride fast behind. Count Raymond gains the ridge to the left of Godfrey, and Bishop Adhemar – the bishop himself leading a force of five hundred knights – appears in the valley by way of a narrow gap in the hills. Suddenly, I see them flying towards us from all sides.

'The startled Seljuqs turn as one to see a new army charging down upon them. One moment they are at our throats, bearing down for the kill – an instant later, the sultan's entire war host is streaming away in wild retreat. Praise God, they are running over one another in their haste to get away!

'Bohemond seizes the chance. Oh, he is not slow. He lofts his sword and sounds the war cry. Then he is charging into the retreating enemy. Reaching for my sword once more, I slip my shield onto my right arm, and grasp the blade with my left. It is awkward, by God, but it will serve.

'Somehow we stir our feet, and rally once more. We wade into the maelstrom, hewing at the enemy horsemen as they pass by. We cut them from the saddle, and impale them on our spears. The blood runs down our upraised swordblades and the hilts became greasy in our hands. Yet, we stand to our work, slashing and chopping, until we can no longer grip our weapons.

'When there is no one else to kill, we look up. The enemy is gone from the field. Godfrey, who has begun the assault, gives charge of his troops to Baldwin. "Pursue them with a vengeance," he commands. "Whatever happens, do not let them regroup." And Baldwin, eager for blood, chases the fleeing enemy through the valley.'

Ranulf paused to swallow, tears in the corners of his eyes as he remembered the great tide of relief at their deliverance. Murdo looked at his father's stump of an arm, feeling the dull horror of the unrelenting day.

'We see no more. The retreat carries the battle from our sight, and we slump down to the ground to catch our breath. Whether wounded or hale, we all hug the earth and thank God we are still alive.

'Later, we are told that the chase led back to where Sultan Arslan had established his camp away over the hills to the east. So swift is the pursuit, the sultan had no time to dismount and change horses before the crusaders were upon him. The sultan's bodyguard put up enough of a fight to cover their master's retreat – then they too fled after him, leaving tents, horses, and all the sultan's treasure behind.

'See, the Arabs are a wandering people. They trust not to palaces nor cities. That is their way, and that is how we get the plunder: we run them off and take it from them. God in heaven, the sultan had a very great treasure hoard, and we took it all.'

Ranulf fell to coughing again. Murdo watched helplessly as the convulsions racked his father's wasted body. Ranulf paused; he touched his fingertips to his lips. Murdo raised the waterskin again, and gave his father to drink. 'Rest a little,' he suggested. 'I will stay with you. We can talk again later.'

But Ranulf seemed not to hear. 'The treasure is vast,' he continued, his voice dry and hollow, 'gold and silver beyond imagining. Baldwin seizes it at once. The battle is over . . . I look around. The cries and shouts still roar in my ears. I can hear nothing for the tumult of war yet raging in my head. I stumble out upon the battleground.

'The dead . . . the dead . . . Blessed Jesu there are more dead than living. I cannot walk for falling over the bodies . . . knights and footmen . . . women and children – their bodies are ripped and torn, their blood and inward parts spilled upon the ground . . . corpses with neither head nor limbs . . . I saw a priest disembowelled, and a baby with hoofprints on his back . . .'

'Father, please,' Murdo begged.

'Seventy thousand!' cried Ranulf, struggling up once more. 'Seventy thousand in one day! That is what they said – add to that women and children, priests and old men – who knows how many more? Seventy thousand knights and footmen went down in death at Dorylaeum. More than twenty thousand were wounded, and many of these lingered in agony only to die in the next few days.

'I searched for Brusi and his sons,' he said, falling back once more. 'I searched the night, but never saw them again. They fell at Dorylaeum with all the rest . . . with all the rest. I never found them.'

The air inside the tent was stifling and Murdo longed for a fresh breath, but dared not leave his father's side. 'Rest now,' Murdo begged, 'you will regain your strength.'

'Nay, son.' Ranulf gave a slender shake of his head. 'I am dying.'

Murdo blinked, trying to hold back the tears. 'Father, I . . .' he began, and could say no more before the tears burst anew.

'Nay, nay,' Ranulf hushed. 'I am shrift and ready. Take word to your mother – tell her how I died.'

'Of course,' answered Murdo. 'I will tell her.'

'Wicked the waste! Wicked!' croaked Ranulf, growing agitated once more. 'Arrogant fools! We paid the price for our folly, by God! We paid with our lives.'

'It is over now,' Murdo said, trying to soothe his father. 'The fighting is finished. Jerusalem is taken.'

But Ranulf would not be calmed. Rising up from his bed, he clutched at Murdo. 'Go home. Find your brothers and go home. This fight is not for us.' He gripped Murdo by the shoulder. 'Tell them what happened here. Promise me, son.'

'I have already promised, remember?' said Murdo, dashing the tears away with the heels of his hands.

'So you have. Good,' said Ranulf. 'Listen to me now. There is one thing more. I leave this to your care, and that of your brothers.' Releasing his hold on his son, Ranulf fumbled at the edge of the pallet with his remaining hand. Strength failing, he fell back, drawing the lumpy mat away from the crude wooden frame.

Murdo gaped in amazement. For there, heaped in a jumbled, gleaming mass beneath the dying man was a treasure trove of gold and silver objects, more valuable, more opulent, more wonderful than anything he could have dreamed.

THIRTY-FOUR

Even in the ochre half-light of the tent, the treasure dazzled. Murdo filled his gaze with the glimmering objects: cups and bowls, plates and platters, armbands and bracelets, bejewelled chests and chalices, caskets, and boxes, necklaces, diadem, and chains of all kinds in heavy gold and fine silver. Scattered in amongst the valuables, like shells or pebbles on the beach, were golden coins, bezants bearing the emperor's image. Some of the surfaces gleamed with the quick bright fire of rubies, the rich green glow of emeralds, and the luxurious milky radiance of pearl. Unable to resist, Murdo reached into the heap and pulled out a gold-handled dagger in a sheath set with sapphires – the sheath alone was more valuable than anything he had ever touched.

Murdo cradled the knife as if it were the frail soul of his father to be snatched away from him at any instant. He held his breath, clutching the knife, trying to comprehend the meaning of such an immense amount of wealth: certainly it was more than Jarl Erlend ever possessed, and doubtless more than many a northern king would amass in a lifetime; probably more than King Magnus himself owned, including all his ships and lands.

'Is it truly ours?' asked Murdo at last, still struggling to take in the immensity of their fortune.

Ranulf, his eyes closed, breath raspy in his throat, gestured to his lips. Murdo retrieved the waterskin and applied it again to his father's mouth. The lord drank but a mouthful before pushing the skin away. 'Even before Nicaea we had decided that any plunder should be shared out equally among the nobles, for the lords to distribute as they saw fit. Everyone agreed. No one knew it could be so much. Nicaea . . . Dorylaeum . . . Antioch . . . ' He coughed. 'What you see is all my share, which I saved. Take it, son,' gasped Ranulf. 'Use it for the increase of Hrafnbú.'

A pang of guilt and remorse pierced Murdo at the word. He could not now bring himself to tell his father that Hrafnbú was gone.

After a moment, Ranulf roused himself. 'Torf and Skuli . . . they have joined Baldwin at Edessa. They were not here when the battle commenced, but you can find them – find them and go home.'

Murdo nodded. 'I will find them, lord, and we will return to Dýrness.'

'Good.' Ranulf closed his eyes again and sank into the mat. 'Leave me now. Let me rest.'

'I will stay.'

'No, son. It is better you go.' He reached out his hand, which Murdo took in both of his. 'Remember what I said.'

'I will remember.' Murdo put the waterskin next to his father's side where he could reach it, and limped painfully to the entrance of the tent. 'I will be outside if you need anything.'

Lord Ranulf's lips framed a ghostly smile. 'I am glad you came, son.'

Murdo nodded, and pushed the tent flap aside. Emlyn was there to support him. Ronan and Fionn, sitting nearby, stood up and came to him. 'He is going to sleep now,' Murdo informed the monks. 'I told him I would stay nearby.'

The priests helped him to a comfortable position in the shadow of the tent. Then Fionn went to fetch the grass mat, and asked Ronan to bring some food and water for them all. Emlyn sat with Murdo, his eyes full of sorrow for his young friend's anguish.

They sat together in silence until they heard footsteps approaching. 'That will be Fionn returning,' said Emlyn rising. It was not Fionn who appeared, however, but a woman. She glanced at him, and hesitated, then saw Emlyn and said, 'Ah, it is you, brother. I am sorry to be so long.' She produced a small stone jar from a bag she carried on her shoulder. 'I have brought him another draught of the potion.'

'He is sleeping now,' the monk told her. 'This is his son,' he said, indicating Murdo.

The woman glanced at Murdo, and nodded. 'I will just put it nearby so he can have it when he wakes.' She pushed aside the flap and stepped into the tent.

'Genna has been caring for your father,' Emlyn explained. 'Her own husband was a knight killed at Antioch. They were on pilgrimage together and –' He broke off as Genna opened the tent flap.

'You should come,' she said simply.

Emlyn was on his feet at once. He stepped to the tent entrance, looked inside, then bent his head. After a moment, he turned to Murdo.

Murdo could tell from the monk's expression what he was going to say. 'Is my father dead?'

'Yes,' replied Emlyn. He stooped to raise Murdo to his feet, and helped him to the tent.

Lord Ranulf lay on his crude pallet as before, but now his features were relaxed and calm, and he was gazing up tranquilly as if contemplating a peaceful sky. He still clutched the waterskin, but it was empty now; he had drained it to the dregs, and the pain-numbing potion had done its final work.

Murdo stood for a long time, trying to make sense of the welter of his emotions, feeling angry, hurt, lost, and alone.

Emlyn stepped to the pallet and, placing a hand to the lord's face, drew down the eyelids. He then stretched his hand over the body, and began chanting softly. 'Our Father in Heaven, most holy is your name. Let your will be done on earth, as in your kingdom. Do not let us fall into the traps of the Evil One, but deliver us from all harm . . .'

Murdo heard the words – he had heard them countless times – but they meant nothing to him. Instead he observed how death had transformed his father's face, returning most of that which the fatal wound had taken from him. His features, gnawed thin and sharp by weeks of hunger and the last days of pain, were relaxed in repose: the tightness around the eyes and mouth eased, the pinched brow smoothed.

In a moment, the priest finished his prayer. He reached down and made the sign of the cross on Lord Ranulf's forehead. 'Sleep,' said Emlyn quietly, 'sleep, friend, in the calm of all calm. Death lies on thy brow, but Jesu of Grace has his arm around thee. Rest in God's peace.'

Genna retrieved the stone jar and turned away. 'I am sorry,' she said softly, then ducked quickly out of the tent.

Arriving a moment later, Fionn and Ronan entered, their faces solemn. 'The woman told us,' Ronan said gently. Fionn crossed to Murdo, and put his hand on the young man's shoulder. 'May God bless you, my friend, and enfold you in his mercy.'

323

'Brothers,' said Ronan, 'let us commend this pilgrim's soul to God.'

The three took their places around the bed – one at the foot, one at the head, and one beside. They then stretched out their hands over the body, and began to chant softly in a language Murdo did not know. He watched and listened, thinking that his mother would want to know every detail; no doubt she would recognize the words of the chant.

The Célé Dé repeated their song three times, and then, folding Ranulf's arms over his breast, they straightened his limbs and began readying the body for burial. The swiftness of the preparations alarmed Murdo. 'Must it be so soon?'

'We dare not delay any longer,' Fionn said, and added, '- owing to the heat, you see.'

'We will see him properly buried,' Ronan assured him. 'Emlyn will stay with you while Fionn and I prepare the grave. We will come for the body when we have finished.'

Emlyn settled down beside Murdo, and the two of them sat gazing at the body. 'It was good you could say farewell, at least,' the monk said after a while. 'I would that we had found him sooner.'

'You were searching for him all this time?' wondered Murdo.

'Aye, we were,' replied Emlyn. 'They told us in the camps that Duke Godfrey's troops had been first on the wall, and Duke Robert's army was with him. The fighting was fiercest there, they said, and those first on the wall had borne the brunt of the attack and suffered heavy losses. So,' the monk concluded sadly, 'we began searching here.'

They fell silent for a time, and Murdo's thoughts turned again to the treasure. 'Emlyn,' he said, 'there is something I must show you.'

The cleric turned his eyes to the young man beside him.

'My father was . . .' Murdo began, but could not find the words. Instead, he simply lifted the edge of the grass mat and revealed his father's treasure.

The cleric stared at the mound of gold and silver on which the dead man lay. 'Oh, fy enaid,' Emlyn gasped. He reached out and touched a golden bowl. 'Then it is true – we have been hearing tales of marvellous treasures, but I never imagined . . .' His hand fell away and he looked at the precious objects, shaking his head slowly.

'It was his share of the battle plunder,' Murdo explained. 'He said I was to use it for the increase of our lands.' His voice faltered; he was suddenly pierced by an ache of longing so intense it took his breath away. 'I want . . .' he said, breathing hard, 'I want to go home, Emlyn.' He bent his head and let the tears fall in the dust.

A short while later, Ronan and Fionn returned to announce that the grave was ready. They brought with them a linen burial cloth in which they carefully wrapped the body, securing the shroud with long strips of binding cloth. Then, as they prepared to remove the body from the tent, Murdo said, 'One of us must stay here.'

Ronan glanced at him in surprise, and Fionn made to protest, but Emlyn said, 'I will remain behind.'

'But why?' said Fionn. 'There is no need. We are finished here and the tent can be of use to someone else. It is – '

'Murdo has his reasons,' Emlyn said firmly. 'You three go. I will wait behind.'

'Are we to know these reasons?' asked Ronan, turning to face the hesitant young man.

Murdo frowned, gazing at the body of his father in its cocoon-like shroud. 'Very well,' he answered. 'I have entrusted the secret to Emlyn already; I will tell you, too, and be done with it.'

Lifting the edge of the mat, he exposed the treasure trove to their view. The astonishment of the two clerics was no less than Emlyn's. Fionn reached in and took hold of a golden drinking bowl with rubies on the rim. 'There is a kingdom here!' he declared.

'Less a secret than an affliction,' observed Ronan tartly. Turning to Murdo he said, 'If you would take my counsel, get rid of it.'

'Get rid of it!' cried Murdo, shocked that anyone would suggest such a thing.

'Truly,' intoned Ronan solemnly, 'wealth such as this is the root of all evil.'

'Surely, brother,' objected Emlyn, 'it is the *love* of wealth which is the root of all evil – not the simple possession of it.'

'It is easier for a camel to pass through the eye of a needle,' Fionn reminded them, 'than for a rich man to enter the Kingdom of Heaven.'

'Quite so,' agreed Ronan. 'So long as you hold to these riches, your soul will be in danger of hell.'

'He is right, Murdo,' conceded Emlyn. 'The treasure will be nothing but a curse to you. Very soon it will begin to poison your life and soul. Unless you are very strong, it will kill you in the end.'

'Give it away,' Ronan urged earnestly. 'Give it as alms to the poor. Get it far away from you as quickly as possible.'

'I will *not* give it away,' insisted Murdo. 'I promised my father it would be used for the increase of our lands. Anyway, my brother Torf-Einar is Lord of Dýrness now, so it is his place to decide what shall be done with it.'

'Never tell him,' Ronan countered. 'Let the secret die with your father.'

'I will honour the vow I have made,' Murdo told them bluntly, 'and will hear no more about it. I have shown you the treasure, and now bind you to secrecy. If anyone learns of this, the blame will fall on your heads, and I –'

Ronan raised a hand in a conciliatory gesture. 'Peace, Murdo,' he said gently. 'No one will hear the smallest breath of a word about the treasure from our lips. Your secret will abide with us for so long as you care to keep it. We will stand by you and do whatever we can to protect you.' Turning once more to the body on the pallet, he said, 'But before we sit down together to decide what is best to do for the living, we must complete our care of the dead. Are you ready, son?'

Murdo nodded; his anger had faded as quickly as it flared. Sorrow claimed him once more.

'Then let us proceed with the burial,' Ronan said. 'Emlyn will remain behind to keep watch over the treasure until we return. Come, it is time to see our brother on his way.'

Together, the priests lifted Lord Ranulf's body and carried it from the tent to the donkey waiting outside. They slung the limp corpse over the patient beast and, leaving Emlyn to stand guard, began a small, somewhat curious procession to the burial ground. Ronan led the way, walking at the head of the donkey; Fionn came behind, bearing Murdo on his back. The priests chanted a low, mournful lament in Gaelic as they went; the plaintive sound of their voices in the bright daylight of an alien land seemed strange and unutterably sorrowful to Murdo.

They proceeded over the hill behind the hospital camp to a little valley where the bodies of dead crusaders were being buried. The whole of the valley was filled with small oblong mounds of newly-turned earth – hundreds upon hundreds of graves, each marked with a crude cross made of sunbleached stones. There were many priests and women at work, digging the shallow graves which would forever hold someone's father, husband, brother, or lord. *At least,* Murdo thought bitterly, *my father will not lack for companions.*

They came to a hole scratched in the dry, desert ground, whereupon the priests ceased their mournful song. Murdo sat on a rock and watched as they lifted his father's body from the donkey and laid it beside the grave. 'Would you speak, Murdo?' asked Ronan.

Murdo shook his head. He could think of nothing to say.

Ronan nodded to Fionn, and the two priests shifted the body into the grave. They began chanting again – a psalm in Latin this time. Fionn took up a handful of dust-dry earth and gave it to Murdo, indicating that he should toss it onto the corpse. Murdo stood, hobbled forward a few steps, knelt down and placed the first handful squarely on his father's chest.

The monks, still singing, then started dragging dirt over the body using the flat stones with which they had dug the grave. They worked from the feet of the corpse upwards, but when they reached the head, Murdo said, 'Wait.'

Reaching down, he pulled aside the burial cloth to reveal his father's face so that he could look upon him one last time. Lord Ranulf seemed to be calmly asleep. The lines of his face were smoothed now with a stillness that suggested he had come to peace at the end of his travail. Murdo looked upon the face he had known and respected and loved all his life. *My lord will never see the green hills of Orkneyjar again,* he thought sadly, *nor delight in the face of his lady wife, his best beloved. His bones will dwell forever in a strange land, far away from the home of his fathers.*

Placing the tips of his fingers to his lips, he then pressed them to Ranulf's cold forehead. 'Farewell, Father,' he whispered, his voice cracking as his throat closed over the words.

He pulled the shroud back into place and pushed the earth over his father's face with his hands. When they had mounded up the earth, they gathered stones from the ground around them and outlined a white cross over the grave. Kneeling at the head of the grave, Ronan offered up a long and thoughtful prayer for the soul of a man cut down on pilgrimage. Murdo listened, but his mind wandered as he raised his eyes from the mound before him to look out over the wide expanse of newly-made graves. There were hundreds, and these were but the few who had even reached their destination. He thought about all the rest, all the thousands upon thousands claimed by starvation and thirst, by the ferocious heat, disease, and the arrows and blades of the enemy.

Wicked the waste, his father had said, and Murdo felt the righteous fury stir in his grief-heavy heart. In that instant he vowed he would never die in a land not his own.

After the prayers, and another psalm, they helped Murdo onto the donkey, and walked slowly back to where Emlyn was waiting. The monks maintained a respectful silence until reaching the tent, whereupon Ronan spoke up. 'Much as I might wish otherwise, we dare not linger here,' he said. 'The tent is needed. It would be best if we left it quickly so as not to arouse interest in our affairs.'

'Let them have the tent,' Murdo answered. 'It is nothing to me. I will find my brothers and tell them what has happened. They will help me protect the treasure.'

'There will be time later to consider what you will do,' the priest suggested. 'First, we must think carefully how to conceal the treasure so that it can be moved.'

'We will need a wagon – a small one, at least . . . ' he began.

Ronan pulled on his chin. 'Every wagon is needed for moving supplies and water to the camps. It will not be easy to find one, and any wagon suspected of carrying treasure will fall prey to thieves. We will have to conceal it somehow.'

The three fell silent pondering how this might be accomplished. Try as he might, Murdo could not think of any way to move the treasure from the tent without letting the whole world know he had it. Perhaps Ronan was right after all, he thought: here, he had not even taken possession of the treasure, and already the curse was beginning to bite.

'Maybe we could find a camel,' suggested Emlyn. 'The desert folk use them as beasts of burden. We could get one to carry the treasure.'

'How would that help?' wondered Murdo. It seemed to him thieves could as easily steal a camel as a wagon full of treasure, and he said so.

'Not if they thought it carried corpses!' Emlyn said. 'Many of the noble families of Jerusalem are carrying their dead to family tombs in the desert. We might pose as one of these and carry the treasure away.'

The idea seemed absurd and ludicrous to Murdo, but he had nothing else to suggest. 'Even if we wanted to, how could we find one of these camels?'

'Leave that to me,' said Ronan. 'Now, we must hurry.' He turned to the waiting Emlyn. 'Secure some more burial shrouds and bindings. The three of you prepare the treasure as you would a body. I will return as soon as I can, and you must be ready.'

THIRTY-FIVE

When all the bodies of the Holy City's former inhabitants had been collected by the few miserable survivors, the corpses were heaped onto great mounds outside the Gate of the Column and the Jaffa Gate. Whether Greek, Armenian, Egyptian, Turk, or Palestinian, all were flung onto the pile; Muslim and Jew and Christian, together in death as they had mingled in life. The corpses had been but one day in the sweltering sun when they began to bloat and burst, spilling a noxious stink into the air which permeated the whole city.

Count Raymond was especially distressed by the horrific stench. In anticipation of receiving the grateful call of his comrades to assume the kingship of the Holy City, he had appropriated the citadel for himself and his entourage of servants and advisors, and was therefore close to the Jaffa Gate, where a large number of bodies had been brought. The wind coming off the sea sent the odour rising up the walls and in through the open windows of the palace fortress. The cackle and cough of the scavenger birds became as constant as the stench was ghastly.

'Burn them!' he cried at last, suffocating from the ripe, putrid smell wafting through his rooms. 'Burn them and be quick about it!'

'Lord count,' counselled his chaplain, 'I urge you to reconsider your command. The smoke resulting from such a fire would be far worse than the stink itself.'

'I do not care,' Raymond snapped angrily. 'At least it will silence those damnable birds! Nothing could be worse than listening to the corpse-pickers day and night. Burn them! Burn them *all*, I say! Do you hear me, Aguilers?'

'I hear and obey, my lord. It shall be done.' The abbot bowed to Raymond's authority, and wished, not for the first time that Bishop Adhemar was still alive. He made to leave, then remembered his previous errand and turned back. 'Forgive me, lord, I was merely wishing to announce the arrival of Count Robert. He is waiting in your private chamber.'

'This soon!' cried Raymond. 'Good! Good!' Leaping from his chair, he strode for the door where he paused long enough to throw another command over his shoulder. 'See to the burning, abbot. I want it begun before I return.'

Raymond's long legs carried him quickly to the inner room he had chosen for the reception of his envoys and intimates. The count had let it be known that, as the lord chosen by the pope himself to lead the crusade, he would not refuse the summons of his peers to govern the Holy City. To this end, he had sent his chief supporter to the various camps to determine the mood of the other lords regarding his speedy accession to the Throne of Jerusalem.

Unfortunately, fever had claimed his most ardent and loyal supporter, Bishop Adhemar; and Counts Hugh of Vermandois and Stephen of Blois had departed the crusade after Antioch, leaving Raymond somewhat deficient in ready companions to champion his cause. Casting his net of favours more widely, he coaxed a reluctant Robert, Count of Flanders, to his side; Robert had quickly become Raymond's closest confidant. Owing to Robert's extraordinary lack of personal ambition, he also enjoyed the trust of the rest of the lords and noblemen. For the last two days he had been flitting from camp to camp, talking to the various leaders, and gaining the measure of each lord's desire for the throne. Having completed his first survey of the field, Robert had returned to report his observations. He now sat slumped in his chair, hands folded over his stomach and legs straight out in front of him, eyes closed.

Count Raymond burst into the room to find his friend asleep, crossed to the table and filled two chalices with wine. Taking them both, he turned and shoved one under Robert's nose. 'This will revive you, sir! Take and drink!'

Robert opened his eyes and accepted the cup. He drank long and deep of the sweet dark wine, and said, 'By the god who made me, Toulouse, it is blistering hot in the camps.' He drank again and held out his cup to be refilled. 'At least the wind is out of the west so it takes away the stink.'

'I have given orders to have the bodies burned at once,' replied Raymond as he filled the cup from the jar. 'But tell me, what have you learned?'

Robert drank again and wiped his mouth with the back of his hand. 'Ah, that loosens the tongue somewhat.' Glancing at the count, he said, 'Now, to business.' He placed the cup on the board. 'This is the way of it: any direct opposition to your taking the kingship has vanished like the dew in the desert sun. Bohemond will no doubt be content with Antioch – likewise Baldwin with Edessa. Both have as much as they can do to hold on to what they have won so far without taking on Jerusalem, too.'

'Let them try!' sneered Raymond. 'The cowardly dogs did not so much as lift a finger to help us win the city. It will be long and long before those two are welcome within these gates.'

'Just so,' agreed Robert. 'There is great sentiment among the other nobles that neither of them should share in the spoils and plunder, since they did not see fit to complete the pilgrimage. No one would support a bid by either of them to become king.' He raised his cup and took another long swallow before resuming his recital. 'That just leaves Robert of Normandy, and Godfrey of Bouillon.'

'Yes? And what is their disposition?'

'My cousin the duke is making plans to return to Normandy even as we speak,' Robert replied, 'and Godfrey is likewise so inclined; his brother Eustace is not well, and they wish to leave as soon as possible.'

'Then this time next week, God willing, I shall be king,' mused Raymond.

'I did not say that,' Robert cautioned.

'You said there was no opposition,'

'I said there was no *direct* opposition,' corrected Robert. 'None of the lords will challenge you, that is true. But the clerics among us are saying that the Bishop Arnulf of Rohes should take the city for the pope. They insist Jerusalem should be placed under ecclesiastical rule, and he is considered the leading cleric since the demise of Adhemar.'

Raymond's eyes narrowed. 'The bishop is a good and steady man, it is true,' he allowed, raising his cup to his mouth. 'And his many preachments have been of great encouragement to the men – never more so than before these very walls. But he commands no army of his own; and unless the pope places a body of troops under his command, I do not see how any churchman can hope to protect the city, much less govern it. No, it is preposterous.' He drank quickly, and asked, 'Is there much support for this ill-concocted view in the camps?'

'Some, it must be said,' the Lord of Flanders conceded.

'What of the bishop? Does he say whether he would welcome a move to place him on the throne?'

'Our friend Bishop Arnulf is keeping his thoughts to himself,' Robert replied. 'He says only that it is a vanity to be king in the city where the Holy Saviour himself reigned.'

'Twaddle!'

'Nevertheless, the sentiment enjoys considerable support,' Robert pointed out. 'Godfrey agrees whole-heartedly.'

'It is a nonsense,' Raymond declared. 'A kingdom must have a king. I take nothing away from our Lord Christ by ascending the throne of Jerusalem. Rather, I should in every way improve that throne which has suffered decline among the infidel so long a time.'

'The bishop could, I believe, be persuaded to become Patriarch of Jerusalem,' suggested Robert, 'if he had sufficient cause to believe the interests of the pope would be best served by the king.'

'Perhaps we can find a way to persuade him.' Raymond smiled and took up the wine jar once more. 'You are a good friend to me, Robert.' He poured wine into both cups. 'But tell me now, what will you have out of this?'

'I am content,' Robert answered. 'To see the Holy City returned to Christian rule is enough for me. I have lands of my own to redeem from my tight-fisted brother.'

'But the whole of Jerusalem is ripe for the taking. You must wish something for yourself,' Raymond suggested.

'What should I have wished for but the success of the pilgrimage? May God be praised, I have that already.'

Just then there came a knock at the door and the Abbot of Aguilers appeared. 'Forgive me, lord, but a messenger has arrived from Jaffa to say that Emperor Alexius' envoy is on his way.'

Raymond's expansive mood shrivelled slightly. 'Is he indeed?'

'Even now, lord,' the chaplain confirmed.

'When is he expected?'

'Before nightfall, I am told.'

The Count of Toulouse considered for a moment, then said, 'When he arrives, he is to be met at the gate and conducted here. I would have him stay with me while in Jerusalem. Is that understood?'

'Certainly,' replied the chaplain.

'Good. Then see that rooms are made ready for his use,' Raymond commanded. 'Alert me when he arrives, and I will welcome him myself.'

The chaplain nodded once and withdrew. As soon as the priest had gone, Lord Robert said, 'This is unexpected. Word of our victory cannot have reached Constantinople so swiftly. They must have been waiting nearby to see how the battle went.'

'Yes.' The count's frown deepened and he stared into his cup. 'I will not pretend delight at his coming. Indeed, I heartily wish the issue of succession had been settled before he arrived. That will not happen now, and we must deal with it as best we can.'

Robert drained his cup and stood. 'I am tired. If you have no further use for me, I will go to my tent and rest.'

'By all means, my friend,' Raymond said. 'But stay here and take your rest until the envoy arrives.'

'With all respect, Toulouse,' Lord Robert replied, 'I find that the stench is far less offensive outside the walls. I think I would rest better in my own tent.'

'As you will,' the count granted. 'But do return when the envoy arrives – we will sup together and discover the emperor's intentions for the Holy City.'

'You are most kind, Toulouse,' Robert accepted with a nod of his head. 'I would be honoured, of course.'

The flame-red sun dimmed to a foul yellow glare as it descended over the dry Palestinian hills. Dalassenus paused to drink from his waterskin and gazed upon the Holy City rising before him on its rock of a mountain. The thick black smoke rolling heavenward seemed like living columns holding up a hazy sky. He had been watching the smoke most of the day, and now he could smell it: heavy and oily, it stank of burned fat and meat and hair and bone. At first he feared the city itself was ablaze, but now that he was upon it, he could see that the fires came from outside the walls, and he knew the source.

'Drungarius?' asked his strategus.

'Yes, Theotokis?' he said, without taking his eyes from the endlessly rolling pillars of smoke.

'You groaned, my lord.'

'Did I?'

'I was wondering if you were feeling well.'

Dalassenus made no reply, but lifted the reins and urged his horse forward once more. A short while later, the imperial envoy and his company of advisors, officials, and Immortals reached the Jaffa road and proceeded directly to the city gate where they were met by Count Raymond of Toulouse's men, who led their party to the citadel where the count was waiting to receive them.

A short while later, the visitors passed through the gates and into the palace precinct where they were welcomed by Raymond himself, and several other nobles – including Duke Robert of Normandy, and Duke Godfrey of Bouillon, who had learned of the envoy's arrival and had come to see the first skirmish of the campaign ahead.

'Pax Vobiscum, drungarius,' said Raymond, stepping forward as the envoy dismounted. The count greeted his guest with open arms, and the two embraced stiffly. 'I trust your journey was uneventful. Now that the road from Jaffa to Jerusalem is in our hands, travellers will find their pains eased considerably.'

'Indeed,' agreed Dalassenus, 'the road was hot and dusty as ever, but it was blessedly free of Turks.'

'Alas, we can do nothing about the heat,' Raymond replied. 'No doubt the emperor has more influence in that domain.' He laughed loudly at his jest, and was joined in his mirth by his nobles, who chuckled politely.

'No doubt,' replied Dalassenus, somewhat awkwardly.

'Come now, you are tired and thirsty. We will allow you to refresh yourselves before supper.' Turning to his servants, Raymond commanded them to lead the envoy and his party to the rooms provided for them.

'It is a thoughtful gesture,' Dalassenus granted, 'but it is unnecessary. My men and I will find lodgings at the Monastery of Saint John. The good brothers provide simple, but adequate, fare and accommodation. We will be more than comfortable there.'

Raymond's face fell. 'That, I fear, will not be possible.'

'No?' Dalassenus regarded the count steadily. 'And why should that be so?'

'Regrettably, the monastery suffered somewhat in the battle.'

Dalassenus' face hardened. 'Are you saying it was destroyed?'

Raymond met the envoy's challenge with a show of pious remorse. 'The monastery escaped destruction,' he explained, 'not so the brothers themselves. They were unfortunately killed.'

This announcement caused a stir among the imperial visitors, who all began talking at once, demanding to know what had happened. Dalassenus silenced them with a word, and then turned once more to the count. '*All* of them were killed?'

'Alas, yes – all of them,' admitted Raymond.

'In God's name, why?' demanded Dalassenus, his face darkening with rage. 'They were Christians, man! Priests! Monks!'

Raymond lowered his head and squared his shoulders to the envoy's wrath. He deeply rued the blind zeal of his fellow crusaders which had purged the Holy City of its entire population, but he did not see what could be done about it now. He had little choice but to meet the imperial ire head on. 'We are all aggrieved by the lamentable incident, to be sure.'

'Lamentable incident!' howled Theotokis, struggling forward. 'You slaughter fellow Christians out of hand, and call it a . . . a *lamentable incident*?' Drawing himself up, he spat at the feet of the Latin lords. 'Barbarians!'

The western nobles, angered at such blatant disrespect, began shouting at the Byzantines. Some few started forth with curses and balled fists.

'Enough!' growled Dalassenus, quickly regaining his composure. To Raymond he said, 'We will make our camp outside the walls. In the name of the Emperor Alexius, I demand that you and the other lords and leaders of the pilgrimage convene in council tomorrow morning when we will discuss this, and other issues arising from the recapture of the city.'

Raymond, eyes hard under lowered brow, met the envoy's anger with flinty obstinance. 'As you will,' he muttered gruffly.

The imperial company withdrew to the Church of the Saint Mary on Mount Zion outside the southern wall, and made their camp within the grounds. Raymond and some of the lords returned to the citadel to drink and discuss the next day's council. Bewildered by the Byzantine response to their offered hospitality, they liberally doused their umbrage with the sweet dark wine of their conquered realm and, as the night wore on, vowed increasingly elaborate revenge on the slight.

For their part, the Greeks spent the night praying with the monks of Saint Mary's church for the souls of their murdered brothers, and for Jerusalem's Christians who had been slaughtered by their supposed liberators. After the prayer vigil, the envoy retired to the cell prepared for him by the monks. Dalassenus slept ill, his spirit troubled by the insidious ignorance and brutishness of the Latin pilgrims; he feared for the day ahead and the demands he must make on behalf of the emperor. The lords of the West had shown themselves truculent and untrustworthy guests, no better than the infidel.

He shuddered inwardly to think what Alexius would do when he learned what had happened at Jerusalem. It would be best for all concerned if the crusaders could be convinced to hand over the Holy City to the rule and governance of the emperor, and as quickly as possible – tomorrow would not be too soon.

Dalassenus had just lapsed into a fitful sleep when he was awakened by the arrival of several monks begging places for the night. It was strange, he thought, for the night was far gone and these were western clerics, but unlike any he had met before. He looked out from the door of his cell and saw them – three robed monks and a fourth, a tall, anxious-looking youth – as they were led across the church's inner yard. The young man started at seeing his face in the doorway, but the four hurried past, and Dalassenus went back to his short and troubled sleep.

THIRTY-SIX

While Raymond was meeting the emperor's envoy at the palace gates, Murdo and the monks were busy binding Lord Ranulf's treasure into corpse-like bundles. Using the rags Fionn had secured, they bound the various items of gold and silver together and stuffed the spaces between them with dried grass and straw – as much to keep the metal objects from clanking together as to fill out a roughly human shape which they then wrapped in a burial shroud.

They worked quickly, gathering and binding, wrapping and tying. At Fionn's urging, Murdo reluctantly withdrew six gold coins from the heap. 'You are not stealing it, Murdo,' the monk chided, 'merely using some of the first fruits to help save the harvest.'

As soon as the last knot was tied, they dragged the bundles from the tent lest anyone become suspicious of their activity. Lastly, Murdo retrieved his father's sword, shield, and hauberk before abandoning the tent to the use of some other wounded soldier. The three of them settled under a nearby olive tree to await Ronan's return.

'What can be keeping him?' wondered Murdo. He cast an anxious eye over the ungainly bundles, of which there were four – three large, which might pass for adults, and one somewhat smaller, which might be seen as a child. Throughout the camp, the monks and women went about their chores, tending to the wounded and dying. No one seemed to notice the little company waiting for the burial cart; Murdo, fearing they might be discovered at any moment, remained ever alert and watchful.

The baleful sun crossed the sky vault to extinguish itself in a blood-red haze, and still Ronan did not appear. 'I suspect camels are more difficult to obtain than horses or donkeys,' Fionn suggested. 'Ronan macDiarmuid will not fail us. Have faith, Murdo.'

'God is ever moving amidst the chaos,' Emlyn added grandly, 'his subtle purposes to perform. Trust not in the works of men, but in the Almighty whose designs are eternal, and whose deeds outlast the ages.'

Despite repeated entreaties from the two priests to calm himself, Murdo could not rest. Even after dark, he found no peace – for, though he was grateful for relief from the heat, the rising moon shed more than enough light for thieves to work. He looked at the night-dark sky. The stars, veiled by a high-blown haze of smoke, glowed like the eyes of skulking hounds caught by torchlight in the dark.

He drew a hand across his face and tried to wipe away the fatigue. He was hungry and tired, and sore, and the first seeds of sorrow were beginning to take root. Murdo did not mind the hunger, nor his scorched skin, nor his hurting feet; those were small pains compared to the sharp, gnawing ache growing in his heart. He missed his father, and he missed his home; he wanted to see the low green islands of Orkney, and feel the cool northern wind on his face again; he wanted to see Ragna, to hold her, and he wanted this miserable day to end.

Fionn nudged him gently. 'Someone is coming,' he whispered.

Murdo sat up. 'Where?'

'Down there.' Fionn pointed to the trail which wound through the valley below. He could see a grey shape moving on the tree-shadowed path, but it was still too far away to see clearly. Closer, the shape resolved itself into two parts, one large, one small. The large shape had long legs and a steeply-humped back; the smaller, walking beside it, was a man.

'It is Ronan,' Fionn confirmed. 'I told you he would not fail us.' Standing up quickly, he said, 'He will not know where to find us. I will bring him.'

Murdo watched as the monk hurried down the tree-covered hill, his pale form flitting in and out of the moonlight. Upon reaching the trail, he saw Fionn approach the elder priest, whereupon they both turned and proceeded towards them. The camel appeared to grow larger with every step; in fact, it was a far bigger animal than Murdo had realized. And it stank of rancid dung.

Indeed, it was one of the most repulsive creatures Murdo had ever seen. The beast was covered with a thick pelt of matted, mangy hair that hung in ragged clumps; bulging eyes gazed lazily out from a small, flat head perched atop a long, ungainly neck; huge flat feet splayed out from bony, scabrous legs, and its great hump sat like a shabby mountain above its distended belly. The thing shuffled when it walked, and folded itself awkwardly when it lay down – which it did as soon as Ronan stopped tugging on its rein rope.

'We must hurry,' Ronan said upon reaching them. From a yoke-shaped wooden frame he withdrew a wad of cloth which he handed to Murdo. 'I brought you some clothes.'

'We have been waiting all day,' Murdo said bluntly, accepting the clothes.

'I thought it best to wait until nightfall,' the elder priest replied, 'when I knew the beast would not be needed.'

'You stole it!'

'Borrowed it, yes,' corrected Ronan. 'As it says in the Holy Scriptures: As they approached the Mount of Olives, Jesu sent two of his disciples ahead saying, "In the village ahead, you will find a camel tied there. Untie it and bring it to me, and if anyone should ask what you are about, tell them the Lord has need of it, and he will give it to you right away." I simply obeyed the Good Lord.' The priest glanced at the sky to reckon the time. 'Still, it would be best for us if the animal was found in its place by morning.'

'But I am going to Edessa to find my brothers,' Murdo declared.

'As to that, I have had a better thought,' Ronan replied. 'For now, get you dressed while the brothers and I secure the treasure.'

The priest hurried away again, leaving Murdo to stew. He quickly shrugged off Emlyn's mantle, and pulled on the clothes Ronan had brought for him – a pair of breecs, with a wide cloth belt, and an ample siarc of a fine, lightweight material, much like the flowing robes favoured by the inhabitants of the region. There were no boots or shoes, but he could not have worn them anyway. While he dressed, the others busied themselves with loading the treasure.

The work was swiftly done, and Ronan hastened to where Murdo was wrapping the belt around his waist. 'Come, we will get you onto the camel's back.'

Murdo regarded the ramshackle creature dubiously. 'I can walk,' he insisted.

'Your stubbornness does you no credit,' Ronan said firmly. 'You will ride, and that is the end of it.'

Together Emlyn and Fionn hefted Murdo onto the front part of the yoke-shaped frame; he perched on the top, his feet dangling either side of the camel's long neck, the treasure bundles bound either side of the saddle behind him.

Stepping to the head of the camel, the senior cleric said, 'Hist! Hist!' The sleeping animal awoke, tossed its head, and stood, unfolding itself awkwardly and shaking its burden from side to side. Ronan, holding tight to the rein rope, pulled hard and the beast gave out a dreadful blaring blat. 'Hist!' said Ronan sharply. The camel blatted again, but turned and started slowly down the hill towards the trail. Murdo held tight to the wooden pommel with both hands as the animal lurched along, its ungraceful swaying threatening to throw off its reluctant passenger with every step.

They reached the trail and turned towards the city. 'Now will you tell me where we are going?' asked Murdo; he had begun to get the rhythm of the creature's jerking undulations.

'Gladly,' answered the priest. 'While searching around the city today, I learned of a monastery nearby – it is outside the walls, so it escaped pillage. I think we will find the good brothers eager to help.'

'A monastery,' grumbled Murdo. He could see the thing drifting from bad to worse. 'How can that possibly help us?'

'Catacumbae,' said Ronan.

Murdo recognized the word as Latin, but could not recall its meaning, and begged an explanation.

'Often in the East,' explained the elder monk, 'the faithful dead are buried in underground chambers. We can bury our secret there, and the good brothers will watch over it.'

Murdo remained unconvinced. Nothing was further from his mind than leaving the treasure in the care of a monastery full of thieving priests. 'And who will watch the monks so they do not steal it?'

'Have a little faith, Murdo,' answered the monk. 'All will be well.'

Murdo drew no comfort from this vague assurance, but lacked the will to argue the matter further. He settled dejectedly against the unyielding hump behind him, and watched the shadows for thieves. Soon the path met a wider way, and they continued on until the road diverged, whereupon they took the southern track and soon were passing beneath the city walls.

Outside the Jaffa Gate they passed a great smouldering mound.

The embers crackled, sending sparks upwards from the glowing pile. Even from a distance, Murdo could feel the heat on his face and hands, and in amongst the flaming coals he saw human skulls – heaped and jumbled one atop another, skulls by the hundreds, and all of them gaping at him with empty-eyed malice. He imagined the heat he felt was that of their rage at the depravity which had stolen their lives. Unable to face them, he turned his eyes away.

The furtive party proceeded along the western wall towards the cragged hump of Mount Zion rising above the Hinnom valley. Upon reaching the southwestern corner of the wall, the dirt track divided once more: the main strand led away towards Bethlehem and Hebron, and the other bent slightly to the east to begin its winding ascent of the mount.

As they approached the Holy Mountain, Murdo could see the pale glimmer of white-washed buildings gleaming in the moonlight, the largest of which had a dome surmounted by a cross. A moment later, they stopped. 'There is someone on the road,' Ronan said, his voice hushed and low. He pointed to a place where the road ahead bent to the left as it rose towards the mount. 'I think they are coming this way.'

'We should get off the road until they pass by,' Murdo said, looking around. Unfortunately, apart from a few small thorn bushes scattered about, the hillside was barren. There was no place to hide.

The priests saw this, too. 'We will have to trust to God for our protection,' Ronan concluded. 'Come, brothers, a prayer for safe passage.' The three began to pray at once, chanting softly. Murdo continued to search the hillside for a hiding place.

Meanwhile, the strangers came nearer and, seeing the wagon, hastened to meet it. Closer, Murdo saw that there were eight or ten of them – some with swords, and some with spears – and, from the way they stumbled and reeled, he guessed most of them were drunk. Murdo braced himself for the inevitable confrontation.

'You there!' shouted the nearest of the warriors. 'Stay where you are!'

Several of his fellows ran to block the path, even though the camel had already stopped.

The priests made no move, but continued to pray until the soldiers had gathered around them. 'Pax Vobiscum,' said Ronan, not unkindly. 'It is late and you are not abed,' he pointed out in ready

Latin. 'Or perhaps you rise early to avoid travelling in the heat of the day.'

Some of the soldiers glanced at one another and shrugged. Others exchanged gruff words in a language Murdo did not understand. Four of the men, he saw now, carried leather bags on their backs, which they swung to the ground as soon as they stopped. By this Murdo knew the bags were heavy with plunder, and the men would not hesitate to add his treasure to their own. He looked down beside his leg, and saw the hilt of his father's sword protruding from under one of the shroud-bound bundles. One quick move and he could have it in his hand.

'Does no one among you speak Latin?' inquired Ronan.

The group muttered menacingly, shifting from foot to foot and grasping their weapons. When no one made to reply, the priest repeated the question in Gaelic. He was on the point of repeating it again, when a figure stepped forth from behind the others. 'I speak a little,' the man said, observing the priests coldly. Turning his attention to the camel, Murdo saw a man of hard countenance; suspicion flowed from him in waves, and lifted the corner of his lip in a sneer. 'What have you got there?'

Indicating the bundles, Ronan said, 'Our dear brother, Lord Ranulf of Orkney, has died from wounds received in Jerusalem.'

The man frowned. 'What about the others?'

'Lord Ranulf had three sons,' the priest explained. 'All were pilgrims like yourself. We are on our way to the Church of Saint Mary. Do you know the place?'

'No,' growled the man. He called something to one of the men standing nearest the camel. The fellow answered, glancing suspiciously at Murdo. He stepped to the side of the animal and began prodding the bundles with the butt of his spear. It was all Murdo could do to keep from snatching up the sword and swinging at the man.

'Why slink around by night if you have nothing to hide?' the foremost soldier asked.

'The sun is hot and causes a corpse to stink prodigiously,' the elder priest explained. 'We hoped to spare our brother this last indignity.' Stretching out his hand in a gesture of friendship, he added, 'We would do no less for you, my friend – or any of your men.'

343

'Do we look dead to you, priest?' scoffed the soldier.

'May God be praised for his enduring mercy,' said Ronan. 'I pray you will live to see your homes once more.'

Emlyn spoke up then, saying, 'Perhaps you would care to accompany us to the church. We could hear your confessions, and offer prayers for your safety.'

'Forgive me, brother,' interrupted Fionn, 'I would but hasten to remind you that the pope has given full absolution for all sins committed while on crusade. These men are obviously pilgrims like the rest of us; therefore, they need no absolution. Hence, no confessions are required.'

'There may be something in what you say,' conceded Emlyn graciously. 'However, I think you are forgetting that the pope's decree of absolution was to remain in force only for the duration of the crusade. Since the pilgrimage is now completed, I believe the decree has expired.'

The soldiers, uncertain what to make of this discussion, shifted uneasily. Murdo could not believe they would choose this moment to pursue a theological discussion.

'Brothers,' said Ronan, adopting the manner of a master curbing the enthusiasm of his wayward pupils, 'this is not the time or place for such debate. These soldiers must be about their affairs.'

'Of course,' agreed Fionn placidly, 'let them go about their business, I say. There is no need to detain them further.'

'Am I to believe what I am hearing?' complained Emlyn. He thrust an accusing finger into the face of the nearest soldier. 'For all we know, their souls may be in danger of hell this very night. Why indulge such a needless risk? Let them be shriven, I say!'

At this the crusaders moved back a pace, suddenly anxious to leave.

'We do not have time for that now,' the soldier grumbled. 'We are on our way to our camp in the valley. Our lord is waiting for us.'

'The church is not far,' offered Ronan helpfully. 'The service would not take long, and you would soon be on your way.'

The soldiers moved back another pace, eager to be gone from these meddling priests; two or three of them began edging away.

'I told you we have more important affairs to attend to,' the warrior muttered.

'What affairs can be more important than the affairs of a man's soul?' demanded Emlyn.

'Our souls are no concern of yours, priest,' the crusader growled. 'Go your way.'

Ronan acquiesced gracefully. 'Come, brothers, we are not needed here.' He tugged on the camel's rope and the beast lumbered forward, almost throwing Murdo off his perch.

The soldiers stood aside, watching the priests and their camel depart. Emlyn turned aside to offer one last homily. 'Remember, my friends, there is no sin too great for God's forgiveness. Our Heavenly Father stands ready to welcome all who truly repent.'

'Move on, move on!' snapped the soldier irritably. He motioned his companions away, adding, 'A bane on all priests!' under his breath.

The monks began chanting their prayer again and continued on their way. They had gone only a few paces when Murdo, unable to help himself, risked a backward glance and saw that the soldiers were hurrying away down the road. 'They are going away,' said Murdo, and realized he had been holding his breath.

'Of course,' replied Ronan. 'Such sheep are seldom eager for their shearing.'

They reached the Church of Saint Mary to find the church precinct paved with bodies. All around the church, covering the slopes from the foot of the hill to the walls of the monastery, people lay upon the ground in knots and clusters; a few were wrapped in cloaks, but most simply sprawled on the bare earth where they had dropped. At first sight, Murdo thought the slaughter must have continued outside the walls of the city, but these were somewhat more fortunate than their countrymen: they were not dead, merely sleeping.

Murdo looked upon the silent multitude and saw among the clustered throngs Jews and Christians and Muhammedans – all massed together, each against the other, having sought refuge from the storm of death in what must have seemed to them the one safe place in the world on that hateful day.

Here and there, he spied a family group, surrounded by a few pitiful belongings snatched from the destruction of their lives. He felt the emptiness of their loss, and understood how very little separated him from them. *All men are fleeing destruction,* he thought dismally; *some make good their escape for a time, many do not. Still, it catches everyone in the end.*

A narrow pathway wound through the mass of bodies to the monastery gate. Leading the camel carefully along the path, the monks picked their way among the sleeping bodies, and arrived at last at the monastery entrance directly behind the huge domed church. The timber doors were shut and barred, but a bell hung from the gatepost, and Emlyn gave the cord a single sharp pull. The sound wakened a few of the sleepers, who grumbled at the disturbance. The door gave forth a creak, and a small door in the larger gate opened. A round, dark face appeared in the gap. 'Who disturbs the peace of this place?'

'Forgive us, brother,' said Ronan. 'We would not trouble you if need were not hard upon us. As you can see, we are priests, too, and we are about a matter of urgency and beg admittance. We desire to speak to your abbot at once.'

The monk regarded them speculatively for a moment, and then said, 'I am sorry, the abbot is holding vigil, and I will not disturb his prayers. You must wait until after terce when the abbot receives his guests – even then, I cannot promise he will see you.' The porter paused, and added, 'These last days have been very difficult for us all.'

'I understand,' replied Ronan equably. 'If that is the best we can hope for, we will abide. But perhaps we might be allowed to wait inside?'

'Again, I must disappoint you,' the monk replied. 'Owing to the sudden arrival of the emperor's emissary, the guest lodge is full to overflowing. Even the yard is full. As you can see, there is room neither inside, nor out.'

'We would not disturb the serenity of this place in any way,' Ronan assured him. 'We require only a place to sit quietly while we wait. You need provide nothing more.'

'Very well,' relented the monk, 'I will let you in.'

'Thank you, brother. May God bless you.'

The little door closed, and they waited. Murdo had begun to think the monk had changed his mind, when he heard a scraping noise coming from the other side of the gate, and a moment later, the door swung open to admit them. They led the camel into the yard, and the gate was closed once more.

The inner yard was a square of hard-packed earth, swept clean, and bounded on three sides by various buildings, and on the fourth by a long wing of cells. Candlelight glowed from the window and doorway of several cells, and from the tiny chapel. There were people sleeping in the yard, hundreds of them, but here the monks had imposed an order on the chaos by arranging everyone in circumspect rows – four ranks on either side of a central pathway.

'I will show you to the stables. You may find a place there to sit while you wait. This way, please.'

They passed along the rows of bodies, and came to a low-roofed open building lined with stalls. There were horses in all the stalls, and picketed outside as well. 'See,' said the porter, 'even the stables are overcrowded. But you may wait here.'

Just then, a tall, white-robed figure emerged from the chapel and started across the yard. Upon seeing the visitors and camel, the figure stopped short and called out, 'Thaddeus? Is something the matter?'

The monk turned. 'No, abbot. I am sorry if we have disturbed your prayers. I was just making these visitors comfortable in the stable.'

'More visitors?' inquired the abbot, starting towards them. 'Truly, we are blessed with an abundance of visitors tonight.' Upon joining the newcomers, the abbot smiled and spread his hands in welcome. 'Greetings, brothers. I see we have the joy of receiving some of our own from other lands. You are welcome here, my friends. I am Philip, abbot of this monastery. Have you travelled far on your pilgrimage?'

'We have come from the land of the Scots at the world's farthest edge, where our monastery rejoices in its labours in the fields of the Lord. As it happens, I am also an abbot of our small, but excellent order.'

'Indeed!' exclaimed Abbot Philip, much impressed by this. 'We must sit together tomorrow when we can talk further. I would hear how the affairs of the church are conducted in the barbarous wilds of which you speak.' He smiled, and made a little bow to the good brothers looking on. 'But you are tired and I will not detain you further. Unless there is something I can do for you, Brother Thaddeus will show you to your rest.'

'Time and circumstance are against us, I know,' Ronan said quickly. 'And I would not trouble you if need were not pressing, but we have begun a work from which we dare not desist until it is completed.' So saying, he indicated the shroud-wrapped bundles on the camel, and invited the abbot to look for himself.

'Ah, I understand,' the abbot said, sorrow shading his tone. 'Are they priests?'

'No, abbot,' answered Ronan. He beckoned the priest a little apart. They spoke to one another in quiet earnest for a moment, and when they returned to where the others were waiting, the abbot raised his eyes to where Murdo sat, still as a stone atop the camel. 'May God bless you richly, my friend. May Our Blessed Lord console you with his loving spirit in your time of grief.'

Murdo made no reply, but nodded his acceptance of the abbot's condolences.

'Brother Thaddeus,' instructed the abbot, 'open the crypt and lead our friends to the catacombs.'

'But abbot, we cannot –' objected the monk.

'Please, the night is far spent,' Abbot Philip told him. 'Do as I say. All will be made clear in God's good time.'

'Thank you, abbot,' Ronan said. 'God willing, perhaps we can sit down and talk together one day soon, you and I.'

'I look forward to that with keenest anticipation,' the senior replied, and departed with a blessing, leaving them to their work.

Brother Thaddeus, none too pleased with the abbot's intervention, nevertheless undertook his duties with good, if somewhat officious grace. 'The crypt is this way,' he said. 'Will you require help with the bodies? If so, I can summon some of our brothers.'

'Thank you, brother, but no,' Ronan declined. 'I fear we have disturbed the tranquillity of your good community enough for one night. The labour is ours; we will shoulder the burden and complete what we have begun.'

'As you wish,' said the monk, and started towards one of the buildings across the yard. 'This way to the catacombs.'

Fionn tugged on the rein rope, and the camel collapsed with a wheezing blat; Emlyn helped Murdo to his feet, and supported him as he limped across the yard, passing back along the rows of sleeping refugees and the line of now-darkened cells towards the chapel. As they approached the last cell, Murdo's eye was drawn by a movement in the darkness. He turned his head and was startled by the sudden appearance of a swarthy, dark-haired man in the doorway.

The man was tall and of regal appearance, and had neither the dress nor the manner of a monk. He glanced at those passing by his doorway and, finding nothing to interest him, stepped back into the shadowed cell once more. Murdo turned his attention to the chore at hand.

THIRTY-SEVEN

Brother Thaddeus led his night visitors behind the chapel to the kitchens and refectory; both were dark and quiet now. Beyond the kitchens stood two large ovens shaped, Murdo thought, like great bee hives. The ovens were still warm from the day's use, and Murdo felt the heat on his tender skin as they passed between them. Thaddeus brought them to a small stone structure which appeared to be a shrine, built against the wall separating the monastery from the Church of Saint Mary.

'Wait here a moment,' the porter said, and disappeared inside. He returned bearing two torches which he took to the nearest oven and lit from the embers. Returning to where the others were waiting, he handed one of the torches to Ronan, and indicated that they should follow him into the shrine.

The single room was bare and without windows, and Murdo soon discovered the reason why: it was not a shrine, but the entrance to an underground chamber; a wide flight of stone steps led down into the darkness below. Passing one of the torches to Ronan, Thaddeus instructed them to have a care for their heads, and started down.

Murdo, hobbling on his sore feet, leaned on Emlyn's arm and the two of them followed Fionn; Ronan, holding the second torch, came after. The steps went down and down, ending at last in a fair-sized room carved out of the stone of the Holy Mount itself. Hundreds of niches, large and small, lined the walls, and in many of these Murdo could see dull grey lumps of bones – given a shadowy life by fluttering torchlight, which made them seem to quiver and shake in their little stone stalls. At the far end of the room stood a low door, its stone posts and lintel framing a black void beyond.

'The entrance to the catacombs,' Thaddeus told them, and led them on.

Cool air wafted over them like a chill breath as, stooping low, they entered a narrow corridor which ended in a short flight of steps. The stone ceiling of the corridor was black from the smoke of torches, and Murdo, bent almost double, descended the steps and emerged to stand upright in a long subterranean gallery. Row on row, and tier on tier, box-like cavities had been cut into the rock walls of the gallery. Some of these were sealed with stone rubble, but most were open, allowing the occupants to be viewed: shrunken dust-grey corpses whose withered brown leathery limbs showed through the ragged holes in their rotting shrouds.

Brother Thaddeus led them along the gallery, through another door and into another gallery identical to the first. They crossed this and entered a third, turned, and passed along this one until they came to yet another door and entered yet another gallery. This last was like the others, except that it was not yet finished; for, at the far end, ladders and tools lay against a wall of half-carved nooks amidst piles of stone-chippings and rubble. From the fine stone-dust which lay thick on everything, it appeared no one had touched the tools for many years.

They came to a row of empty niches. 'I believe one of these should serve your purpose,' Thaddeus said. 'If you wish, I will summon brothers to help you move the bodies.'

'You are most thoughtful, brother,' Ronan replied. 'But we have disturbed everyone enough for one night. We will undertake this duty ourselves.'

'That is your decision,' Thaddeus replied, manifestly grateful that his offer had not been taken up.

He led them back the way they had come, and upon reaching the end of the first gallery, Ronan passed his torch to Murdo, saying, 'Perhaps it would be best if you waited here to light our way.'

Murdo accepted the torch, and watched the others disappear up the passage leading to the crypt above. He heard their footsteps fade quickly, swallowed by the great stillness of the catacombs. He stood for a while, looking around, and his eye fell on a nearby niche; there was an inscription carved into the side of the box-like hollow. Holding the torch closer, he made out the curious scratchings of Greek letters; the inscription on the next one was Greek, too – as were most of the others. He did, however, find one or two in Latin, and of one of these he was able to make out the name and the year of death: Marcus Patacus . . . Anno Domini 692.

Here was a man who had lived and died more than four hundred years ago. Murdo could not comprehend such a vast amount of time, but the discovery sparked in him the desire to see if he could find another, perhaps older still. He began hobbling along the gallery, holding his torch to the carvings. Upon coming to the end, he turned and entered another room which he had not seen before. This room was filled with columns and pillars of various kinds supporting a high, many-vaulted roof. As in the other galleries, there were many hundreds of corpse niches, but also a goodly number of larger, more ornate tombs, some carved into the walls, others free-standing. Most of the tombs boasted flat-featured carvings of men and women in flowing robes, seated or reclining, their faces serene and dignified.

He was examining his sixth or seventh tomb when he heard the patter of footsteps in the room behind him, and remembered that he was supposed to be waiting for the others. Turning quickly, he started limping back the way he had come and, upon reaching the doorway, saw the reflected glow of torchlight moving along the gallery beyond.

'Here I am!' he called, shuffling forward as fast as his sore feet would allow. He ducked through the door and came face to face with a tall, dark-haired monk robed in white. The monk carried a torch which burned with a bright light which seemed to fill the gallery. 'Oh!' Murdo said in surprise. 'I thought it was ... I was just –'

Murdo's explanation died in the air as the realization broke upon him that he had seen this priest before. 'You!' he gasped. Upon saying the word, his mind instantly returned to the little chapel he had found when wandering the streets of Antioch trying to find his way back to the marketplace and citadel.

'You were in Antioch,' Murdo said. 'I saw you there – in the chapel. You showed me how to find my way.'

'Did you find the way?' asked the white priest.

'I did,' answered Murdo. The air seemed to have become heavy and difficult to breathe. He stared at the monk, and noticed the torch burned with a silent flame which inexplicably produced no shadows. 'Are you the one called Andrew?'

The priest regarded him, his quick dark eyes gleaming with a disconcerting intensity. 'I am,' he said. He held his head to one side, as if listening. After a moment, he said, 'Night is far gone, and time grows short. Will you serve me, brother?'

Murdo swallowed hard. 'Forgive me, lord,' he said, 'I fear I must disappoint you, for I have no wish to become a monk.'

The priest laughed at this, and his voice echoed among the tiered ranks of bones and shrouds. Murdo felt a shock at the strangeness of such mirth in the silent realm of the dead. He glanced around quickly, as if fearing the sudden onslaught of that joyful sound might be enough to rouse the dead.

'I have monks enough, my friend,' the priest told him. 'But I need kings also.'

'I am no king,' Murdo replied, 'nor ever likely to be. Indeed, I am but a farmer.'

'A farmer without a farm?' Andrew mused. 'That is something new. But then all the world is turned upside down.' Holding Murdo with the strength of a gaze which pierced him to the quick, he said, 'But tell me now: when the king seizes the farmer's fields, may not the farmer assume the king's throne?'

Murdo shifted awkwardly under the intense scrutiny of the man's gaze.

'All you possess was given you for a purpose, brother. I ask you again: will you serve me?'

The question hung between them, demanding an answer. 'I will do what I can,' replied Murdo.

'If all men did as much,' the white monk declared, 'it would be more than enough.' He raised a hand to Murdo's shoulder. Murdo, fearing for his sunburn, winced in anticipation; yet, the touch was so gentle it caused no pain. Instead, as the monk's grip tightened on his shoulder, Murdo felt as if he were held in place by a mighty and exalted strength. Moreover, he sensed an ardent vitality of purpose flowing through the touch. Powerless to move or speak, Murdo could only watch and listen.

'Build me a kingdom, brother.' Brother Andrew gazed upon him, urging him, willing him to accept what he had heard, and believe. 'Establish a realm where my sheep may safely graze,' the earnest cleric continued, 'and make it far, far away from the ambitions of small-souled men and their ceaseless striving. Make it a kingdom where the True Path can be followed in peace and the Holy Light can shine as a beacon flame in the night.'

353

Before Murdo could think what to say to this extraordinary request, a voice called out from the catacomb entrance in the room beyond. 'Murdo! – are you there? We need the torch!'

'Ronan!' gasped Murdo. 'I forgot.' He turned towards the sound, and found that he could move again. He ran two steps, remembered himself, and looked back.

The priest was gone, the gallery lit with the light of Murdo's lone torch. The radiance of the vision had already vanished.

Murdo darted away; he ran down the narrow passage to the doorway which joined the two galleries. He ducked his head to pass through the low door, and ran back along the length of the first gallery to where Ronan was waiting at the entrance, holding a single torch.

'I am sorry,' Murdo said quickly. 'I was looking at some of the tombs.'

'Lead the way,' Ronan said. 'Our friends are anxious to return to their rest.'

At these words, Murdo glanced up and, looking behind Ronan, made out a line of monks stretching back up the steps to the crypt above. They were carrying the corpse-shaped bundles. Seeing Murdo's grimace of dismay, the elder priest bent his head towards him. 'The abbot insisted,' he whispered. 'I could not refuse. This way, we may finish before dawn.'

Straightening once more, Ronan called to those behind him. 'We are ready now. Follow on.' To Murdo he said, 'Go – I will stay here to light the passage.'

Retracing their footprints in the dust, Murdo led the line of monks to the gallery they had chosen. He did not like so many strangers entangled in his affairs, but with their help, the work of stowing the bundled treasure was quickly accomplished. When the others had been dismissed, Murdo and Ronan made certain the treasure was tucked well out of sight. Murdo then placed his father's shield below the niche to mark the place. When he was at last satisfied that nothing unusual could be seen by anyone, he allowed himself to be pulled away.

'Come along,' Ronan urged, 'it is getting on towards dawn, and we must return the camel to its owner.'

They quickly retraced their steps to the crypt and hurried out into the thin grey light of a fast-fading night. They crossed the yard, collected the camel and passed back through the gate, and it was not until they were well down the road that Emlyn noticed the smoothness and strength of Murdo's stride.

'Look at you now!' he exclaimed. 'You are running!'

Murdo had to admit that it did appear to be so; he could not explain it, but his feet no longer hurt him, and his sunburned skin was no longer painful to the touch. 'I suppose I am feeling much better,' he allowed.

'Oh, to be young again,' sighed Fionn, labouring along beside the disagreeable camel.

When they came again to the road leading past the Jaffa Gate, Fionn turned the animal westward and they began climbing towards a small cluster of farms nestled in the hills. Murdo fell into step beside the senior cleric. 'Are you truly an abbot?' he asked.

'Yes,' Ronan confirmed, 'but among our brotherhood, such distinctions are not so important that we make much of them.'

'What did you tell the priests?'

'Which priests?'

'Back there – at the monastery. They were not about to allow us to use their catacombs. But you spoke to the abbot. What did you tell them to make them change their minds?'

'The truth, Murdo,' replied Ronan. 'I simply told them the truth – that generally produces the most satisfactory result, I find.'

'You told them about the treasure?' cried Murdo, stopping in his tracks.

'Calm yourself,' the priest replied. 'Have a little faith, son. How could I have told them any such thing, when I vowed to uphold your secret? No. I simply said that these were the last remains of a very wealthy family, and that I had every confidence that you – the youngest surviving member of that noble family – would be most happy to give the monastery a handsome reward in exchange for keeping them safe until you return to take them away to your own country.' Ronan smiled. 'Was I wrong in any of this?'

Murdo shook his head at the priest's audacity. 'No,' he allowed, 'you were not wrong.'

At the first house they found a post in the yard, where they tethered the animal. They were just finishing this task when the farmer appeared in the doorway of the house. He shouted something at them, whereupon Ronan turned and spoke to him in his own language.

355

The man moved into the yard, clutching a stout wooden staff. Ronan spoke again, putting out his hand towards Murdo. The farmer stopped, regarded them coolly for a moment, and then answered, speaking quickly and harshly.

'What does he say?' asked Murdo.

'I have told him that we borrowed his beast, and have returned it. He does not believe me, however; he thinks we were trying to steal it.'

'Ask him if thieves pay for the things they take.' Murdo instructed.

Ronan obliged, and then said, 'He says the crusaders have taken everything else, and paid him nothing. Why should he think us better than the rest?'

Murdo reached into his belt and produced a gold coin. While the monks stood looking on, he stepped before the man and placed the coin in his open palm. 'Tell him we are not thieves.'

The man looked at the coin, but did not close his hand. He spoke to Ronan, who interpreted, saying, 'Neither is our friend here a thief. He says it is too much for the use of his camel; he cannot accept it.'

'Tell him he can keep it,' Murdo said. 'We want nothing more from him but to leave quietly.'

Ronan spoke again, and the man smiled quickly and whipped the coin out of sight. He then loosed a rapid babble of words, snatched up Murdo's hand and pressed it to his lips.

'He says that he is most grateful,' Ronan explained, 'and that if we have need of his animal again, or his house, or his barn, or anything he might possess, however large or small, we are to come to him and it will be given with immense joy.'

The sky was glowing pink in the east as they started back down the hill. Murdo, hungry, and exhausted by the events of the day, wished only to find a cool place to sleep before facing whatever trials lay ahead.

'I suppose King Magnus will wonder where we have been so long,' Emlyn said, moving up beside him.

'I suppose,' Murdo agreed. In the turmoil of all that had happened in the last days, he had forgotten about the king and his war band, of which he was a member. 'Do you think he will be angry?'

'He has been busy with his own affairs,' the priest suggested lightly. 'I expect he will not have missed us very much.'

'The farmer,' Murdo said, 'what language was he speaking?'

'Aramaic,' the cleric replied, 'a very ancient tongue. It was the speech of our Lord Christ. Many still speak it hereabouts. Does it surprise you that Ronan should know it?'

Murdo shrugged again. 'I do not know what priests are taught.'

'My friend,' Emlyn reproved gently, 'you should know by now, those who follow the True Path are not at all like other priests.'

BOOK IV

January 21, 1899: Edinburgh, Scotland

As I think on it now, I am convinced that I was chosen to replace Angus. In saying this, I do not mean to degrade my own selection, or belittle my worthiness to accede to the honour and status granted me by my initiation into the Brotherhood. I mean, simply, that if Angus had lived, in all likelihood I would never have been asked to join the Benevolent Order in the first place.

The plain truth is that Pemberton was Angus' friend, not mine. I believe the old gent had been grooming him for several years; I have no doubt that in due course, Angus would have made a tremendous contribution to the Brotherhood. I know *I* have missed his boundless enthusiasm, his easy nature, his wit and loyalty. But life is rarely predictable; destiny scorns even the best intentioned plans. Angus was taken, and I was left behind.

In a way, one might say Angus passed his birthright on to me through our friendship. Upon his death the Brotherhood began the search once more; because of our close affinity, I suppose, they happened to light on me as a possible successor. Or, perhaps I am mistaken, and there is more to it than that.

Be that as it may, the night of my initiation I returned home with my cape and blackened fingerbone, and knew beyond any doubt that my life had once more undergone a deep and profound change, the effects of which I could not fully imagine or anticipate, but would, in due course, discover.

Indeed, it would be years before I began to appreciate the sheer scale of the Brotherhood's interests and involvements throughout the world, and yet more years before I fully understood them. Nor did I realize that, far from having arrived, I had merely embarked upon the first few halting steps of a long and eventful journey – a pilgrimage of phenomenal lengths.

Nevertheless, I returned home to Cait and the children that night feeling as if I had downed a keg of burning pitch. I was aflame with an excitement I could not contain. I did not sleep.

Instead, I paced the floor from hall to den and back, clasping my hands and murmuring a babble of half-remembered prayers and liturgies. It was all I could do to keep from running through the streets, shouting at the top of my lungs. One moment I was laughing, and the next would find me dissolved in tears – the one emotion as wholly surprising and inexplicable as the other.

All I know is that something had taken place during the initiation, something genuine and rare, extraordinary and unique – perhaps 'sacred' is the word that best conveys my feeling. For when I knelt to kiss the sword and don the cape, God help me, I *did* feel as if a crusader's mantle had been draped over my shoulders. I felt as if I had joined a circle of fellowship that stretched back and back through the centuries to the first rough knights who had taken the cross and pledged their lives to champion Christ's name. I had joined their number and could no longer look upon the world in the same way.

In that sacred instant, I glimpsed, however imperfectly, the shape of the sacrifice required of me. I saw the burden to be borne, and without hesitation accepted it. I had come so far already, to turn aside would have been not only an act of low cowardice, but betrayal as well. When so many before me had given all to the Brotherhood, could I refuse? Could I hold my life higher than theirs, and still think myself an honourable man?

I could not; neither could I forsake the trust that had been placed in me by those who had shielded me and supported me over the years. Thus, I gripped the naked blade in my hand and kissed the swordhilt with my lips – the ancient sign of knighthood taking on the burden of the cross – and in doing so, took my place beside those worthy knights of ages past.

Upon receiving the cape and talisman, I had succeeded to the First Degree. There was no way, of course, that I could have known there were six more degrees of fellowship to attain; each following grade was guarded with such secrecy as to prevent anyone who was not already a member learning anything about it. In retrospect, and at long remove, I can say with absolute certainty that no more than half the members of the Brotherhood ever understood that there were higher degrees of any sort at all.

I hasten to point out that the secrecy was not employed in order to create an élite – as is sadly so often the case – but for the protection of those whose lives would be endangered by the knowledge. For each initiation was accompanied by greater revelation, and therefore greater risk. While I have no wish to sound melodramatic – like some beetle-browed hack of the penny dreadfuls – it is a plain fact that the enemies of the Brotherhood are legion, and it only stands to reason one cannot betray a secret one does not possess.

My first year as a new initiate was taken up with study. I learned much about the many involvements of our Order, and the subtle ways in which we brought our influence to bear. I learned the lore and teaching of the Temple and a few of its secrets. Sadly, the very nature of the secrets we protected often meant that we were not at liberty to reveal our full powers, nor could we interfere with the natural course of events in the world at large.

We could but stand aside and watch as the manifold catastrophes of man and nature wreaked havoc great and dire upon the world. In this, I began to learn something of the heroic patience of the saints. To stand aside and watch while the worst mistakes were made again and again – and always, always to the cost of those who could least afford it – was almost more than I could take. Often was the time I sought retreat, sickened in my soul over the inhumanity rampant around me.

I watched and learned, and slowly mastered the arcane history of our clandestine Order. The years passed, and Annie and Alex grew, attended school and, eventually, flew the nest to begin families of their own. Cait and I continued in all happiness, and looked forward to grandchildren, in good time, and a leisurely life as a couple once more.

Meanwhile, I advanced in the Order, passing on from one unknown level to the next until arriving at the Sixth Degree, which I erroneously assumed was as high as one could attain. At each stage of this long journey, there were fewer companions. For example, when first inducted into the Benevolent Order, I learned there were upwards of seventy thousand members in various Temples throughout the world. Upon becoming a member of the Brotherhood, I discovered there were only seven hundred First Degree brethren; when I attained the Second Degree, that number diminished by more than two hundred, and so on. With each ascending rung of the invisible ladder, the numbers decreased accordingly. No more than thirty members ever hold a Sixth Degree membership at any time.

The reason for this is, again, protection. The fewer the number of people who know a secret, the greater the security. Until three weeks ago, however, I could never have imagined that the magnitude of the secrets guarded at the highest level increased astronomically. That is to say, what was shown me but a few nights ago in the Inner Temple has convinced me beyond all doubt of the necessity for our secrecy. In this I am utterly sincere.

How then, you might ask, is it possible for a man who believes in the righteousness of his cause, and the crucial necessity of secrecy to protect and advance it – how is it possible for that man to reveal its most confidential information? How is it possible for that man to divulge the very secrets he has sworn to protect with his life?

Allow me to reiterate: I would gladly suffer death a thousand times rather than betray the Brotherhood, or endanger the Great Work.

How then, this document? The answer is that, as the most recent initiate of the Inner Temple, and therefore the most receptive to the remarkable methods employed in the dissemination of the knowledge I have lately acquired, I have been given the task of chronicling the development of the Order from its very beginnings.

The purpose of this task is twofold. In committing to paper all that has been vouchsafed to me, I will gain greater mastery over it. Secondly, the Inner Temple has, in its wisdom, foreseen the day when the preservation of that which we hold so jealously at present will best be served not by secrecy and stealth, but by outright proclamation. One day, they say, the surest way to protect a secret will be to shout it from the housetops.

If this seems a ludicrous paradox, I can only say that the particular circumstances which make this extremity of purpose necessary, though not yet fully apprehended, are drawing inexorably nearer. Friends, we live in troubled times. The day is coming when the whole world will be tried in the crucible of war.

By God's will and by his hand, we may emerge from the fiery furnace. But if we are destroyed, then this record may be all that is left of our illustrious order, and it will fall to those who come after us to complete the Great Work we have begun.

Thus, in the very first days following my Seventh Degree initiation I began the occupation which has been urged upon me. I confess I have written in haste; my chief desire has been to capture the bright images just as they appeared to me in the white heat of the vision. Loath to let the dream fade, or allow time to cloud my memory, I have secluded myself in my study at the top of the house, and I have not stirred, save for infrequent meals. Scarcely have I rested.

Dear Caitlin fears I am losing my sanity. 'Far from it,' I tell her, 'I am rescuing sanity's last remnant.' And that is true. I do believe that if I desisted even for a day, the chaos of my thoughts would overwhelm me. So long as I work, I make sense of the strange double life I have acquired. If I lose myself in these pages, it is only so that I may find myself again. Thus, I have no choice. I dare not stop until my work is finished.

Even so, the end is in sight.

If my poor chronicle should in future find any readers, I would like it known that I have, in so far as possible, striven for the truth in every particular. Any triumph belongs to those whose story is here related. Any failure is my own.

It is the story of the Sanctus Clarus, yes, but it is also the story of the men and women who strove to keep that Holy Light burning through the ages. I ask you to remember this when weighing out our failings. We are but flesh and blood, and not angels after all.

THIRTY-EIGHT

Bohemond, Prince of Taranto and Count of Antioch, arrived in Jerusalem with two hundred knights. He wasted not a moment, but established himself in the palace recently vacated by the commander of Amir Iftikhar's bodyguard. The high-walled house, with its numerous columns and floors of polished stone, was swiftly converted to an armoury and stables. The generous courtyard and gardens were given to the prince's horses which were allowed to drink from the white marble fountains.

King Magnus quickly joined his avowed lord in the palace, and the two began scheming how best to get their hands on a healthy share of the city's newly liberated wealth. Towards this end, Bohemond let it be known through various subtle means that he would be inclined to support the claim to kingship of any noble who supported his claim to plunder.

The lords and noblemen whose sweat and labour had secured the Holy City were not pleased with the late-comer's demands, and resisted all attempts to persuade them otherwise. There were harsh words and hard feelings on each side, and rising tension among the lords as they anticipated the next day's council.

Murdo and the monks came to hear of this when they returned to the king's war band. It had taken most of the day following their midnight visit to the monastery of Saint Mary outside the walls to find their comrades; the place where they had been camped was vacant, and no one in the area had paid any attention to the movements of the long-haired Norsemen. Despite Murdo's aversion to returning to the city, they had no choice but to continue the search inside Jerusalem.

The streets along which they passed were eerily silent, the houses vacant and, for the most part, quiet – except where looters still worked: furniture, clothing, and valuables of the dead were often hurled from the upper windows into the street below, to be more easily collected and carted off. The Temple Mount had been turned into a huge repository for the treasure hoard prior to its division and distribution.

Dark stains still marked the paving stones, and the stench and clouds of flies were formidable, but the number of corpses to be found lying untended in alleyways and courtyards was not so many as Murdo had feared. In all, they encountered only five wagons piled with bodies, each making its slow way to the bone fires; the disposal of Jerusalem's dead had been accomplished with remarkable efficiency.

They came upon a procession of monks who had already commenced the reconsecration of several of the city's smaller chapels and churches which had fallen into disuse under the Muhammedan occupation. Upon inquiring of the bishop, they learned of Bohemond's arrival and his seizure of Iftikhar's commander's palace. 'Find Bohemond,' Ronan declared, 'and there we shall find our king and companions.'

A short time later, they arrived at the palace of Jerusalem's former warlord – a handsome and imposing edifice, which the other crusader lords deemed unsuitable, owing to its former association with the Muhammedan infidel. Bohemond had no such scruples; his brief residence in Antioch had given him a taste for Arabian opulence. Murdo and the monks found the Norsemen firmly ensconced in the apartments lately occupied by Amir Iftikhar's physician and his retinue of advisors.

Murdo, tired from the previous night's activities, found himself a quiet corner and promptly went to sleep. He was roused some time later when King Magnus returned to the palace with Bohemond. While the king dined with his liege lord and benefactor, his house carles sat at meat in the hastily-altered hall, discussing the day's inconclusive events.

'Mark me: it will come to blows. The kingship will only be settled by combat.' Lord Orin took another swallow of wine from his cup.

'Hey-hey,' agreed Jon Wing. 'But it is not Bohemond's fault that he was not here. It is a long way from Antioch to Jerusalem. If the siege had lasted longer, he would have been first through the gate, I think.'

This sentiment was greeted by a general growl of approval from all those looking on and listening. More than one cup was lofted to drink the prince's singular courage.

'It is not his bravery they are doubting,' pointed out Magnus' pilot, a man named Sven Horse-Rope. 'Rather, it is his right to share in plunder he did not help to win. If it was *my* place, I do not know that I would be so quick to divide my treasure with him.'

The Norsemen rejected this line of reasoning with loud grunts of protest – not because it was wrong, but because, if followed rigorously, it would deny them their own share of what they reckoned was an immense fortune. King Magnus, in siding with Bohemond, had bound himself to the rise and fall of the prince's fortunes. They had gained but little for themselves out of the fall of Jerusalem, and were hungry for more. For better or worse, Prince Bohemond promised to be the most likely source for gaining a portion of the vast hoard of Jerusalem's wealth to be carved up among the western lords.

'The fighting lasted but a day;' Tolf Bent-Nose pointed out, 'many of Count Raymond's men did not lift a blade, either. Yet, they still claim a full portion. Also, we have collected as much plunder as anyone else –'

'*And* as many bodies!' grumbled Sven, frowning at the stink, still fresh in his memory. This sentiment was shared by one and all around the board.

'This fact should be put to the lords at the council tomorrow, I think,' said Tolf, to which everyone heartily concurred.

The next day's discussions were followed with keen attention by the king and his mercenary vassals. Each feint and counter-thrust in the subtle struggle of swagger and bluff was duly noted and reported that night in the hall over cups of raw Palestinian wine. Murdo, too, listened to all the talk, although it failed to ignite in him the same fiery itch that inflamed the others. He already possessed a fortune in plunder and, as he was not interested in the crusade or its leaders, cared nothing for their interminable squabbles over position and power. He viewed them all with the same weary indifference – save one: Baldwin. Whenever that name was mentioned, Murdo drew near to hear.

His brothers were with Lord Baldwin, he knew, and he was anxious to join them as soon as possible. To this end, he listened to all that was said, and learned that Lord Baldwin was brother to Duke Godfrey of Bouillon. Godfrey, it seemed, was a truly pious man and a fierce warrior – the same who had gained and held the wall during the first assault of the recent battle, and his fearless action did more than any other to bring about the fall of Jerusalem.

Younger brother Baldwin's esteem had slipped considerably lower, because he had not fulfilled his crusade vows, preferring instead to assume the rule of Edessa, a city a few days' march to the north. Murdo spent much of the next day pondering how he might undertake the journey to find his brothers, when word arrived at the palace that Baldwin and his war band had arrived at Jerusalem and were encamped on the Mount of Olives. He wasted no time finding Emlyn to tell him.

'My brothers are here,' he said, 'I am going to find them.'

'It will be dark soon,' the priest pointed out. 'Perhaps you should seek them tomorrow.'

Murdo would not contemplate even the slightest delay. 'I am going now,' he insisted. 'If I hurry, I can be there before nightfall.'

'I will accompany you,' Emlyn said. 'Only give me time enough to take our leave of the king.'

The monk hurried away, returning a short while later with a staff for himself, a spear for Murdo, and a waterskin to share between them. Leaving the palace, they entered the street outside the amir's residence, and hurried down through the city to the Jaffa Gate. Owing to the lateness of their start, Emlyn thought it best to find their way to the Mount of Olives *outside* the walls, rather than try to navigate the tangle of unfamiliar streets in the dark. So, they departed by the western gate and, once outside the walls, struck off onto the road which encompassed the city. This track was continually joined and divided by other roads which led off to various settlements and cities – Hebron, Bethlehem, Gethsemane, Damascus, and others – and was ringed by clusters of little farms, each with its tiny patch of green behind low white walls, or dense hedges of thorn and cactus.

The heat of the day was slowly releasing its hold on the land, though the sky was still flame-coloured in the west. The air was warm and still, and held an arid, woody scent which seemed to emanate from the small dusty shrubs all around. The road was nearly deserted; they met only the occasional farmer or labourer, and these, seeing Murdo's spear, recognized the couple as Franks, giving them a wide and wary berth. They walked along, keeping the city wall on their left hand, their eyes on the olive-planted hills rising before them. The hills were dull purple in the evening light, and the gnarled trunks of the olives pale blue, their leaves black.

They walked along in silence for a time, and Murdo found himself thinking about all that had taken place in the last two days. He thought about their midnight flight to the monastery, and his vision of Saint Andrew in the catacombs. *Build me a kingdom, brother,* the apparition had said. *I will do what I can,* he had promised. His cheeks burned with shame as the weight of his unworthiness descended over him – like a mountain shifting and settling full upon his soul.

In a little while they came to the place where they had met the soldiers two nights before, and Murdo asked, 'Is it true what you told those men the other night?' he asked, trying to sound indifferent.

'About the pope's decree of absolution?' Emlyn gave him a side-ways glance. 'Well,' he sighed, 'it is how I feel. No doubt our Latin brothers would have a different view, but those soldiers last night did not know we were not of the same order as the rest. Men like that are rarely eager for spiritual counsel; the guilty are reluctant sheep at best, I find.'

'Is it that you do not agree with the pope's decree?'

'You and I are friends, so I will speak freely,' Emlyn replied. He paused, gazing at the twilight sky; when he spoke again, his voice was thick with condemnation. 'The pope is a fool if he believes sin and forgiveness are commodities to be bartered in the marketplace of men's souls. The sins committed here will corrode the spirit just as surely as any others, and the lack of confession will haunt the heart through all eternity.'

These words produced a peculiar sensation in Murdo; he heard in them the ring of truth, and felt himself moved to confess his part in the wickedness perpetrated on that evil day. He saw again the smoke-dark sky and the leering faces of the soldiers, the blood sluicing red and hot from the wounds, the small mutilated bodies in the street. He could feel the suffocating oppression and revulsion of all he had witnessed that day, and knew it was not a burden he cared to shoulder the rest of his life.

'I am as guilty as anyone,' Murdo declared, his voice low.

'Yes?' Emlyn's voice was gently probing.

'I have done wrong,' he said and, with halting words, described the carnage and destruction he had seen in the Holy City – the

371

burned temples filled with blackened corpses, the streets filled with bodies and flowing with blood, the poor drowned child, the insane slaughter of defenceless people. He told how he had come upon three soldiers chasing a woman and her babies, and how, after killing the woman and her children, the crusaders had turned on him. 'They would have killed me, too, but they were careless, and I was quicker. I killed the leader and the others ran away.' He then described how he had stripped off the mantle of the dead crusader and put it on himself. 'I was afraid,' he concluded. 'I wanted only to get away from there – from that. On my life, I did not mean to kill him. But he attacked, and he was so sloven, so thoughtless . . . the spear was in before I knew it. In truth, I might have avoided killing him, but I did not care. He died in the street, and I was afraid the others would come back. I took his cross so I would not be attacked again.'

'I see,' replied Emlyn after a moment's thought. 'You killed only to save yourself. You acted out of fear, perhaps, but no more. Had the soldiers given you another choice, you might have acted differently, yes?'

Murdo nodded.

'There is little sin in this, if any,' the priest told him. 'You acted merely to preserve your own life. There is no condemnation in that.'

'I did not care!' Murdo countered miserably. 'If I had acted sooner, the woman and her children might have lived. I stood there and watched and did nothing to help them. I was afraid!'

'Fear is ever the great failing of Adam's race, to be sure,' the monk replied. 'While it is true that fear sometimes leads us into sin, it is rarely a sin in itself.'

'I knew what I was doing,' Murdo countered. 'That is why I took the killer's cross for myself. That woman died trying to protect her children, but when the blades turned on me, I was a coward. I should have died defending her – instead, I stole another man's cloak so I could escape.'

'I am beginning to understand,' replied Emlyn. 'Perhaps, as you insist, you might have saved that poor woman and her babies. If nothing else, you feel you should have resisted deceit. You should have refused to allow wickedness and iniquity to outwit and over-power you. Yes?'

'It is true,' confirmed Murdo, feeling worse by the moment.

'You are a man of high integrity, my friend,' Emlyn observed. 'You demand it of yourself no less than of all those around you.' At Murdo's cautious look, he said, 'This is true as well – I know, otherwise you would not feel these things so deeply. You believe that you should have remained faithful to the truth that was in you, rather than relinquish your honour to the great lie all around you. These things you did not do, and for these things you stand condemned – in your own heart, at least.'

Murdo, in full agreement with the priest's impeccable judgement, felt his failure anew. Misery descended over him in thick, black waves. His throat tightened and he could not speak.

'Listen to me now, Murdo. I am a priest, and I am your friend,' Emlyn declared. 'And I will do what any friend might do: I will raise you from the pit into which you have fallen. And I will do what only a priest can do: I will redeem you and set your feet on the True Path once more, and guide you towards the Holy Light.'

'Please,' he begged, hope rising in him again. Only a heartbeat ago he had glimpsed himself so lost and utterly bereft of virtue, it did not seem possible that he could be redeemed. 'Tell me what I must do, and I will do it. Shrive me, Emlyn.'

'Very well,' agreed the monk. He halted and, taking Murdo's arm, turned him around. 'Kneel down and bow your head.'

The road was empty; there was no one around. Murdo did as he was told, bowing his head and folding his arms across his chest. Emlyn, placing a hand on his shoulder, began to pray, interceding on Murdo's behalf and begging forgiveness for him. He then said, 'Murdo, do you renounce evil?'

'I renounce evil,' answered Murdo with conviction.

'Do you cling to Christ?'

'I cling to Christ.'

'Do you repent of your sins?'

'I do repent of my sins.' In that instant, he ached to be rid of them and make a clean start.

'God save you, Murdo,' said Emlyn. Then, placing his hands on Murdo's head, he spoke a rune of blessing over him, saying,

> 'May the Great King, and Jesu, his Holy Son,
> and the Spirit of All Healing,
> Be shielding thee, be upholding thee, be abiding thee,

Be clearing thy path and going before thee,
On hill, in hollow, over plain,
Each step through the stormy world thou takest.'

The priest then clapped his hands and said, 'Rise, Murdo Ranulfson, and rejoice! Your sins are forgiven, and remembered no more. You may resume life's journey with a pure and unblemished soul.'

As Murdo climbed to his feet once more, he did feel the burden roll away from him. There was a lightness in himself he had forgotten; he felt calm and reassured and, for the first time in a very long time, at peace with himself.

He looked with astonished eyes at the round-shouldered monk before him. 'How did you do that?' Murdo asked, astounded at the suddenness and intensity of the feeling.

Emlyn regarded him curiously. 'I suspect you have never been properly shrift before. Oh, it is a splendid feeling, is it not?'

Murdo agreed with all his heart. Certainly, nothing any other priest had ever said or done had ever produced such a remarkable and profound effect on him. It occurred to Murdo that perhaps for the first time in his life he had, however fleetingly, brushed against true holiness, and the result was wondrous. His spirit fairly bubbled inside him like a fountain overflowing a too-narrow container. He felt as if he could lift mountains with a single word, as if he could reach out and pluck the rising moon from the sky and hold it in the palm of his hand, as if he had but to stamp his foot to send whole legions of the Enemy fleeing back to their darksome dens.

They continued on then, but Murdo, no longer content to walk, wanted to run. He wanted to fly!

'Come along, Emlyn!' he cried, dashing a few steps ahead. 'My brothers are waiting! Hurry! We are soon there! Hurry!'

'I am hurrying,' the cleric insisted, lumbering into a stiff-legged trot. 'Patience is also a virtue, you know.'

They proceeded along the road through the valley beneath Jerusalem's high walls. When the path began to rise towards the hills, Murdo was persuaded to take a slower pace. 'If you did not believe in the pope's decree for the crusade, why did you come to Jerusalem?' he asked, falling into step beside his friend once more. 'If not for the crusade, why did you undertake the pilgrimage?'

374

'There are as many reasons for pilgrimage as there are paths and pilgrims,' answered Emlyn.

Murdo was not to be put off. 'What was *your* reason?'

Emlyn pursed his lips. 'We were . . .' he hesitated, 'commanded to come to Jerusalem.'

'By King Magnus,' Murdo assumed aloud. 'I remember.'

'No,' Emlyn answered. 'We were commanded in a vision. King Magnus' appeal came later.'

Murdo looked sideways at the monk to see if he had heard him correctly. 'What sort of vision was it?'

'A very ordinary sort, I believe,' the cleric said. 'We were commanded to come and wait upon God to tell us what to do.'

'Well?' demanded Murdo. 'Has God told you?'

'He has,' answered Emlyn. 'What we learned in Antioch confirmed our calling beyond all doubt.' When he appeared inclined to let the matter rest there, Murdo grew impatient with his reluctance.

'You said you were my friend,' Murdo reminded him. 'I have entrusted you with the shriving of my soul. I will not betray your secret.'

'We were commanded to rescue the lance.'

The reply was so far from what Murdo expected, it caught him out of step. 'The Holy Lance?' he said, as if there might be some other.

'To be sure,' answered the monk. 'We have been told to rescue the sacred relic from those who would make of it a curse and a blasphemy.'

'Who told you to do this?' inquired Murdo, already sensing the reply before it came.

'Saint Andrew,' Emlyn said, and explained that Ronan was the only one who had seen the saint. 'In a vision, as I say. Fionn and I trust Ronan's judgement in these matters. Brother Ronan is a most holy and devout man.'

'I do not doubt it,' Murdo replied, his heart burning within him. Should he tell Emlyn about his own encounter with the mysterious saint?

Before he could work up the courage to say anything, the monk sang out, 'There! On the hillside! I see Baldwin's camp.'

THIRTY-NINE

The Count of Edessa had established his camp atop the Mount of Olives, erecting his own tent on the crown of the hill. The campfires spread out on every side, spilling down the western slope overlooking the walls of the Holy City which rose straight and tall across the Vale of Kidron. As the night was warm, the fires of the soldiers were small – merely lights to illumine their faces while they talked and supped and drank the dark wine of Palestine.

Baldwin had brought four hundred knights and footmen, as many as he could spare from the defence of Edessa. They had arrived just after midday and he had proceeded into the city to hold close council with brother Godfrey, leaving his nobles to arrange the camp as they saw fit. As usually happened, the various groups – the Franks, Scots, Flemish, Normans, and others – had clumped together with their own kin and countrymen, pitching their tents together around a fire or two. Thus, it was a fairly simple matter for Murdo and Emlyn to locate the Dark Islanders.

'Pax Vobiscum, friends,' said Murdo, stepping up to the first group of soldiers they met. 'We are looking for the sons of Lord Ranulf of Orkneyjar. Can anyone here tell us where they might be found?'

This brought a few mumbled suggestions and much shrugging of shoulders, but no firm answer. Murdo thanked them and moved on. At the next clump of men, they received a better reception, and the information that the Orkney men were most likely with the Danes – although no one had seen them after arriving at Jerusalem. They might be camped anywhere, they said, why not try near the horse pickets?

The two proceeded to another campfire a little further on, and learned that the Danes were up at the top of the hill. 'They are near to the count's tents,' one of the knights told them. 'I saw them there before dark.'

As the count's tents were closer, they decided to try there next. They climbed the hillside in the dark and came upon the count's encampment – a cluster of large tents before which stood the count's standard and those of two other noblemen, the gold and silver trim glimmering in the fireglow. Below the encampment was a group of smaller tents. Murdo and Emlyn heard laughter from the camp, but the mirth died away quickly as they approached.

'Pax Vobiscum, friends –' began Murdo once more, breaking off as two large soldiers rose from their places.

'Move on, move on. We need no priest here tonight,' said one of the men.

'Torf?' The soldier, his face half in shadow, glanced towards him.

'Torf-Einar,' said Murdo, coming into the firelight. 'It is me – Murdo.'

The soldier stared as recognition slowly transformed his scowl. 'Murdo?' he asked in amazement. 'Is it you?'

'Torf, I –'

'God bless us, it *is* Murdo!' cried another voice as a third man rose from among those hulking at the fire.

'Skuli!' cried Murdo, stepping quickly over the fire to join his brothers.

Torf slapped him on the back in rough welcome, and shouted to the others looking on. 'Here now! It is our brother come to join us!'

'Murdo what are you doing here?' asked Skuli, thumping his back happily. 'How did you find us?'

'Look at you now,' said Torf, breaking in. 'Almost as tall as me. I never guessed it was you. How did you get here?'

'Skuli . . . Torf,' replied Murdo, shaking his head. 'I am so glad I found you. Are you well?'

'When did you arrive?' asked Skuli. 'Have you been here long?'

'What news from home?' said Torf. 'Father is in Jerusalem. Did you know that?'

'Have you seen him?' said Skuli. 'We parted company at Ma'arra.'

'Where is Paul?' asked Murdo glancing around quickly. 'Is he here with you?'

Torf's smile faded. 'Paul did not make it to Edessa,' he explained. 'The fever at Antioch took him, and he died there. That was when we decided to join Count Baldwin.'

'Who is the priest?' wondered Skuli, brightening the mood once more. He turned towards Emlyn who stood looking on across the campfire.

'This is my friend, Brother Emlyn,' Murdo answered. 'We have been travelling together.'

'Murdo and a priest on pilgrimage together!' hooted Skuli. 'I never would have believed it. Do not tell me *you* have taken vows, Murdo. You *hate* priests more than Torf even.'

'No,' laughed Murdo, 'I never would. There are two others – they are counsellors to King Magnus. They allowed me to join them.'

'King Magnus is here, too?' asked Torf. 'How many men did he bring?'

'A fair many,' Murdo said. 'Nearly four hundred in all.'

'Then he should join Baldwin,' Torf said. 'The count is paying his soldiers well.'

Emlyn spoke up then, saying, 'Perhaps we might find a place to talk among ourselves. You all have much to say to one another, and I would like a drink after our long walk.'

'Yes! Yes, to be sure,' agreed Torf. 'This way – there is a tree just here. Skuli, fetch us a jar and cup.' To Murdo and the priest, he said, 'It is wine only – there is no ale hereabouts, but we are growing used to it.'

'I have found a taste for wine,' the fat cleric remarked. 'It is wet, after all, and goes down tolerably well.'

Torf laughed at this, and led them away from the campfire to a twisted old olive tree a few paces away. The view across the valley to the Holy City – pale as bone in the moonlight, and silent as a tomb – brought the solemnity of his purpose to Murdo's mind once more.

They settled themselves beneath the branches. Emlyn rested his bulk against the trunk, and Torf reclined on the patch of dry grass around the gnarled and twisting roots; Murdo sat crosslegged opposite his brother, suddenly silent. All the things he had to say bubbled in a strong ferment inside him – but where to begin? What to tell first? There was so much, he could not think what to say, so merely stared at his brother, willing Torf to understand the need that had driven him over oceans to search them out, to lay his plea before them.

'How do you like Jerusalem?' asked Torf after a time. 'They say the fighting was good. Were you here when the city fell?'

'We were here,' answered Murdo. Not caring to refresh the memory of that day, he asked instead, 'Is it far to Edessa?'

'Aye, far enough,' replied Torf-Einar. 'It took us ten days to get here. If they had prolonged the siege, we might have joined the battle. We got word four days ago that the city was taken.'

'There is a lot of plunder, they say,' remarked Skuli as he rejoined them. He filled the cup with wine and passed it to the priest.

'Sláinte!' said Emlyn, raising the cup. He drank deeply and passed the cup to Murdo, who took a mouthful and passed it on to Torf; he drained it and gave it back to Skuli for refilling.

'Murdo,' said Skuli, shaking his head in disbelief. 'You are the last person I ever thought to see here. But how is our lady mother to do with the farm? Is she to take care of it all herself now?'

Murdo, loath to darken the mood with bad tidings, nevertheless decided it could not be put off any longer. 'That is why I have come,' he said. 'Hrafnbú is lost.'

'Lost?' wondered Skuli over the rim of his cup. 'Hrafnbú gone? Murdo, how could you let –'

Torf held up his hand for silence.

'That is not the half of it,' Murdo continued. 'Father is dead – two days ago. I was with him when he died.'

This last was received in stunned silence, which Murdo allowed to endure. After a long moment, Torf said, 'Tell us what happened.'

'He was wounded. Emlyn here, and the other monks – they found him in one of the tents,' Murdo said, and went on to explain how they had found Lord Ranulf, his death, and burial in the valley outside the walls of the Holy City. Torf and Skuli listened quietly, alternately frowning and shaking their heads. Murdo then told them how he had come to Jerusalem so that their father might return to Orkney and set about reclaiming their estate.

'You are Lord of Hrafnbú now,' Murdo concluded with a nod to Torf-Einar. 'It is for you to come back to Orkneyjar and settle our affairs once and for all.'

Torf stroked his chin thoughtfully. 'I am sorry to hear of your bad luck,' he said at last. 'But I am not going back.'

'We can get a boat at Jaffa,' Murdo said, 'I know many of the nobles are going home now, and we can get passage with one of them. We can leave at once, and –'

'Murdo!' Torf said, raising his voice. 'I said I am not going back to Orkney. Skuli and I have sworn fealty to Count Baldwin. We are staying here to fight for him.'

'But the crusade is finished,' said Murdo, struggling to understand. 'We can go home now.'

'The count has taken Edessa,' Torf told him. 'He has made it the first city of a great kingdom, and he has promised that any who stay to help him will be rewarded with gold and lands of their own. There is much wealth here, and we mean to get our share.'

'It is true, Murdo. We will soon have enough plunder to become counts, too,' Skuli added. 'We will have a realm of our own, with palaces and horses and treasure beyond counting. Baldwin has done it – and Bohemond – and we will do it, too.'

'We have lands in Orkney,' Murdo protested weakly. 'There is wealth enough there once we reclaim it. I know who it is that holds the land – he is one of Magnus' men and he is in Jerusalem. We could –'

'What we had in Orkney was nothing,' Torf said bluntly. 'Compared to the wealth of the East, we were beggars. Hrafnbú is gone maybe, but it is not worth fighting over. And it is never worth travelling all the way back to Orkneyjar just to take it away from some fool of a Norseman who wants it. Let him have it, I say. There is more *here*. And it is ours for the taking.'

'You should stay with us, Murdo,' suggested Skuli. 'We will all be kings together.'

Murdo stared at the men before him. Were these really his brothers? How could they talk so? The death of their father had not even raised a sigh of regret, and the loss of their lands produced nothing but scorn.

'Kings!' Murdo mocked. 'No king would refuse to fight for his lands and people. You want treasure? I have treasure, and wealth enough for all of us. Lord Ranulf saved all his share of the plunder won from the enemy, and I have it. We can go home and use it to win back our lands.'

'You do that, Murdo,' Torf said. 'You take whatever Ranulf saved, and go back home.'

'We know about our father's treasure,' Skuli said. 'A few bits of gold and silver – we've seen it. I tell you the truth, Murdo, there are men here – not lords, but soldiers like us – who have amassed more treasure in a single battle than any jarl of Orkney ever saw. We have gold and silver, too, and we mean to get more.'

'Take Hrafnbú if that is what you want,' Torf told him. 'While you are scratching a living on your rock of an island, I will be Count of Tyre and Sidon. Think about that when you are wading in pig shit on your grand bú!'

Murdo shook his head in dismay. He had travelled from one end of the Earth to the other for the sake of his home and family – only to be told he was a fool for caring.

Anger, frustration, and humiliation warred within him. Anger won the fight, and he rose slowly to his feet, fists balled, arms trembling to contain his rage. 'I have heard enough,' he said through teeth clenched so hard his jaws hurt.

He glared at his brothers – Skuli sitting smug-faced and superior, Torf sneering with derision – the moonlight making their features pale, like the corpses he had seen in the streets of Jerusalem. It came to him that he was looking at dead men, and that this was the last time he would see them.

'I have done what was required of me,' Murdo said. 'I am going home, and I am taking the treasure with me.'

'Take it,' Torf said hotly. 'Take the lordship, too. Lord of Hrafnbú – I give it to you, and it's not worth a fart. Hear me: we have offered you a chance to make something of yourself. If you cannot see that, then you deserve whatever you get.'

'Stay with us, Murdo,' offered Skuli. 'Baldwin will give you a place in his war host. We will soon be getting lands of our own, and we will make you a duke.'

'I want nothing from you,' Murdo answered, his voice thick with disappointment and regret. 'Fare well . . .' he hesitated over the word, then said, '*Brothers* . . . we will not see one another again.' Turning to Emlyn, he said, 'We have done what we came here to do, let us be on our way.'

He turned his back and started down the hill.

'Murdo,' pleaded Skuli behind him, 'stay the night at least. We will talk, and you will see the thing differently in the morning.'

When Murdo made no answer, Skuli rose and started after him. 'Wait! Listen to me! Murdo, wait!'

'Let him go, Skuli,' said Torf. 'He always was a sneaking little coward.' To Murdo he shouted, 'Go on, coward! Run away home like you always do.'

The words were hateful; once they would have stung, but he felt nothing from them now. Murdo held nothing but pity for the man who had spoken them.

Emlyn fell into step beside him, but said nothing. They walked for a long time, descending to the valley where they found the road once more. The walls of Jerusalem loomed over them, black and imposing, and though the moon was fading as it drifted lower towards the hills, the sky was still bright with stars. 'That did not go well,' the monk observed after they had resumed their march along the southern wall.

'No,' said Murdo. 'It did not go well.'

'What will you do now?'

'I will do what I said I would do.'

'Return home and claim your farm?'

'Yes.'

'You said the man who holds your lands is in Jerusalem now,' Emlyn mused, 'is that so?'

'He is,' Murdo muttered. Having just lost his brothers to greed and covetous ambition, he did not feel like discussing the finer points of his grievance.

'Who is it?' enquired the monk.

'What difference does it make?' Murdo snapped.

'God knows,' answered Emlyn amiably. 'I merely thought that if I knew more about this affair, I might be able to help you.'

'No one can help me,' Murdo declared. 'I am alone in this, and that is the way of things.'

Emlyn desisted then, and they resumed their walk in silence – which Murdo much preferred. By the time they reached the Jaffa Gate, he had decided that so there should be no bad blood between himself and King Magnus, he would redeem his oath of fealty – beg it, if possible, buy it, if necessary. Then he would return to the monastery, retrieve his fortune, and hasten to Jaffa where he would arrange passage on the first ship leaving the Holy Land to return to the West.

What he would do when he reached Orkney – that was less certain. But, inasmuch as he had a long, long time aboard ship to ponder the question, he was certain the answer would occur to him long before he saw the blue-misted hills of the Dark Isles.

FORTY

The lords of the West met in council the next day in the Church of the Holy Sepulchre. There, in the chapel built over the rock-cut tomb where the carpenter Jesu was laid to rest following his execution by the Romans, the leaders of the crusade met to decide who should hold and protect the city for all Christendom.

Several long boards had been set up end-to-end below the chapel's altar, forming a single long table to accommodate the crusaders and their companions. The chapel was not large; there was room only for sixty men at table, and the remaining two hundred or so were made to stand behind their respective lords. Other curious onlookers filled the vestibule, and still more stood out in the yard, straining to hear what passed within.

Raymond of Toulouse, accompanied by his chaplain, the Abbot of Aguilers, Count Robert of Flanders, and various other noblemen in his company, took the chief places at the table. Next, Duke Godfrey, and his brother Baldwin, Count of Edessa, arrived and assumed their places on Raymond's right, leaving Bohemond and his company of noblemen and advisors no choice but to claim the left side of the board. Robert, Duke of Normandy, last to arrive, joined the company at the foot of the table alongside the Bishop of Bayeux, his chaplains and counsellors; for once, he did not mind facing Raymond – since his men were already making preparations to leave the city, by this time next week he would be well on his way home no matter what happened in council.

'God bless you, and be gracious to you,' Raymond began. He folded his long hands before him, and gazed solemnly down the length of the board at the many faces turned toward his. 'This day, all thanks to Our Lord, we meet in the Holy Shrine of Our Saviour's Tomb to decide among us who shall ascend the throne of Jerusalem. For this purpose, and towards this end, I have asked the abbot to lead us in prayers of thanksgiving for our victory, and supplication for our guidance in the weighty matters before us.' Lifting a hand to his chaplain, who rose from his place beside him, he said, 'Abbot, we wait upon you.'

The count then pushed back his chair and knelt on the stone floor. Godfrey was quick to follow his lead – out of genuine piety, for it was how he always prayed – and the others, not to be thought impious, drew back their own chairs and benches, and put their knees to the floor as the cleric faced the altar, stretched forth his hands, and began to pray.

Mercifully, the abbot confined himself to a half dozen well-chosen prayers and psalms, and then pronounced his benediction, allowing his congregation to resume their places at the table with unaccustomed haste. Raymond then opened the proceedings with a blunt, but truthful appraisal of their position. 'My lords,' he said, 'the death of Bishop Adhemar has left us with a question: who is to rule over the Holy City? Adhemar was not only our friend, he was the pope's legate, and therefore the likely successor to the throne of Jerusalem. We may be bereft of our friend, and his judicious guidance, but our cause is well-served by the men who have gathered around this board today.'

He let his gaze sweep the length of the table before continuing. 'The throne of Jerusalem is reclaimed, and now it is for us to choose who will ascend that throne. The rule of the Holy Land is not to be lightly assumed,' Raymond warned, his voice growing stern, 'for the man who would wield authority in Christ's city must himself be blameless, upright, and able to defend the holy places from the enemies of our faith.'

The Lord of Toulouse nodded to himself. He had put the thing fairly, and now it was for the others to say what they would. He sat down, letting his eyes rest on Robert of Flanders, who manfully stirred himself to his duty. 'My lords and dear companions,' he said, rising to his feet from his place near the head of the table, 'if you would allow me to speak, I will presume on your attention for the briefest of moments.'

'Speak! Speak!' the lords answered. 'Speak, man. Say it out.'

'Thank you.' The count bowed, as if acquiescing to the will of the assembly. 'As is well known among you, I have no personal interest in the rule of this city. Even now, I am carrying forth my plans for a swift return to my lands and home . . .'

384

'Yes, yes,' muttered the noblemen. 'Get on with it, man.'

'Therefore,' continued the count, taking no heed of their impatience, 'my only interest is to see this city – this city whose freedom has exacted such a heavy price from us all, a price which we have all borne with . . .'

'Move on, move on,' murmured the voices.

'. . . price which we have all borne with selfless – nay, *sacrificial* – forbearance and endurance, counting the cost daily, not only in the material wealth granted us, but in the lives of our kinsmen, friends, and men at arms who follow . . .'

'For God's sake, get on with it!' shouted a nobleman from Bohemond's entourage.

Robert glared coldly at the man, and continued, 'My only interest is to see this city well provided with leadership, protection, and government, both temporally *and* spiritually, for the safety, not only of its citizens, but for the many pilgrims who will follow in our footsteps . . .'

'Hoo! Hoo!' bawled Bohemond's supporters, some of them banging on the board with the flat of their hands.

'Lords and noblemen!' barked Count Raymond, leaning forward sharply. 'This is not seemly. We are here to choose the next king of Jerusalem.'

'We are here to divide the plunder!' called a voice from among Baldwin's entourage.

'All in good time, my friend,' Raymond replied imperiously. 'Those who only care for the wealth of the world shall have their reward, but we will deal with higher things first.' Turning his approving gaze upon Robert, he said, 'Pray continue, my friend. We are listening.'

Robert, growing flustered by the repeated interruptions, decided to cut short his discourse, and strove resolutely towards the end. 'Therefore, I find it fitting that we should come together in the place where Our Lord rose from his grave, to assist in the resurrection of the Holy City, that from this day forth . . .'

'The king! The king!' shouted another of Bohemond's men. 'Who will be king?'

'Silence, everyone!' cried someone in Godfrey's camp. 'Or we will be at this all day!'

Robert, fumbling for words now, cut his losses and made a hasty retreat. 'To this end, I submit that we could not choose a better man to assume the throne of Jerusalem than Raymond, Count of Toulouse and Provence.' He sat down so quickly that it took a moment for the rest of the assembly to realize he had indeed finished.

The Duke of Normandy seized the opportunity. 'Friends and comrades, as a warrior and a nobleman, whether on the field of battle, or in the court of rule, I yield nothing to anyone who holds not my respect; and that respect must be earned, by God. I say Duke Godfrey has earned my highest respect, and that of all crusaders. Therefore, he should be king.'

'Hear! Hear!' shouted the duke's supporters and advisors. 'It is God's will!'

Bishop Arnulf, who was chaplain to the duke, added his voice to the acclaim. 'The man who was first on the wall, and first to set foot in the city, and first to draw blood in defence of the faith – should not that man be made ruler of the city? What say you, Godfrey?'

The Duke of Bouillon, looking suitably solemn, rose and turned pious eyes towards the altar. After a moment, he made the sign of the cross over himself, then turned to the assembly. 'I am humbled that you should deem me worthy of the honour you propose. Yet, whether I am granted the rule of the city, or whether it shall pass to another, I believe that it should here be established that the throne of Jerusalem shall remain empty until Christ himself shall come to resume his reign. Brothers, we would do well to await that glad day with keen anticipation. Until our Lord Christ returns, I should be honoured to hold this city for him, but never let it be as king. For no mortal monarch should wear a crown of gold, where Our Lord and Saviour wore a crown of thorns!'

Raymond, alarmed at the speed with which the kingship was receding from his grasp, waded back into the fray. 'Well said, my friend!' he called loudly. 'You speak my own thoughts admirably well. Allow me to propose, therefore, that the ruler of the Holy City should own a title befitting his humility and devotion.'

This sentiment met with the acclaim of the assembled lords, who shouted their support so loudly that Raymond allowed himself a small, inward smile at how well he had steered the tide of opinion back to his favour.

But he had not reckoned on Bohemond. 'My lords, and esteemed and worthy comrades, we have braved many dangers on our pilgrimage, the successful completion of which is now contemplated. It only remains for us to choose an honourable ruler, and make division of the treasures which God has placed in our hands for the benefit of our troops and the on-going protection of his Holy City.'

His listeners were rapt. Here was a new wrinkle in the argument; what did the wily prince have in mind?

'I speak not for myself,' Bohemond continued, 'but for those who have no voice at this assembly, yet who nevertheless have given of their sweat and blood as much as anyone here. Were we to hear those voices, I doubt not they would tell us that he who would be ruler of Jerusalem must be seen to be just, fair-handed, and generous. They would say that it should be the Lord of Jerusalem's first duty to see to the division of the treasure seized in plunder. To this end, I will uphold the man who will shoulder this burden with all equity and impartiality.'

So saying, the prince then sat down. He wished Tancred was with him; his cousin's support would have helped sway the balance of opinion. Still, he had an ally equally eager to see an evenhanded division of the spoils: King Magnus. The Norse lord was on his feet before the crowd had yet tumbled to the implications of Prince Bohemond's proposal.

'My lords, friends, and brothers-in-arms,' said the king in rough Latin. 'I am not known to many here, but like you, I have taken the cross and, like you, braved the dangers of pilgrimage to see the Holy City liberated. I agree with Bohemond: we must choose the man who will support those whose blood and muscle made the conquest possible – wherever they fought, and wherever they fell.'

Magnus then took his seat, to much noisy acclamation. To Raymond's chagrin, the noblemen liked this plainspeaking barbarian lord and his outrageous suggestion that the latecomers should share in the plunder.

'The prince and his liegeman are right to remind us of our duty to the men on whom we all depend,' Raymond said, desperate to repair the breach to his carefully constructed campaign. 'Let me add my voice to those who say that we should honour them. But I ask you: would it not be a disservice to those who gave their lives to include men who were not here, who by their very absence caused those on whose shoulders fell the burden of liberation to labour more greatly for the lack?'

Before his voice had died away, Magnus was on his feet once more. 'Please, my lord, I mean no disrespect, but men where I come from are used to simpler fare. Are you saying that you would not abide by the agreement, made by every nobleman around this table, to divide the plunder equally?'

All eyes turned to Raymond to see the count's face grow red with anger and exasperation. The count's discomfiture pleased Bohemond greatly. In the short time he had known the King of Norway, Bohemond had grown very fond of his new vassal. Of Northern blood himself, he understood Norsemen and their unaffected ways. Of all his mercenary host, he valued their courage, skill, and fearlessness most highly. These were men he could count on to dare anything for gain – something Bohemond appreciated, and wholeheartedly approved.

Thus, the two questions hung in the air like storm clouds poised to collide and inundate all beneath with thunder and torrent. King Magnus had forced the count to declare his intentions regarding the division of spoils, and had let the assembly know where his sentiments lay. Raymond, insisting on the narrowest interpretation of their agreement, had let them know he would withhold the spoils from anyone who had not fought in Jerusalem.

Now, it was for the other contender to make his position known. Bishop Arnulf spoke up, 'Forgive me, lords, if I speak where I ought to pursue silence. But as I have voiced my support for Godfrey of Bouillon, I would hear his answer to the questions posed before us.'

'Indeed! Indeed!' shouted the noble assembly. 'What say you, Godfrey? On your feet, man!'

The Duke of Bouillon rose and smiled at his questioners, and at Raymond, too, to show there were no hard feelings on his part. 'Again, I am honoured that my fellows and peers should consider me worthy to occupy the most important seat of government in all Christendom. Therefore, let me reassure any who, through no fault of their own, were unable to reach Jerusalem in time to aid in its liberation, that I recognize their invaluable contribution to the crusade. Out of appreciation and gratitude for the unity of our purpose, I would see that selfsame unity extend to the apportioning of the plunder.'

He inclined his head towards the bishop, and resumed his seat to the acclaim of his supporters. To any who yet wavered in their convictions, it quickly became apparent that the question of who should sit on the throne of Jerusalem would only be answered by including Bohemond and Baldwin in the allotment. For their part, both noblemen professed themselves well-pleased with the conquest, and loudly lamented the fact that they had not been able to reach Jerusalem in time to aid in the city's release from Muhammedan domination; and, of course, neither saw any reason why, as recognized leaders of the crusade, they should not extract a generous portion of the spoils.

Raymond remained stoutly against the latecomers' inclusion, resisting all suggestions that the city's plunder should be shared by any who did not actively aid in making possible its acquisition. Much to his surprise, this position did not enhance his position among the noblemen. When placed aside the wider generosity of Godfrey, the Count of Toulouse seemed grasping and mean-spirited.

In a last desperate attempt at winning the favour of the undecided peers, Raymond proposed a compromise which advocated that, as the cost in men and arms had been borne by those who freed the city, this cost should be repaid first, and the remainder of the treasure divided up equally, as they had all agreed in Constantinople.

On another day, this compromise might have been seen as a wise and just settlement by a competent ruler. But it was already too late. The lords and noblemen who had been roused by Godfrey's supporters were eager to get on with the proceedings; and the prospect of wading through the interminable wrangling over how much each lord and lordling should take out of the common purse filled them with tepid dread. Raymond's wise and just suggestion was regarded as demeaning the great charity of Godfrey's open-handed offer to include all equally.

Baldwin, sensing the opportune moment had come, rose amidst the noise and clamour of the assembly as they proclaimed their approval of Godfrey's plan. 'My esteemed lords and fellow Christians,' he said, rapping on the board with the handle of his dagger. 'It gratifies me right well to hear your praise of my brother. Therefore, it is with great good pleasure that I commend to your affirmation, our comrade and friend, Duke Godfrey of Bouillon.' He looked down the length of the table on both sides. 'What say you, my lords?' He thrust out his hand towards his brother. 'I give you King Godfrey!'

The chapel rang as the gathering roared its confirmation. The nobles pounded the board with their hands and knife handles; some drew their swords and lofted them in the air. They cheered and shouted his name, and those nearest him raised him to his feet to address the acclaim. Smiling, gesturing benevolently, he received the jubilant tribute and, when the roar had abated, said, 'I am stirred to my soul by your kind adulation, and declare before this lordly council that, with God's help and guidance, I will accept the charge you have laid on me.'

There were more cheers, and shouts of adulation. 'God wills it!' they cried. 'Godfrey is king! God wills it!'

When the shouts had subsided once more, Jerusalem's new monarch said, 'Please, it is not fitting that any mortal should bear a sovereign's title in the city where the King of kings holds sway. Therefore, I beg you, do not lay upon me a greater rank than any mortal has a right to assume. If I am to reign in this place,' he turned pious eyes towards the altar, 'let me rule by this title: Advocatus Sancti Sepulchri!'

Of all the things he might have said, this was by far the most fitting, and the gathering admired him all the more for it. In a stroke he had disarmed any remaining opposition and swept the field. 'Hail Godfrey, Defender of the Holy Sepulchre!' they cried, and the chapel shuddered in thunderous acclaim.

Because all were preoccupied with the celebration of Godfrey's ascension, no one noticed the arrival of a small group of warriors dressed in battle array; their arms and legs were encased in figured metal; their burnished helmets were surmounted by white horsetails; gleaming loricas of overlapping metal plates encased their bodies; and each one carried a long, double-bladed lance. They were led by a man dressed in the same way, but wearing no helmet, and carrying no spear; instead, his lorica had gold fittings, and he wore a purple cloak.

The sudden appearance of the strange warriors silenced the lords in full cry. They turned as one, and were startled to see this solemn apparition in their midst. Some drew swords and prepared to fight; others urged peace and calm. Only one or two of the crusade leaders recognized the figure at the head of this invading force. Godfrey was one of these.

'Peace and welcome,' he called, extending his hand towards the young commander and his Varangian troops. 'I give you good greeting, Drungarius Dalassenus. Your presence here has somewhat taken us unawares.'

The commander bowed stiffly towards the altar, and to the western lords. 'In the name of Alexius, Equal of the Apostles and Vice-Regent of Heaven, Holy Roman Emperor, Supreme Sovereign of All Christendom, I bring you greetings and congratulations on your estimable victory.' His thin smile faded as he proceeded directly to the reason for his abrupt intrusion. 'The emperor has sent me to convey his laud for your magnificent achievement, and to prepare the way for the Holy City to be returned to the dominion of the empire.'

Jerusalem's new ruler stared at the intruder. Return the city to the emperor? Godfrey could see his prize receding as quickly as it had arrived. He had not even taken up his office, and already he was being deposed by the emperor.

Dalassenus pressed the slender advantage surprise had afforded him, and said, 'Naturally, the emperor is pleased to offer you and your troops due reward from among the treasures you have secured. In token of his gratitude and good will, he has decreed that he will gladly undertake the payment of all expenses incurred by his vassals in the defence of the Holy City. What is more, Emperor Alexius has given me a free hand in determining how best to reward those who aid in the swift establishment of the imperial rule.'

A sound like the growl of a dog warning an intruder rumbled around the table as the drungarius' demand sank in. The council bristled with menace and drew breath to shout the audacious interloper down. But Count Raymond, more mindful than most of their sworn obligations to the emperor, rose and said, 'By your leave, Duke Godfrey, I beg the boon of answering this dictate.'

'Pray speak, sir,' replied Godfrey, glad for some help.

'Lord Drungarius,' said Raymond coolly, 'it is right to remind us of the emperor's felicitous regard. Now that the crusade has reached its successful conclusion, it is right also to reflect on our obligations, and consider the aid we have had from the emperor.' Spreading his hands wide, the tall Frankish count said, 'I know I speak for every man here when I say we are beholden to Emperor Alexius for all he has done on our behalf. Truly, we never could have finished the pilgrimage without his many thoughtful kindnesses.'

'Hear! Hear!' muttered some of the lords.

'Nevertheless,' Raymond continued, 'I insist before this assembly that we must decline your demand. We, who have won this city, will undertake its protection and governance.' Raymond drew himself up full height. 'In short, sir, the city will *not* be surrendered to imperial rule.'

Dalassenus stiffened. The moment he had feared more than any other had come. 'I will ask you but once, and plainly: do you refuse to honour your vow?'

The lords around the board prepared for the clash that would come. Oath of fealty or no, they had no intention of giving up Jerusalem, any more than they had given up Antioch or Edessa, or any of the other towns they had won from the Turks and Saracens; indeed, many still felt aggrieved that they had returned Nicaea to Alexius. They had won the Holy City, no thanks to the emperor, and they would be damned if they would hand it over to him without a fight.

But Raymond was shrewd. 'As many here can attest, I would be the first to urge us all to uphold the vows we swore before the imperial throne in Constantinople,' he said smoothly. 'Yet, I feel I must beg your pardon, drungarius, but I am compelled to point out that Jerusalem never belonged to the emperor in the first place.'

Dalassenus' face darkened. 'You would think to conceal your obscene avarice beneath such a flimsy shroud? The authority and jurisdiction of the Holy City have always been the duty and concern of the church. The emperor, as Supreme Head of the Church, is therefore the rightful sovereign of Jerusalem. Any attempt to with-hold the Holy City from imperial control will be seen as an act of war against the church itself.'

Godfrey, picking up Raymond's argument and waving it like a banner, entered the fray then, saying, 'We are all of us grateful to the emperor for his many gifts in support of the crusade. And I, like my brother lords, readily recall our oath and freely attest that we have promised to return to the emperor all cities, goods, and citizens formerly held by the empire. But Raymond is right: Jerusalem has ever remained beyond imperial authority and jurisdiction. Naturally, we cannot be expected to return something which was never lost.'

Dalassenus knew the crusaders would never willingly relinquish their prize; as they had demonstrated at Antioch and Edessa, they had no intention of giving up anything unless by force. As Grand

Drungarius he could declare war on the Latin lords, but in doing so he would place the empire in the indefensible position of fighting against the Holy City. How could the Emperor of All Christendom be seen to make war on the defenders of his own church? However desirable it might be, the prospect was not one he could pursue, and he knew it.

Conceding he must abandon the field, he loosed the one arrow left in his quiver. 'The emperor will be informed of your decision,' Dalassenus told them, hoping the implied threat would weaken their resolve. 'No doubt he will be delighted to hear that you recognize the letter of your agreement, if not the spirit. And since you obviously value precision so highly, I will assume that even now you are making plans for the return of a certain valuable to the imperial treasury.'

The lords glanced guiltily at one another. It fell to Godfrey, as the new ruler of Jerusalem, to discover which valuable the envoy meant. 'If we have taken anything which did not belong to us,' he replied magnanimously, 'then rest assured it will be returned with all haste.' He saw Baldwin glaring furiously at him, but continued nevertheless. 'Only tell us what this valuable might be, and we shall gladly deliver it to you.'

Dalassenus smiled. These crusaders were like children in many ways. 'Do you not know?' he asked wonderingly. 'Why, it is on everyone's lips. Indeed, every Christian from Jerusalem to Constantinople is talking about the Holy Lance.'

FORTY-ONE

Since their triumphant return from the council, Bohemond and King Magnus and their noblemen and advisors had closeted themselves in Bohemond's private chambers. Like the rest of Magnus' war band, Murdo was anxious for the king to emerge from the deliberations; and, like the rest of the men, he was growing restive and bored. Unlike everyone else, however, he cared nothing for the final result of the council. His only reason for staying was to redeem his vow of fealty to the king – so that he might take his leave with the king's blessing and a clear conscience.

At first, the rumours had flown thick and fast. There was to be an equal distribution of plunder, some said; there was to be no division at all, others said. The lords had chosen a king for Jerusalem; the lords had failed to choose a king. The emperor was on his way with ten thousand Varangi; the emperor was already here! The emperor demanded the city and its plunder; the lords were getting ready for war . . .

As the day dwindled and no further information was gleaned, speculation eventually ceased and the waiting men grew increasingly sullen and peevish. The Norsemen were now grumbling and moaning openly, their former mood of high expectation turning sour as the day sped away. Murdo thought to escape the sombre mood, but it was too hot for wandering around the streets and, anyway, the city stank. He considered going outside the walls where the air was somewhat better, but he feared missing his first opportunity to speak to the king.

'They have had no food or drink brought in,' Fionn pointed out. 'We will not have much longer to wait.'

'I, for one, am through with waiting,' declared Murdo, rising abruptly. 'I am leaving.'

'Do not wander far,' the cleric advised. 'I will fetch you when the lords have finished their deliberations.'

'Farewell,' replied Murdo, already striding away.

With that, he left the courtyard and hurried along the columned corridor, passed quickly through the entrance and out into the street. Brother Emlyn caught up with him just before he reached the Jaffa Gate. 'Murdo, wait!' he called, hurrying along behind as the young man made for the gate. 'I saw you leave the palace. Where are you going?'

'I mean to collect my father's belongings, and then I am going home.'

'Once the council has made its decision, we will all be leaving – a few days at most, I should think, and then –'

'I have no reason to stay even a day longer,' Murdo said sharply. 'I did what I came to do. Now I can leave this place for ever.'

'Your brothers –'

'They are no longer my brothers,' Murdo replied bitterly.

'What I was going to say was that your brothers treated you very badly, but that is no reason to –'

'Torf and Skuli have made their decision, and I have made mine. In fact, they have done me a valuable service. I know now that I am alone in this and cannot count on anyone else. Very well. That is how I began; that is how I will carry on.'

'Do not talk so,' the monk chided gently. 'Come back with me, and we will speak to the king. It would be well to allow him to release you from your vow.'

Murdo started walking again. Emlyn fell into step beside him. '*You* go back if you wish,' Murdo told him. 'I will not be persuaded to return.'

'How will you reach Orkneyjar?'

'Many crusaders are leaving now. I will get a place aboard one of the ships at Jaffa.' When the monk asked what he would do if all the places were taken, Murdo said, 'Then I will *buy* a ship. One way or another, I mean to leave this place far behind.'

'Then I am going with you,' the cleric declared.

'You are one of the king's advisors; you cannot leave him like this.'

'So,' observed Emlyn, 'my vow prevents me, but yours does not? Explain this to me.'

Murdo sighed. 'What do you want me to do?'

'Come back and beg a proper leave-taking of your king. Allow him to offer you his blessing.'

'And if he does not?'

'That is his choice. He is the king, and you are his vassal,' Emlyn replied; taking Murdo by the arm, he turned the headstrong young man. 'Come, do not think the worst. Magnus is a reasonable man, and a most generous lord if you permit him to be benevolent.'

Murdo returned to the palace precinct, and to restless waiting. At midday, the lords emerged from their vigil to proclaim their hopeful assurance of a swift and just settlement of their demands. They spoke of their renewed zeal for one another's support and loyalty, and their eagerness to demonstrate their prodigious gratitude for the services of their warriors. Bohemond then departed with his noblemen to his quarters, leaving Magnus to hold court with his men.

There followed still more waiting while the king, besieged by anxious Norsemen, answered their questions and allayed their fears. At last, Murdo's turn came; with Emlyn at his side, he stepped before the king and said, 'Lord and king, I beg the boon of your indulgence.'

'Speak freely, my friend,' Magnus invited. 'But, pray, speak quickly. I am to rejoin Bohemond, and we must soon return to the council.'

Succinctly as possible, Murdo explained his wish to return home by the swiftest means. He asked the king to release him from his vow of fealty, yet pledged his continued loyalty and friendship, to which the Norse king replied, 'I, too, share your desire to return home. I ask that you lend me your patience yet a little longer. We will all be leaving Jerusalem soon enough, and when we do, we will depart as wealthy men.'

At hearing his request denied, Murdo's heart fell. The prospect of remaining in Jerusalem, even a day longer, filled him with dread. Plucking up his courage, he said, 'Forgive my boldness, Lord Magnus, but I will gladly barter my share of the treasure for your permission to leave for Jaffa at once.'

Magnus paused to consider this a moment. 'Your offer tempts me,' he conceded. 'Yet, I would be a false and unworthy lord if I agreed. The road between here and Jaffa is not safe, and I could not spare so much as one man to go with you. Therefore, I think you must stay, and content yourself with a goodly share of the plunder which Count Bohemond and I hasten now to secure.'

The king turned and started away again. Murdo, risking all he might gain, made one last attempt to change the king's mind. 'If I found someone to travel with me, my lord, would you agree then?'

Magnus made a dismissive gesture with his hand. 'If you can find anyone willing to forfeit his portion of the plunder, then you may depart with my blessing.' He chuckled mirthlessly. 'Even so, if I know my men at all, you will still be trying to convince them the day we sail from Jaffa.'

'I will go with him,' offered Emlyn, stepping forward.

Magnus frowned.

'If you would permit me, lord,' the monk hastened to add, 'I might accompany him as far as Jaffa, and await your arrival there. It would be no hardship to me, since, as a priest, I would not gain a share of the treasure anyway.'

'Very well,' agreed Magnus impatiently, 'let it be as you say. I will bow to my wise counsellor's judgement. Go, both of you, with my blessing. May God grant you safe passage. Now, if you will permit me, I must join Lord Taranto.'

As the king and his nobles went on their way, Emlyn said, 'Come, we will tell Ronan and Fionn, and bid them farewell. Then, we shall be on our way.'

They found Ronan as he prepared to attend Lord Magnus, and Murdo bade him farewell. 'Why farewell?' he asked. 'It cannot be that you are leaving.'

'I am,' said Murdo adamantly. He explained the bargain he had made with King Magnus, and Emlyn's offer to accompany him as far as Jaffa. 'The good brother will see me safely on a stout ship, but I would go with a better heart if *you* would give me a blessing.'

'You need never ask, Murdo, my heart,' Ronan told him. 'The High King of Heaven holds you in the hollow of his hand, and his angels stand ready to defend you.' He regarded Murdo fondly. 'If I thought anything I said could change your mind, I would counsel you to stay. It would be a waste of breath, I fear.' Stretching his right hand over the young man's head, he said, 'The Good Lord bless you and keep you, and be gracious to you, and may the light of his countenance shine upon you and give you peace wheresoever you may go.'

He embraced Murdo then, bade him farewell, and said, 'Have you told Jon Wing your plans?'

'You say fare well for me,' Murdo answered. 'He has gone off with the others.'

'Find him, Murdo,' Ronan urged. 'He will want to see you well away.'

'Tell him I am grateful for his care, and that if he should find me when next he comes to Orkneyjar I will fill the welcome bowl with good brown ale.'

The heat rising from the bare ground met the walkers' faces like the blast from an oven as they moved out from the shadowed tunnel of the gate. The sun was a harsh yellow glow in a sky bleached pale by the heat and dust. Black columns of carrion birds still wheeled in the dead air above the city; their screeks and squawks could be heard falling from on high with an abrasive incessance.

Upon passing through the gate, Murdo turned quickly onto the Hebron road rising towards Mount Zion and the Church of Saint Mary. 'How will you get your father's belongings to the ship?'

'You will see,' replied Murdo, and would say no more.

In a short while they came in sight of the little farming settlement where Ronan had borrowed the camel and Emlyn received his answer. Murdo turned off the road and onto the track leading to the farm. 'So, you think to borrow the fellow's camel again. Do you think he will give it to you?'

'He will when I show him the gold.'

They walked on, and arrived at the cluster of small, white-washed, baked mud buildings. As they entered the yard, a skinny brown dog came from around the side of the house and started barking. The farmer appeared in the doorway a moment later and started to shout. Then he saw who it was, and ran out into the yard, seized Murdo's hand and kissed it – all the while babbling in the queer speech of the Holy Land's peasants.

'What is he saying?' demanded Murdo.

Emlyn looked at the farmer and shook his head. 'He is speaking Aramaic, I believe. Ronan knows Aramaic, not me.'

Murdo rolled his eyes. Retrieving his hand from the farmer, he dipped the fingers of his right hand into his belt and withdrew a gold bezant. He then pointed to the camel which was kneeling beside the post in the yard. The farmer babbled something and pointed to the beast, nodding enthusiastically. He turned and shouted towards the house, whereupon his brown wife emerged and, with a shy sideways glance at Murdo, bustled off towards the camel. She took up a stick, and struck the animal on the foreshoulder, clucking her tongue and hissing at it. The animal rose leisurely and, while the woman untied the tether, the farmer gibbered at Murdo, who merely nodded and smiled.

The task finished, the woman then joined her husband, and she, too, kissed Murdo's hand, whereupon Murdo produced a second gold bezant and gave it to her. She snatched the coin away and hid it in a knot in her mantle almost before her husband knew she had it. The farmer's eyes grew wide at his great good fortune, and he began babbling more ecstatically than ever.

With difficulty, Murdo extracted himself from the zealous veneration of the farmer and his wife, and set off again, leading his purchase. He bade the peasants farewell as they passed from the yard, though he knew they would not understand him.

'I wonder if they know they will never see their camel again?' mused Emlyn as they started down the hill towards the road once more.

'That is what the second coin was for,' Murdo replied.

'Yes, I thought as much,' Emlyn agreed approvingly.

'Look there,' said Murdo, pointing to the road below where a company of knights were just then passing. 'I wonder if it means the council is finished at last.'

'Who is it? Can you tell?' asked Emlyn, squinting his eyes. 'Is it Baldwin?'

'No, not Baldwin,' answered Murdo. 'I do not know who it is.'

The mounted soldiers passed out of sight long before the two on foot reached the road, and no more were seen as they climbed the steep slope of the Holy Mountain. They passed the church, and moved through the crowds huddled around the walls to find the gates flung wide and the yard within filled with horses and armed men. Murdo did not hesitate, but went in straight away before anyone could stop him.

They had taken but two steps past the threshold however, when they were met by a very distracted gatekeeper. 'I am sorry,' he said. 'No one must enter. We are closing our doors for the night by order of the emperor.'

'Please,' said Emlyn, 'we will not disturb anyone. We wish only to retrieve the remains of this man's family from the catacombs, and we will be on our way.'

The gateman frowned. 'It is the emperor's command!' he insisted, trying to push them back out.

'You did not open the gates to us,' Murdo told him. 'The gate was open and we came in. If anyone asks, you can tell them we were already inside.'

'I dare not!' shrieked the man. 'The emperor –'

'Is the emperor here?' wondered Emlyn, looking at the commotion in the yard.

'It is the Grand Drungarius, the emperor's personal envoy,' the worried gateman replied. 'He has just returned from the council at the Church of the Holy Sepulchre. Now you must leave at once. Please, it will be on my head if anyone finds out.' He clutched at Murdo's sleeve as if to pull him out.

Murdo whirled on the porter; his hand snaked out and caught the fellow by the wrist and gripped it hard. 'I am going to fetch my father's remains from the catacombs,' he said, putting his face close to the gateman's. 'When I have done that, I will be on my way. You can help us, or you can stand aside.'

The porter blanched and looked to his fellow cleric for help. 'You see how it is,' said Emlyn. 'It will only take a moment, and no one will even know we are here.'

The gateman relented then. 'God have mercy,' he muttered, and flapped his hand at them. 'Go on . . . go on – and hurry!'

Keeping to the perimeter of the yard, they made their way through the confusion of soldiers. Off to one side, surrounded by a group of tall soldiers in gleaming armour, Murdo saw the abbot and the dark-featured man he had seen the night they came to the monastery. As he hurried by, the man looked up and stared directly at him, and Murdo knew he had been recognized. The man turned his attention once more to what the abbot was saying, and Murdo and Emlyn continued on to the small building behind the refectory and kitchens. Murdo ducked inside and fetched a torch from the box beside the door, lit it from the embers of one of the ovens, and then they both descended to the darkness of the catacombs below.

The air cooled wonderfully as they went down into the earth.

Murdo stepped from the staired passageway and was met by the scent of dry mould and ancient dust. In the flickering light of the torch, he saw their footprints from their previous visit on the floor, and followed them through the first two galleries and the next and into the one beyond – the unfinished gallery where they had laid the treasure.

Murdo saw his father's shield below one of the niches where they had hidden the treasure; he squatted down and, when he did not see anything, he thrust the torch inside. The shroud-wrapped, corpse-like bundles were still there, along with the sword and belt, and hauberk. He quickly checked the other niche as well, and saw that all was as they had left it. He realized he was holding his breath, and exhaled a long, slow sigh of relief. 'All is well,' he told Emlyn. 'They are still there.'

'What did I tell you?' said the monk. 'There is no place safer than the catacombs.'

'I will remember that,' Murdo replied, pulling the first of the bundles from the niche.

They worked quickly and quietly, dragging the bundles up from the catacombs and binding them with cords to the camel's saddle frame. Lastly, Murdo retrieved his father's sword, shield, and hauberk, and tied them on as well. Satisfied that his treasure was secure, Murdo led the camel back out into the yard again.

The commotion had abated somewhat, and they hastened along, unnoticed by any save the gatekeeper, who was greatly relieved to see them. He opened the gate as they approached. 'Hurry! Hurry!' he said, beckoning them through.

Murdo paused a few paces outside the gate. 'Do not stop!' said the gateman, rushing towards them. 'Move on. No one knows you were here. Move on before they find out.'

Turning to Emlyn, Murdo whispered, 'Talk to him. Keep him occupied for a moment.' He pushed the priest forward. 'Make certain he looks the other way.'

Emlyn scurried forth. 'Thank you, brother,' he said, taking hold of the gateman's arm and turning him around. 'Truly, you have rendered us a divine service, and we are grateful for your kindness.' He walked the gateman back towards the gate. 'Never fear, you will not see us again.'

'It is not myself who has made this command, you understand,' said the worried cleric. 'It is the emperor's envoy. We must do what he says, and –'

'I am certain of it,' said Emlyn, breaking in. 'Rest assured, we bear no ill feelings.'

'On the contrary,' said Murdo, stepping up beside him, 'I want the monastery to have this as a remembrance of our gratitude and thanks for your help.' With that, he placed a fine golden bowl into the astonished gateman's hands.

'What is this?' whined the porter. He gaped fearfully at the bowl as if a world of fresh trouble opened before him.

'A gift,' Murdo assured him. 'I want you to take it to your abbot and tell him that this is my thanks for the brief use of the catacombs. Will you do that?'

'It will be in his hands before vespers,' replied the gateman, relieved to have the matter resolved.

'Then we will trouble you no more. Come, brother,' he said to Emlyn, 'we are away.'

They left the gateman standing before his gate, clutching the golden bowl and gawking after them. They passed the church and started back down the hillside. Murdo looked out across the valley to the Holy City, now misty in the haze of a hot day's rosy twilight, and, for the first time since leaving home, felt as if he had finally, at long last, arrived.

They descended into the valley, passing beneath the city walls once more. Upon reaching the Jaffa road, Murdo looked for the last time at David's Tower, and then turned his face to the west and put Jerusalem at his back. 'We will find a place to sleep beside the road,' Murdo said. 'Are you hungry?'

'A little bread and wine would sit nicely with me,' Emlyn said. 'But I am content.'

'Maybe we can buy some bread and wine from a farmer,' Murdo suggested. 'Or find some water at least.'

'If not, we will fast like true pilgrims – until we reach Jaffa,' Emlyn offered amiably.

After a while the road bent a little to the north, and they could see the fires of the crusader camps on the hillsides and in the valley along the northern walls of the city. The sky was almost dark now, and the first stars were glowing overhead. The path began to rise to its climb into the heights, before beginning its long descent to the sea. Once up from the valley floor, the air was cooler, and the light breeze felt good on their skin. Yes, and it felt good to be on the road, thought Murdo, to be going home.

FORTY-TWO

'Most imprudent of you, Godfrey,' observed Baldwin, holding out his cup to be refilled. 'How could you promise to forfeit the treasure to the emperor without knowing what it was you were being asked to surrender?'

'Would you rather have him take Jerusalem?' Godfrey, in a surly humour, glared at his brother and at the noblemen holding vigil with him. The day, begun with a towering victory, had ended in ripe disaster. In his first act as ruler of the Holy City he had succeeded in losing its most holy and sacred relic.

The lords of the West were angry at him, and baying for blood. Some of them were for refusing to honour the promise and declaring war with Byzantium instead. The fact that the empire's troops now outnumbered their own vastly diminished armies had not yet occurred to anyone.

Jerusalem had been won. The heady days following the city's fall were giving way to a season of sober reflection – for Godfrey, Defender of the Holy Sepulchre, if for no one else. In the short space between this day's glorious beginning, and its cruel, regretful end, Godfrey had pondered deeply over his unenviable position; his unhappy meditations had borne bitter fruit. The lords of the West had liberated the Holy City, but the cost had been ruinous. And now, with nearly all the crusaders returning home, he would be ruler of a city surrounded by hordes of crafty and relentless enemies – Turks and Saracens, to be sure, but also Greek and Armenian Christians whose people had been slaughtered in the blood frenzy – all of whom knew the land and tolerated the unbearable heat far better than his own war-weary troops.

The sad truth, and Godfrey knew it well, was that the crusaders would very soon be in desperate want of imperial aid. Continual and close friendship with Alexius was the only way to guarantee that help remained forthcoming. Unless he thought of something now – this night! – tomorrow he must deliver Jerusalem's most valuable object to the emperor's envoy as a peace offering and sign of his reign's good will, and his recognition of Alexius' supremacy. The prospect made him squirm. Why, he would become the laughing-stock of the entire Christian world: the Lord of Jerusalem a mere vassal of the Greeks.

'Oh, cheer up, brother,' Baldwin said over the rim of his cup. 'The night is young. We will yet think of something.'

'So you say,' Godfrey sneered. 'Tomorrow you can ride back to Edessa and begin your reign in all pomp and glory. Meanwhile, I begin mine in shame and disgrace – and all because I must give the Holy Lance to the emperor!'

Baldwin, growing bored with his brother's rant, swigged down another mouthful of wine, and said, 'Then give it to someone else. Give it to Bohemond. Better still, give it to Sultan Arslan. Ha!'

Godfrey stared at his younger brother. 'You are an ass, Baldwin. Worse, you are a drunken ass. If that is the best you can suggest, go back to Edessa. I will face my humiliation alone.'

'Now, see here –' Baldwin made to rise, but found his legs were not as steady as he imagined them. He fell back in his chair. 'I was only trying to help. If you cannot see that, then maybe you deserve your humil . . . miliation.' He called loudly to the servingman standing by. 'Wine, you sluggard. More wine!'

'You have had enough, brother,' Godfrey said. He put his cup down with a thump, and rose. 'I am going to bed. You would do well to do the same.'

'Splendid,' muttered Baldwin. 'The emperor claps his hands and you cry "Thunder!". Well, if it was my place, I would send the thing away. Let Alexius get it from someone else.'

Godfrey bade his inebriated brother and noblemen good night, left them to their cups, and went to his bed chamber. Dismissing his servant, he lay down on his bed, but found he could not rest. He rose, crossed to the window and pulled it open to allow some fresh air into the stuffy room. He looked out to see the moon was rising over the olive groves; the Jaffa road was a silver river trickling towards the city, and away to the north, low and dark on the ground, lay the camps of the crusaders. In a few days, the soldiers would be gone, and the abandoned camps but one more execrable memory in the long, turbulent existence of this ancient city.

Fool! he thought. Had he come this far, dared this much, only to become the butt of jokes and japes? Feeling the weight of his failure, Godfrey knelt at the window and began to pray. He remained long in this posture, and when he rose at last it was with a better heart. He would accept his indignity and shame as a chastisement from God's hand for the errors he had made on pilgrimage.

Thus resolved, he stretched himself once more on his bed. Night was far gone when sleep finally found him, and then it was an uneasy, fitful rest. He awoke to the croak of crows from the rooftops below his open window, and Baldwin's last words of the previous night tumbling restlessly in his mind: *Let Alexius get it from someone else!*

For the first time since the council's disastrous conclusion, he saw the palest glimmer of hope: if the Holy Lance must be relinquished, let it be surrendered by another. But who?

The answer burst upon him with all the force and urgency of a battlecry. As on the field of war numerous times, he felt the familiar stirring in his blood. In the space of a single heartbeat, the plan was arrayed before him. Any lingering gloom of doubt was banished by the fierce light of his certainty: there was only one person in all the world able to resist the demands of the emperor, and that was the pope. If anyone could protect the Sacred Lance for the crusaders it would be Pope Urban. Let Alexius get the relic from someone else: let him get it from the pope.

He came up from the bed like a lion rising to the attack, his mind filled with all the things he must do. Before anything else, he must delay the envoy. He must buy himself some time if his plan was to have even the slightest chance of succeeding.

Godfrey bolted from the bed chamber, calling, 'Baldwin! Where is my brother?' He grabbed hold of a sleepy servant, and shouted. 'Find my brother, and bring him to me. I want to see him at once.' He then charged off to the chapel for his morning prayers. He would send for the abbot as soon as he was finished, and put the plan in motion.

Murdo and Emlyn had spent a short, wakeful night beside the trail, moving on before dawn. As the sun crested the hills behind them, they looked down the road, descending in a series of long, gentle slopes all the way to the sea. A sprinkling of farms and fields lay before them and, as the sun threw their shadows before them, they started for the nearest of these, hoping to beg some water for the day, and perhaps a handful of fodder for the camel.

Emlyn was already drenched with sweat by the time they came into the dusty yard. There seemed to be no one around, so they went to the well and dipped the dry leather bag down and down into the cool dark hole. At first, Murdo feared the well must be empty, but the bag came up half full of murky water – which he poured out into a nearby trough for the beast. He poured out another, dipped again, and offered Emlyn the first drink. The monk sniffed, then drank a few mouthfuls. 'I have had worse,' he declared, wiping his mouth with his sleeve. 'It will keep us until we can get something better.'

'Even so, we need more waterskins,' replied Murdo, looking towards the mud-brick dwelling. Flies buzzed in the yard, but no other sound could be heard. 'I wonder if the house is abandoned.'

'That we can soon discover,' said Emlyn, moving towards the building.

A dirty, ragged cloth hung across the doorway so Emlyn slapped the rounded timber post with the flat of his hand, calling out in a loud voice, 'In the name of Christ, I bid thee, come and greet a weary pilgrim.' He waited, and called again. Receiving no answer, he turned to Murdo. 'I think there is no one here.'

Tying the camel at the trough, Murdo crossed the yard in quick steps, while Emlyn pulled aside the rag at the door and looked in. 'Empty,' he said as Murdo pushed in beside him.

Murdo scanned the single room, his eyes quickly adjusting to the dim interior. There was a small, low table, and a three-legged stool beside the door, and in the centre of the room, a hearth. He put his hand to the ashes, but they were cold. There was no telling how long ago the inhabitants had deserted the place. Beside the hearth was an assortment of clay pots of various sizes, cracked and blackened from the fire. There was nothing else in the humble room; most likely the farmer and his family had taken anything of use or value with them.

'See here!' said Emlyn, pointing to a rough cloth bag hanging from a wooden peg on the far wall. He crossed to the bag, lifted it from the peg, and peered inside. 'Praise God, for his faithful provision!'

'What is it?' asked Murdo impatiently. The empty house made

him uneasy; he did not like it and wanted to be on his way once more.

'Grain,' answered the monk; he reached inside and brought out a fistful which he let slide back into the bag. 'Enough for the camel, and for us, too, if we find nothing better.'

'Good,' said Murdo. 'We will take some of these bowls, too, for water.' He collected the clay vessels, retraced his steps to the well, and began filling the pots. Meanwhile, Murdo tied the grain bag to the camel's saddle, and then retrieved the filled jars, replenished the waterskin, and stowed everything among the treasure bundles as carefully as he could.

'We should be on our way,' said Murdo when he finished, 'before it gets too hot.' He glanced at the sky, already white in the east with the heat of the day to come. 'We will stop and rest later.'

They left the farmhouse and, somewhat refreshed, began the day's journey in earnest. The countryside was quiet; there were no people in the fields, nor did they discern any activity around the houses they passed, whether near or distant. Murdo seemed to recall having seen labourers and farmers, women and children, sheep and dogs and chickens, too, when he had passed this way before.

They walked all through the morning and, when the sun grew too hot, found an olive tree near to the road and rested in the shade. They drank from one of the bowls, and Emlyn fed the camel a few handfuls of the grain. Murdo was dozing lightly when he felt Emlyn's touch on his arm. 'Listen! Someone is coming!'

The sound of horses moving on the road reached him in the same instant, and he came fully awake. The company was soon on them, and they huddled beneath the olive branches and watched the long double rank of soldiers gallop past.

'They are certainly in a hurry,' observed the monk.

'It is the emperor's envoy,' replied Murdo, looking at the distinctive armour. 'They must have been getting ready to leave when we were at the abbey.'

The soldiers moved on and the silence descended upon them once again. They then stretched themselves beneath the tree and slept through the heat of the day, rousing themselves and moving on again as the sun drifted low in the west.

Emlyn chanted a verse in praise of light and warmth, and offered up a travelling prayer for the protection of wayfarers. When he finished, Murdo asked, 'How did you come to serve King Magnus?'

'Well now,' said Emlyn, 'that is one of our secrets.'

'Yet another secret?' scoffed Murdo. 'It is a wonder you find anything to talk about at all.'

'The Célé Dé have become a secretive order, it is true,' allowed Emlyn. 'Believe me, it was not always so. But now it is our best protection. This is why we chose King Magnus.'

'*You* chose *him*?' laughed Murdo derisively. 'Then Magnus is like no king I ever knew.'

'We needed a protector and a benefactor,' the monk explained, ignoring Murdo's scorn. 'We are few, and the power of the Anti-Christ is strong. It was either take up swords ourselves, or find someone who would shield and defend us. King Magnus was the strongest lord in the north, so –'

'Wait – what was that? Anti-Christ? What in God's name is that?'

'You would do well to speak that word softly,' Emlyn warned. 'The Célé Dé know that in every age a spirit of immense evil arises to work its wicked will on mankind. Very often this vile spirit seeks refuge in the Church itself, where its wickedness can work the greatest woe and destruction on the poor and needy spirits of this world; when this happens, we call it the Anti-Christ – the opposite Christ. Whatever Our Blessed Redeemer may be, the Anti-Christ is the opposite, the reverse.'

'So then, who is this Anti-Christ?'

'It is rarely a single person,' Emlyn replied. 'Sometimes, perhaps. Most often it is more like a sickness, a plague which suddenly assails the Body of Christ and seeks to destroy it.'

'If that is so, then what good is a king, no matter how many swords and shields he has at his command?'

'Oh,' remarked Emlyn quickly, 'do not misunderstand. Though the Anti-Christ might be a spirit, albeit of wickedness, the power he wields over those in his service is extraordinary. Make no mistake, in the last extremity the servants of the Anti-Christ must be fought with sword and spear.'

Murdo regarded the monk beside him – stocky legs stumping rhythmically, red face dripping with sweat. Once again, as so often happened when talking to the unassuming cleric, the discussion had abruptly taken an unexpected turn. He felt like the fisherman who sees his prize catch suddenly disappearing into unknown depths with a glinting flash of its silver sides. 'Tell me about the True Path,' he said.

'I have told you all I can. If you would learn more, you must become a Célé Dé,' the monk replied.

'I will never become a monk,' Murdo said with a flat slash of his hand.

'Did I say anything about becoming a priest? Most of the Célé Dé are priests, it is true. Most, I say, but not all.'

This roused Murdo's interest; he asked what he would have to do to become a Célé Dé. Emlyn answered, 'Better to ask what would be required of you *after* joining our number.'

'Does that mean you will not tell me?'

'It means,' replied the monk, 'that you would do well to count the cost of following the True Path.'

'How can I count the cost,' complained Murdo, 'if no one will ever tell me what it is? Who are the Célé Dé anyway, that you treat everyone with such suspicion?'

Emlyn sighed wearily, as if a sleeping dog had woken to snap at him once more. 'Ever since King Oswy – that poor benighted man, weak-minded and easily led by his pernicious wife and that grasping Saxon bishop – we have been made to suffer Rome's insults. The Célé Dé, longer in the land than any Saxon, have everywhere been hounded by the pope's noxious minions and driven to the wastes and wilderness.' The priest's hands clenched at the ends of his arms.

'We, who established the church among the pagan folk from the first, are reviled and rebuked by those who received salvation from our hands,' Emlyn continued, his voice rising steadily. 'We, who should sit at the banquet table with our noble brethren, are forced to stand in the yard with the lepers and malefactors! Almighty Rome gluts itself on the rich food of power in the realm of kings, yet our modest portion is denied. Having brought light and life to those who long dwelt in darkness and death, we are made wanderers and outcasts in the very lands that once rejoiced to speak our names.'

Murdo stared at the monk. He knew that there was some contention between Rome and the Célé Dé, but never had he heard any of the brothers complain so forcefully. 'So that is why you chose King Magnus to be your protector,' mused Murdo, thinking about what he had been told earlier.

As Emlyn drew breath to reply there came a distant rumble like the sound of a storm far away. Both he and Murdo turned instinctively to look behind them on the road. In a moment the sound came again, a little louder this time.

'More soldiers, I expect,' surmised Emlyn. 'It seems we will never be lonely on this road.'

The drumming of the hooves, rolling relentlessly towards them, sounded ominous. 'They are coming this way fast,' Murdo said. 'And there are more of them.'

'Perhaps we will have some company on the way.'

'No,' Murdo countered, swiftly scanning the land around for a place to hide. 'Get off the road.' Further on, the road passed through the remnant of a cedar and pine forest, but they would never make it. The last farm was too far back to be seen now, and there were no others ahead. Save for rocks of various sizes, and the occasional lonely olive tree and thorn bush, the land around them was barren.

'Over there –' Murdo pointed to a thorn bush growing from a little heap of rocks; together the bush and pile protruded above the surrounding landscape. Perhaps if they could get the camel to kneel, they might have a chance of hiding there.

Taking hold of the animal's harness, Murdo urged the beast off the dusty track towards the rock pile. They had just left the path, however, when, with a jerk of its head the camel stopped. Murdo pulled on the harness, but the beast refused.

'They are coming!' shouted Emlyn. 'I can see them!'

Murdo whirled to look behind them. The riders could be seen now as they came up over the hill, but they were still too far away to be counted; there might be six or sixteen, he could not tell.

'Help me!' Murdo called, pulling hard on the rope rein. Emlyn dashed to the grain bag and dug in his hands. Then, holding his hands before the camel, he succeeded in coaxing the beast forward a few more steps. But precious moments had been lost; the riders were now much closer.

There were not six or sixteen – there were more than sixty – and they were neither crusaders, nor Immortals. Murdo glimpsed the white-turbaned heads of the riders and his heart quailed. 'Turks!'

The rock pile stood little more than a few dozen paces, but already it was too late. For although he and Emlyn might reach it in time to get themselves out of sight, the foul beast never would.

'Leave it!' said Emlyn.

'No!' shouted Murdo defiantly. 'They will have to kill me to get their hands on my treasure.'

'They *will* do just that, and think nothing of it.' The monk tugged on his arm. 'Come away, Murdo.'

'No!' Murdo darted to the camel's side and reached for his father's sword. 'Hide behind the rocks. I will hold them off —'

'Murdo, stop!' said Emlyn, his voice taking on a note of authority Murdo had never heard him use before. 'Think! It is not worth your life, son.'

'It *is* my life!' spat Murdo. 'You cannot know what it means.' He drew the sword, and then unloosed the shield.

Emlyn stepped beside him and gripped him hard by the arm. 'No, Murdo,' he told him. 'Do not imagine that you will defeat them. Put aside the sword.'

'This is our only protection,' Murdo said, quickly strapping the sword belt around his waist.

'Listen to me closely; there is not much time. I can protect you,' the cleric said. 'I can protect us both, but there can be no weapons.'

This was said simply, but with such confidence that Murdo felt his conviction wavering. He gripped the sword hilt in his hand, feeling the comforting heft of the blade. He glanced again at the onrushing Turks; there were over a hundred, and still more appearing over the hill.

'You have trusted me in small things; will you trust me in this?' asked Emlyn. 'Will you do what I ask of you?'

Still watching the enemy's approach, Murdo reckoned that, at best, he would only be able to strike three or four times with the sword before the enemy drove him down with their spears.

'What must I do?' asked Murdo.

'Stand next to me,' Emlyn instructed, 'and take hold of my mantle.'

Although it made no sense, Murdo did as he was told. 'Now give me the sword,' the monk directed.

Murdo hesitated.

'Hear me, Murdo: we do not need it. You must trust me now.'

Emlyn took the sword in both hands, closed his eyes and spoke a few prayer-like words, then began scratching the rough outline of a circle in the hard-baked, rocky dirt. Murdo watched as the Turks raced nearer. The monk completed the circle, joining the ends so that it now enclosed them; he then drew back his arm and let the sword fly. It spun once in the air and landed with a dull thud in the dust a few dozen paces away.

'What are you doing? They are almost here!' he said, unable to keep the fear from edging into his voice.

'This is the caim,' said the monk. 'It is a powerful symbol.'

'Symbol!' Murdo almost shrieked. He knew better than to trust a priest. Why had he given Emlyn the sword?

'It represents the all-encompassing presence and protection of God. Now do not let go of my mantle, and do not step across the circle – understand?'

Murdo nodded.

'Our Lord Christ said that wherever two or three are gathered in his name, he would be with them.' Closing his eyes, he raised his hands, palm outward, and began to chant.

The Seljuqs were almost upon them now. Murdo could see the foam gleaming on the horses' sides, and the dark, unfriendly eyes of the riders. It took all his courage, but Murdo closed his eyes, too, and listened as Brother Emlyn said, 'In the holy name of Jesu, I invoke the powerful protection of the Three to encompass me even now. I stand within the circle of the Great King's might, and place my life, my spirit, my soul in his loving care. Dearest Lord and Saviour, be to me the Swift Sure Hand of deliverance in danger. While enemies gather round about me, hide me in the hollow of your hand.'

The invocation finished, the two opened their eyes as the foe thundered past; the horses' hooves cast up clouds of grey dust as the riders hurtled by only a short spear's thrust away. The horses, nostrils wide, legs stretching and gathering, raced on as their riders, faces dark beneath white turbans, stared straight ahead, looking neither right nor left.

On and on they came, and Murdo and the priest, absolutely still inside their protecting ring, stood and watched. Murdo held tight to Emlyn's mantle, feeling that any moment one of the riders would see them and attack. But the Turks streamed by without so much as a sideways glance.

Finally, as the last of the enemy warriors flew past, Murdo released his grip on the priest's garment and turned to look for the camel. He glanced around quickly, disbelief turning quickly to alarm. He couldn't see the camel anywhere; the vile creature had vanished.

'The camel is gone.' Murdo's head swivelled this way and that, trying to locate the beast.

'Stand still,' hissed the monk, taking hold of Murdo's arm to hold him in place.

Even as he spoke, another band of Seljuq warriors appeared on the road. Murdo turned to look, and the movement must have been seen, for suddenly a group of enemy warriors swerved from the main body, left the road, and reined to a halt before them. The foremost Seljuq spoke a quick word and twenty spears swung level.

FORTY-THREE

The eyes of the Turks glittered black and hard as chips of jet. The horses tossed their heads, their mouths and flanks speckled white with foam, their slender, almost delicate, legs shifting and restless in the settling dust. Behind them, Murdo saw the main body of the Seljuq war host galloping by; he saw the silver tracings on the horses' tack and the riders' saddles, and the glint of gold-handled knives in their wide cloth belts. He saw the ivory flash of teeth behind black beards, and the snowy mounds of bulbous turbans above lean faces the colour of bronze.

The leader of the war band spoke, and he saw the man's mouth twitch out the incomprehensible words; flecks of spittle flew from his lips, each beaded droplet agleam like a mote of dust caught in the sunlight, his chin thrust up and out in contempt, in menace, in judgement.

All this Murdo saw with a dreadful heightened clarity – made all the more terrible by the dire pounding in his ears. The roar of blood pulsing through his veins filled his head with a booming thunder which drowned out all other sound. His mouth was sticky and dry. His scalp tingled and his heart raced, leaping wildly in his chest like a captive thing trying desperately to free itself. His legs trembled, his muscles aching to run, to flee; it took every last grain of courage to stand within the circle of the caim.

The leader spoke again and as the blade of his lance darted forth, the point came to rest at the base of Murdo's throat. He felt the honed steel bite into his soft flesh, but he did not flinch. He stood to the blade, wishing only for a quick end. His last thought would be of Ragna, and he tried to see her face in his mind. To his dismay, he could not remember how she looked.

How fitting, he thought in disgust. His life had been ruined by priests, and now he would die having trusted one. Despite his resolve never again to believe a priest, that very thing would be his demise.

Sweat trickled down his forehead and cheeks. *Just finish it,* he thought. *Kill me and be done!*

The Seljuq commander spoke again, and Murdo drew a deep breath, preparing for the lethal stroke as, beside him, Emlyn slowly raised his hand as if in greeting.

'La ilaha illa 'Llah,' said the priest. He spoke clearly and slowly, and the effect was extraordinary.

The Turks stared at the monk. 'La ilaha illa 'Llah,' the commander replied, repeating the strange words. The spear blade dropped instantly from Murdo's throat, and the enemy leader shouted a word to his men.

The Turks turned their mounts and instantly the warriors were galloping away, following their war host down the road. The commander glanced over his shoulder at Murdo and the monk, and cried, 'Muhammadun rasulu 'Llah!' Then he put spurs to his horse and raced after his men.

Murdo watched with mingled relief and amazement as the troop joined the last of the Seljuq host. From the many banners and flags streaming from upraised spears and standards, Murdo guessed the amir himself was passing with his bodyguard. There must have been two hundred or more, each on a white horse with black harness and tack, and each warrior wearing a pointed helm with a white plume, and bearing a round shield with a silver rim. Some of the warriors were leading horses laden with boxes and chests. Murdo stood and watched as rank after rank passed, disappearing at last over a rise further down the road.

When the Seljuqs had gone, he stirred and made to step from the caim. 'Wait,' cautioned Emlyn.

Murdo looked down at the circle scratched in the dirt. Emlyn knelt and put his hands together, spoke a silent prayer, and then put his hand to the circle and rubbed out a portion of the mark, breaking the caim. 'Now we can go.'

They stepped from the broken ring, and it seemed to Murdo as if he were waking from a dream. Emlyn, on the other hand, raised his hands and began a paean of praise for God's wide mercy and saving power. 'We are alive, Murdo!' he cried. 'Rejoice and praise God!'

'You said you would save us,' Murdo agreed, 'and you did.'

'I did nothing but call upon God,' the priest corrected mildly. 'It was Our Lord who delivered us out of the hands of the enemy.'

'What did you tell him?' asked Murdo. 'The Turk battlechief – what did you say to him?'

'La ilaha illa 'Llah,' repeated the monk. 'It is all the Arabic I know. It means: "there is no God but God alone," and it is the one point on which all Christians and Muhammedans agree. I learned it from the brothers at Arles. You should rejoice in your good fortune, Murdo. It is God's good pleasure that we should yet remain in the land of the living. We were spared! Allelujah!'

Murdo nodded, still trying to comprehend what had happened. Had the charmed circle – the caim – saved them? Or, had the Turks simply had more urgent affairs to pursue? Perhaps the lives of a half-mad monk and a ragged, unarmed youth were not worth taking. Perhaps there was nothing more to it than that.

'We were rescued out of the hands of Death,' Emlyn continued, his face glowing with delight. 'Our Good Shepherd has brought us through the Valley of the Shadow; he has shown favour to us according to his great and generous mercy. Today is a day to rejoice in the Lord and be glad.'

'I am glad,' Murdo insisted, and turned to look for the camel.

They found the lazy animal at rest in the scant shade of the little brush-topped hillock they had been making for when the Turks came upon them. The beast was asleep, motionless, its head upright, eyes closed, its dusty colour blending into the dun-coloured land around it – which is why, Murdo decided, he had not seen it when first he looked.

Murdo took hold of the rein rope, and began yanking at it to rouse the creature. It was then he noticed all the water had been spilled; the clumsy animal had sloshed every last drop from the pots as it swayed and tilted to fold its long legs under its belly.

'There is no more water,' Murdo said, indicating the empty pots as the monk joined him. 'Do you have a charm for that, too?'

Emlyn gave him a disapproving frown. 'O, ye of little faith.'

Murdo made no further comment and, with both of them yelling and tugging on the rope, they succeeded in rousing the reluctant beast. The camel gave out a loud blatter of complaint as it climbed awkwardly onto its legs. Emlyn led the animal to the road, and

Murdo walked beside, pausing to retrieve his sword; they continued on – the priest rejoicing in God's saving power, and Murdo in a more reflective mood. As the sun dipped below the horizon, they reached the rise over which the Turks had disappeared.

It came into Murdo's mind that now he knew why the road had been so lonely, why they had seen no sign of anyone at any of the farms and settlements they had passed. Most likely, the Seljuq army had been travelling this way for some time, driving the inhabitants into hiding.

Upon arriving at the top of the rise, they paused to look down the other side. In the glare of the setting sun they saw the road falling away in a long, gently rolling descent to the sea which gleamed as a thin silver strip on the horizon. Away to the left, still far off but easily visible as a lighter glimmer amidst the shimmering sea, was the port of Jaffa. They stood for a moment and gazed upon their destination.

'It looks as if *they* are making for Jaffa, too,' observed Emlyn, pointing down the slope to the white cloud of dust which marked the passage of the Seljuq war host.

'I suppose so,' said Murdo.

'Maybe we should go back to Jerusalem,' the monk suggested helpfully.

'We cannot go back to Jerusalem,' Murdo told him. 'We have no water. Jaffa is closer. We can make it that far at least.'

'But if there is going to be fighting at Jaffa –'

'We have no choice,' replied Murdo, moving off.

The sun set and the evening twilight gathered around them. For the first time since leaving Jerusalem, Murdo felt the gnawing ache of hunger in his empty stomach. His mouth was dry and his tongue stuck to the roof of his mouth; he wished he had drunk some more when he had the chance.

The air began to cool as the last glimmer of twilight left the sky and night closed around them. They walked on through the night, until fatigue at last overtook them and they found a place beside the road to rest. They tethered the camel without unloading it, and then settled themselves for the night. Exhausted by the rigours of the day, Murdo took a stone for his head and slipped into a deep dreamless sleep, awaking only to the rumble of distant hooves.

Murdo lay for a moment, listening to the sound seeping up from the ground through the stone on which he rested. The rumbling increased even as he listened, and he knew the riders were not far off. He rose quickly and looked around; the sky was already light. The sun had risen, but could not yet be seen from where they were below the ridge.

Rolling to his knees, he took Emlyn by the shoulder and shook him hard. The sleepy cleric came awake with a start. 'What? What?'

'Horses,' Murdo said. 'We should get out of sight before they see us.' Casting a glance up the long slope, he spied a little rocky outcrop behind which they could hide. Leaving the camel to sleep, they hurried up to the rocks, lay on their stomachs, and waited. It was not long before the first riders came into view. 'Who are they? Can you see?' asked Emlyn.

'No, they are too far away, and the light is not so good.'

Hunkering down behind the rocks, they waited. The jingle of the horses' tack could be heard easily now – a light tinkling sound above the drumming of the hooves. The riders came on at a quick, yet measured pace – not as if they were chasing anyone, nor trying to escape. Murdo raised his head and looked again towards the road. At that moment, the sun broke over the ridgetop, sending its rays down the slope and illuminating a large company of riders.

'Crusaders!' cried Murdo. 'Emlyn look! We are saved!' He leapt to his feet and gave a shout, waving his arms. 'Here! Here!'

But the riders, if they saw him, took not the slightest interest. Not one of them so much as slackened his pace, but the whole company – perhaps a hundred knights in all – continued on towards Jaffa.

'They do not see us,' Emlyn said. 'We must warn them about the Turks! Murdo, hurry! Run and tell them!'

Murdo ran to the road as quickly as the rough ground allowed, and stood waving his arms and yelling for the crusaders to stop. Aside from drawing a passing glance from several of the riders, he received no response. Emlyn joined him and added his voice to that of Murdo's. Perhaps because the pair of them, so far from any habitation, presented such an unlikely prospect, they succeeded only in arresting one of the last of the knights, who reined aside to glare down at them and demand what business they had accosting soldiers in the service of the Defender of the Holy Sepulchre.

'We are trying to warn you,' Emlyn said quickly. 'We have seen Seljuqs on this road.'

'There are always Turks around,' sniffed the knight. 'Raiding parties. It means nothing.'

'It was more than a raiding party,' maintained the cleric.

'Are you a chief of battle that you know about such things?' demanded the crusader. He pulled on the reins and made to spur his mount away.

'He is telling the truth,' said Murdo. 'There were Turks – *hundreds* of them – on this road yesterday. We both saw them. They were heading for Jaffa.'

'Did you see them ride into the city?' the soldier challenged.

'No,' said Murdo, pointing back the direction they had come, 'we were on our way from –'

'Worthless beggars,' sneered the knight. 'Be gone with you!' He lashed the reins across his mount's shoulders and the horse lurched away.

'Wait!' called Murdo. 'We need water – a drink only. We have lost our wat –'

'Drink piss!' shouted the knight as he rode to rejoin his companions.

Thirsty and disappointed, they turned their attention to rousing the camel and, after repeated threats to flay it alive, succeeded in getting the belligerent creature onto its great flat feet. They then started off once more, following the crusaders' dust.

They walked along, and Emlyn began saying prayers in Gaelic to occupy himself. Murdo listened, picking out a word here and there which he recognized. Hearing the familiar sounds put him in mind of his mother. He wondered how she would take the news of her husband's death, and her sons' refusal to come home and fight for the return of their land. He wondered how Ragna was faring, and what she was doing, whether she missed him as much as he missed her, and whether they would ever see one another again. He vowed, not for the first time, that if he ever got home, he would never leave her side.

The sun gained strength as it ascended, and the morning warmth gave way to an oven-like fire which baked the arid hills and rocks all around, and caused the lowlands before them to liquefy and run in the heat haze. When they could not stand to walk any longer, they stopped to look for a place to rest and escape the sun. There were no trees nearby; a fair-sized thorn bush not far from where they stood offered the only shade for leagues around.

Leading the camel to the bush, Murdo flicked its forelegs with a stick and the beast knelt down. Next, Murdo stripped off his sweat-soaked siarc and draped it over the bush. He settled in the bone-dry dirt beside Emlyn, and the two of them rested in the combined shade of the siarc, stinking camel, and thorny bush. It was too hot to talk, or think, and they were beginning to feel the loss of their water. Murdo's mouth felt as dry as the stones on which he lay, and his tongue as if it was swollen to twice its size; his lips were cracking, and his eyeballs were cinders in his head.

He closed his burning eyes and rested his head on his arm. In a moment, he heard Emlyn's breath slow and deepen as the monk drifted off to sleep. Though he tried, sleep eluded Murdo; his mind kept returning to the awful moment when he thought the Turks would kill him while he stood there clinging to Emlyn's mantle like a toddling child. He felt again the sharp spear point bite into his throat, and he heard the warrior say, 'Build me a kingdom, brother'.

The voice was so clear and lifelike, he opened his eyes and looked around. There was no one nearby, of course, and Emlyn was still asleep, so he knew he must have imagined it. Though the voice was imagined, the words were those of Saint Andrew, and he had promised to do what he could. Perhaps, he thought, the same lord who honoured the circle in the dirt – the caim of protection – could deliver him safely home.

'Only get me home, and I will build a realm for you,' Murdo said; 'I will build it next to my own.'

His mumbling roused Emlyn who opened his eyes drowsily. 'Did you say something?' he asked, yawning.

'No,' whispered Murdo. 'Go back to sleep.'

The monk yawned again and closed his eyes. 'It looks like smoke,' he said, his voice falling away as he drifted off to sleep again.

Murdo lay for a moment before it occurred to him to wonder what Emlyn had said. Turning his head, he looked in the direction that Emlyn was facing, and saw the hard-baked land, white with dust, beneath a heat-riven sky so bleached it appeared almost grey. A thin thread of darker grey was snaking up through the cloudless heights. Yes, concluded Murdo, it *did* look like smoke. What could be burning in this God-forsaken place?

He raised his head and looked again. The thread was slightly thicker now, and a little darker, rising out of the west. It was Jaffa!

Rolling to his knees, Murdo looked out, shielding his eyes with his hands. The sun was beginning its long, slow slide into the west, its fierce light all but drowning out the faint smoke trail. He dragged himself to his feet, and climbed to the top of the gulley for a better look – only to find that he had to go all the way back to the road in order to see down to the distant horizon.

One quick look confirmed his suspicion: the smoke was coming from the walled city.

Hurrying back to the thorn bush, he quickly pulled his siarc off the branches and drew it back on. He then knelt and shook Emlyn awake. 'You were right about the smoke,' Murdo told him. 'Jaffa is burning.'

'They must be fighting there,' the monk said.

'Maybe,' Murdo granted. 'It is still too far to see.'

'I hope the ships are not in danger.'

'The ships!' It had not crossed his mind that the ships might be at risk in any conflict. What if the Turks were attacking the port? 'Hurry!'

'Murdo, wait!' Emlyn called after him. He struggled to his feet and started up the side of the gulley, remembered the camel, and paused to untie the rein rope.

Their short rest had far from restored either of them, and here they were, starting out again in the heat of the day. It was madness, thought Murdo; even if he reached the fighting in time, what could he do?

'Murdo, slow down,' called Emlyn, struggling up out of the gulley and onto the road. He held tight to the camel's rope, all but pulling the beast after him.

Ignoring the monk, Murdo charged on, head down to keep the sun out of his eyes. Though more desperately thirsty than ever, he kept his mouth shut, and concentrated only on putting one foot in front of the other. How long this continued, he could not say. Time seemed to melt into a stagnant pool; he was no longer aware of its passing. This strange state persisted until he heard Emlyn say, 'Look, Murdo! I can see the harbour.'

Murdo raised his head and was amazed to see how far they had come. The city lay on the shelf of the sea plain below them, its white dwellings shimmering pale gold in the light of a low-sinking sun. The sea stretched out on either hand in a broad band of shining white silver. Smoke rose in a dark column from the city walls in the vicinity of the central gate, where, judging from the darkly writhing stain on the plain outside the city, the battle still raged. But the ships rode at anchor in the bowl-shaped harbour, as yet untouched by the fighting outside the walls.

'Can you see who it is?' asked Emlyn, toiling up beside him. The cleric sank to the road and rested on his haunches in the dust.

'No,' answered Murdo, 'they are still too far away. I suppose it is Godfrey's troops – the ones that passed us earlier. No doubt the Turks were waiting for them.'

With that, he started off again.

'Murdo, for the love of God, man, can you not wait even a moment while I catch my breath?'

'Catch your breath later,' Murdo called back to him. 'We must get down there.'

'Murdo, stop!' cried the monk. 'We can await the outcome here.'

He hastened down the track leading to the city. Behind him he heard Emlyn call out, 'Murdo, if you cherish your life at all, do not go down there!'

He stopped and looked down upon the broad plain. Emlyn was right; there was nothing he could do down there except get himself killed. He returned to where the priest was waiting, took the rope from his hand, and led the camel off to the side of the road where they found another low bush and settled down to watch and wait until the battle was over.

FORTY-FOUR

From their high vantage they watched as the movement on the plain gradually ceased, whereupon the greater mass separated itself from the lesser, and moved off, skirting the city and disappearing up the coast. Murdo stood slowly. 'It is over. The Turks have gone.'

They then started down the hill track once more. By the time they reached the plain, the battlefield had been invaded for a second time – by a host of people from Jaffa, many of whom were yet streaming out of the city and onto the plain. Murdo and the monk hurried to meet them, proceeding to the edge of the battleground where the first corpses they encountered were those of crusader knights, struck down by Seljuq arrows. There were more horses than men, and several of the animals were still alive, thrashing in agony on the ground as they hurried by.

Closer to the centre of the fighting, the corpses became more numerous. They came upon the body of a knight who had fallen beneath his mount. The horse still lay upon its rider, whose arm extended from beneath the animal's neck, the hand still clutching the sword. Murdo paused and regarded the unfortunate, then looked at the waterskin on the horse's saddle.

'He has no further use for it,' Emlyn said, 'and is past caring in any event.'

Murdo nodded, stooped quickly and untied the strap holding the skin; he removed the stopper and put the skin to his mouth. The water slid over his parched tongue and down his throat in a cool deluge. He drank down great greedy gulps, pulling the waterskin away reluctantly and passing it to Emlyn with a gasp of relief.

They shared the water between them until the skin was empty, whereupon Emlyn replaced it. He made the sign of the cross over the fallen warrior, and offered a death blessing. The water revived them wonderfully well, and they moved on towards the centre of the field where the battle had been most fierce. The dead became more numerous, the parched ground beneath them black with spilled blood. Though they looked, they could see no wounded. Most of the soldiers had suffered both arrow wounds and sword cuts. 'Felled by arrows and finished with the sword,' Murdo observed grimly. 'The enemy showed no mercy.'

'It is because of Jerusalem,' remarked Emlyn. He stood gazing sadly upon the slaughter, his round shoulders bending under the weight of a terrible vision. 'Now begins the season of revenge, when Death reigns, and evil is loosed upon the world.'

At these words, Murdo saw again the ghastly carnage unleashed upon the Holy City in a veritable storm of hate and greed and butchery. He saw himself wandering through the blood-rich desolation, fearful, lost, and alone, while high above him, sailing through the smoke-filled air with leathery wings outstretched, laughing with wicked glee, the Ancient Enemy rejoiced in the slaughter and chaos.

Murdo looked around him and saw the same grisly destruction, and heard the same demonic laughter streaking through the empty heights. What was begun in Jerusalem will last a thousand years, he thought; of war and revenge there will be no end. These dead, still warm upon the blood-soaked earth, are but the first of a blighted race whose population will grow more numerous than the stars.

Somewhere, thought Murdo, there must be a refuge, a haven from the storm of death and destruction. Somewhere there must be a place of peace and prosperity – if only to remind men that such qualities could still exist this side of heaven.

Build me a kingdom, Saint Andrew had said. *Establish a realm where my sheep may safely graze, and make it far, far away from the ambitions of small-souled men and their ceaseless striving. Make it a kingdom where the True Path can be followed in peace and the Holy Light can shine as a beacon flame in the night.*

As Murdo stood gazing upon the field of death, the words of the ghostly monk quickened in his heart: *All you possess was given to you for a purpose. I ask you again,* said the voice from the catacombs, *will you serve me?*

At the time, he had pledged to do what he could. Now, looking upon the wanton, senseless waste of life in the ignorant service of rapacious, power-mad avarice and ambition, he knew, *knew* beyond all doubt, what he was being asked to do.

I will do what I can, he had vowed, at the time. No, he decided, I will do more. I will build that haven from the storms of death and destruction. I will build a kingdom where the Holy Light shines as a beacon flame in the darkness of that terrible night.

At Emlyn's touch, Murdo came to himself with a start. 'What were you saying? It sounded like Sanctus Clarus – are you well, Murdo?'

The young man nodded.

'We should see if there is anything we can do,' the monk said, moving on. Murdo followed, leading the camel, his heart and mind churning with the certainty that he had been called to this place and this moment.

Picking their way among the bodies, they came at last to the place where the crusaders had made their stand. Here, the corpses were heaped one upon another on the ground, and there were few horses. The unhorsed knights had been no match for the mounted Seljuqs. Arrows bristled from every corpse; most had been struck many times.

Here also, the people of Jaffa had begun their work. A number of them were removing the harnesses and saddles from the horses, and others were skinning the animals and butchering them where they lay. Their red, raw carcasses glistened in the harsh light, and the rank smell of their entrails mingled with the sweet stink of blood already thick in the air. A little apart, other groups of townsfolk were separating the crusaders from the Turks – flinging the Seljuqs onto a heap, and dragging the Christians off to be placed in long ranks on the ground, where other men and women were moving along the rows, stripping the dead knights of valuables, weapons, and any useful items of clothing.

These articles were then taken to waiting wagons where they were loaded under the watchful eye of a man in a tall black hat with a staff in his hand. He was standing before a small heap of objects on the ground.

As this man appeared to be giving orders to the others, they went over to him to learn what they could of the battle. Emlyn greeted the fellow politely, and he turned his face towards them, frowning. 'What do you want?' he asked, eyeing the camel suspiciously.

'We saw the battle,' Emlyn said. 'We were on our way to Jaffa and saw –'

Black Hat turned away and shouted at a fellow standing in one of the wagons. 'Only the weapons in that one!' he cried. 'How many times must I tell you?'

Turning back to the priest, he said, 'It was not much of a battle. The Turks were waiting for them.' Indicating the pile of valuables at his feet, he said, 'Have you anything to sell?'

'We saw smoke,' said Murdo. 'Was the city attacked?'

'Aye, they tried to burn the gates,' the merchant told them. 'Third time this month. But we put the fire out.' He shouted at his helper in the wagon again, then said, 'If you are going to stand here, you might as well make yourself useful. I pay good silver for their belongings.'

'What about the wounded?' asked Emlyn looking around.

The merchant shrugged. 'If you find any, you can give them last rites.'

There came a clatter of steel from the nearby wagon. 'Careful with those!' the merchant roared. 'Can I sell broken blades?'

A woman came up to the black hatted merchant; she was holding a belt with a silver buckle – a knight's sword belt. The man took the belt, looked at it, and threw it down on the heap in front of him. Reaching into a purse at his side, he drew out a fistful of coins and counted a few of them onto the woman's palm. She bowed her head and scurried away, returning eagerly to her work.

Murdo and Emlyn moved among the fallen, searching for any who might yet be saved. They had not gone far when they heard a soft, moaning sigh. 'Over there!' said Emlyn, hurrying towards the sound, calling encouragement as he went. Murdo quickly tied the camel to the pommel of a dead horse's saddle, and removed the waterskin hanging there; he joined the priest as he knelt beside a knight with an arrow in his chest and another in his thigh.

The wounded man struggled up onto an elbow as Murdo handed the priest the waterskin. 'Turks . . .' he gasped as the priest knelt over him.

'Rest easy, friend,' Emlyn said gently. He drew the stopper and offered the skin. 'Drink a little. We will help you.'

The knight, a fair-haired young Norman, grasped the skin clumsily and tipped it to his mouth. He drank, the water spilling from his mouth and down his neck to mingle with the blood oozing from the wound in his chest. He drank too fast and choked; water gushed from his mouth and he fell back.

The monk quickly retrieved the waterskin, replaced the stopper, and said, 'We must remove these arrows. Murdo, give me your knife.'

'The Seljuqs attacked us . . . They took it . . .' said the knight. Seizing Emlyn by the mantle, he jerked the monk forward. 'They were waiting for us –' He grimaced, gritting his teeth against the pain. 'Tell Godfrey the lance is gone . . .'

Murdo reached into his siarc and brought out the slender knife Ragna had given him. The knight, his face twisted in his agony, reached his hand towards Murdo. 'Tell Godfrey . . . they took it!'

'Peace,' soothed Emlyn. 'Be still. We will soon have those wounds bandaged.'

Before Murdo could ask what he meant, the knight closed his eyes and passed from consciousness. Emlyn lowered his face to the wounded man's, and then sat back. 'He sleeps.' Turning worried eyes to Murdo, he said, 'It will be dark soon. We must work quickly.'

Using the knife, the monk carefully sliced through the soldier's siarc to expose the wound. The arrow had entered at the top of his chest, below the bones of his left shoulder. 'This one was fortunate,' Emlyn observed.

Taking up the waterskin, the monk dashed water over the wound to wash away the blood. Then, holding the blade gingerly in his fingers, he carefully pressed it into the wound beside the arrow. The knight groaned, but did not wake.

'Grasp the arrow firmly,' he directed. Murdo did as he was told, and the monk said, 'Now, on my command, I want you to pull upwards on the shaft. Ready?'

Murdo gripped the arrow in both hands. 'Yes.'

'Pull.'

Murdo gave an upwards tug and Emlyn, pressing down on the shoulder with his free hand, twisted the knife blade at the same instant, and the arrow came free. The knight jerked his arm, and then lay still.

'That was well done,' breathed Murdo, tossing the arrow aside.

The monk handed him the knife. 'Cut strips from his mantle to bind him,' he said, dashing more water over the wound. Reaching into the pouch at his belt, he took out a small bag and withdrew a pinch of yellowish stuff which he sprinkled over the shoulder, before binding it with the strips which Murdo handed him.

That done, Emlyn turned his attention to the wound in the knight's thigh, repeating the procedure with a deft efficiency which caused Murdo to marvel anew. Twice in this eventful day he had been surprised by the monk; he wondered what else the priest could do that he did not know about.

They were just finishing tying up the leg wound when the sound of horses reached them from the hills east of the plain. Murdo turned towards the sound, expecting to see the Seljuq horde sweeping down upon them. Instead, galloping towards them in the yellow afterglow of the setting sun, he saw two long columns of knights.

'Who are they? Can you see?' asked Emlyn, rising to stand beside him. 'The banners – can you see them?'

'Black and yellow, I think,' replied Murdo.

'The yellow and black – that is Prince Bohemond,' said Emlyn.

The crusaders skirted the battlefield and came on to where their comrades had made their final stand. They reined up along the fallen front line, whereupon many of the knights dismounted and began moving quickly among their dead comrades. Their leaders, meanwhile, rode on to where Black Hat stood directing the scavengers.

'Stay with him,' Murdo told the monk. 'I want to hear what they are saying.'

'Greetings, friends,' called a tall, broad-shouldered man to the Jaffa merchant as Murdo edged near. The knight's freshly burnished helm and hauberk glimmered golden in the fading light. His long fair hair curled from beneath his helm, and his arms bulged with knotted muscle as he struggled to hold his mount still. From the man's easy authority, Murdo knew it must be Bohemond himself who addressed them.

'I see no surviving warriors of Lord Godfrey's war band.' He regarded the small gathering with grave dark eyes. 'I pray you, tell me I am wrong.'

The Jaffa merchant took it upon himself to answer for everyone. 'Alas, lord,' he replied, 'you are too right. The Turks were waiting in ambush. Their victory was complete; there are no survivors.'

'If you saw the ambush,' said the man with Bohemond, speaking up, 'I wonder that you did not send soldiers from the town to aid in the fight.'

'They set fire to the gate,' the merchant countered. 'What could we do?'

'Has the city no other gates?' demanded the knight angrily.

Bohemond held up his hand for silence. 'Desist, Bayard. The deed is done.' He gestured towards the wagon into which the weapons were being loaded. 'Go and see what they have found.' The knight rode to the wagon, and while he began questioning the townsfolk working there, the count turned once more to the merchant. 'These men were coming from Jerusalem. Am I to assume they did not reach the city?'

'No, my lord, they did not,' Black Hat confirmed. 'Unfortunately, they were attacked before they could reach the safety of the walls.'

The Prince of Taranto nodded and looked around. He saw Murdo standing nearby, and said, 'You there. Is that the way you saw it?' The question held neither suspicion, nor judgement. Bohemond gazed mildly at the young man before him, his handsome face ruddy in the dying light.

'We saw it only from a distance,' Murdo answered, pointing to the hills away to the east. 'By the time we arrived here, the battle was over. But there is –' he began, intending to tell the prince about the lone surviving knight they had found.

Before he could say more, the nobleman Bayard returned from his inspection of the wagons. 'It is not among the weapons,' he called, reining in his horse. 'I say the Turks have taken it. They cannot have gone far. We can catch them.'

Bohemond turned his attention to those searching among the dead. He called to the warriors, and asked, 'Have you found it?'

'No, lord,' shouted the nearest soldier; the others answered likewise.

'Return to your mounts,' Bohemond commanded. 'Come, Bayard, we will discover where the accursed Seljuqs have gone.' He thanked the merchant and townspeople for the help, turned his horse, and rode away. Within moments the battle host was streaming after him; they passed by the walls of the city and headed south along the coast.

Murdo returned to where Emlyn was waiting. He had spread a cloak over the wounded soldier, and was sitting beside him, praying. He looked up at Murdo's approach. 'What did you learn?'

'You were right – it was Bohemond,' the young man confirmed. 'They are looking for something. They said the ambushed troops belonged to Godfrey, and that . . .' Murdo paused and gazed at the wounded soldier. 'I know what it is.'

'Well?' asked the monk.

'*He* said it,' Murdo replied, indicating the unconscious knight. 'He said, "Tell Godfrey the lance is gone." He meant the Holy Lance.'

'They have lost the Holy Lance,' Emlyn said, his voice growing suddenly bitter. 'These ignorant, foolish men! Blind and stupid, every one – from king to footman, not a brain among them. Cast them all into the pit and be done with it, O God!'

Once, such an outburst from the gentle monk would have alarmed Murdo, but not now. He knew exactly what the monk was feeling; he felt the same way himself.

Sinking to his knees, Emlyn raised clenched fists in the air. 'They have made of your great name a curse, O Lord,' he cried, 'and their deeds are blasphemy in your sight. Who will restore your honour, Great King? Who will overthrow the wickedness of the mighty?'

Murdo heard these words, felt his heart stirred to anger within him, and answered, 'I will.'

Emlyn, hands still raised, looked at his young friend. 'Murdo?' Seeing the light of a strange and powerful determination in the young man's eyes, he said, 'You have seen the vision, too.'

'I have,' confirmed Murdo. 'A curse and a blasphemy, you said – you were told to rescue the sacred relic from those who –'

'– from those who would make of it a curse and a blasphemy, yes, but –' the monk began.

'I am going after it,' Murdo said, his confidence growing by the moment. 'It is not right that they should use that holy relic as a trinket to be bartered for position and power. One way or another, I will bring it back.'

The priest rose quickly and stood before him. 'Hear me, Murdo: once in every life the choice is given,' Emlyn said quietly, his voice taking on the tone he used when telling the stories that moved Murdo's heart, 'to follow the True Path, or to turn aside. Your time has come, Murdo, and here is where it begins. You may lose everything you have worked for – you may even lose your life; but once you have begun, you can never turn back. Do you understand?'

Murdo accepted this with a nod. In that instant, he saw the path stretching out before him; he had taken the first step of a journey that would take a lifetime to complete. And for once in his life, he felt truly free. 'I am going,' he said again.

431

'Give me your sword,' Emlyn said. 'Men are forever taking up swords in spiritual battles. They forget who upholds them and delivers them; they trust instead to their own strength, and they fail. I do not want that to happen to you.'

Murdo hesitated.

'Look around you,' the monk instructed, indicating the corpses spread out upon the field. 'Godfrey's best warriors could not avail; why believe one more blade will make any difference?' He held out his hand for the weapon. 'It is not by might or skill at arms that this battle will be won, but by faith and the will of God.'

Unbuckling the sword belt, Murdo handed the blade to Emlyn. 'You are right,' he agreed. 'Besides, it would only slow me down.'

'May God bless you, Murdo, and send a flight of angels to surround you and guide you safely home once more.'

Murdo thanked the monk, embraced him, and said, 'Once you get inside the walls, go to the harbour. Find Jon Wing's ship and wait for me there. I will join you as soon as I can.'

Murdo drank some water then, and quickly refilled the waterskin from the contents of others he retrieved from among the belongings of the dead nearby. Meanwhile, Emlyn pawed around in the pouch behind the wounded knight's saddle, and brought out a chunk of dried meat and a bit of hard bread. Taking a cloak from behind the saddle of another dead knight, he returned to Murdo. 'You will need this tonight, I think,' the priest said, handing him the cloak. 'And take this bread and meat.'

Murdo slung the waterskin over his shoulder, and drew on the cloak. 'I will return as soon as I can,' he promised, accepting the small hard loaf and scrag of meat the monk offered. He glanced up at the sky and saw the stars already shining over the hills to the east. 'It will be a clear night and a good moon. I will be able to see the way. You should hurry, too, before the gates are closed for the night.'

He started off, making for the trail Bohemond and his war band had followed. 'Fear nothing,' Emlyn called after him. 'God himself goes with you.'

'See you do not lose the camel,' Murdo called back, lifting his hand in farewell. Then, turning his gaze quickly to the south, he saw the broad backs of low hills; he could make out their smooth slopes in the twilight. These were the leading edges of the grassy dunes which ran along the coast south of the city. It was from there that the Seljuqs had sprung their attack, and that was where he had seen them disappear. Somewhere among these dunes, thought Murdo, he would find the Holy Lance.

FORTY-FIVE

Murdo reached the edge of the sand hills as the first numbing pangs of fatigue seeped into his bones. He paused only long enough to catch his breath and swig a few mouthfuls of water before he climbed the nearest dune for a better look around. Sea grass, tough and dry, covered the top of the hill, and hissed at him as he waded through the tall stuff to see over the other side.

The moon was rising above the line of the hills so he had a good view of the bay spreading out before him. Directly ahead, no more than half a league distant, stood the nearest walls of Jaffa. To his right, there were more dunes, marching off along the coast in staggered ranks that formed a series of little valleys whose mouths opened towards the sea. Away on his left, he saw the silver arc of the coastline beyond the city, gleaming in the moonlight.

As he stood looking, he heard the unmistakable sound of a battle taking place far away to the south. So! he thought, Bohemond has found the Seljuqs. Before he knew it, his feet were moving towards the fight.

He moved along at an easy dog-trot, alert to the sounds around him. Though it would have been easier to walk along the water's edge, he considered he would be too easily seen, so Murdo decided to keep close to the dunes where he would be more difficult to spot and catch. After a while, he came to a place where the coast bent sharply to the right. As he could not see around this bend, he decided to climb up one of the nearby hills to discover what he could of the way ahead.

The moment he crested the hilltop, he knew what he would find – the battle sounds grew instantly louder as he stepped up to look over the top. Stretching below him was the long outward curve of the shoreline and the flats of a shallow beach. Midway between the glittering water and the sandhills was a dark swirling mass of men and horses where the battle was taking place. The sound of the clash echoed up from the sand, making it seem as if there were battles taking place in every wrinkled hollow and fold.

Uncertain what to do next, he hunkered down in the long seagrass to watch and wait. While watching, he became aware of a movement on the sands below – a company of men on horseback was fleeing the fight and riding directly towards him. Murdo lay down on his stomach in the tall grass and waited.

Closer, this dark shape resolved into a band of warriors – perhaps twenty in all – riding hard for the dunes. From the sheen of moonlight on their plumed helms, and from the quickness of their horses, Murdo could tell they were Turks. He pressed himself still closer to the sand and held his breath.

The enemy warriors raced by, disappearing into one of the little valleys between the sandy hills – only a few hundred paces further on from where Murdo was hiding. He watched and waited, and when the Turks did not appear again, he decided to find out what they were doing.

Creeping slowly, he moved along the sandy ridges, pausing to listen every few steps, until reaching the place where he had seen the enemy vanish. There he stopped. Down in the valley between the dunes, he could make out the large dark mass of something hidden in the shadows. No sound came from the object; nothing moved.

'*The Arabs are a wandering people,*' his father had told him. '*So they always travel with their tents and treasure – even in battle they keep their treasure with them.*'

There were a dozen or more horses picketed directly beneath him, and he first thought the warriors must have quickly dismounted and tethered their animals there. Yet, upon glancing quickly to the valley entrance, he saw that the warriors themselves were still mounted. The Turks' backs were to him, they all appeared to be watching the battle taking place further up the beach.

Murdo gazed at the dark object hidden in the valley – with the extra horses ready and waiting – and knew he had found the amir's treasure tent.

When he was certain no one else lurked nearby, Murdo slid over the crown of the dune and down the other side. He crossed to the tent quickly, flitting out of the moonlight and into the shadow to squat before the odd-shaped tent – like a great black wing resting on the sand – its entrance rising to a single opening tall enough for a man to enter standing up.

He stepped cautiously to the opening and peered inside; from the little he could see, the interior seemed to be filled with boxes and chests of various sizes and shapes. He paused, listening for a moment, and then went in, nearly falling over a wooden chest just inside the entrance. The chest was large and bound with an iron chain which rattled slightly. As his eyes adjusted to the darkness, he could make out still more articles in the gloom – rolls of cloth, numerous jars and basins, and caskets. Fumbling over these, he found a box that was not chained, opened it, and reached inside.

His fist closed on a quantity of coins. He withdrew a handful and held them before his face. They were golden bezants, and the chest was full to overflowing with them.

Straining into the darkness of the tent, Murdo began searching for the Holy Lance. The amir's plunder had been thrown into the tent in haste, and lay in a haphazard jumble. Crouching, crawling, Murdo picked his way among the chests and caskets, praying he would know the lance when he found it, all the time working his way slowly towards the back of the tent where he discovered a shambling mound of hastily-stored loot taken from the crusaders. His hopes rose as he waded in and began carefully pulling mail hauberks and long swords from the heap.

The voices outside the tent took Murdo by surprise.

Mind whirling, he ducked down and glanced towards the tent entrance and saw the dark shapes of horses moving outside. Murdo squeezed himself further back in the tent, hoping against hope that they would not come inside.

As Murdo shrank away from the entrance however, one of the guards entered, took up a box and backed out quickly; another guard followed and likewise took up a chest, and backed out of the tent.

Murdo's heart fell. The Turks had begun loading the treasure, preparing to carry it away. He edged further back into the tent, his mind whirling furiously, trying to think how he would escape.

Four more guards entered the tent in rapid succession and retreated with boxes, which they took to waiting pack horses. There came a little space while the chests were bound into place on the pack frames.

Murdo realized what this meant: of the twenty or so guards protecting the treasure, only six were loading and packing it. Judging from all the boxes and chests, it would take them a fair while before they worked their way to the back of the tent. Murdo steadied his faltering courage; he still had time to work.

The guards returned for more chests; Murdo counted them off one by one and, when the sixth had gone, sprang into action. Feeling with his hands in the dark, he seized upon various objects – bowls and cups, bags of coins, silken garments, banners, small aromatic boxes rattling with loose gemstones – discarding them even as he touched them. All the while, he listened to the Turks talking outside, trying to discern from the sound of their voices when they would return to the tent for more treasure.

The third time the guards returned, he heard their steps in time to hide again; but the fourth time, he had no warning at all. He had worked his way towards the centre of the tent, and was on his knees, feeling among the boxes, when the first of the guards entered the tent.

He froze in place, hoping he would not be seen in the dark. The man stooped, picked up a chest and backed out. Murdo crouched swiftly, trying to hide before the next guard entered. As he went down, his elbow knocked against a long rod-like object which was leaning against the top of the chest beside him. The thing slid down and struck against a box with a solid thump. Murdo's hand snaked out and caught the staff as it fell.

The slender object, cold and hard under its splendid winding cloth, filled his hand with such a familiar weight that he knew, even without looking beneath the silken cloth and braided cord, that he had found the Iron Lance. In the same instant, the Turks outside stopped talking. Murdo's heart clenched in his chest. Had they heard him?

One of the guards shouted something, and Murdo, clutching the ancient relic, edged further back towards the rear of the tent. He watched the entrance and saw a flicker of flame kindle outside: torches.

He was out of time. Gripping the lance, he rolled to the side of the tent where it sloped down to the ground. The thick woollen fabric was secured by stakes at the corners and along the edges, but the sandy ground was soft and he easily loosened the nearest stake and wormed his way under the heavy tentcloth and out.

Murdo found himself between the tent and the foot of the dune. A swift glance towards the valley entrance confirmed what he had already guessed – a dozen or more Turks on horseback stood guard there; six more were loading the pack horses on the other side of the tent, and one of these had a torch.

He drew a deep breath and pressed himself into the shadow at the foot of the dune. It took all his nerve to stay there, still as a stone, while the Turk searched the tent with the torch – only the thickness of the tentcloth separating him from discovery and death.

After a hasty search, the guard emerged once more, threw the torch onto the sand, and called to his fellows. They entered by turns to collect more treasure. As the last guard ducked into the tent, Murdo made his escape.

Moving in the shadow, he slipped along the steeply rising foot of the dune, keeping the tent between himself and the Turks as much as possible. He ran with an easy, silent, gliding lope, holding the lance low at his side, and making for the end of the little dune valley where he crouched to wait. He watched while the guards carried out six more chests, and then untied three horses and brought them to stand with the others.

The instant they turned towards the tent, Murdo was away again. With a last backward glance, he moved into the light, crossed the valley floor, and started up the opposite face of the dune. He had taken no more than ten steps when one of the Turks cried out behind him.

In midstep Murdo turned, leapt back, and ran for the shadows once more. He reached the opposite dune and, without a quiver of hesitation, bounded up the shadowed slope. There were more shouts coming from the tent, and two Turks on horseback pounding after him. He reached the top just as the nearest rider started up the dune. Murdo caught the glint of moonlight on upraised steel, vaulted over the edge and down the other side.

Halfway down the slope, he changed direction, running along the face of the sandy hill to a crease formed by the meeting and merging of two nearby dunes. There he dived into the fold of the hill and hunkered down in a knot of tall seagrass, tucking the lance under him while the horse and rider crested the dune and plunged down the other side, passing within a few paces.

Upon reaching the bottom, the rider spurred his mount towards the mouth of the valley. Murdo watched him go, and in that moment his fear left him. This would be, he thought, just one more game of hare and hunter – the game he had played so often with his brothers in Orkney.

Murdo waited until his hunters had passed, and then, swift as any hare, he skittered up the sand hill to the top and crouched in the long grass. Taking the hem of his cloak, he teased out a few threads from the ragged edge and, pulling gently, he twisted them into a sturdy line and wound it around his fingers. He tied one of the threads to one of the tough stalks and, using all the stealth at his command, he crawled through the grass, back towards the valley entrance, paying out the line as he went. After a few paces, he paused and tied the other end of the string to a second stalk and continued, edging his way along slowly, slowly.

When his thread gave out, he stopped and waited. In a little while, one of the guards on foot appeared at the mouth of the valley and started forward. Murdo waited until he had passed by, and then gave the second line a furious pull. The grass stalk jerked and rustled. The Turk whirled to the sound. Murdo saw his face in the moonlight as he opened his mouth and shouted to his companions. The fellow turned and started for the place where the grass was yet quivering.

Murdo allowed him to get half-way up the dune face and then gave the first thread a tug, paused and tugged again. The Turk shouted, and his cry was answered by the others as they came running. Murdo gave the string a final tug for good measure and, as the two on foot passed below him, he rolled to the other side of the dune.

The guard on horseback was already galloping away as Murdo slid down the slope behind him. No sooner had he gone, than Murdo started up the opposite slope and made good his escape. He worked his way eastward, away from the coast and, when he reckoned he was no longer being followed, he turned and skittered away over the tops of the north-lying dunes.

Upon reaching the last dune, he paused. He could see the broad plain of the first battleground stretching out on the eastern side of the city; it was bathed in moonlight. The still unburied corpses of the fallen knights and the butchered carcasses of their horses appeared as a great black stain over the plain, but the open ground stretched wide and without cover – anyone following would spot him long before he could hide himself among the dead.

Closer, the city's southern wall swept down to the sea. It, too, was awash in moonlight – save for a narrow strip of shadow cast by the tower surmounting the corner of the wall. There was no cover between the dunes and the wall, but he would be in the open only a short time; if he could make it to the wall he could hide there in the shadow of the tower, at least until the moon had moved on.

With a last backward glance, he started down the broad, banking slope of the dune and out across the open ground, heading for the base of the wall. He ran, keeping his head down, stretching his long legs, fighting the urge to look behind him. Better not to know if he was being followed, he thought; there was nothing he could do about it now.

The distance was further than it looked; he reached the base of the tower, exhausted, his lungs burning, and staggered into the shadow, collapsing thankfully into the darkness to lie with his back to the great stone blocks, and gaze at the dunes he had left behind. There was no sign of anyone, however, and as he lay there, slowly regaining his breath and strength, he began to think that he had eluded his pursuers.

He looked at the long, slender length of cloth-bound iron in his hand, and decided to take a look at the prize for which he had risked his life. He pushed himself up and sat crosslegged, holding the lance across his knees, he untied the golden cord and unwound some of the silken covering.

For all that he could see, sitting in the dark, the holy relic was a simple shank of ancient iron, rust-spotted, and slightly crooked along its length. Despite its age, the crude weapon seemed sturdy still. True, it had lost its wooden shaft, and binding – all that remained was the iron haft and the short, tapering, three-sided blade – still, it did not appear beyond repair. It was simply an old iron lance, and a wholly unremarkable example of its kind at that.

He carefully pulled the winding cloth back into place, and retied the binding cord. This finished, he leaned back against the wall once more. He was tired and hungry, and wished only to be far, far away from this wretched desert land. God, he thought, I want to go home.

He closed his eyes, thinking only to rest a moment, but awakened with a start to find the night far gone. He looked around quickly, and made to run. But all was quiet. The moon had disappeared, and from the look of the sky to the east, he reckoned it was near dawn.

Rising, he began walking stiffly along the wall, using the lance as a staff. His over-tired muscles were sore, his back ached, and he was hungry and thirsty. He wondered how Emlyn had fared, and whether the monk was waiting for him at the harbour. Murdo walked around the tower, and started along the western wall making for the main gate. The plain where the battle had taken place the previous day was still in darkness, but he thought he could see figures moving on the battlefield – scavengers early to their work, he thought.

The gloom faded as he walked on towards the massive gate tower. Upon reaching the entrance, he darted quickly around the base of the tower – only to find the huge doors closed. Scorched and blackened from the fire of the day before, they had not yet been opened by the gatemen.

He turned and looked out at the battlefield again and saw that he had been mistaken: the figures he had taken for scavengers in the dim early light were actually those of knights and their horses moving slowly among the dead. They seemed to be searching for something . . . *They, too, seek the lance,* he thought.

Stepping quickly back against the great gatepost, he pressed himself against the stone, hoping someone had not noticed him already. Once beyond the walls, he would not be caught. If he could just avoid being seen until the doors opened – was that too much to hope?

Making himself as small as possible, he squatted down in the corner formed by the door and post to wait. He lay the lance down beside him, and kept his eye on the soldiers moving out on the plain. While he was watching, he heard the jingle of horses' tack; the sound seemed to be coming from the wall to his right. Keeping low, he leaned out from the doorway and looked down along the city wall. Three riders were approaching at a fast trot; they were making for the gate.

It was too late to hide, and he would never outrun them. He would have to brazen it out. He kicked dust over the lance and hoped to God they would not see it.

In a moment, the riders came around the side of the gate tower to find a young man leaning against the gatepost, head down, half-asleep.

'You there!' said one of the riders.

Murdo raised his head and regarded the three men sleepily. All were knights and, judging from the quality of clothing and horses, at least one was a nobleman. 'Greetings, my lords,' Murdo replied. 'Pax Vobiscum.'

'What are you doing out here?' demanded the second knight, who seemed to be superior to the other two.

'I was late coming home,' Murdo explained, 'and the gates were closed.'

'You spent the night outside the city alone?' inquired the knight suspiciously.

'Aye, for a fact I did,' answered Murdo directly; he gazed honestly into their faces. 'I am waiting for the gates to open now.'

The rider's eyes narrowed. 'Why were you so late coming home?'

Murdo hesitated. 'I was watching the battle,' he said, deciding to tell as much of the truth as he dared.

'What battle?' demanded the foremost rider. He glared at Murdo, and all three were frowning.

'Out there,' Murdo replied, pointing away to the south. 'Bohemond's troops engaged the Turks who slaughtered Godfrey's war band.'

'Bohemond here?' wondered the other knight. 'How do you know this?'

'I saw him,' Murdo answered vaguely. 'I took it you were men of his war band. I see I must be mistaken.'

'We are from Count Baldwin's camp,' replied the nobleman.

'What is Bohemond doing here?' demanded one of the others.

'I cannot say,' replied Murdo, trying to sound helpful but ignorant at the same time. He did not care for the tone of accusation creeping into the nobleman's voice.

Just then he heard a scraping sound on the other side of the huge timber door; it was followed by a clanking, jangling noise. Murdo guessed the gatemen were drawing the bolts. All he had to do now, was to keep the riders occupied until he could get through.

'We saw the first battle, too,' Murdo volunteered helpfully. He pointed out towards the plain. 'The Turks ambushed the knights and killed them. It was a terrible fight. The crusaders fought well, but there were too many Turks, and they –'

While Murdo was speaking the rider to the left of the nobleman leaned close to his companion and whispered, 'Look! He has it, by God!'

Murdo saw the knight's gaze shift to the lance behind him on the ground.

'What have you there, thief?' shouted the nobleman.

There came a clunk from the door, and a muffled voice on the other side called out. Murdo took a slow step backwards.

'Stop! Stand where you are!'

The door gave out a creak. Murdo glanced to the side to see that a smaller door cut in the larger was opening. He took a half-step towards it, away from the lance.

'Stand still!' shouted the knight, handing his reins to the rider next to him as he made to dismount.

Murdo waited until the knight had begun sliding his leg over the saddle, and then leaped forward, throwing his hands in the horse's eyes, and shouting as loudly as he could. 'Hie!' he cried, waving his hands. 'Hie-yup!'

The frightened animal tossed its head and reared back, lifting its forelegs off the ground and sending the unbalanced knight sprawling, his foot still caught in the saddle. The other horses shied, too. Murdo jumped back, snatched up the lance, and dived for the door, which was yet but half-open. He heard the sharp ring of steel as the knights drew their swords, and then hit the door with his shoulder. The gateman was thrown back off his feet, and Murdo was through.

Gathering his feet under him, he dashed for the nearest street.

An instant later, the first of the knights burst through the door. 'Stop, thief!' cried the knight, his voice loud in the quiet of the morning. 'Thief! Thief! Stop that man!'

FORTY-SIX

Keeping the sun at his back, Murdo darted quickly along the twisting, narrow streets, working his way down through the city of Jaffa to the harbour. Every now and then, he paused to look for his pursuers, but he neither saw nor heard them, and began to feel he had left them far behind.

As he ran on, he noticed there were more people about in the streets now as the morning's business began to occupy the towns-people. Lest he draw any unwanted attention, he slowed to a purpose-ful walk, and crossed an empty market square in which merchants and traders were beginning to gather. Once across the square, he entered a covered street stuffed tight with tiny stalls from which the ring of hammer on brass could be heard. Several of the traders called out to him in Greek as he passed, but he ignored them and hurried on.

The sudden sight of the bay brought him up short. He stopped and stepped quickly back, hiding in the early shade of a pillar for a good look around before proceeding. Among the scores of ships anchored in the harbour below – Genoese and Venetian for the most part, along with Greek of various kinds – small fishing boats plied the still water. Here and there along the wharf scatterings of crusaders lazed, waiting, no doubt, for ships to take them home.

At the far end of the wharf, he saw the imposing imperial galley, its tall yellow masts and folded red sails towering over its nearest neighbours: the low-hulled longships of King Magnus' Viking fleet. He searched among the tall, upswept prows for the one he knew best, and quickly found it; *Skidbladnir* was second from the last, which was nearest the emperor's ship.

Leaving his hiding place, Murdo started down to the wharf, where he made his way quickly towards Magnus' ships, forcing himself to appear calm and unhurried, just one more eager home-going pilgrim.

He drew near the Norse fleet, and saw several hulking figures he recognized; men left behind to guard the ships. He had almost reached the first friendly hull when the dreaded cry sounded behind him.

'There he is! Stop him!' the cries went up. 'Stop thief! You there! Stop that thief!'

Two men reclining on the planking jumped to their feet as Murdo fled past. They made a grab at him, and one of them snagged a piece of his sleeve and spun him around. But Murdo was ready. Even as he turned, he swung the iron lance down hard on the man's forearm. The fellow yelped and released his hold, falling back with a curse between his teeth as Murdo leapt away.

He put his head down and ran for Jon Wing's ship, and was up and over the rail before anyone else could lay a hand on him. He dived for the prow, his fingers searching under the rail for what he had hidden there. When he did not find it, dull panic seized him in its icy grasp. Had it been found? Had someone removed his handiwork?

The shouts on the wharf were louder. His pursuers were almost upon him. He ducked out of sight beneath the upswept prow, swallowed down his fear, and searched again.

Cold iron met his touch. He grasped the metal, and pulled the spear he had made in Arles from its hiding place. The weapon now wore a thin coat of rust from the sea air and damp of its long stowage beneath the rail. This gave it a much older appearance, thought Murdo, which was no bad thing.

Hearing footsteps on the deck behind him, he turned and saw the familiar face of Jon's pilot. 'Gorm!' he called. 'Keep them off the ship!'

Without a word, the leather-skinned pilot swung around, seized a spear from the holder and levelled it on the nearest of the advancing pursuers. The men, unready to face this challenge so early in the morning, hesitated and fell back.

Swiftly, swiftly, Murdo's hands flew over the golden cord and binding cloth of the Holy Lance, stripping it away – and just as quickly rewrapping it. He could hear the voices shouting from the wharf. They were calling for him to come out and show himself. He also heard the clatter of hooves on the dock timbers, and knew that his ruse was all but finished. He could not hope to hold them off

445

any longer. He tied the last knot on the golden cord, carefully lay the lance on the deck, took a deep breath and stood to meet his fate.

A sizeable crowd had gathered on the quay. The knights who had raised the pursuit stood on the wharf, weapons drawn, staring at him. At Murdo's appearance, the shouting had ceased; it now began again. Murdo calmly raised his hands – for silence, and to show that he held no weapons. 'Please!' he called. 'In the name of Our Lord Christ, I beg you, let me speak.'

'Silence!' roared the foremost knight. When quiet reclaimed the crowd, he said, 'What do you have to say, thief?'

'Who is your lord?' asked Murdo. He knew, but he wanted those looking on to hear it for themselves.

'We are Count Baldwin's men,' the nobleman replied. 'We demand that you return that which rightly belongs to him.'

'What is it that you believe I have stolen from Count Baldwin?'

The nobleman glanced quickly at the crowd around him before answering. Clearly, he did not like the direction the proceedings were moving. Flinging his hand at Murdo, he shouted, 'He has stolen the Holy Lance!'

The crowd on the wharf murmured in astonishment. The Lance of Christ! Here? they wondered. How can this be?

'I have stolen nothing from you,' Murdo answered directly. 'What I have, I obtained not from you but from the amir.'

'Liar!' shouted the man. 'Seize him!'

The crowd, inflamed by the knight's accusations and a desire to involve itself in this interesting conflict, surged forward in a rush towards the ship. Murdo stooped quickly and retrieved the lance and lofted it above his head. 'Halt!' he shouted.

Amazed at the sudden disclosure of the relic, the crowd lurched to a stop.

'Stay where you are,' Murdo warned. 'If anyone takes so much as one step nearer, I shall throw the lance into the sea.'

'Do it!' challenged the knight. 'We will find it again easily.'

'You might,' allowed Murdo. 'Then again, you might not. Shall we put your faith to the test?'

The knight glared at him. 'I will gut you like a fish and throw the bloody pieces to the dogs if you drop that lance.'

The crowd began muttering again, and several made bold to

446

advance a step nearer. Murdo took one hand away from the spear and let it slip. The throng gasped and shrank back in horror.

Murdo frowned. The thing was not going as he had anticipated. Moreover, the length of iron was heavy and his arm was starting to tire. He did not know how much longer he could hold it outstretched with the weight of the lance at the end. He would have to put it down soon, and then what?

'Hear now,' said the nobleman. 'If you but give the lance to me at once, I will see you absolved of your theft.'

'I did not steal –' Murdo began, but never finished. He heard the wet splosh of water spilling onto the deck and whirled to see two men slip over the side and into the boat. 'Gorm! Help!' he cried as the two men rushed upon him.

Murdo threw the end of the lance into the face of the first one, who ducked the blow. He jabbed at the second, who made a grab and somehow caught hold of the silk-wrapped iron and tried to yank it from him. Murdo hung on, and the two pulled him into their grasp. They heaved him up onto the rail where he thrashed and squirmed, clinging desperately to the lance.

The crowd, seeing the fight, began clamouring for the two attackers to throw him in. Those nearest the boat made swiping lunges at him from the wharf, trying to pull him down.

'Peace!'

Even above the outcry of the crowd, Murdo heard the shout. It sounded twice again before it had any effect, and by then Murdo, like everyone else on the wharf, knew that someone of unassailable authority had arrived.

'In the name of God, I pray you cease and desist this unseemly display.' The voice was deep and resonant, and loud enough to be heard from one end of the wharf to the other.

The crowd calmed under its stern admonition, and Murdo turned his eyes to see the throng parting to make way for a tall man on a warhorse. There were half a dozen or more knights with him, and all had swords drawn and shields at the ready.

'You there, on the boat,' the man called. 'Release him and stand easy, or answer to me for your disobedience.'

The soldiers reacted instantly to the stranger's command. Much to Murdo's relief they pulled him back aboard the boat and eased their hold on him.

'Step away from him,' the tall man instructed, and the two reluctantly obeyed.

Murdo straightened and found himself looking into the quick, intelligent eyes of Count Bohemond. He sat his saddle easily at the edge of the quay where he calmly regarded Murdo. 'God be good to you, friend,' he said. 'I think we know each other do we not?'

'Yes, my lord,' replied Murdo. 'We met yesterday outside the walls.'

'It seems you have roused the ire of half the people of Jaffa, and this before the sun has quartered the sky. I would hear how you performed this prodigious feat.'

'That is easily told,' Murdo said. 'I have the Holy Lance, and *they*,' he indicated Baldwin's knights, 'would take it from me by force.'

'Indeed!' exclaimed Bohemond. 'Your tale fascinates me, I confess. I would hear the whole of it. Pray, continue.'

'I will, my lord, and gladly,' Murdo replied. 'Give me but space enough and time, and I will tell you all you wish to hear. Nor will you call me thief when I am done.'

'Good man,' answered the Count of Antioch. 'You speak well for yourself. Indeed, I would suggest that you speak very like a certain nobleman who has earned my highest regard in these last weeks. Can it be that you and he are kinsmen?'

'I cannot think it likely, lord count,' Murdo replied. 'There are few pilgrims from the northern isles, and fewer still from Orkneyjar.'

'But he is the king of the northern isles,' the prince declared. 'I am speaking of my vassal, King Magnus – do you know him?'

'I know him – that is to say, I made the pilgrimage with some of his men,' Murdo answered.

Bohemond smiled broadly at this. Raising himself in his stirrups, he turned and called out, 'Here! Magnus! I have found one of your countrymen!'

There was a shifting movement of the crowd behind Bohemond's horse, and the familiar figure of King Magnus stepped out from among his bodyguard. Crowding in behind him, Murdo recognized the round figure of Brother Emlyn, trying desperately to squeeze through the tight-pressed throng.

'Hey-hey,' said Magnus by way of greeting. 'What have we here?'

'This fellow tells me he came to the Holy Land on one of your ships. Do you know him?'

Magnus cocked his head to one side and studied Murdo for a moment. 'He does appear familiar. If he says he sailed with me, I take him at his word and claim him as one of my own.'

'I sailed with Jon Wing, my lord,' Murdo told the king. 'It was his ship that brought your priests – one of whom came to Jaffa with me.' Murdo pointed into the crowd below. 'He is here now; you can ask him if you do not believe me.'

At that moment, the foremost of Count Baldwin's knights interrupted with a shout. 'Enough of this! Serious business lies before us, and you prattle away like spinsters over a pie.' Flinging out a hand to point at Murdo, he said, 'This man is a liar and a thief. He has stolen the Holy Lance, and we will see it returned to its rightful place.'

Bohemond looked at the man, his expression placid and good-natured. 'Why do you call him liar? He has freely admitted possessing the sacred relic; where is the lie?'

The nobleman glowered at Bohemond. 'The lance belongs to Lord Godfrey, and you know it.'

'The Holy Lance belongs to the Holy Church and her people. But, leaving that aside, do you deny that it was taken from your comrades in the battle?'

'You know well that it was,' the soldier spat. 'Godfrey's troops were attacked within sight of the walls and the lance carried off.'

'Are you saying that this unarmed youth defeated Godfrey's army all by himself and stole the relic for himself? Is that what you imagined happened?' Bohemond inquired innocently.

'You twist my words,' the knight growled. 'You know it was the Turks.'

'That is the first true word you have spoken,' Bohemond said. 'Yes, it was the Turks. We have laboured long against them this night, and have come fresh from the battlefield.' Raising his hand to Murdo, the count concluded, 'If this fellow has risked his life to recover the lance which was lost at your comrades' hands, it seems to me that instead of seeking his skin, you ought rather to be thanking him and heaping rewards and praise upon his head.'

The knight grumbled at Bohemond's assessment, but made no outright challenge to the count's version of affairs. He and his companions glared their displeasure, but held their tongues. Turning once more to Murdo, the Count of Antioch said, 'It would be my pleasure to sit with you and King Magnus, and discuss this matter with the propriety it deserves. If you would allow us to come aboard, I give you my word nothing ill will befall you.'

'Very well,' agreed Murdo, 'only allow the priest to join us, and I will tell you all I know.'

The count dismounted and placed his men along the quayside to guard the ship; meanwhile, Gorm quickly produced the plank to allow the lords and their noblemen to board the vessel more easily. Murdo soon found himself clutching the lance and standing face to face with his unanticipated defender, and a dozen or more noblemen – including Orin Broad-Foot, and the ever-suspicious Bayard. Brother Emlyn bustled up the plank and came to stand breathlessly beside him.

'I waited all night, and when you did not return, I thought to go to the gate to see –'

'Never mind,' said Murdo. 'Where is the treasure?'

'You recovered the lance, praise God!' He swallowed a gulp of air. Lowering his voice to a whisper, he said, 'There are too many nobles here for my liking. What are we to do about them?'

'Trust me,' replied Murdo. 'Now tell me – my father's treasure, where is it?'

The priest leaned nearer. 'It's here, aboard this very ship – where else should it be?' Glancing around, he said, 'Maybe you should give the lance to me. I could –'

'Hear me, Emlyn,' warned Murdo, 'say nothing. Whatever happens, hold your tongue.'

'Be careful, Murdo. These men will stop at nothing to have their way. Do not give in to them.'

'I mean it!' Murdo growled sharply. Grasping the priest by the wrist, he squeezed hard. 'Whatever I say or do, just keep quiet and stand aside. Understand?'

Stunned, Emlyn nodded and stepped away, rubbing his wrist.

Turning from the monk, Murdo faced Bohemond. 'Thank you for saving me,' he said, lowering his head in dutiful respect. 'I fear I would be drowned now if you had not arrived when you did.'

'And that would have been a great pity,' Bohemond told him. 'To lose both the Holy Lance *and* its most ardent protector at a stroke – it does not bear thinking about. Therefore, let us pass on to happier fields of discussion.' He put out his hands to Magnus and Murdo. 'Sit with me, friends, and let us decide what is best to do.' They settled themselves on rowing benches. Indicating the silk-wrapped object in Murdo's lap, the count said, 'Now then, I would hear how the Sacred Lance came into your possession.'

Murdo nodded, and began his tale; he described how, after Count Bohemond and his troops had departed to engage the Turks, he had followed and heard the clash on the strand. He told how, upon climbing the hills for a better look, he had discovered the tent hidden among the dunes. 'The amir's treasure was inside the tent,' he concluded simply. 'I found the Holy Lance and came away with it. The Turks returned before I could get more.'

'Remarkable,' said Bohemond, shaking his head slowly. 'You have rescued the holy relic from its enemies – both Turk and Christian. I commend you . . .' he hesitated. 'Please, I still do not know your name.'

'I am Murdo, son of Lord Ranulf of Dýrness,' he answered, glancing at Magnus, who regarded him thoughtfully, but showed no recognition of the name.

Bohemond received the name with a gracious nod, and continued, 'I commend you, Murdo, Son of Ranulf of Dýrness. Your bravery shall be rewarded. I pledge a thousand pieces of silver for the return of the lance.' So saying, he extended his hand to take possession of the weapon.

'Murdo, no!' cried Emlyn, unable to help himself. 'Please, for the love of God, you must not –'

Murdo silenced him with a single sharp look, and turned once more to Bohemond. 'Again, lord, you have my thanks,' he replied, maintaining his grip on the iron lance. 'Forgive me, but I will take nothing from your hand for the return of the relic. I have my own reasons for what I did, and it is not right that anyone should amass profit upon the sacrifice of Christian lives. It will be enough for me to see the lance returned to its rightful place.'

Bohemond's expression became shrewd. 'More remarkable still,' he murmured.

King Magnus, who had taken in everything in silence, now leaned forward and, speaking in Norse, addressed Murdo directly, 'Son, think carefully about what you are saying. Jarl Bohemond here is a powerful man, and here he stands ready to give you anything you ask. Only give us the spear, and I will see you live to enjoy your reward.'

Murdo perceived the implied threat, but had already decided to brazen out his plan come what may. 'I thank you for your concern, lord,' he replied in polite Latin. 'Pray, do not think me disrespectful if I refuse your kind reward. For, what good is silver when a man's land has been stolen, and his family turned out of their rightful home?'

King Magnus was not slow to grasp Murdo's meaning. 'If this is what troubles you, my friend, then your hardship is at an end. As I am King of Norway and Orkneyjar, I will see justice served.'

'Very well,' replied Murdo, inclining his head in assent. 'I ask for no more than that.'

'Splendid!' cried Bohemond, slapping Murdo on the back. 'It is agreed.'

'Now then,' the king said, 'tell me who has perpetrated this offence, and when we return to the Dark Isles I will have the man summoned and demand an accounting for his crimes.'

'There is no need to wait for our return to Orkneyjar,' Murdo answered bluntly. 'The man I speak of is here among us even now.'

'Here!' wondered Magnus, drawing back suddenly as if suspecting a trap. Casting a quick, worried glance at his liegemen, he said, 'Certainly, you must be mistaken.'

'There is no mistake,' Murdo assured him. Pointing to the rank of onlooking noblemen, he declared, 'Orin Broad-Foot is that man.'

Magnus, aghast and dismayed, stared at Murdo, and then at his vassal lord, who was as surprised as his king at this startling accusation. Bohemond appeared bemused; he regarded Murdo wonderingly, as the Norse lord rose and stepped quickly to his nobleman. The two held close conversation for a moment while all those about them shuffled and murmured in restless anticipation.

'This is a most difficult matter,' Magnus announced, turning from his consultation. 'It seems my son, Prince Sigurd, is responsible for taking your lands. Naturally, Lord Orin knew nothing of your family's plight and he is not to blame in this matter.'

'God knows it is true,' Orin swore. 'If I had known the bú belonged to your father, I would never have taken it. But I had it on good faith from the bishop that those lands had fallen forfeit when Jarl Erlend was dethroned.'

Magnus nodded, satisfied with his lord's declaration of innocence. 'For this reason,' he continued, 'I do not think justice would be accomplished by punishing a good man for a crime which he neither knew nor intended.' Murdo opened his mouth to protest, but the king, anticipating his complaint, raised a hand to stay him. 'Still, it is not right that you and yours should bear such ill-fortune. I would be a worthless king indeed if I did not offer some remedy for injuries caused by my son's inexperience.'

Bohemond nodded approvingly, and the noblemen added their endorsement of the king's judgement with grunts and growls of support. 'Therefore,' Magnus resumed, 'I would make amends to you and your family and vassals by offering you other lands on which to build and settle.' He paused to take in Murdo's sour disposition, and then added, 'However great your lands in Orkneyjar, ten times that much again shall be given to you.'

'There is no estate in all Orkneyjar so big as that,' Murdo observed somewhat warily.

'That may be as you say,' answered Magnus. 'So I will give you land in Caithness – a portion of the kingdom granted me by Malcolm, King of the Scots. I give it right freely, and welcome you to take it.' He offered his hand to Murdo – the gesture of a Norseman when striking a bargain.

Realizing he had achieved a boon far greater than anything he would have dared ask, Murdo rose to his feet. 'My father, Lord Ranulf, fell at Jerusalem,' he said. 'But if he were standing here before you, I know he would accept your generous offer, freely forgiving any grievance or ill-feeling towards Lord Orin, or Prince Sigurd. Therefore, in honour of my father, I accept.' He grasped the offered hand, thereby sealing the bargain. 'Know, too, that my father would want to see the Holy Lance placed in safe and trustworthy hands for the good of all.'

With that, Murdo delivered the lance to Count Bohemond, who received it gladly, then stood at once, crossed to the rail, and lofted the silk-wrapped weapon above his head to the rapturous delight of the crowd who yet stood waiting to see how the confrontation would be resolved. 'The Holy Lance is recovered!' he called. 'Praise God, and give thanks for its swift return.'

Murdo heard a loud sigh behind him and turned in time to see Emlyn crumple to the deck. Overcome by the sight of his trusted companion delivering the lance to the adversary, the priest had swooned.

FORTY-SEVEN

Bohemond wasted not a moment summoning the imperial envoy to deliver his prize. Like Godfrey, he understood his survival depended on the good will of the emperor. Unlike Godfrey, he was not afraid to make the sacrifice which would secure Alexius' support. In his brief and prickly appearance before the council in Jerusalem, Dalassenus had left little doubt that the emperor's future co-operation depended on the return of the lance.

The wily count had decided that if the lance could secure the emperor's support, it was a price he would gladly pay. In order to derive the maximum benefit from the gift, Bohemond must be seen to be the agent of its return. Even as he and Magnus walked from the council chamber, he had begun scheming as to how to get the relic away from Godfrey.

The instant Bohemond learned that Godfrey's men had departed Jerusalem, he put his spies to work. Upon discovering that Godfrey intended sending the sacred lance to the pope for safe-keeping, he had set off in pursuit with his best knights. True, he had not reckoned on fighting the Turks all night, neither had he foreseen Murdo's intervention. And if the gatemen had not been telling everyone about the youth who had stolen the Holy Lance, he would have despaired of ever finding it again. Life in the eastern empire was full of surprises, however, and he was learning to seize each opportunity as it arose.

Grasping the iron lance in his hand, he marvelled at his own good fortune. 'Take word to the Grand Drungarius,' he said, turning to Bayard. 'Tell the envoy that Count Bohemond comes bearing the Holy Lance of Christ, and that we would be pleased to wait upon him for the relic's delivery at his earliest convenience.'

Bayard and two of Bohemond's nobles were despatched to the imperial ship with the count's message.

Murdo knelt beside the stricken priest, and shook him gently. After a moment, the priest woke with a moan and sat up. He saw Murdo and clutched at his sleeve. 'You gave the lance to Bohemond!' he gasped. 'We must try to get it back – it is not too late. We must –'

He struggled to rise. 'Shh!' Murdo warned, pushing him back down. 'Be still.'

'The lance!' Emlyn hissed. 'He means to give it away!'

'All will be well,' whispered Murdo, bending near. Gripping the monk by the arm, he helped him slowly to his feet. 'Listen to me, there is not much time. Magnus is here – which means Ronan and Fionn cannot be far away. The less they know about this, the better, I think.'

Emlyn searched the young man's face for a reason, found none, and shook his head sadly. 'I do not understand. Last night you said you would follow the True Path and rescue the lance, yet today you give it away. What has changed you, Murdo?'

'Nothing has changed,' Murdo told him. 'We have to see this through.'

At that moment, Bohemond, standing at the rail with King Magnus beside him, lofted the Holy Lance in the air, and called out in a loud voice so everyone on the wharf could hear, 'Make way! Make way, my friends, for the emperor's envoy. He comes to receive this most holy relic into his care.' The sailors and crusaders near by looked up to see the golden cord and silken wrapping flash in the sun; they saw the emperor's emissary moving towards them, and backed away, uncertain as to what was about to happen.

Bohemond put his hand out in a conciliatory gesture. 'Join me, drungarius,' he called. 'Let us stand together and pledge troth before all gathered here.'

While the Grand Drungarius made his way through the throng to the dragon-prowed ship, Bohemond delivered a high-sounding speech to his onlookers, speaking eloquently about the suffering of the crusaders and their noble achievement in securing the Holy City for all time. He spoke of God's great design for his people, and the supremacy of the emperor as the Almighty's sole representative on Earth, and how it was good to reflect on the suffering of all those who had died in the struggle, and how the Good Lord himself had blessed their great enterprise by revealing the Holy Lance as a sign of his favour.

From his place beside Murdo, Emlyn gazed longingly at the lance in the count's hands. 'He is giving it away!' The monk started forth.

'Peace, brother,' Murdo muttered, taking his arm and holding him to his place. 'Be still.'

The monk, growing desperate, squirmed in Murdo's grasp. 'We cannot stand by and let him give it away!'

'That is exactly what we will do.' Murdo jerked hard on the monk's arm. 'Now stand still and be quiet.'

Dalassenus, with four Varangian guards on either side, mounted the plank to the ship and came to stand before Bohemond. The prince embraced the emperor's envoy like a long-lost kinsman. Taking the Holy Lance across his palms, he extended it towards Dalassenus, saying, 'In the name of Our Lord Jesus Christ, I charge you to place this most sacred relic under the keen protection and loving care of the Supreme Ruler of all Christendom, Emperor Alexius. Let him know by this, that the lords of the West honour and revere him, and that we bend the knee to his authority, joining with him in the upbuilding of the Christ's great kingdom.'

With that he delivered the Iron Lance into Dalassenus' hands. The Greek commander inclined his head regally and accepted the sacred relic with the grave respect due the occasion. 'On behalf of the Emperor Alexius, Equal of the Apostles, God's Vice-Regent, and Life of the Church, I welcome the charge laid upon me, and swear before these gathered witnesses that this holy relic, sacred to Our Saviour's memory, shall be given all the care, veneration, and protection deserving of its eminence.'

Those looking on – aboard the ship, and below on the quay – greeted this bestowal with a muted, if not puzzled, response. While some called out to know what was going on, others gave out half-hearted cheers of acclaim; most simply went about their business once more.

The Grand Drungarius then thanked the count for returning the lance and upholding the vows sworn before the emperor's throne. 'Rest assured, Emperor Alexius will wish to thank you himself. Perhaps, when your duties permit, you will return to Constantinople and allow the emperor to reward you himself.'

Bohemond, looking suitably deserving, smiled benevolently at the prospect of meeting the emperor once more, and beckoned his nobles to share in his glory. King Magnus stepped beside him, and the two lords embraced; other crusaders or the prince's entourage were invited to bask in the reflected glory of their lord's triumph.

Lastly, the magnanimous count turned to Murdo and motioned him to join them, but he refused.

He declined politely, saying, 'I thank you, lord, but I have my reward. I am content.'

The noblemen exchanged vows of eternal brotherhood, and eagerly accepted Dalassenus' invitation to join him on the imperial ship for wine and a service of thanksgiving. Murdo and a much-subdued Emlyn retreated to the prow to watch as Bohemond and Magnus, flushed with pride at their salutary accomplishment were conducted to the imperial ship by an honour guard of Immortals, led by the emperor's emissary. They were escorted onto the emperor's ship, where they were served with wine and a lavish selection of local delicacies.

'It is not right that they should glory so,' Emlyn grumbled sourly. 'It is an offence against heaven.'

'Heaven can take care of itself,' Murdo answered. 'We still need the good will of kings.' Scanning the wharfside activity, he found what he was searching for. 'Look, there is Jon Wing – Ronan is with him.'

Murdo called to them, and saw that the sea lord and priest were leading a small procession which snaked its way along the edge of the crowd on the pier, with Fionn and the sailors of the *Skidbladnir* bringing up the rear. Many of the seamen seemed to be labouring – dragging or carrying something as they came.

Ronan and Jon reached the edge of the quay and started up the plank. 'Hail, Murdo! Emlyn! God be good to you,' called the elder monk. 'We hoped we might find you before you sailed.'

'Behold!' said Jon Wing, stretching his hand to those coming on behind. 'Today you see the making of a king!'

Murdo looked where the Norseman was pointing, and saw the first of the sailors as they came swaying up the plank carrying open baskets of gold and silver objects. In all, six baskets of plunder were carried aboard to be carefully stowed within the tent on the platform behind the mast. One of the sailors helping secure the treasure emerged from the tent, and called out, 'Jon, there are some dead people here! What should we do with them?'

'Leave them in peace,' replied Jon. Turning to Murdo he said, 'Ronan told me about your father, and I was sorry to hear it. I knew you would want him to accompany you to Orkneyjar. Do not worry. Unless he begins to stink, I will not put him off the ship.'

Murdo thanked the sea lord for his thoughtfulness, and asked, 'How did you come to get so much treasure?'

'Bohemond chased off the Turks who ambushed Godfrey's troops,' answered Jon Wing. 'We arrived with Magnus in time to aid in the rout of the Turks. The amir's treasure was taken for spoils.'

'They had the treasure with them,' put in Fionn, joining the group as the last of the baskets was brought aboard and placed in the tent. 'King Magnus' men helped liberate the treasure and were granted a sizeable portion.'

'Would that you had joined us just a few moments ago.' Emlyn said, speaking up at last. 'You might have saved the Holy Lance as well.'

This occasioned a much-interrupted explanation of all that had happened to them since leaving Jerusalem – their narrow escape from the Seljuqs, the battle before the city walls, Murdo's recovery of the sacred lance, and his extraordinary bargain with King Magnus for the return of the relic. The others agreed with him that the bargain was extraordinary indeed.

'The king is known to be a fair and generous lord,' Jon Wing declared. 'I suppose he was at pains to prove it – with Bohemond and his noblemen looking on.' To Murdo he said, 'You had him in a very tight place, if only you knew it.'

'If not for Bohemond's intervention,' Murdo replied, 'I have no doubt it would have ended otherwise. Baldwin's men were for slitting my throat. I still do not know why the count acted as he did.'

'No doubt it was to do with the council.' He told Murdo how the emperor's envoy had appeared before the Latin lords and demanded the Holy Lance as a sign of the crusaders' recognition of Alexius' supremacy. 'When Bohemond learned that the lance had been sent from the city, he set off with a force of men to help protect it.'

'If you had but lingered half a day longer in Jerusalem,' added Jon Wing, 'you would have learned all this. What is more, you could have travelled to Jaffa with us.'

'Alas,' sighed Emlyn, 'it was *this* close.' He pinched his thumb and forefinger together. 'We had it in our grasp...' He glanced reproachfully at Murdo, and shook his head.

The three priests fell silent, reflecting on how near they had come to realizing their divinely-ordained vision. Murdo steeled himself against their benign disapproval, and held his tongue.

'Maybe it is not so bad,' said Jon, trying to console them. 'Such a secret is difficult to keep. It would have been nothing but trouble for you. It is better this way, I think.'

Jon Wing moved off, and the monks, disheartened, went to the stern to pray and seek the good Lord's direction following their failure to rescue the valuable relic. Murdo longed to go and comfort them, but held himself apart. In a little while, one of the king's house carles returned and summoned Jon. Murdo watched while the two spoke together, whereupon Jon called Gorm, and the two put their heads together in close consultation.

'The emperor's envoy is anxious to return to Constantinople,' Jon informed Murdo when he saw him standing alone at the rail. 'It seems our generous Count Bohemond has pledged the king's fleet to sail with him to help guard the treasured relic. Magnus has sent word that we are all to be ready to sail at first light.'

'And then what?' asked Murdo. 'What happens when we get to Constantinople?'

'I do not know what the others will do,' replied the sea lord, 'but as for me and my ship, we are going home.'

At these words, relief swept through Murdo with such a force that his knees buckled and his throat grew tight. He had intended finding a ship, but had not dared hope he might sail with his friends. This, together with the stringent demands of the last days, combined to make him light-headed; he swayed on his feet, and if Jon had not put out a hand to steady him, Murdo might have fallen over backwards.

'Here, Murdo,' said the great Norseman, patting him on the back, 'a drink will restore you. Gorm! Bring us a jar!' When the bowl arrived, Jon put it in Murdo's hands, saying, 'It is a shame we have no öl, but wine is not so bad.'

The wine did revive him, he drank deep and passed the bowl to Jon, who hailed his friend, saying, 'You are a good man, Murdo. You can sail with me any time.'

'When I get home, I will sail no more,' Murdo vowed, taking another good swig of wine, 'but if I did, I would not think to go to sea with anyone but you.'

'It is a long way to Orkneyjar,' Jon pointed out. 'You might change your mind.'

The rest of the day was spent readying the ships and amassing the necessary supplies and provisions for the journey. As the kegs, casks, and baskets came aboard, Murdo helped store everything and make sure it was tied down securely. Although Jon Wing bade him to rest and let the sailors do the chores, he declined; the work kept his mind off the long journey ahead. Still, every time he thought of it, his heart gave a leap inside his chest and he felt a quiver of excitement in his stomach.

As the sky sank by ever deeper degrees from flame red to the purples of night, Murdo found himself staring westward at the dying light, and imagining that it was the cold northern sea he was staring at, not the warm Mediterranean; and that it was the low Dark Isles lifting their sleek heads from the still waters, not clouds drifting on the far horizon. The yearning to be home grew in him like an ache and consumed him. 'Ragna . . .' He whispered her name to the sea and to the gentle twilight. 'Ragna, I am coming home.'

That night Murdo curled up in his customary place at the prow, and fell asleep with his beloved's name on his lips. Dawn found him awake and waiting for the call to shove away from the pier. The call finally came, and Murdo took up an oar and settled himself on the bench as the emperor's ship slid slowly out into the harbour, to be followed by the smaller, faster, Norse boats. One by one, they pushed away from the wharf and followed the envoy's vessel into open water. Once clear of the harbour, Jon Wing gave the call to up sails, and the return journey commenced.

The tawny sail rose and stretched – as if stirring itself from a long sleep. The heavy cloth flapped slowly and shook out its creases, then caught the wind, filled, billowed, and the ship began to glide away.

As Jaffa dwindled slowly behind them in a haze of gleaming, sun-bright white, Murdo lifted his eyes to the arid hills east of the city and looked his last on the Holy Land. He felt a fleeting pang of sadness for leaving his father and brothers behind. He breathed a silent farewell to them, and then turned his face once more to the west, and to the long voyage home.

FORTY-EIGHT

Grey mist scudded low, billowing on the sharp-gusting wind, obscuring the sea and all upon it. Overhead, the sky remained bright and blue, untroubled by haze and mist. Murdo, after so long a time at sea, stood at the prow gazing into the dense grey wall, refusing to accept defeat by anything so insubstantial as fog. Somewhere on the sea ahead lay the whale-like humped backs of the Orkney islands, and he meant to see them.

The voyage from Constantinople, though long, had been uneventful. For most of the journey, they had enjoyed the company not only of King Magnus' fleet, but of Venetian and Genoese ships as well. Now that the Holy Land was secured, the merchant princes were eager to establish trading ties with the new Latin kingdoms. Their cargo-laden ships were already plying the sea of Middle Earth in increasing numbers.

Magnus, intent on inducing more men to help him carry away the wealth of the East, took leave of Count Bohemond in Constantinople, vowing to return as soon as he could arrange his affairs and acquire more ships. He then pursued a relentless course west and north, sailing always by the shortest routes and making the best running whenever the wind obliged – which gratified Murdo, and saved Gorm from a plague of incessant demands for speed from an impatient passenger.

Upon reaching the Caithness coast, the doughty king made landfall near his principal Scottish residence at Thorsa. Little more than a mud-and-timber fishing settlement, it nevertheless boasted a large and lordly hall, and a new stone church. Within moments of his arrival, the king ordered a feast to celebrate his safe return. While the ale vats were being set up outside the hall, he called Murdo to him and bade the young man to stay. 'I will make you one of my house carles,' Magnus offered. 'Together we could win much plunder in the Holy Land, you and I.'

462

'My place is here, and here I mean to stay. But if I ever return to Jerusalem, I will not undertake the journey with anyone else,' Murdo declared. 'Despite the trouble between us, no other lord has treated me half so well as you, King Magnus. For that I am grateful, and will erect a shrine in your memory as soon as I have established myself in my new lands.'

'As to that,' the king replied, 'come to me when you are ready, and we will set out the boundaries of your realm.'

'That I will, lord,' Murdo replied. He stayed one night on dry land, and set off the following day for the Dark Isles, having tempted Jon Wing with the promise of a substantial reward for delivering him swiftly to Hrolfsey.

Dawn was still a mere rumour in the sky as Ronan, Fionn, and Emlyn walked down to the strand with Murdo to see him away. 'The king will remain here gathering men and provisions until mid-summer,' the elder priest informed him, 'and then he plans to go to Norway and do the same. He hopes to depart for Jerusalem before winter and, unless God intends otherwise, we will go with him.'

'I will come back as soon as I can,' Murdo promised.

'Do that,' the elder priest advised. 'I would see you settled before we leave.'

'The sooner we are away,' Jon Wing said, starting towards the boat, 'the sooner we can return.' He moved on, shouting to his pilot. 'Gorm! Make ready to sail!'

'We will say farewell then, Murdo, and pray for you a swift and safe return.' Ronan raised his hand in benediction. 'Bless you, my friend. May the Lord of Life shield you and protect you until we meet again.'

Murdo thanked the priests and added, 'Save some ale; we will lift a jar together when I return.'

Jon Wing called him then, and Murdo bade the priests farewell and started towards the ship, only to find Emlyn by his side once more. 'Why farewell?' asked the monk. 'Am I not going with you? How will you find your way back without me to guide you?'

Murdo smiled, and accepted the priest's offer. Jon Wing clapped his hands loudly. 'Over the side those staying behind!' he cried, then leaned over the rail and called to the men waiting on the shore. 'Here now! Stand to! Push us away!'

The ship lurched awkwardly and Murdo heard the keel scraping against the pebble shingle. 'Heave!' shouted Jon Wing to the shoremen. 'Heave away!'

The men groaned and all at once the shingle dropped away and the boat glided into deeper water. 'To oars!' called Gorm from the tiller. Murdo, Emlyn, and the three crewmen snatched up long oars from the holders at the rail, and set themselves to rowing. In a few moments, the dragon-prowed longship was sliding through the dark waters of the bay.

Upon rounding the protecting headland, the ship turned north and onto the open sea. The sails were raised at Gorm's command, and the rowers shipped their oars as *Skidbladnir* began its run to the islands.

The day broke dull and murky with a dense sea mist on the water and thin grey clouds high above. All morning long Murdo stood at the prow searching through the shifting sea mist for the first glimpse of his homeland. His vigilance was rewarded when, just after midday, the sun burned through the hanging overcast. The sudden warmth banished the mist and all at once Murdo found himself gazing at the smooth, shapely hills of the Orkney isles.

From the direction of their approach, he thought he could make out the low flat rise of the Dýrness headland, and beyond it, pale blue in the distance, the steeper hump of Hrolfsey. Murdo's heart beat faster, and he at last allowed himself to contemplate the homecoming he might receive – a craving he had not dared indulge all the long months at sea. Now, with home in sight, and his journey swiftly nearing its end, he could no longer hold back the flood of images that rose within him: Ragna with her hair long and glinting golden in the sun, her arms outstretched in glad welcome; his mother, smiling through her tears to see him, hurrying to gather him into her loving embrace; Lady Ragnhild, warmly extending her hands in the blessing of her daughter's betrothal . . .

Oh, but there were less happy moments to come. It would be his sad duty to tell the women that their husbands and sons would not be coming home.

At Murdo's direction, Gorm held *Skidbladnir* on a steady course for Hrolfsey, rounding the Dýrness peninsula and passing swiftly along the wild eastern coast. Murdo stood at the helm with the pilot, guiding him by old and familiar landmarks through the narrow straits between the mainland and the scattering of islands and islets. From a distance they could see Kirkjuvágr, which, after the shimmering white port cities of the East, now seemed small and impossibly colourless and crabbed to Murdo. The sleek ship carried them swiftly on and soon Hrolfsey loomed into view.

The sun was low in the west when they finally slid into the deep-water bay below Cnoc Carrach. Murdo pointed out the house, observing that all appeared quiet and in good order; he would have leaped from the ship then and there, but Jon Wing advised caution.

'It has been two years, you know,' the seaman warned lightly. 'Maybe things have changed a little. It might be good to let them know you are coming before bursting in upon them.'

'Changed?' demanded Murdo as if he had never heard the word. 'They are *waiting* for me.'

'Maybe they are,' allowed Jon sagely, 'but maybe they are busy with other things.'

'What other things?' Murdo stared at him as if the Norseman had lost his mind.

'Two years is a long time,' Jon answered with a shrug.

'He is right,' put in Emlyn. 'Perhaps it would be best if we went ahead of you.'

'Then you must catch me first,' replied Murdo. With that he was over the side and flying up the steep path as if all the Seljuqs in Palestine were baying for his blood. Jon Wing shook his head as he watched him go. 'He is stubborn, that one.'

'He is young,' Emlyn said. 'Come, we will go and share in his welcome, and pray that it is all he hopes.'

'You pray,' suggested the seaman, drawing a spear from the bundle at the rail. 'I will carry this – should his welcome be less than he expects.'

Murdo heard Jon Wing's call behind him as he entered the yard, but refused to wait for the Norseman to catch up with him. He strode towards the house and called out loudly. 'Ragna! Niamh! I have returned!' He paused, and when his cry produced no effect, he shouted again, more loudly. 'Ragna! Niamh! It is Murdo! I have returned!'

Receiving no answer, he started for the house.

'Wait!' shouted Jon Wing, puffing up behind him. He looked at the house and empty yard. 'Is there no one here?'

'Most likely they are busy inside,' Murdo replied, trying to convince himself.

They moved to the door, but found it barred. Murdo stood on the step and shouted again. He beat on the door with the flat of his hand. There came no answer.

'It is very quiet for such a big steading,' observed Jon.

'Perhaps they have gone to the market,' suggested Murdo, frowning now. 'Or, maybe they are in the fields.'

'Everyone?' The Norseman shook his head. 'The sun is up and a farm this size should be busy.'

They moved quickly across the yard between the barn and the granary and past empty livestock pens; the pigsty was empty, too. The fields, however, were well planted and neatly tended, the early greens bright against the rich black earth. Still, they saw no one at work anywhere, and Murdo, fighting down his desperation, started back to the house. They were crossing the yard when they heard someone sneeze. 'Listen!' Murdo turned this way and that. 'It came from the kitchens.'

Murdo darted off on the run. Jon Wing followed at a slight distance, the spear ready in his hand. Upon reaching the squat building behind the house, Murdo started for the door. Jon's shout brought him up short. 'Wait!'

Murdo hesitated, his hand reaching for the door.

'Come out!' called Jon Wing sharply. 'No harm will come to you if you show yourself now.'

Silence. Nothing moved. Murdo started forward again, but Jon shook his head. Instead, he called, 'We are not robbers, or raiders. We only wish to speak to you. Come out and answer our questions, and then we will be on our way.' He paused. 'But if I must come in after you, it will be with a spear in my hand.'

In a moment, the door cracked open, and a small, wrinkled face appeared in the narrow gap. 'Please, we want no trouble,' said a shaky voice. 'We are afraid. Go away. I have a dog with me, so do not try to rob us.'

'Come out where we can see you,' commanded Jon Wing in his seaman's voice. 'If you do as we say, and do it quickly, there will be no trouble. We have not come to rob anyone.'

The door swung a little wider and a small, white-haired old woman stepped out quickly; she was slightly hunched, and wizened, and Murdo was certain he had never set eyes on her before. A big grey dog pushed out beside her and stood looking warily at the newcomers.

'Jötun!' said Murdo. 'Come, Jötun.'

The dog cocked his head to one side, but remained steadfastly beside the old woman. Murdo realized the dog no longer recognized him. Everything was changed, he thought, including himself.

'That is better,' said Jon Wing to the woman, resting his spear. 'Now then, old mother, who else is with you?'

'No one,' she said, 'just my Jarn – and the dog here.'

'Where is Jarn?' asked the sea lord. 'We did not see him. Where is he?'

Pointing vaguely towards the fields, she replied, 'With the cows, I suppose. He was tending the cows.'

'We saw no cows,' said Jon mildly.

'Where is everyone?' demanded Murdo, starting forward, his fists clenched. 'The people who live here – where have they gone? Where is Ragna?' The old woman's eyes grew wide, she whirled on her heels, and scuttled back into the kitchen, slamming the door behind her.

'Perhaps it would be best if just one of us asked the questions,' Jon proposed.

'You were asking about cows!' Murdo blurted angrily. 'What do we care about cows? Ask her what happened here – where is everyone?'

'Calm yourself,' soothed Jon. 'We will not leave until we have heard all there is to tell.' A voice called out from the yard just then. 'There now, Brother Emlyn has arrived. You go and bring him here while I coax the old one into giving us something to eat.' Murdo stared at the door. 'Go fetch the priest, Murdo.'

Murdo moved off reluctantly, and Jon turned his attention to persuading the old woman to come out once more. By the time Murdo returned, the Norseman was sitting on a stump beside the kitchen door with half a loaf of buttered black bread in his hand. 'She makes good bread,' he said, chewing contentedly. He passed the loaf to Murdo, who tore off a chunk and passed the remaining portion to Emlyn.

'Is there any ale?' wondered the monk.

The old woman appeared just then with a dripping jar in her

hand. 'Bless you, good woman!' exclaimed Emlyn, rushing to relieve her of the burden. He raised the jar to his lips and drank deeply, then passed the jar to Murdo, proclaiming the brew divine, and its maker a very angel. This pleased the old woman, who chuckled to herself. 'It is the best beer I have tasted in many months,' he told her. 'Your good husband is certainly a very fortunate man to have you to cook. But is it only yourselves you have to feed?'

'I was just about telling this one here that my Jarn and me are all that's left. Everyone is gone – the lord and lady, the vassals, too – all of them gone.'

'Where did they go?' asked Murdo impatiently.

The old woman eyed him suspiciously. 'Do I know?' she snapped. 'No, I do not! I was never told. We were brought here to keep the cows for the bishop –'

'The bishop!'

'Aye, Bishop Adalbert,' answered the woman. 'Is there another hereabouts?'

'But why –' began Murdo. The old woman drew back.

Jon Wing reached out with the jar and shoved it into Murdo's hands. 'Fill the jug, Murdo, and stop pestering the good wife.' Murdo took the jar and disappeared into the kitchen. 'My young friend is anxious about his mother,' Jon explained. 'We have been on crusade with King Magnus, you see.'

'And his mother was the lady here,' deduced the woman incorrectly. 'Then his father must be the lord. But I never heard what happened to any of them. We were just told that the property here was under the care of the church, and the bishop was loath to let the fields fall idle. Nor is it meet to let a good house suffer neglect.'

'Indeed,' agreed Emlyn, 'and I am certain the house is well in hand with you and Jarn here. But the fields are too much for the two of you, I think. You must have help with those.'

'Oh, aye,' answered the woman quickly. 'The vassals take care of the crops still.'

'Where are the vassals?' inquired Murdo, stepping from the doorway with the jar. 'They would know what happened here, but we saw no one in the fields.'

'They are working on the other island today, are they not?' answered the woman smugly. 'The bishop has many such estates he must care for now. So many of the men went away on the crusade, you see, and left him with all the work – fields to plough, cattle to raise, crops to be harvested, and what all.'

'A shame that,' observed the monk, taking up the jar once more. He drank a long, noisy draught. 'Ahh, yes, a very joy and a blessing to restore the inner man!'

'You have travelled far then,' the old woman said.

'All the way from the Holy Land,' answered the monk.

'As far as that . . .' the old mother shook her head and clucked her tongue. 'Well, you can stay here the night, I expect. The bishop would not refuse you hospitality, nor will I.'

'We thank you, good woman,' agreed Jon, much to Murdo's annoyance. 'It would be fine indeed to spend a night on solid ground. We accept your kind offer.'

'Gladly,' put in Emlyn. 'But do not burden yourself on our account. Simple fare, for simple travellers. Bacon and black bread – we expect nothing more.'

'Pish!' cried the old woman, her wrinkled features taking on a glow of excitement. 'We can do better than that! This is a bishop's house, you know.'

FORTY-NINE

Murdo glowered into the puddle of gravy in his bowl. Despite the warm praises heaped on the meal and its maker by Emlyn and the hungry sailors, he had not tasted a single bite. Never in all the time he had been away had he considered that he would not be met on his return by those he had left behind.

Hardly a day had gone by in the last two years when he had not imagined sitting before this very hearth. And now at long last, here he was – but in every important way he was no closer to his destination. He was angry with himself for allowing his hopes to soar so high; and he was angry with his companions for refusing to sail straight away to Kirkjuvágr to pull the bishop out of bed and demand an explanation at swordpoint. Most of all, he was angry with the grasping, scheming bishop – for using his holy office to prey on the weak, and for failing his sacred trust to protect and defend the people in his care. Which of the two was the worse, Murdo could not say, but he meant to hold the churchman to account for his crimes.

Unfortunately, the old woman could shed no further light on the matter. Nor could Jarn add anything beyond what his wife had already said. A quiet man, he had finally returned with his cows for the evening milking, and though he was agreeable enough, he knew less about the affairs at Cnoc Carrach than his wife. Under Emlyn's gentle probing, it emerged that they had been vassals of Jarl Paul, and had lost their small holding when Magnus placed his son over the islands. Thrown upon the charity of the church, Jarn and his wife, Hannah, had been brought by the bishop's men to look after the cows and keep the house; that was all he knew.

While the others sat at their ale, talking of their travels and gathering what news they could from the old folks, Murdo, restless and fretful, went outside to walk and think. He stalked the cliffs above the sea in the long, late twilight, gazing out across the strait to Orkney's mainland, where he imagined the greedy bishop sitting at his supper, smug in his comfort, ignorant of the fearful vengeance soon to break upon his devious head.

Midnight found Murdo sitting on the rocks above the bay, watching the starlight glinting in the calm water of the cove. He could hear the voices of *Skidbladnir*'s small crew as they reclined on the strand around their driftwood campfire. He could smell the smoke as it drifted up the cliff face, but felt not the slightest inclination to join them. The solitary discomfort of his chill perch suited him better.

He slept little, his heart aching for the dawn when they would up sails and make for Kirkjuvágr. By the time the sun broke above the sea's flat horizon, Murdo was already aboard ship, cursing the laziness of Emlyn and Jon Wing who had stayed the night at the house while he had slept on stones.

The two errant sailors appeared on the clifftop as the dawnlight filled the cove. They stumbled stiff-legged down the steep path and greeted the crew with the easy banter of the content and well-rested. Murdo protested their belated arrival, but Jon Wing said, 'If it is a fight you are wanting, save it for the bishop. He will be standing before you soon enough. Why not let *him* feel the sharp edge of your tongue?'

With that, the sea lord strolled off along the rail to talk to Gorm. A moment later, the call came to push away, and the crew took up oars to push the ship off from the wharf. 'Never fear, Murdo,' said Emlyn, leaning over the rail with his oar, 'we will find out what has happened and see it put right. We have the support of King Magnus, remember. I doubt this bishop of yours can easily afford to anger the king.'

'This bishop is a pig-stealing rogue,' Murdo replied, shoving hard against the oar. 'He cares for no one and nothing but the size of his purse.'

'That I heartily doubt,' remarked Emlyn. 'Instead of believing the worst, we should rather pray for the best.'

'If anything has happened to either Ragna or my mother,' Murdo vowed, 'the bishop will believe the worst is only beginning.'

The low-hulled ship left the quiet cove and sped across the strait towards the big island. Upon reaching the centre of the channel,

Gorm turned south to follow the undulating coast to the wide bay of Saint Ola below Kirkjuvágr. There were a dozen or more boats of various sizes in the harbour, but Gorm piloted the ship on a smooth straight line directly to the wharf. Murdo was out of the ship and half-way up the street to the cathedral before the mooring rope was tied.

'Murdo! Wait!' called Emlyn, waddling up the beaten earth track. 'Wait, son, let us help you!'

Murdo had no intention of waiting for anything or anyone. He raced up the slope without looking back, reached the cathedral and darted through the small door and into the dim, cavernous nave to a side door leading out into the cloistered gallery and the chapter house beyond. The door to the chapter house was closed and barred, so Murdo began pounding on it and shouting at those inside to open up.

'I want to see the bishop,' Murdo said to the first face to peer through a crack in the door.

'His reverance is at table breaking fast,' answered the monk. 'He sees no one until after prime. Come back then.'

'I do not care if he is at his window breaking wind,' growled Murdo. 'I want to see him now!'

'He sees no one –' was all the monk got out before Murdo kicked the door into his face. The unlucky cleric gave a yelp and fell back.

'I believe he will be seeing me,' said the young man, stepping quickly through the gap. The monk was rolling on his back, clutching his head and moaning.

Murdo raised the stricken priest roughly to his feet, and pushed him into the room. It was early yet, and most of the brothers were at their morning meal; there was no one else about.

'Now that we understand one another better,' Murdo said, 'tell Adalbert that Murdo Ranulfson has returned from the Holy Land. Tell the old thief that his day of reckoning has come.'

The monk stood in wounded silence, glaring uncertainly at his attacker.

'Better still,' said Murdo, moving to take the cleric by the arm, 'I will tell him myself. Show me to his majesty the bishop's chamber.'

Murdo marched the reluctant monk across the darkened room to another door. 'Through here?' he asked.

The monk nodded, but refused to speak. Murdo put his hand to the latch and pushed the door open. The room they entered contained a wide table surrounded by six large, throne-like chairs; the table was covered with a cloth of gold, and cushions of the same gleaming fabric rested on the chairs. Silver candletrees glimmered in the darkened corners of the room, and here and there, glints of gemwork and precious metals lit the darkness. Bishop Adalbert, however, was nowhere to be seen.

Murdo tightened his grip on the cleric. 'Where is he?'

The monk winced and pointed to a wooden stairway at the far corner of the room. 'Show me,' commanded Murdo, pushing the priest before him. They mounted the wooden treads and ascended into a small room with two narrow windows with panes of stained glass in red and yellow, making the room glow with a rosy colour in the early morning light. A table covered with parchments, quills, and ink pot occupied the centre, and on the wall opposite the windows stood a large, curtained bed.

Murdo crossed the room in two strides and yanked the curtains aside. Adalbert's eyes flew open and he gave a little startled cry as Murdo seized him by the arm and dragged him out of bed; he landed on hands and knees with a grunt. 'Stand up!' ordered Murdo, grasping the bishop's arm and jerking him upright.

'Unhand me!' answered the bishop. Recovering some part of his ecclesiastical decorum, he rose slowly in his siarc, legs and feet bare. 'Who are you?' he demanded. 'How dare you accost a prince of the church on holy ground!'

'I think you know me, bishop.' Murdo stepped nearer, staring into the churchman's face.

'I have never seen you in my life,' declared Adalbert stiffly.

Murdo's hand snaked out and caught the churchman on the side of the face with a resounding slap. 'I have no time for your lies,' Murdo told him.

'What do you want from me?' demanded the bishop, pressing a hand to his cheek.

'Lady Ragnhild and her daughter Ragna – where are they?'

'I have no idea what you are talking about.'

Again Murdo's hand flicked out, stinging the rattled clergyman on the cheek. 'Think carefully before you answer next time,' he warned.

Thrusting a hand towards the silent monk cowering at the top of

473

the stairs, Adalbert pleaded, 'Brother, fetch help. Quickly! I want this brigand seized at once.'

'Stay where you are,' snapped Murdo. The monk remained standing. To the bishop he said, 'Lady Ragnhild and her daughter – where are they?'

'Again, I can only say I have no idea what you are talking about,' replied the bishop petulantly. 'You are deceived if you think that I –'

Murdo's hand caught him on the cheek once more, harder this time. The sharp slap brought a new light of fear to the churchman's eyes. 'Who are you?' he murmured. 'Why are you doing this?'

The fearful monk seized the opportunity to run for help. He fled in stumbling haste down the stairs. Murdo gripped the bishop's arm and raised a warning finger. 'For the last time of asking: what have you done with Lady Ragnhild and her daughter?'

'I have the entire flock of the islands under my care. It is difficult to know what is hap –'

Murdo drew back his hand, higher and further this time, giving his victim a chance to see the blow coming.

'No! Wait!' Adalbert shouted quickly. 'Lady Ragnhild and her daughter! Of course, I remember them now.'

'Where are they?'

'Lady Ragnhild is dead,' the bishop informed him bluntly. 'Fever, I believe. I know nothing about anyone else.'

Murdo stared hard at the oily churchman, and decided he was telling the truth. 'Her daughter and the others – the Lady Niamh who lived with her – what happened to them?' he asked, dreading the answer.

'Am I now to assume responsibility for every wayward woman in these islands?' Adalbert sneered. 'You must be insane.'

The blow caught the bishop full on the mouth and rocked him back on his heels. Blood trickled from Adalbert's split lip, spilling down his chin. At the sight of his blood, the cleric began whimpering.

'The lady is my mother, you grunting pig.' Murdo drew back his arm once more. 'Must I ask you again?'

'No! No!' The startled churchman thrust his hands before him. 'The convent – any women were taken to the convent. I can tell you where it is.'

'I have a better idea,' replied Murdo. He started towards the

474

stairway, pulling the bishop roughly with him. 'You will *show* me where it is.'

There came a commotion from the room below and footsteps sounded on the stair.

'Salvation is at hand,' remarked Adalbert with a superior smile. 'I am not going anywhere with you. Indeed, you will soon wish you had never perpetrated this outrage against the church.'

Murdo turned to meet the first of the bishop's defenders. It was Jon Wing's head and shoulders that appeared in the opening, however. 'They are coming, Murdo.' Indicating the bishop, he asked, 'Has he told you anything?'

'Some, not all.'

'Then bring him. I will hold them off.'

The Norseman disappeared at once, and Murdo tightened his hold on the unrepentant cleric. 'Move!'

'There is no need to –'

'Move!' shouted Murdo, yanking his stumbling captive towards the stairwell.

'I cannot go like this – I am undressed. I must have my mantle at least – and shoes.' He turned and tried to squirm back into the room. 'I cannot be seen like this; it is undignified.'

'We will have a care for your dignity,' Murdo retorted, placing his hands firmly on Adalbert's back and forcing him down the stairs. 'The same measure you granted to others shall be granted to you.'

Upon reaching the room below, Murdo pushed the resisting cleric to the door and out into the anteroom where Jon Wing was standing, spear in hand. 'Hurry! Someone is coming.'

They ran for the outer door, tugging the bishop with them. Just as they reached the gallery, the door opposite the bishop's quarters opened, and a voice shouted, 'You there! I demand you stop at once!'

Glancing behind him, Murdo saw Abbot Gerardus hastening towards him. He took one look at the odious priest and called to Jon Wing, 'Bring him, too.'

The Norseman whirled around, raising the spear in the same motion. Gerardus, his voice loud in protest, saw the spear levelled at his throat and promptly closed his mouth.

Murdo poked his head out into the gallery to see Emlyn standing before a group of monks; from the intent looks on their rapt faces, he seemed to be explaining something to the brothers. 'Come along, and keep your mouth shut,' Murdo said, drawing the bishop out into the gallery; Jon Wing followed with the abbot firmly in his grasp and the four started down the cloistered gallery towards the sanctuary.

They reached the sanctuary, crossed the nave quickly and made for the great outer door, which one of the brothers was just opening for the day. Murdo thanked the startled monk and shoved the door wider; Jon Wing pushed the two priests through, and they started down the path leading to the harbour.

Once away from the church, the bishop, still in his night dress, halted. 'Kill me if you wish. I am not taking another step.'

Jon Wing crossed to Adalbert in two strides. Handing his spear to Murdo, he said, 'Take this and lead the way. We will be right behind you.'

Murdo prodded Abbot Gerardus in the ribs with the butt of the spear and, as they started off once more, Jon Wing turned to the churchman and said, 'Allow me, bishop.' Stooping quickly, he caught Adalbert around the knees, and hoisted him over his shoulder like a sack of mutton.

In this way, the four men hurried through the town – to the laughter of the citizens going about their early-morning chores. The bishop, struggling weakly, called for help and pleaded to be released. Upon reaching the harbour, Murdo turned to look behind them, expecting to see monks boiling out of the cathedral. To his surprise, however, all he saw was Emlyn bustling down the hill to the harbour, his short legs stumping.

'Get him aboard the ship,' Murdo told the Norseman, who hurried onto the wharf, bearing the near hysterical bishop.

'You cannot hope to gain anything by this,' the abbot sneered. 'You are only making things more difficult for yourself. Let us go and we might yet consider granting a pardon for your sins.'

'My sins are not so heavy that I cannot bear a few more for a worthy cause.' Murdo jabbed the abbot once again. 'Move along; there is a good wind, and it would be a shame to waste it.'

So saying, Murdo bundled the abbot aboard, and then turned to wait for Emlyn. In a few moments, the monk arrived, puffing and sweating from the exertion. 'I think it best that we cast off as soon as possible.'

'What did you tell them?' asked Murdo, helping Emlyn over the rail.

'The truth,' wheezed the monk. 'I said that we have come from King Magnus on urgent business with the bishop. That satisfied them for the moment, but if we linger here, I fear they may become curious and come down to see what is happening.'

They clambered over the rail and joined the others on deck. Abbot and bishop stood together, glaring balefully at their captors. At first sight of Emlyn, the abbot spat. 'I might have guessed there would be Célé Dé behind this.' He said the word as if it was the worst slander he knew. 'Heretics and blasphemers to a man.'

The butt of the spear clipped the abbot on the side of the jaw and sent him sprawling to the bottom of the boat where he lay writhing in agony. 'Forgive me, abbot,' said Murdo, brandishing the spear, 'it seems I have developed the regrettable habit of striking churchmen.'

Gerardus glowered at him. 'You dare raise your hand to me?' he rasped, shaking with rage.

'Perhaps I am at last outgrowing the natural tolerance of youth,' Murdo replied evenly, 'but I will raise my hand to anyone who demeans this good man. The Célé Dé have shown me nothing but kindness and respect, and I will not hear their benevolence impugned by the likes of you.'

The abbot sat glaring and rubbing his jaw, but made no further complaint. Turning to Jon Wing, Murdo said, 'Our passengers are settled; let us be on our way.'

At Murdo's word, Jon Wing called the order to cast off; Gorm and the three-man crew leaped to the ropes and oars. A moment later, *Skidbladnir* began gliding away from the wharf and into the quiet water of the bay.

'Where are you taking us?' demanded the bishop.

'That is for you to say,' Murdo told him. 'Where is the convent?'

Adalbert grew belligerent. Folding his arms defiantly across his chest, he growled, 'King Magnus will hear of this!'

'Hey-hey,' agreed Jon Wing cheerfully. 'Hear of it he will indeed, for I am telling him myself. I will tell him, too, about all the farms and lands you have stolen from the families of the crusaders while the menfolk were away.'

'I have done nothing wrong,' declared the bishop indignantly. 'Those estates were placed in my care freely and forthrightly.'

'Lord Brusi's lands were under the care of his lady wife and daughter,' Murdo told him. 'My mother was with them.'

'I know nothing of your mother,' the churchman insisted.

'Oh, you would well remember Lord Ranulf's wife, I reckon,' Murdo told him.

The bishop stared at him for a moment, and his expression slowly wilted. 'Young Ranulfson,' he sighed, as if remembering an old and painful irritation. 'I heard you followed your father on crusade.'

'That I did,' Murdo confirmed, 'and I tell you the truth: it sickens me to see what you have done. While others died for Christ at your behest, you could not wait until they were cold in their graves before swooping in to plunder their lands.'

The young man drew himself up and looked the larcenous bishop in the eye. 'Your days of thieving and treachery are finished, priest. Murdo Ranulfson has returned, and now you will take us to this convent of yours.'

'I will not,' declared Adalbert defiantly.

'You will,' said Murdo. 'And bishop,' he warned, his voice falling to a whisper, 'I suggest you pray we find the women well and happy.'

'I will agree to take you to the convent,' the scheming cleric retorted, 'but I cannot be held responsible for any injury to befall the unwary. That is the Almighty's concern, not mine.'

'Those estates were in your care,' Murdo retorted. 'That makes it *your* concern. I intend to hold you accountable.'

'You overreach yourself; God is my judge, not you.'

'Then we will send you to your judge,' Murdo said softly, putting his face near the grasping cleric's, 'and we will let *him* decide whether I killed an innocent man.'

FIFTY

Murdo and Emlyn paused before the gate. The monk put his hand on the young man's arm. 'Allow me to serve you in this,' he said gently. 'I will go and speak to the abbess and bring you word.'

Murdo gazed at the large timber door. 'I have not come this far to turn aside now. I will see it through.'

'As you will.' Emlyn stepped to the door, lifted the iron ring and swung it down with a hollow thump. In a moment, a small slit door opened in one of the beams and a plump, good-natured face appeared. 'Good day, sister. I am Brother Emlyn of St Aidan's Abbey, and this is Lord Murdo Ranulfson.'

'Good day to you, brother, and God's blessing be upon you both,' the old woman replied. 'What is your business here?'

'We want to see –' blurted Murdo.

Emlyn swiftly interrupted. 'We have come to enquire of the abbess. I pray she is well.'

'She is well indeed,' answered the nun. 'A moment, if you please.' The door closed, and they heard a long scraping sound as the bar was withdrawn.

'Why did you do that?' demanded Murdo. 'Are we here to find my mother and Ragna, or not?'

'Patience,' chided the monk. 'All in good time. It is best to proceed with a little propriety and discretion if we expect to receive their help. Also, I believe we should confine ourselves to finding your mother. It would be best not to mention Lady Ragna just yet.'

'Why?' It made no sense to Murdo and he said so.

'We do not know what the bishop told the abbess when the women were brought here – not the truth, I think. Therefore, I urge caution until we see how the thing stands.'

Murdo nodded curtly and kicked the dirt with the toe of his boot. After a few moments the door in the gate jerked and swung open.

'I am surprised to find the abbey gates closed. Are the doors barred the entire day?' asked Emlyn.

'Alas, they are, brother,' replied the nun. 'We are little more than prisoners in our own abbey, for there has been raiding already this year. We were set upon three times last summer. It is that the lords and knights are gone away on pilgrimage, you see. The Sea Wolves know they can plunder the weak who are left without protection.' She smiled, her wrinkles framing a kindly face. 'Thank you for asking. Enter please, and I will take you to the abbess.'

The monk offered a small bow and stepped over the threshold. Murdo turned and looked back to the ship waiting in the bay below. In the near distance he could see the broad, curving inlet of the firth the Norse sailors called Dalfjord; away to the south was a smudge of smoke which he took to be Inbhir Ness. Turning back to the door, he took a breath, squared his shoulders and stepped through.

The abbey was a small settlement enclosed behind stone walls, with dwellings of various kinds: a church, gardens, an orchard, livestock pens, storehouses and work shops. There were almost as many buildings inside the walls as outside, and the place seemed especially busy. Murdo was surprised to see plenty of men around – some were monks, but there were craftsmen and labourers as well; he had expected a convent to contain only women.

'The convent is only a part of the work God has given us,' Abbess Angharad explained upon receiving them in the lodge beside the chapter house. Following Emlyn's advice, Murdo was trying to engage in polite conversation while all he could think about was finding Ragna and his mother. 'Subduing a wild and savage land is a toilsome occupation; we turn away none who are willing to earn their crust by the sweat of their brow.'

'And to all appearances, you have succeeded admirably well,' remarked Emlyn. 'The settlement thrives, I see. Verily, it flourishes.'

'It is God who prospers us, dear brother,' the abbess replied tartly. Thin-faced, her wrinkled skin brown from the wind and sun, she was wiry and vigorous despite her years, and proving to be more awkward than Murdo had expected. 'If we thrive,' she continued, as if lecturing wayward children, 'it is only through obedience. We ask no more than to shine as a beacon flame in a dark and treacherous land.'

'And yet,' offered Emlyn lightly, 'there is joy in the journey, no?

Obedience is good. Esteem is better. Love is best of all. The Great King is ever a gifting giver.'

The thin old abbess regarded him stonily, her grey brows puckered. 'I see you and your brothers are yet slaves to the old deception. We continue to pray for your enlightenment,' she informed him primly.

'Even as we pray for yours, abbess,' Emlyn said. His sudden laugh induced the sober lady to raise her brows and purse her lips severely. 'Forgive me,' he said quickly, 'but it suddenly occurred to me that if our ardent petitions were to be answered at the same time, the resulting enlightenment would certainly make Scotland the brightest realm in all the world.'

The abbess did not share the gentle monk's amusement. Folding her hands before her, she said, 'Now then, I do not believe you have come to enquire after my soul's well-being. Was there perhaps another purpose to your visit?'

'We have come seeking –' began Emlyn.

'Lady Niamh of Dýrness,' put in Murdo, his patience at an end. 'Is she here? Is she well?'

Abbess Angharad regarded him as if he had uttered a blasphemy. 'And who are you that you should concern yourself with her welfare?'

'I am her son,' he answered, and explained how he had followed his father on crusade, and had just returned. 'We have been told that my mother was brought here in the company of some others. I have come to take her home.'

'I can tell you that she is here, and she is well,' the abbess replied. 'It may be, however, that she has no wish to go with you. Nor will I compel her.'

Murdo stared at the woman. The resistance he felt was as solid as the grey granite hills above the firth, and he began to see why Emlyn had counselled politeness and caution.

'But she will want to see me,' insisted Murdo. 'She has been waiting for my return.'

'Perhaps,' allowed the abbess. 'But it may be otherwise. This will be determined.'

'I do not understand,' said Murdo, growing more confused and frustrated by the moment.

'It is not so difficult,' the abbess replied, offering a brief, superior smile. 'Women come here for many reasons. Oft times a woman will find that her fortune or, God knows, even her very body, has

481

become an affliction to her. Whatever the reason, we take them in and provide a haven for them, and protect them as best we can.' She paused, pressing her mouth into a firm line. 'Do you expect me to hand over one of my charges on your command when I know nothing of you? Indeed, for all I know, it might easily be that you are the one she has come here to escape.'

'But, I am her son,' countered Murdo feebly, looking to Emlyn for help.

'There are murderous sons, just as there are lusting and covetous husbands,' the abbess replied crisply. 'And the fact that you have come here in the company of a monk of a disreputable order does not commend your cause in the least.'

'Sister abbess,' said Emlyn gently. 'Your vigilance would do good Saint Peter credit, but I stand as God's witness to the plain truth that this young man has travelled to the Holy Land and back for the sole purpose of righting a terrible wrong perpetrated by cruel circumstance upon his family. His father, the Lady Niamh's husband, was killed in the taking of Jerusalem, and –'

'Jerusalem is won?' The abbess gasped. 'Are you certain?'

'As certain as the sun and stars, good abbess,' replied Emlyn smoothly. 'We were there, and saw the victory with our own eyes.'

'All praise to the Almighty,' declared the nun. 'We had not heard.'

'Forgive me,' Emlyn said. 'I thought word had reached you here, or I would have told you at once.'

'Jerusalem is reclaimed out of heathen bondage,' sighed the old abbess. 'Christ is triumphant at last.'

'It is this very thing we have come to tell Lady Niamh,' the monk continued. 'That Jerusalem is won, but at fearful cost, including the life of her husband – sad tidings for the lady, to be sure. Yet, it is our hope that we might mitigate the severity of the lady's grief by reuniting her with her surviving son.' Placing a hand on Murdo's shoulder, he said, 'All we ask is the opportunity to speak with her for a moment, and then whether she stays or goes will be her decision to make, and hers alone, as you suggest.'

The monk's mollifying tone produced the desired effect. In fact, his address worked so well that Murdo suspected the abbess had been waiting to hear those precise words before proceeding further.

'Very well,' Abbess Angharad promptly conceded, 'I will arrange for you to see Lady Niamh. You will wait here, please.'

The dutiful abbess departed, leaving them to themselves. Murdo, anxious and indignant at being made to wait some more, stalked back and forth across the floor. In an effort to distract him, Emlyn talked about the convent and its useful presence in the place, and the sisters' tireless good works on behalf of the people.

Murdo waved him to silence as Abbess Angharad pushed open the door just then. She entered the room, hands folded, pursing her lips and regarding the fat brother with rank disapproval. Turning to Murdo she said, 'Lady Niamh will see you. Follow me, and I will take you to a place where you can speak privately.'

The sister led them out across the yard to a wooden door set in one of the walls. Here she paused, and indicated that Murdo was to enter. 'I will give you a few moments to yourselves.'

Murdo thanked the abbess, and stepped through the doorway. 'You go ahead,' Emlyn said. 'I will await you here.'

Murdo found himself in a small orchard, walled on every side to protect the trees from the cruel northern winds. But this day, in the full flower of spring, the air was warm and full of the sound of bees working among the pear and apple trees. The sunlight was bright, and it took him a moment to see the figure bending low in the shadow of one of the boughs.

Dressed in the grey, shapeless robe and mantle of the nuns, her hair wrapped in the same cloth, she knelt over something on the ground, her back to him. Murdo took two awkward steps and stopped. 'My lady?' he said, his voice low, so as not to frighten her.

The figure straightened instantly, and froze.

'My lady,' he said again, 'it is Murdo. I have returned.'

The woman turned her head and Murdo's heart clenched in his chest. 'Ragna?'

The slender young woman stood slowly, and took a hesitant step towards him, a multitude of emotions playing over her features. She gave out a cry and rushed into his arms. 'Murdo!'

'Ragna . . .' he said, and then her mouth found his and he wrapped his arms around her and crushed her fiercely to him, as if to make up in one embrace for all the times he had yearned to hold her, but could not. Ragna kissed him again and again, raining kisses on his face and neck, her hands clutching him so that he would not escape again, tears of gladness streaming down her cheeks.

'Ragna . . . my heart . . . how I have missed you,' he said, burying his face in the hollow of her slender neck. 'I am here. I am home.'

'My love,' she whispered. 'They did not tell me you –'

'They said I was to see my mother, I did not know –'

'She is here –'

'I have come for you. We will leave this place at once. We will go –'

'Shh!' she whispered, placing her fingertips to his lips. 'Do not speak. Just hold me.'

They stood still, eyes closed, their bodies pressed tightly to one another, and Murdo felt a warmth descend upon him, and his heart quickened – as if a shard of ice which had pierced his heart had begun to melt away in the heat of Ragna's loving embrace. Murdo would have been content to stay like this for ever, but he slowly became aware of another presence in the orchard. He opened his eyes and looked over Ragna's shoulder to the place where she had been kneeling.

There, in the long, green grass, sat a chubby, round-faced infant, staring at him with wide brown eyes. At Murdo's glance the babe let out a spirited yelp, drawing Ragna's attention. Taking Murdo's hand, she led him to the child, then stooped and gathered the babe into her arms.

'Eirik,' she said softly, putting her lips to the child's round cheek. 'Your father has come home. See? This is Murdo. He is your da.'

'Da!' exclaimed the child, reaching out with a plump little hand.

Murdo, awestricken, took the tiny hand in his own and the strength of the tiny grip filled him with wonder. 'Mine?' he gasped. 'I have a child?'

'Ours,' corrected Ragna. 'Yes, my love, you have a son. His name is Eirik.'

Raising a hand to touch the child's pale yellow curls, he put his face near the babe's and whispered, 'My son . . .' That was all he could get out before the lump in his throat took away his voice.

He gathered Ragna and the child to him, kissing them both, and the three were yet standing together when he heard a soft footfall in the grass. He turned his face to see his mother approaching swiftly through the grass. 'Oh, Murdo . . . Murdo,' she said, her eyes shining with tears. 'When abbess told me you were here, I . . . I knew you would come back.'

He turned to take her hands, and drew her near. 'Mother . . .' he said, as she kissed him on the cheek.

'Welcome home, Murdo, my heart, I knew you would come for us.' Looking to Ragna, she said, 'We both prayed every day for your safe return.'

'Mother,' he said gently, 'I am the only one to return.' He then told her of Ranulf's death.

Niamh, clutching her hands, bowed her head and began to cry. Murdo put his arm around her, and let her weep. When the first wave of grief had passed, Murdo told her, 'I saw him before he died. We talked long and he told me everything. I will tell you all he said, but now is not the time.'

'I feared he would not be coming home,' she said, her voice trembling. 'I thought I was prepared for the worst, but . . .' She broke off, drew a deep breath, and said, 'Tell me now – I must know, what of Torf-Einar and Skuli? Were they killed, too?'

'No, they are alive and well,' Murdo said, glad to be able to relate some better news. 'They have taken service with Count Baldwin – brother to the new King of Jerusalem – and they have both chosen to remain in the Holy Land to gain their fortune.'

'And my father?' asked Ragna, her eyes searching his for an answer other than the one she guessed already. 'Was he killed, too?'

Murdo nodded. 'I am sorry. He fell at a place called Dorylaeum – and your brothers with him in the same battle.' He paused, allowing Ragna to take this in, then said, 'Your mother will be spared this unhappiness at least. The bishop told me.'

'That bishop,' said Niamh angrily, 'is well informed of everything that passed in the islands. He was the first to know when Ragnhild died. Not a day passed before he got his claws into Cnoc Carrach.'

'But now that you are here,' Ragna offered hopefully, 'we can go home.' She grasped Murdo's hand tightly. 'We will have our marriage vows completed in the chapel, and you can be Lord of Cnoc Carrach now. We can –'

'No, Ragna,' he said, shaking his head. 'That is not to be. Neither your father nor his heirs will return; the estate will fall forfeit to the church. But I have my own lands, my own fortune, and we will make a new place for ourselves.'

He then told how he had confronted King Magnus with the injustice perpetrated in his name, and how the king had offered him land as settlement of his grievance. He explained that he had the bishop and abbot with him, and that they would be made to stand before the king and face judgement for their actions. 'The king is a fair and honourable man,' Murdo assured them. 'He will see justice done.'

'My father and brothers –' Ragna began, 'there is no doubt? Perhaps you are mistaken and they are still alive. Perhaps –'

Murdo shook his head gently. 'There is no doubt. I am sorry.'

The door in the wall opened just then and the abbess appeared; she walked quickly towards them. 'Well,' she said briskly, glancing at Ragna who was still clutching Murdo's hand, 'I might have known you were the father of this child.'

Dismissing the couple with a jerk of her chin, she turned to Murdo's mother. 'Lady Niamh,' she said, 'this man has confessed his desire to take you away with him. What is your decision?' Before Niamh could answer the abbess added, 'I hasten to remind you that you are free to choose as you will. While you remain within these walls you shall not be made to go anywhere against your own volition or desire. Do you understand?'

'Thank you, abbess,' Niamh answered coolly. 'It is good of you to counsel me. Yet, I must confess your charity baffles me – all the more since you well know I was brought here against my will by Bishop Adalbert of Orkneyjar.'

The abbess stiffened. 'I had hoped your time among us here would have softened your heart, my lady. I prayed you would come to understand and accept that what was done was only ever for your own good.'

'I understand better than you know, abbess. It was done for the good of the bishop's purse. And if I had him and his covetous abbot here before me, I would tell them the same.'

'Mind how you speak,' Abbess Angharad protested. 'The Bishop of Orkney is God's own servant, and must be treated with all respect.'

'Rest assured Bishop Adalbert is receiving all the respect he deserves,' Murdo told her.

Taking the child into his arms, he led Ragna and his mother from the orchard. They paused to collect a few small things from their quarters, and then crossed the yard to the gates. 'We are away,' Murdo called as they approached.

'Where now?' asked Jon Wing.

'Thorsa,' replied Murdo. 'The king wishes to make me a lord, and

I would not keep him from his heart's desire even a moment longer.'

'What about these two?' The Norseman indicated the sullen and angry churchmen with a twitch of his spear. The bishop scowled at them, his arms crossed defiantly over his chest; the abbot stood beside him, more subdued, his hands hanging at his sides. 'Shall we take them with us?' asked Jon.

'By all means, let them accompany us,' Murdo answered. 'I think King Magnus will be interested to learn just how many of his vassals' estates and farms have passed into the church's possession. Who better to explain it than the two men responsible?'

Adalbert made to protest, but Jon Wing spun him around and pushed him towards the gate. Emlyn took the abbot by the arm and began leading him away, saying, 'Cheer up, my friend. Lord Magnus is a fair and honest king. You will have ample opportunity to explain yourself to him.'

Abbot Gerardus glared at the monk, but made no reply. Jerking himself free of Emlyn's grip, he stumped off alone. The kindly monk turned to Murdo's mother, bowed and offered his arm, saying, 'My lady, I would be honoured to escort you to the ship.'

Niamh smiled and accepted his arm, and walked away, leaving the abbey without a backward glance. Ragna, however, paused briefly in the doorway looking her last at the place of her captivity. Murdo stood beside her for a moment. 'I will never leave you like that again,' he vowed. Taking her hand, he led her away, saying, 'We will make a place for ourselves where we will be together always.'

FIFTY-ONE

King Magnus greeted his newest vassal lord with a ready and genuine welcome. Splendid in a yellow siarc and breecs, new brown boots, and a wide belt of red leather, he met them, cup in hand, at the door of his great hall at Thorsa, saying, 'Hail, Lord Murdo! Good greeting and good ale await you in my hall. Come, drink with me.'

Murdo, pleased to find the king in an expansive mood, greeted the lord respectfully, and accepted the proffered cup. The ale was cool and frothy and rich, and tasted like liquid smoke on the tongue – reminding him of the Dark Isles, and his home at Hrafnbú. He passed the cup back to the king, who drained it and promptly called for more; a servingboy appeared to take the cup, and Magnus confided, 'We have been drinking a little öl already, but never fear, there is plenty for everyone.'

'I hope your journey has borne fruit,' the king replied; handing his cup to the servingboy, Murdo beckoned to the women waiting a few paces away to join him. 'But tell me now, who are these ladies?' asked Magnus. 'For, despite their drab habits, I cannot think they are nuns. Although, if such beauty were more common in the cloisters, I might be tempted to don monk's robes myself.'

'Lord and king,' replied Murdo proudly, 'your eye is keen as ever. Allow me to present my mother, Lady Niamh, and my wife, Lady Ragna.' Taking up the infant, he said, 'And this is my son, Eirik.'

While the king greeted each of his guests in turn, the rest of the landing party arrived in the yard. The king called to the sea lord and said, 'Jon Wing! Welcome! Who is this with you? Can it be the Bishop of Orkneyjar and his esteemed abbot?' The king spread his hands, 'I am honoured indeed. Never has such an illustrious company gathered in Thorsa court. My friends, I give you good greeting, and bid you to take your ease beneath my roof. You will want for nothing while you are my guests. Come, let us share the welcome bowl.'

Bishop Adalbert and Abbot Gerardus, however, decided to take the opportunity to declare their outrage at having been dragged from the cathedral like criminals. 'You are mistaken, O king, if you believe we have come here of our own volition,' declared the bishop.

'These men,' the abbot said scornfully, 'have taken grave and unlawful liberties for which we expect them to be soundly punished.'

'Are you telling me you did not come here to pay homage to your king, and offer thanksgiving for his safe return?' wondered Magnus.

'Your safe return was ever upmost in our minds, of course,' confirmed the abbot. 'Even so, we were carried away by force and have been brought here very much against our will.'

'I demand you take these men at once and make them answer for their crimes.' The bishop waved his arm to include Murdo, Jon Wing, and his men, in the accusation.

The king frowned. 'As it happens, I have made it my concern to discover what has been happening in my realm while I have been away on crusade.' He drew himself up. 'I was willing to allow you a respite from the journey before bringing the matter to judgement, but you have forced my hand. Therefore, we will deal with it here and now.'

He turned and called to his counsellors to attend him. Hearing the summons, the house carles and warriors in the hall came to see what commotion was taking place outside; they crowded the doorway, spilling out around those standing judgement before the king. In a moment, Ronan and Fionn pushed through the throng and took their places either side of Magnus. 'Tell out,' he ordered. 'Tell us all what you have discovered.'

'At your command, and on your behalf, O king,' said Ronan, speaking gravely, 'we have made inquiries of your subject lords and vassals. From these we have discovered that no fewer than eighteen holdings, estates, and properties have been taken by the bishop and placed under the control of the church.'

'How so?' asked the king. 'Word of the crusade's victorious conclusion has yet to reach these shores. As we ourselves are the first to return, I cannot see how the bishop can know which of the many landholders will return to resume the possession of their lands.' Addressing the churchmen, he said, 'Enlighten us, if you can.'

The bishop grew indignant. 'Am I to be made to answer this rumour-monger's gossip?'

'Come now, Bishop Adalbert, it would be a mistake to dismiss these accusations so lightly,' said Ronan. 'I myself have spoken with more than one whose lands have been seized.'

'No one's lands have been *seized*,' the abbot said. 'At most, we have simply extended the protection of the church to those who, through unfortunate circumstance, required our aid.'

'Aid and protection,' sneered Murdo. 'A curious kind of protection, when you cast a mother and her newborn child out of a warm house and force them to take ship in the dead of winter. Or, perhaps it was the house and lands you were wishing to protect.'

'We acted only in accord with the provisions of the decree of remission and conveyance which Lord Brusi signed before his departure,' the bishop replied haughtily. 'You will find the documents all properly attested.'

'It was my home,' declared Ragna. 'And you took it from me.'

'You are mistaken,' said the abbot. '*You* were not among the heirs listed in the decree. Your father included only your mother and brothers. An unfortunate oversight, no doubt, but that cannot be laid at our feet. As the lord and his heirs are all deceased, those lands belong to the church now.'

'But you took the estate anyway,' Murdo pointed out. 'The king himself has said it: you could not have known Lord Brusi would not return.'

'We know it now,' replied the abbot smugly. 'At the time, we were but offering the church's protection to people in need of it.'

Murdo felt his once-solid certainty beginning to crumble. The oily churchmen were squirming from their grasp.

'Yet,' replied King Magnus tightly, 'it seems to me you did act with unseemly haste to secure your right to the estate.'

'What about my father's estate?' he countered. 'Lord Ranulf signed no decree, yet Hrafnbú has fallen under the *protection* of the church.'

'That is a far different matter,' asserted the bishop staunchly. 'The former estate of your father fell forfeit to King Magnus himself and was given to Lord Orin Broad-Foot. It was Lord Orin who placed your lands under the protection of the church while he was on crusade.'

'Ah, now we come to it,' said Ronan. 'I have been wondering how it is that the only lands to fall forfeit to the king belonged to landholders who did not sign the pope's decree. Nor were any of the unfortunate noblemen given opportunity to swear fealty to Prince

Sigurd, which would have secured their holdings. Perhaps you could explain that, bishop?'

The bishop's mouth clamped tight in a frown.

'We do not have to answer to you, heretic!' Abbot Gerardus sneered.

'Yet, I will have an answer,' said the king.

'Then ask Lord Orin,' answered the bishop. 'He was the one who took the lands, not me.'

'Very well,' agreed the king, 'we will ask him.' He nodded to Fionn, who disappeared inside the hall, returning a moment later with Orin Broad-Foot at his side.

Magnus greeted his nobleman, and said, 'We have been discussing how so many estates have been claimed by these zealous men for the church. They are telling me that *you* are responsible, Lord Orin. Can this be true?'

'My lord and king,' answered Orin, 'it is true that I led the seizure of certain holdings in order to gain fealty for the king and Prince Sigurd. The estates we took were those of rebel lords whose loyalty to Jarl Erlend and Jarl Paul prevented them from taking the prince to be Jarl over them.'

Murdo opened his mouth to object, but the king raised his hand to silence him, and asked Orin to continue, saying, 'How did you know these estates were those of noblemen who would not own Prince Sigurd for their Jarl?'

'Bishop Adalbert offered us his counsel,' Orin answered matter-of-factly. 'He came to us saying he feared the peace which had been long obtained on the islands would be broken if the rebel lords were allowed openly to defy the prince. He said he had learned of a plan to kill the prince and return Jarl Erlend to the throne. He urged us to act swiftly to put down the rebellion and preserve the peace at all costs.'

The bishop glared ahead in rigid defiance. The abbot, however, brow creased in thought, appeared to be composing a different song than the one he had been singing.

Turning next to Lady Niamh, the king said, 'Good lady, I would hear you speak of your husband's loyalties in this matter.'

Before she could speak, the bishop objected. 'Ask a woman? The affairs of kings and lords are beyond her understanding, certainly. She can tell us nothing.'

'I disagree,' answered the king, sobering now. 'Indeed, who knows the moods and desires of a man better than his wife?' Looking to Niamh, he said, 'What say you, my lady? Was Lord Ranulf loyal to Jarl Erlend, or was he willing to support Prince Sigurd?'

'You ask her to denounce her husband, or to condemn me,' the bishop protested. 'Which do you imagine she will choose?'

'Yet, I will hear the answer,' insisted Magnus. He nodded to Niamh. 'Proceed.'

'My lord and king,' answered Niamh, 'you ask whether my husband's loyalty to the Jarl would have prevented him from supporting the prince. In truth, I cannot say.'

'There!' the bishop cried. 'It is as I said. She knows nothing.'

'I cannot say,' continued Niamh firmly, 'for the reason that my husband joined the crusade long before the jarls were dethroned.'

'Are we to believe her?' demanded the bishop. 'She would say anything to demean us.'

'I do not beg belief of anyone,' Niamh answered, cold fury edging her voice. 'The fact is self-evident: the lords left on pilgrimage before the harvest, and Prince Sigurd did not arrive in the islands until the following Eastertide.'

'Your recollection is entirely correct, Lady Niamh,' declared the king. Turning once more to the churchmen, he observed, 'It seems to me that you have become so used to trimming the truth to fit your covetous designs, Bishop Adalbert, that you no longer know or remember its original shape.'

At last the bishop felt the sand washing away beneath his feet. He stared at the king, and at Lord Orin. 'You brought me here not to seek justice, but only to condemn me.'

'If I condemn you, it is my right,' Magnus retorted. Suddenly fierce with indignation, he drew himself up full height. 'Hear me, you two low serpents! You have used my son in his youth and innocence as a tool for your purposes – in effect, stealing in *my* name. Even so, I would not have you imagine yourselves unjustly accused and punished. Therefore, I have decided that you will both be taken to Jorvik to explain your dealings to the archbishop. Lord Orin will accompany you to make certain your crimes receive their full hearing.'

The abbot made bold to challenge the king's decision, claiming he had only acted on his superior's command. But the king would not hear it. 'As you have so bravely supported your bishop in his acquisitions, do not be cowardly now. Where is your loyalty, man?'

The king summoned several of his house carles then, and ordered them to make the bishop and abbot comfortable in the storehouse until a ship could be found to take them to Jorvik. While the bishop and abbot were led away Magnus brought Murdo and his family into his private quarters within the hall to share the welcome bowl. Lord Orin and Jon Wing joined them, and the king's counsellors as well.

When custom had been more than satisfied, the king bade Ronan to fetch the parchment that had been prepared. The elder priest left the chamber, returning quickly with a large rolled skin tied with a fine leather strap. Taking the scroll, the king unbound it and spread it across the table. He called everyone to gather around and see what he proposed.

'This,' he said, tracing a wavy black line on the bleached skin, 'is my realm in Caithness. And this,' he said, indicating a red line dividing the kingdom almost in half, 'shall be Lord Murdo's realm if he will have it.'

Murdo gaped at the vast extent of his lands. 'My lord, it is far more than the bargain we struck.'

'Cannot a king treat his nobles generously?' asked Magnus. 'Still, you should know that this is a gift which will demand the best of you and your people. This is no easy wealth I give you; in truth, of all the realms I possess, Caithness is the least in many ways. For the land is wild, and there are neither settlements nor holdings, less yet fine estates like those you have lost. It will fall to you to decide where the settlements should be built and how. It will be the work of a lifetime, and more.' He regarded Murdo with a dare in his eye. 'Well, what say you? Will you take it, and be my liegeman?'

'If it shall please you, my lord, I will take it,' he replied, and quickly added, 'and so that my ignorance and lack of wisdom does not prove a hazard to us all, I would beg the use of the king's wise counsellors to aid me in the establishment of my realm.'

King Magnus smiled approvingly. 'You need have no fear of ignorance, I think. And anyone with the prudence to secure the services of my advisors lacks nothing in wisdom.' Turning to the monks, he said, 'I leave it to you, priests. Stay with him and help him, or sail with me to Jerusalem. The choice is yours.'

The three held a quick consultation, and the matter was swiftly decided. 'If it pleases you, lord,' answered Ronan. 'We would help Murdo establish his realm. But so that the king should not lack for advisors on his return to the Holy Land, I will summon the learned Brother Monon from the abbey to join you.'

The king professed himself well pleased with this decision, and hailed the new arrangement as a boon and blessing for all Caithness, and commanded a feast to be prepared for his guests. Noticing the ladies' drab convent clothing, Magnus called for some of the noblewomen of the settlement to come forward. 'These ladies will be attending the king's feast tomorrow. Find them attire more befitting their rank, and see that they are well-arrayed for the celebration.'

Niamh thanked the king for his kindness and consideration, and said, 'Your queen is a fortunate woman to have such a thoughtful husband.'

'Alas,' Magnus replied, 'my wife and queen has not yet arrived from Norway, so I will not have the pleasure of commending you ladies to her acquaintance. Yet, I would be honoured if you would take her place at table.'

'My lord,' Niamh replied, inclining her head gracefully, 'the honour would be mine.'

The ladies took their leave and hurried away, whereupon Magnus declared himself parched, and called for ale to quench a thirst greatly inflamed by the incessant demands of kingcraft. 'Noble friends, let us sit together and drink the sweet öl of brotherhood.' He led them into the hall where the vat had been filled to overflowing with sweet dark ale.

After the cups had made the circuit a fair few times, Murdo found the chance to slip away. Begging leave of the king to borrow his counsellors for a small duty, he asked Jon Wing to join him and the five left the hall together. He led them across the yard, out of the settlement, and down to the cove where the *Skidbladnir* had been pulled up onto the shingle.

'This is a day to settle accounts,' Murdo told them. He climbed over the rail and onto the deck, beckoning the others to follow him. Stepping to the platform before the mast, he entered the tent and untied one of the four shroud-wrapped bundles. Gathering it in his arms, he emerged and presented the sea lord with the plunder.

'I promised you a reward for helping me,' Murdo said. 'There are three other bundles like this, and they are all yours.'

'You paid for your passage with six silver marks, remember?' Jon Wing said.

'Even so, I can never repay your care and protection, less yet the debt of friendship I owe you. Take it,' he urged.

Lowering the bundle to the deck, Jon took his knife, cut into the windings and began pulling out objects: a golden bowl, two silver cups in the shape of horns, a gold bracelet with a plaque in the shape of a horse, and a gold chalice with two rubies and two emeralds set in a silver band around the base, and handfuls of coins.

Rising from the treasure, the sea lord said, 'I cannot take it, Murdo. The plunder I got from the amir's tent is enough for me. And if I return to the Holy Land with the king, I will get more. Besides, you will need your wealth if you are to build a realm here.'

'Please,' Murdo said, indicating the hoard, 'take something at least, so that I can say I began my rule with an easy heart and an open hand.'

At this, the Norseman relented. He stooped and retrieved the two silver cups shaped like horns. 'As you insist, I will take these,' he said. 'And I will keep them full so that when you come to visit me, we can drink together like kings.'

'That we shall,' agreed Murdo happily. 'No doubt it is thirsty work building a kingdom.'

'You are always welcome on my ship,' the Norseman vowed happily. 'A lord always needs men with ships to serve him. Who knows, maybe we will sail together again one day, hey?'

'I would like nothing better,' Murdo agreed. Turning to the monks, he said, 'I have something for you, too.'

'We have no need of gold or silver,' Ronan demurred. 'It is enough for us to see you reunited with your family and befriended by the king. We are well content, my friend.'

'Be that as it may, I would reward you,' Murdo insisted. Moving quickly to the ship's prow, he motioned to the others to follow. When the four had joined him there, he asked Jon Wing to witness the giving of the gift.

'I kept waiting for a good time to give this to you,' Murdo told them, 'but there were always too many people around, and I was afraid of what Magnus would do if he found out. But that does not matter anymore.'

The monks, puzzled by his words, looked on as Murdo knelt and began running his hands along the underside of the railing. After a moment, his fingers closed on the prize. 'Here it is,' he said, bringing out the long, slightly bent iron spear.

Ronan took one look at the relic and lapsed into an awe-stricken silence.

Emlyn was not so afflicted. 'God save you, Murdo!' he gasped. 'What have you done?'

'The Holy Lance!' Fionn murmured in amazement.

Ronan sank to his knees. 'Can it be?' he whispered. He clasped his hands and raised hopeful eyes to Murdo. 'Is it truly the sacred lance?'

'It is,' confirmed Murdo. 'I wanted to tell you sooner, believe me. I could not risk losing it.'

'But I saw you give the lance away,' Fionn insisted. 'With my own eyes, I saw it.' Seeking the consensus of the others, he added, 'We all saw it.'

'You saw me give away the spear I made in Arles,' Murdo corrected. 'Remember Arles?'

'Ah, yes,' nodded Jon Wing thoughtfully. 'I had forgotten Arles.'

Murdo explained how he had eluded Baldwin's soldiers in Jaffa, reaching the ship in time to exchange one iron lance for the other. 'I wrapped the one I made in the bindings of the other. That was the lance I gave to Bohemond.'

'You lied to the lords.' Emlyn's eyes grew wide at Murdo's audacity.

Murdo shook his head. 'No, brother, I told them the truth. Bohemond's arrogance and greed did the rest.'

'But Magnus gave you land in exchange for the lance. You have tricked him, Murdo,' Fionn pointed out. 'That is a very great sin.'

'That is not precisely the way it happened,' answered the young man. 'As Emlyn will doubtless recall, I told Bohemond and the king that I would accept nothing for the lance, nor did I. Magnus gave me land because Prince Sigurd seized my father's estate and gave it to Lord Orin. I only demanded justice, and that was my right.'

Silence descended over the group as the strength of the young man's determination, and the deftness of his cunning broke over them. Jon Wing, however, revelled in the brazen courage of the deed. 'Such daring will be sung in kings' halls throughout Skania and Daneland!'

Murdo dismissed the praise, and said, 'No one will ever know of this save us alone.' He paused, looking at the rough Iron Lance;

then, holding it across his palms, he offered it to Ronan kneeling before him. 'This is the Lance of Christ. I place it in your safe keeping.'

Ronan, still struggling to comprehend the magnitude of their good fortune, gazed upon the Iron Lance, and all speech fled.

'When I was standing on the Jaffa plain,' Murdo continued, 'I decided to follow the True Path, and I have you to thank for showing me how to find it. You have been better to me than my own brothers, and I am grateful. If anything good were ever to come of that wretched crusade, I wanted you to share in it. The Holy Lance belongs to you, and I cannot believe anyone else could revere and protect it half so well.'

Brother Ronan accepted the lance. 'It is a very miracle,' he said, gazing lovingly upon the ancient relic and shaking his head slowly. 'All this time I thought it was gone forever, and that our pilgrimage to Jerusalem had failed.' He looked at Murdo, his eyes filling with tears. 'In truth, I had begun to doubt the vision we were given. I confess I doubted God.'

'Now you can fulfil the vision.'

Ronan, clutching the spear to his breast as if it were his very soul, stood and gathered Murdo under his arm. 'You have shored up an old man's weak and tottering faith, and brought peace to an uneasy heart.'

Passing the lance to Fionn, the elder priest placed his hand on Murdo's forehead, and said, 'May your fortunes increase with your wisdom, and may you live long in the land your lord has given you . . .'

At Ronan's touch, Murdo felt a sudden stirring in his soul, and he heard in the priest's blessing, the echo of Brother Andrew's words: *All you possess was given you for this purpose, brother. Build me a kingdom.*

In that instant he was in the catacombs. He smelled again the dry dusty closeness of the monastery tomb, and he saw the mysterious white priest before him, posing his question and waiting for his answer. *I ask you again: will you serve me?*

His own reply came back to him. *I will do what I can.*

Build me a kingdom, Brother Andrew had said. And now it seemed the question was before him again. Once, not so long ago, nothing would have given him greater pleasure than to renounce his promise, to walk away as if it meant nothing to him. Once, but not now. He had chosen the way he would go, and he would abide by his decision. Besides, this was the day for settling accounts, a time to pay debts and honour vows. On such a day, when he demanded justice of others, he could not himself be false.

'. . . May the Holy Light shine for you,' the priest continued, 'and may your feet never stray from the True Path all the days of your life.'

Murdo thanked Ronan for his blessing and, accepting the burden of his vow, declared, 'With your help, I will make my realm a haven for the Célé Dé, far away from the ambitions of small-souled men and their ceaseless striving. Together we will make it a kingdom where the True Path can be followed in peace, and the Holy Light can shine without fear of the darkness.'

'Do that,' Emlyn told him, clapping him affectionately on the back, 'and you will be a lord worthy of the name.'

'That,' said Murdo, 'is all I ever wanted.'

EPILOGUE

We are the Seven, and we are the last.

Our long, lonely vigil is drawing to an end. A thousand years have come and gone since our illustrious order began – a thousand years of watching and waiting. In that time nations have risen, flourished, and crumbled, kings and potentates and dictators have strutted and preened and vanished, and the very stars have come within reach. But many things – **most** things – never change: children are born; they grow and marry, and raise families of their own in a world where the sun yet rises day by day, and the seasons make their sacred round. Tribes forever make war on their neighbours, goods change hands in gainful trade and wealth circulates the globe in an endless, ever-widening river. Always, always the tides of power sweep the world end to end.

So it has ever been, but soon it shall be no more. For the consummation of the age is at hand, and the True Path will be revealed at last. That time is hard upon us, friends. Whether in New York or Paris, London, Madrid, or Moscow, I look out of my hotel window to the busy streets below and I see the world dissolving, crumbling away before my eyes. The old world is fast returning to the chaos from which it was formed. Yet, the Holy Light, though dim, is not extinguished; the flame shall be renewed. The birth pains of the New World have begun.

Listen to the sirens in the night; listen to the bombs and the guns, and the screams of the victims, the angry shouts of the mobs in the streets. Listen! In all these things is heard the galloping hoofbeats of the swift-flying steed: the Winged Messenger is coming. The Day of Reckoning is upon us. That which exists will not long endure.

So be it!